Eleanor Dark was born an married Dr Eric Dark an
Katoomba.

Eleanor Dark publishe
1920s, and her first novel,
Her other novels are *Prelu
Coolami (1936), *Sun Across the Sky* (1937), *Waterway* (1938),
The Little Company (1945), *Lantana Lane* (1959) and the
historical trilogy, *The Timeless Land* (1941), *Storm of Time*
(1948) and *No Barrier* (1953).

Eleanor Dark died in 1985.

Also by Eleanor Dark
and available in Imprint Classics

Return to Coolami

The Timeless Land

Waterway

Storm of Time

IMPRINT CLASSICS

NO BARRIER

ELEANOR DARK

Introduced by
Barbara Brooks with Judith Clark

An imprint of HarperCollins*Publishers*

AN ANGUS & ROBERTSON BOOK
An imprint of HarperCollinsPublishers

First published in 1953 by William Collins Publishers
A&R Australian Classics edition in 1980

This Imprint Classics edition published in 1991 by
CollinsAngus&Robertson Publishers Pty Limited (ACN 009 913 517)
A division of HarperCollinsPublishers (Australia) Pty Limited
Unit 4, 31 Waterloo Road, North Ryde NSW 2113, Australia

HarperCollinsPublishers (New Zealand) Limited
31 View Road, Glenfield, Auckland 10, New Zealand

HarperCollinsPublishers Limited
77-85 Fulham Palace Road, London W6 8JB, United Kingdom

National Library of Australia
Cataloguing-in-Publication data:

Dark, Eleanor, 1901–1985.
  No Barrier
  [New ed.]
  ISBN 0 207 17325 7
  I. Title
A823.3

Cover: J. H. Carse 1819–1900
        Wentworth Falls 1873
        Collection of the Warrnambool Art Gallery
Printed in Australia by Griffin Press

5 4 3 2 1
95 94 93 92 91

INTRODUCTION

In August 1953, Eleanor Dark had just published *No Barrier*, the third in her series of historical novels. Exhausted when she finished the novel, she was also feeling quite disturbed and pessimistic about the political climate in Australia. It must have been a comfort when Helen Palmer wrote a thoughtful letter to her about the novels. Writer, school teacher, and political activist, Helen Palmer was the daughter of Vance and Nettie Palmer, writers who had advocated the need for a sense of history in Australian writing. "Thinking back over the three books," Helen Palmer wrote,

> I felt I wanted to pass on to you my conviction of how immeasurably valuable to us all it is to have the period they cover imaginatively recreated in the terms you have established . . . [I] feel very strongly about the very poor historical sense we give kids at school . . . strange that the problems of the period seem too relevant and so little dated today . . .[1]

In *The Timeless Land, Storm of Time* and *No Barrier*, Eleanor Dark had written a fictionalised but historically accurate account of the early settlement of NSW, based on letters and journals and government records. These novels were the first accurate account of the early settlement to be accessible to most Australians. In the absence of written histories, her work was important and influential — her audience was wide, schoolchildren and teachers, library readers, historians . . . In 1963 Manning Clark would send her a copy of his *History of Australia* saying that his work "comes in part from the inspiration of reading *The Timeless Land*".[2]

Eleanor Dark had published five novels during the 1930s. By the time she started on *The Timeless Land*, her name was known. She had found a voice as a writer. She was one of several women writers of the time dealing with the changing lives of women in the period between the wars, and the developing sense of what it meant to be living in Australia. She had been experimenting with form and structure. The voice she had settled on was an interior voice, the voice of consciousness, moving backwards and forwards through time, focusing on a moment of crisis and change. In the later novels of the 1930s, rather than the single authoritative voice of a central consciousness there were several interwoven voices, narratives that balance as well as question each other.

Why did Eleanor Dark turn to a completely different genre, the historical novel? Why did she spend years researching and writing, reading letters and journals in the Mitchell Library? After *Waterway* was published in 1938, she spent most of the next 15 years on the historical novels, stopping only when she was overcome by writers block during the war. She broke through by writing out her concerns in *The Little Company* (1945), a novel about the position of writers and intellectuals during the Second World War.

These novels are important because of her intellectual approach to the history, because of her politicised consciousness. She wasn't the only one of her contemporaries turning to history, she was one among many — Barnard Eldershaw, and Katherine Susannah Prichard, for example. But look at the scope of what she achieved. She took on the project of looking at the country in its historical, political, and ecological environment. Where did the impetus come from?

> Sat Dec 5th (1936): . . . I began to work but got reading History of NSW instead.[3]

In December 1936, Eleanor Dark was working on *Waterway*. She and Eric Dark had been living in the Blue

Mountains since 1923. Her writing had to be fitted in around her domestic commitments — the children, the housework, the phone that, because Eric Dark was a doctor, always had to be answered. Her son and stepson were at school. She had a housekeeper a lot of the time, and a husband who admired and encouraged her writing. But her diaries record the living room curtains to be washed, the gardening, the jam to be made, walks, visits, as well as the early mornings when she wrote before breakfast and the nights when she worked on her writing until she was too tired. Time for writing was always an issue.

There were political and social changes taking place that would change the lives of the Darks, and all of the liberal intelligentsia. In December 1936, when she wrote in her diary that she was distracted from *Waterway* by reading the history of New South Wales, Franco was talking about victory in Spain. That year, the Nazis went into the Rhineland, the Fascists were marching in London, Italian troops invaded Abyssinia, Japan invaded China. Trotsky left for Mexico after Zinoviev and Kamenev were executed.

> The disruption of the bourgeois world, its disorders and anomalies, the frightful insistence on economic questions, leaves the writer, whatever his origins, quite at sea.[4]

The 1930s depression made the Darks reassess their political ideas. Eric Dark was affected by what he saw happening to his patients during this time. He began to move to the left and by 1938 was writing about the connections between medicine and society, poverty and disease. Eleanor Dark already called herself a socialist; she had grown up in a leftwing household.

> Of course I'm a socialist . . . Everybody of any intelligence is a socialist nowadays.[5]

A combination of economic issues, fascism in Europe and what dissenting voices called fascism at home made a comfortable liberal humanism seem inadequate. By the late

1930s the Darks, like so many others, were looking back to the First World War and fearing another war.

> If we don't find the true causes of this thing and destroy them it will happen all over again.[6]

Writers like the Palmers, Barnard and Eldershaw, Katherine Susannah Prichard, and the Darks believed they were living in a country where they could influence the course of change. They needed a sense of the past in order to understand the present and talk about the future. In Melbourne, Brian Fitzpatrick was laying the foundations of a left-wing historiography. The Palmers had been talking up cultural nationalism for years.

> We have to discover ourselves — our character, the character of our country, the particular kind of society that has developed here . . . through the searching explorations of literature.[7]

Eleanor Dark lived a fairly secluded life in the Blue Mountains, despite letters and visits from Miles Franklin, the Palmers, Fitzpatricks and others. She looked out with interest on what was happening in the outside world. She looked out from a house perched on the end of a ridge, where, if it wasn't for the trees that enclose the house, she could almost watch over the stillness and space of the Jamieson Valley. Even today, when the Blue Mountains is a commuter belt, developed, heavily touristed as the reports say, that view takes you away from urban development, civilisation or what passes for it, and makes a lot of things seem irrelevant. It takes you to thoughts of something else . . .

> Out of silence mystery comes, and magic, and the delicate awareness of unreasoning things.[8]

The Darks lived where they did because they loved the bush. They went on long walks most days, took their visitors on picnics, spent weekends and holidays walking, climbing, camping, exploring. They had a cave they used as a weekender, and even now if you go to Katoomba someone will tell you that Eleanor Dark wrote *The Timeless Land* in a cave. She didn't. But she must have been thinking, as she walked through that country, about its stories, the dreamings of the original Aboriginal inhabitants, and what it was like when the first European settlers came.

> I do not want to be taken for a 'back-to-nature' advocate, nor for one who, in these disillusioned times, regards our own civilisation as inevitably doomed; but I do believe that we, nine tenths of whose progress has been a mere elaboration of the technique, as opposed to the art of living, might have learned much from a people who, whatever they may have lacked in technique, had developed that art to a very high degree.[9]

By 1936 Eleanor Dark had already made some forays into the records in the Mitchell Library. In the description of Sydney in *Waterway* there is a subtext about history and the land and the past. In 1937, she was researching an article on Caroline Chisholm, for Flora Eldershaw and the Women's Committee for the Sesquicentennial, who were doing a book on women pioneers. Shades of the Bicentennial; the Sesquicentennial celebrations glossed over the more controversial aspects of history — the aboriginals, the convicts, even the women.

In 1937 she began three solid years of work. She was working in the Mitchell Library, travelling down from the mountains by train, sometimes leaving home so early it was still dark. There was so much transcribing she had pains in her arm. She was working from primary sources. What she was doing was collecting a huge mass of facts, interpreting them, and then trying to rise above them with an appropriate narrative. She was writing *The Timeless Land*, which was published in 1941.

She brought to the account of early history the critique of the intellectual, as well as the imagination of the creative writer. It was an enormous task. But as time passed — 1939 and the declaration of war, the introduction of press censorship, encroachments on civil liberties, the sense of crisis — she, like her contemporaries, felt powerless in the face of the history they were living through. What could a writer do that was useful? She and Eric Dark were active in local community politics in Katoomba during the 1940s. She decided to keep writing, that was the most important thing for a writer to do.

> I think that because we are living in such times of stress, there's an intellectual striving. The writer feels this like everyone else, his business is to express it. So when people are searching for an understanding of their problems, they naturally turn to their literature, which gives — or ought to give — a reflection, and perhaps an interpretation, of themselves and their community.[10]

Her interpretation takes into account imperialism, class, gender, race and ecology. She asked: Who were the convicts? Why were they transported? What was it that the British government transported to their penal colony?

> The greed, the brutality, the strife and the suffering were not born here. They were brought.[11]

She asked, what were the consequences? If the convicts rebelled, what kind of freedom did they want?

> He thought of freedom that could strike shackles not only from his own feet but from the feet of all men everywhere. And he thought not only of shackles made of iron, but of others, invisible, which held men's minds imprisoned.[12]

The contending forces in these novels are not only the colonial powers, the government officials and convicts, the free settlers, the women, but also the Aboriginal people.

> Am I to convince these people that it was necessary to steal their land from them? That it is "necessary", having

stolen it, to hunt their game, to haul nets in their waters? That it is "necessary" now to send an armed force against them? What is this "necessity"? The necessity for a distant jail in which to herd our criminals! The necessity for another colonial possession! The necessity for empire and dominion, for power and glory . . .[13]

Anyone who thinks seriously about the history of Australia without blinkers on has to think back further than 1788. Australia has a history, still largely unrecognised and unwritten, going back perhaps 60,000 years. Eleanor Dark understood that. Her representation of the Aboriginal people caused a controversy at the time. It needs to be reassessed now. But she wrote these novels 50 years ago, and some of the issues she raised are not settled yet. The Aboriginal people are still seeking a treaty, their history is only beginning to be taught in schools and colleges and universities. No wonder she felt demoralised in the 1950s, when she saw, not the progress they had wanted, but the possibilities of change evaporating . . .

In the Mitchell Library she had met Brian Fitzpatrick — historian, man of letters, civil libertarian — doing his research. He and his wife Dorothy became firm friends. Dorothy Fitzpatrick was an interested reader and perceptive critic of these novels.

The adjustment of the Aboriginal to his environment (which you show extraordinarily well) throws into relief the weakness of the British social organisation more clearly than any description of those weaknesses could do.[14]

But she was critical of the characterisation of the historical figures . . .

I feel that if you were quite certain about these people you would let them out more often without their adjectives.[15]

The Fitzpatricks were also critical of the use of Stephen

Mannion, the Irish landowner, as a literary device.

> You wished to round off your story by showing the type of
> man who exterminated the Aborigines and raped the
> countryside . . . Mannion was not a really satisfactory way
> of telescoping this historical process. He was not a type
> known in Sydney till the late 1820s at least.[16]

But it was the relationship between the people and the
country that was the real centre of the historical novels.

> Man's immemorial urge to be identified with his environ-
> ment was here frustrated. He could, as yet, neither claim
> this place, nor permit it to absorb him; neither call it his,
> nor yield to it. Every white man and woman in the
> community suffered the spiritual malaise of humanity
> uprooted — felt a curious sense of impermanence, of
> illusion, of drifting, as though they were ghosts, or
> clouds, or blown shreds of smoke between earth and sky.
> And so, resist it as they might, and cling as they would to
> memories of the soil from which they had been torn,
> they were obsessed with this unresponsive land.[17]

Eleanor Dark was writing *Storm of Time* in the late 1940s,
during the period of postwar reconstruction. The political
climate had changed considerably from that of the late
1930s. The Darks were both accused of being underground
supporters, if not active members, of the Communist Party.
Eric Dark, who had been active in local politics, received
poison pen letters. There were threats on his life. There was
graffiti on the walls in Katoomba saying "Lynch
Communists!"

The times had changed and her concentration faltered.
In September 1947 she wrote, "the book is floundering
along with the end in sight now, but I'm making a frightful
mess of it as I'm too tired to think straight . . ."[18] Her arm
was "crippled with cramp as usual". She finished *Storm of
Time* in December 1947. "Your economic history is good,"
Dorothy Fitzpatrick wrote, "but the book is heavily written

and too close to the documents." Had the effort of mastering the facts exhausted her? A successful historical novel, Dorothy Fitzpatrick said, should get further than the documents "by showing the documented facts outlined in the light of strong feeling . . ."[19] Still, she said, it's a milestone in the popularisation of Australian history.

When the novel was published, the Darks took a holiday. They went "walkabout" and spent six months travelling around Australia. Soon afterwards they bought a farm in a small community in south-eastern Queensland. They spent part of each year there from 1951 till 1957. She finished writing *No Barrier* on the farm in Montville.

Her working title for *No Barrier* was *Land of Plunder*, making it clear that the idea of exploitation of the land, a theme that runs through all three of these novels, was strong in her mind.

> You intend to exploit this land; have a care, Sir, that it does not end by exploiting you.[20]

Storm of Time and *No Barrier* continue to develop the ideas in *The Timeless Land*, but they were harder novels to integrate. In *The Timeless Land* the focus was on the settlement. There were Bennelong and Phillip, representatives of two contending cultures, to set against one another. In *Storm of Time* and *No Barrier*, she had to deal with the expanding settlement, with a diverse community, with complex political intrigues. There was her version of Bligh, probably influenced by Evatt's "Rum Rebellion", her critical portrait of Macarthur, also Hunter, King, Macquarie. The novel had to move between Sydney and the outlying settlements to show what was happening to the Aboriginal people. Her fictional characters, Johnny Prentice and the Mannions, made some of the connections. Prentice provided the link she needed between the convicts, the Aboriginal people, and the settlers. Then there was the attempt to cross the mountains . . . They weren't easy books to write. She had used parallel narratives in her earlier novels, but here she had no single crisis to draw the threads together.

Karl Shapiro, the American poet, had written warmly about *The Timeless Land* in 1943.

> *The Timeless Land* has left a wonderful flavour with me. It's andante, acrid, blue, warm as sky, inwoven like tapestry, hung in the space of the Australian atmosphere, not quite tragic, wiser than nostalgia, full of peace . . . I imagine that after living in such a mood you find modern Australia with its American influence a bit rasping. Or do you?[21]

She did. One of the things she was trying to do in the historical novels was not only to question but also to reinforce the sense of what it meant to be Australian, to stand against the onslaught of American-based mass culture that she hated. It was a post-colonial nationalism she and her contemporaries had advocated, a progressive nationalism; but now, when an independent nation became a kind of colony by choice, when the progressive position was marginalised once again, nationalism was thrown into question.

No wonder her morale was low when she finished *No Barrier*. The Darks and their friends had been under attack. Despite what she had achieved, it was no time for celebration. She had a wide readership for her novels; she had recognition of her contribution to Australian historiography. She saw the trilogy used in schools broadcasts, to encourage schoolchildren to imagine themselves in the position of the Aboriginal people when the first fleet arrived. *The Timeless Land* had been a Book of the Month Club choice in America. She would make more money from these three than any other novels. But she had not been able to do what she set out to do, because the tide of history had turned against her.

Eleanor Dark always felt a special relationship with history. She was "born with the century" in 1901. She felt a connection with the country through her family history.

History is to the community as memory is to the individual, she said. Now, after the optimism of the postwar phase of reconstruction, she and her contemporaries were living through a period of disintegration, the conservative backlash of the 50s had fragmented the connections they had all been trying to make. She felt there was no place for her in these times.

But she hoped she was writing more than an account of history. There was the history she had reconstructed from the documents. Then there was her interpretation, history as propaganda, if you like. There was also an attempt to relate it all to herself, her readers. To place her fictional characters at the centre of historical conflict was to try and imagine the dialectic of history and the patterns of human life . . .

> Nor is the average person more than dimly aware of himself as a part of a pattern. He will probably recognise this pattern of his personal life quite vividly, of family life quite clearly, of town life less clearly, of national life rather vaguely, of human life hardly at all; but to relate them all is an exercise he rarely attempts. The single thread of his own existence is soon lost to view in the vast tapestry of history — yet the tapestry would be lost without it, and it is this that the story-teller must not only assert but demonstrate. It is this which lends any story that quality which alone can give it "greatness" . . .[22]

I'm writing this in a cabin in the bush north of Sydney, looking out the window at a screen of gum and banksia branches moving in the wind, and behind them a cloud-streaked blue sky. I come up here to get away from Sydney, and I go back refreshed after walking in the bush. Reading and thinking about her novels here seems appropriate. To think about these novels now, at another time when political structures, both national and international, seem to be cracking around us, seems appropriate. What is our position as writers now? Can we provide the kind of interpretation that Eleanor Dark talked about? It's a time when we look at things in fragments. Perhaps it's a good time to try to retrieve and share some of the optimism and sense of purpose she must have felt when she began *The Timeless Land* in 1938.

BARBARA BROOKS WITH JUDITH CLARK
Bucketty March/April 1991

REFERENCES

1. Helen Palmer to Eleanor Dark 1.8.53. Eleanor Dark papers NLA 4998
2. Manning Clark to Eleanor Dark 22.8.63. Eleanor Dark papers NLA 4998
3. Eleanor Dark papers MLMSS 4545 Box 10
4. Christina Stead, quoted in Drusilla Modjeska, *Exiles At Home* (Sydney: Angus & Robertson) 1981, p. 13
5. *Waterway* (Sydney: Collins Angus & Robertson) 1990, p. 63
6. *ibid.* p. 192
7. Vance Palmer, 'The Future of Australian Literature', the *Age*, 9.2.35
8. *The Timeless Land* (Sydney: Collins Angus & Robertson) 1990, p. 23
9. *ibid.* Introduction, p. 9
10. Australian Writers Speak Series, interview with Eleanor Dark, 7.10.44. Eleanor Dark papers, MLMSS4545 Box 10
11. *Storm of Time*, (Sydney: Collins), 1948, p. 279
12. *ibid.* p. 296
13. *The Timeless Land*, p. 424
14. Dorothy Fitzpatrick to Eleanor Dark 2.12.41. MLMSS 4545 Box 24
15. *ibid.*
16. *ibid.*
17. *Storm of Time*, p. 295
18. Eleanor Dark to Margaret Kent Hughes, 29.9.47. MLMSS 4545 Box 15
19. Dorothy Fitzpatrick to Eleanor Dark, 1.4.49. MLMSS4545 Box 24
20. *Storm of Time*, p. 188
21. Letter from Karl Shapiro to Eleanor Dark, 7.6.43, in the possession of Michael Dark
22. Eleanor Dark papers, MLMSS4545 Box 10.

CONTENTS

1808-1809

Extracts from the Journal and Letters of Conor Mannion

February 9th, 1808. I have written nothing in my Journal since that terrible Day two weeks ago, feeling myself much Confused and wearied by recent Events. It has for so long been my only Confidant that I commonly write in it with great Freedom, as I might speak to one so close and dear that the necessity to guard the Tongue would never be thought of; but sometimes I find my Pen hesitating of late, even over these pages which are for my eyes alone. Yet I feel that it is good to open the Heart, and without some living person to confide in, blank paper may serve.

I have been thinking much of these eight years past, in which I have become by turn a bride, a stepmother, twice a mother, and now a Widow. I have been recalling that day when I came here with Cousin Bertha for the first time—how hot it was!—and all the household was assembled on the viranda by my Husband's direction to bid me welcome. First my stepsons were presented—Patrick a tall boy of fifteen, and Miles a hand-some, cheerful lad of nine, who pleased his Papa—and me!—by throwing his arms about my neck in that impulsive manner which I came to know so well. "And this, my love, is Mr. Harvey, who is Tutor to my sons." He bowed (so diffident as barely to raise his eyes to mine) and I did not dream that he would in time fill my thoughts as he fills them now.

And then Ellen. "My housekeeper, Ellen Prentice." What a little Booby I was, to be sure! How long it was before I realised that she, having lived so many years under my Husband's roof, had been something more than his Housekeeper! And even after this had been revealed to me, and after I had learned something of her History, how blind I remained to the violence and turbulence of her emotions, and how little I dreamed that there were Tumults in her soul which would in time make her an Assassin! No; I saw only her black eyes, so cold and without expression, fixed upon me, and felt a sudden bewilderment at finding myself disliked. And when Emma, and the overseers, and the outside Servants had been presented, and Ellen's two children were drawn forward, I tried to soften that for-bidding look of hers by praising them. La, it was difficult, for they were the most uncomely children—Maria but a couple of years older than Miles, yet already unchildlike with her clumsy Frame, her heavy face, and her pale eyes and hair; and Andy, a year younger, lumpish and ugly, his hair flaming red, and his face blotched with freckles. Yet I thought she must love them, and sought to please her by asking their ages, and exclaiming how large they were.

What does a woman feel for a daughter whom she has unwillingly conceived in the wretchedness of convict quarters on a transport, and fathered by one whose face, even, is unknown? Or for a son born in a convict hut—legally fathered, indeed, but by one so devoid of either husbandly or parental Tenderness that he could, at the first Opportunity, abscond into the Bush, abandoning wife and children to their Fate? How can I know these things? In Ellen there was at least a fierce sense of duty and protection; and if, to protect and provide for them, she ensured her livelihood by means offensive to Morality, am I to condemn her, and excuse my Husband, who was her Partner? Nor is it true that love was wholly a stranger to her heart, for she often betrayed a softness towards Miles, who was her foster-child; and she cherished the memory of her elder son, Johnny, who vanished at eight years old into the woods—or into the harbour—or into some pond or river—who knows? Poor Ellen!

And last of all—quite forgotten, had I not observed her peeping round a doorway with the whites of her great eyes gleaming in her dark face—appeared Dilboong. A Native child, my Husband informed me carelessly, whom he had procured in Sydney to learn domestic work under Ellen's guidance. "But is she not very young?" I enquired, astonished—for she was not a day older than Miles, and looked younger. But no one was greatly interested in Dilboong, and I had but time to pat her cheek before I was escorted indoors to view my new home.

How shallow can kindness be! For though I was ready to pat her cheek, I did not think to regard her as one with a history of her own, and it was by mere Accident, from gossip heard later in Sydney, that I learned she was the Daughter of that famous Native called Bennilong, who was Gov'r Phillip's Favourite, and accompanied him to England, and who, since his return, has been much given to drinking, and to quarrelling with his Compatriots. I could find no one who recollected her Mother until I spoke with Mrs. Macarthur, who declared she was a woman called Burrunguroo (or some such name) of fierce and shrewish Temperament, and who died soon after Dilboong's birth. Whence, I wonder, does the Offspring of two such fiery-tempered Parents derive the gentle and Affectionate nature of our Dilboong? I recall, too, my interest upon learning from a chance remark of Mrs. Macarthur's, that this Bennilong had been, in his time, a notable maker of those songs which his people sing during their corrobaris; for I have many times come upon Dilboong crooning words to herself or to the Children which appear to be rambling Tales, made up as she proceeds, of the small incidents of her daily life. Yet when I first set eyes upon her I saw only a little, black-skinned Creature, so strange as to seem more fitted to take her Place among the odd animals of the Country than among human beings. Such Ignorance as mine was

6

then is a poverty of the Spirit, and it is no matter for surprise that at first I found life dull, and time passing slowly.

Dear Cousin Bertha—though my husband's kinswoman, and not my own—was my solace, but so old, and even then so deaf, that she could not afford the kind of company desired by a restless, active, chattering and impatient young Woman. How I fretted as I loitered about the House with no occupation to fill the hours, sometimes attempting to find some small domestic task, only to be thrown into confusion by Ellen: "Is there anything you require, Ma'am?" How often, sitting on the viranda with my needlework, I was tempted to beg Mr. Harvey's permission to join Patrick and Miles at their lessons. I could have done so with advantage, for I fear I was, at nineteen, a shocking ignoramus, and am little better now.

But this is Idle. I must think not of what is past, but of the present and the future. Now that poor Ellen has been taken away to suffer the penalty of the Law for her dreadful Deed, I am much engaged with household Duties, which indeed have served to distract my Thoughts, and restrain me from useless Brooding upon the horrors I have Witnessed. Maria has besought me with tears not to dismiss her because of her Mother's Crime, and though Patrick at first disclosed some reluctance to keep her, he has yielded to my Persuasions; the poor Creature is so grateful that she uses every endeavour to give Satisfaction, and were it not for my Admonitions, would neglect her own Cottage to labour here from Dawn till dark. Her assistance is the more welcome since our Housemaid could not be prevailed upon to remain, declaring the House will be Haunted, and much other nonsensical Stuff. Have observed Dilboong looking ill at ease, and wonder if she has been disturbed by these tales, since all agree that the Natives are very prone to Superstitious beliefs.

It is rumoured that the *Dart* is to sail for England shortly, so I must summon my resolve to write to dear Grandpapa, and also to my late Husband's Mother and Sisters, giving them the dreadful news of his death, a Task that I shrink from, feeling myself unable to express that sense of grief in my Bereavement which they will naturally expect. I have begged Patrick to write to his Brother on the same subject, and trust it is not heartless in me to hope that dear Miles' sanguine temperament, and the many interests and diversions of his life in London, will aid him in bearing this blow with Fortitude. . . .

* * * *

Beltrasna,
New South Wales,
February 10th, 1808.

My dear Grandpapa,

I write to you in great Distress and some Confusion, owing to the many disturbing Events with which I must make you Acquainted. In my last letter, written when I was still confined to my room by illness following the loss of my unborn Child, I told you of a Plot discovered among our Convicts. At some later date I may describe the details of this Affair more fully, but for the present I have other things to tell you of, and will confine myself to saying that the expected rising did take place, apparently by the agency of that same convict, Finn, whom I have mentioned to you, and whose escape from here occurred some three years ago. In the course of this rising an Encounter took place in one of our fields, when several convicts were killed or wounded, and one of our Overseers barely escaped with his Life. The convict Finn was taken, and the same day died in a manner so painful and shocking that I cannot yet bring myself to relate it.

I speak of these events only because they took place on the same day as another, to apprise you of which is the main Object of my letter; and though no connection between them can readily be discerned, I cannot altogether rid myself of a suspicion that a connection did exist.

In the evening (my Husband having despatched a messenger to summon a military Detachment, since he feared that other escaped Convicts were still at large in the Neighbourhood) I had retired to my Room, and he and Patrick were in the study awaiting the soldiers. Patrick having finally left him, Mr. Mannion stepped out on the viranda, for what purpose is unknown, but probably to assure himself that the men guarding the House were at their posts. Of what passed we have no knowledge, but we were all aroused by the sound of a Shot, and, rushing to the scene, discovered my Husband lying dead, and our Housekeeper, Ellen Prentice, standing over him with a pistol in her hand. At some little distance the body of one of our overseers, who had been patrolling that side of the house, was discovered lying among some bushes; we conjecture that this was the work of a Native, since he had died of a spear thrust, and that it may have been some sound or faint cry from him which caused Mr. Mannion to step out on to the viranda.

You will naturally ask, my dear Grandpapa, what can have inspired Ellen to so terrible a Deed. I cannot reply; but I must now reveal to you what I have mentioned to no one before, namely that there was an association between her and my Husband before our Marriage, which has been renewed during at least one Period since. Whether the motive for her crime may lie concealed in that Circumstance I know not; yet I have learned that the relationship between men and women, whether sanctioned by Marriage or not, can arouse emotions which are not always Tender.

I am persuaded that I need not describe to you the horror and dismay of this situation. Patrick, who immediately assumed the direction of affairs, had Ellen confined in the cellar to await the arrival of the Military, meanwhile maintaining a strict guard upon the House. The detachment, however, did not come—the reason for which I shall reveal later—but towards midnight Mr. Harvey arrived from Sydney, having heard of our Plight from the overseer who had been sent to summon the soldiers, and having at once ridden to our Assistance. This was not needed, since no more was heard of the escaped convicts (if, indeed, there were ever others besides Finn, for none was seen save him).

I must now pass to the second series of events which had been simultaneously taking place, unknown to us, at Sydney, and which accounted for the Military not having answered our summons. You will doubtless have heard from other Sources besides my letters, of the opposition Gov'r Bligh has met with from many of the leading inhabitants of the Colony, and in particular from the members of the New South Wales Corps. Mr. Harvey now brought us the astounding Intelligence that the Corps had mutinied, marched upon Government House, and forcibly deposed the Gov'r, whom they had placed (and still hold) in confinement. Rumour says that this business has been in Agitation for some time, and though Captain Abbott (who is Commanding Officer at Parramatta) denies having had knowledge of it until after it had taken place, the tale told by our Overseer of his reluctance to send a Detachment to our aid, and the nervous inattention of his Manner, incline me to suppose that he must have suspected, at least, that something was afoot.

You will wish to learn what effect all this will have upon my return to Ireland which, as you know, was decided upon before Mr. Mannion's death; and you may also suppose that now, deprived of my Husband, I shall be the more eager for departure, but this is not so. I am seriously inclined to the notion of remaining in the Colony for a time at least, and perhaps removing with the Children and Cousin Bertha to Mr. Mannion's house in Sydney, when Patrick has had time to arrange his domestic affairs here. This is a Course which may not meet with your approval, and will, I am sure, be Opposed by Mr. Mannion's Family, but I can see no grave obstacle to my adopting it.

Julia and Desmond grow fast and are both exceedingly Robust, which I attribute to the excellent Climate of this place; indeed neither of them has known a day's Illness. Dear Cousin Bertha, despite her age and Infirmities, remains cheerful, and her goodness and Affection have greatly comforted me during this distressing Time.

I know not when this letter may reach you, for we have no certain news of any vessel sailing, and indeed it is said that those now in Power here are not anxious for news of their actions to reach England before they shall have arranged their Plans. I shall entrust it to our good friend Mr.

Robert Campbell, who will forward it by the first safe Opportunity, and meanwhile beg you to believe me, my dear Grandpapa,

With all love and duty,

Your affectionate grandchild,

CONOR MANNION.

P.S. Upon reading this I fear you will discern a want of Feeling, and perhaps be surprised that I do not more openly disclose a degree of Grief which might be expected in one so recently and tragically Widowed. I trust I am not wanting in natural Sensibility, but cannot pretend that my regard for Mr. Mannion exceeded that sense of duty which is proper in a Wife.

*   *   *   *

March 25th, 1808. To-day I learned that Ellen has suffered Execution for the murder of my Husband. Here where no eye but mine shall see the words I write, I confess my pity for her, and my comprehension, in some part, of her unhappiness; for my Husband was not a kindly man. Yet I still feel that there was some Mystery in this affair which we have been unable to fathom. There has been that in Patrick's distress and Agitation which, I believe, goes beyond what would be natural in a son suddenly deprived of his Father. I cannot now prevail on him to talk to me. He is moody and silent, and keeps himself much secluded.

We have been so much occupied here at Beltrasna with our own Troubles that we have paid but little regard to the extraordinary Occurrences at Sydney, and indeed throughout the Colony, in the past two months. When Mr. Harvey rode hither on the night of Mr. Mannion's death, and informed us that Gov'r Bligh had been overthrown, I must confess that the news made but little impression on me, shocked as I was by the events which had taken place here on that day. But now, as time passes, I am disturbed by the tidings which come to us, and wonder how all this Tumult can end.

Gov'r Bligh, it appears, is still held a Prisoner in his house, and all those who have been his supporters are in fear of Persecution. Letters I have received from Mrs. Palmer and Sophia Campbell tell of Interrogations undergone by their Husbands at the hands of the rebel Faction, and express the gravest fears for the future. They say that Mr. Macarthur (whom they regard as the prime mover, and Col. Johnston as but his Tool) desires to send the Gov'r to England in Mr. Macarthur's ship, the *Dart,* which he, fearing for his safety, declines, demanding to be put in possession of H.M.S. Porpoise, and great Arguments are in train upon this Matter. . . .

April 18th, 1808. To-day Patrick returned from a visit to Sydney. He says that Mr. Macarthur, whom he saw there, was somewhat distant in his

Manner at first, which Patrick attributes to the fact that he, Patrick, had declined to sign a document calling for the deposition of the Gov'r after that event had already had taken place. However, he later became more Cordial, at which Patrick was relieved, for he is sensitive to Discord. For myself, I suspect that Mr. Macarthur conceives that he may yet win Patrick to his Party, in which I judge he will be disappointed; for Patrick—though he is of a somewhat pliable Nature, and might well come under the influence of so vigorous and determined a character were he in Sydney, yet has so great a dislike of being embroiled in argument and Dissention, that I feel sure he will embrace the Seclusion offered by this place, and remain aloof from all Publick quarrels.

Upon his return journey he called upon Mrs. Macarthur at Parramatta to deliver a note from her Husband, who appears to be greatly involved in affairs at Sydney. She read aloud a sentence from the note, in which Mr. Macarthur declared he had been deeply engaged in contending for the liberties of the Colony; but it would appear that different people have different ideas upon the subject of Liberty, for I learn that the settlers at the Hawkesbury have prepared an Address to be forwarded to Col. Paterson at Port Dalrymple, praying him to return and assume the Government, and speaking of Mr. Macarthur in terms of the strongest Reprobation. Patrick himself, though unwilling to censure such friends as Mr. Macarthur, Col. Johnston, the Blaxlands and Dr. Townson, appears disturbed by some of the measures which have been adopted, and which I cannot but feel to be highly Illiberal, and even Tyrannous. . . .

May 5th, 1808. Have received a letter from Sophia Campbell in which she informs me that Mr. Campbell has sent our letters by the *Dart,* which, after many delays, sailed the 17th of last month, and in which Mr. Edward Macarthur, together with Mr. Grimes, travelled to England, taking despatches from Col. Johnston. She also tells me that Gov'r Bligh, though greatly anxious to get his own despatches home, feared to send them by the *Dart* owing to its being Mr. Macarthur's ship, lest they should be landed again, and given to Col. Johnston instead. They have now been sent by the *Brothers,* which sailed a few days ago. The Gov'r also entertained doubts of this vessel by reason of its being the Blaxlands', but Sophia confides in me that her husband gave them into the care of the Master in the guise of a packet of mercantile Papers for which he obtained a Receipt, and by this Ruse they will probably arrive safely. It appears that the Usurpers are already at Odds among themselves. . . .

June 24th, 1808. We hear that the *Cumberland* has arrived, bringing intelligence that Col. Foveaux is on his way hither from England, and, as Col. Johnston's superior officer, will take the Command on his arrival.

Things remain greatly disordered, and we hear much disquieting news. Gov'r Bligh is still under restraint. Mr. Gore, who has long been imprisoned owing to his having been of the Gov'r's Party, has now been transported to the Coal River; Mr. Campbell has come to the relief of his wife and children, who would otherwise be left destitute. . . .

August 2nd, 1808. Col. Foveaux has arrived in the *Sinclair,* and I trust may restore some degree of Order, though already it seems evident that he inclines to the Rebels. We learn that upon the arrival of the vessel Gov'r Bligh immediately sent Mr. Palmer, Mr. Griffin and the Rev. Mr. Fulton to wait upon him, but they were not permitted on board, though Col. Johnston, Mr. Macarthur, and others of their Party were received, and remained on board the greater part of the Day. Am at a loss to understand why Col. Paterson does not return from Port Dalrymple and assume the Command, he being the Lieutenant-Governor, and surely the proper Person to do so? Patrick declares that he prefers to remain out of Trouble, which I suspect may be the Truth, remembering his peaceable Nature, and his former strained relations with Mr. Macarthur when he was wounded in a Duel, and also his indifferent Health.

It appears that while Gov'r Bligh's adherents are being harshly used, those who support Col. Johnston are being rewarded in a manner which seems to indicate an improper Partiality, receiving large grants of Land and other Indulgences; which, to the reflecting Mind, cannot but suggest the existence of Motives other than those of Duty, which they profess. . . .

Sept. 6th, 1808. The *Estramina* has sailed for Port Dalrymple, and it is said that Col. Paterson may return on her. Much argument is taking place between Gov'r Bligh and Col. J. on the subject of the former's return to England—he still declining to go save on the *Porpoise,* and they being unwilling to permit him the command of that Vessel.

Sept. 8th, 1808. One of our overseers, having this day returned from Sydney, where he delivered a letter from me to Sophia Campbell, brought back a reply from her containing news of poor Mrs. Putland, who suffers great anxiety from the plight her Father finds himself in, and expresses violent indignation against his Opponents. Sophia writes: "Mrs. P. says the Governor is as well as his Circumstances permit, deprived as he is of his Liberty and his Command, and harassed every day by impudent demands and insulting Communications from his Usurpers. He would much like to return to England, there to lay the details of this terrible Affair before the proper Authorities, but his strong sense of Duty urges upon him the question: How far a Governor can with Honour quit his Post until he receives permission from His Majesty? Mrs. P. declares that this thought weighs heavily upon his Mind; and that conceiving no purpose can be served by further Negotiations with the Villains who have deposed him, nor with Foveaux, who supports them, he has written directly to Colonel Paterson, calling upon him to suppress the Mutiny in his Corps." I hope that this may bring some results, but hardly expect it.

October 12th, 1808. I am greatly disturbed about Patrick who, for the last month, appears to have grown increasingly Moody. Before the Winter set in I had already suggested to him that I should remove from here with Cousin Bertha and the Children to the Sydney house, but noting that he seemed in poor spirits did not press the Matter, thinking that Solitude would only add to his Melancholy. Was therefore much surprised to-day when he mentioned the subject himself, and conveyed, without actually saying so, that he would prefer to be alone. I feel, though not without some Misgivings, that it will be best to fall in with his wishes; nor can I say with Truth that it would be against my own inclinations, since such Seclusion as we experience here has never been to my Taste. This Property, moreover, passed entirely to Patrick upon his Father's death, the Sydney house and an Income being mine so long as I remain a Widow, and the Irish Estates being divided between Patrick, Miles, and my own two dear Children upon their coming of Age. So I shall shortly say farewell to Beltrasna, and though its beauties have often given me pleasure I shall leave it without a Sigh. The liveliness and interests of a Town are more suited to my Temperament, as they are to Cousin Bertha's, despite her age. Moreover, the Children will in Sydney more easily find Playmates. But as I write these things I am aware of dissembling even to myself, and compel my Pen to confess that my desire to live in Town is not unconnected with my desire to see Mr. Harvey. . . .

October 16th, 1808. The *Estramina* has returned—but without Col. Paterson, the reason given being the bad state of his Health, and the poor Accommodation on that Vessel; he requests that the *Porpoise* be sent for him, which will be done.

November 2nd, 1808. Have been occupied in arranging matters here so that Patrick will have no household Difficulties when we are gone. I travelled to Sydney last week where I not only effected some preparations in the House there, but engaged and brought back with me a very suitable Sort of Woman called Mrs. Emmett as Housekeeper and Cook. She has a daughter of about eighteen years called Hattie who will act as Housemaid, and with the assistance of Maria, Patrick will have a modest Establishment which will be sufficient for his Needs—at least until he marries, which I trust may be soon. Met with some slight Trouble from Mrs. Emmett by reason of her disinclination to associate with poor Maria, she saying with Indignation that she has not been accustomed to mix herself with the Daughters of Murderesses. This attitude I was bound to oppose, and was supported by Patrick, for Maria's Husband is a useful Man; and indeed Maria herself has changed much for the Better since her Marriage, and particularly since the birth last year of her little boy, Simeon. I flatter myself that I have allayed Mrs. E.'s fears, and that all will go along smoothly.

I had assumed that Dilboong would be one of my Household in Sydney, but she begs to be permitted to stay here. This surprises me, for she has always shown a great Affection for the Children, and also for Cousin Bertha. She asks me repeatedly for news of Miles, to whom she was passionately devoted when they were both Children, and it occurs to me that her untutored Mind may harbour some thought that only by remain-ing here will she see him when he returns. Patrick declares himself in-different upon the Matter, but says she should stay if she wishes it, and that Natives become profoundly attached to a place where they have lived for a long time. This may be so, and I shall not attempt to persuade her further. . . .

*   *   *   *

MRS. MANNION TO MRS. ROBERT CAMPBELL.

Beltrasna,
November 30th, 1808.

My dearest Sophia,

All is arranged, and we are to remove to Sydney next week, when I promise myself the great pleasure of seeing you again. The Children are much excited, and Julia asks frequently about your little Boys, and when she shall be able to live with them. I have promised that she shall have a Party on Christmas Day; as you know, this is also her Birthday, which makes it an especially great occasion, and I trust you will bring little John and Robert to share its Delights with her. . . .

MRS. MANNION TO MR. MARK HARVEY.

Beltrasna,
December 3rd, 1808.

Dear Mr. Harvey,

I write to apprise you of the news that I am shortly to be in Sydney, not merely for a brief visit, as hitherto, but to reside there with Cousin Bertha and my Children. You will easily imagine that I look forward with Pleasure to this Change, and the opportunities it will afford me of seeing more of my Friends, among whom I number yourself.

The Harvest is going forward here, and Patrick is, of course, greatly occupied. Cousin Bertha remains as well as can be expected, and not even Julia speaks with more Animation of our Removal. I trust the disturbing Events of the past Year have not had an adverse effect upon your School? But I shall hope to hear a full Account from you before long, and in the meantime subscribe myself

Your sincere Friend,
CONOR MANNION.

*   *   *   *

January 1st, 1809. In the bustle and disorder of our departure from Beltrasna my Journal has been again sadly neglected. Now we are settled in our new home (to which I have given the name of Moore House, in remembrance of my Father) and upon this first day of the New Year I am resolved to be more regular in my entries.

I have secured a Mrs. Bodley for Cook, and Patrick has insisted that I bring with me young Shawn Morgan for Coachman, who, by a fortunate chance, is but lately married to a young Woman named Flora, the daughter of a respectable Settler in the Toongabbee district, and she performs the duties of Housemaid with great Willingness, if but little Address, though I doubt not she will improve. These, with Bessie for the Children, and an elderly convict called Holmes who comes each day to tend the Garden, make up my little Establishment. Sophia tells me that the Girls at the Orphanage are trained for Needlework, and take in plain sewing for such Ladies as desire it, about which I must enquire further soon.

Julia's Party passed off very well on Christmas Day, and she was greatly delighted with her Presents, and still more with her young Guests. I fancied that Patrick (who rode hither to spend Christmas with us) looked a little put out when I told him that I had invited Mr. Harvey to be among those to sit down to dinner; but I am now my own Mistress, and shall do as I please. Mrs. Bodley acquitted herself well, but I suspect that the roast Turkeys and Mincemeats and plum Puddings appropriate to the Christmas festival at home, are hardly suited to this Climate. The day was very hot.

I made an Occasion for some private conversation with Mr. Harvey, and am consumed with a burning Indignation on account of certain Matters which he revealed to me only upon my most urgent Questioning. I had been troubled to find him looking thin and unwell, and was still more so to learn that for months past his School had been Closed, which leaves him with barely any means of Subsistence beyond the small sum he receives from Mr. Campbell for his services as Clerk. This (though he obstinately denies it) cannot be adequate, and indeed it is plain that his Health has suffered.

The reason for this change in his fortunes is, it seems, that he declined putting his name to that same Document which Patrick also rejected, and this (together with his being in the employment of Mr. Campbell) has marked him as a supporter of Gov'r Bligh. If he is right in this, which I greatly fear, what fresh and dreadful Light it throws upon the methods which may be employed by those in Power to bring about the Downfall of their Opponents! And with what Malice they pursue even those who, by reason of obscurity and modest Circumstances are in no position to embarrass them, but are nevertheless marked down for Persecution merely because they are suspected of Sentiments which are not Approved! For it appears that, having no just cause for hostility towards Mr. Harvey (who, indeed, is modest and self-effacing to a fault) they have moved against him in a sly and hidden Manner which to me seems even more unworthy than open Oppression. The man who owns the little building where Mr. Harvey conducted his School approached him the day following his refusal to sign the Paper, and declared that the Building might no longer be rented, since it was required for other Purposes. In great Concern (but at first suspecting nothing) Mr. Harvey urged that he might be permitted to retain it at least until he had secured other Accommodation, representing the needs of his Scholars, and the ill effects of an interruption to their Studies. Upon this, the man (who appears to be a worthy enough Fellow) drew him aside, and protested that, for his part, he would be willing to leave Mr. Harvey in possession; but he owed a considerable Debt to an Officer, by whom he had just been informed that he would not be pressed for repayment if he immediately made available the Building in question, in which the Officer desired to store some of his possessions. Mr. Harvey, whose simple and Upright nature makes him slow to scent Villainy, begged to know whether some other Place might not serve the Officer as well for a storeroom; whereupon his Companion laid a Finger to his Nose, and, regarding Mr. Harvey with a strange Look, enquired: Whether it were not true that he had yesterday declined to sign a certain Paper? and added in a tone of great Meaning: "Nowadays it's best not to cross the Lobsters, Sir!"

Thus, for almost a year, Mr. Harvey has had no place to house his School, several other buildings (though none near so well adapted for the Purpose) having been refused to him on various Pretexts. He speaks with gratitude of Mr. Campbell, who has continued to employ him as a clerk, and who—being a prominent and active supporter of Gov'r Bligh— himself suffers much under the present Rulers. Not only has he been dismissed from his post as Naval Officer, but he is continually harassed and annoyed in his business Concerns, and his Debtors are withholding moneys owed to him, conceiving that they may safely do so now that he is out of Favour with those in Power.

I found Mr. Harvey also deeply concerned for his friend, Mr. George Suttor, who has been thrown into gaol for a term of six Months. I had read of the trial of this Gentleman in the *Gazette*, and could not forbear to admire the spirited Manner in which he denied the legality of the Court, and stated that his allegiance was to Gov'r Bligh. The Cause of the Trial was given out to be a Letter which he wrote to Col. Foveaux, protesting that he and his Labourers should not be summoned to attend a Muster at the height of the Harvest; but Mr. H. considered that the Animosity with which he had been pursued is connected with his having been chosen as a Delegate to proceed to England on behalf of the Hawkes-bury settlers, there to set out their Complaints against the present Rulers. I begin to learn a little of these Political Matters, in which it appears that even those who loudly denounce Tyranny, themselves readily become Tyrants when the reins of Government are in their hands.

At last, after much reluctance and many delays, Col. Paterson has only this day arrived on board H.M.S. *Porpoise* to relieve Col. Foveaux; but there is much comment upon the manner of his arrival, which was not in the usual way at Sydney Cove, but near the entrance of the Harbour, whence he was driven to Town by Lieutenant Lawson. It is supposed that he had reason to believe that the Gov'r would order the Captain of the *Porpoise* to put him under an Arrest, and therefore took this means to disembark before it could be accomplished.

I have seen Mrs. Putland but once; she is so very vehement and passionate that I do not feel it easy or profitable to converse with her upon the present state of affairs. She now numbers Col. Foveaux one of the worst of her Father's enemies, and expects no better of Col. Paterson. Yet I recall my voyage hither when Col. P. was my fellow-traveller, and find nothing in my memory save a mild and amiable Gentle-man, truly desirous of performing his Duty faithfully. It would appear that there is that in Publick life and Office which often causes mild-natured men to act against their true Inclinations; I suspect this may also be true of Col. Johnston, whom I think a Booby, but a harmless one were he left to himself. Yet the man of strong mind and Purpose who gains Office by his ambitions uses that Office for his own Advancement. Who, then, is fit for Office? Surely only he who does not desire it, but accepts it in a true spirit of service; who possesses principles sufficiently firm to withstand the pressures of those who would use him, and acts always in conformity with his Conscience? Must contrive an opportunity to speak of this with Mr. Harvey. . . .

January 28th, 1809. Much gossip and speculation in the Town con-cerning the Conflict now taking place between the Gov'r and Col.

Paterson regarding the disposal of the *Porpoise*. The Gov'r is very anxious to keep control over this ship, which his enemies are equally determined to prevent, and he therefore wrote to the Captain (immediately upon the vessel's arrival here at the beginning of the month) directing him to place himself and his Ship under the Gov'r's Command, and to take Orders from no other Person. Now, however, Col. Paterson directs Captain Porteous to proceed to Norfolk Island, which the Capt. declines, and which has so incensed Col. P. that he has forbidden any further communication between Captain Porteous and the Governor. Yesterday, so I am informed, Captain Porteous waited upon the Gov'r at Government House, but was turned away by the centinels, and there are rumours that the Gov'r is to be sent home in the *Admiral Gambier*. . . .

January 30th, 1809. Sophia Campbell has quitted me but half an hour since, having disclosed to me the most remarkable proceedings of this day. In the forenoon Major Johnston and Captain Abbott were sent by Col. P. to Government House, bearing a Communication to Gov'r Bligh. Sophia is not in any certain Manner aware of the contents of this Document, but from her knowledge of the situation she surmises that it took the form of further pressure upon the Gov'r to release the *Porpoise*, that it might be sent to Norfolk Island. She declares that the Rebels are apprehensive that Assistance for the Governor may arrive from England at any time, and are therefore impatient to get him away from this place; but not in command of an armed Vessel. Gov'r Bligh, for his part, wishes to get possession of the Ship (his authority as a Naval Officer being now all that remains to him) but is still reluctant to quit the Colony without orders from home, and also because he conceives that his presence here, though in so helpless a State, is an embarrassment to the Usurpers, and places some slight restraint upon their Conduct. Thus Sophia is persuaded that the purpose of this morning's visit was to urge the Gov'r upon pain of harsher Confinement, and separation from all his friends and Supporters, to abandon his claims upon the *Porpoise*. In this Design they evidently failed, for the Gov'r was about midday brought forth without ceremony, and forced to enter the Chaise in which Major J. and Capt. Abbott had arrived, which then drove away. Immediately afterwards poor Mrs. Putland, suffering the most intense distress and Agitation at this treatment of her Parent, ran hatless and distraught from Government House, crying out: "I am going with my Father!" In the burning heat of the day she ran after the Chaise, which fortunately proceeded no farther than Mr. Finucane's barrack, and here, seizing hold of the Gov'r's arm, she accompanied him into this poor lodging where centinels were placed to guard them, and where Col. Johnston and Col. Foveaux directed the proceedings.

Sophia was almost in Tears as she disclosed to me this Ordeal which her friend had suffered. Upon hearing of it, her brother, Mr. Palmer, ordered his Carriage and drove to the place with his wife, demanding admittance to the Prisoners, but they were rudely driven off by the Centinels, one of whom is a certain Sergeant Whittle who, so Sophia informs me, was conspicuous in the deposition of the Gov'r a year ago, and whom she describes as a Nasty Villain.

It appears that Captain Porteous is now hand in Glove with the rebels and, while taking pains not to set down in writing anything but what shows him obedient to the orders of his Commodore, he has been quite won over to the other Party, while grants of land have been made to him and other officers of the Ship, and every Indulgence given them in order to divide them from the Gov'r, and unite them with the Rebel cause.

February 4th, 1809. To-day Governor Bligh and Mrs. Putland returned to Government House from the Barrack where they had been confined. Do not know whether this signifies that some Accommodation has been reached between him and the rebels. Trust I shall soon learn more of it from Sophia. . . .

February 7th, 1809. This morning I drove out with Sophia and the Children in our Carriage, and she confided to me the events of the past few days. Daily expecting succour to arrive from England for Governor Bligh, Col. P. is in great haste to get him away, which it is believed he intends to compass at all Costs. During his confinement in the Barrack the Gov'r had agreed to embark on the *Admiral Gambier,* but learning that Major Johnston and Mr. Macarthur were also to be passengers, he strongly objected to sailing in their Company, and thus his enemies were once more at a loss. Sophia declares that a Plan was then hatched to permit the *Gambier* to sail without the Gov'r, but with orders to bring to off Botany Bay, where the Gov'r would be conveyed by night, and forced on board. It was, however, abandoned, Col. P. being afraid, in his delicate Situation, to resort to Force unless all other means failed. Governor Bligh was therefore presented with a Paper (already signed by the Colonel) in which he was to agree to embark with his Family on board the *Porpoise* on the 20th, and sail as soon thereafter as the wind and weather would permit. He was also to undertake that he would proceed direct to England without touching at any other port in this Colony, and that he would in no manner interfere with the present Government; Col. P. for his part agreeing to permit him to return to Gov't House, to communicate with his friends, and to take to England with him such people as he may require to give evidence on his behalf.

Among these, of course, will be Sophia's brother, and perhaps her husband also.

In this Predicament, and fearing that should he decline to sign the Paper he would be put forcibly on board the *Gambier,* thus losing the last opportunity of gaining the Command of his ship, the Gov'r put his name to it, and is now engaged in making his preparations for departure. . . .

February 10th, 1809. To-day, during a drive abroad with the Children, came upon Mr. Harvey walking near the Fortifications, and allowed the Children to alight and play while I talked with him for a while. I took this opportunity to open my Mind to him upon a subject which has occupied it during the last few days since I heard of a Cottage for sale near the Common, and past which I had directed Morgan to drive me only an hour before. It is by no means handsome or commodious, yet for lack of something better it would serve for a School, and my Plan is to purchase it, and then make it available to Mr. Harvey. This he at first declined with some heat; but upon my pointing out that he could pay me a Rental equal to that paid for his other building, and that I could again sell it when he no longer had need of it, he agreed with some reluctance, though with many expressions of gratitude, to consider the Proposal. . . .

February 13th, 1809. I have this day received a note from Mrs. Macarthur inviting me to visit her, and, though greatly inclined to do so (not having seen her for many months), have excused myself. How painfully these Publick turmoils act upon private Friendships! For I have indeed a regard for Mrs. M., yet cannot feel the same for her Husband, and therefore do not wish to run the risque of meeting him in her Presence, lest my disapprobation of his Conduct should reveal itself, and cause a Coolness between us. When he has sailed for England I shall feel more free to renew my pleasant association with her. She tells me that her two remaining boys, James and William, who are but eleven and nine years old, are to go with their Father; what fortitude she displays in thus parting with her Children for such long periods! Edward and John are already in England, and she will be left with her three Girls only; and poor Elizabeth, who is now a young Woman, and would in happier Circumstances have been a great Support to her, is so gravely ill as to be but an additional source of Anxiety. Mary, I trust, will be her Mother's aid and companion. Little Emmeline I have not seen since soon after her birth; she is said to be her Father's Darling. How strange a character is that Man—all fondness and softness towards his Family, and yet so ruthless and unyielding in his conduct towards others! . . .

February 16th, 1809. . . . . Yesterday I consulted with Mr. Campbell upon the question of the Cottage I wish to purchase. Was greatly encouraged to find that he regards the Plan with approval, not merely as a means of providing Mr. Harvey with a School, but to advance my own Fortunes! He declares that the value of Property in the Town must increase, and that such a purchase would in time prove a good Investment. How fortunate that I have as my Counsellor so shrewd and astute a man of Business, for these arguments, which I have endeavoured to memorise carefully, are surely such as will persuade Mr. Harvey to accept my Proposal!

February 22nd, 1809. To-day it is common Gossip that Mr. Palmer is not permitted to go with Gov'r Bligh—nor any others! Recalling Sophia's account of the Agreement made between the Gov'r and Col. Paterson, I find this very Strange, and hardly to be believed. . . .

*　　　　*　　　　*　　　　*

MRS. MANNION TO MR. PATRICK MANNION.

Moore House,
Sydney,
March 6th, 1809.

My dear Patrick,

It is now more than two months since we have seen you, and I trust no untoward Circumstance has prevented you from coming to Sydney, for we had hoped to receive a Visit from you before now.

In my last letter I informed you to the best of my Ability upon the state of Affairs here, but there is so much Rumour, and most of it so clearly informed by self-interest and the spirit of Party, that I do not always know what to believe.

The *Porpoise* still remains in the Harbour with the Gov'r on board, which causes much talk and speculation, suggestions being made that Col. P. and his Friends now regret having permitted him out of their Custody, and that they are concerting Plans with the Officers of the Ship to remove him, but I cannot speak as to the Truth of this.

I trust that Mrs. Emmett continues to your Satisfaction, and that your Harvest being now completed, you may have more leisure, some of which I hope you will employ in visiting us. I am deeply interested in your remarks concerning the Narrative Poem on which you are engaged, and which I hope to read when it is completed. . . .

*　　　　*　　　　*　　　　*

Monday, March 13th, 1809. To-day Mr. Harvey called upon me at my request that I might consult further with him on the subject of his School. As I had anticipated, the arguments provided for me by Mr.

Campbell have prevailed, and with that Gentleman's kind Assistance, the business will now go forward.

I learned from Mr. Harvey that there is much hidden Activity among the Governor's party and their opponents, both sides ceaselessly intriguing to gain the Advantage. Mr. Harvey has himself on several occasions rowed out to the *Porpoise* in a Boat at dead of Night to deliver papers and Messages to the Governor, and declares that the other Party also sends emissaries on board to confer with the ship's Officers, all of whom support them, and are willing to combine with them in any Strategem save direct disobedience to the orders of their Commodore, which would of course bring about their Ruin. Thus the Gov'r, though in possession of his Ship, has no person on board upon whom he can Rely, and can therefore accomplish nothing by remaining here. Mr. Harvey says the *Porpoise* has already left her former Moorings, but says he has information that she will not leave the Harbour yet. . . .

Saturday, March 18th, 1809. Mercy on us, what next! Have to-day received a visit from Sophia who is in great distress at the sudden Arrest of her Brother, and also of Mr. Hook, who is a partner in her Husband's mercantile Business. It appears that last evening, having Intelligence that the Gov'r was about to sail, and that before doing so he wished to issue a Proclamation, these Gentlemen went out to the *Porpoise* and received copies of this Document, which they distributed among all the Masters of the ships in Port. Sophia left with me a copy of this Proclamation, which I now transcribe:

"I hereby publickly proclaim the New South Wales Corps to be in a state of mutiny and rebellion, now under Colonel Paterson's command; and I do forbid any master or masters of ships, at their peril, taking any person or persons connected, or supposed to be connected, in the rebellion out of the country or its dependencies to any place whatever, either in or out of His Majesty's dominions, particularly any Officers of the said Corps, or John Macarthur (settler), Nicholas Bayly, Garnham Blaxcell, Richard Atkins, Gregory Blaxland, John Townson, Robert Townson, Robert Fitz, Thomas Jamison, Thomas Hobby, Alexander Riley, d'Arcy Wentworth, James Mileham, Thomas Moore, and Walter Stephenson Davidson.

Given under my hand on board His Majesty's ship *Porpoise*, Port Jackson, New South Wales, this 12th day of March, 1809.

WILLIAM BLIGH."

For distributing this Paper, Mr. Palmer and Mr. Hook were taken into Custody and brought before a Bench which has committed them for

Trial before a Criminal Court. (Sophia, in a great Passion, declared: "A court of Criminals, is what they should say!")

The Governor also left in Mr. Palmer's charge a letter to the Commanding Officer of the force which, he confidently expects, will soon arrive from England to overthrow the Rebels. In this he declares his intention of removing to the Derwent in order to frustrate the design of his enemies to sieze his Person; but this Sophia revealed to me only under a pledge of the strictest Secresy.

Greatly astonished, I recalled to her the Agreement which the Gov'r had signed, whereby he undertook to proceed directly to England without touching at any other port in the Colony, but Sophia says he conceives that in order to regain his Liberty he is justified in any expedient; that the good of His Majesty's Service is not to be put in jeopardy by keeping faith with unscrupulous Rogues; and that he will not quit the office or the territory entrusted to him without clear orders from his Sovereign. At this I was deeply shocked and confused, and am still reluctant to believe that any solemn undertaking should not be Honoured. Upon my expressing this view, Sophia exclaimed: That Col. Paterson had already broken the Agreement by refusing to permit her Brother to sail; which must be allowed. Yet to what a Pass would Morals be reduced were we to concede that the Perfidy of others excuses our own! Nevertheless, I am bound to admit that the course taken by the Governor, if not in accord with the highest Principles, is yet, in his desperately embarrassed situation, an instance of human Frailty which the understanding Mind will not too harshly condemn.

Sophia also reveals that it has been known for some time among the Governor's closest Adherents that he did not intend to sail for England, but on the contrary to delay here as long as possible in the hope that Assistance would arrive, which she believes he may still do for some days, cruising outside the Heads. But by reason of the Disaffection of his Officers, and fearing that they may combine with the rebels to take him out of his Ship, he will probably soon feel himself compelled to retire to Hobart Town. This, she declares, will cause great Astonishment and Chagrin among some on board, who believe themselves bound for England.

Sunday, March 19th, 1809. Col. Paterson has issued a Proclamation forbidding any person to hold any communication whatever with the Governor, and denouncing "certain wicked and evil-disposed persons" (by which he means Mr. Palmer and Mr. Hook) for distributing what is described as a "libelous and inflammatory paper".

There was a time when I should, upon reading such phrases, have believed them, merely from Ignorance that during periods of violent

Dissention, words, no less than Deeds, are employed by each Faction to incite hatred of the other among the common people. Yet when each Party cries Villain at the other, and each man denounces his opponent as a Liar, and statements are held wise and just if they emanate from one's own Party, but wicked and inflammatory if from the other—is not the Publick mind thrown into dangerous confusion, and Truth entirely confounded? . . .

Tuesday, March 21st, 1809. Have but an hour ago returned from Sophia's house, whither I hastened upon hearing that the Criminal Court has sentenced Mr. Palmer to three months' Imprisonment, and Mr. Hook to one month, together with fines of Fifty pounds for each. They denied the competency of the Court, but this was of course not attended to, and they are now in Gaol. Mrs. Palmer was also at Sophia's house, and I was able in some measure, I hope, to calm their fears.

A signal from the Lookout Post on South Head reports the *Porpoise* still in the vicinity of the Harbour, and therefore Col. Paterson has for-bidden the *Perseverance* to sail, this vessel being owned by Mr. Campbell, and the Colonel no doubt fearing some communication with the Governor by his friends. . . .

March 23rd, 1809. The *Admiral Gambier* is ready to sail, but its principal passengers (who are Mr. Macarthur, Major Johnston, and Messrs. Harris, Jamison and Davidson) are in a state of considerable Alarm lest the *Porpoise* should intercept them when they leave the harbour, and the sailing is thus delayed. . . .

March 28th, 1809. . . . . The *Gambier* has sailed at last, from which I judge that Gov'r Bligh's ship must have quitted these waters. I cannot but feel some Doubt as to the wisdom of the Governor in thus permitting his Enemies to reach England with their Story before him. Mr. Macarthur is a master of so many arts and stratagems. . . .

It is said that Col. Paterson has learned by some means that the *Porpoise* is proceeding to the Derwent, and that he will send a copy of his Proclamation to Lieut.-Governor Collins at that place by the *Æolus.* If Col. Collins pays attention to it, I fear the Governor's situation at Hobart Town will be hardly more easy than here. . . .

May 27th, 1809. . . . .. Many reports are coming in to the Town touching the calamitous rising of the Hawkesbury River in the last few days, whereby stock is said to be lost, and much of the ground recently cropped laid waste. This Disaster is attributed to the bursting of a Cloud in the Mountains, since but little rain has fallen in the Hawkesbury district of late. Have heard nothing from Beltrasna of how they are faring, but trust that the elevated situation of the property may save all but the lower fields from Inundation. . . .

May 29th, 1809. More trouble for poor Sophia! Mr. Campbell is now brought before a Bench upon an absurd Pretext, and committed for Trial, but is liberated on bail. Sophia (her Brother being still in Gaol) now fears that her Husband may be similarly confined. Indeed I cannot imagine what the Authorities at home are about, that they permit the Colony to remain so long in this alarming and disordered State!

June 7th, 1809. Mr. Campbell this day brought before the Court, and declined to plead, or to acknowledge the legality of the proceedings. To the surprise and relief of his wife and his friends, he was sentenced only to a fine of £50. Although it is said that Col. P. is angered because no term of imprisonment was ordered, the release a few days since of Mr. Palmer (who had not yet served his full sentence) inclines me to think that the rebel Party fears to act in too arbitrary a Manner as the time approaches when it must be called to Account. . . .

Sunday, July 2nd, 1809. . . . To-day's *Gazette* contains an interesting account of Brigadier Nightingall, who has been appointed to succeed Governor Bligh, and who is expected to sail from England shortly. To my own way of thinking, he should have been here months ago, if they were resolved not to reinstate Governor Bligh.

I have received letters from my Grandpapa, from Miles, and from Mr. Mannion's Mother. From Mrs. Mannion's I learn that Grandpapa visited her a week or two before his letter was written, and though he does not mention this himself, I perceive in it a reason for expressions of opinion which would otherwise cause me some Astonishment. He has never liked that old Lady, calling her a Tyrant in Petticoats, Madam Midwinter, and other disdainful Names; and thus I surmise that, finding her mind implacably set against the notion of my remaining in the Colony, he has chosen to take the opposite View, and now applauds my decision, and even declares that he may himself come to visit me! Save for the Gout, he appears to be in robust health, despite his seventy-five years.

Mrs. Mannion's letter caused me some agitation at first, being written in a tone of cold censure, and accusing me of indifference to the welfare of *her grandchildren* (who, I shall make bold to point out, are also *my children!*) by detaining them in a place which she describes as "a Haunt of Vice and Violence, wholly unsuitable for Gentlefolk, other than those whose Duty compels their Presence." May kind Heaven forbid that she should ever have the moulding of their Minds!

Dear Miles, though expressing very proper sentiments of grief and horror at his Father's death, seems nevertheless to find great Entertainment in London (as indeed he would do anywhere, but makes no mention of his Studies). He assures me he does not forget the Colony, however, and looks forward to his return in a few years. He writes: "As you know, I leave Poetry and such Stuff to my Brother, but I have several times recalled some lines from the Poem by Mr. Scott which Patrick admired so much when it was printed here some few years ago, namely:

"Breathes there the man with soul so dead
Who never to himself hath said
   This is my own, my native land!
Whose heart hath ne'er within him burned
When home his footsteps he hath turned
   From wandering on a foreign strand!"

I can only trust that in his letters to his Grandmama he does not speak in such a Strain, or refer to this place as his own, his native land, for it would surely cause her to suffer a Paralytic Stroke!

Have also received a letter from Mrs. Marsden, who was in Yorkshire at the time of writing it, and who has added yet another Babe to her Family—a little Girl called Jane. Much of the letter devoted to this Infant, but she says her Husband has been ceaselessly employed in seeking suitable Clergymen to be sent hither. Also describes his Agitation at hearing of the Rebellion, when he immediately set out for London to lay his Views before the Authorities. It is well known that he has long entertained a vehement dislike of Mr. Macarthur, and his wife tells me he declares that either he or that Gentleman must quit the Colony, for it will not contain both. For my part, I should not greatly lament the loss of either. . . .

August 6th, 1809. . . . A grave scarcity of grain prevails in the Colony, which the present rulers attribute entirely to the recent Floods. No doubt these have played their part, but many declare it to be as much due to the measures pursued by the rebel Government in taking labour from the farms during the Harvest. Some go as far as to state that the Officers have desired to impede the development of Agriculture, since the farm of a ruined Settler may be more cheaply purchased, and since they are able to sell their own grain at a better Price if but little is produced by the settlers who are in a small Way. . . .

August 15th, 1809. Yesterday came in the *Boyd* from Cork, bringing me a letter from my Uncle Denis with the sad Intelligence of my dear Grandpapa's sudden death as the result of a severe Fall. This news, following his last letter in which he wrote with such Animation, has caused me much distress. My Uncle goes on to inform me that although the Estates are, of course, entailed upon him and his sons, my Grandfather has directed in his Will that much of his Furniture, Plate and China shall be mine, and asks if I wish it to be sent to me. He hopes, however, that I shall soon return to Ireland, and offers me the small house on the estate where, as he declares: "your Aunt and I would be ready to afford you and your Children our love and Protection." This is kindly meant, and I must frame my reply with care; but the truth is that I do not wish to be protected.

By the *Boyd* there also came a detachment of the 73rd Regiment, which is to replace the New South Wales Corps, bringing news that owing to illness Brig.-Gen. Nightingall will not come out as Governor after all, and a certain Colonel Macquarie is appointed in his stead. The present Expectation is that he will arrive in about a Month. . . .

Friday, August 18th, 1809. Another Vessel arrived to-day—the *Indispensable* from Portsmouth. I learn that there is a new clergyman come on board this ship with his wife and a young Family. His name is Cowper, and he comes with the recommendation of Mr. Marsden, who is himself expected to return shortly. . . .

Saturday, August 19th, 1809. . . . How I wish Patrick would come to Town! Such determined seclusion is not natural in so young a man. . . .

Saturday, September 23rd, 1809. The arrival of Col. Macquarie is now expected hourly. Have heard no more of how Gov'r Bligh fares at Hobart Town, but, recalling his confidence before sailing from here in March that aid from England was close at hand, I conclude that after six months his impatience must be almost transformed into despair! Col. Paterson spends most of his time at Government House, Parramatta, leaving the direction of affairs to Col. Foveaux; it is said that Col. P. is indulging himself too freely with Liquor. It will be a good day when Colonel Macquarie arrives, and I pray that he may be the kind of man who can restore order and tranquillity to this unhappy place.

Mrs. Macarthur has had word from her Husband at Rio, at which place he heard that Col. Macquarie had sailed from England, but was compelled to leave that port before his arrival. . . .

Thursday, December 28th, 1809. To-day the Town in an indescribable Tumult of excitement following the news that Colonel Macquarie has arrived! . . .

1810

ONLY the wind, blowing steadily from the West, failed to welcome the new Governor. H.M.S. *Hindostan* and the storeship *Dromedary* made the entrance to Port Jackson early in the morning of December 28th, 1809, and by ten o'clock they were anchored inside the Heads. A few miles up the harbour the news was greeted with joy by the inhabitants of Sydney, and by none more than by Lieutenant-Governor Paterson, to whom release from responsibility for this disorderly Colony could not come a moment too soon. But the wind, rushing strongly out of the heart of the continent, forbade their nearer approach, and dragged the vessels on their anchors as if it would blow them out to sea again.

His gracious Majesty King George the Third, having taken this lonely place for his own twenty-two years ago, had found himself under the tiresome necessity of maintaining it. Those of his Ministers who were, from time to time, charged with the duty of directing its progress, had conceded it a somewhat grudging and absent-minded attention, for events in the civilised world had been treading fast upon each other's heels, and, by comparison, the fate of a remote penal colony seemed trivial. Strange, potent doctrines were abroad; the long shadow of Napoleon lay over Europe; there was, naturally, little thought to spare for an insignificant outpost muddling through its early years so far from all that mattered.

Yet, like the troublesome, undisciplined infant that it was, it persistently claimed notice, and asserted (with what successive Secretaries of State considered a deplorable and unnecessary importunity) its turbulent and demanding existence. It struggled, it quarrelled, it starved, it recovered to struggle and quarrel again; it razed the trees and ploughed the virgin earth, it reaped its scant harvest and went hungry; it razed more trees and ploughed more earth, and sowed again, and fared a little better; it reared its first handful of livestock—and lo!—by degrees, entangled with the clamour of disputes and recriminations, there emerged the rumour that it was growing wool of quite excellent quality. . . .

At last! His Majesty's Ministers, though still finding it an embarrassment and an encumbrance, dared to hope that it might not remain an encumbrance for ever. They had need of this small comfort, for never a Governor's despatch arrived which was not loaded with requests. In the early days it had been food; stores, stores, stores—send us stores, or we starve! And throughout the years the demands had continued. Send us clothing, send us tools, send us medicines and blankets, send us beds, stoves, kettles, tubs, ploughs, lanthorns, ropes, handcuffs, legirons, paper, paint, candles . . . did they think the Treasury was bottomless? A procession of Secretaries of State, reading between the lines of these documents—so carefully phrased by a procession of Governors to reveal the difficulties under which they laboured, while stressing their own zeal and competence—faced the fact that the colony remained always on the verge of chaos. From their London offices (and always with one eye upon events nearer home) they instructed these harassed gentlemen; they admonished, they advised, they commended, they rebuked; they ordered, exhorted and deplored, they recalled and appointed. And still the colony went on struggling and muddling, went on working, idling, rebelling, trafficking, quarrelling and, above all, drinking.

But there it was, somewhere on the wrong side of the world—a distant, uncouth, unpredictable, unresponsive land whose effect upon transplanted Englishmen appeared to be disturbing; and it must be attended to, Napoleon or no Napoleon. And then, two years ago, that perpetual state of simmering turmoil in which it lived had suddenly boiled over; its fourth Governor, Captain William Bligh, had been deposed and imprisoned. . . .

Authority was scandalised into attention as complete as it could humanly be, with the Napoleonic challenge nearing a crisis. Rebellion against the King's representative! Yet even here, in its most stormy episode, the cantankerous place would not conform to pattern. For the classic form of rebellion—and even in this Authority liked tradition to be observed—was the uprising of the lower orders against their superiors. But there, in that upside-down world of Botany Bay—or New South Wales—or Australia, or whatever its name might finally turn out to be —it was the military force which rebelled; it was the soldiers, the official supporters of the Governor, who overthrew him. Confound the place, and its untidy uproars!

My Lord Castlereagh was greatly occupied with the appointment of Sir Arthur Wellesley to the command in Portugal. It was therefore not without some difficulty and annoyance that he was able to detach his mind from this urgent matter for long enough to appoint Brigadier-General Miles Nightingall to the command in New South Wales, and to decide that the 73rd Regiment, under Lieutenant-Colonel Macquarie, should accompany him to replace the mutinous Corps. Yet it appeared that no arrangement made for this perverse colony could run smoothly; the Governor-elect, after a period of waning enthusiasm for the honour bestowed on him, declined it, and all was to do again. In the gloomy pause that followed the voice of Macquarie was heard offering his services, and a sigh of relief ran softly round the Colonial Office. Well—why not? Clearly this post was unlikely to attract many candidates, and—considering the nature of the place, its distance from the amenities of civilisation, its unsavoury repute, and the fact that Governors were apt to return from it in a chastened mood—one could hardly be surprised. My Lord Castle-reagh, meeting Lieutenant-Colonel Macquarie by accident in the street, hastily informed him that he was the new Governor of New South Wales.

And so, in the month of May, while all England had ears and thoughts for nothing but the triumphant campaign in the Peninsular, the *Hindostan* and the *Dromedary* had set sail for the Antipodes.

*   *   *   *

Now the voyagers, seven months out from Portsmouth, found them-selves immobilised on the very threshold of their goal. There was nothing to see about them but the harbour and the surrounding hills, yet the scene, by its very unobtrusiveness, nagged at the eyes and mind. The great, indented expanse of water was just water, and they had seen too much of that to observe it now with any freshness of appreciation. Whipped into white-topped waves, and glittering restlessly under the midsummer sun, it broke against piled rocks on the shore, or upon golden, crescent-shaped beaches; and beyond it the hills rose.

These were the land; to these the eye turned, seeking climax, and fell away, puzzled. For Nature, here, had not employed her customary techniques for the fashioning of beauty and grandeur. She had flung up no towering mountains, nor had she splashed the landscape with vivid and dramatic colour. She had worked not only quietly, but (so one seemed to feel) with incredible deliberation, subduing line and tint to produce those low hills, clothed in a monotone of dull green, as if to prove that between the blues of the sea and heaven common to all lands, she could create a new beauty, and an unfamiliar grandeur.

Held there by the inhospitable wind, and denied for the moment a sight of the town, the newcomers almost felt this place as its first colonists had felt it twenty-two years ago. True, their feeling was modified by the knowledge that some sort of civilisation did exist only a few miles away, and by the sight of boats rowing down from it to bring them official greetings. But when the visitors had departed, and the brazen glow of sunset had faded from the water and the sky, the ancient quiet of centuries descended—so compelling that the land seemed to reveal itself more strongly in darkness than in daylight. Macquarie, recalling that he had once described it as "that land of exiles", felt suddenly that he knew what exile meant.

*   *   *   *

Among the many visitors from the outlying settlements who made their way to Sydney on the last day of 1809, young Mr. Patrick Mannion would probably have been counted the most blessed by Fortune. Not yet quite twenty-six years old, handsome, well dressed and well mounted, he was the owner of one of the most flourishing estates in the colony. He had set out very early, having a long ride before him, and the summer morning was not yet too hot. Sunlight lay brightly over the undulating, wooded countryside, and the curious, aromatic scents of the bush came pleasantly to his nostrils. Yet he frowned as he rode, and his blue eyes were sombre; this expedition to the capital—which most young men would have welcomed as an agreeable diversion—was something which he had forced himself to undertake, having fallen during the last two years into habits which were making him something of a hermit.

To a young man of sensibility, of a contemplative nature, and inclined to introspection, they had been painful years. Since that terrible night in January, 1808, when his private life and the social order which contained it had been simultaneously thrown into chaos—since the military faction had arrested Governor Bligh, and Mr. Stephen Mannion had fallen dead on the verandah of Beltrasna with a bullet in his heart—peace had forsaken him.

This memory was always like the stab of a knife, and now it sent a shock through his body so that his hand twitched on the reins, and his horse baulked in its even pace. He spurred it to a canter, as if by riding faster he might leave the thought behind, but he could not outdistance it. Since that time, he reflected, there had been nothing but conflict and disorder, both in his own mind and in the affairs of the colony. He abhorred conflict and disorder. He asked of his mind only that it devote itself to philosophical thought and the composition of poetry; and of society only that it function quietly, leaving him free to indulge his liking for such gentlemanly intellectual pursuits. His overpowering instinct during this time of chaos had been to retreat; the isolation of his property at the Nepean afforded him physical seclusion, and his nature turned only too easily to spiritual solitude. He was a conscientious young man, drilled from childhood to respect property, so he attended to the business of his estate, but in all those aspects of it which demanded trips to the larger settlements, and intercourse with his fellow-men, he had delegated responsibility more and more to his overseers, himself remaining invisible at Beltrasna. It had kept him out of the turmoils of the colony, but delivered him perilously to the turmoils of his own mind.

Who had fired that shot? Ride he never so fast, the question kept him company, and the answer would not be evaded. For he knew, if no one else did, and he had remained silent. He had obeyed the command in the eyes of a convict woman, and allowed her to hang for a crime she had not committed. At the last moment, when she was being taken from his house to certain execution, he, overcome with horror, had tried to speak. And she, watchful, had turned upon him like a fury, screaming imprecations against his father, reiterating her guilt, building up against herself such evidence that his own uncertain half-glimpse of someone else vanishing in the darkness while his father lay dead at her feet, could seem nothing but nonsense.

And yet he knew. Any lingering doubts which he might have cherished for his own comfort had been slain by the very frenzy and determination of her confession, and by the fierce, challenging demand in her eyes as they met his. He and she, and no other living soul, knew of a certain evening ten years ago when their conversation had ended with a promise. *"A secret, you said, Master Patrick . . . ?" "It's a secret, Ellen . . . I shall not speak of it. . . ."*

He had kept his promise, and his conscience would be tormented by it until he died, but it was not his only source of mental conflict. Dilboong, the native girl, Dilboong the black, ugly, awkward, docile member of an inferior race. . . . He had tried to see that business as a man of the world would see it; he was not the first white man to take a native woman for mistress, and he would not be the last. It was a mere incident, and one that was common enough. Yet it continued to trouble him. He, the eldest son of an old, proud, and wealthy family, cohabited with a black heathen, not even beautiful; and in a few months his child, a half-caste, would open its eyes upon the world. . . .

Again he tried to force his mind to a contemplation of more pleasing things. He had got his harvest in. He could flatter himself that he had done well enough in the management of his property, even if he did turn from it with relief to the more congenial world of books. And from to-day matters were surely going to improve for the colony as a whole. At last a new Governor had arrived; at last there would be an authority to which he could give his dutiful support with a clear conscience. He was still not sure that he entirely condemned Colonel Johnston and Mr. Macarthur and their followers, but he was disturbed by the incontrovertible fact that their administration was illegal. It was irregular, and he disliked irregularity. Now all that would be changed, and he had emerged from his retirement on this bright summer day to witness the transformation.

Arrived at Sydney, he found evidences of jubilation and excitement. As he came into the town itself he could hear the thunder of guns from the ships in the harbour answered from the battery on Dawes' Point, and knew that His Excellency must be coming ashore. He did not hurry. He called upon the postmaster, and, among a small bundle of letters just arrived from England, found one from his father's sister, his Aunt Frances, in whose London home first he, and then Miles, had been received. He rode up the hill past the Parade Ground and spent a few minutes watching the harbour—a scene of animation this morning, with flags fluttering, and small boats rowing busily about the two newly-anchored ships. He dismounted at last, found a rock to sit on, and read his letters. His Aunt Frances informed him in her exquisitely sloping hand that there was every reason to believe that a baronetcy would shortly be conferred upon her husband; gave him some gossip of her London life; demanded to know when his stepmother proposed to return to civilisation with her children; bemoaned his own decision to remain in the colony; begged him to send her a parroquet and a bronzewing pigeon; and declared at length that Miles was wholly irresponsible, ". . . though I must say that your example has encouraged him; I declare that young men nowadays seem to have no sense of their obligations to Society. . . ."

Patrick shrugged and opened his other letters. By the time he had finished he had begun to be aware that he was hot and thirsty, so he mounted reluctantly and set off again down the hill. To find himself once more among crowds of jostling, eager people after his long solitude at Beltrasna disturbed him, but he was determined, now and at all times (little as Aunt Frances might believe it), to perform those social gestures which were right and proper. It was proper that he, as a gentleman and a large landowner, should be present to greet the King's representative, and pay his respects; but he would get it over as fast as possible.

Among the colony's leading inhabitants who thronged the big drawing-room at Government House he stood morosely, answering salutations from his acquaintances with a forced cordiality, and studying the great man and his wife whom he could glimpse now and then through the crowd surrounding them.

Colonel Macquarie, tall and broad-shouldered, was a sufficiently impressive figure in his scarlet and gold braid. Many years of service in India had darkened his complexion; his unpowdered brown hair was plentiful, brushed up upon his head, adding to his appearance of height; and beneath thick eyebrows his dark eyes were keen and quick. Something (Patrick decided after staring for a while that it might be a strong growth of beard which partially defied the razor) gave his face, despite its sunburn, a curiously grey appearance. He looked a practical and determined man, and yet his expression was genial. Paterson, at his elbow, performing the introductions as Lieutenant-Governor, seemed more gloomy and cadaverous than ever beside him.

A feminine voice spoke at Patrick's side.

"Well, Mr. Mannion, this great event has tempted even you to Sydney!"

He turned hastily. Mrs. Robert Campbell, gay in a lavender gown of floating muslin, was tapping him playfully on the arm with her fan. Her husband and her brother stood behind her with a gentleman who was, to Patrick, a stranger.

"It's very wrong of you," Mrs. Campbell was continuing, "to be so unsociable. Pray allow me to present our new Judge Advocate, Mr. Bent —he is just arrived, you know, with the Governor. This is Mr. Mannion, Sir, who hides himself away on his farm at the Nepean, as if there were no diversions and no charming young ladies in the colony worthy of his attention!"

Patrick, as he bowed, formed an impression that such pleasantries would not be well received by Mr. Bent. He seemed a very old young man. Was it because his figure was decidedly portly? Or because his hair was sparse? Or because his short-sighted eyes looked out so peeringly from behind his spectacles? Or was he, perhaps, cultivating an air of weighty and dignified reserve which he considered appropriate to one of his exalted judicial position? Patrick remarked politely:

"I understand that you have had a long and trying voyage, Sir?"

"During the latter part of it I have been extremely ill," replied Mr. Bent glumly. "I am still far from recovered."

"Oh," cried Mrs. Campbell airily, "our climate will soon remedy that!"

Mr. Bent looked at her austerely and shook out a large, spotless handkerchief. "I find it exceedingly hot, ma'am." Wiping his pale face as if to emphasise his discomfort, and rebuke Mrs. Campbell for her misplaced cheerfulness, he turned to Colonel Foveaux who was bustling up with a brace of officers to be presented. Immediately, with a fading of smiles, a slight turning of shoulders, and a barely perceptible movement of withdrawal, Mr. Palmer and Mr. and Mrs. Campbell contrived to isolate themselves and Patrick, leaving Mr. Bent to the Colonel and his friends.

"The air is certainly a trifle oppressive," remarked Mrs. Campbell clearly. "I had not noticed it till this moment." Her fan vigorously dispersed the contamination of Foveaux' presence. "You know," she whispered to Patrick, "Mr. Bent has been to look at Mr. Atkins' house, and it's not at all to his liking! Not that I blame him—for we all know that ménage, do we not?—but I believe he's very put out at not finding a residence equal to his great importance!"

Her husband shrugged.

34

"I'm told his legal qualifications are of a high order. In that respect at least—and I hope in others—he'll be an improvement on Atkins."

Palmer observed sourly:

"I should hope so! And he appears very friendly with the Governor, which should make for tranquillity. Where's his wife, Sophy?"

"Were there a little less of her she would be totally invisible. There she is, with Mrs. Paterson. You see, Mr. Mannion? The gentleman talking to them is Dr. Arnold—but he'll be returning to England with his ship, of course. Yonder near the window is the new Lieutenant-Governor—Colonel O'Connell, you know, who commands the 73rd. And the young man with him is Captain Antill—he's to be the Governor's Aide-de-Camp . . . no, no, you're looking in the wrong direction!"

Patrick was studying a man of forty or thereabouts whose observant eyes, as he stood close beside the Governor, seemed to be collecting and docketing the faces about him for future reference. "That's a namesake of ours," Mrs. Campbell explained. "I've not yet discovered if he is related to Mrs. Macquarie—she was a Miss Campbell, you know—but at all events they met him for the first time at the Cape on the voyage out, and he's to be the Governor's Secretary. La, the place is full of Campbells, is it not?"

Patrick made her a little bow.

"We can't have too many of them, ma'am."

"You are quite a flatterer! Have you observed George, pray?"

"George?"

"The black boy in livery who remains always so close behind His Excellency."

"I had noticed him—he's not one of our colonial natives, surely?"

"Oh, dear me, no! He has been with the Colonel since he was but a child of six or seven. Mrs. Macquarie tells me that her husband purchased him in India, and he's more faithful than a dog! Is it not romantic? You are acquainted with Mr. Cowper, I suppose?"

"I have not that pleasure."

"No? But he has been here four months at least! You are indeed a stranger to our Sydney society! That is he yonder—the tall, excessively thin young man with his back to us. I don't see his wife for the moment, but she is quite an amiable person. Their little boy, Charles—*his* son, you know, for she has no family as yet—has become a playmate of your own little brother, Desmond. What a delightful child Desmond is, to be sure! And as for little Julia, there will be some hearts broken . . ."

Patrick smiled and murmured mechanically. The room was now uncomfortably crowded, and the day approaching noon. Hot and restless, he noticed with relief that Mrs. Palmer had come up and engaged her sister-in-law in conversation, so he began to edge through the throng in the direction of the vice-regal pair.

Mrs. Macquarie, with Mrs. Paterson at her elbow, was acknowledging the stream of introductions with a valiantly sustained smile. He thought, as he stepped forward to receive his share of it, that she looked a sensible and agreeable young woman, whose blue eyes suggested a certain quiet humour. He made his bow, and passed on to pay his respects to the Governor.

Mr. Mannion, Paterson explained, was one of the colony's very early settlers, having arrived here in childhood. Macquarie bent a benevolent eye upon him.

"Indeed? You can almost be called a native, Mr. Mannion."

"Very nearly, Sir. I have a brother, and also a half-brother and a half-sister who were born here."

"Excellent! I trust I shall make their acquaintance. I'm particularly interested in the emergence of a new generation native to this land, and there will be by now many of them nearing the adult state. They must receive every encouragement—must they not, Colonel?—to acquit themselves worthily in the service of their birthplace."

"Quite, quite," murmured Paterson. Patrick, preparing to withdraw, was detained by His Excellency.

"In what part of the colony is your property situated, Mr. Mannion?"

"On the east bank of the Nepean, Sir, but somewhat removed from the main centres of settlement. I trust your Excellency will do me the honour of visiting it some day."

"You may be sure of it. I intend to make myself familiar with the whole colony as speedily as possible."

Patrick, his duty done, bowed and retired. He made his way slowly but with determination to the door, and emerged thankfully into the open air. People were still thronging the streets and chattering about the gates of Government House, so he mounted and turned uphill towards the open expanse of land usually known as the Common, which bounded the eastern side of the town, and rode briskly to his stepmother's house.

She greeted him affectionately, her two children at her side.

"You have just come from Government House, Patrick? What excitement there is! You must tell me all about Colonel Macquarie and his wife. But first you shall have some rest and refreshment, for you must be hot and tired. We are rejoiced to see you again, are we not, Julia? See, Desmond, here is your big brother whom you must almost have forgotten, since he comes so seldom to visit us!"

"I have much to occupy me at Beltrasna," Patrick defended himself from her gently implied rebuke, "and I have little liking for Sydney, with its endless disputes and intrigues."

"There have been many of those," she agreed. "Julia, my love, tell Flora to bring refreshments for your brother, and then run to Bessie; take Desmond with you, and watch him on the stairs. Now, Patrick, sit down, pray, and tell me all the news of Beltrasna."

"There's not much to tell." He sat down in a high-backed chair and stretched his booted legs out wearily. "All goes on as usual."

Watching her seat herself on the sofa opposite and take up her needlework—a complicated design of roses and pheasants—he felt an old constraint, and a slightly aggrieved anxiety. Last time he had seen her she had still been in the black of her widowhood; now, though the gown she wore was grey, simply and soberly cut, the very fact that she had discarded her mourning added to his uneasiness. She was still young—only three years older than himself—and her beauty was not less, but different. She was paler, and the eager vivacity of her girlhood now only glimmered beneath a controlled quietness. It made him apprehensive. He had not greatly loved his father himself, and he suspected that his step-mother's marriage had not been a happy one, but he was a conventional young man, and he would have appreciated a more conventional attitude in her. Yet even as this thought formed, he was bound to admit that she had nowhere transgressed the rules of decorum since her husband's death—except . . .

Except that she was still here. That, he acknowledged, was what disturbed and irritated him. For the fact was that there was no place in this colony for gently-born ladies save as appendages to their husbands; an unattached lady, especially if young and handsome, was . . . conspicuous. . . .

He asked abruptly:

"How is Cousin Bertha?"

"She seems wonderfully well. For an old lady she has a remarkable liveliness; she's all agog to see the Parade to-morrow."

"You propose to be present, then?"

"But of course! The whole town will be there. I've ordered the carriage for one o'clock. You'll come with us, Patrick—no, pray don't refuse—we see you so rarely!"

"I had intended to leave early in the morning. . . ."

"There is no need, surely? We shall have company to dinner to-morrow—Mr. Cowper and his wife, and Mr. Harvey also, whom I'm sure you would be glad to see again. . . . ?"

He glanced at her quickly. With her dark head bent over her needlework she looked a pattern of demure womanhood, but he was teased by

37

a suspicion that she was not as guileless as she looked. There had been one or two hints dropped that she was seeing a good deal of Mr. Harvey. Did she know of them, and guess his disapproval? He perceived uneasily that this might be more than a simple invitation to dinner. It was as if she were saying: "My dear Patrick, I propose to see as much as I please of Mr. Harvey; how much pleasanter for us all if it should be with your public sanction and approval! I invite you, then, to join us at dinner, but should you decline, the Church still lends me its countenance."

He said a trifle sulkily:

"I shall be happy to stay, then. I've not yet made Mr. Cowper's acquaintance, though he was pointed out to me this morning." Irked by his own acquiescence, he turned suddenly to the one subject upon which he could feel himself unassailably in the right: "You know, ma'am, it's really time you were thinking of sending Julia home."

The moment he had said it, and seen the distress in her eyes, he was contrite. But he persisted stubbornly:

"She's nearly nine. . . ."

"No, no—only just eight. . . ."

"All the same, it's time she went—I'm sure you recognise it. Before my father died it was understood that you were all to return—he had already arranged . . ."

"I know, I know, but . . ."

"And his main reason for wishing to delay no longer was Julia. He spoke of it to me. Had he not been . . . were he still with us, you would all have been home by now, and Julia receiving the education and training which are her due. Indeed I feel it my duty," proclaimed young Mr. Mannion, a little carried away by finding himself for once so confident of his rightness, "to urge that his wishes in this matter should be respected."

Conor rose and moved about the room restlessly.

"Believe me, Patrick, it's not *only* my own selfish desire to keep her with me—though I confess that may play its part. But . . . I cannot feel certain that the education and environment which you call her due are indeed the best for her."

He stared.

"Not the best? They are the best that the civilised world has to offer."

"You believe so? Upon that point I am still confused. They are the same that I knew as a child, but I did not find them very helpful to me when I was confronted by—by the difficult problems of maturity."

He avoided her eyes, slightly embarrassed. Always lurking in his memory was the shocking, incredible picture of her on that evening two years ago, stumbling like a drunken woman across the field at Beltrasna on her husband's arm—dirty, dishevelled, splashed with the blood of the dead convict, Finn, her feet shoeless, her stockings torn, her hair wild across her white, smeared face. . . . He had seen her then with her whole being shaken by some emotion which had swept her from her safe and sheltered world; had she ever quite returned to it . . . ?"

He shifted his ground.

"There's no need for you to be separated from her; you know very well that my grandmother asks nothing better than to receive you as a daughter. . . ."

He stopped dead, for she had—yes, she had actually shuddered! He felt no particular affection for that domineering old woman himself, but she *was* his grandmother, and his family pride was affronted. He added stiffly:

"The notion seems to be unwelcome. You could, alternatively, establish yourself in London. . . ."

"No. If I return at all it would be to Ireland—to my own old home, where my Uncle and Aunt have offered to receive me. And this I may do—someday. But not yet."

He demanded bluntly, in exasperation:

"Why not? What is there to keep you here?"

He saw the colour flood into her cheeks, swiftly though she turned away to hide it.

"My inclination," she said shortly.

He threw out his hands in despair.

"I don't understand you!"

But he thought he did, and became uneasier than ever. Mr. Harvey? A penniless tutor? He began to be tormented by memories which now, it seemed, could bear a disturbing interpretation. Years ago, when he himself was in England, and Mr. Harvey still at Beltrasna, news had come to him from his father that the young tutor had been summarily dismissed. "I have had occasion to dispense with his services, owing to his insolence and presumption. . . ." How had that "insolence" manifested itself? What had been the form of that "presumption"? He looked frowningly at the slender figure standing by the window, and found his thoughts turning to the wild, never-to-be-forgotten night of January 26th, 1808. . . . When it was all over—his dead father lying indoors, the guarded house quiet, but not sleeping, all ears stretched for the coming of the detachment from Parramatta—who was it, in fact, who came? Not Captain Abbott at the head of his soldiers, but Mr. Harvey, alone, on a borrowed horse which he had ridden as if the devil were at his heels; Mr. Harvey with only one question on his lips: "Mrs. Mannion . . . she is safe, she is well . . . ?"

Patrick could no longer avoid the conviction that he did understand after all, and the conflict between his natural kind-heartedness and his acquired respect for the conventions was printed so clearly on his face that Conor, turning back from the window, was sorry for him.

"Let us not speak more of it just now, Patrick. Tell me something of yourself. Is all well at Beltrasna? Is the harvest in?"

"All save a few acres of maize."

"The same overseers are with you?"

"Toole and Evans. Allen has left me to set up for himself as a black-smith. He has been restless, and drinking overmuch, ever since that day. . . ."

He left the sentence unfinished. There was a brief silence while they both unwillingly recalled that day when Finn had so madly returned to attempt the liberation of other convicts; when shots had rung out on the Beltrasna fields, and men had fallen dead or wounded; when Allen had collapsed beneath the blows of men maddened by the chance of freedom; and when Finn—so close to death that he had accepted without surprise the aid and support of his former master's wife—had driven his lashed and tortured body to one final bid for liberty, and died beside her in the sunset light that lay over the deserted fields. Conor, her head bent closely over her work again, and her fingers tight on the embroidery frame, asked at last:

"And the new men you got out from Ireland?"

"They are well enough." He frowned. "But there's a curious laxity. . . . I can't trace its source, or even describe very clearly how it shows itself. . . . It's as though nothing remains quite the same here—neither people, nor events, nor customs. . . ."

She raised her head to look at him attentively.

"You have felt that too? Yet wouldn't it be strange if it were not so? It is a different land—a different society . . . ?"

"A different land—yes, of course. But why, merely because the place is different, should the whole form and spirit of society change? Can we not," he demanded with some annoyance, "shape a society as we please? There are certain factors—things within the realm of nature—to which we must adapt our customs, it is true . . . but . . . there's more than that. . . ."

"You speak of changes in people themselves, I think. There have been many—and deep ones—in me. In yourself too, perhaps? Why not in others?"

He stood up and walked over to a picture hanging on the opposite wall, and she watched him out of the corner of her eye while she stitched. It had touched him—that suggestion of change in himself—and she wondered why. She had a question ready, but she did not ask it until he was facing her again.

"How is Dilboong?"

"Dil . . . ? She is just as usual . . . She is very well."

The over-fast reply, the bitten-off word, and his quick turn from her to the window, all tended to confirm a suspicion which she had been harbouring now for some time. She allowed the silence to extend until he looked at her, and she looked at him, and they mutely understood each other. Dropping her eyes to her needlework again, Conor was a little surprised by her own anger. Dilboong—that ignorant, docile, loving-hearted child . . . ! She resolved that—welcome or unwelcome—she would pay a visit to Beltrasna, and view this situation for herself. In the meantime it was best to allow the matter to pass.

*   *   *   *

Elizabeth Macquarie, escaped for the first time during an eventful day from the formalities and obligations of her husband's new office, hesitated for a second on the threshold of her bedroom, as if momentarily daunted by its unfamiliarity. It was in some disorder still, for though her maid had already unpacked a few trunks and boxes, more had been brought in, giving it that air of a temporary habitation which the paraphernalia of travelling bestows.

She moved forward slowly, looking about her, for the day had so far been too full of events to allow her time for anything but the most cursory inspection of her new home. It was a pleasant enough room, she noticed, with windows overlooking the harbour; already a few of her possessions had been disposed about it, and she paused here and there to touch them, as if finding their presence reassuring in a place still so far from seeming her own.

The sun had almost set, though it was mid-summer, and not yet seven o'clock; the indoor light was fading, and she could see no lamps, but felt disinclined to ring for them. She crossed the room, picking up from a table as she paused the little brown leather-covered book in which she had recorded, day by day, the events of the voyage; and finding a chair placed near the window, sank into it with a sigh, admitting that she was tired. She sat still, her hands clasped over the book in her lap, and looked out the window at the *Hindostan* and the *Dromedary,* anchored off the Government Wharf. It was good to be ashore again, though she had enjoyed the voyage for the most part, and was just a trifle nervous about what the future held for them in this remote, and really very odd colony; obviously, the deposition of Governor Bligh had caused great confusion, and the fervour of Colonel Paterson's welcome left no doubt that he was overjoyed to relinquish his responsibility. . . .

However, Mrs. Macquarie reflected, her dear and altogether excellent husband was now in charge—and thus the troubles of the place were as good as ended. To be sure, Governor Bligh was still uncomfortably close; she would not, somehow, feel quite tranquil until she knew that that possibly ill-used, but certainly difficult man, was well on his way to England. Doubtless he would return here post-haste from the Derwent the moment he received news of their arrival, and all Macquarie's tact and patience would be required to deal with him. But for the present things should go well enough, with their own regiment to replace that most irregular New South Wales Corps, and their own friends about them—Colonel O'Connell, and the Bents, and Henry Antill, and John Campbell as Secretary, and Major Cleaveland as Brigade Major. . . . Yes, on the whole matters seemed favourably arranged. . . .

Yet she sighed again, staring out the window. The air was still now, and the sky, with the setting of the sun, had taken on the colours of a subdued rainbow—pale pink and blue and green merging into each other, and shedding a faint, opalescent light on the glassy water. Here at last was the wonderful harbour of which she had heard so much; and during the days when they were anchored down near its entrance, she had—as an intelligent traveller should—compared it with the fabulous harbour of Rio, whose beauties she had eulogised in her Journal. But now, tired after the long, hot day, she accepted it without conscious pleasure, merely grateful in a vague way that its new mood of tranquillity should be so soothing.

There was a light showing on the *Dromedary*. Noticing it, she felt a sudden nostalgia for the little cabin which had been her home for seven months. It was not the first time she had recognised her affection for it as the scene of an interlude in her life which had held qualities of happiness not to be expected elsewhere; and she opened the book on her knee, turning its pages till she found the entry she wanted, and holding it towards the window's fading light to read.

". . . *on coming on board I always feel now as going home, the ship appearing to me in the place of a house which has long been my habitation, and a very happy one it has been to me. I have spent my time in a manner which entirely suits my inclination, having the great comfort of my Husband's company uninterrupted all the morning, when we read and write in a social manner which I shall never enjoy on shore, as when he has it in his power he shuts himself up alone all the morning to business; but here I am admitted from necessity. . . .*"

She laid the book down, and looked round the darkening room. Would she ever again know that comforting sense of close intimacy and companionship—illusory, perhaps?—which had for a short time been vouchsafed her "from necessity" . . . ? When this rare mood of sadness threatened, she had learned to bring forth her sense of humour to repel it, and she did so now, driving the droop from her lips with a smile for her husband's solemn, and even laborious romanticism. So dear, so good, so kind, so much to be respected—and so funny! Having buried his heart for ever in the grave of his first wife, with what puzzled guilt and uneasily restrained ardour had he found it, ten years later, still available to offer to herself! Yet her humour—she admitted it—had not quite sufficed to curb the exasperation she had felt at being won only to be deserted for three years. And all for a ridiculous vow which the fair ghost who had inspired it would doubtless, in life, have considered as silly as she did herself. But that vow was Macquarie—romantic, yet canny; impulsive, yet cautious; binding himself, in the first abandonment of his grief, by a passionate vow—with a loophole! Having sworn never to re-marry in India, he could not have been tempted by any woman under Heaven to re-marry—in India; having pledged himself never to take a wife to India, he would postpone, if not abandon bliss, and the newly-betrothed Miss Campbell must watch his departure for that land, and await his return from it before they could be united. Miss Campbell, half irritated (for a visit to India would have been most interesting, after all) and half amused, had acquiesced; but she had asserted herself to the extent of ignoring his directions as to the disposal of her time during his absence, and by permitting the tone and infrequency of her letters to cause him a little salutary uneasiness. . . .

Yet she loved him dearly, and still dared to hope that he might some-day cease to hug those bonds in which his true devotion for her lay so awkwardly restricted. She knew—none better—that it was not his lost Jane who stood between them, but his own sentimentality, oddly in league with his stubborn sense of rectitude. Indeed she had sometimes felt a flash of resentment on behalf of the unknown, but doubtless very human girl whose memory was becoming, with the passing of the years, merely the means for a man's determined vindication of his own con-stancy. But that was Macquarie. So benign, and yet so inflexible; so shrewd, and yet so ingenuous; so solemnly conventional, and yet, beneath his sober and imposing deportment, always seeing visions and dreaming dreams—always bubbling with excitement and enthusiasm, like a miss at her first ball!

Would she have him different? She knew that she would welcome difference only if it were wrought by the slow hand of time; and mean-while, she thought, rising briskly and patting her curly, reddish hair into position before a darkening mirror, they would both be far too busy to watch the time passing. He had gone with Lieutenant-Colonel Foveaux for a drive about the town, but he would soon be back, and it was not to be desired that he should find his Elizabeth—whose greatest virtue in his eyes had always been her robust good sense—moping by a window in the twilight.

She rang the bell for lights.

*   *   *   *

By half-past one next day the Parade Ground was crowded; everyone was there, everyone was excited, and everyone was hot. The populace stood waiting, defenceless, under the glare of the midsummer sun; the din of drums, the roar of guns firing salutes, and the brand-new scarlet of the brand-new regiment (beside which the uniforms of the New South Wales Corps looked sadly faded) were exhausting to the ear and eye, and made the heat seem hotter.

The brand-new Governor, however, had lived in India, and when at last, surrounded by his retinue, he took his place in the centre of the square, he seemed unaffected by the temperature. He stood tall and stiff, surveying his subjects who looked, to be sure, very like a crowd anywhere else—shuffling, murmuring, gaping, ready to be entertained or impressed by a spectacle. He was thinking that if—as past events seemed to suggest—his difficulties were to come from the higher stratum of society, the excellent Proclamation which Mr. Bent had already drawn up for him would surely have a restraining effect. This he had reserved for an occasion later in the day, when, at Government House, it would be read to a more select assemblage; he reflected with satisfaction that its first sentences went straight to the point, and left no room for misunderstanding. "*His Majesty having felt the most urgent regret and displeasure on account of the late tumultuous proceedings in this his colony, and the mutinous conduct of certain persons therein towards his late representative William Bligh, Esq. . . .*"

That should give pause to anyone still feeling tumultuous. It was perhaps unfortunate that the opportunity for driving the point home by ceremoniously reinstating Bligh for twenty-four hours should have been lost by that gentleman's absence; nevertheless His Majesty's views had been made plain—and all things considered, the occasion would pass off more smoothly without him.

A suitable hush of anticipation having descended, Macquarie opened the proceedings by handing his Commission to the Judge Advocate, who unfolded it and, with a flourish, displayed to the crowd the Great Seal of the Territory. The troops presented arms, the officers saluted, the band played God Save the King, and everyone uncovered. Macquarie viewed this well-rehearsed reverence with approval; Patrick Mannion bared his head, but stepped back a pace into the shade of the carriage from which

44

Desmond watched, round-eyed, struggling with some memory of a picture in a Bible which showed just such a scroll of parchment being displayed to an awed multitude. His notion of the functions of a Governor was vague, but he had understood enough from the remarks of his elders to realise the importance of this commanding, majestic being in scarlet and gold, and was quite prepared to concede him divinity. But Cousin Bertha, who was uncomfortably hot, and too old for reverence, nudged Conor and whispered: "La, it seems a great to-do about a bit of paper, does it not?"

She dozed then—more fortunate than Mr. Bent, over whose bald head an orderly sergeant unfurled a large umbrella while he ploughed his way through the reading of the Governor's, his own, and the deputy Judge Advocate's Commissions. The citizens shifted restlessly on their tired feet, and wiped their sweating foreheads, but new interest was aroused when Mr. Bent retired—plainly exhausted and in an ill-humour—and the Governor stepped forward to speak.

"Fellow-citizens and fellow-soldiers. . . . !"

Those first words underlined the difference between him and his predecessors; no Governor before him had thus been able to claim professional fraternity with the military force. The assurances which followed of his intention to exercise authority with strict justice and impartiality were accepted as routine pronouncements which any Governor might be expected to make; the crowd was still digesting the implications of that "fellow-soldiers".

"I am sanguine," Macquarie declared, "in my hopes that all those dissensions and jealousies which have unfortunately existed in this colony for some time past will now terminate for ever. . . ."

No tremor of expression disturbed the faces of his audience. Lieutenant-Governor O'Connell, erect and impressive in his uniform, Mr Bent, perspiring beneath his umbrella, Mrs. Macquarie, Captain Antill, Mr. John Campbell—in fact any of those but newly arrived—might possibly have shared His Excellency's optimism. But through the old residents of the colony—from Colonel Paterson down to the lowest convict, and from Mrs. Mannion down to the youngest of the orphan girls—there ran a little shock of startled wonder, pitying, and half amused. Dissentions and jealousies terminate for ever . . . ? In New South Wales . . . ? It was as though the Governor had affirmed his belief that in future the gum trees would shed their leaves in winter, and snow lie thick in the Sydney streets on Christmas Day. They continued to listen patiently, however, acquiescing in the convention that such pious hopes must be confidently expressed, and decorously received.

The upper classes, His Excellency continued, must show a good example to the lower by readily conforming to the colony's laws and regulations. At this certain well-barbered faces beneath tall, glossy hats became studiously blank, and there appeared among the convicts and the humbler inhabitants a few sour, fleeting smiles. Yet as Macquarie approached his peroration they were all aware of listening to something which was more than a formal expression of sentiments proper to such an occasion. It was not his assurance of the King's wish to promote the welfare of the colony which made their apathetic gaze grow more attentive, nor his assertion that it would be their own faults if they were not comfortable and happy. These were mere words, and he might have garnished them with all the arts and graces of fine oratory without lending them conviction. What kept their eyes upon him with growing intentness was that note, subtle and compelling, which sounds only when a man's mind and heart endorse what he is saying. They stared, wondering. "Comfortable and happy . . . ?" In bondage, in poverty, in disgrace, in exile . . . ?"

"To make them so, as far as depends on me," declared the new Governor, looking round upon them with the firm benevolence of a father, "is not only my duty but will at all times constitute my chief happiness; and the honest, sober, industrious inhabitant, whether free settler or convict, will ever find in me a friend and a protector."

"Aye," muttered one convict to another, "as far as depends on him, maybe—but he'll find that ain't far!" Yet when the citizens grabbed off their caps and opened their mouths to cheer, there was a warmth in their huzzas. Unlikely as it was that this optimistic Viceroy could achieve their comfort and happiness, he really seemed to desire it.

The acclamation which followed His Excellency's speech aroused Cousin Bertha, and the roar of guns from the battery and the ships rudely completed her awakening. "I cannot understand," she declared rather petulantly, "why ceremonies should always be made the occasion for so much intolerable banging. Is it over, my love?"

"Yes, the crowd is beginning to disperse, Cousin. We shall drive home immediately, for the children are tired from all this excitement— poor Desmond is almost asleep. Well, Julia, have you enjoyed the Parade?"

But Julia's mouth was drooping. Mama was making no attempt to be presented to the Governor, and the Governor had not even set eyes upon Miss Julia Mannion. She pulled crossly at her blue sash so that it came off and fell upon the floor of the carriage, and she kicked at it with the toe of her little black slipper and said: "No, it was silly!" Desmond raised his head from the hot leather upholstery, and murmured vaguely: "Was that man God?"

*   *   *   *

Two lights burned late in Government House on the following Sunday night. One was in the room where Mrs. Macquarie lay in bed, but not asleep. The interlude of constant companionship with her husband had, indeed, ended with the voyage, and he was involved in affairs which must make him, more and more, "shut himself up alone to business".

Now he had retired to his study where the other light burned; though he was not working in any official sense, he still sat in the high-backed, red leather chair at his desk, and there was a paper before him over which he pored. A devout and God-fearing man, it was not his custom to profane the Lord's Day with more work than was avoidable, but he had much to consider, and he had sat for the past hour considering closely, and scribbling for his own greater mental clarification, stray notes and memoranda.

Years of habit had made it almost indispensable to him to pin down his thoughts and emotions on paper—not only with words, but with symbols—with dashes, question-marks, and points of exclamation extravagantly multiplied, with the wavering scrawls of abstraction, the black, erasing strokes of rejection, and the vigorous underlinings of determined emphasis. The sheet of paper before him was a chaos of scribbling which reflected not only the tenor of his thoughts, but the moods of his thinking. The word "Bligh", followed by a series of question marks, stood high upon it. Only yesterday he had composed a careful letter informing his predecessor of his arrival, explaining that the "deranged affairs and critical state" of the colony had compelled him to assume office at once, and lamenting the impossibility of fulfilling that part of his instructions which commanded Bligh's temporary reinstatement as a mark of His Majesty's displeasure at the mutinous conduct of the usurpers. And he had concluded with the hope that he might soon have the honour of seeing Captain Bligh at Sydney, "where you may rest assured I shall be most happy to pay you every respect and attention in my power to bestow while you find it necessary to remain in the settlement."

There were the question marks. How long would Captain Bligh find it necessary to remain? How would he conduct himself while he did so? What effect would his explosive presence have upon the brawling, easily ignited community into which Macquarie desired to introduce harmony as soon as possible? Well, the letter was already on the way; the *Estramina* had set forth with it only a few hours since, and time alone could provide the answers.

He had left that thought, therefore, and followed another, expressed by three words in a column—"barracks", "hospital", "stores"—tied together by a vertical line which shot off, arrow-like, to an uncompromising comment: "inadequate—*falling down!!*" Invisible, but clear, the train of thought ran from here to the expression of something which was as much a dream as a statement of necessity. "Government architect?" said his pen, writing slowly, reflectively, almost lovingly, and enclosing the words in a carefully drawn rectangle, as if, perhaps, recognising their dream quality, and isolating it. The dreamer, then, made way for the moralist. "Intemperance and concubinage", written with firm, black disapproval, hardly needed the support of the heavily underlined *"deplorable!!!"* which flanked them. Alone, segregated by two horizontal lines, stood, ominously, the words "spirituous liquors"; over these he had pondered for a long time before passing, with evident animation, to fluent phrases betraying that, so far as one problem at least was concerned, he had already a settled conviction, and a solution. "Illiberal policy towards emancipists unwise and inhuman", and "reward of good conduct should be re-admission to respectable society" were expressions of a mind both just and generous; its conventionality, and its core of native caution were apparent in the warning note of qualification: "Difficult matter—proceed with *great delicacy!!*"

But this paper he now thrust aside, and drew towards him a map of the colony. He had already explored the town; there was not so much of it that a few excursions undertaken in the spare half-hours of a busy week could leave much of it unrevealed. What he had seen had inspired a certain grieved disapproval, mitigated by the knowledge of his power to mould and alter. He was an emotional, but not—except in a closely circumscribed sense—an imaginative man. Such imagination as he possessed was rather a product of his emotions than an extension of his intellect; he could imagine what he desired, and he desired Order, Dignity and Rectitude. Thus his first glimpse of the town had inspired visions—still lingering in that half-absent reference to a Government architect—if not admiration. It had, clearly, neither order nor dignity, and he feared that rectitude also was an insufficiently honoured guest within it. All this, however, he would change.

In one glance from any eminence the eye could take in what seemed the whole range of human existence, from the primitive—expressed in human terms by a native loitering on the shore, but more strongly by the landscape itself—to some manifestation of the civilised world—a fine house, a carriage and pair, or even a feminine toilette which displayed all the sophistication of the world's great cities. Between these two extremes, these points of wonder and surprise, lay the town itself. Its buildings were mostly of wood, with here and there a few still of wattle-and-daub to remind the observer that hardly more than a score of years ago the place had been a settlement of mud and clay huts. Some were of brick, and a few of stone, but all were roofed with shingles, and most stood isolated in a small patch of ground, protected from the street—in theory at least—by a low, paling fence.

The first Governor's dream of wide and noble thoroughfares had been defeated, for improvisation had been urgently dictated by the necessities of the early years. Possibly, Macquarie had reflected, staring with distaste at the crooked streets, a flatter terrain would have produced (even if equally by accident) a plan which more established times could have seen developed, and upon which some dignity could have been imposed. But this place was hilly. It was evident that the town had been born in haste and squalor—a furtive, illegitimate birth, for which no proper provision had been made. Buildings had been put up somewhere, somehow, as fast as possible, over an area which here sloped one way, there another, and yonder thrust up a forbidding outcrop of rock. There had been neither time nor labour for levelling ground or removing obstructions; often, therefore, a building must sidle backward or forward from its line, edge a few feet this way or that, perch itself here or squeeze itself in there, observing none of that disciplined regularity which a Governor with a long military career behind him could have desired. The harbour, too, was at fault. Picturesque it undoubtedly was, but—unrestrained. Its bays bit deeply into the shore, forcing the town to withdraw, and deflecting its streets; obviously, as the years passed, and settlement spread—doubtless even to the north shore opposite, whose trees now grew in almost unbroken ranks over the hills—it could still be a town planned only to the extent permitted by that wayward sheet of water.

His Excellency, having seen all this, and decided that, bad as it was, it could be bettered, had now turned his attention to a wider field. Measuring with his pen from the scale of miles upon the map before him, he noted that the settled part of his domain was bounded by the ocean and three rivers—or, more correctly, by two, since the Hawkesbury and the Nepean were in fact one. Some thirty miles inland the Nepean came down from the mountains, swinging in a wide arc across their foothills before it became the Hawkesbury, and plunged eastward to join the sea some fifteen miles north of Sydney; and, about the same distance south, the much smaller George's River emptied itself into Botany Bay. Within these limits, then, he would find the greater part of his eleven thousand people.

His eyes remained on the map, but his mind extended it to another, much larger, taking in a grandiloquent sweep of the coastline and the vastness of the Pacific Ocean. Norfolk Island had, since the foundation of the colony, been a settled dependency of New South Wales, though the removal of its inhabitants to Van Diemen's Land was under way, and must be hastened. New Zealand and Lord Howe Island also came beneath his eye—convenient landfalls for whalers and other merchant ships. There were the Feegee Islands, from which sandalwood could be obtained; and Van Diemen's Land, with communities well established at Hobart Town and Port Dalrymple. But there was no need to pause so soon, for the Commissions of all Governors had, with a fine lavishness, authorised them to take jurisdiction over "all islands adjacent in the Pacific", within specified latitudes which included even the four-thousand miles distant Otaheite....

His Excellency's thoughts lingered pleasantly upon this spacious realm. It was a far cry from the little boy, scion of an ancient, but impoverished clan, obscurely born in the bleak isle of Ulva forty-nine years ago, to the commanding figure of a Viceroy taking up his sovereign rule over an ocean and a continent.

He entered upon his reign with energy and enthusiasm, issuing orders, receiving reports, making new acquaintances, and always, interminably, hearing in a word, or a phrase, or a long, circumstantial harangue, the echo of old feuds and enmities. These he turned aside with determination. The past was past; henceforward, with himself as its paternal head, showing, like a wise father, no favouritism to any person or class, this community would leave at peace.

He held long conferences with Foveaux, for it seemed abundantly clear that Paterson, even if nominally in command, had been of small consequence compared with this vigorous, masterful man, whose knowledge of local affairs seemed endless, and whose unbounded efficiency in such matters as repairing roads and damaged buildings compelled Macquarie's admiration. He possessed, too, another advantage which recommended him to His Excellency: he was out of favour with both the main protagonists of the rebellion. He had been in England when it took place, and on his return had speedily clashed with Macarthur; the fact that he had so readily accepted the situation he found—thus incurring the bitter enmity of Bligh—did not impress Macarthur as a crime, for though he understood something in theory, he could have no first-hand knowledge of the powerful motives which, for eighteen years, had maintained a state of warfare between the Corps and the Governors. His one aim was to restore peace, and keep it; he felt but little inclination to probe too deeply into the origins of conflict. He found in Foveaux an alert, clever man who, while awaiting the departure of the vessel which was to take him back to England, could be, and was, most useful to him.

On the Thursday of that week a ship was sighted off the coast, battling with contrary winds. It was not until Sunday that a boat was able to reach her, and return with the news that she was the *Mary Ann* from Bengal, via Hobart Town; by a vessel from England which had reached the Derwent while she was there, Governor Bligh had learned of his successor's departure for the colony. He was, therefore, about to return himself with all haste. . . .

"H'm!" remarked Macquarie to his wife. "We shall have him here at any time. We had best have all this junketing over by then."

For Sydney was still deliriously *en fête*. For the first time in two years the inhabitants were able to relax; for the first time warring factions were able to combine—at least outwardly—in common rejoicings. If His Excellency's prompt dismissal of all those who had taken office under the rebel regime, and his reinstatement of those whom Bligh had appointed, caused some heart-burnings, it was discreetly concealed. The revocation of all grants or leases of land, and all gifts of stock made since the rebellion was harder to bear, though a grain of hope remained to some in the proviso that the Governor might, at his discretion, renew such as he found to have been made justly. The declaration that all trials and investigations held by the rebel Government were illegal, was no more than a salutary gesture; it could not give back to Mr. Suttor, and other intransigeants, the months they had spent in gaol, nor—though it was the signal for his release—could it obliterate from Mr. Gore's life the two years he had endured in the ill-omened settlement at Coal River.

Nevertheless, the inhabitants found these measures more than welcome, and they made merry. The celebrations reached their climax on the night of January 16th, with bands playing, bonfires blazing, liquor flowing copiously, and the townsfolk standing, in happy bemusement, to gape at the illuminations displayed in the homes of the wealthy.

Mr. Howe, publisher of the *Sydney Gazette,* roamed the streets, and found himself embarrassed by a wealth of copy. Mr. Underwood's mansion, glittering like a whole firmament of stars, contributed a spectacle before which all others paled. Front and back, every window was ablaze, and as the evening wore on a bonfire was lighted, fireworks spat and sparkled, and a band on the verandah played Rule Britannia. Nor was Mr. Underwood yet content, for as midnight approached the doors of his house were thrown open, and the spectators crowded in to find tables groaning under the weight of choice and lavish refreshment. Mr. Howe, observing all this, permitted himself a faint, sardonic smile; it was clear that, whatever discomfiture might await the leaders of the rebellion, many of its supporters would now spare neither pains nor expense in dissociating themselves from a party whose star was on the wane.

As the fires died down, and the surfeited revellers turned reluctantly from Mr. Underwood's ravished tables, a ship, making ghost-like up the coast, was nearing the entrance of the harbour.

*   *   *   *

The Governor, benignly as he had watched the rather feverish celebrations in his honour, was tempted to feel next morning, when informed
of Governor Bligh's arrival, that they had ended only just in time. He
found the thought reflected in the eyes of his wife, his secretary and his
aide-de-camp as they confronted each other across the breakfast table.

"Mercy on us!" exclaimed Mrs. Macquarie. Mr. Campbell raised his
dark eyebrows and grinned at her.

"You're right, ma'am. To arrive and find the town in so festive a
mood . . . yes, it would have been a devilish provoking situation for a
touchy man. It's indeed a mercy upon us that he was not a few hours
earlier—eh, Antill?"

Captain Henry Colden Antill—before long to be nicknamed "the cold
one"—agreed.

"No doubt it would have seemed the turning of a knife in the wound.
You'll wish me to go down to the harbour to greet him, Sir?"

Macquarie pushed his chair back and rose hastily; Campbell and
Antill were immediately on their feet.

"Yes, yes—you must go down at once and present my compliments.
Send word to Colonel O'Connell first that I want to see him without
delay—we must take pains to show Captain Bligh every attention.
Campbell, prepare an order for the troops that he's to be received by all
guards and sentries with the same honours as when he was Governor. My
love, I don't know what arrangements he'll wish to make for his stay
ashore, but you had better have rooms prepared for him and his
daughter. . . ."

Their eyes met, but the apprehensive thought they shared remained
unspoken. A difficult guest; it was to be hoped that he would speedily
find quarters for himself elsewhere. . . .

But it would take more than ceremonial courtesies to provide balm
for Bligh's wounded and embittered spirit. His nine months' sojourn at
Hobart Town had been one long fury of frustration, and now he had
returned too late to claim that token reinstatement which might have
assuaged, if only slightly, the torments of his angry heart. His successor
was already installed in office, and he, when he stepped ashore, would
step into a kind of void where he had no standing or authority.

He stood on the deck of the *Porpoise* wtih his widowed daughter,
Mary Putland, and his secretary, young David Griffin, and watched a
boat putting out from the shore; he felt that pang which strikes the heart
when an old scene is re-played in different and unhappier, circumstances.
Not four years ago he had stood thus with Mary on the deck of the *Lady
Madeleine Sinclair,* but the boat then approaching them from the shore
had borne a welcome to a Governor-elect; this one, however civil the

message it might convey, came to an ex-Governor, defeated and discarded. Then his thoughts had all looked forward, full of confidence; now they were chained to the last two years, and those years stretched out in his memory like a century. He, whose temper was direct and aggressive, had been forced to scheme, intrigue, and manœuvre. He, whose whole nature craved action, had been compelled to wait . . . and wait. . . .

He put his hand over his daughter's where it lay on the rail, and hers turned upward to clasp it. He was thinking of her illness when they had arrived at Hobart Town (poor child, she would never make a sailor, and that was a damnable stretch of sea across the strait!) and with what relief she had landed to take up her abode in the miserable building which served for a Government House. Oh, yes, Collins had been all civility then, receiving them with deference, insisting on vacating his wretched dwelling for them. . . .

But Bligh had known, for all this outward parade, that he was still alone among enemies, and he had slept on board his ship every night. That—having been won single-handed after months of argument and by a final stroke of duplicity for which he, at least, felt no need to apologise —should not be taken from him again! But there had been less than a month of that precarious peace before Paterson's insolent Proclamation arrived, shattering all pretence of harmony, forcing him—and poor Mary too—back permanetly on board the ship—his one remaining foothold of authority.

And then nothing to do but wait, suffering an endless succession of outrages and pin-pricking insults, and writing desperate letters to his superiors in England. Wait, wait . . . *"until succours might arrive from your Lordship. . . ."* Wait, wait . . . *"I have no resource but patience until some of His Majesty's ships arrive, which I am daily looking for. . . ."* Wait, wait . . . *"I now remain, my Lord, under the most embarrassed situation that can be conceived. . . ."* Wait, wait . . . *"my succours cannot be far off. . . ."*

Well—the ex-Governor's blue eyes snapped angrily—while he waited he had dealt back his enemies trouble for trouble! He had defied and harried them to the best of his considerable ability—and he was not finished with them yet! The King had seen fit to appoint a new Governor, and William Bligh would never question the orders of his Sovereign, no matter how abominably his own might be disregarded by violent and unscrupulous villains like Macarthur and Foveaux, by dull-witted nincompoops like Johnston, by vaccillating weaklings like Paterson and Collins . . . ! Yet his sense of injury had swollen in him like another self, a giant inhabiting his body, filling it to suffocation till he could speak no word that was not coloured by resentment, and hardly frame a thought untouched by vengeful bitterness. His expression was darkly unresponsive as he received the courteous message of welcome which Antill presently presented, and his voice was brusque as he replied:

"My compliments to His Excellency. My daughter and I will land at ten o'clock to-morrow."

*　　　　*　　　　*　　　　*

Nothing should be left undone, Macquarie resolved, which could underline the disapproval with which Authority viewed the mutinous proceedings of that memorable night when His Majesty's Governor had been deposed by His Majesty's troops. Not only his explicit instructions, but his own dour, Scottish sense of propriety, would insist on that. He realised that he had to deal with a man in whom bitterness had been mounting throughout a long period of stubborn, but helpless resistance; a man whose fierce pride had been outraged by this second mutiny in his turbulent career. The parade of ceremony and respect with which the new Governor prepared to greet and surround him during the time (Heaven send it might be short!) while he remained in the colony, would perhaps partially soothe and placate him; but that, so far as Macquarie was concerned, was incidental. The military, the merchants, the populace at large, must be shown beyond any possibility of misunderstanding, that His Majesty's late representative was answerable only to His Majesty's Ministers; how else could His Majesty's present representative rest secure?

Two companies of the 73rd marched in from the encampment that mid-January morning when Bligh once again set foot on the soil of Sydney Cove. He came ashore from the *Porpoise* to the salute of guns, and Lieutenant-Colonel O'Connell, as His Excellency's deputy, awaited him at the landing stage, surrounded by a retinue of officers and gentlemen. Bligh's expression was forbidding. His daughter's was haughty, and she kept her chin well raised. Poor Papa! How abominably he had been treated! He felt the pressure of her small, gloved hand on his arm, and remarked grimly: "We return with at least more honour than we left, my love."

Then the boat scraped the wharf. Mary Putland, handed ceremoniously ashore, found herself presently confronting an impressive, scarlet-coated figure, and responding to her father's introduction. "Lieutenant-Colonel O'Connell, Mary; my daughter, Sir, Mrs. Putland."

"Your servant, ma'am." This somewhat awkward occasion suddenly assumed, very pleasantly, a new interest; and for a second, as he looked at the beautiful, dark-eyed face shadowed by its bonnet, the Colonel was in danger of forgetting his responsibilities.

*　　　　*　　　　*　　　　*

Mr. John Campbell found, as others had before him, that the post of Secretary to the Governor of New South Wales was no sinecure. Letters, orders and proclamations flowed from his pen, for Macquarie was losing no time in letting his views be known—and the burden of them all was "Peace, my children, peace, peace. . . ." Feuds must cease, injuries must be forgotten, and angry passions subdued. Attention must be paid by all, high and low, to "the necessity of forbearance, and the importance of that union, tranquillity and harmony in the present crisis so essential to the welfare of the colony."

In the little brick cottage to which Bligh had retired with his daughter, his secretary and his household, this dove-like policy of conciliation was held to be applied too indiscriminately. The ex-Governor had been shocked to find many of his enemies—headed by Foveaux—on terms of friendliness with Macquarie, basking in the warmth of his all-enveloping goodwill. For himself, he was not prepared to forgive and forget so easily; his good name was yet to be cleared. But he strove to set a guard upon his temper and his unruly tongue, and his relations with Macquarie continued civil, if not cordial.

Yet every soul in the colony knew that he was angry, hurt, consumed by resentment at his wrongs, touchily jealous of the dignity which had been so brutally affronted. The guard of honour which mounted daily over his dwelling was continually springing to attention, saluting and presenting arms as he passed in and out upon his purposeful occasions; the citizens who touched their caps to him in the streets could recognise—either with sympathy or malice—the bitter resentment which lent sharp-ness to his irascible response.

Only to his wife, staunchly fighting his battle in England with the powerful support of his friend, Sir Joseph Banks, did he reveal his whole heart and mind. "*You must not, my dearest Love, be uneasy about us. . . . Marsden arrived a few days since and gave us the most cheering accounts of you all . . . it is a hard trial of my temper to be here just now, to see all the poor loyalists in the background. . . . I have the greatest comfort and happy reflections on the good I have done the country. . . . It is no vanity in me to say to you, altho' it would be to any person else, that the good of the Colony and the happyness of the people depended on my remaining with them another year. . . . Adieu, my dearest Life. . . .*"

She, at least, could see beneath his uncompromising manner a man who had always done his duty as he saw it; a man to whom the tumul-tuousness of his life, the trouble that dogged his footsteps and the enmities which assailed him, were perpetual sources of aggrieved astonishment. Only to her would he betray his vulnerability. Even to his supporters, who now once more gathered round him, he would show nothing but the

mask of aggressiveness with which he covered it. Through long conferences with them—young David Griffin scribbling notes and memoranda
at his elbow—he prepared his exhaustive evidence of the rebels' misdeeds
against that day of reckoning, the thought of which had never ceased to
sustain him.

Many of his documents were gone. The room at Government House
where they had been kept, and which had been sealed by the rebels after
his arrest, was now opened; but it yielded nothing of value or importance
to his case. He had not expected it. Johnson and Macarthur had taken
what they wanted; the rest . . . well, there had been many bonfires. . . .

But throughout his captivity he had written and written. While each
successive outrage was fresh in his mind he had captured it on paper. He
had copies of his correspondence with his captors, sheaves of letters from
his friends, loyal addresses from settlers in the various districts of the
mainland, and in Van Diemen's Land. Now he laboured to arrange his
evidence, and collect his witnesses.

Yet there were interludes of merriment and social pleasures. *"We
have our Parties once a week, which are made up of our old Friends, and
some officers of the 73rd. . . ."* To these, occasionally, came Conor
Mannion with the Campbells, and a whispered conclave soon take place
between Sophia and their hostess. Mrs. Putland, deeply interested, recalled one morning at Government House some years ago when she had
surprised a blush upon Mrs. Mannion's face as a young schoolmaster
entered, bringing his pupils to be presented to Papa. . . . She gave Mrs.
Campbell a conspiratorial glance, and rustled across the room to Conor,
who was being greeted by her host.

"Pray, dear Mrs. Mannion, will you not persuade Mr. Harvey to give
us the pleasure of his company next week? I shall send him a card—shall
I not, Papa?"

"By all means. I learn from Mr. Campbell and Mr. Palmer, ma'am,
that Mr. Harvey has been of much assistance to them—and to me."

Thus Mr. Harvey appeared, quiet and unassuming in his well-brushed,
shabby clothes. The gentlemen found him an attentive listener, and one
who, when he spoke, did so with good sense; the ladies observed that his
eyes strayed with remarkable persistence to that corner of the room where
Mrs. Mannion was seated.

Mrs. Putland's interest in this romantic situation was, however, soon
eclipsed by an overriding preoccupation of her own. Starving for society
after months on board the *Porpoise* (which she declared to be the most
odious ship, carrying the most disagreeable set of officers in the world)
she delighted in the dinners and card parties which she now arranged,
and found, as the weeks went by, that an especially exciting and delicious

quality was pervading them. She would recollect her first sight of Lieutenant-Colonel O'Connell, waiting on the wharf to receive them as they came ashore. Had he not, even then, paid her a little more attention than was strictly necessary . . . ? Had he not invited them to dine with him that same day . . . ? Was he not continually contriving opportunities for meeting her . . . ? Surely she was not deceiving herself in believing that his glances, and the tones of his voice, conveyed more than mere courtesy . . . ?

She was young, and even her enemies allowed that she was handsome; she had no wish to remain for ever a widow, and the Colonel, though considerably her senior, was an eligible and pleasing suitor. But having shared her father's humiliations, she now shared his ardent desire to see his foes confounded, and she was not slow to realise that this situation provided her with an opportunity to contribute, in an oblique, feminine way, to their discomfiture. The villains who had deposed Papa were, no doubt, consoling themselves for having incurred His Majesty's displeasure with the thought that they had, at least, succeeded in ousting the Blighs from the colony. It was an alluring notion that one Bligh, if she wished, could remain—not in defeat and obscurity, but in triumph as the wife of the Lieutenant-Governor. . . .

Her father, obsessed by his own problems, was oblivious. He found nothing in the despatches from England which Macquarie had handed him to suggest what penalties were to be visited by an outraged Government upon those who had defied it. Macquarie himself could tell him nothing save that Mr. Atkins was to be sent home, and that Macarthur was to have been tried on the spot by a Criminal Court. But the age and excesses of Mr. Atkins had so impaired his health that Bligh gloomily doubted whether he would survive the voyage; and Macarthur was not on the spot to be tried. He corresponded at length upon the subject with the new Judge Advocate, who gave it as his opinion that the crime of high treason did not attach to the colony, and was doubtful upon what other charge an indictment could be laid against those of the rebel party who remained in it. Mr. Bent, indeed, found the whole business extremely tiresome. For one thing, he was ambitious for wealth, and he had already discovered that New South Wales was a place where such spare moments as he could command might be very profitably employed. Moreover, he had formed an unfavourable impression of the Blighs. "They are a pretty pair," he wrote peevishly to his mother, "and I cordially wish they were in England, for he is eternally troubling me." Captain Bligh was shrewd enough to see that the last thing his successor wanted was a local trial which would arouse once more the violent passions of partisanship which were now beginning to subside, and he sometimes suspected that if there were some alternative legal measure which could be invoked, Mr. Bent was not anxious to discover it. But he was himself no lawyer, and he realised that the weight of his vengeance must be reserved for the arch-criminals, and meted out to them in London.

He chose the witnesses whom he desired to take with him when he sailed, and laid their names before the Governor. Macquarie was shocked. Sixteen of them! He trusted that Captain Bligh would consider the great expense to Government of paying passages for so many people—the great inconvenience to themselves and their families . . . ! Captain Bligh contented himself, finally, with ten.

Midway through March he set out, accompanied by a small party, upon a farewell tour of the Hawkesbury districts. Here he felt himself among people who were, almost to a man, his supporters, and prepared to acknowledge with gratitude the benefits of his much-condemned regime; and to them, whether in the townships or scattered among the outlying farms, he was determined to make his adieux. He had ground to cover which forbade the use of his carriage, so he went on horseback, and suffered for it. Worry had sapped his once abundant energy, and lack of exercise during two years of enforced activity had increased his cor-pulence. Soon he lay with a fever and a badly-swollen leg at Green Hills, and Dr. Arnold—who had fortunately embraced this opportunity of seeing the country—found himself with a difficult patient, and unburdened himself in a letter home. ". . . although he was sufficiently grateful, yet on the whole he is so uncertain in his manners, so violent in his conduct, but at the same time so eloquent in his diction, that he overpowers and affrights every person that has any dealings with him. . . ."

Still imperfectly recovered from his illness, the ex-Governor returned after three weeks not only to a round of entertainments which he con-templated without enthusiasm, but to a gathering storm of which he must pretend to be unaware, though he had known it to be brewing. His partisans, wishing once more to demonstrate their loyalty, had long ago sought the Governor's consent to a public meeting; here they would vote Bligh an address declaring their sympathy, their indignation at his depo-sition, and their detestation of the usurpers.

His Excellency sighed. He had been trying assiduously to smother the dying sparks of dissention, and he foresaw that such a meeting would fan them once more to a blaze. He could not refuse, but he could, perhaps, delay. Would not these gentlemen, he soothingly suggested, defer the meeting until shortly before Captain Bligh's departure—surely a more suitable time . . . ? The gentlemen had agreed, and now the time had come.

"Confound it!" Macquarie exclaimed privately to his wife. "This business will set them all by the ears again! The place is poisoned with this deplorable party spirit—no compromise, no forbearance . . . !"

"Never mind," replied Mrs. Macquarie, producing for the hundredth time her formula of comfort. "He will soon be gone."

The meeting was, indeed, tumultuous, and fulfilled the Governor's worst fears. Nothing emerged from it but a resolution passed by Bligh's supporters, four counter-resolutions—which the other party declared carried "unanimously", though their opponents had left the meeting—and a couple of difficult half-hours for Macquarie. The decent veil of tranquillity with which he had been striving to clothe naked hatred being thus rudely stripped away, the leaders of each faction proceeded to a round of farewell parties from which those of the other were carefully excluded. Only Government House and the officers of the 73rd—the new-comers, observing with slightly superior astonishment the unforgiving enmities of the past—were able to adorn all functions with impartial amiability.

Mr. John Palmer, preparing for departure as one of Bligh's witnesses, welcomed their Excellencies and a large company of ladies and gentlemen at his Woolloomooloo mansion. The news, received only that day from Hobart Town of Colonel Collins' sudden death, did nothing to damp the spirits of those guests who had resented his treatment of the ex-Governor. But Palmer himself felt a momentary and unexpected pang. Through the glitter of this elaborate and sophisticated function he glimpsed, sud-denly, the Sydney Cove he had first seen twenty-two years ago, all virgin bush, mysterious and unresponsive. He saw the chaos of the first landing, the rows of tents, the convicts huddled in their miserable mud huts. He saw the first Governor—now living, old and ill, at Bath; he saw young George Johnston—now middle-aged, facing trial on a charge of mutiny; he saw young King—now dead; young Collins—now dead. . . . Time, he thought, had dealt strangely and variously with that little band; and in a moment of abstraction he forgot the lights and music, oppressed by a vague, unformed regret.

*　　　　　*　　　　　*　　　　　*

It was the end of April before the ex-Governor, his welcome long worn out, at last embarked, his daughter still beside him. It would be some time yet before they sailed, but O'Connell would countenance no further delay in breaking the news to him that his daughter would remain. Bligh received it with blank incredulity.

"My daughter . . . ? Consent . . . ?" His puzzled voice was suddenly a roar. "Certainly not, Sir!"

But the denial, and the violence of its utterance, were automatic—an instinctive resistance to something which had hit him like a physical blow. His dear child to leave him—remain behind . . . ? It was an idea so entirely outside his calculations that he was bewildered. He dismissed the Colonel and summoned her. She wept, answering his questions in confusion and distress. It was true; she had received the Colonel's addresses, welcomed them, given him her word. . . .

Even as he questioned, warned and protested, he knew himself help-less, not even convinced by his own arguments. When she left him, his consent had been unhappily given, and he sat alone for a long time, his head bent, his hands hanging limply between his knees. His mind was already trying to frame the sentences in which he must send this news to a mother eagerly awaiting her daughter's return; he could form only fragments, incoherent and disconnected. "In the highest feelings of comfort and pride in bringing her to England. . . . my heart devoted to her . . . in the midst of most parental affections and conflicting passion of adoration for so good and admired a child . . . I found what I least expected . . . I could not believe it . . . What will you not, my dear Betsey, feel for my situation at this time . . . overwhelmed with a loss I could not retrieve . . . overwhelmed, overwhelmed. . . ."

But he must not speak only of his own sense of desolation. He must add words of reassurance. "The honour, goodness and high character of Colonel O'Connell . . . they remain persons of the utmost importance and consequence . . . beloved by all . . . my dear Love, I had thought nothing could have induced her to have quitted me. . . ."

It was his own grief crowding back into his mind. He thrust it away and turned again to preparations for his lonely voyage. He had no heart for the final festivities; he looked strangely old, tired and subdued as he gave his daughter away in the magnificently-decorated drawing-room at Government House where Mr. Marsden performed the marriage ceremony. He saw her drive off to Parramatta with her husband, and four days later he sailed.

Never before had there been such an exodus, nor such a frenzy of farewells. Among the crowd gathered on South Head to watch the three ships leave the harbour, that party spirit which His Excellency so much deplored was still high and vociferous. The New South Wales Corps was divided between the *Porpoise* and the *Dromedary*. On the former travelled Mr. Atkins, old, apprehensive, and entirely unlamented. On the latter Mrs. Paterson shed a tear or two, less for the colony she was leaving than for the memory of the many trials it had inflicted upon her weak, peace-loving husband, now lying below in his cabin, too ill to give it a last glance. Dr. Arnold, a shipmate of Bligh and his witnesses on board the *Hindostan,* heard the cheering and counter-cheering which sped them on their way, and reflected that neither in the voyage before him, nor in the colony they left behind, was there much prospect of harmony. One Governor too fierce; the next—unless he was much mistaken—too mild. Well, it was not, thank God, any affair of his.

The *Hindostan* was turning to breast the long swell between the Heads. On its deck Bligh stood apart, struggling with a sensation of defeat. Again, for a second time, to go home with a task unfinished . . . again to face the world as one whose command had been wrested from him by mutineers . . . ! Yet as he turned from his last sight of the harbour and faced the ocean, something had already begun to revive in him. Defeat? He was on his way to another battle!

*   *   *   *

The Governor and his wife drove home alone from South Head. Captain Antill and the rest of the vice-regal entourage were returning on horseback, and Mrs. Macquarie, no less than her husband, was glad to relax in pleasant silence, and admire the picturesque glimpses of the harbour that presented themselves from this high and winding ridge.

What a whirl it had been these last few weeks! Balls, dinner-parties, fêtes, and a wedding to crown it all! In a way it had been enjoyable, and might have seemed entirely so had it not been for the knowledge of their own peculiarly delicate situation; of jealous eyes watching to see upon whom she smiled, with whom Macquarie exchanged a handclasp, and whether this smile or that handclasp were warmer or more cordial than those bestowed a moment since on someone else. . . .

Oh, la, how tiresome! But now that brawling set had departed the colony would surely regain its disordered wits. She looked pensively out over the harbour, hoping that dear Macquarie's optimism and confidence would not be too rudely shaken. He possessed, she reflected, a certain simplicity of character which assumed—despite all worldly protestations to the contrary—an equal forthrightness in others; a noble trait, of course, but one which left him, perhaps, a little vulnerable . . . ? On the other hand, his wisdom and energy must rapidly produce excellent effects; she felt cheered, turning over in her mind the many measures he had already adopted. He had naturally forbidden the most improper custom of working on the Sabbath, and ordered the closing of all public houses during Divine Service. He had threatened punishment upon persons enticing girls from the Orphan School, and seducing them from the paths of virtue. He had invited such men of the New South Wales Corps as desired to remain in the colony to volunteer for service in a Veteran Company attached to the 73rd. He had voiced anew the perennial complaint of all Governors—that the inhabitants not only persisted in washing their clothes in the Tank Stream, but threw their dirt, garbage and offal into it, and allowed their swine and cattle to stray upon its banks. (Mercy, how foolish and improvident!) He had observed with displeasure the great number of public houses, and pruned it ruthlessly to twenty in Sydney, three in Parramatta, six at the Hawkesbury, and—as an indulgence to thirsty travellers—one half-way between each of these points. (And quite enough, too!)

He had imposed an extra duty on all spirits imported into the colony. (Heaven send that he might be able to overcome the evils raised by this terrible intemperance!) He had deplored the failure of children to enrol at the free school, and directed Mr. Howe to assure parents that if their literacy were unequal to the task of filling in application forms, they might receive assistance at the *Gazette* office. (But even children could earn a few pence; might not poor parents think this more important than pot-hooks and spelling?) He had prohibited the use of guns in the town and about the Government Domain. He had issued a truly thunderous procla-mation against vice, condemning the careless colonial custom of dispensing with the formality of a marriage service; and he had threatened the keepers of brothels, and urged upon everyone the proper observance of morality and decorum. He had despatched Colonel O'Connell upon a tour of the country to make a general muster of its inhabitants. (And how he had stared when she slyly hinted that three weeks' absence from Sydney at that time was a cruel interruption of the Colonel's wooing!) Yes, he had certainly done much already, and no person of unprejudiced mind could fail to see in all this the determination of a wise and benign ruler to improve the lot of his subjects. ("Subjects . . . !" How easily the word came! But he was, indeed, like a king, and had several times himself spoken jestingly of "my reign". . . .)

Yet one must not suppose that all would be easy. There was the question of deserving emancipists, for example, and here it was already plain that his benevolent policy would meet with some opposition. There was that very worthy person, Mr. Andrew Thompson, who had made such a favourable early impression by coming forward to offer his Sydney house to the Bents just when—more than a little disgruntled—they were about to retreat to the ship again, rather than suffer the discomforts of Mr. Atkins's mean and most unsuitable residence. Macquarie would cer-tainly not be so foolish and unreasonable as to dwell upon the youthful indiscretion of so industrious and capable a man—and a brother Scot, as well! Dr. Redfern, too, was clearly a person of superior education and attainments; and Mr. Simeon Lord had been most helpful on several occasions. As for the Acting Surveyor-General, Mr. Meehan, he was perfectly indispensable. How could anyone of good sense fail to allow that diligence and upright conduct should suffice to restore an emancipist to respectability? Yet there were many who opposed the idea with quite remarkable vehemence—and none more bitterly than the Reverend Mr. Marsden. (Was not this odd, in what might be termed a professional Christian . . . ?)

Ah, well, it did not really signify, for Macquarie would not be deterred by such harsh and illiberal views. Mr. Thompson, Mr. Lord and Dr. Redfern had all been received at Government House; Mr. Thompson was already appointed a Magistrate and Justice of the Peace at the Hawkesbury; Dr. Redfern's post as Assistant Surgeon would, she trusted, be officially confirmed from home; and Mr. Lord would also be elevated to the Magistracy when a vacancy occurred. And, thought Mrs. Macquarie, tilting her nose, let the malcontents say what they pleased!

The Governor said suddenly:

"A fine, fair wind!"

His wife smiled. It could not blow his predecessor away too fast for him! Already she was aware of a slackening of tension in him which matched her own, and the glance she stole at his face revealed the expression of a child left alone at last to its own devices. His voice translated it into words:

"Well, they've got off, and God be thanked for it! Impossible to settle down whilst they were about, darting their black looks at each other, ready to fly at one another's throats! I'm glad to see the back of them. There'll be some noise in England when the trial comes on, and they'll all afford fine food for the lawyers! An extraordinary character, Bligh . . . ! Though I confess I can't see anything he has done to bring such a thing on him—except to be himself!"

She wondered: When are we ourselves? Are we not all moulded by events taking place about us? Do we not find certain of our qualities developed by a situation, and others modified? In a serene and orderly society are we not calm, reasonable and amiable, and in a disturbed one do we not feel our calm assailed, our reason less firm, our hearts closing doors of anger and suspicion? She said slowly: "We have known one Captain Bligh. Perhaps there is another whom we could hardly have expected to find revealed to us in this curious and difficult situation . . . ?"

But his next words showed that her comment had passed unregarded. He was occupied with another train of thought, and it was folding a worried crease between his eyes.

"Matters are in a very ill-ordered state here—I fear I'll be compelled to considerable expenditure. I trust the Colonial Office will see the necessity for it."

But upon this Mrs. Macquarie felt herself unable to offer a reassuring opinion. She contented herself with laying a hand for a moment on his arm, and hoping fervently that it would.

*   *   *   *

Mrs. Mannion, having summoned Flora to make up a fire in her bed-room, had drawn her chair close to it, and, with her Journal on her knee, was writing fast.

"*May 12th, 1810.* To-day Gov'r Bligh sailed, but I was not here to witness his Departure, having made my farewells a few days since. Have but this evening returned from Beltrasna, whither I went yesterday with-out apprising Patrick of my Intention, being disturbed in my mind by certain suspicions, and wishing to discover if they were well founded. Upon alighting from my Carriage at the door, the first person my eyes rested upon was Dilboong, and my fears were at once confirmed. She is very near her Time.

"Upon seeing me she ran forward with every expression of Joy, and was soon followed by Mrs. Emmett, whom I dismissed after some con-versation, and retired with Dilboong to the Parlour. I at first wondered whether the father of her Child might be some overseer or labourer about the Place, but that it is Patrick's I was not long left in doubt, though it was soon clear that Dilboong regarded the coming Event as the most natural in the world, and felt no apprehension that she had done wrong in entering upon such a Union, but believed that in such a matter, as in all others, she must be acquiescent to her Master. Indeed, I found it difficult to fix her attention upon this business, for she continually broke in upon my questions to ask: When would Mr. Miles return? Upon my telling her that there was no time fixed for it, her eyes filled with tears, and her face assumed an expression of sadness, yet of patient Resignation which moved me deeply. How faithfully she recalls the playmate who left her seven years ago! The affection and docility of her nature, together with her Ignorance and simplicity, quite dispelled any thought of Censure from my mind so far as she was concerned, though I felt my anger rising against Patrick.

"It was, as I think now, fortunate that he was abroad in the fields when I arrived, since the interval before his return enabled me to Compose myself, and consider the matter more calmly. It is, after all, I fear, an occurrence which is far from uncommon, and can often claim less excuse than I am able to discern in this instance. So that when he appeared, and I taxed him with it, I was able to speak without that heat which, I believe, would have made him close his heart to me.

"He readily admitted the Circumstance, and indeed seemed somewhat relieved to speak of it, expressing, as I was glad to hear, some concern for Dilboong herself, and assuring me that it was not his intention to cast her Off, but always to provide a home and protection for her and the child. Perhaps observing that I entertained some doubt as to whether this might for ever be possible (or indeed proper), he added: That he thought he should never marry. I did not pursue this question. If he is indeed resolved, no arguments could prevail; but the appearance someday of a suitable young Woman will afford more potent Persuasion than any I could apply. I contented myself, therefore, with assuring him that a shelter for Dilboong and her child would always be available beneath my roof, and addressed myself to discovering the reason for this Melancholy, and that hermit-like Habit which he had imposed upon himself.

"In this I encountered much resistance, he asserting that he had no taste for Society, and preferred a seclusion which afforded him time for reading, meditation, and literary Composition. This I allowed to be True, for Patrick has ever been of a mild, quiet, and studious disposition; yet from his manner I was persuaded that it was but part of the truth, and continued to press him, when, after much Hesitation, he disclosed to me a story which filled me with pity and Amazement.

"He declares that eleven years ago, before I came to the Colony, he was riding alone one day on the river bank some miles above Beltrasna, when he came upon Ellen's son, Johnny Prentice, whom all had long believed dead. The boy (for he was then but fifteen years old, being of the same age as Patrick) had been living seven years among the Natives, and like them went naked, armed with spears, and was so accustomed to speaking in their tongue that he had almost forgot his own. This astonishing Circumstance Patrick at once revealed to Ellen, who persuaded him into a promise to preserve the secret. Upon my asking in surprise why she did not rather wish her son restored to her, Patrick told me much of the child's early life. It appears that once before he had run away to join the Natives, with whom he had lived some time before being discovered, and returned to the settlement much against his Will. He possessed a rebellious Spirit, which constantly brought Trouble upon him, and cherished an inveterate hatred of my late Husband, who imposed upon him arduous Tasks, and severe punishments. Ellen feared, so Patrick believes, that such a youth would have been for ever in conflict with my Husband and with the Authorities; and that the fact that the boy claimed to possess Firearms alarmed her, lest he had already, or should in the future, commit a Crime which would bring him to the Gallows.

"How deep in the past may the roots of an event lie buried! And how little we may know of those who live beside us! I had learned in a general way of this child, but only yesterday was it revealed to me how deeply Patrick had been affected by the Association. From their first meeting as children of six years old, his gentle nature was strongly influenced by the more independent and resourceful character of Johnny Prentice. And how Melancholy is the picture of that character which emerges from Patrick's accounts—one in which the admirable qualities of independence and resource were, in a mere infant, bent by harshness to evil ends; to theft and lying, and bitter, unchildlike knowledge. (I was much struck by certain passages about Johnny in a Journal which Patrick had begun to keep some time before this chance meeting with his old playmate, and which he brought out and showed to me. "I have shown it to no one else," he said, and upon my replying that I also have for many years found pleasure in a Journal for my own eyes alone, he seemed calmer, and spoke more freely, and confessed that he has himself continued the practice to the present time.)

"Overwhelmed as I was with wonder and Dismay at this strange Tale, I could not descry in it anything which should account for Patrick's behaviour; for even a young man of great Sensibility would surely not continue to be so affected by something which happened very long ago, and for which no blame could be apportioned to him? I therefore sought to cheer him by saying: That if the boy (though he would be a man by now, if he still lives) could be found, we could befriend him; but if not, Patrick must not for ever permit something irrevocable to depress his Spirits and govern his life. Upon which he looked at me in a strange manner, and replied: 'You think that is all?'

"Observing that his agitation increased again, I besought him to continue if there were more to tell, and he at once burst into words, saying Wildly that he was responsible for two deaths, and perhaps even for three; that had he reported his meeting with Johnny, and caused him to be returned to Civilisation, much tragedy would have been averted; concluding in a desperate fashion, and beating with one hand upon the other: 'Yet I could not, for it would have seemed a betrayal!'

"Quite aghast at the Distress he revealed, I thought it best to speak with some Sharpness, declaring it absurd for him to presume the course events would have taken had be behaved differently, this being something which cannot come within any man's Knowledge; and seeing him something more Composed, I begged him to explain himself, when he drew a chair close to mine, and said in a low voice: 'He is still alive—I know it!' This appearing to me a happy rather than a disturbing circumstance, I was about to repeat that we must find him, and recompense him for his Misfortunes; when Patrick, leaning forward to whisper (though we were alone in the room, and no one near) declared with great abruptness: '*It was he who killed my Father!*'

"I do not recall having screamed but once before, nor swooned from any cause save bodily ill, yet a cry did escape me upon hearing this, and I felt a momentary faintness, so that my memory of that instant is a trifle confused. I recall clutching at Patrick's sleeve and uttering the words: 'Ellen? Ellen?' and he broke away from me in a kind of fury and walked

66

up and down the room muttering as if to himself: 'Yes, I let her die, I let her hang though I knew she was innocent. Her eyes commanded me to say nothing and I was silent.'

"What is the truth of this terrible Story? For Patrick says that upon that night he saw nothing save a faint shape vanishing into the darkness from the viranda where my Husband lay dead, and Ellen stood over him with the Pistol in her hand. I am appalled by the dilemma in which he found himself, for of evidence such as I imagine a Court of Law would accept, there was not a shred. And poor Ellen Proclaimed her guilt with a Passion and earnestness which I well remember, but which now bears a new and dreadful light. Anything that Patrick could have said would surely have been fruitless in the face of that confession, and the well-known history of the unhappy woman's relations with my Husband. I endeavoured to comfort him with this Thought, yet to his Sensitive nature I fear the comfort was cold.

"I have been reflecting much, and I cannot but believe that this Johnny was the Assassin. I have considered the Thefts and other depredations which took place over a long period at Beltrasna, and whose Author was never discovered. There were the firearms stolen from my Husband's study, and Cousin Bertha's footstool from the Viranda, and even my silk scarf which so mysteriously vanished. It is true that those articles which disappeared from outside the house might well have been taken, as was supposed at the time, by natives, but the firearms were inside the house, and I believe my scarf also, though it is possible that I may have dropped it from the Carriage. Yet if we once assume the presence of this young man who, though going barefooted and using spears like a Native, is still a white man, familiar with the use of keys and firearms, do not all these things become at once more comprehensible? Might he not by some means, either with or without his Mother's knowledge, have obtained her key to the House, and effected an entrance to it in the dead of Night? And would not this supposition explain the fact that it was one of these same Pistols which poor Ellen held in her hand when she was discovered by my dead Husband's body? I have considered also the murder outside her Cottage long ago of the overseer, Merrett, which it was at the time natural to attribute to Natives, owing to the prints of bare feet which were found, and to the spear with which the Deed was committed. Yet again, if we assume the presence of this youth, does not all wear a different aspect? Can we not find in all these otherwise bewildering Events a constant and terrible Motive—that of an embittered and revenge-ful Outlaw, bent upon harassing those whom life has taught him to detest?

"And I have pondered another possibility which disturbs me strangely:

Could this Johnny have been associated with the convict, Finn? Could it have been by his agency that the man escaped? Why not? Finn was working by the river, and no doubt Johnny, in his native life, must have learned from his dark Friends their art of fashioning and paddling canoes? And if this be so, and they had been long in association, may not the murder of my Husband have been revenge not only for Johnny's own wrongs, but for the torture and death which was meted out to that unhappy Man?

"I feel greatly wearied. This morning, before anyone was astir at Beltrasna, I went out to the little hillock where Finn lies buried. Was he a good man, or an evil? I have just taken from their places between the pages of this Journal those half-burned leaves of the book my Husband once took from him. *'O ye that love mankind!'* Surely the man who cherished and studied these words was not evil? *'Tyranny, like Hell, is not easily vanquished.'* *'I thank God that I fear not.'* Can the man who copied down such sentiments have been a villainous and stony-hearted Rogue? I can by no means account for the certainty with which my heart answers these questions.

"I have agreed with Patrick to reveal nothing of Johnny's continued existence, nor of the terrible suspicions we harbour concerning him. Is this Wrong? Should the Law, having hanged the wrong person, now hang the right one—if it can discover him? What is guilt, and what innocence is this coil of misery? Though I am confused in my thoughts, something clearly bids me leave this door locked upon the past."

        *   *   *   *

The Warragombie River was little frequented, even by natives. The deep, precipitous gorge through which it cut its way harboured no game save a few rock wallabies; though good fishing in its deeper pools some-times tempted hunters, the tribes regarded it as a place to look down at from above, and not for use in the comings and goings of daily life. It gathered, as the white men had yet to discover, the flow from many creeks coming down from the heights to join the Wollondilly and the Koornong Rivers, which met above it, and poured their accumulated waters through its dark, majestic ravine to join the Nepean.

It was familiar enough to Johnny Prentice, who had lived during his boyhood partly with the native tribes, and partly in a secluded hut beside a small, tributary creek of the Wollondilly. He rarely saw it now, how-ever, for white settlement had moved too close for the liking of his friend, Matthew Finn, whose escape from Beltrasna he had contrived. Together, four years ago, they had retreated farther inland with their goods and livestock to establish themselves in a quiet valley above the Koornong. Here they had later brought Johnny's native wife, Ngili, and her baby

68

son, Kooree; here Johnny's half-brother, Billalong, had also joined them for such short periods as his restless temperament allowed; here they had built their new hut, and cleared their land, and sowed their grain; here they had jealously tended the few fowls and goats stolen from Green Hills, the cattle descended from those stolen by Andrew Prentice long ago from the wild herds at the Cow Pastures, and a handful of sheep taken from Mr. Macarthur's flocks at Camden. And from here they had set out one summer day upon the desperate adventure from which only Johnny had returned. Ngili, cradling her child upon her knee, had seen him come up from the river alone, and when she looked into his face she had no need of words to tell her that the man her people had named Coo-mal, brother, was dead. It had been his plan to release other convicts as he himself had been released—to bring them here to share the freedom and the possessions with which a new life was being built. He and Johnny were to have returned with these others whose arms would lighten the burdens of toil, and whose presence would make a tribe, where there had been only a family before. This last, to Ngili, was the most comprehensible part of the undertaking, for she suffered from her isolation. If more men came, she reasoned, there would soon be, in the natural course of events, more women; and if more women, then more children. Thus the proper pattern of life would be re-established, and this high, cold, lonely valley would seem no longer a place of exile.

But no more men had come, and Finn himself had not returned. She wailed for him—for his cheerfulness, for his ready tongue, for the gaiety of spirit which he had possessed, and which seemed among her people so necessary for living. It was something that Dyonn-ee, her husband, had never been able to sustain alone, and now could hardly summon even for a passing moment. Though he was not of her race, he had lived with it for so long that she had sometimes been able to forget his difference; now it was hard to forget, for he had become wholly a white man, driven—as all white men seemed to be—by an insatiable desire to work. Finn, too, had betrayed this curious obsession, and had implanted it in Dyonn-ee, who formerly had accepted the native custom of working only when the immediate necessities of life must be provided; yet Finn had leavened work with laughter, and thus it could be endured. Now that he was gone, and there were but two to work where three had worked before, toil had become a kind of madness. From sunrise to darkness Dyonn-ee worked —and she worked too. Even Kooree, who was not yet six years old, was given endless tasks; and though his father never struck him, neither did he caress nor play with him, but moved through the long days hardly speaking, grim, unsmiling, and unyouthful.

There were things in the hut which always lay on a high shelf, out of reach of Kooree's exploring fingers; things which Ngili herself was not permitted to touch, though she made good use of them. All children, she knew, must learn the legends of their tribe, the stories of ancestral heroes and great deeds. Bewildered and disturbed as she was by the thought that her child had no tribe, she was at least able to provide him with his legends. Here on the shelf lay material for the legend of his father, Dyonn-ee, and of his father's father (whose name was of course forbidden now that he was dead) and often she would lift the child that he might look at a key threaded on a loop of kangaroo hide, and at a necklace made of human hair and tarnished metal buttons.

The tale began, as legends must, with the words *"berrugen korillabo"* —long, long ago—and upon hearing these words Kooree would cease his fidgeting, abandon his mischief, and relax into a state of tranced receptive-ness.

Long, long ago, then, before she herself was born, there had come to this land a strange, pale-skinned tribe called the Beerewolgal, the men come from afar, who had made a great camp on the seashore, far from the *towri* of her own people. But at last, after many seasons, there had come to the *towri* of the Boorooberongal, who lived not far distant from her own tribe, one of these people—a teeri-yeetchbeem, a red-headed one —alone, fleeing from his fellows who would have captured and slain him. Being ill, he was tended in the camp of the Boorooberongal, and when the sickness left him he had taken a woman of the tribe named Cunnem-beillee, and departed.

About this time, also, there had appeared near the river great beasts such as had never been seen in the land before, ". . . though you know them well, my little one," Ngili would say, "and drink the good milk that comes from them." The *teeri-yeetchbeem*, finding these beasts, had taken them for his own, and journeyed up the river to a place where he had made his camp in the towri of her own people, and there he had lived with Cunnembeillee, who had borne a son, ". . . and this son you also know, for he is Billalong, who teaches you to throw your spear."

Now it happened—so the tale went on—that one day while Cunnem-beille was out looking for food, she came upon two other members of the Beerewolgal, both dead, and wearing strange, bright coverings to which were fixed the round, hard objects now strung upon this necklace which Cunnembeillee had made from her own hair. This necklace she always wore, and was envied by the other women, who had none so fine—though some said now that it was the cause of the illness which brought about her death.

The *teeri-yeetchbeem* had at last begun to fear that his enemies would discover him, so he had found another retreat beyond the river, well hidden, and to this place he had moved some of his beasts and all of his possessions; for he now had many things which he had taken from a great man of his own tribe named Man-yun, who had come to dwell farther down the river. In this new place, which she herself had never seen (for it was a place of death to which only white men would go) he had built a hut such as this one in which they now lived, with a door, and a key; and the key was this very one which Kooree could now behold with his own eyes. The red-headed one had worn it always round his neck.

But before he could remove his wife and child to the hut, Gheegher-Gheeger, the wild, cold wind whose home is in the mountains ". . . up yonder, at the top of those high cliffs which you can see . . ." had burst from his hiding-place, bringing a great rain with him which had caused a flood in the river; and into its rushing waters the little Billalong had fallen. . . . (Here it was always necessary for Ngili to pause, in order to remind the round-eyed and tremulous Kooree that since he had himself seen Billalong a grown man in his full health and strength, the story must end happily.) He would, indeed, have been swept away and drowned had not his mother plunged into the river and swum to his rescue; but the waters were too strong for her to regain the bank, so she had clung to a floating tree which had been guided by the good spirit until it came to a place where the *teeri-yeetchbeem* was, and he had saved them.

Now, with the introduction of magic into the tale, it became very solemn; Ngili's voice was hushed, and Kooree's eyes grew rounder than ever. For though the red-headed one had saved Cunnembeille and Billa-long, he had himself been killed; a great log, borne down by the force of the waters, had crushed his body against a rock, and he had sunk beneath the yellow flood, and died. Yet when Cunnembeillee—cold, sorrowful and exhausted—had staggered up from the river with Billalong in her arms, she had almost immediately found him again, sitting waiting for her beside a bright fire, and wearing round his neck, as he had always worn it, the key. But he was no longer a man; he was now a *birahlee*, not much bigger than Kooree himself, and his name was—Dyonn-ee!

This was a climax unfailingly gratifying to Kooree, who was proud that his father should be the hero of so fine a tale. He well understood from his mother's careful explanations that it was customary for the spirit, after death, to take once more the form of a child, and in this form to ascend by the tree-tops to the sky. In this case the child-spirit had remained on earth to live its life over again, which was undoubtedly strange, but no stranger than many other things told of the Beerewolgal.

There were also other tales, sequels to this one of the key and the necklace, and they were all tales of the exploits of his father, Dyonn-ee.

There were tales of the time when, still a boy, he had lived in the hut with Cunnembeillee, and Billalong, and Milbooroo—who had become Cunnembeillee's new husband, and to whom she had borne two little boys and a little girl, whose names were Gooradoo, Balgundra, and Gooburdi. But at last Cunnembeillee had died, so that the hut became a place forbidden to the dark people, and Milbooroo had returned to the tribe with his children, and only Billalong had remained there for a time with Dyonn-ee. There was the tale of how another member of the Beerewolgal, escaping from his own tribe, had arrived, sick and starving, at the hut, and of how Dyonn-ee had given him shelter and food until he too had died. There were tales of how Dyonn-ee had gone far down the river in his canoe, sometimes accompanied by Billalong and other natives, to a place where the white men had made one of their large camps, there to exchange beef for many of their goods. That small, silvery object, for instance, which (so Dyonn-ee had told her) was placed by the women of the Beerewolgal upon their fingertips—doubtless as a spell against some kind of evil; and that curious implement which Dyonn-ee sometimes used to trim his hair and beard; and that pile of white, fragile sheets called paper, ". . . some covered as you can see with lines of black marks which were made upon them with that small, straight stick. . . ."

Who, Kooree would enquire, had made these marks, and what were they for? He-who-is-gone, Ngili would reply rather doubtfully, had tried to explain their purpose to her, seeming to say that they were message-marks; and he had made most of them himself, though Dyonn-ee, who also understood the art, had made some. Privately, however, she was not satisfied. Among her own people marks were often made to convey messages from one tribe to another, but they were quite different. Indeed they were much more pleasing to look at than these thin, monotonous black lines, being burned or painted upon flattened sticks especially prepared, which were then carried to their destination by a ceremoniously-decorated bearer. These papers had never been carried anywhere save from the old hut to the new one; and why, argued Ngili to herself, should Dyonn-ee and the one now dead, who had lived together, and had only to open their mouths to speak to each other, make message marks? She was inclined to believe that paper was, rather, a kind of sacred *churinga* of the white man, in which his very spirit was contained; for she had observed that never were Dyonn-ee and that other more solemn—never more clearly engaged in wrestling with the deeper mysteries of life—than when they were making, or speaking of, these marks.

She would pass on to tell of those small, hard discs which stood in a pile at the back of the shelf. These, she explained, were called money, and she had heard it said that they could be exchanged for food—though it was difficult to believe that anyone would give good food for objects so small and useless. She would tell, too, the story of how Dyonn-ee had saved him-who-is-gone from captivity, and brought him to the old hut, from which he had often come to visit her people; and of how he had joined the men in their hunting, and talked with the women, and played with the children, ". . . but always saying that you, the son of his friend Dyonn-ee, were the finest of them all. . . ." This tale, however, she did not tell very often, for it brought tears to her eyes. More exciting, in any case, was the tale of how Dyonn-ee went sometimes at night to the great house of the white man, Man-yun, who was his most hated enemy, to take or destroy his possessions; and even, once, to enter it, and take Man-yun's weapons, his sticks of fire, and this beautiful thing which was now her own. . . . And Ngili would spread out proudly all that was left of a long, silk scarf, still soft and pleasing to the touch, still showing beneath its grease and grime patterns of coloured flowers wreathing two mysterious—(and no doubt magical) marks—C.M.—which, from long familiarity, she could have traced in the dust if she had dared.

Thus, though he had no tribe, Kooree had his tribal legends, and knew them by heart. Having no recollection of other children, he did not miss their company, but took the chickens, the kids, the long-legged calves and the new-born lambs for his companions. He had friends, too, among the birds and animals of the country, and once Dyonn-ee had brought home a baby wallaby which he had found in the pouch of its dead mother. What little he knew of hunting, and the lore of tracking in the bush, he had learned from Billalong—for Dyonn-ee, though he had once been proficient in these arts, rarely troubled about them now. His light, coppery body naked in summer, and clad in an odd assortment of improvised clothing in winter, Kooree trotted soberly about performing the tasks allotted to him. He spoke in a mixture of his father's tongue and his mother's, ate well, grew fast, loved Ngili, obeyed Dyonn-ee, and was happy enough.

* * * *

It was almost three years since Johnny, in the first agony of his fury and grief at the death of Matthew Finn, had determined to turn his back for ever upon his own race. This resolve he could have kept easily enough had the decision been, as he supposed it to be, entirely his own; for a kind of dull, stony indifference had replaced the nagging and hostile curiosity which had disturbed his earlier years. It was as though all the tormenting memories and the shapeless resentments which had haunted his boyhood had been concentrated into that one hot, terrible afternoon which saw the recapture and death of Finn. On that day hatred had filled him like a poison from which he felt that he must have died had he not, by one action, purged himself. For, despite all that Finn had taught him, he was still, in moments of emotion, governed by the spiritual lore of the natives, whose symbolism had merely extended the symbolism of the child he had been when he joined them; and therefore, seeking a symbol at which to direct his hatred, he had clothed all evil in the person of Stephen Mannion, and shot it down. He was still living in the curious, empty lethargy which —when passion was at last exhausted—had followed that action; for him, emotionally, his own society was dead, and his brain, when he heard tales of it, was only half attentive.

It was, however, so far from dead in fact, that his native friends on the banks of the Nepean were feeling its impact on their own life more and more, and from Billalong, Gooradoo and Balgundra, when they came to visit him, Johnny heard news of his countrymen from time to time. When he did, on rare occasions during those years, follow his river down to its junction with the Wollondilly, and thence, by old, familiar routes, across the high ridge to descend into the Cow Pastures, he went neither from curiosity, nor for company, but for spoil. He made no attempt to spy upon the doings of the white men; he even avoided, as far as possible, the sight of their dwellings. Billalong and a few other native youths who had frequented the huts and stockyards since childhood could still come and go unchallenged, and they were able to steal for him various useful things —a lanthorn, a tinder-box, small quantities of seed, a butcher's knife, an old pair of boots—and, having got what he wanted, Johnny would turn his back once more upon a life which no longer seemed real.

But of late Billalong had reported that he and his companions were not now as well received as formerly by the labourers and shepherds who called them thieves, and displayed an indignation which (said Billalong) seemed remarkable in men who, year by year, stole ever more land from the tribes whose ancestors had dwelt upon it since the dream-time. In many ways, he complained, life, which had once been so simple, was growing complex and disturbing. Some of the natives had left their camps and gone to labour on the farms of the white men, causing great distress and forboding among the elders. More and more of the Beerewolgal were coming about the Cow Pastures; settlers often grazed their horses and cattle on the rich pasturage of that favoured spot, though it was said to be forbidden by their Law. Clashes between black men and white men were becoming more frequent; indeed, the time seemed to be approaching when friendly · association could no longer be continued. Milbooroo, declared Billalong, and Murrah, and Narrang, and Kurringy, and many others, were now saying that it was impossible to live at peace with white men who were not content with taking vast tracts of land, but ordered the black men off it, broke their spears and canoes, insulted them, stole and ravished their women, and fired on them with no more thought than if they had been wallabies. The tribesmen were becoming very tired of all this, and it was freely said among them that they, too, could kill.

*   *   *   *

Nature was friendly to the new Governor in this first year. The sun shone, the rains fell, and the crops stood high and green in the fields, but as he drove or rode abroad, listening to the tales of the farmers and land-owners, he determined not to be lulled into an unwise complacency. There were long, dry seasons; there were sudden and torrential rains, and fabu-lous hailstorms; there was fierce heat which scorched the pastures and brought raging fires; and the Hawkesbury was clearly a capricious river.

He conferred, therefore, with that prosperous merchant, Mr. Simeon Lord, and negotiated with him for a cargo of two hundred tons of Bengal wheat to be delivered by the following January. True, Mr. Lord sought permission to import also twenty thousand gallons of rum, but—as he explained—this indulgence would permit him to supply the wheat at a very low cost, and His Excellency was ready to allow the justice of this argument.

Thus secured against the vagaries of the climate, he permitted himself to relax, and enjoy its present halcyon mood. He found it difficult, how-ever, to devote his whole attention to his surroundings while his carriage jolted over the shocking road which stretched for some forty miles between Sydney and the Hawkesbury settlements. This must be one of his first undertakings—a fine, smooth, turnpike road upon which the carts of the farmers and the carriages of the gentry might roll along in speed and comfort. The cost of it must first be met from the Colonial Fund, but the toll-gates would soon reimburse this; he would be able to assure my Lord Castlereagh that the home Government would be put to no expense.

Interwoven with new scenes were the plans he made for them, and he felt a stir of excitement at having so much empty space to fill. There must be new roads, new stores, new barracks, new churches, whole new towns . . . He would build, and build. . . .

His days, so full of preoccupation with things and places, brought him face to face with people too, and whether he encountered them in the streets or in the fields, whether formally in his study or socially at his dinner table, he felt that they were not only what they seemed, but much more, unknown to him. Every man, of course, must have a past—always at his elbow, guiding his movements and prompting his tongue—but the pasts of which he learned were so dissimilar, and often so fantastic, that their convergance on this spot seemed perplexing, and even ominous. For he must stabilise a present which would be common ground for all these pasts; he must at least indicate a future which would create a common purpose. Never, he declared to his wife as new faces and new stories passed before him in procession, had a stranger collection of human beings congregated in so small a compass.

The problem of making a pattern for all these people was a bewildering one. Fate—Justice—Providence—whatever guiding principle might be invoked—seemed here to operate with a blind and monstrous inconsequence. There appeared to be no fixed relationship between crime and punishment, virtue and reward. Wealth or poverty, joy or grief, love or loneliness, could come to the just or the unjust; ability or ineptitude appeared in bond or free; the arts—never, indeed, greatly concerned with respectability—dwelt unashamed in convict garb; good or ill fortune struck here or there with careless impartiality. A place so financially, socially and morally untidy might have confused and exasperated the Governor to the point of panic if it had not been for that saving streak of simplicity, and that almost naïve geniality of temper which allowed him to recognise the common pattern of humanity in all these ill-assorted, and incongruously placed people. Instinctively, he fell back on that.

Throughout a year which continued reassuringly peaceful, his moments of misgiving were more than counterbalanced by a growing optimism. The place, he declared to his wife, was not near so bad as it had been painted. "What a climate!" he exclaimed again and again, as mellow autumn passed gradually, and with but little change upon the face of nature, into a winter of crisp nights and clear days.

There was a wet spell early in July, and for a few days reports from the Hawkesbury made him fear another flood. South Creek rose high; Mr. Andrew Thompson was again—as he had been on previous occasions—indefatiguable in aiding the removal of people, animals and goods from endangered areas. But the rain ceased, the weather cleared, and the waters subsided. The Governor breathed easily once more.

His subjects, too, were on the whole behaving well. There had been difficult and provoking incidents, of course. Mr. Marsden had haughtily declined to act with Mr. Thompson and Mr. Lord as a Trustee of the new turnpike road; there had been awkwardness when some turn of conversation re-awakened old animosities; and there were, of course, instances of crime, idleness and insubordination among the lower classes. But for the most part the inhabitants went about their business in a manner sufficiently orderly.

Satisfactory as his public life seemed, however, he suffered his private disappointments. From his supreme position as Viceroy, holding the fate of the colony and the lives of its citizens in his hand, he sometimes looked with an emotion verging upon envy at some humble settler or tradesman, surrounded by a lusty progeny. Since the death in infancy of their first child, a malevolent fate seemed determined to frustrate the desire of the Governor and his wife for parenthood, and it was with a heavy heart that he took up his pen one evening to record another blow to his fondest hopes.

"*7th August!!! Mrs. Macquarie had the misfortune of having a mis- carriage this Night after going to Bed which caused us both a great deal of uneasiness and mortification. . . .*"

But Elizabeth, though indisposed for a few days, soon recovered her health and spirits, and was ready to take her place beside him when, at the end of August, he journeyed by water to Parramatta. The interest of the inspections he must make there and in the surrounding districts soon turned his thoughts to other matters, and a week later he was back in Sydney, more confident than ever that the material of a model colony lay to his hand for the shaping.

As if his very passing had been a benediction, gentle rain fell during the week following his return, and the farmers watched their fields give green promise of an abundant harvest. But in the towns rain meant mud; Macquarie determined not to rest until he had tamed the undisciplined streets of Sydney, across which the citizens must pick their way, and down whose steep slopes the yellow water rushed in angry little torrents.

Streets, indeed, were never far from his thoughts, for they meant buildings, and buildings were his passion. Since the future of the colony depended upon its agricultural progress, he reminded himself constantly that the country was of pressing importance; but he was more at home in urban life. His care for both would be assiduous, but his approach re- mained different. He planned for the country, but he dreamed for the town.

In the heart of it once more, and secure in the feeling that all was running smoothly, his geniality expanded. He stood by the font at St. Phillip's in the rôle of godfather, and heard the baptismal names of William Macquarie bestowed upon the Cowper's newborn son. He visited and entertained, he smiled, conversed and jested. It was, he believed, only proper that a town—*his* town—should provide gay functions and popular diversions. It pleased him to grace the magnificent Bachelors' Ball with his hearty presence, to approve the holding of a race meeting, and to grant a three-day holiday to the Government labourers, that they might join in the races, sports, cocking, and other innocent amusements of the festival. He watched the races with the zest of an urchin; he shed his most fatherly smile upon the crowd, and chuckled at its antics. He beamed with pride upon his wife as she presented the Ladies' Plate, and was visibly affected by the ovation she received for her little speech. His laughter was clearly to be heard among the joyous shrieks of the onlookers as a few daring females raced in sacks for a cheese. He felt a warm satisfaction when a smile accompanied a curtsey, when a hand flew to a cap more willingly than dutifully, when a child approached him without fear, when some small favour was asked, and could be granted. Jealous of his dignity and conscious of his authority, he was, nevertheless, in his unguarded moments, like a child offering goodwill, and innocently happy to receive it.

But towards the end of October, the merrymaking just over, came news from the Hawkesbury which saddened him. Mr. Andrew Thompson had been ailing since his exertions during the threatened flood two months ago, and now—at thirty-seven, reputedly one of the colony's wealthy men, and assured by the Governor's benign policy towards emancipists of ever-increasing stature in the community—he was dead. To those who saw in the brand of felonry a stigma more ineradicable than the mark of Cain, His Excellency's expressions of grief seemed unbecoming, and his eulogies of the deceased deplorable. But some days later, when the elaborate funeral was over, and Mr. Thompson's executor had bowed himself out of the Governor's study, Macquarie was left with an even higher opinion of Mr. Thompson than before. He hastened upstairs to acquaint his wife with the remarkable news just conveyed to him.

"A fourth of his fortune . . . ?" cried Elizabeth. They stared at each other in gratified excitement; she added delicately: "He was supposed an opulent man, was he not?"

"As fortunes are regarded here," Macquarie said cautiously, "he would assuredly be counted opulent. Mr. Williams thinks that when all his affairs are properly adjusted there may be some twenty or twenty-five thousand pounds. A very handsome sum—and his leaving a fourth of it to me is a truly extraordinary instance of friendship and gratitude."

There were, however, those who saw it in a very different light. Mr. Marsden pursed his little mouth. Mrs. Macarthur, faithfully informing her absent husband of all that passed in the colony, was now compelled to report that the Governor had become a beneficiary of an ex-convict who had been laid to rest with as much honour as any respectable gentleman. Throughout the colony—and, in due course, among the temporary exiles in London, the circumstances surrounding the death of Mr. Andrew Thompson became, for the exclusive circle, symbolical of an alarming change.

*　　　　　*　　　　　*　　　　　*

Mrs. Macquarie alone (and she with some slight sense of guilt) discerned in the Governor at work, the child at play. He had been given a new toy, and its manipulation occupied his every waking hour. She told herself that the remodelling and development of a colony was a serious work of adult administration; yet she could not but be reminded of a small boy with his bits of wood and string, his busy fingers, his secret vision, his absorbed and blissful sense of creative power. She cherished the silly fancy even as she rebuked herself for it.

For weeks, now, she heard little from him but the streets and the hospital, the hospital and the streets. For the main thoroughfare, of course, only one name was possible—that of His Majesty King George the Third. The Queen's name could with great propriety be given to the open ground about the church. "I think Charlotte Square sounds well, don't you, my love?" She agreed; but it startled her a little to learn that the unoccupied area at the top of the hill—hitherto known with characteristic colonial fecklessness as the Common, the Exercising Ground, the Cricket Ground, or the Racecourse—was to become Hyde Park. It was but a wide, irregular expanse of rough grass, fringed by native scrub and trees—was he not conscious of a certain incongruity . . . ? He was not; more than ever she realised that secret visions were at work.

The names of six royal Dukes provided for the barely-formed streets and tracks about the Barracks. Chapel Row became Castlereagh Street. Mr. Pitt's name, naturally, must remain, but to His Excellency's ear Pitt Street was more dignified than Pitt's Row. Two more Rows made way for the names of Phillip and Bligh, and the steep streets plunging down the hill to the Tank Stream were henceforth to immortalise Hunter and King. Having done his duty to his vice-regal predecessors, Macquarie considered his own claims.

There was need and promise of an exceedingly handsome street along the hilltop from behind Government House to Hyde Park; this, he decided, should be Macquarie Street. For good measure he would also bestow his name upon that little space near the foot of Bridge Street, where Mr. Lord's imposing building, a few disreputable cottages, a well and a patch of bush were at present tumbled together with unseemly irregularity. He would tidy all this, clear away the oldest buildings and the bush; it would be the heart of his town, the spot from which he would measure all the streets and roads in the colony. His vision pictured them spreading fanwise over hundreds of miles, tying the whole land together, converging upon this point, the hub of colonial civilisation, Macquarie Place. . . .

"And Bridge Street . . . ?" enquired Elizabeth. Her husband pondered. Bridge Street had named itself twenty-two years ago when someone, in the first days of the settlement, had thrown a log across the Tank Stream. The log had vanished long ago, but Macquarie, the Highlander, had his mystical moments, and was aware of a reluctance to obliterate its memory. "I think," he decided, "that we may perhaps leave that name unchanged."

But those two most important gentlemen, his Lieutenant-Governor and his Judge Advocate, must have their names immortalised in the town whose infancy they had helped to guide. Near the head of Sydney Cove, in that regrettable tangle of small streets which could never now, he feared, be reduced to symmetry, he named O'Connell and Bent Streets, and then permitted himself to indulge a momentary nostalgia. It was no accident that Argyle Street, named for his wild, mountainous native county, should scale the craggy heights of The Rocks.

There was still his dear wife to be considered, and he declared that he had reserved for her a street that might be worthy of her name. What more fitting Elizabeth Street than one forever bordered graciously by Hyde Park? What more delicate compliment to her lively spirit than a road which would lead the citizens to their innocent revels—their fêtes, races, fireworks, games and rambles?

His satisfaction with all this was enhanced when, towards the end of the year, he began to see the way clear for the establishment of a General Hospital. It was a project which lay very near his heart, but the tiresome question of expense had been, as ever, exercising his mind. So many new buildings were required that the resources at his disposal could not be stretched far enough to provide the dignified edifice his soaring fancy painted. It was no less than providential, therefore, that Mr. Blaxcell and Mr. Alexander Riley, two wealthy and influential citizens, should come forward with a proposal which seemed to eliminate all difficulties at a stroke. He was even more gratified when—the negotiations being at a difficult stage—these gentlemen were joined by Dr. Wentworth, whose opulence gave greater security to the plan, and whose character the Governor conceived to be a happy blend of zeal and rectitude.

The building they offered to erect would be an adornment to the city; none finer, His Excellency confided to his wife, would be found in any of the colonies. And the only recompenses the three public benefactors required in exchange for their labours were twenty oxen, and the right to import forty-five thousand gallons of rum over the three-year period during which the hospital would be completed. Four thousand of it was already in their possession, and they would pay duty on the rest within six months of its landing. They would be permitted the use of twenty draught oxen from the Government herds, returning them upon completion of the contract; and they would be allowed twenty male convicts, whom they would maintain at their own expense.

"It seems quite an advantageous arrangement," observed Mrs. Macquarie, pleased to see her husband looking so jubilant.

"I venture to say no arrangement ever made in this colony has been more advantageous! The expense to Government will be trifling, and we shall have a building which will not only be a boon to the sick, but an ornament to the town. Picture it, my dear! Can you not see it standing up there on its elevated site where it will immediately catch the eye, and lend an air of elegance to the whole place . . . !" He waved his hand in the direction of Macquarie Street, and his expression was rapt. "It's to accommodate two hundred sick, so you may have some conception of its size. . . ."

"Two hundred and eighty feet long, I think you said . . . ?"

"No, no—two hundred and eighty-seven and one half. There will be stone pillars, and a flight of stone steps, stone chimneys and chimney-pieces—everything done in the most handsome manner, and with every sort of judicious ornament—and a Surgeons' Barracks attached, and a fine kitchen, and a stables with coach houses. And a stone-flagged path leading to the kitchen and necessaries, so that the patients won't get their feet wet. And a fine well. . . . But you must study the plans with me, and then we shall drive out and inspect the site together. You'll agree that we have made a highly beneficial agreement with these gentlemen, and I must say they've been most handsome and liberal in their manner of coming forward. Of course," he added, "I've been under the necessity of promising to grant no other permissions for the importation of spirits while this contract is in existence—but without prejudice, you understand, to what Government may require for its own use, or what has already been given permission for, or what promiscuous ships may bring." He seated himself beside her on the sofa, patted her hand, and sighed contentedly. "Yes, I flatter myself this is something that will meet with a full measure of approval from Lord Liverpool!"

*   *   *   *

One day toward the end of the year, an imposing little cavalcade was to be seen mounting the hill towards Beltrasna. The vice-regal carriage was preceded and flanked by a guard of dragoons, and behind it trotted Captain Antill and several other gentlemen. Mrs. Emmett, having been informed of its approach by Hattie, peeped through a window and cried: "Lawks, the Governor—and the master out in the fields!" But Patrick was fortunately not far distant; the message, conveyed to him by a panting servant, brought him hastening to the house, from which he was just in time to emerge, smoothing his hair, as the carriage drew up at the door. Summoning a hovering overseer and a couple of servants with a crook of his finger, he descended the steps to bid his guests welcome.

His Excellency alighted, his retinue dismounted, and Patrick handed Mrs. Macquarie ceremoniously from the carriage. The Governor was all amiability.

"We have ventured to hope that we may claim the hospitality of your house for an hour or so, Mr. Mannion."

"I am honoured, Sir."

"You're acquainted with Captain Antill and Captain Cleaveland? And Dr. Redfern, of course? And our good friends Mr. Evans and Mr. Meehan? Excellent! We have for a long time looked forward to seeing your celebrated estate, Sir."

"Your Excellency is heartily welcome." Patrick offered his arm to Mrs. Macquarie. "Allow me, ma'am. . . ."

At the top of the steps she turned to face the view, while the carriage and horses clattered out of sight, escorted by the Beltrasna servants.

"I see that it is very justly celebrated," she remarked. "Why, Mr. Mannion, what an admirable prospect you have! No, no, pray don't take us indoors, for I see that you have chairs set out here on your beautiful verandah, and no pleasanter place could be imagined!"

"My wife," said the Governor with a fond smile as she accepted the chair which Patrick drew forward, "has become so partial to the outdoor life in these last weeks that the comforts of a house hold no further attraction for her. With such a verandah as this, Mr. Mannion, I daresay you spend but little time indoors yourself?"

"Most of the time I find it more agreeable here, Sir. Pray be seated, gentlemen; refreshments will be brought immediately."

Captain Antill stretched his legs out with a sigh of relief, and ran a handkerchief over his forehead.

"They'll be welcome—we'll not deny it, eh, Redfern? We have travelled so far, and seen so much that I'd confess to fatigue were it not for being shamed by the superior endurance of the only lady in our party."

"Nonsense, Henry!" cried Mrs. Macquarie. "I have travelled at ease in the carriage, Mr. Mannion, while my husband and these gentlemen have gone on horseback or on foot over I don't know how many miles."

"Nevertheless, ma'am, such a journey as I understand you have been engaged on is something of an ordeal. I trust you have found compensation in the interest of the tour?"

"It has been quite delightful! The beautiful and romantic places we have visited—the tranquil scenes of the forest—this noble river with its lofty banks, so wild and picturesque! I have been entranced, Sir!"

The refreshments were brought and handed round. The guests, at ease in the grateful shade, recounted their adventures with all that retrospective pleasure in past exertions which present comfort and idleness inspire. They compared the spots where they had made their camps, and the farms they had visited; they argued about the fertility of the soil in different areas, estimated the number of miles they had travelled, described the nosegays of native flowers which Mrs. Macquarie had gathered, and gently teased her about the traces of sunburn which—despite veils and parasol—had reddened her fair skin.

"I'm deeply impressed," the Governor declared, "by what I have seen during this tour—and I think I may say that I have seen everything except the settlements at the Hawkesbury, for which we are now bound. Most of the farms appear to be in a highly promising state, though the buildings are frequently of a meaner sort than I had hoped to see. And the inhabitants are poorly clothed, which in many cases I cannot ascribe entirely to poverty. In some instances they seem to consider a rag or two sufficient to cover them."

"For that, Sir, perhaps the climate may be responsible," suggested Redfern, running a finger round inside his high collar.

"Some attention to personal neatness is necessary, however. I thought also that many of them appeared to be ill-fed—less robust than might have been expected. Yet you consider the population healthy on the whole, Doctor?"

"Decidedly. There are no indigenous diseases. Dysentery is prevalent particularly among the poorer classes, but infantile diseases are almost unknown. The rising generation of native born is remarkably robust."

"You have lately been in the Cow Pastures area, I understand?" Patrick asked, and Mr. Meehan replied: "We have, Sir!" in a tone of rueful emphasis which set them all laughing.

"Poor Mr. Meehan," Mrs. Macquarie explained, "had the misfortune to dislocate his arm while hunting the wild cattle, and his memories of the spot are not entirely happy. And I myself must confess that the lowing and bellowing of the beasts all round my tent at night alarmed me a little. Oh, we have had many adventures! We visited Mr. Davidson's farm—what is it called, Mr. Evans . . . ? Menangle, or some such name . . . ? And we met Mrs. Macarthur, also, who was inspecting her husband's property nearby. And we were entertained by numbers of natives, who performed a dance for us—la, it was amusing, was it not, Henry?"

"Not even dancing dervishes could surpass them," replied Mr. Antill lazily. "I can't recollect ever having seen dancers more full of animation and spirit."

"Spirit, Sir—or spirits?" enquired Mr. Meehan, and set them laughing again.

"We primed them with a glass or two, Mr. Mannion," remarked His Excellency, "and it had a wonderful good effect. You're well acquainted with them hereabouts, I expect?"

"We see them constantly passing up and down the river, Sir, but they don't often come about the property, except during the maize plucking. . . ."

"Ah?" The Governor leaned forward. "I've been told that. It seems that such instances of hostility as have occurred between them and our own people have mostly taken place at that season. You find them troublesome then?"

"In my father's time, Sir, he most strictly forbade them coming about the place at all, and the overseers had orders to drive them off if they approached. When they did appear it was usually during the maize harvest."

"You still find them troublesome at that time?"

"No, Sir, I can't say that I do. In the last two years I have adopted the practice of approaching them and handing out a few cobs to each. I find that they accept these—with expressions of pleasure and gratitude— and go away perfectly content."

Mr. Evans interjected dryly:

"You'll have the whole tribe encamped on the edge of your fields next year, Mr. Mannion." Patrick shrugged slightly.

"It's possible, Sir. Yet there are not so many of them that a little freely given by all settlers might not prove less expensive in the end than their marauding, which causes them to be fired on—this in turn creating ill-will, and causing hostilities in which lives are lost on both sides."

Macquarie nodded emphatically.

"You are right, Mr. Mannion. Patience and forbearance must be exercised towards these poor, ignorant children of nature. Yet we must not be content with allowing them to become mere mendicants. From your experience, Sir, would you consider them capable of acquiring some degree of civilisation? Might they, perhaps, master the rudiments of education?"

Only Mrs. Macquarie noticed the faint flush that rose on Mrs. Mannion's face. He replied briefly:

"I think it quite certain, Sir; though whether this would of itself be sufficient to draw them from their savage state, is another question."

"It is, of course, quite indispensable that they should learn at least sufficient of our customs to respect the laws of property. They must be made to comprehend that they, like ourselves, are His Majesty's subjects, and that his laws will protect them so long as they, in turn, obey his laws. You think we might attempt this with some measure of success, Mr. Mannion?"

Patrick, looked at him, and then away across the river.

"I think, Sir," he replied carefully, "that it may take some time to convince them of our title to property which was so recently their own."

The Governor's easy, genial laugh reduced this answer to its proper place as a whimsicality.

"We may, however, be permitted title to our maize crops, I trust? For the rest we must be thankful that tolerably good relations exist, and exert ourselves to improve them still further. We had some intercourse with a couple of the race when we were exploring the entrance to the river which comes in from the west—the one we have called the Western River, but which we must now remember to call by its native name, the Warra . . . Warra. . . ?"

". . . gumba," supplied Antill.

". . . gumbie," corrected Redfern.

". . . gamba," declared Evans and Cleaveland simultaneously.

". . . gombie," announced Mrs. Macquarie with decision.

"The Warragombie," His Excellency ordained. "You are familiar with it, Mr. Mannion?"

"Only for the first mile or two, Sir. It is very wild and precipitous, and much impeded by rocks."

"So we discovered. We were soon stopped by falls, and compelled to turn back. I think we shall find no passage through the mountains by that means. Mr. Blaxland, who was with our party then, kept casting his eyes towards the summit of the north bank—he had some notion that a route might be found across the highlands by following a system he explained to me. Ah, well, for the present we have more pressing matters to claim our attention. From your elevation here I judge you are not much incommoded by floods?"

"My buildings have never suffered, Sir, though the lower fields have been inundated on many occasions."

"I mean to establish new townships on higher ground in the Hawkes-bury districts—I shall attend to this immediately. We have already marked out one on George's River which will be excellently situated for trade and navigation; I've called it Liverpool. Places of security and retreat are urgently needed for those Hawkesbury settlers whose lands lie within the influence of floods. Which serves to recall to me, Mr. Mannion, that we have yet much ground to cover. . . ." He rose, and his entourage be-stirred itself reluctantly. He extended a hand to his wife who, with a little grimace, allowed herself to be pulled from her chair. "Come, my love, duty does not permit us to loiter, whatever inclination may urge! Mr. Mannion, at some future time you will perhaps allow me the pleasure of inspecting your estate more closely? Are there messages we may convey from you to the charming Mrs. Mannion?"

The carriage was summoned, the gentlemen mounted, the farewells were made. Mrs. Macquarie, peeping from the window as they bowled down the curving drive, caught her husband's arm, and said quickly:

"Look! The girl yonder—the native girl with the child. . . . You recall the story we have heard?" Dilboong, with her baby in her arms, bobbed an awkward curtsey as the carriage passed. "It must be she—the baby looks much lighter, does it not? They say she's the daughter of that wretched Bennilong who repaid Governor Phillip's kindness so ill, and is now so troublesome and ferocious when he's in liquor. . . . How strange it is . . . !"

Her sentence remained unfinished, but her husband did not ask her to complete it. He found it strange indeed that the grandchild of a drunken savage should be also the child of that handsome, wealthy, well-born young gentleman who had just entertained them so courteously. So strange—and so distasteful—that it was best ignored. There were, after all, some things which even a Governor could not regulate.

*   *   *   *

Billalong, meanwhile, was visiting Johnny, and regaling him with the latest news of that frontier where white settlement was halted by the river and the mountains. The Bereewolgal, he revealed, had recently acquired a new Gub-na whose name was Ma-gor-ee. He had just made a great journey throughout the country, accompanied by many men, carts and horses, and had even brought his woman with him, and camped across the river in the mia-mias which white men commonly erected out of doors. And he had held fabulous feasts, at one of which Billalong had himself been present. This man, he assured Johnny, appeared friendly and much given to laughter, which was undoubtedly a sign of a good heart; so it might be that he would restrain his people from those outrages which were so gravely affecting their relations with the tribes.

Johnny hunched his shoulders sceptically, and uttered an impatient grunt. He hardly knew (so imperceptibly had the implications of Finn's tales taken root in his mind) whence he had acquired his bitter knowledge that the personal goodwill of Governors counted but little in a clash which was, basically, between the possessors and the dispossessed, regardless of the colours of their skins. A Viceroy, however genial, was but the tool of enemies whom his thoughts could not identify save, vaguely, as "Them". "They" were the possessors; and against the dispossessed, whether white or black, they would wage an implacable war in which, to him, the laughter of this new Governor rang with a note of mockery. He listened gloomily to Billalong's animated account of this pleasant and even hilarious encounter, searching for words to express, or even reasons to support, his own fierce refusal to abandon his mistrust.

Ma-gor-ee, Billalong was saying, had asked the tribe to perform a corroboree for his entertainment—a request which they had, of course, found very amusing, since corroborees were not lightly performed before strangers, and particularly before a woman. However, he explained, they had known that he would not be able to tell the difference between a corroboree and a few meaningless routine steps and gestures, so they had improvised a little dance of no particular significance, and he had seemed well satisfied. He had given them some of the fiery drink before they began, so that their tongues had been loosened, and they had accompanied their movements with derisive and satirical words of such purport that it was perhaps as well they had not been understood. Some of the old men had been gravely scandalised, saying that such behaviour was dis-courteous towards people who, however ignorant, were guests; and if this fiery drink had the effect of making men not only forget their manners but their art, so that they stumbled clumsily through a few steps which any untaught child could perform, then it was to be hoped that the white men would bring it no more among them. But the young men—though a trifle shamefaced next morning—had enjoyed themselves immensely. "My laughter," declared Billalong, laughing heartily again at the mere memory, "nearly burst my sides!"

"Guests, eh?" Johnny remarked dourly. "Don't make no mistake, boy, it's their guests ye are from now on."

Billalong sobered suddenly; his brows dropped low over his eyes, and his mouth grew sullen. He picked up his spear and touched its sharp point reflectively. "How much they want?" he asked suddenly, and neither of them paused to wonder why he had lapsed into English to utter that bald question. He had chosen to be native rather than white, preferring the rich, crowded tribal life with its intricate and colourful social affairs, its merriment, its ceremonials and its periods of care-free idleness, to the more narrow and austere life which he might have shared with Johnny; but there were times when he realised the difference of his thinking, and felt the burden of the future. Johnny answered him grimly with one word:

"Everything!"

Billalong nodded slowly. It was true; and since he had another tale to prove it, he reverted to the tongue in which tales could be most fittingly clothed. The man, Ma-gor-ee, he said, was clearly intending to explore still farther, and to take more land. With his woman and some of his companions he had journeyed in two boats some distance up the Warragamba. . . ."

"Eh?" interrupted Johnny sharply. "What's that ye say?"

Billalong's shoulders lifted in a shrug. As Dyonn-ee well knew, not

even a native canoe could go far up that stream, and the white men—
encumbered as they always were with clothes, boots, and all kinds of gear
—were unlikely to wade, swim, climb and scramble their way through
the deep and precipitous ravine which would bring them to the place
where the Wollondilly joined the Koornong. Not by that route would
they come upon Dyonn-ee's *towri*; indeed they had immediately abandoned
all thought of further progress by that means. They had done no more
than disembark not far from the mouth of the river, point and exclaim,
eat one of their enormous feasts upon the rock, and return whence they
had come. All this, explained Billalong, had been reported to him by a
friend of his who had been invited by Ma-gor-ee to join his party. Yet
it was his own opinion that the Bereewolgal would not be content to
remain on the seaward side of the mountains; they would seek another
route.

Johnny only grunted. But with that hint of a fresh move in his
direction his compatriots had begun to seem real to him again. Looking
at his domain, he felt the cold shell of his indifference cracking, and the
small, hot flame of an old hatred beginning to break through as from some
hidden, unextinguished furnace.

1811

To Mrs. Mannion the cottage which she had purchased for the accommodation of Mr. Harvey's school might be poor and mean, but to Mr. Harvey it seemed a palace. It boasted four rooms, a verandah, a kitchen, a scullery and an outhouse; the soldier who had been its previous occupant had made a small vegetable garden, and in an earlier stage of its history someone had planted three peach trees which now, in the first month of 1811, were bowed with fruit.

With such a dwelling at his command, Mr. Harvey was no longer compelled to live in lodgings. The largest room, equipped with desks, benches and a blackboard, served him for a schoolroom. In another he set up his bed, and a third, furnished with a table, a couple of chairs, and his books set out on shelves, became the parlour. From his verandah he could look across the open expanse of Hyde Park—over whose new name his tongue still sometimes stumbled; it was a pleasant place to walk when school was over, particularly since Mrs. Mannion not infrequently chose to alight there from her carriage, and permit her children to play and ramble in the fresh air.

Never a demanding young man, Mark Harvey hardly expected complete happiness of life, but cherished, with a kind of wondering and anxious gratitude, that measure of it which had been meted out to him. And when he compared his present situation with what had gone before, he was almost nervously amazed by his felicity. He had a house, a school, and a livelihood which, if still close to penury, at least promised to mend; and from the black fate which had hung over him, he had been miraculously delivered, for *she* had not left the country after all. She was here, and he saw her often. It was enough.

He would have been less than human had he not sometimes reflected with a mad quickening of his heart that she was now free. But though he had gained much confidence since his rebellious exit from Beltrasna six years ago, and increased the independence of his thought, he was still —and would remain to the end of his days—a man of incorrigible personal diffidence. Though he had his pride, it functioned only in defence of a few—but sufficient—inviolable convictions; it lay deep, and no power could it bring forth to beguile him into the notion that the heights of glory, wealth or bliss were for him to scale.

Upon this trait in his character Mrs. Mannion had for long been brooding with a somewhat exasperated tenderness. That he should ask so little of life, that he should stand by while others—so much less deserving —snatched its prizes from beneath his nose, would not at all have disturbed her had she not felt that she herself was one prize at which he might stand gazing for ever. The colony had provided her with so many unedifying spectacles of how men bore themselves in scrambling for what they wanted, that she observed Mr. Harvey's detachment from the *mêlée* with approval. Yet she could not but reflect rather indignantly that while it was, no doubt, an admirable indifference to worldly advantage which held him back from such sordid pursuits, it was surely a superabundance of respect, and an excess of modesty, and an altogether absurd superfluity of scruple which held him back from her.

She had done her best. She had contrived, as if by accident, a score of meetings; she had invited him to her dinner-parties, and to the little soirées which she held occasionally in her drawing-room. By voice and glance and smile when they were alone, she had invited him to abandon his careful formality; and with tears and burning cheeks she had lain wakeful at night, recalling her manœuvres.

It was upon one day early in January, when she went—discreetly accompanied by Cousin Bertha—to inspect his new abode, that she became actively rebellious. La, how bare and ugly and ill-arranged and comfortless! Her imagination fell upon the place and transformed it; nor was she more than momentarily halted by the realisation that in seeing her carpet with the rose garlands here, and her little walnut cabinet there, and her escritoire placed before that window, and dear Mama's old chair in this space by the fireplace, she was literally kidnapping Mr. Harvey from his bachelor estate. She drove home in a concentrated silence, broken only once by Cousin Bertha:

"That young man, my love, requires a wife."

Of course he required a wife! Conor escaped to her room in something approaching a tantrum, made furious by the sudden revelation that she had been wickedly and improvidently wasting time. She was nearing her thirtieth birthday, the days were racing past, and there was so much to do with life! She paused in her restless pacing to study herself sternly in the mirror; it might tell her that she was still beautiful, but it supported the assertion of the calendar that her first youth was past. She turned from it in a mood of reckless determination. Matters must be set right without delay. She fetched her journal, unlocked it with the little key which hung about her neck, and sat down to unburden herself of the tumult in her heart.

"*Have made a RESOLVE which I trust is not unwomanly, though* one which might be held in accord with strict notions of female Propriety. Yet when I am persuaded that the happiness of another, as well as my own, is at stake, I cannot hold it blameworthy to Act. A diffidence altogether proper and Honourable may stand indefinitely in the way of happiness unless some occasion is made, and some strong encouragement given to overcome it. Gentlemen are somewhat difficult to Move. I shall therefore beg Mr. H. to call upon me upon the Pretext of seeking his advice upon some points concerning Julia's education, and intend employing the Opportunity to bring him to a Declaration, since I fear that his honourable Motives may else constrain him for ever to Silence."

There! It was written, and as good as done. She closed the book defiantly, locked it with a sharp click, returned the key to her bosom, and was surprised to find herself trembling.

* * * *

She awaited her visitor on the appointed day in a mood which was still determined, but not free from agitation. She had equipped herself with specimens of her daughter's calligraphy (which Mr. Harvey dutifully attempted to view with a proper professional interest), and a series of questions upon the standard of spelling and figuring proper in a young lady of nine. These preliminaries concluded, she took up her still-unfinished roses and pheasants, and addressed herself with a fast-beating heart to the real business of the interview.

"I'm relieved to know that you think the child makes progress. But there is much more, is there not, to education than this . . . ?" Her gold thimble indicated the slates and books on the sofa beside her. "Patrick, you know, is greatly concerned about her. He thinks the colony is no fit environment for either of the children, and urges me to take them home. . . ."

"And . . . and you think of going, ma'am . . . ?"

She heard the sharpened tone of his reply, but remained silent, keeping her eyes upon her work. It was a calculated silence, timed to permit a gathering of suspense, and while it lasted she was wondering wearily if conversations between men and women must always be conducted in this tiresomely devious way. Men, she reflected, by reason of their experience and wider opportunities, amassed a much greater store of knowledge than women, and their mental processes were, perhaps, more thorough—but— oh dear!—how slow! And since custom decreed that not only in matters such as this one which was now engaging their attention, but in nearly all matters, the initiative must be taken by the more slowly cerebrating half of humanity, it seemed inevitable that women should spend much of their time mentally hovering, waiting for men to catch up. . . .

She had no intention whatever of returning to Ireland. She intended to stay here and marry this exasperatingly obtuse young man; for a moment the impulse to tell him so plainly almost overcame her. But she knew that men—even the best of them—had their little vanities, chief among which was the illusion that they were always the pursuers, and women always the pursued. And women themselves (she admitted it with a sigh) found it pleasant to be wooed. . . .

She glanced up, and found such an intensity of fear in his eyes that her own smarted suddenly, and she fixed them hurriedly upon her work once more. She did not want to cause him pain—oh, no! But left to himself, how long might he not continue to hesitate, to stand at a respectful distance, and adore? She perceived very clearly that a man may indefinitely refrain from laying hands upon his treasure while it remains stationary at his side; but upon the first hint that it may be wrested from him, he will be in a mood to grab. . . .

She said, therefore:

"I feel I must consider it very seriously. Do you not think I should do right to go, Mr. Harvey?"

He answered slowly:

"You ask me a difficult question, madam."

"Difficult? How so?"

"If you feel that you have a duty to your children, it is not for me to dissuade you."

She cut a thread with a sharp snip, and replied:

"It's upon that point that I do not feel quite sure, Sir. Is it indeed desirable to remove them? And you speak of dissuading me; does this mean that you think there are arguments in favour of remaining?"

"The question of a suitable education does arise, ma'am, undoubtedly. Yet year by year the colony will improve in this regard, and it should not be difficult for you to obtain a suitable governess. And the climate here is allowed to be most beneficial to children—their health is of the first importance, is it not . . . ? And of course," he added with a rush, "there is Mrs. Herbert to be considered . . . I hardly think so old a lady would support the discomforts of the passage, and I think you would not care to leave her. . . ."

Conor laid her embroidery frame on her lap and looked at him, marvelling. With what remarkable diligence he marshalled every reason except the true one! And in Cousin Bertha he had hit upon an argument difficult to evade . . . but wait . . . not impossible. . . . She said sadly:

"I greatly fear that problem may be soon most unhappily solved, Mr. Harvey. Cousin Bertha grows very frail—oh, you would not notice it, I daresay, for her spirits are so lively, but there are signs . . . I fear she may not be with us much longer . . ."

He took an impulsive step towards her, and she saw so much concern and distress in his expression that she rose in sudden agitation, and went to stand at the window, half ashamed of herself, and half furious with him. He came to stand beside her, and she thought, almost in tears: "La, why doesn't he put his arms about me? Does he not know how to comfort a woman?" But his hands remained at his sides as he said earnestly:

"Believe me, I'm deeply grieved to hear of this. I know your affection for her, and I understand how anxious. . . ."

Now she was really weeping with shame and self-reproach, but her tears only fell the faster with the knowledge that he imagined quite a different cause for them. Suddenly she could not bear this fencing any longer; she threw subtlety to the winds, and interrupted him with the crudest of leading questions:

"Would *you* not miss me if I went, Sir?"

"*Miss* you . . . ?"

His hands wavered up from his sides, he stared and stammered. "How can you ask? M-miss you . . . ! You have m-made this wilderness a garden . . . without you I d-don't know how . . . I dare not think . . . !"

She reached out blindly for his hand, and with the first contact of their fingers her battle was won. She knew, as she relaxed thankfully into his arms and finished her weeping on his shoulder, that though the issue was no longer in doubt, some further struggles with his scruples still lay ahead of her; and indeed he was already holding her away from him to stare down into her face and say distractedly:

"I am mad! Forgive me! What have I done . . . ?"

She felt inclined to answer tartly: "Very little—almost nothing, in fact!" But his extreme agitation seemed so endearingly comical that she replied instead, smiling as she dabbed her wet eyes: "Something that I found . . . very pleasant."

He snatched her again with an inarticulate, despairing murmur, but she pushed him away, and cried vehemently:

"Stop groaning, Sir! It is painful to my vanity that you should groan at such a time!"

His smile was so doubtful and bewildered that she felt near to tears again. He said slowly:

"I have always been over-serious, and no one save yourself has ever teased and laughed at me, and made me feel, for a time, lighthearted and —and young. Yet now, when I'm closer to youth and happiness than I have ever been before, I must be older and more serious than ever. For this—this joy you seem to offer me, ma'am . . . how can I accept it? I am nobody. I am penniless. . . ."

She said—her hands on his shoulders and her face invitingly uplifted: "Shall we speak of that another time?"

"No!" he cried angrily. "We shall speak of it now, before I give way utterly to madness. I can offer you no home, no life that is suitable."

She passed him, returned to the sofa, sat there and patted the seat beside her.

"Come, then, and let us talk. I think these terrible obstacles you mention can be overcome. Sit down, pray, and . . . must you be so far away? Well, no matter. You reject my offer, Mr. Harvey?"

He smiled again, unwillingly.

"You're determined to jest, ma'am. . . ."

"My name is Conor. Pray do not call me Mrs. Harvey when we are married, for I think it an unfriendly custom, and we. . . ."

He said absently:

"I have many charming names for you in my private thoughts. . . ."

"Tell me!" she cried eagerly. He jumped.

"No! Be serious . . . I *beg* of you, be serious."

"Very well," she sighed, "I am serious. What have you to say?"

"That I earn barely enough for my own support, and am in no position to marry anyone, and least of all a lady who . . ."

"Who loves you dearly?"

"Who has all her life," he continued doggedly, "been accustomed to every comfort that money can buy."

She looked at him reproachfully.

"I think men are often strangely selfish, Sir."

"Selfish?"

"For the sake of a foolish pride they will sacrifice not only their own happiness, but that of a woman whom they profess to love. Spare me your protestations, Sir—I don't do you the injustice of imagining that it is *only* such pride which disturbs you, though I think it is not altogether absent. You are truly apprehensive lest I should suffer the hardships of poverty. Let us consider this prospect. If I marry again, I shall have no money from Mr. Mannion's estate, and I shall be poor in comparison with my present position; but I shall still have a small income left to me by my father. I do not doubt that you can continue to support yourself from your school, nor that in time, by our united efforts, it will prosper so that you can support us both. I merely point out that since I possess this small, but adequate income, you need not fear that I should be altogether deprived of my comforts."

Her tone was dry and slightly disdainful. He said sadly:

"I have angered you."

"It always angers me that money should be placed so high in importance."

He answered that with a hint of sharpness.

"I trust I shall not anger you again by saying that I think those who have never lacked money disdain it most easily."

"That is true, no doubt. I have often found myself in the position of being rebuked for lack of experience by those who would do most to keep experience away from me. I have never been poor, and I cannot say how far love may make poverty supportable. But in our own case, Sir, this question would not arise. We should be far from wealthy, but we should not be poor in the sense that so many miserable people in this place are poor. And I am well tried in one experience which I think you are ignorant of—idleness. Have you thought of that?"

"No." He looked at her frowningly. "I don't understand you."

"Only the rich can afford to be idle. The poor, knowing nothing of it, and toiling too hard, think of it as a pleasure, but to one who is by nature active, it can be a very heavy burden. I have found it so. If I had lived in Ireland after my marriage, I should most likely have learned to fill my days as so many women of my kind do, with social pleasures and distractions, and perhaps some charitable activities. But I came here, Sir, to Beltrasna, where there was no society, where all domestic duties were performed for me, and where my possibly ill-judged attempts to—to understand the lot of the unfortunate, and to comprehend the world I lived in, met with nothing but bitter opposition from my husband. Yet here—I have always felt it—there are opportunities even for a woman of my class to live usefully. You cannot guess with what envy I have watched Mrs. Macarthur assuming so many responsibilities in her husband's interest. You may find it hard to believe that I have even envied the wives of poor settlers whom I have seen working in the fields. Yes, yes, I know what you would say—it is easy for one who has never known the weariness of manual toil to see it as something desirable, and were I in their position I should soon learn to feel differently. It may be so; there can be too much work—but there can also be too little." She put her hand on his. "I am asking you for something more than a romantic association, Sir. I am asking you for an opportunity to live other than emptily—idly—uselessly. . . ."

The hand that had clasped his was now crushed in his grip. She tried to pull it away, and added stormily:

"Nevertheless, I am not a suppliant! Don't dare to laugh at me! I declare to you, Sir, that with you or without you, I shall remain here and find some means of filling my days. I—I shall take up land, and have a small farm . . . yes, I am ignorant, but I can learn . . . from

Patrick, from Mr. Campbell, and Mr. Palmer, and Mr. Suttor. I have friends who will assist me. . . ."

The struggle for possession of her hand ceased suddenly as his pull on it became too insistent to be denied. She collapsed against his shoulder, sobbing. He said stroking her hair:

"Your arguments are too strong for me, my love, my love. That you should feel even some small need of me to set against my great need of you, leaves me with no more objections, and few fears. Shall we be married soon?"

*　　　　*　　　　*　　　　*

The Orphan School, charitably established by Governor King, had conformed to the usual custom of such establishments by being less suc-cessful in practice than in theory. Its inauguration had been auspicious, beginning with a religious service, and ending with a feast; Mr. Marsden had delivered a sermon in which he described the ruin and depravity from which the orphans were being rescued, and exhorted them to gratitude, humility, industry, modesty and obedience. Thus spiritually fortified and encouraged, the congregation had adjourned to the school itself, where, as the missionary, Mr. Hassall, had recorded: "We was highly delighted with seeing the girls in the greatest order feasting on an excilent sort of pork and plumb puddin' and seemed very happy in their new situation."

Happiness, thereafter, was assumed, and those entrusted with the direction of the refuge devoted their attention to the inculcation of the virtues enumerated by Mr. Marsden. Governor King's part was to make it financially secure without adding to the expense accounts which were apt to be so querulously received by the home Government, and to this end he had exercised his considerable ingenuity; there was hardly a crime or misdemeanour in the colonial calendar, from manslaughter to smug-gling, using short measures, holding unlicensed auction sales, failing to register boats, or allowing goats to stray unattended, which was not at some time punished by a fine which added to the coffers of the Orphanage. Even large tracts of land were set aside for its endowment, and the most respectable ladies of the colony, headed by Mrs. King herself, had formed a committee of Trustees to guide and prosper its destinies.

Nothing which good intentions could devise had been neglected. The orphans not only received spiritual direction, but were instructed in spinning, needlework, the domestic arts, reading, and even, in some cases, writing. They were dressed neatly in black, and escorted to Divine Service every Sunday; they were duly exhorted, punished, and shielded from the degrading influences of idleness and levity; they were fed regularly, and in a manner quite sufficient for their station in life. Mr.

Marsden never wearied of recalling to their minds their indebtedness to His Majesty, His Excellency, their charitable benefactors, and God.

They were mostly parentless, but from time to time some had been admitted whose parents, from poverty or some other cause, were unable or unfit to care for them; this practice, however, had now been forbidden by the new Governor, who decreed that the Orphanage was to be reserved for orphans only. Their ages ranged mostly from nine to fourteen years, though there were some younger and a few older. Swept willy-nilly under the shelter of its roof, they were at least removed from the streets, where their presence would have been an embarrassment and a reproach to the citizens, but once there they remained a problem which was only less disturbing to the extent that it was also less visible. For even the most charitable were forced to admit that they were not admirable little girls. Despite continuous admonishment, they were seldom modest, pious, humble, industrious, obedient, or even grateful; indeed they commonly displayed quite shocking tendencies—noisiness, impudence, rebelliousness, a deplorable vocabulary, and, worst of all, a familiarity with certain matters about which females of such tender years would properly be ignorant.

Emily was one of the original inmates. If anyone knew who her parents had been, they had neglected to inform her. When it was necessary for the purposes of the institution's records, her surname was set down as Rocks, this being the name of the neighbourhood where, at the age of six, she had been found wandering alone, hungry and neglected.

She could still dimly remember the cold and loneliness of nights she had spent huddled behind some boulder at the edge of the rough, precipitous streets, and her fear of the stars when she woke to see them pricking the black vault of the unfriendly sky. She remembered, too, that sometimes people had questioned her, and given her food, and that one lady had reproached her for her torn frock. "You must go home and have it mended." Home? She had had no home, but merely a mammy who slept here and there as opportunity offered, and now—as she had tried to explain to the lady—her mammy was dead.

She had accepted the food, but fled as quickly as possible from questions which, instinct told her, might lead to adult interference in her affairs; for her life had fallen into a cycle—misery by night, which must be, and was, exorcised by happiness during the daylight hours. With sunrise she was afoot, putting loneliness and terror behind her, to embark with all the singlemindedness of childhood upon her daily search for joy.

It had not been difficult to find. There were many children about the streets, and always some who would play with her. She still kept, along with the memory of solitude and darkness, or of rain which sent her scuttling for such shelter as she could find, a much clearer memory of sunny days when the hilltop beyond the Observatory was her playground and sanctuary. Here the rough grass was dotted with scrub and huge boulders which furnished a hiding place from officious adults. There was always something to watch on the harbour—boats plying to and fro in the Cove, native canoes putting out from the tree-clothed shore opposite, sometimes a ship from England coming into view round Bradley's Head, far down the glittering path of water. Occasionally a party of natives would go by with fish in nets over their shoulders to barter for bread in the town; they would pause to greet her with words which she did not understand, or with smiles which she did. Down by the shore there were crabs to watch, and in tiny rock pools left by the high tide, strange shells which moved, and soft, growing things which closed tightly on the tip of her exploring finger. Children whom she came to know would slip out to join her, and one little boy never failed to bring her a crust saved from his meal, and sometimes even a pasty.

All that was nearly nine years ago. The eye of authority had spied her out at last, and she had been brought, rebellious and resisting, to the Orphanage. Since then her intervals of happiness had been few, and pale beside that knowledge of ecstasy which had no shape in her mind, but was merely a stored-up memory of sun, and play, and freedom.

She was now a thin girl with alert dark eyes, and a cloud of brown curls forever escaping from the ruthlessly combed confinement considered suitable for orphans. There were no mirrors in which she could see herself—vanity being a snare of the devil, as Mr. Marsden constantly reminded them—so she did not know, as yet (though she was beginning to suspect it) that she possessed the promise of comeliness. She was not without enjoyments, for she housed in her small, skinny person a great zest for life, and a capacity for happiness which, lacking its true nourishment, must be fed with pleasurable excitements. Of these there were many, for the Orphanage stood on a corner facing George Street, with Bridge Street running down beside it, and much of Sydney's street life could thus be observed by little girls pressing eager faces to its upper windows.

From here, looking across Bridge Street and over the high wall of the Lumber Yard opposite, it was possible to see something, and hear much of what went on inside. There was no busier place in the town, for it contained the Government workshops where the carpenters, sawyers, locksmiths, tailors, cobblers and harness-makers toiled all day in a veritable chaos of noise. Here the gaol-gangs came tramping and clanking each morning in their chains; here the drays laden with timber discharged their loads, and the piles of planks and beams rose high in the yard to the accompaniment of clattering and shouting. Here the forge contributed its metallic clangour, and from here, too, could not infrequently be heard the screams and curses of some convict being flogged.

Next door to the Orphanage on the other side was the big, white mansion of Mr. Joseph Underwood, where there was also much coming and going, but of quite a different kind. The orphans (who understood fine shades of social distinction very well) knew that Mr. Underwood was an ex-convict, and thus respectable only to the extent that his opulence could make him so. Not everyone would visit him, but many did, for he entertained handsomely, and obsequious tradesmen ran constantly with full baskets between his gate and his back door.

A little farther along the street on the opposite side, the gaol provided another point of interest, and the orphans were often enlivened by the spectacle of some man or woman being dragged to imprisonment, sped by jeers and witticisms from passing citizens. It was but three years ago that they had seen Mr. Underwood himself, along with his partners, Mr. Lord and Mr. Kable, escorted thither for a month upon the orders of Governor Bligh. With delighted awe they had witnessed the incarceration of the great Mr. Macarthur, and watched the crowd of his partisans and Bligh's exchanging blows and insults in the street outside. All sorts of people, in their experience, might find themselves in gaol for all sorts of inscrutable reasons; anyone, from Governors to murderers, might be arrested; imprisonment bore no discernible relation to justice, but happened as capriciously as a thunderstorm. The lack of a pattern, so much deplored by authority, was a source of delighted wonderment to orphans.

Farther down Bridge Street, just beyond the stone bridge now being repaired, there was still a small patch of bush, often frequented by aborigines, and here, one night only a few weeks ago, Emily had witnessed an interesting but oddly disturbing scene. With two other girls she had scaled the Orphanage wall, and set forth in search of dubious adventure —the first time that she had taken part in such an escapade. Gaining the shelter of the trees, they had come suddenly upon a native man in the act of stunning a native woman by a blow on the head with his waddy. As they watched him drag her off, apparently senseless, Emily— already rather apprehensive of the rendezvous for which she was bound— succumbed to panic, and scuttled back to the Orphanage; thanks to this incident she was still a virgin, though the contemptuous laughter of her companions made her ashamed of her cowardice.

From the bridge, the street climbed the hill to Government House, the view of which, from the upper windows of the Orphanage, was somewhat obscured by the tall, square block of Mr. Simeon Lord's stores. Along the upper end of Bridge Street were the residences of the Judge Advocate, the Surveyor-General and the Chaplain, the last of which was a small cottage with a verandah, an orchard, and two fine orange trees standing on either side of the path. These, planted long ago by the Reverend Mr. Johnson, now yielded their harvest to the Reverend Mr. Cowper and his wife, and the orphans were very familiar with the sight of this tall, thin young clergyman hastening past on a Sunday morning to take the first of his three services in the gaol yard, and proceeding thence to the eleven o'clock service at St. Philip's.

The Church stood on the crest of the hill looking straight down the Old Parade at the Orphanage, so that the progress of the Governor's carriage, when he and his lady set out punctually every Sabbath, could be followed all the way down Bridge Street, across George Street, and up the opposite hill; and a fine, colourful sight it was to see His Excellency, magnificent in his uniform, acknowledging the salutes of the citizens, and his lady bowing graciously from beneath her parasol.

Thus, with all their little world beneath their eyes—with everyone to watch, from scarlet-coated soldiers to yellow-clad convicts, from toiling artisans and tradesmen to sailors loudly enjoying their idleness ashore, from ministers of religion to malefactors, from the virtuously sober to the uproariously drunk, from gentlemen on horseback to shabby citizens on foot, from naked aborigines to ladies *en grande tenue*—life could not be said to be dull for the orphans, and Emily did not find it so. Of course they were always being dragged away from the windows—having, as was well known, their code of signs by which they could make clandestine appointments with willing passers-by—and the Governor was already pondering the removal of the institution to some site at Parramatta which should command a view less damaging to their morals. But besides the spectacle of the world outside, there were excitements to be manufactured and enjoyed within—rules to be broken, teachers to be baited and defied, punishments to be evaded or endured, things to be thrown and broken, stories to be whispered, quarrels to be pursued. There was much alleviation of their lot in such activities; but Emily, haunted by shadowy memories, and taught by certain rare, illuminated moments in her present life, half knew that happiness was something different.

She could recognise no common factor between these moments now experienced, and those others, so dimly remembered; she only knew that occasionally they came, at times when she would have least expected them. Reading, writing, spinning and plain sewing comprised her education, if one ignored—as she certainly did—the moral precepts and exhortations of the visiting Chaplains, and it was always during these periods of instruction that she felt the benison of happiness descend upon her. For her brain was quick, and her fingers deft; it was not always possible to remember that tasks were imposed upon her, and therefore to be hated. In those rare, unguarded moments she forgot it, and knew the happiness of her small achievements.

For the past two years these moments had come more frequently, and acquired a new poignancy, for she, as one of the best and neatest semp-stresses the establishment could boast, had been chosen to execute the plain sewing of Mrs. Mannion. Usually this was delivered and collected by a servant, but now and then Mrs. Mannion came herself, and Emily was drawn forward to make her curtsey. This beautiful and elegant lady was kind; she smiled at Emily and bestowed words of praise. Love was an emotion in which orphans were unpractised, but at the age of fourteen Emily had discovered it in herself, ready after years when it had lain unused and unrecognised, to flame into a wild passion of adoration. It was her treasure, to be guarded from the sly, searching eyes and the sharp tongues of her companions—yet it must be expressed. Into the long hems of Mrs. Mannion's sheets, and still more into the tucks and ruffles of her fine cambric petticoats and chemises, went Emily's minutest and most even stitches; and in this small act of service to her idol the pent-up love of her heart found its secret and blissful release.

*   *   *   *

Only to Patrick—who, as the head of the house, must of course be immediately informed—had Conor at first disclosed the secret of her betrothal to Mr. Harvey. The news brought him post-haste to Sydney in the middle of January, disturbed, and, as always, torn between the con-ventions of his upbringing and the natural generosity of his heart.

"You understand, ma'am, I don't wish to suggest any personal objection to Mr. Harvey. He is a man of gentle birth and of education. You will do as you please, of course, but you must know very well that your position as his wife will be inferior—both in a monetary and a social sense—to that which you occupy as my father's widow. And I confess that I dislike the notion of my brother and sister living in. . . ." Patrick was not a brutal young man, and he bit off the words "a hovel". But what else was it—that miserable cottage at which he had looked with horrified distaste only an hour ago? ". . . In the conditions you contem-plate," he finished gloomily.

She looked worried.

"I don't know—indeed I don't! I must tell you that Mr. Harvey is himself inclined to your opinion; he believes I should send the children home for a few years at least."

"I commend his judgment," Patrick replied stiffly. She sighed.

"I place great reliance on it. But mark me, Patrick, if I act upon it in this case it will be for reasons of my own. I realise my own sad incapability, and I should not wish them to suffer from it. I have much to learn, and it may be that in a few years I shall have learned enough, and our affairs will have sufficiently improved, for me to be able to provide a home to which they could return, and find that order and tranquillity which are so needful."

"Does Julia know that this change is to take place?"

"I have not spoken of it as yet."

"You may find that she herself would wish to go."

"To leave me . . . ? Conor's voice was incredulous, but her eyes were frightened. For the first time she allowed herself to see plainly what she had refused to see before, being so newly wrapped in a happiness which could not bear to be disturbed. A beautiful, imperious child, long the spoiled darling of an indulgent Papa, so fastidious, so careful of her dainty frills and ribbons, so impatient of discipline, so conscious of her importance as Miss Julia Mannion—suddenly transplanted from a handsome house, from servants and wealth and deference, into a life which would seem to her squalid beyond words. . . .

"I don't know," she repeated, shaken. "I must think carefully, I must consider. . . ."

The fear haunted her, but could not quite overshadow her joy. She was in a mood for gaiety, and she had prevailed upon Patrick to remain for a few days and escort her to the Queen's birthday ball at Government House, to which Mr. Harvey also had been bidden. Colonel Macquarie's hospitality was more generously all-embracing than his predecessors had deemed wise, and if there were a few who might once have looked askance at a poor and shabby young schoolmaster, they would now find him much more socially acceptable than others whom they were likely to encounter beneath the vice-regal roof.

Conor and Patrick had dined with their Excellencies before the ball, in a party which included the Bents, the O'Connells and Dr. Redfern, and early in the evening, before the other guests had arrived, they invaded the ballroom to inspect the decorations. Conspicuous among these was a transparent painting by Mr. Lewin, which occupied the whole of one wall. The room was deserted save for the Editor of the *Gazette,* who sat on one of the chairs flanking the walls, scribbling notes. Mrs. O'Connell, her arm linked in Conor's, led the exclamations of surprise and admiration.

"How clever, is it not? I declare, the figures are all speaking likenesses! See, my love . . ." she drew her husband to her side and pointed with her fan, ". . . don't you recognise that native called Nanbarru? And the one near the front of the group, holding a shield—that is undoubtedly Bennilong."

"Yes, yes," O'Connell agreed, giving the picture an amiable if perfunctory glance. "Excellent! Very well executed, and expressing a most proper sentiment. Ah, Mr. Howe, good evening! You're preparing an account of this happy occasion for your paper?"

The editor rose to make his bow, and as the party passed on to view the decorations in the supper room, he sat down again and resumed his writing rather hurriedly, for the guests would soon be arriving. He gazed earnestly at the picture. *"Highly finished style,"* he scrawled, *"appropriate design—representative of Native Race in happier moments of festivity—contrasting their rude amusements to recreations of Polished Circle. . . ."* It was true, he thought, studying the picture again, that in each separate figure Mr. Lewin had captured a remarkable resemblance to some well-known native; but whether the sentiments he appeared to attribute to them, and which Colonel O'Connell had found so edifying, were as accurate as his portrayal of their physical characteristics, Mr. Howe took private leave to doubt. It even occurred to him that Mr. Lewin might be indulging in a little satire, for artists were notoriously irreverent. . . . His own part, however, was not to doubt, but to describe. *"Striking full-sized figure,"* he wrote hastily, *"in one of the most animated attitudes of CORROBORI, points with waddy at Church of St. Phillip of which accurate perspective view given—symbolical of Christian religion inviting them to happiness. . . ."*

But the first carriages were drawing up outside; he must make himself scarce, and remember to secure from Mr. Robinson the copy of his new Ode written for the occasion, which would doubtless have been prepared for the *Gazette*. As he slipped out of the door and bowed his way round the party of ladies and gentlemen re-entering the room, he was reflecting that it was not often one saw young Mr. Mannion in town, and wondering whether his appearance to-night had any particular significance. It was Mr. Howe's business to be well abreast of the news, and there were already rumours circulating about Mrs. Mannion and Mr. Harvey; it was whispered that this would be a mésalliance of the first order, and that the late Mr. Mannion's eldest son could hardly be expected to approve it. Mr. Howe, who had enjoyed an acquaintance with Mr. Harvey for many years, was hopeful that young Mr. Mannion's appearance in public with his stepmother at a function which his ex-tutor was also to attend, might be taken as evidence that, whatever his private thoughts upon the matter, he was prepared to lend it his countenance.

*　　　*　　　*　　　*

On that night the Governor, as he moved among his guests, was aware of a faint uneasiness. There were indications that Colonel O'Connell was being influenced by his wife in a direction which could do nothing to promote harmony, and obliterate the memory of old feuds. It was natural, he allowed—and even proper—that Bligh's daughter should remain her father's partisan; but she was a young woman with decided views, and a tongue which she (like her choleric parent) did not always control, and it was unfortunate, not to say confoundedly embarrassing, that his Lieutenant-Governor should be infected by her partiality. He had tried to tell himself that a man of mature years, marrying late in life a woman considerably his junior, was apt to be led by the nose; the realisation that this could apply also to himself and his Elizabeth had compelled him to abandon the thought in some haste, but he remained rather glumly censorious of his second-in-command.

He had reflected, too, that in a small and restricted society it was but natural that ripples of discord should stir the surface of social life; he had seen it often enough in India. Yet he could not avoid the suspicion that here it was less the surface than the depths which were disturbed; that he was not confronted by a mere clash of personalities, but—far more seriously—by a conflict of policy.

He could not, as yet, quite believe it. He, the benevolent autocrat, stood among these people as the living symbol of a fresh start. Now the slate was supposed to be wiped clean; now there could be no policy save his. It seemed so simple, and he was not so much alarmed as wounded by hints that it might not be as simple as it seemed. He was compelled to realise that there were still many of his subjects ready to catch fire and blaze into argument and recrimination about that deplorable rebellion if even a spark of a reminder were applied. Though Mrs. Macarthur and Mrs. O'Connell ostentatiously did not meet, it was inevitable, in this pocket-sized community, that chance should throw them together occasionally. Superbly unaware of each other's existence as they then appeared, it was clear that though Jack Bodice and Bounty Bligh were twelve thousand miles away, their fierce and unforgiving spirits were still turbulently present. Recognition of this quarrel as being itself but a manifestation of some profounder conflict was, as yet, permitted only to hover on the outer fringes of his reluctant thoughts.

Ah, well—patience, patience! He moved on, a tall, impressive figure, through the swelling, talkative crowd. Patrick, conscious that his step-mother's eyes were on the door, felt himself more than ever alone, and a stranger. Stepping back to make way for Mrs. Palmer, who was rustling amply across the room towards Mrs. O'Connell, he collided with someone behind him, and turned with a hasty apology.

"Your pardon, Sir—very clumsy of me. . . ."

"Not at all—my fault entirely. Mr. Mannion, I think?"

"Yes. I regret, Sir, that I don't . . . ?"

"You could not be expected to recall me, for I think we have never spoken before, and I have been absent from the colony for some time. Wentworth, Sir—William Wentworth."

Conor had turned upon hearing the name, and Patrick hastened to perform the introduction.

"But there's no need, Patrick, for I remember Mr. Wentworth very well, though it's many years since I saw him. You came with your father once to Beltrasna, did you not, Sir, when Patrick was ill, and we had sought the benefit of Dr. Wentworth's advice?"

"I'm honoured, ma'am, that you should remember a mere child for so long." She laughed.

"We were not permitted to forget you, for you and Miles formed great schemes for crossing the mountains together, and he spoke of nothing else for weeks!"

"You must have misunderstood him, ma'am. Rivalry was the essence of our plan, not combined endeavour. He swore he would be first, and I swore I would. We shall see!"

She replied smilingly:

"You had best make haste then, Mr. Wentworth, before Miles returns. You are yourself but recently returned from home, I believe?"

"Almost a year ago, ma'am—though in my case it was a return to home. I was born at Norfolk Island, and England, though dear to me, is not my native land."

Patrick enquired:

"You have returned to settle permanently, then?"

"My plans for the immediate future are uncertain. But my home is here."

"My brother mentioned in one of his letters that he had seen you in London."

Conor glanced at Patrick, wondering if he recalled as clearly as she did the wording of that careless reference. *"My Aunt Frances to whom I presented him, declared him an uncouth colonial, and made him the occasion for further exhortations to me to remain in a civilised society. . . ."* In the light of that recollection she studied the young man with interest. Standing a full head shorter than Patrick, Mr. Wentworth was thickly built; his hair, whose brown showed a reddish tinge, was untidy, though the night was young, and despite the formal clothes suitable for a vice-regal ball, he achieved a general air of dishevelment. Yet his manner, if it were not polished, was completely self-possessed. A slight cast in one eye was responsible, perhaps, for the odd detachment of his stare; his composure and his air of maturity were such that she found it difficult to believe him younger than Miles. Even Patrick, who must be more than half a dozen years his senior, looked slender and boyish beside him. He was replying:

"I met him a couple of times, quite briefly. He was—as I imagine is his habit—in excellent health and spirits." The cool, crooked gaze seemed to turn to Patrick and just miss him. "He told me," continued young Mr. Wentworth with a casualness which made his remark doubly shattering, "that you are something of a poet."

To his anger and confusion, Patrick felt his cheeks burning, and Conor was overwhelmed with sympathy for his embarrassment. Poor Patrick! His father, and his father's family, she knew, had always treated his penchant for scribbling verses as a pitiable eccentricity, so that he himself had come to regard it as something to be privately—and even guiltily—indulged.

"Poet . . . ?" he was saying hastily. "I . . . ? Oh, a pastime of my youth, merely . . . I have but little time for such . . . my property claims all my attention. . . ."

Wentworth observed him from beneath his heavy brows with a mild curiosity.

"Indeed? I had thought to find a kindred spirit—or should I say a fellow-slave? I find the Muse an exacting mistress, Mr. Mannion, but I should not wish to escape from her."

"You write poetry?" Patrick was so astonished that he blurted out the question like a child.

"Incessantly," replied Mr. Wentworth. But Conor, who had just seen Mr. Harvey entering the room, heard nothing more. For her, the evening had begun.

* * * *

The early months of the year had been hot and dry. Patrick returned to Beltrasna and wrote gloomily to his stepmother of the failure of his maize crop. The Tank Stream dwindled; Sydney's inhabitants began dipping their pitchers into small hollows above the tanks, and hawkers went about the streets selling water at sixpence a pail.

But to Conor nothing seemed quite real which did not concern the new, personal life towards which she was advancing. She shut herself up with piles of *Gazettes* and studied prices, astonished to observe their incomprehensible weekly fluctuations. Why should maize increase suddenly by one shilling a bushel, and potatoes fall by two and sixpence? She had never enquired the price of those foodstuffs which, on the way from the back door to the dining-table, were transformed into a meal—for whatever it was, the food would appear. Even here in Sydney, where she had congratulated herself upon her capacity for household management, she had done no more than order meals, supervise cleaning, and count the linen. She had conscientiously checked the bills and paid them, but she had never queried, or even particularly observed, the prices. All this, she realised guiltily, must now be changed, for the remarkable instability in the cost of food might concern her very much.

She astonished the worthy Mrs. Bodley by asking floods of questions. What did this saddle of mutton cost? How much sugar did the household consume in a week?˙ Were cabbages less expensive than peas? "I hope, ma'am," said Mrs. Bodley at last, with some stiffness, "that I'm giving satisfaction?"

She was mollified by Conor's reassurances, and since rumour came as easily to the kitchen as to the drawing-room, soon able to guess the reason for her mistress' sudden passion for domestic enlightenment. She even acquiesced with a kind of pitying benevolence when Conor invaded her kitchen, and demanded instruction in the art of cooking. "It's not what I'm used to," she confided to Flora, "having the mistress under my feet when I'm getting the dinner, and there's many cooks would give in their notice for less. But if it's true she's for marrying that schoolmaster she'll need to know a sight more than she does now."

"There, ma'am," she would say, transferring an exquisitely browned sirloin to a hot dish. "As nice a little joint as ever I see!"

"It looks excellent," Conor would reply, crouching to thrust her hand tentatively into the oven. "But this matter of the heat still perplexes me, Cook. I can feel cool, or warm, or hot, but I declare I cannot judge these fine degrees of heat with my hand. It seems no different now from the heat you used yesterday for the pastry."

"Law, ma'am, it's a trick that comes with practice—though I can't for the life of me see what a lady wants with it . . . ?"

But Conor made no response as yet to such oblique hints. She was approaching the time when she could no longer ignore the threat of grief which she felt lying in the heart of her happiness, and one evening she closed the drawing-room door and drew Julia to her side.

"My love," she began a trifle nervously, "I have an important piece of news to tell you. . . ."

"We're going to Ireland? Mama, are we really going to Ireland?"

"No, no, it's not that. . . ."

"But that's all I want, Mama," Julia protested, wriggling. "I don't want anything else, and I've been waiting and *waiting*. . . ."

"Sit still, child, and listen, for this is something which I hope will please you. I am going to be married, Julia, and. . . ."

"But you *are* married, Mama." Julia's blue eyes were round and uncomprehending. "You're married to Papa."

"I'm a widow, my love, now that . . . now that your Papa is not with us any more. And I'm to marry Mr. Harvey, so you and Desmond will soon have another Papa. . . ."

Before the words were fairly out of her mouth she felt Julia stiffen.

"I don't want him! I don't want a new Papa!"

"But Julia. . . ."

The child strained against her mother's arms, tore herself away, and burst into tears.

"I won't, I won't! I want my real Papa—I don't like Mr. Harvey!"

She stamped and sobbed. Conor, distracted, caught her hands. She pulled them away and screamed:

"I hate him! He's only a tutor! He's not a real gentleman like Papa!"

"Julia!" Conor spoke sharply. "Mr. Harvey is a gentleman, but what is much more important is that he is a kind and honourable man whom your mama loves dearly. You must not speak of him like that, or I shall be seriously displeased with you." She held out her arms. "Come, child, you wish Mama to be happy, do you not?"

Julia held back stubbornly.

"I don't want another Papa. I—I want my real Papa. . . ." Her tears overflowed again; she yielded at last to the pull of her mother's hands, and collapsed in a storm of sobbing. Conor, gathering the small, shaking body in her arms, stared over the dishevelled curls at the floor, her own heart pounding with agitation. Her mind produced desperate phrases of reassurance. "It is the shock . . . I was too abrupt . . . she was quite unprepared . . . she was so devoted to Stephen . . . she will become reconciled in time. . . . But at a deeper level where it refused all comforting self-deceptions it was admitting that this child, however loved, had always seemed a stranger. She said at last:

"Should you like to go to Ireland, Julia, and live for a time at my old home with your great-uncle Denis, and your great-aunt Millicent and your cousins? They are grown-up cousins, you know, not children for you to play with. . . ."

"Oh, Mama, yes! I like grown-up people best. May I go, Mama, truly?"

"Without me, my love? For I should stay here."

"Yes, I want to—all the other children go to England—James and William Macarthur went, and John and Robert Campbell, and even those silly Marsdens! I'm the only one that stays here, Mama. . . ."

"Don't be foolish, child—there are many hundreds who will always stay here. But if you wish it I shall consider . . ."

"When shall I go, Mama? Soon? Will there be a ship soon?"

"Quite soon, I expect. Come, now, it is late, and Bessie will be waiting for you."

When Julia was at last in bed and asleep, Conor went into her own room and stood at the window. The drought had broken at last, and rain was drumming through the darkness against the glass. It was not possible after all, she thought, to begin life quite anew.

*   *   *   *

The marriage of Mrs. Mannion and Mr. Harvey was celebrated so quietly that many heard of it only after it was over. The ceremony took place one morning late in March at St. Phillip's, being performed by Mr. Cowper, and attended only by young Mr. Mannion and old Mrs. Herbert.

Though the Sydney house was no longer Conor's, being forfeited by her re-marriage, Patrick had implored her to remain in it.

"I see no reason at all why you and Mr. Harvey should not occupy it, using the cottage for his school. I must maintain it in any case for Cousin Bertha, and continue to employ Mrs. Bodley and the Morgans. . . ."

But Conor was obdurate, and he reluctantly desisted from persuasions. But he said restlessly:

"My brother and sister. . . ."

"Julia and Desmond will do very well—and I shall send Julia to Ireland when a suitable opportunity offers."

"Then let me at least take them to Beltrasna until you are settled in the cottage. . . ." Seeing her hesitate, he added quickly: ". . . but perhaps you consider my house no longer suitable. . . ."

"Don't be absurd, Patrick—you are altogether too sensitive. How is Dilboong?"

"She is well."

"And her little girl?"

"The child seems to thrive." His tone dismissed it, but his eyes were troubled, and he continued at last, uncertainly: "It is very active, and already makes some attempts to stand. Dilboong has called it Mary. It seems much fairer in colour . . . indeed it is in some respects a not unattractive child. . . ."

"I shall see her quite soon, I hope," Conor said gently, "when I come to visit you. In the meantime, dear Patrick, your proposal to take the children for a time seems an excellent one, and I hesitated only because it would be the first time that Desmond has left me. But it would solve the problem of Bessie—I have found her a new situation, but . . ."

"You're dismissing Bessie? The children will have no nurse? You will have no assistance at all? I do protest . . . !"

"Calm yourself, Patrick. I shall have assistance. There's a girl at the Orphanage who has been doing my needlework since I came to Sydney, and who is now at the age beyond which they are not usually kept there, so. . . ."

"I hear no good reports of these girls. Her influence on the children. . . ."

"Mercy, how weary I am of all this talk of influence! Mark me, Patrick, keeping children from all knowledge of any kind of life other than their own can influence them quite as evilly as any connection with other classes." She suppressed her irritation with an effort. "But Emily is a good child, I assure you, and eager to come to me—pray trust my judgment. What I was about to say is that Bessie's new employer is to remove to the Liberty Plains district, and cannot receive her just now; so if you would take the children for a few weeks she could accompany them." She laughed, and patted his arm. "Come, Patrick—smile! Your misgivings are but a poor compliment to me!"

So, the wedding over, Patrick departed with Bessie and the children for Beltrasna, and Mr. and Mrs. Harvey, having seen Cousin Bertha safely disposed upon her sofa after the morning's excitements, returned alone to the cottage near Hyde Park. In the evening Mr. Harvey came upon his wife seated at the rosewood escritoire which had been her mother's; he felt a pang when she looked up and hastily closed the book in which she had been writing, but he said only:

"You are occupied, my love—I shall not disturb you."

She caught him before he reached the door.

"Disturb me—how could you? No, no, I was merely startled—you must forgive me. . . . It is a Journal I have kept for many years. . . ."

"A Journal . . . ?"

"I felt the need to express my thoughts—silly and confused as they often are—and had no one to whom I could talk. It has become a habit, my love, and though I shall not need it now, I . . ."

"All your thoughts are precious to me—might I not read them?"

She blushed vividly, and he added in hasty reassurance:

"No, no, I'm wrong, of course. We all cherish and need our privacy —I should not ever wish to intrude. . . ."

"Oh, don't speak—*pray* don't speak of intruding! Indeed you shall see my Journal—yes, every word of it—someday. . . . Someday when we have been longer together, and you know my failings better, my con-fusions, my impatience, my—yes. . . ." she blushed again, ". . . my duplicity . . . !"

He began to laugh.

"Your impatience is as nothing to mine. I can hardly wait to learn of this duplicity of yours! Yet I shall wait—for why should I need Journals to study you, now that you yourself are at my side?"

          *   *   *   *

The children's few weeks at Beltrasna extended to two months. Patrick, they discovered, was a somewhat capricious guardian; he could be stern, but only when it occurred to him, as it occasionally did, that he had been over-indulgent, or when he realised guiltily that he had forgotten their existence for a time. Bessie, as one recently come from the capital, was well primed with gossip about the great ones of the colony, and able to recount (with an accuracy and detail which would have astonished Conor) the progress of her mistress' romance. She was, therefore, extremely popular in the housekeeper's room, and the children were left mainly to the care of Dilboong.

Julia queened it happily among them. Desmond, chubby and serene, had always been her follower; Maria's three-year-old son, Simeon, was soon her willing slave; Samuel Dawson, son of Patrick's newest overseer, was torn between admiration of her and respect for his elder brother, the ten-year-old Timothy—for it was only Timothy who ever questioned her sway. Nevertheless, when all else failed, she was able to confound him by assuming her most imperious air, and transforming herself in an instant from a playmate into a young lady who was, when all was said and done, the master's sister. There was only one other girl—Dilboong's baby daughter—who was far too young to be a rival even if it had not been for her natural inferiority as a native. Patrick, riding back across the fields from some inspection of his property, or emerging from his study after hours of absorbed communion with his latest poem, would observe the little group with a hint of uneasiness. Yet it seemed not so long ago that he had himself been a child, roaming these same fields with Miles and Dilboong, and Andy and Maria Prentice. It was one thing, he told himself, for well-born children to associate on a large estate with the children of its servants; quite another for them to rub shoulders with an Orphanage girl and the sons of convicts in a mean town cottage. He sighed, and left them to their play.

It was while they were still at Beltrasna that a chance incident again set an old wound in his mind aching fiercely. They had gone down to the river with Dilboong, and he, finding them there, paused idly to watch them playing at the edge of the water. A canoe, paddled by two native youths, came into sight round a bend, but he observed it at first without any particular interest, for the sight was common enough. As it approached, however, his gaze became intent. Was not the elder the same youth who, on the day of his father's death, had come running and yelling with two little native boys to declare that they had been set upon by white men in the woods south of Beltrasna . . . ? Patrick was convinced by now that their appearance had been a ruse to decoy his father, himself and the overseers from the property, and leave the way clear for the escaped convict, Finn, to free other prisoners. If that were so, they had been in league with Finn—and perhaps with Johnny Prentice . . . ?

He called peremptorily, beckoning them to the bank. Rather un-willingly, he thought, they paddled the canoe nearer, and he demanded of the elder youth:

"You—what is your name?"

Billalong understood English perfectly, and spoke it with some fluency, but now he only stared, smiled, and shook his head. Patrick asked:

"You come here once? You come with two little boys?" He sketched their height with his hand. "You tell us white men hurt you?"

Billalong continued to stare blankly. Patrick hesitated, and then shot out the question which he almost dreaded to hear answered:

"You know Johnny Prentice?"

Billalong was ready for it. The broad, white streak of his uncompre-hending grin did not alter, but Patrick saw his companion dart a strange look at him. Julia, agog with curiosity, scrambled up the bank and stood beside her brother; Dilboong, carrying Mary and dragging Simeon by the hand, followed, with Desmond and the two Dawsons at her heels. Julia demanded:

"Who's Johnny Prentice?"

Patrick felt a sudden panic. What had he done? No living soul among the white people, save himself and Conor (and perhaps, by now, Mr. Harvey) suspected that Johnny was still alive; he had no wish to be the means of betraying that secret—even to Maria—through the chatter of children. And, he thought, if this youth were indeed in communication with his old playmate, had he not given warning that he not only knew of Johnny's existence, but suspected him of complicity in the death of Mr. Stephen Mannion? Would not this intelligence, when conveyed to him, make him more desperate an outlaw then ever? Yet he could add no message of reassurance without confirming to the curious ears of the children about him that there did exist, somewhere, a person called Johnny Prentice. Julia was repeating persistently:

"Who's Johnny Prentice, Patrick?"

Inspiration came to him. He looked straight at Billalong and replied with careful distinctness:

"He was a boy—Maria's brother—who ran away, Julia, and was lost. No one ever saw him again. He died—many years ago. . . ."

The grin had faded from Billalong's face, and his eyes watched Patrick intently. Then, with a word to his companion, he swung the canoe round and paddled it into the open stream. Julia was asking: "Why did he run away? How old was he? What made him die?" But Patrick had already turned to leave them, confused and bedevilled by the thought that once again he had lied to shield his father's murderer. Julia watched him go, wondering why he paid no attention to her questions, and why he walked so fast.

Early in June—Bessie's new employer now desiring her presence and Mama declaring that the children had already been away too long—Shawn Morgan arrived from Sydney with the carriage. Next morning Bessie, wrapping her charges in ulsters and scarves against the frosty air, took them back to the capital with a reluctance which was no less than Julia's. Both children had become homesick for their Mama, but while Desmond acknowledged it at bedtime with forlorn enquiries and a few tears, Julia would not admit it even to herself. For Mama was no longer Mrs. Mannion, but Mrs. Harvey, and she felt that this was in some way a betrayal of her beloved Papa. Beltrasna seemed very much his place. Above the mantelpiece in the dining-room hung his portrait in oils, executed during his last visit to Ireland; his handsome face looked out of it commandingly over the immaculate ruffles of his shirt, his hand with its signet ring clasped the lapel of an elegant coat; the artist, seeking an appropriate setting for a gentleman pioneering the wilderness, had per-mitted his fancy to improve upon tales of New Holland, and placed his subject against a background of sunlit fields, dotted with negro labourers and backed by towering peaks of malevolent aspect. To Julia this was Papa, and it did not occur to her to contrast the peaks with the low, quiet, dull green foothills across the river; perhaps she felt that their splendour, like the splendour of everything else, had shrunk and faded with his death, and though she had long ago shed the poignancy of her grief as children will, the mere memory of his omnipotence lent her a feeling of security in a world which seemed, just now, threatened by sinister change. She wept as they departed, and moped throughout the long, tiresome journey.

She found her new home bewildering and uncongenial. Even com-pared with Moore House it was small; compared with Beltrasna it seemed contemptible. Why, she thought in dismay, even Maria's cottage is as big as this! Mama was very busy doing many things which were usually done by servants, and Mr. Harvey was occupied with the dirty little boys who came every day to the schoolroom. It was strange to find that she was now expected to perform for herself and Desmond many little offices which had always been performed by their nurse; but most strange of all strange things in this new home was Emily. She was a servant, but oddly unlike any servant Miss Mannion had known before. In rare intervals between cooking and scouring she would join Julia and Desmond in the long grass of the little yard behind the cottage, and play with them— not indulgently and perfunctorily, like Bessie, but earnestly and with ardour, entering into their discussions with serious passion, sharing their arguments vehemently, and telling them, occasionally, the most surprising stories of her life in the Orphanage.

For the first time, Julia learned that the gentry were not always regarded with respectful awe by the lower orders. Shocked, and more than a little resentful, but still held attentive by a kind of fascination, she watched Emily's irreverent mimicry not only of the matron and the schoolmaster, but of many much more important people, including, even, the Governor himself. She heard the very voices of Mrs. Marsden, Mrs. Macquarie,. Mrs. O'Connell and other ladies of the colony wickedly parodied in high, mincing tones. And while Desmond fairly rolled on the grass with his laughter, she felt her own involuntary enjoyment in-hibited by indignation. Were not these orphans mere paupers, existing on the charity and benevolence of those whom one of them was now so mercilessly deriding? Should not Emily be grateful to these highly-placed people? "I suppose," she said fiercely one day, "you think my Mama's funny too!"

But Emily turned on her in a fury.

"I never said nothing about her, did I?"

And indeed it was clear even to Julia that Emily served Mama with a veritable passion of devotion.

Her greatest shock, however, came when she learned that Mr. Harvey proposed to give Emily lessons, and that he and Mama were actually considering whether Julia might not share them. She, Julia Mannion, share lessons with a servant . . . ? The temptation to demonstrate that she, though so much Emily's junior, was a more proficient scholar than an ignorant orphan could ever be, almost overcame her reluctance until she discovered, to her incredulous amazement, that Emily already surpassed her. "You see, child," Mama explained, "you have only had me for a teacher, and I fear you have not taken any great pains either, whereas Emily is very eager to learn. If you would but apply yourself seriously with Papa. . . ."

"He's not my Papa," objected Julia crossly.

She was half relieved and half affronted to find that the matter was not pressed. Sometimes she would peep into the schoolroom in the evening when Mr. Harvey and his new pupil retired there with books and slates. She would watch Emily bent over some task; and because Papa had never tired of praising her own blue eyes and golden curls, she was not altogether pleasantly surprised to observe that the servant-girl, with the lamplight burnishing her brown hair and throwing the shadow of long lashes on her cheeks, was pretty too. But it was at Mr. Harvey that she looked longest. He was not nearly as handsome as Papa—not nearly! There was about him none of the careless magnificence of dress and bearing which had made Papa such an exciting figure. She had been but four when Mr. Harvey left Beltrasna—too young to form an opinion of her own concerning him, but old enough to have absorbed her father's, whose cold, contemptuous references during the following years had taught her to despise a dismissed and penniless tutor. Now she was confused and angered to find herself in a house where he was "the master". She scolded Desmond for calling him "Papa". She rejected his friendly advances, and then sulked when he ignored her. She pretended unconcern for her mother's distress, met her rebukes with a show of defiance, and cried herself to sleep at night.

Her greatest treat was to spend a day at Moore House. There, talking to Cousin Bertha about Ireland, dressing up in the old lady's shawls and scarves, or seeking the company of Cook and Flora—who were real servants, and treated her with a proper blend of indulgence and respect—she felt at home.

*   *   *   *

Conor, meanwhile, was busy establishing a domestic routine which, though more exacting than she would have believed possible, still pleased her by being something of her own creation; had it not been for the irreconcilable Julia, she would have said that she knew perfect happiness for the first time since childhood.

Each week-day morning, when the pupils had arrived, and sounds from the schoolroom proclaimed that lessons had begun, she addressed herself to a series of unfamiliar tasks, marvelling that so much time and effort should be required to produce effects of neatness and cleanliness which she had hitherto taken for granted. On Market days Emily was despatched with money in her pocket, and a basket on her arm, to lay in stores for the coming week—a duty in which she took great pride, relating to her mistress on her return the fierce arguments she had conducted with villains who desired to cheat her. In the evenings there were sometimes guests; Dr. Redfern—himself lately married—would bring his wife; Mr. and Mrs. Cowper were frequent visitors; Captain Antill and Captain Piper would arrive and sit talking over a glass of port; and occasionally young Mr. Wentworth would appear to enliven the conversation with his uncompromising views upon controversial questions. It was but rarely, now, that Conor went into society; neither their house nor their means permitted the giving of formal entertainments, and she declared that she had lost the taste for attending them. But one day in July, summoning Shawn Morgan with the carriage, she drove with Julia to visit Mrs. Macarthur at Parramatta. Her friendship with the Campbells, and her frequent appearances at Captain Bligh's parties had caused a certain constraint between herself and the mistress of Elizabeth Farm; but time had already done something to calm the tempests of partisanship, and she herself had retired so much from the colony's society that she now ventured to hope that a once pleasant association could be resumed. And besides, she thought, it would be an agreeable excursion for Julia, who now so rarely drove out visiting with Mama.

Mrs. Macarthur, for her part, was happy to receive Mrs. Harvey. She recalled one bright morning many years ago when the late Mr. Mannion had begged her friendship for the young lady who was to be his bride, and she had observed the subsequent indiscretions of one who was thus, in a sense, her protegée, with an almost maternal disapproval. Mrs. Harvey's choice of friends in the past might have been unfortunate, but it could be ascribed to an ignorance of colonial politics, in which she herself, as the wife of John Macarthur, was naturally so soundly informed. It was not too late, perhaps, to instil better judgment. Upon his return, Macarthur would still need supporters; for the present he certainly needed information upon all that passed in the colony, and the very fact that Mrs. Harvey visited where she herself did not . . .

But she found Conor singularly barren of gossip. She had not been at Government House for a long time; she had exchanged only a few words with Mrs. O'Connell in months; she had heard little of the projected hospital; she was but slightly acquainted with Mr. John Campbell; she had not seen the Marsdens of late; but Captain Piper had called upon them several times. "It is pleasant to have him in Sydney again, after his long absence at Norfolk Island, is it not?"

On this point the ladies were able to agree, for Captain Piper contrived, in the most amiable fashion, to remain on good terms with everyone. The absence which his friends deplored had saved him from embroilment in the rebellion, and he had returned—debonair, sociable and obliging as ever—still qualified to claim unique distinction in Sydney society as a man with no enemies.

"We shall not have him long, however," remarked Mrs. Macarthur, "since he goes home in the *Providence*. And speaking of the *Providence*, we're in great excitement here, are we not, my dears . . . ?" she appealed to her three daughters, ". . . over the letters and boxes that came by her from Macarthur. Mary, my love, take Julia and show her all the pretty things Papa has sent us. Elizabeth, you had best go too, and take Emmeline with you." Watching them disappear, she added: "He has forgotten nothing! Everything that is necessary, or that could give us pleasure, is there! Though of course . . ." her fingers strayed to a bulky package of papers on her lap, ". . . most welcome of all is the news he sends us of himself."

"He is well, I trust?"

"So he assures me, though he is compelled to keep to the most rigid diet. And naturally the uncertainty of all this business about Captain Bligh preys upon his mind."

"I hear that Captain Bligh reached England in October." Conor, recalling the three shiploads of hostility and intrigue which had set out from Port Jackson, could imagine the frenzied activity which must have animated the voyagers when they set foot in England—the pouring out of conflicting stories, the buttonholing of friends, the manœuvres to reach the ears of the influential. . . .

"Yes," her hostess was saying, "and Macarthur went down to Portsmouth the moment he heard the ships had arrived. You'll be interested to learn that he escorted Mrs. Paterson up to London."

"Ah, poor Mrs. Paterson! It was sad that the Colonel should die during the voyage—just when he had escaped from a place which I fear was never congenial to him."

But Mrs. Macarthur could be implacable. In the storms and stresses of colonial life over many years, Colonel Paterson had failed to co-operate with her husband, or to use his authority boldly in support of his plans. Therefore, though Macarthur himself had magnanimously chosen to behave civilly to the Colonel's widow, Mrs. Macarthur would not concede him even a sigh.

"It was hardly to be wondered at," she remarked briskly, "and my husband says that Mrs. Paterson appeared in good spirits. For his own part, he's conferring with his lawyers from morning till night. He sees Colonel Johnston constantly, of course, and he has made his peace with Foveaux—as you know, my dear, there were many dissentions between them. But this business requires that all those opposing Bligh should be united. What Macarthur has had to suffer from the ingratitude and pusillanimous conduct of those who should be giving him firm support . . . ! But by now I trust it is all over, and justice done."

Conor thought it time to give the conversation a new turn.

"And your sons? What do you hear of them?"

"Oh, they are in excellent health. Their father sees much of them, and it's some consolation to me for these dreadful delays to know they are together." She sighed. "How I wish it were all over, and Macarthur home again! Apart from missing his companionship, dear Mrs. Harvey,

I find the responsibilities of caring for our stock and property cause me great anxiety."

In a brief interval while the girls returned to display their gifts, and little Emmeline leaned against Conor's knee with a handful of ribbons to be admired, their mother fell silent, fingering her husband's letters, and pondering his instructions. *"Do not sell any estate or any part of the breeding stock . . . send home by every opportunity what wool you can . . . be CAREFUL of the Spanish sheep and let no pains be spared in culling the flocks . . . you have never sent me a return of stock since I left home. . . ."*

Had she ever been an ignorant, idle, dreamy girl? What would have become of her had she married some quiet, easy-tempered man of un-ambitious disposition? Perhaps she might still have known the cares attendant upon bearing eight children and rearing seven of them—but she would not have been responsible, also, for rearing thousands of sheep! Yet how dull that might have been in comparison with the life she had led as John Macarthur's wife—a life always full of projects, always sharp with crisis, always tense with the need for a watchful eye and a dis-ciplined tongue, always lit by the beacon light of ambition . . . ! *"Act with your accustomed prudence, and preserve a guarded silence on the measures of your new Governor . . . be patient and all will be well, for I have found a powerful body of friends in this country . . . I think I shall be obliged to procure a seat in Parliament—the expense will be great . . . we must therefore be very economical. . . ."*

She started. The girls had gone away with their treasures, and her guest was addressing her.

"Forgive me, my love, my thoughts were wandering—you were saying . . . ?"

"I merely mentioned that the arrival of the *Providence* was a matter of some excitement for me also. My uncle in Ireland has sent out some furniture and other things which my Grandpapa left me, and I have been busy arranging it. To be sure, much of it is altogether too large for our little house, and will have to be stored or sold; but it has given me a strange pleasure to have these things about me again—the things I recollect from my childhood."

"How well I understand that! I have myself many little relics from my home in England, and they're my dearest possessions. And how in-terested your pretty Julia must have been to see them!"

"Yes, indeed." But Conor's animation had faded. The time she had been dreading was upon her, but her dread was now mixed with a sad conviction that her daughter's world was not, and might never be, hers. For Julia still refused to accept even a temporary place in the new life which her mother had undertaken, rejecting it, child as she was, with a strangely mature and bitter persistence. In these last weeks a home and a country which had been legendary had been made real by visible and tangible objects they had harboured, and her impatience had become feverish.

"Mama, I could go home in the *Providence!* Couldn't I, Mama? Why not?"

Why not, indeed?

When her guests had departed, Mrs. Macarthur returned immediately to the letters she had been studying when they arrived. Macarthur was an exacting correspondent. Not only must she keep him informed of how his business affairs progressed, but she must also let him know the temper of the colony, whether the new Governor seemed friendly, what kind of policy he was developing, who his associates were, and how all this might be expected to affect the fortunes of John Macarthur. And she must give him, too, the detailed family news for which he so clearly hungered. The pile of papers covered with his firm, black writing, seemed a poor, but precious, substitute for his physical presence; she was tormented by feeling herself close to him, and knowing herself far away.

For she knew him so well that even without his admissions she would have guessed his restlessness, his nervous impatience, his fits of acute depression. They were caused not only by his unfortunate tendency to dyspepsia (indeed she had often suspected this ailment of being less the cause than the result of his abrupt plunges into gloom); nor by separation from herself and his daughters; nor by anxiety about the outcome of his legal battle with Bligh. All these, no doubt, played their part, but the real truth was, she told herself, that he was enduring a kind of temporary death. He was so much the architect of his own life; he had fought, wrestled, worked, schemed and contrived to make it, and it was all here, in this colony, from which he was now banished—for how long?

She dared not dwell upon that question. During the voyage to England he had been still sanguine. *"In two months I hope to be in England, and in three months after on my way back."* But it was almost two years since that was written, and still there seemed no prospect of an early return. She pored anxiously over passages whose tone had changed, as the months went by, from an earlier optimism. *"How thankful I should be if the business were settled, for to live in such a state of suspense is dreadful. . . ."* *"Would to God the time were come, for I am weary of doubt and anticipation. . . ."* This was the most recent letter—how long before she could hope for another? She sat staring at it absently, and her eye was caught by that paragraph which had most vividly betrayed his nostalgia. *"Often in my walks about the pleasant Commons and Roads*

. . . do I think of your probable employments, and calculate the difference of time. When I come home about ten o'clock I suppose you are seated at your breakfast table, and pray God you may be enjoying your repast in peace and happiness, and in health. At my own breakfast hour I picture you all seated round a cheerful fire sipping your tea, and when I think of the immense distance that separates us, and the labours I must perform before I can flee to you, my philosophy is scarcely sufficient to enable me to bear my hard fate without desponding. Had I some employment to occupy my time, my situation would be less painful. . . ."

Yes, yes, she thought, that was it! It was not his habit to wait upon events, but to create them. He saw life as his life, and here he had been able to make this conception a fact, gathering the life of the colony about him, holding himself firmly in its centre, agitating, manipulating and directing it for his own purposes, watching it revolve about him. New South Wales was small enough to be dominated by his energy and ambition; London was not. London knew little of John Macarthur, and cared less. It had its own life in which he could find only precarious foot-holds—a few friends who might gain him the ear of influential people, a few acquaintances who might well temper their geniality towards one apparently under a cloud owing to his participation in some obscure colonial rebellion. . . . And so he must wait on the fringes of London's life —restless, ill, homesick, frustrated, anxious, and bitterly alone. . . .

Yet no—not quite alone, she thought, for the boys were there, and all his letters breathed parental pride in them. She was comforted by a vague notion that she was, in a sense, with him after all in the sons she had borne him, and she told herself sharply that she must not repine. She must redouble her efforts to keep all his colonial affairs in order— and she must really be more careful about sending him returns of stock. She must write cheerfully to sustain his spirits, and she must see that the girls wrote often too. She rose energetically, calling: "Elizabeth— Mary—have you begun your letters to Papa?"

*　　　*　　　*　　　*

Macquarie had proceeded through his second year of office with un-abated confidence. So far the climate had not seriously embarrassed him with excesses. Quarrels—which of course continued to rage—had not involved him personally to any uncomfortable degree. The indignation aroused in some quarters by his lenience towards convicts and eman-cipists was as yet no more than a muttering, and if his contract with the builders of the hospital had caused envy and resentment, it found little open expression. On points of law he was able to refer to a Judge Advocate whom he still regarded as a paragon of good sense, and pro-found legal knowledge. Crime, of course, was to be expected in a penal colony; but he had effected a vigorous reorganisation of the police force, and if what had been nightly examples of theft, rioting and drunkenness were not—as he liked to declare—almost totally suppressed, they were at least driven from the streets. No spectre of starvation threatened him; the harvests had been good, the stores were filled with provisions for those who must be victualled by Government, and the poor were accustomed to poverty.

Yet he had his problems and his worries. Foremost among them was a lively apprehension that the home authorities would find his expenditure too lavish; he lost no opportunity of pointing out economical devices which he had adopted, and which would, he hoped, soften the impact of the Commissary's accounts.

He was concerned, too, about the Code of Civil and Criminal Law, unrevised since the establishment of the colony, and now, in his opinion, unsuitable to its altered conditions; long consultations with Mr. Bent upon this subject revealed that the Judge Advocate fully shared his views. Yet whenever this comforting thought crossed his mind, he was aware of a barely visible shadow skulking behind it. His relations with Mr. Bent continued cordial; Mr. Bent was an able lawyer: Mr. Bent attended to his duties. Mr. Bent behaved with propriety. Nevertheless, the Governor seemed to catch now and then in his manner an undercurrent of some emotion not altogether friendly. There was a hint of resentment, sometimes, and an occasional word from his lady which—however playfully uttered—seemed to express injured, but dutiful, acquiescence in some nebulous injustice or disadvantage.

Under what possible injustice, the Governor asked himself irritably, could they imagine themselves to labour? Thanks to the good offices of the late Mr. Thompson, they occupied a house which was, in many ways, far more comfortable than the leaking and white-ant-ridden Government House itself. Mr. Bent's salary was good, and his position was one of the utmost respectability. He had servants allotted to him, and he was, from all reports, on the way to making a fortune for himself out of his cattle. What more could the man want? As a tiny thorn embedded in the flesh stabs sharply at a careless touch, so this half-formed impression hurt His Excellency every time he thought of Mr. Bent.

But he had neither time nor inclination to examine it more closely. Among his problems at the moment was the Cow Pastures—that tempting tract of land which had been adopted years ago by the wild cattle. These, he estimated, would now number between four and five thousand, without allowing for others which had probably strayed into areas as yet untrodden by white men. So considerable an asset to the Crown must be safeguarded; from it could come hides and tallow, to say nothing of large quantities of beef for the stores. Yet they were something of a liability as well. When a convict escaped, he made, if he could, for the Cow Pastures; beyond them, in the high, rugged hills intersected by deep ravines, a man might lie safely hidden, and descend at night to kill a beast for food. And who knew how far beyond that place some of the beasts might have strayed—or been driven? Moreover Mr. Macarthur and Mr. Davidson had already secured properties in the area, and Macquarie was convinced that their stockmen and shepherds, as well as settlers from farther down the river, killed numbers of the cattle for their own advantage. Secure in solitude, able to shift blame from their own shoulders to those of natives, or conveniently invisible outlaws, they were ideally situated for committing such depredations. Those cattle, valuable as they might be, were an ever-present temptation to lawlessness, and as such the Governor viewed them with mixed feelings.

The *Providence* had added some hundred and seventy convicts to the felonry of New South Wales, and the *Admiral Gambier* and the *Friends,* which reached Port Jackson that spring, brought almost three hundred more; but the time appeared to be past when Governors must dread the arrival of new prisoners, seeing them merely as so many more mouths to feed from an inadequate store. By now only almost inconceivable disaster could seriously endanger the food supply, and labour was welcome. Macquarie, inspecting them when they came ashore, saw them as hands which would help to transform his realm from a few makeshift settlements to a colony which could boast of its towns and buildings with the best.

In the meantime he was busy preparing an exhaustive despatch which the *Providence,* as the first direct conveyance to England for nearly a year, must bear to the Earl of Liverpool. In the Secretary's office Mr. Campbell and his clerks compiled documents setting forth the results of the latest muster, returns of stock and of land under cultivation, of persons holding civil and military appointments, of births, marriages and deaths, of trials, pardons, and grants of land. They penned the usual regrettable but inevitable requests for tools, implements, stores and clothing; they transmitted memorials from various people soliciting various indulgences; they enclosed a copy of the contract for the hospital; they set out His Excellency's appeal for trial by jury and other revisions of the Criminal Code, his plea for the inviolability of the area inhabited by the wild cattle, his report on the insufficiency of labour at Hobart Town, his description of the new roads and the new Market; and many other matters. Their hands ached from writing, and the piles of paper rose higher on their tables.

At last it was time for the *Providence* to sail, and Captain Piper embarked with his family, quite undismayed by the remarkable assortment of commissions with which his many friends hastened to entrust him. The Governor's despatches were delivered into his charge, together with a bundle of *Gazettes*. A deluge of black swans—birds which had proved acceptable presents to great personages from whom colonial gentlemen might hope someday to receive favours—descended upon him. He was made the bearer of countless boxes, packages, letters and verbal messages. Colonel and Mrs. O'Connell were sure he would have the goodness to convey cages of parrots to Captain Bligh, and shells to Mrs. Bligh; in China he would no doubt be so kind as to purchase silks and scarves for the Misses Bligh, and ivory fans upon which he would cause their initials to be suitably engraved. *"I have to offer you every apology, my dear Sir,"* wrote the Colonel deprecatingly, *"for giving you so much trouble, but have availed myself of your very obliging disposition. . . ."*

So well known was the obliging disposition of the genial Captain, that for months past a hundred plans had been in agitation among high and low to make him unofficial messenger and courier for the whole colony. "Ask Piper to take it for you," said this gentleman to that. "Tell Piper to get it," "Ask Jock to deliver it." And "Why, my love," cried the ladies to each other, "our dear Captain Piper will be only too happy to take charge of anything you wish to send!"

Conor had protested to her husband:

"I declare I'm ashamed to ask him—for what with letters, and birds, and boxes, and shells, and swans, and despatches, and children of his own. . . ."

But if these were the penalties of popularity, Captain Piper was accustomed to accepting them with a good grace, and as he stood on the deck of the *Providence* with his family on one warm, Spring evening in October, it seemed the most natural thing in the world that Julia Mannion should be committed to his care along with everything else.

The Governor and Mrs. Macquarie had come aboard with a large party to make a festivity of the departure, and Macquarie, with his despatches off his mind, and the prospect of a pleasant little voyage of inspection to Van Diemen's Land now imminent, was in his most jovial mood. There was much talk and laughter from all save Mrs. Harvey, who seemed to find difficulty in reflecting the general mood of merriment. Julia, whose cheeks and eyes were bright with excitement, wished that Mama would not stand so close to her, obscuring from view her new frock and her new bonnet with its curled feather and cherry red ribbons. She looked a trifle enviously at Desmond, who was running up and down the deck with Hugh and John Piper; she would not, of course, behave as noisy little boys did, but if Mama were not holding her hand so tightly she could have walked about feeling grown up, conversing, and being admired. Captain Piper—who had a way with the female sex at any time, and knew a ten-year-old coquette when he saw one—had won her heart by treating her with polished gallantry, but for the moment even he was ignoring her, giving all his attention to Mama and Mr. Harvey. More than an easy good-nature and social aplomb were needed to account for the readiness with which everyone confided in "Jock"; Julia, looking up restlessly, saw her mother press a handkerchief to her eyes, and caught a few words of the Captain's consoling murmur:

"Pray have no fears, my dear ma'am. . . . Mr. Harvey, you must convince her . . . as one of my own, I promise you . . . already the darling of the ship, upon my word. . . !"

The darling of the ship! Julia smoothed her skirt and touched her curls happily. If *only* the visitors would go ashore! If *only* the voyage would begin. . . !"

*   *   *   *

With the *Providence* gone, there was only one more public duty for the Governor to perform before he himself set sail for Van Diemen's Land, and on one bright, breezy afternoon he drove ceremoniously up to Macquarie Street with his entourage to lay the foundation stone of the new hospital. There he was received by the gentlemen entrusted with the work, plied with refreshments in a marquee, handed a box encased in lead to be embedded in a cavity of the foundation stone, and presented with a silver trowel. When the stone was laid he stood back to read the inscription with pride and pleasure. Already he could see his big completed hospital, handsome and imposing on its hilltop. What was man without buildings? What was the human community without cities? Perhaps the neat fitting of timbers, and the clean laying of brick on brick, the raising of austerely simple walls and smooth columns, and the dedication of these things to righteous human uses, were symbolical of that Order, Dignity and Rectitude which were so much more easily achieved in buildings than in the intransigeant hearts of men. At all events, he felt a new access of confidence; surely the appeal for official commendation with which he had ended his despatch, would meet with a warm response!

Yet that night, when a remark from his wife recalled to him that Mrs. O'Connell was expecting a child in January, and when memory thrust at him a picture of Mrs. Harvey, obviously anticipating a similar event, he was swept by an old, familiar melancholy. He was nearly fifty, and still childless. Must he always be content to see his name bestowed upon streets, buildings, and the sons of other men?

*   *   *   *

It was but a fortnight later that Mrs. Macarthur sat down to write to Captain Piper, for the departure of a vessel next morning might enable her letter to catch up with him at one of the ports of call—and how surprised the dear man would be to hear all the gossip of the colony so soon! "*We experience a great blank in the loss of your society,*" she assured him. "*For the first week there was nothing but lamentation. . . .*" Her pen raced, and her little touches of malice were as delicate as her handwriting. "*The Govr. and Mrs. Macquarie embarked and sailed for Hobart Town on Monday week. Capt. COLD ONE, John Maclean and Jimmy Meehan attended them, leaving Mr. Campbell here. . . .*" She delivered a little two-pronged stab at the influential Secretary and the husband of her enemy, Mrs. O'Connell: "*I am sure the Lieut.-Govr. is restricted from exerting much prerogative. . . .*" The *Gambier* and the *Friends,* she reported, had not yet sailed; it was rumoured that Mr. Marsden had sold his Brush Farm; Mrs. Marsden and the children were still at the Hawkesbury, "*. . . where I believe Mr. M. would willingly leave them. . . .*"

Her pen was momentarily halted by a thought never far from her mind since the arrival recently of a whaler bringing news which had been received with widely varying emotions in the colony. She continued more slowly: "*. . . we have recd. a few letters and some papers containing an account of Col. Johnston's Trial—the sentence not known, how very tantalising and disturbing to me who am so much interested in the event. The Commodore is finely exposed, however the affair terminate. You will probably know before this reaches your hands . . . I will not dwell on this subject which so much bewilders and disturbs me. . . .*"

She turned again to social gossip. "*On Friday night we dined at Mr. Bent's . . . Mrs. Bent has been much indisposed since you departed. She is in very bad humour about the Governor's absence, having, as you know, no manner of respect for the little great Lady, who is still in statu quo. . . .*"

Strange! She sat there biting her pen and reflecting. The Judge Advocate and his wife were really not at all well disposed towards the Governor and Mrs. Macquarie—as Captain Piper knew, as she knew, as almost everyone in the colony knew . . . except, apparently, the Governor himself. . . .

*　　　　*　　　　*　　　　*

In response to a letter from Conor, Patrick journeyed to Sydney early in December. Cousin Bertha, she told him, had been ailing of late, and Dr. Redfern believed that her condition gave cause for grave anxiety.

Young Mr. Mannion took the minor responsibilities of his position as head of the family the more seriously for obstinately evading the major one; if he would not return to his rightful place in the ancestral Irish home, he would at least inconvenience himself to the extent of making a dutiful visit to his aged kinswoman. He embraced the opportunity, too, as he was passing through Parramatta, of paying a courtesy call upon Mrs. Macarthur, who seemed, he thought, less ready than usual to talk about her absent husband. Yes, she had received long letters by the *Gambier*. Yes, she was happy to say that her dear boys were in good health. For the rest, she turned the conversation to agricultural matters.

She had been, in fact, greatly worried by these letters, though less by their news than by their tone—for Macarthur's confidence was clearly ebbing. In imagination she could follow the incessant, striving restlessness of his thoughts, the interminable, but inconclusive planning, the anxious weighing of pros and cons. Should he withdraw himself and his family from the colony altogether? No; living had become too costly in England, and taxes were too heavy. And would this indeed be a wise course, even if expenses could be met? Who could say how matters would shape in the colony?

And then, upon his already troubled mind, must have burst the incredible tidings she had been compelled to send him of the way they seemed to be shaping. She could almost see him pacing the room in his agitation—almost hear his voice uttering the words he had written. "*Every paragraph increases my amazement . . . God alone knows how such a state of things as you describe may terminate. . . . I am interrogated on all hands about the affairs of the Colony, and know not what to reply. . . . Is it possible, it is said, that Governor Macquarie can associate with, and bring to the table, men who have been Convicts . . . ?*" Truly the colonial pattern which he knew, showing its bold, irrevocable lines of cleavage between the felon and the free, must be wholly disintegrating! How could the respectable maintain their advantage if cunning rogues with the brand of felonry upon them were not only permitted to amass wealth, but even admitted to the society of the Governor himself? The news that his old enemy, Andrew Thompson, had so won Macquarie's regard had plainly horrified him; it was, he declared, but the interposition of Providence which, in removing this artful knave by death, had saved the colony from utter ruin. Moreover, thought his wife indignantly, some of his friends were as much trouble to him as his enemies—too fearful, now that the time of reckoning was near, to stand boldly by their leader; Colonel Johnston himself was but a broken reed, and Lieutenant Lawson, it appeared, had literally fled from the impending trial upon the same vessel which had brought her husband's letters.

Unaware of the train of thought behind it, Patrick saw in her sudden question a mere conversational politeness:

"Do you never feel a desire to return to England, Mr. Mannion?"

"I feel none at present, ma'am. I find the life here well enough to my taste."

She sighed. The longing for a glimpse of her native land was never quite absent from her heart, yet though there was a faint wonder in her mind that this wealthy and foot-loose young man should of his own choice remain here, she was determined to do the same. Yearn as she might for England, her roots had gone deep into the soil of New South Wales, and at least one of the problems which beset her husband was already resolved for her. It was not merely the estates to which she would cling; nor the merino flock, valuable as it was; nor even the house, surrounded by the garden she had made, and filled with familiar objects whose gradual acquisition formed a kind of history of her colonial life. She had a woman's respect for concrete achievement, a woman's instinct to hold fast to what the years had built. One did not create only to abandon.

Patrick took his leave, and rode on to Sydney. Arrived there, he went first to the office of the Postmaster, where he found a letter from Miles awaiting him, and then called briefly at Government House to offer his condolences upon the bereavement suffered by His Excellency in the death of his mother, news of which had recently reached the colony. He rode up George Street to the Market Place, where he paused for a few moments to watch an unhappy miscreant who had spent the last hour in the pillory being taken down and hustled back to gaol. The sight depressed him, but the welcome of Shawn Morgan as he ran out to take the horse, the deferential greetings of the worthy Mrs. Bodley, the cool, ordered ease of the drawing-room, where Flora hastened to set refreshments before him, and the leisurely perusal of Miles' letter restored his spirits. Cousin Bertha having been prepared to receive him, he presently ascended the stairs to pass a dutiful hour at her bedside, before setting out once more to walk to the Harvey's cottage.

"I have a letter from Miles," he said when Emily had cleared the dishes from the dinner table, and he was seated with Mark and Conor in the little parlour. "You would like to read it, perhaps?"

"Yes, indeed!" cried Conor, settling down with her needlework. The roses and pheasants had been set aside, Patrick noticed; it was some garment of Desmond's which now occupied fingers betraying signs of menial work. She was far advanced in pregnancy, and something—the departure of Julia, no doubt, and anxiety about Cousin Bertha—had shadowed her face with sadness, and painted a darkness under her eyes. Her husband said:

"Pray read it aloud to us, Patrick. If Miles' penmanship is still as I remember it, you would be doing us a kindness."

"It's much the same," Patrick replied, pulling the letter from his pocket, "so you'll bear with me if I stumble. It's dated April 10th, from London.

" '*Dear Patrick,*

I have been in Ireland since you last heard from me, and found our Grandmother well enough, though, like so many persons of her age, full of Complaints about the younger Generation, of which, according to her, I am a striking Example. However, by putting on my most agree-able manner and paying her every Attention, I was able to win from her before I left some degree of grudging Approbation, and—what pleased me more—some pecuniary Assistance of which I stood much in need. Though we indulged in some passages of Recrimination, I found the old lady preferable to our Aunts, who never ceased to commiserate me for the Misfortune of having been born in Botany Bay (as they persist in calling it), and towards whom in consequence I appeared in my most Ungentlemanlike guise, in order that they might have the pleasure of feeling their worst Fears confirmed. The whole Family clamours for your return, and, fearing your Obduracy, endeavours to prevail upon me to stay; for I truly beleive. . . .' You recall, Sir, that Miles could never spell 'believe', and he has not yet learned to, '. . . that they imagine the Heavens will fall if no Male Mannion remains at the Irish Beltrasna. I assure you, my dear Patrick, that I cast the responsibility back upon you with enthusiasm, and fervently embrace my Inferior position as the younger son.' "*

"How like Miles that is!" laughed Conor, and Patrick, sorting the thick, crackling pages, looked up to say with a shrug:

"He would have made a more satisfactory elder son than I, never-theless; he is at least preparing to perpetuate the family line."

"*What?*" Conor dropped her needlework on her lap and stared at him in amazement. "Miles? Why, he's a mere child . . . !"

"No, no," Mark objected. "He must be—let me see. . . ."

"Twenty-two next birthday," supplied Patrick. "Well, hear what he says:

'*I am in fact contemplating an early return, and perhaps if my wishes are realised, as a married Man. I have made the acquaintance of a young lady called Laetitia ffoulkes, of good Family and some Fortune, who, I think, would make an agreeable Wife if I am able to persuade her—and her parents—of the eligibility of a Colonial. I am at present addressing myself to this delicate Task, and am sanguine enough to think that I make some progress, despite an Inauspicious beginning.*

128

The occasion of my first meeting with my Angel was at a Dinner during which the conversation turned to the Colony, when my Host desired to know: Whether I were not happy to have left it for ever? Upon my replying that I was, on the contrary, eagerly anticipating my return, there arose a great clamour of exclamations, and it was protested on all sides that surely no person of education and sensibility could endure to live in a society composed of degraded and immoral Wretches. To which I made reply that degradation was indeed to be found there, having been introduced at some pains and Expence from England; and as for immorality I had yet to learn that it was unknown among the highest and most Illustrious circles of the Mother Country. . . .'"

"Mercy!" exclaimed Conor, "how rash the boy is!" She looked doubtfully at her husband, who was shaking with silent laughter. "And yet there is some truth . . . pray go on, Patrick."

" 'This remark caused a rather cold Silence to fall, into which Mr. ffoulkes interjected the observation that the immoral Wretches referred to were Felons, and appeared (as did the rest of the Company) to consider that no more remained to be said. And there you would perhaps feel that Prudence should have persuaded me to leave the matter. . . .'"

Conor shook her head. "Prudence is not a quality which has ever been marked in Miles, I fear." Mark said emphatically:

"I recall, Heaven forgive me, that I once endeavoured to instil it into him, and I begin to be happy that I failed. Come, Patrick, let us hear the rest of his indiscretions."

"They are on a fine scale. *'I did not feel disposed to do so, however, and quoted Mr. Wilberforce's words upon the subject, in which he declared that corruption and profligacy take their rise among the rich, and spread their destructive poison through the whole body of the people. This, also, was not well received, particularly by Mr. ffoulkes, whose face assumed an alarming Hue (he being a corpulent and full-blooded Man) and by another Gentleman who was seated next to the lovely Laetitia and had been paying her more attention than it pleased me to see. This Person now declared in a haughty Manner: That if a proper respect for the upper classes were not insisted upon, all Society would be brought down in Ruin; adding that this was, perhaps, what Mr. Mannion desired? To this I made reply that Society was apparently on the path to Ruin without any Assistance from me, the main*

Cause of its tottering State being that Hypocrisy among the upper classes which held excusable in themselves what it condemned in the lower Orders. My Host then enquired: Whether Mr. Mannion disapproves the humane and Moral motives which led to the establishment of his native Colony? Does he not commend the efforts being made there to instil habits of industry and virtue into criminals? I answered without heat (and observing with Satisfaction that Miss ffoulkes' lovely orbs were now fixed upon me with flattering attention): That it was a common failing among human beings to discover the noblest of Motives for actions which, in fact, were performed but to serve their own Interest; and I judged that the establishment of New South Wales had been resolved upon less from motives of moral reformation than to rid the country of those whose presence was becoming an embarrassment— nay, a danger—to polite Society. Whereupon Mr. ffoulkes declared in a Passion: You are no better than an Anarchist, Sir!

" 'You will allow that this was not a propitious introduction to Miss ffoulkes' Papa, and I am therefore the more pleased to be able to inform you that I have nevertheless advanced my Suit with some success by paying Court to her Mama. In her presence I take particular pains with my Dress, and assume my most polished Manner, by which means I have prevailed upon her to believe that my indiscreet utterances are no more than the ebullitions of Youth. She has also, I learn, made herself acquainted with my worldly Prospects, and, finding these to her Satisfaction, she smiles upon me, as does my Angel herself, and I dare to hope that Mr. ffoulkes' consent will in due course be secured. But no more of this for the present.

" 'As I told you in my last letter, the arrival of Governor Bligh caused some little Stir here when it was first known, but most people seem to have lost Interest in the Business; though the Proceedings are said to be imminent, they cause no great curiosity in any save those directly concerned, and some, like myself, who have connections with the Colony. Bligh goes about like a Lion seeking whom he may devour, and urging the prosecution of everyone associated with Macarthur's Party, and is strongly supported by Sir Joseph Banks. Johnston and Macarthur are in London, and rumour says they are less confident than they would wish to appear. Poor Mrs. King, whom I have seen once or twice, is, I imagine, too greatly absorbed in her own Misfortunes to think much about the Uproar. I understand that King left her in considerably straitened Circumstances.

" 'You ask me, as an elder Brother should, of my aims in Life. My dear Fellow, they are the simplest in the World. I propose to spend my time in satisfying my curiosity about men and places, and in sampling with due appreciation, the many agreeable things which Providence has provided. The Navy and the Army are, I assure you, out of the question: I possess no talent for accepting Orders. The Law I regard as a device for employing some thousands of words to say Yes, in order that they may be subsequently proved to mean No. Neither reverence nor Modesty permit me to say more than that I feel myself unsuited to the Church. To take up land is something I shall consider, but merely to provide a home for the wife I hope to acquire, the numerous family with which I hope to be blessed, and as a Refuge for the old age which will doubtless overtake me in a future as yet too remote to be contemplated over seriously. For the present London pleases me, but my thoughts turn often to the Colony, and (if Miss ffoulkes and her Papa prove amenable) you may expect to see me there within a year or so. However, it is in my mind that Sydney forms but a very small part of my Native land, and I do not propose to remain stationary in that neighbourhood, I assure you. I still intend to pursue my old project of crossing the Mountains, though the same notion appears to have taken possession of other minds; I am told that Lieut. Lawson has spoken of it with several people here, Mr. John Blaxland declares that his brother also considers it, and of course William Wentworth's resolve is as old as my own. But such an expedition would by no means exhaust the possibilities; I have been studying the available maps and charts, and propose to see much of the Country before I die. Flinders, as no doubt you know, arrived here in November of last Year after more than six years imprisonment at Isle de France, and is said to be busy preparing his Charts for publication, which should afford much enlightenment. Wealth, I confess, attracts me, but I beleive it to be attainable in the Colony—by one with some Capital to invest—without the necessity for tedious application to one fixed Pursuit. . . .' "

"Tedious application," interjected Mark, "was something that never did appeal to Miles. "Yet he could apply himself well enough to pursuits he did not find tedious, and there should be sufficient of those to keep him occupied. But continue, Patrick."

"There's not much more. 'Pray send me all your news. I trust Mr. Harvey is well, and finding his present Pupils more diligent than at least one of those he taught at Beltrasna. Convey my affectionate Greetings to our Stepmother, inform her that I view with the liveliest Sympathy her refusal to accept Sanctuary under the Grandparental Roof, and beleive me, my dear Patrick,

Your affec't Brother,
Miles Mannion.' "

"Never," said Mark reminiscently, "was there a less diligent pupil than Miles. Yet he has what no one can teach—and I, perhaps, less than most—a great capacity for enjoyment, a great confidence, a great zest for the mere business of being alive. I shall be glad to see him again."

"Dear Miles!" sighed Conor. "How I hope this Miss ffoulkes is a young woman of good sense—and patience. . . ."

      *   *   *   *

It was just dawn of a mid-December day when Mark stood at the gate of his cottage and watched Dr. Redfern out of sight along Elizabeth Street. Late last night Cousin Bertha had died—and this morning, but an hour ago, his son had been born. There would be much to do when the day began, but this was a poised moment in which, released from anxiety and the demands of daily tasks, he could be still, admitting his fatigue, and tasting his joy.

The eastern sky towards the Heads was reddening; the early morning fog which lay over the harbour and dimmed the town with its soft, shifting vapour, was already warmed by it, and would soon be dispersed. In the one night both death and birth had come close to him, and the scene —at once sad and luminous—matched his mood. He remained for a moment watching it, and then turned back to the house.

      *   *   *   *

Billalong, with his half-brothers, Gooradoo and Balgundra, paid a visit to Johnny Prentice when the year was dying in a fierce blaze of heat. They climbed the steep hill from the river, and came, about sundown, to a spot overlooking the clearing, only to halt abruptly, held by the solemn and familiar sound of a woman wailing for her dead.

They could see the hut below them, standing in a long shaft of evening sunlight which made it look peaceful and serene. Yet Billalong and the two lads—hungry as they were, and eagerly as they had been anticipating a substantial meal—stood motionless, looking at it with uneasiness as they listened to the distant sound of lamentation, and feeling that awe, that awakening of excited anger with which their people always confronted the mystery of death.

The wailing came not from there, but from the slope rising out of the valley floor to meet the base of sheer cliffs. It was in the minds of all three natives that this was a terrible way for Dyonn-ee to die—alone, tribeless, with only a woman to mourn him; thus their relief was profound when they saw Dyonn-ee himself, alive and well, coming up from the stream below the hut with a pail in his hand. Billalong's held breath released itself in a little grunt; clearly it must be only Kooree whose spirit had departed for the eternal dream time. But still they did not move. It was well known that death was caused by an evil magic, and the place where it struck forever accursed; no person with a due respect for the malignant powers of spirits would approach too near to such a spot. Therefore Billalong cupped his hands about his mouth, and sent the native summoning call echoing across the valley, and Johnny, hearing it, looked up to see them standing among the low ferns and undergrowth of the hillside. He carried his pail to the hut and set it down beside the door. He looked up again, his eye finding his visitors only with difficulty in the failing light, so still did they stand. He beckoned, but they did not move. He shrugged, and began to walk slowly towards them.

The degree of mourning for one dead was naturally determined by his value to the tribe. A man of great wisdom—an accomplished hunter —a courageous warrior—a celebrated maker of songs and corroborees— a noted medicine-man—these were the men for whom a tribe must pour out the full passion of his grief; for a woman, less; and little indeed for a child. Yet for any death there must be sorrow and the shedding of tears by those individuals who, through relationship or close ties of friend-ship, felt themselves bereaved; though Billalong and his companions re-joiced that their first fears were unfounded, and that the spirit of a man had not departed without suitable ceremonies, their faces expressed a kindly melancholy, and they exchanged a few gravely sympathetic com-ments as they watched Johnny approaching.

"The spirit of the little one has left you?" Billalong remarked as he came up to them, and Johnny replied briefly in the same native tongue:

"Three suns ago. A sickness came upon him."

They did not pursue the matter further. Kooree, though a fine little *birahlee* whom they would all have gladly seen playing in his accustomed haunts again, was of real importance only to his mother, whose long, sad wailing still sounded thinly through the gathering dusk. Soon, no doubt, his spirit would be re-born. They looked expectantly at Johnny, for they had remembered their hunger again; but he seated himself on a charred log, his head bent, his face sombre, and he said only:

"Ngili will not return to my hut. She has not come near it since the child died."

Billalong frowned slightly, and glanced at the others. They all found it hard, sometimes, to remember that Dyonn-ee was—different. Of course Ngili would not return—and if it were not for this difference in Dyonn-ee, he too would leave the place of death for ever. Had he been a true black man it would have been a simple thing to destroy a bark shelter, gather up the few family belongings, and depart. But the dwell-ings of white men were not so easily left, and they knew, uncomfortably, that he would never abandon his stout log hut, his heavily-built table and benches, the yards for his beasts, the laboriously-cultivated plots of earth. . . . To the white man, his material possessions were of more importance than the spiritual possession of a Law which must be observed. . . . They were awkwardly silent, and Johnny, who understood native custom as well as they did, looked up and read the lack of an answer in their troubled eyes. Not only to Ngili, but to them also, the hut was now forbidden ground.

Yet presently he drew Billalong aside. He knew that it would be as useless to argue with Gooradoo or Balgundra as with Ngili herself; they were wholly native. But Billalong—his own half-brother, with the blood of Andrew Prentice in his veins . . . ? Billalong, who years ago had already once defied the tabu when he continued to live at the other hut with Johnny after his mother's death . . . ? Might he not be persuaded to remain? For Johnny was afraid of the solitude he could see closing about him. He tried to tell himself that he feared it because he needed help; one pair of hands could not adequately tend his beasts and cultivate his land. But the truth was that he had lost the taste for solitude; first Finn, his friend, then Ngili, his woman, and lastly his little son, Kooree, had forced a way into the stubborn self-sufficiency of his life. He was now capable of loneliness.

But Billalong was not to be persuaded. This was not his *towri;* indeed, it should not now be the *towri* of any man. Johnny became angry.

"Listen, y' fool!" he stormed, reverting to English in his agitation. "The boy was sick—anyone can get sick! Devils! Spirits! Magic! Would y' heed such stuff? Did they ever harm ye when ye stopped with me before? Where are they? Can ye see them? I tell ye there's no sech thing as spirits . . . !

Billalong kept his eyes on the ground, and shuffled his feet. Some part of him was shocked by this mad, foolhardy talk, though his emotion was less fear than the embarrassment of being compelled to listen to remarks in execrable taste; in the same mood many highly civilised people might have studied the floor while some firebrand blasphemed the sacred usages of their society. It was true that his long association with Johnny, and later with Finn, had disturbed if not destroyed his faith in many tribal beliefs and customs. On the other hand, his life was with the tribe, and he enjoyed it. Moreover, he now had a pleasing young wife of his own whom he was not anxious to leave, and who would never, of course, forsake her people to live in this distant, death-haunted place. No; he would perhaps disregard the tabu to the extent of coming from time to time to visit Dyonn-ee, but he would not cut himself adrift from his tribe by permanently defying it. Gooradoo and Balgundra would also continue their visits if it were understood that they approached no nearer to the hut than this. Yet his heart bled for Dyonn-ee in his predicament. Tribeless, and now womanless, he was indeed in a pitiable plight—but where was a woman who could now be persuaded to share his hut with him, and brave the malignant powers which would doubtless prevent the birth-spirit from favouring her? He offered, lamely and without convic-tion, the only possible suggestion: would not Dyonn-ee return with Ngili to the tribe?

"Me?" shouted Johnny. "Leave my place for such a thing? Leave all this . . ." his arm swept round in fierce indication of his domain, ". . . because a woman's afraid of devils? Go back there and live under a bit of bark? Go back there to be hunted down like a wallaby by the soldiers? What d'ye think I came here for? What d'ye think we was workin' for—me and Finn . . . ?"

Billalong's eyes darted in consternation towards the others; Johnny had crowned his indiscretions by uttering the name of a dead man—and his voice had been loud. Now, more than ever, he, Billalong, must demonstrate his allegiance to his people's laws by withdrawing from one who violated them so recklessly. He turned away, and Johnny watched him go.

Next morning he watched again from the hilltop behind his hut while the three young men scrambled down towards the river with Ngili. They knew he was there, and once Ngili turned to look at him, but he made no move or gesture. When he could see them no longer he turned to face his possessions. For what, now, did he hold them? For whom would he work? "Myself"—once big enough to fill the world—seemed strangely small.

1812

It was so long since Mrs. Harvey had appeared at any of the elegant assemblies which now occurred with great frequency in Sydney, that she stood before her mirror one afternoon in February and studied her reflection rather doubtfully. Her gown of grey taffetas, its bodice cut low and square over her bosom, and its skirts descending to her feet, was, she feared, no longer in the very latest fashion, but she was consoled to find that it still fitted her to perfection. Mark, whose coat had been new seven years ago, but whose shirt frills—thanks to Emily's care—could pass muster with the best, was awaiting her at the gate where the carriage was standing, and Conor whispered, as she took his hand and lifted her skirts to enter it:

"We're eclipsed by Shawn, I fear—he has a new livery!"

It was a large and highly respectable gathering which sat down at five o'clock to the table of the Lieutenant-Governor and his lady. With her re-marriage Mrs. O'Connell had set all troubles behind her; the news that Colonel Johnston had been cashiered for his part in the rebellion, thus bringing about the discomfiture of Mr. Macarthur and the vindication of her dear Papa, had delighted her, and increased the little air of triumph she had worn since assuming her position as the second lady of the colony. This dinner-party, to celebrate the christening that morning of her six-weeks-old son, found her glowing with the pride of motherhood, pleasantly stimulated by her return to society after a period of enforced retirement, and happily conscious that her mature, fair, soldierly husband made an excellent foil for her own dark and youthful beauty.

The Governor, in his genial manner, related many amusing anecdotes of his recent tour in Van Diemen's Land, and the conversation proceeded —as it always did at any table where His Excellency sat down—with animation and much laughter. Nevertheless, his gaze sometimes paused reflectively on his host and hostess, and his thoughts strayed from the chatter about him.

His study of the colony's brief history had revealed that Lieutenant-Governors, far from being the faithful right hands of their vice-regal superiors, had been, to put it bluntly, a confounded nuisance. Since O'Connell's marriage he had felt with increasing uneasiness that this tradition might be maintained, for Bligh's daughter possessed much of her father's implacability. As for O'Connell himself, it was the Scottish

Governor's opinion that if, under his wife's influence, he were becoming less able, or less willing to assist in promoting harmony and concord, it merely indicated a lightness and instability of temperament which might have been expected of an Irishman educated in France. All the same, it was disturbing, and Macquarie had already taken such steps as he could to ensure that when the time came for the regiment and its Commanding Officer to be transferred, the new Lieutenant-Governor would be one from whom the Governor would receive absolute support and co-operation. His own brother, Charles, had notions of coming to the colony as a settler; agreeable as that would be, how much more agreeable to see him established as Lieutenant-Governor, either here or at Hobart Town! True, there seemed no likelihood at present of O'Connell's removal; but a successor to Collins had as yet to be appointed to Van Diemen's Land. . . . As he talked and smiled, therefore, His Excellency was recalling the private letter he had already written to Lord Liverpool upon this subject, and dreaming pleasantly of the halcyon calm which would descend when Governor Macquarie was assisted by Lieutenant-Governor Macquarie. What an inestimable boon to the colony such a fraternal combination would prove . . . !

The light had faded and the candles had been lit before the ladies rose. In the drawing-room Mrs. O'Connell, having discharged her duties as hostess, and seen that Mrs. Macquarie sat enthroned in the best chair, sank with a rustle on to the sofa beside Conor, and unfurled her fan.

"Mercy, how hot it is! Or am I merely overcome by the exertions of the day? Dear Mrs. Harvey, I must take this opportunity to offer my condolences upon the sad death of Mrs. Herbert. You must miss her sorely."

"I do indeed, ma'am."

"The house is unoccupied, I believe? Perhaps Mr. Mannion will offer it for sale?"

"I think he has no intention of doing so. He says it is convenient for him to have a residence in Sydney—and I believe it is also in his mind that his brother may return from England shortly, and wish to live in it."

"Indeed? I'm not acquainted with Mr. Miles Mannion, but I assure you the society of Sydney would rejoice to see Mr. Mannion married and living in it himself. He's far too eligible and handsome to cling so obstinately to the single state."

"I daresay he will forsake it someday."

"A man is not truly human until he is married, my dear—and a father. It's remarkable the change I have observed in O'Connell these last weeks—and you should have seen him at the church this morning!

The christening passed off very well—but my love . . ." the fan flew up to guard her whisper, ". . . did you notice the Governor's face at dinner when our dear babe's health was drunk? I declare, I felt near to tears! Only yesterday I told O'Connell I was almost ashamed to ask him to stand Godfather, for he so greatly desires a child of his own. And poor Mrs. Macquarie. . . ."

"I know," murmured Conor. "I understand there have been several. . . ."

"Four!" whispered her hostess. "Is it not sad? Yet see her now—so smiling and animated! She conceals her feelings better than he does, poor man! But pray tell me of your own new babe? It is a boy, I believe?"

"Yes—we have called him Robert. And your own child, ma'am— what a fine boy he is! I trust your health . . . ?"

The fan flew up again. Dr. Redfern, entering with the other gentle-men, touched Mark's arm and indicated the two ladies in their secluded corner.

"There, Sir, is a conversation in progress such as no man is ever permitted to overhear. Nevertheless," he added with an indulgent smile, "I wager I could give you the substance of it."

*   *   *   *

Though Patrick rarely sought company, he had been finding of late that company more frequently sought him. With the development of Windsor, Richmond and the other hamlets of the Hawkesbury, with the appearance of new farms scattered along the banks of the river, and those of its tributary, South Creek; with the establishment of Mr. Macarthur's and Mr. Davidson's properties in the Cow Pastures area, and with the general improvement of the roads, a neighbourhood once remote and in-accessible was becoming more frequented. An excursion to the river was no longer a major adventure, and those gentlemen who found themselves in that part of it which was overlooked by Beltrasna, were apt to ride up the hill, pay their respects to Mr. Mannion, and accept the refresh-ment and hospitality of his house.

One such visitor, early in the year 1812, was Mr. Gregory Blaxland, whose cattle grazed over a large tract of land between South Creek and the river, and who, with his elder brother, had applied himself for some years to the selling of beef and milk. It was no secret that the relation-ship of the Blaxland brothers with the two Governors preceding Macquarie had not been cordial. Mr. John Blaxland was, however, absent in Eng-land, and a truce prevailed at present between His Excellency and the younger brother. All the same, as he sat on the verandah of Beltrasna, rather hot and dusty after his ride, his conversation with Patrick turned mainly upon the mismanagement of the colony in general, and the persecution of the Blaxland brothers in particular.

. "We had high hopes of this country," he declared, "and we did not come to it empty-handed, as so many have done. We were astonished to find that settlers of substance and respectability were so poorly received —even when they were armed with the highest recommendations from home. What was given, was given grudgingly, with an ill grace; and much that we had a right to expect was withheld. I have still some hopes that Colonel Macquarie may prove more liberal and enterprising in his policy—though his tenderness towards convicts and emancipists is as marked as was Bligh's partiality for the small settlers. Free men of our kind, Sir, having respectable connections and monetary resources, seem to be the least regarded." He leaned forward to flick a black and yellow caterpillar from the edge of the verandah with his whip. "These creatures even invade your house, Mr. Mannion!"

"They have been very troublesome this year. Toole thinks we should delay our sowing till the plague is past."

"I'm told many farmers are doing so. This morning as I rode here I saw fields eaten bare as your hand."

"I turned a flock of turkeys into my barley field with good effect— this morning there were few of the insects left. However, when they come in such numbers over what is, after all, but a limited area, they must be expected to cause serious damage."

Mr. Blaxland nodded. "A limited area—there you've touched the heart of our problem, Sir—and not only with regard to insect plagues. It has been much in my mind that there's too little scope for us here, penned as we are between the sea and the river—to say nothing of being harassed by all the petty restrictions that emanate from Government House. . . ." He broke off, and then added abruptly, gesturing with his whip at the climbing hills beyond the river: "There, on the other side of the mountains, may be the answer."

"They'll be passed some day, no doubt. But all those who have so far attempted it agree that the country is so rugged as to make the crossing an arduous business—and, what's more, to give but little hope that it would be worth the effort."

Blaxland rubbed his hand reflectively over the side whiskers which adorned his plump cheeks.

"It may be that no proper plan has been pursued. I've given the matter considerable thought, for it's become plain to me that the land I now occupy will not much longer serve my needs. As you know, Mr. Mannion, I kept my stock at first in the more closely settled part of the colony, but when I found they did not thrive there as I had hoped, I removed them to my present area around South Creek, where they had what appeared to be almost unlimited pasturage. Yet the grass here too dies away when hard fed, and the land becomes ever less productive, and settlement closes in and circumscribes the area. . . ."

"But even if there were good pasturage across the mountains," Patrick objected, "wouldn't it be an almost impossible task to move your beasts through such country? Wild, precipitous country, too barren to support them?"

"I'm not persuaded of that," Blaxland interjected quickly. "Oh, yes, I've talked with Caley and others who have attempted it. 'Impossible,' they say. But I've made some experiments myself, Sir, and my view is that the proper method has never been employed." He tapped his open hand with an outstretched finger to emphasise his points. "What has been done? Some party has set out—following a river-bed, as Grose did, only to be halted by unscaleable cliffs; or it has plunged into the hills and attempted to follow a straight course—leading down into ravines from which it's almost impossible to find a way out. This is to wear oneself out for very little result. Some time ago, as you may have heard, I made an expedition to the ridge running behind the Cow Pastures, following the plan of keeping always at the head of the different runs of water which emptied themselves down the slopes—and by this means I was able to proceed at a good pace, and with very little difficulty. It was of no importance save as a demonstration, for my course was turned by the lie of the land ever more south by east—towards the sea again— but it has confirmed me in my belief that this is the method which should be adopted."

"You think it would prove equally successful in a Westerly direction?"

"Why not? When I accompanied the Governor a year or so ago on an excursion which took us some distance up the Warragombie in boats, we were soon stopped by rocks and boulders; but it seemed plain to me that if one were to climb the heights north of that stream, keeping the heads of those that feed it on the left, and those that feed the Grose on the right, one must inevitably be carried into the interior of the country. And, Sir, without that fatigue, and that useless waste of time which attend incessant plunges down into ravines from which one must climb out again."

"You think of making the attempt?"

"I have considered it seriously. If I can get some support and countenance from the Governor—and some assurance of a suitable reward for my exertions. . . ." He glanced sideways at his host. "You would not care to join my party, Mr. Mannion, when the time comes . . . ?"

Patrick shook his head.

"You approach the wrong Mannion, Mr. Blaxland. It's my brother, Miles, who has always, from childhood, cherished a resolve to cross the mountains. For myself, I have no particular taste for exploration, and never had."

But as he spoke the last two words he knew that they were not the truth, and suffered one of those painful, vivid moments which reveal a man's hidden mind to himself. For once, as a lad, he had found great pleasure and interest in exploring; on many a day, with a pocketful of bread and meat begged from Ellen, he had saddled his pony and ridden off alone up or down the river, through country then virtually unknown to white men. And on one such occasion, he had come upon Johnny Prentice. . . .

Mr. Blaxland was saying:

"When does your brother return from England?"

"I don't know." Patrick, looking down at his hands, twisted his father's signet ring on his finger. "In a year or thereabouts, I expect. I have no certain news of it as yet."

"For such an expedition I should wish for companions fired with my own enthusiasm. Young, too, for it would be no journey for men past middle age. . . ."

"You should see William Wentworth," Patrick suggested idly. "It was he who joined with Miles many years ago in forming a resolve to cross the mountains when they were grown up. . . ."

"Young William, eh?" said Mr. Blaxland thoughtfully. "Well, I shall continue to turn the matter over in my mind." He rose. "I must be upon my way, Mr. Mannion, pleasant as it is here. My thanks, Sir, for your hospitality."

When he had gone Patrick returned to his chair and sat watching the sun sink down towards the hilltops across the river. He knew now what his mind had never before admitted to him—that it was the fear of meeting Johnny which had killed his taste for exploration, and the knowledge was so painful that he immediately attempted to deny it. Absurd! After that one meeting had he not returned often to the same place, no longer exploring, but seeking? Calling and searching for the lad who had once been his playmate, and even, in some unhappy and precarious way, his friend . . . ? That, replied his new knowledge of himself, was when you were still a lad yourself; before you went away for years to England, and grew out of childhood in another kind of life, and returned at last, a man, knowing the gulf that yawned between yourself and those like Johnny Prentice to be too wide and deep for any call to span. So that you forgot—because you wished to forget it—that you had once had a friend on the other side. . . . Until one night there was a shot fired here on this verandah, and your father fell dead, and you saw the shadows move out there in the dark as someone slipped away. . . .

He sat motionless in his chair facing a further truth—that Johnny had become identified in his emotions with all the tragedy, the cruelty and the suffering of life. No taste for exploring! Was the habit of retirement which had grown upon him merely an extension of the fear of meeting Johnny? And this fear nothing but the fear of confronting life in all its ruthlessness and desolation? How deep and dark the caverns of the mind! He saw now that his relationship with Johnny was but an echo of his relationship with life—the tale of a desire to be united, and of struggling, tentative advances always brought to nothing by the failure of self-confidence. Life—and Johnny—had always been too fierce and intractable for him; but no matter how he retreated, they pursued.

Mrs. Emmett, peeping from a window, said to Hattie:

"It's a wife he wants. Sitting around thinking and writing poetry—it's unnatural, that's what it is!"

And, almost as if he had heard, Patrick rose abruptly and entered his study by the long windows from the verandah. "See?" remarked the housekeeper with gloomy triumph, "he'll be there till supper time now, you mark my words!"

But Patrick was not engaged upon his poem; he was writing a note to the Governor.

"*Sir,*

Having a desire to make myself better acquainted with the country immediately west of the Nepean, and being aware of your Excellency's order that no Person save the families of Messrs. Macarthur and Davidson may cross the river without a written pass, I have to request that I may be furnished with such a pass for myself and one attendant. I am at all times desirous of observing those Regulations which your Excellency may deem it proper to impose, and trust that my Conduct during my long residence in this Colony may be such as will persuade your Excellency of the propriety of granting this Indulgence.

I am, Sir,
Your obed't Servant,
Patrick Mannion."

*   *   *   *

Devoted as Emily was to her master and mistress, she found her situation in their house a little lacking in excitement, and the summons of the Market bell on Saturday mornings was one which she always heard with delight, and obeyed with alacrity. The new Market Place which the

Governor had established on the spot not long since occupied by Mr. Blaxland's stockyards, could be relied upon to present a scene of noise, movement, colour and confusion which she found entrancing. Within its high walls the cries of vendors, the babel of voices raised in greeting, protest, argument and badinage, mingled with the lowing of cows, the bleating of sheep and goats, the grunting of pigs, and the agitated squawking of poultry; the stalls were piled high with pumpkins, melons, peaches, figs, oranges, apricots, and a profusion of such other fruits and vegetables as the season might offer; late-coming carts trundled through the crowd to lodge their wheat, oats, barley, hops and potatoes at the Market Store; there were baskets of eggs, casks of butter, sides of bacon, and great slabs of red meat, around which the hungry flies buzzed.

The Governor had done his utmost to ensure decorum and seemly behaviour by commanding that the Clerk of the Market and his assistant should be sworn in as constables, with authority to impose order, regularity, peace and quietness. But the citizens of Sydney had other views. If there were order and regularity they could be found only in the neat lines of the new buildings ranged with precision round the inside of the hollow square. The peace was frequently shattered by brawls, and Emily was always an eager spectator where the altercation was hottest, contributing a word or a taunt herself when it threatened to cool, and delighted beyond measure when words gave way to fisticuffs. Quietness was not even attempted; from the moment when the bell rang and the gates opened, until the moment when it rang again to end the day's transactions, Bedlam reigned triumphant in the Market Square.

Into this stimulating pandemonium Emily stepped briskly on a bright Saturday morning in April. It was not to be expected that so comely a girl could walk unnoticed and unaccosted, and indeed she would have felt greatly disappointed if she had not been compelled to ward off advances, meet too bold a stare with a tilt of her nose, or snap out a sharp answer to some ribald jest. Not only men of the humble sort approached her. Soldiers, elbowing their way cavalierly through the crowd, would turn to ogle and follow; several times respectable gentlemen—and not all of them young—had sidled up to seek an assignation with the bright-faced, quick-stepping girl who always had a smile on her mouth, and an invitation in her eyes.

While enjoying their attentions, Emily felt a profound contempt for all these men. The invitation was for life itself—life which had become suddenly and intoxicatingly her own after years when it had been but a passing show beneath the Orphanage windows—and some vague comprehension of this made her disdainful of the male vanity which could see it as an invitation to any one man. "Ah, be off with you!" she would cry, waving an importunate optimist aside. "Leave me be, you old wretch!" "Put y' hands back where they belong, sojer!" "Mercy on us, what would I want with the likes o you?" And she would pass from stall to stall, examining the wares with a narrowness which was not all by-play (for she was astute, and would not allow her mistress to be cheated) and haggling long so that the delights of Market Day could be protracted.

Throughout the week while she scrubbed, cooked, sewed, and tended Master Desmond and Master Robert, she lived on memories of the past Saturday, and anticipations of the one to come; for though she knew that she was fortunate beyond her dreams in being taken beneath the roof of Mr. and Mrs. Harvey, she could not deny that unrelieved industry, virtue and respectability were sometimes dull.

She was ashamed to find them so, and wondered if she were indeed as wicked as all the girls from the Orphanage were reputed to be. There were times when she desperately missed the feverish companionship of her contemporaries, and the breathless excitement of some perilous, forbidden escapade; yet she burned with guilt and gratitude when her mistress showed concern for her moral well-being, gently warning her against the perils of the streets, and the misery which lay in wait for girls who surrendered their virtue. There was a happiness in her new life which she treasured almost unbelievingly; in the schoolmaster's house she was important—she was even valued! "What should I do without you, Emily?" the mistress would exclaim. But it was not only her knowledge of housewifery which earned her praise, for the master showed his pleasure when she was diligent at her lessons. "You have a quick mind and a good understanding," he told her. "You will be quite a scholar some day." It was no easy situation that she had, for she must be up at daylight, and it was often late before she could seek her bed again. Sometimes she would become so bored that she neglected her tasks to prink at a mirror, or flirt with the butcher's boy at the kitchen door, and then the mistress would say: "Yes, child, you have a pretty face, though for your own sake I could wish it not so pretty; but the master needs his clean shirts, all the same." And sometimes in the evening, tired yet restless, she would escape into absent-minded dreaming and stumble over her lesson so that the master, patient as he was, would shake his head and say: "You're not trying, Emily; I'm disappointed in you." Yet she valued such admonitions and rebukes, for she could feel the difference between this kindly concern for her welfare and education, and the harsh, routine exhortations and punishments of the Orphanage. Heedless as she might often be, she strove to deserve their commendation. She could not help flirting now and then, but she attacked the ironing with redoubled energy afterwards; she could not always discipline her day-dreams, or resist the still novel allurements of a mirror, but she studied the more diligently, and scrubbed the harder for every lapse; she could no more subdue the ardour of her response to life than a plant could subdue its response to the sun, but she was fiercely determined to remain chaste—not because she felt any strong prejudice in favour of chastity, but because Mrs. Harvey wished it.

She paused now to watch an irate stallkeeper pursuing a small, naked native boy who was making off with a couple of stolen eggs. The chase had reached a dramatic stage, for the child, having darted between the cheering onlookers, dodged behind piles of crates, ducked beneath the legs of horses, and set every dog in the square barking furiously, was now penned in a corner, with retribution advancing upon him.

A stock pen set against the wall offered a last hope of escape; but the spoils must be sacrificed, since one cannot climb with an egg in each hand, and the absence of pockets clearly pointed the disadvantages of nakedness. A scream of delight arose from the bystanders as the pursuer fell back smearing a stream of slippery yellow fluid from his face; a roar of laughter and cheering broke out as a soldier, cursing, wiped egg-yolk from the scarlet glory of his coat; a small black form flickered up the posts as if untrammelled by the laws of gravity, stood poised for a moment on top of the wall, and dropped out of sight.

"Ah-h-h!" breathed Emily ecstatically, entranced by the spectacle of authority discomfited and lawlessness triumphant. "Oh, my, the sojer—how comical he looked!"

She spoke aloud, but to no one in particular. All round her people were contributing their comments, and conversation did not stay for introductions in the Market Place. But as she glanced about at them to share her enjoyment, she met so strange and intent a stare from the eyes of a man beside her that she was put out of countenance, and stared back, startled.

He was neither young nor handsome, but she felt a stir of interest and excitement which disconcerted her, for there was no change in his expression as their eyes met—no hint of the sly smile, the light, lewd, questioning glance which normally accompanied such encounters. He had an air which was at once indifferent and aggressive, as if, while challenging life and his fellow-men, he still despised them. His hands were thrust into the pockets of his coat, and a short, clay pipe was clamped between his lips; he wore a red handkerchief knotted round his throat, and his cloth cap well back on his head—almost as if he wanted to flaunt the long, fresh scar on his forehead, which, in a subtly macabre fashion, seemed to duplicate the line of his long, thin, unsmiling mouth. Emily found it hard to break away from his gaze; intolerable to keep on meeting it. She turned her back on him hastily, and pushed her way to a stall on the far side of the square. Here, in lively argument with the vendor, she had quite recovered her composure when she glanced up to find the man once more at her elbow, listening to the brisk bargaining which had now left her in possession of the finest lamb chops in the market at the price of the poorest.

There was something about this fellow which made her at once uneasy and resentful. Admiration she was accustomed to; appraisal was unfamiliar. She flounced past him angrily, her colour higher than ever, calling him in her mind an impudent old rogue (for he could not be a day under forty) and resolved to let him see the contempt in which she held his senile attentions. She could not, however, resist glancing back presently, and when she found him following again her temper flared, and she paused, pretending to adjust the contents of her basket, giving him time to overtake her, and preparing a suitable remark with which to blast his first attempt at a verbal approach. He asked as he came up to her:

"Are ye as good a hand with a cooking pot as ye are at a bargain, lass?"

It was not what she had expected, but she snapped out:

"What's that to you? Ye'll find I'm a good hand at a box on the ear if ye keep followin' me around!" She was turning her back on him when his next remark took her breath away:

"I'm lookin' for a wife. And by all the signs—whether ye know it or not—I'd say ye were lookin' for a husband."

She retorted furiously:

"If I am I must be lookin' further. Be off home to y' grandchildren!"

Unmoved, unsmiling, and speaking past the pipe still held between his teeth, he replied: "I ain't got grandchildren—yet."

She seized the opening.

"Then ye've surely left it too late. Now will ye take y'self off, for I've better things to do than to waste me time talkin' to an old goat with grey in his beard."

He fingered the stubble on his chin, still calm.

"Ye're well-favoured enough," he observed, studying her at his leisure, "but that don't trouble me—much. There's plenty such to serve when a man wants his pleasure. And if there's grey in me beard it means I've lived long enough to know what I want—and get it. Me own land with a bit of a house on it, and some beasts, and a trifle o' money put away that'll be more one day. And as for grandchildren—well . . ."

his tone still held no hint of anything save bare statement, ". . . ye could find out for y'self if I've left it too late."

She slapped his face. Immediately they became objects of absorbing and delighted interest to the passers-by; jests, witticisms, and cries of encouragement or reproof came from all around them, but for once Emily did not enjoy the commotion. The man appeared not to notice it; he stood looking at her, and for the first time his expression was altered by something like a smile, though it did not move his scar-like mouth. Emily, her palm still tingling from its contact with his rough cheek, noticed the curious implacability of his light-grey eyes, and felt frightened. She pushed her way through the crowd and fled.

Once out in the street she walked fast, her heart beating uncomfortably, tears scalding her eyes. When she looked back and saw him following again she walked faster than ever, but when she reached the gate of the Harvey's cottage he was still behind her. A last panic-stricken glance as she hurried indoors showed him passing slowly along the street, his eyes fixed upon her with that intent, disturbing, appraising stare.

"Why, what ails you, Emily?" Conor asked as the girl set her basket down on the table. "You are quite pale and breathless!"

"Nothin', ma'am," Emily declared hastily. "I been hurryin', that's all."

But she had left behind her some food for gossip. Joseph Dean was well known, if not well liked, and the episode had been observed with sly amusement. Some seven years ago he had reached the colony as a settler, but no one knew his history, for he volunteered no confidences, and in New South Wales questions were not asked. His first grant had been a small one in the Baulkham Hills district, and there, with the aid of a convict woman who had been assigned to him, he had toiled from dawn till dark, appearing in the townships only to sell his produce, and in the wine shops and brothels not at all. Later, as his farm began to prosper, he had employed a young convict labourer who, it was noticed, grew thin, haggard and wild-eyed. Rumour had it, as time went on, that the woman was frequently heard screaming, and it was understood that she had become half crazy. The convict servant was found dead one morning in the bush a mile from Dean's dwelling, with his head battered in. Natives, Dean said. Perhaps, and perhaps not. As for the woman, she had been removed to the Government Lunatic Asylum at Castle Hill, and Dean had soon afterwards sold his grant and bought another, much larger, in the vicinity of Eastern Creek. Here, so the gossips related, he drove his three convicts so mercilessly that one of them had recently attacked him with a knife, laying his forehead open, and was now paying the penalty in one of the road-gangs. Here he conducted a feud with the local natives, firing upon them if they so much as showed their faces on his property, and even, on occasion, going out armed with a musket to hunt them from the neighbourhood. These were not his only expeditions; sometimes alone, and sometimes with any other white man who could be persuaded to accompany him, he spent a day upon a different kind of hunting, for whatever his aversion to the native men, it did not extend to their womenfolk. He would end, it was freely prophesied, with a spear between his shoulders; but in the meantime the dislike he inspired was mixed with a kind of sour envy and admiration of his bulging muscles, his harsh, but striking features, his obviously increasing prosperity, and his air of relentlessly and successfully pursuing—what . . . ?"

Here the gossips became confused. Some said it was wealth, and no one was found to argue that this was not a thing sought by all men. If it were the quarry of Joseph Dean, he was surely hot upon its trail, for his new farm flourished, and it was no secret that he also acted profitably as agent for several gentlemen in the sale of stock and liquor. Yet others, more perceptive, shook their heads. More than wealth would be needed, they felt, to assuage the hunger that drove this man; when one remarked that he was the sort to make a fine flogger, a brief silence fell, and the conversation turned—as if by unspoken consent that some dark aspects of human nature were better undiscussed—to other matters.

So, as he drove in along the turnpike to Sydney on Saturday mornings, he exchanged few greetings with others on the road, nor did he pause to carouse with them at the Halfway House. At the Market those who knew him did not waylay him to discuss the price of wheat, the state of the crops, the affairs of their neighbours, or the Governor's latest edict, but passed by with a brief salutation. His pursuit of Emily, therefore, and his subsequent public rebuff, had caused some small sensation; that he should make advances to a bit of a girl, and have his face slapped for his pains, seemed to reduce him nearer to the level of ordinary men. One or two of his acquaintances were even moved to call a jesting word of commiseration, and all watched with interest the next Saturday to see whether the comedy would develop.

They were disappointed. On the following three Saturday mornings Emily appeared as usual, and though it was observed that she glanced often in Dean's direction, he seemed unaware of her. When—with her basket filled, her colour high, and her eyes fixed with determination straight ahead of her—she passed him on her way to the gates, he paid no attention. Only when the bell rang at noon to close the Market for the day did he set about his pursuit once more, being no impatient youth, but a man who could afford to take his time, and amuse himself in his own way.

And Emily, peeping from door or window during the afternoon and evening, could always see him somewhere—standing idly in the street, strolling past the gate, lounging on the rough turf of the park opposite, supporting himself on one elbow and chewing at a blade of grass. Mrs. Harvey found her increasingly neglectful of her duties; Desmond found her absent-minded when she played with him; Mr. Harvey was compelled more frequently to rebuke her for inattention at her lessons; at night she tossed restlessly in her bed, and her sleep, when it came, was no longer sound and dreamless. She felt that she was waiting for something, but could not tell whether the tense anticipation of her mood were painful or pleasurable. She only knew that soon something would happen, and thus she was not really surprised one evening when she slipped out the back door to go to her tiny room off the kitchen, and saw a dark figure standing beneath the peach trees. True, the sight of it almost stopped her heart-beats, and forced a gasp of terror from her lips; but it seemed that some part of her had always known that he would be there one night, and as if obedient to a force beyond her own control, she put her hand into the one he held out, and allowed herself to be drawn into the deeper shadows.

*   *   *   *

The Governor's levee in honour of His Majesty's birthday was an annual event from which no gentleman of the colony cared to absent himself, and Patrick Mannion duly rode in from Beltrasna, and accompanied Mr. Harvey to Government House. The levee concluded, there was still His Excellency's dinner to attend at five o'clock in the large and handsome dining-room recently completed. This year, however, the seventy-three guests who sat down were all men; Mrs. Macquarie had been ailing for the past three weeks following another miscarriage, and was not yet well enough to entertain.

Mr. Harvey found himself beside young Mr. Wentworth. As they talked he recalled his first encounter with the young man's father many years ago, and reflected that the fond, parental pride and ambition which had then made themselves so evident, might well prove justified. It was not easy to say what caused the impression. True, Mr. Wentworth had been appointed at a very early age as acting Provost Marshal—a civil post of some responsibility, but still, when all was said and done, only a minor colonial office. He displayed few of the graces and little of the polished sophistication which commonly marked men for advancement, and Mark found himself at a loss to discover the source of that self-confidence which sounded so clearly in his remarks—uttered with an impressive if slightly florid command of language, and finely edged with satire. They were speaking of the evacuation of Norfolk Island, and Mark said:

"It was your birthplace, I understand—in fact I recall your telling me so on the occasion when I first had the pleasure of making your acquaintance. You have some regrets, perhaps, to think of it as totally abandoned?"

"Perhaps." Mr. Wentworth appeared to consider, with a trace of amusement, this evidence in himself of sentimentalism. "All the same, Sir, it must be allowed that the measure is justified. And I left it at such an early age that I'm well able to feel myself a native of this country—in which I foresee plentiful opportunities for any ability I may possess."

"In what direction do you think of employing it?"

"When I look about me," replied Wentworth—and did so, with a reflective glance which took in the odd assortment of men who composed the élite of His Majesty's colonial subjects—"and consider the avenues which lie open, my difficulty is not to choose, but to reject. What would you advise, Mr. Harvey?" His pause was brief, and Mark, realising that the question was rhetorical, did not attempt to fill it. "Shall I join the ranks of the landed gentry, and retire to my estates—'retire' being understood, of course, to apply in a physical sense only, since the power and influence of the large property-owner make themselves felt at the seat of Government, be he never so invisible. Shall I brave the ocean or the wilderness in search of new country—so that others, from strict attention to their own affairs during my absence, will reap the benefit of my exertions? Shall I challenge the worthy Mr. Robinson, and snatch from his brow the laurel wreath placed there by the Muse of Poesy? (By Heaven, when I saw old Pomposity preparing to inflict his inevitable Ode upon us this morning, I was sorely tempted by the notion!) Or shall I follow my father's footsteps and tend the bodily ailments of my fellow-men? Or minister to their souls in the manner of our friend, Mr. Cowper? (Concerning Mr. Marsden's labours in this direction you'll observe that I remain silent.) Or perhaps . . ." the note of irony, Mark noticed, was momentarily subdued by an undertone of genuine reflection, ". . . I might study the ills of society itself, and attempt to remedy certain defects which appear in our methods of conducting its affairs . . . ?"

"You have ideas as to the measures which might be necessary?"

"Some thousands," confessed Mr. Wentworth imperturbably, "at present ill-digested, no doubt, and certainly ill-arranged; but affording me food for thought." He paused for a moment to address himself to his meal, and continued at last: "Yes, Sir, I might do worse than spend some time in observation of that small fragment of society in which my lot is cast, and. . . ." He let fly suddenly a direct question: "How does it strike you, Mr. Harvey?"

Mark pondered for a moment.

"Its growth has been remarkable—but I must admit that at times it has struck me as . . . alarming. . . ." He hesitated, searching for words, but Mr. Wentworth, whose tongue was never at a loss, supplied them.

"You use the word 'growth', Sir, and whether by accident or design, it's the just word, in contradistinction to the one you might have used—'development'. In the planting of a colony much more is needed than the mere introduction of human beings into a given area."

"There was a plan . . ." began Mark, but this neighbour waved a dissenting hand.

"There was an intention, Sir, which was merely to remove from the shores of the Mother Country those people who were considered redundant or undesirable. This was the motive which brought the colony into existence, and all plans and wordy schemes for its ordering, and for the moral reformation of its inhabitants, were but by-products. And what plans! The banished undesirables were to be controlled by a military force which—as might have been foreseen—proved no less undesirable than they. Thus we were set upon our way with two distinct classes—the felon and the free—of which the free consisted entirely of civil and military officers. From this circumstance *grew*—I embrace your word, Sir—those attitudes which to-day produce so marked and deplorable an effect upon our society; for in due course there began to emerge (as a moment's mature consideration would have revealed to be inevitable) a third class—the emancipists. Could it be supposed that this would fail to create conflicts? That those who had for so long enjoyed pre-eminence over men whose sentences deprived them of all civil rights and rendered them helpless tools in the hands of their masters, would *welcome* their reinstatement when those sentences had expired? Were they expected to arise and embrace their potential rivals?"

Mark smiled rather ruefully.

"When you frame the question thus, the answer must be No. But suppose you were to ask whether it would not be reasonable in them to arise and embrace fellow-citizens whose efforts could now combine with their own to create a new and prosperous country, to their mutual advantage . . . ?"

Mr. Wentworth let out a hoot of laughter.

"Your abode should be Utopia, Sir!"

"Perhaps. Yet it's surely but the course dictated by commonsense not to spend strength opposing what will be, despite all one's efforts. The emancipist class cannot for ever be kept down, since it becomes month by month more numerous."

"Oh, I agree. You have only to glance round this table to see that the Governor has shown his political wisdom, no less than his liberal mind, in recognising the necessity for restoring these people to a place in our society. However . . ." he shrugged, ". . . it's not to be expected that he could introduce so novel a change without arousing the hostility of those who have gained their present ascendancy by monopolising the colony's trade. To this junta, Sir, a felon should remain a felon, not only till the termination of his sentence, but for ever. Nay, more than that— these individuals would make felonry an hereditary defect, raising an eternal barrier between their own children and those of convicts. You protest? Yet that would be the effect of the policy they support."

"You feel, in fact, that the moral opprobrium which they cast upon the felon smells of pecuniary jealousy?"

"Precisely, Sir. And it's this, I think, which causes the alarm you confess to feeling when you contemplate the rapid growth of the colony. A rational and orderly development would excite no such sensation. But the increase of our population, the enlargement of our settlements, the extension of our mercantile activities and the accretions of capital in our midst surely can't be contemplated without misgiving when it's plain that the tares of dissension were sown along with the seeds of progress, and both *grow* together—with but little to control them in the way of effective husbandry."

"Must that not always be so?" suggested Mark. "Is not the recon-ciliation of differences a problem to be resolved by the individual's con-science and goodwill?"

Wentworth gave him a sideways glance, and replied rather dryly:

"No doubt; yet a little administrative wisdom would aid the process. I have long felt disinclined to believe that we come into this world endowed with any innate sense of morality whatever. Conscience, in my opinion, is a habit acquired, as all other habits are, from long associations. The nature of the associations prevalent in this place do little to stimulate it. You read the *Gazette*, Mr. Harvey?"

"Yes; it does not occupy me long."

"How should it? When it prints nothing but what has first passed beneath the eye of Government, it can afford but little exercise for the enquiring mind. It has its merits and its uses, no doubt, but they are negative, at best. A paper which would voice the opinions and the aspirations of the colonists themselves, and ventilate their wants and grievances, would have uses of a positive and beneficial kind."

"The same thought has occurred to me," Mark admitted, "only to be followed by doubts. If one paper is but the mouthpiece of Government, Mr. Wentworth, what is to prevent another from becoming but the mouthpiece of some strong opposing faction? Between the one and the other, the voice of the colonists might well remain inaudible."

"It's unlikely that many of the general run would possess opinions worth voicing."

"Valuable opinions, it's true, are not fostered in ignorance. But you spoke also of aspirations—of wants and grievances. . . ."

"Their expression," declared Mr. Wentworth firmly, "would be use-less unless accompanied by concrete proposals which would further the one and rectify the others. No, Mr. Harvey, it must be left to those whose education, property and attainments qualify them for the task to expound policies which would be beneficial to all. Of one thing I become more and more persuaded—that the present system of Government cannot be much longer maintained. The Governor's powers—wisely as they may chance to be exercised by any individual—are excessive, and must ulti-mately be replaced by a Legislative Assembly. This, Sir, is a privilege— nay, a right—to which we are entitled as British subjects. This land is now native soil to many of us who cannot for ever remain content with a system designed for a penal settlement. Even should we ignore this argument," he added, "it must be clear that in mere physical size it is already becoming too extensive to be governed by such means. Consider the areas already explored by sea and by land, Sir; ask yourself whether, having been discovered, they can remain unsettled; and then attempt to envisage the military establishment necessary to maintain order under such a system as we have at present."

"True," said Mark, and then, recalling a conversation with Patrick only that morning, he enquired: "And speaking of exploration, have you heard anything of a plan of Mr. Blaxland's for crossing the mountains? Mr. Mannion mentioned to me that he hopes to make an attempt."

"There has been some talk of it, I believe. But when has there not been talk of it? Indeed, Miles Mannion and I formed our own schemes as long as a dozen years ago. And I'm told that of late Mr. Mannion himself . . . ?"

He paused enquiringly Mark, glancing across the table to where Patrick sat beside the Judge Advocate, said slowly:

"No. I think Mr. Mannion's excursions are not so ambitious, Mr. Wentworth."

Patrick, meanwhile, having spent some time in conversation with Mr. Cox on his left, now turned to his other neighbour. Mr. Bent was in a poor humour, for the day's ceremonies had involved much standing, and his corpulence made this something of an ordeal to him. He held a low opinion, moreover, of Government House dinners and stared gloomily about the table noting the dishes, that he might provide his wife with a detailed and derogatory account. This meal, he allowed, was better than the one served to farewell the Patersons—when, as he had written to his mother, one might have danced a reel between the dishes—but still inferior to the feasts dear Eliza provided at his own table; nor was it disposed with that taste and elegance which he valued above all things. The absence of their hostess, he decided, was no loss, for she was deficient in those polished and graceful manners by which ladies of fashion and breeding promoted the ease and merriment of their guests. As he picked disdainfully at his boiled turkey, he was thinking it strange that the Governor could not do better than this on so great an occasion as the King's birthday. But when his neighbour turned to him with a civil question he roused himself to reply with amiability, for young Mr. Mannion was a gentleman of birth and position, and reputed extremely wealthy.

"You are finding colonial life agreeable, Mr. Bent?"

"Tolerable, Sir. There are many inconveniences not easy to put up with, and we find our circle of congenial acquaintances somewhat restricted. It's very difficult to get good servants, as no doubt you know— though perhaps in your remote situation they are not so spoiled as they are here by the distractions of the town. The convict nursemaid we have now for my little boy—by Heaven, she's the merest dawdle in Nature! And the others—well, we put up with them for fear of getting something worse. But it has added to my wife's trials, and I may say to mine, particularly during the time when I was gravely unwell, and in no condition to be troubled by such matters."

"I hope your health is now quite restored," Patrick responded politely. "The climate is generally considered very fine, and many people have found it beneficial."

"Oh, on that score I have no complaint—though I find it very necessary to avoid exposure to the sun. Certainly I'm far more robust than at the time of our arrival." He helped himself from a proffered dish of sucking-pig. "But pray tell me, Sir, what is your opinion of the country about the Nepean for grazing?"

"I am told that parts of it are good. My own pursuits are mainly agricultural, though I have a few sheep and cattle."

"I've lately got a grant in the district, you know, adjoining Birch's. He and I have bought a flock of breeding ewes and a hundred head of horned cattle. It's my belief that grazing is the most profitable pursuit in this country, Sir—no trouble or expense, boundless pastures, and every calf worth ten to fifteen pounds the moment it's dropped."

He folded his hands across his ample stomach and stared absently at the epergne in the middle of the table, reflecting that by the time he returned home in a year or two he should have amassed a tidy little fortune which would compensate for the shortcomings of colonial life. There were profitable sidelines to be pursued, as he had proved soon after his arrival when fifty-seven gallons of brandy which had cost him seventeen pounds at Rio found a ready sale in Sydney at a hundred and forty-two, and twenty pounds' worth of Cape wine returned him six times that amount. He abandoned his pleasant musings to answer another question from Patrick.

"The people? You ask how I find them? You are referring to the general run of colonists? My dear Sir, I naturally associate with them only in the line of duty, but there can surely be but one reply—they are the most immoral set I ever met with in my life! Prostitution is not even concealed—they avow it with open shamelessness as 'the custom of the country'! As for drunkenness, it's beyond anything I could have conceived! They'll buy spirits at any price—I repeat, Sir, at *any* price, for I've seen five shillings given for a glass of brandy, and nothing thought of it!"

Patrick looked at him and felt a sudden uneasiness. Of Mr. Bent's own transactions he was not aware, though the traffic in liquor was so universal, and so generally accepted as something inextricably woven into the pattern of colonial life, that they would not have caused him a moment's surprise. But he was reminded of certain receipts and invoices he had found among his father's neatly arranged papers which had shown that even Mr. Stephen Mannion of Beltrasna had not disdained to profit by it. That, too, had seemed natural at the time; he had himself continued the practice for a year or so when opportunity offered, and the fact that he did so no longer was due merely to his own distaste for trading, and his preference for a secluded life. He had even felt a trifle guilty when he realised that under his management the colonial income shown in the Beltrasna books was diminished, and heard an echo of his father's voice accusing him of incorrigible indolence and inattention to affairs.

Yet he was learning painfully that the habit of heart-searching may reveal sins quite other than those which are being sought. His sense of guilt had been, at first, only for his part in the death of Ellen Prentice; yet stumbling through the dark places of his own mind and heart, he had come upon other matters which gave him pause. Dilboong and her child confronted him, mutely accusing. Johnny Prentice was looming up ever more largely from the shadows, at once a victim and a judge. And now the chance association of Mr. Bent's diatribe against intemperance with his own memory of those carefully filed papers seemed to illumine another ugly corner hitherto comfortably obscure.

But the Judge Advocate had returned to the subject at present most interesting to him.

"Yes, from all that I can learn, grazing offers the surest and quickest road to wealth. Wheat, on the other hand, would appear to be hazardous;

should there be a flood much of it is ruined or swept away, and should there be no flood the harvest is so great that the farmer finds himself ruined by the cheapness of the grain, since there's no market for his surplus produce. Indeed that might apply to most articles, for the colony is so distant from other countries that the market seems to be always either empty or overstocked. Tea, for example—we may pay five guineas the pound for it—and then the arrival of a ship from China will reduce the price to as many shillings. But all this must be an old tale to you, Sir. And I must suppose that you find the life here has its compensations, since you remain from choice, and not, like most of us, because duty compels it."

"It suits my taste well enough."

Mr. Bent, having received a plate of tartlets from an attentive servant, fell to again with a shrug and a sigh.

"Perhaps I should be equally content in your sylvan solitudes, Mr. Mannion, for no society at all might be preferable to the associations I am compelled to endure in the course of my professional occupation. The work in my department is very arduous indeed, and I've had to make many reforms, for everything seems to have been conducted in a most slovenly and irregular way. And such duties as mine are often singularly unpleasant to any man of sensibility."

"That," agreed Patrick, "I can well understand. I have often thought that to pronounce sentence of death upon a fellow-man must . . ."

Mr. Bent paused with a mouthful of pastry poised in mid-air, and looked at his neighbour in mild surprise.

"Oh, that. . . . No, Sir, I've found myself quite able to perform that part of my duty with remarkable coolness. Quite soon after my arrival such an occasion arose, and though I'm aware that Judges in a similar situation are sometimes so overcome that they burst into tears and are compelled to turn their heads aside, devil I tear could I squeeze out! Much depends, you know, upon the circumstances and surroundings. Give me a handsome Court and a handsome salary—give me on my left a fine, smart fellow with a silk coat, a sword and a white wand, and on my right a jury-box, and below me a crowd of big-wigs, and above me an assembly of ladies, and then, Sir, I'll weep with any judge on the bench! But to sit as I'm obliged to in a bit of a hovel, with no one to remark my agitation—no High Sheriff, none of those appendages which lend dignity to a Court, and stimulate emotions of awe and solemnity in the breast—that's very different, I assure you."

"Indeed?" Patrick's tone was strained; for a moment he had glimpsed Johnny Prentice standing before this judge, and a kind of panic had seized him. For if that playmate of his childhood still lived—and there seemed little doubt of it—he would, sooner or later, find the society he had abandoned overtaking him, and he would turn upon it. He had killed already; he would not hesitate to kill again. And there would come, as surely as the sunrise, a day when he stood face to face with Mr. Bent. . . .

But Mr. Bent's thoughts had turned once more to his property, and Patrick, hardly hearing him, murmured vague assents when a pause in the flow of words seemed to demand them. His attention was recaptured by a reference which brought Dilboong to his mind, for the Judge Advocate was saying:

"It's a pity that the natives of the country are so totally uncivilised that they can't be trained in habits of industry. On such remote estates as yours and mine, Mr. Mannion, they might be extremely useful, whereas they are now nothing but a nuisance. However there's little to be ex-pected of them, for they're surely the lowest in the scale of human existence—no better than Baboons, in fact. Yet we can't plead on their behalf that they're incapable of understanding what's required of them, for most of those about the town speak English very well. . . ."

"An accomplishment," interrupted Patrick with sudden irritation, "not common among Baboons." He was a trifle startled by his own burst of asperity, and as Mr. Bent turned his large, pale, offended countenance upon him he noticed with relief that the company was rising. "Pray excuse me, Sir," he said briefly, and turned away, feeling glad that His Majesty's birthday occurred but once a year.

*　　　　*　　　　*　　　　*

Meanwhile, as the autumn faded and the first frosts whitened the grass outside his hut, Johnny had grown increasingly restless. Physical activity seemed the only antidote to the silence and the solitude which had closed about him, but he could no longer find contentment in the labours of cultivation and the development of his domain. He had no need, now, for anything but what his own subsistence demanded.

He saw no one save, occasionally, a few natives from the tribe which dwelt at the northern end of the valley, or from others further up the river. Their tongue differed from that of the coastal tribes; they were taller, rather lighter in colour, and wore their dark locks tied high in a bunch behind their heads. They had long accepted the white man with his native wife and child, and in pairs of groups, roving through the valley, they would sometimes pause on the outskirts of his strange *towri* to watch him toiling in his fields, and approach when, by a gesture, he acknowledged their presence. He had learned enough of their language to talk with them, and gave them melons, potatoes, cobs of maize, or a coolamon of fresh milk—a courtesy which they returned by bringing, from time to time, a duck or an eel from the river, or a young wallaby which they had speared. But such visits were rare—almost as rare as the visits of Billalong—and every passing day increased his loneliness.

His eyes turned to the high cliffs surrounding the valley. Only once, years ago, he had climbed them with Finn, but now he climbed them again, driven less by curiosity than by the need for occupation. At first he went only for a couple of days, carrying food and a musket with him. Then, as the long, high, winding ridges tempted his feet farther and farther, his interest was awakened. He walked mile after mile, only to come always to the head of some rocky spur overlooking a gorge hundreds of feet deep, across which the cliffs reared up again to country no different from what he had just put behind him. He retraced his steps to try another spur, and found himself similarly halted. He discovered perilous ways down the cliffs through cracks where a few shrubs and trees gave handholds, into damp, dim gullies where the only sound was the rush of streams pouring through their rocky beds. He stood in green-shadowed places where his feet sank deep into the rotting mould of centuries, and huge ferns towered above his head. He climbed out to find himself on another spur which led him to another cliff, another chasm, another halt; there seemed no end to these meandering ridges, no limit to the number of vast gorges and small, secret gullies they enclosed.

Once, despite the expert training he had received in childhood from his native friends, he was lost for a full day and night. He was shocked and startled, but the incident only strengthened his desire to learn an area which could, incredibly, make him feel so helpless. It was not only bewildering, but exhausting country, and, in his determination to master it, he began to abandon his white man habits, and revert to the techniques of natives on the march. He dared not set out wholly unprovided with food, for he soon saw that there was little worth hunting on this high tableland; but such as it was, it sufficed to keep him from hunger when supplemented meagerly by food he carried with him, so he diminished his provisions, left his musket behind, took his firesticks and a spear, and travelled more easily.

Billalong, coming to visit him, still could not be persuaded to approach the hut, but he agreed to accompany Johnny on one of these expeditions. Though he protested that the high country was well known to be barren, worthless, probably infested with evil spirits, and certainly the home of Gheeger-Gheeger, the wild, bitter wind of winter, he enjoyed his half-brother's company, and felt that such evils as might be encountered in the mountains were more easily braved than the death-evil which undoubtedly brooded over the hut.

There was one high, bleak, boisterous plateau from which, with exclamations of surprise, they found themselves looking down across miles of sinking hills to the plains where the settlements of the white men were. They could see a glimpse of the river, and the roofs of houses near it; perhaps, said Johnny, his face suddenly dark with bitter memories, it was Green Hills. . . .

He would go no farther in that direction, and it was plain to Billalong that the mere sight of the white men's habitations—even at so great a distance that they looked but specks upon the plain—disturbed him. They turned their backs, and followed the westering sun until, after two camps, they came level with Johnny's own valley again. But to Billalong's surprise and chagrin (for he was tired by now of this purposeless journey, nostalgic for his tribe, his wife, and a good, belly-filling meal of fish) Dyonn-ee did not here turn southward and clamber down the steep pass which gave access to his domain. He was determined to go on, and Billalong, not without grumbling, agreed.

For two more days they walked, keeping always to the highest ground except when the need for water drove them down into a gully, and on the evening of the second day they came quite suddenly to a halt. The spur they followed ended, like all the others, in sheer cliffs, but it looked out over comparatively open country. Johnny stood for so long looking at it that Billalong grew impatient. It was a good place, he acknowledged, but of what interest to them? They had their own places, and this was the *towri* of other tribes. He reeled off a string of tribal names; all these, he said, had at one time or another—perhaps in his own lifetime, or perhaps so long ago that even the old men knew of it only from legends— sent emissaries across the mountains to his own and the coastal tribes. There were several accepted routes, though—since the high country was a place of hardship and bad hunting—they often preferred to travel along the river. . . .

"Along the river . . . ?" Johnny's eyes and voice were sharp.

Certainly along the river, Billalong assured him. He himself had never followed its course farther than was necessary to reach Dyonn-ee's *towri*, but it was well known that it had its source beyond the mountains.

"Ye mean," Johnny said slowly, "that there's a river rises down there and runs clean through the mountains? My river . . . ?"

Billalong, looking up at a leaden sky fast darkening with night and lowering clouds, repeated impatiently that there was. He was less interested in the river than in the problem of finding shelter for the night, and dining as well as might be from a large lizard which they had found basking unwarily in a patch of mid-day sun; but he began to understand the disapproval of the tribal elders who had shaken their heads over

Dyonn-ee's irregular boyhood, and his long periods of segregation from the tribe. It was not from so undisciplined a mode of life, they had grumbled, that a young man could learn all that was necessary—and indeed it now appeared that there were serious gaps in Dyonn-ee's mastery of legends with which every beardless lad should be familiar.

That night it was bitterly cold, and Gheeger-Gheeger was abroad. He roared and raged through the treetops that overhung the rock shelter where Billalong and Dyonn-ee crouched by a small fire; towards morning he retreated, leaving a strange, unnatural hush behind him, and at dawn Billalong, with a sharp exclamation of wonder and fear, saw plain evidence of sorcery in the sky. It was not rain that was falling, but something white, soft and soundless which had covered the ground while they lay shivering in an uneasy half-sleep; the naked flesh, touching it, recoiled from a coldness which seemed to burn. He was reassured—though not reconciled—when Dyonn-ee told him that he had seen such a thing before when he had come with Finn to these heights; he gave it a name, and declared that in the lands from which the Beerewolgal came it was frequently seen. He pointed out that Billalong's own tribe knew of it, and told of it in songs and legends. That, Billalong admitted rather sulkily, was true; but he still felt, shuddering over the small pile of glowing sticks, that legendary matters were best left in legends.

He agreed eagerly when Johnny decided that they would seek a way down on to the plain, for he wanted nothing so much as to escape from these inhospitable mountains, and from the sharp, slippery crunch of that white substance under his bare and shrinking feet. It took them the greater part of the day to discover and negotiate a route down through the cliffs on to the still steeply-sloping talus where no snow lay, and the temperature was many degrees warmer, though a light, drizzling rain fell steadily. It was not till the next afternoon that they came to running water which—though it bore little resemblance to the stream which curved below Johnny's valley, and was still less like the deep and noble river which swung north on the other side of the mountains—must surely, from its direction, be the Koornong.

To Billalong's disgust, however, Dyonn-ee did not turn to make his way homeward along its banks. His eyes were on the hills which rose from the plain where the sun was setting in a blaze of vermilion, and his desire to explore was not yet exhausted. Where, he demanded of Billalong, did the waters begin to flow westward? For though the formidable heights of the first range were now behind them, they were clearly not yet across the watershed. But Billalong had no further knowledge to yield; why should he be familiar with rivers which were no part of his own *towri*, and which found no place in any tale he knew? If Dyonn-ee wished to learn of these, he said rather sulkily, they had best seek out some of the tribes that dwelt in the area.

They came upon the ashes of a fire next day, and soon afterwards upon a few natives who received them warily and with wonder, but showed no hostility. In company with these they went on at leisure, sharing in the daily activities of their hosts, and Billalong's spirits rose again, for the hunts were exciting and successful, the meals lavish. This, he exclaimed several times to Dyonn-ee, was a rich *towri*, and when they came at last over the hills and down to a vast plain through which a river did flow westward, his interest was less in its direction than in the incredible abundance of fish and ducks which it provided.

Now the expedition was enjoyable indeed. The local tribe, having learned from Billalong that Dyonn-ee was one who had died long ago, and returned in the form of a child to re-live his life, accorded him a suitable respect in which Billalong, as his familiar companion, shared. The undulating plain was wide, and teeming with game; its grass was long and thick, though scorched in some places by frost; every little valley and hollow had its stream, or its pool alive with waterfowl. Yet Dyonn-ee did not seem pleased. His face was grim, his tongue silent. It was he, now, who wanted to turn back.

So they set out at last, accompanied for the first two days by their hosts, and, when these had left them, travelled eastward again by easy stages until they came once more to the banks of the Koornong, and followed it downstream. It widened as they progressed, gathering the flow of many rivulets. As they passed from open country into hills they had to wade or swim it sometimes, but for the most part the banks were flat, and they moved at a good pace. Prepared as he was for the sight, it was with a shock of wonder that Johnny, rounding a bend on the evening of a crystal-clear winter's day, saw two of his own cows feeding placidly by the water's edge. Here the river was his own; a hundred yards ahead was the spot where he often fished; some sixteen hundred feet above him, at the top of that steeply-sloping hill, was the floor of his own valley, and his home. He bade Billalong farewell, watched him out of sight, and climbed slowly up the hill, thinking hard.

Did *They*—the detested masters of his own race—know of that fine country west of the mountains? His mind went back to a white man whose footsteps he had dogged throughout an exploration years ago; a man who had pushed up the Wollondilly valley for many days before he turned back; a man who had written words in a foreign tongue upon a scrap of paper left by an abandoned camp fire, and now lying with other treasures on a shelf in Johnny's hut. . . .

That man had erred by turning upstream instead of down—a natural error, since one does not think to penetrate the interior of a country by following a river towards the sea. The short, but wild and impassable gorge of the Warragambie which forbade a direct approach, and sent explorers over the ridge to join the Wollondilly some miles above its junction with the Koornong, had been all—and was still all—which kept his own river unknown. But it could not remain unknown for ever. Some-day, Johnny thought, sitting alone in his hut and feeling all the accumu-lated hatred of the rulers of his own people burning up in him anew, They would stumble on it. Someday they would follow it—not to return after a few days with a report of more barren, rugged land, but to find it a road through the mountains to rich country, ripe for plunder. Then they would come, bringing their muskets and their floggers, their laws and their legirons and their convict gangs, their wealth, their greed, their cruelty and their arrogance. . . . And against these things there would rise up in the dispossessed the black hatred which he had once seen burst out in rebellion . . . and the black despair in which rebellion died. . . . They would come, they would come—and he could not kill them all, as he had killed Stephen Mannion. . . .

In this mood of smouldering hatred and foreboding, he pursued his lonely life. Twilight closed in early, and dawn came late; the nights seemed endless, and solitude increasingly a burden. He took down the stack of papers from his shelf and pored over Finn's clumsy writing, wrestling with the meaning of disconnected sentences and struggling to relate them to his own fragmentary knowledge of white men's affairs; the temporary illusion of communion with his friend left him the more wretched when it faded. He missed Ngili's ministrations, her cheerful, docile presence, her warm body in his bed; he even missed Kooree, and walked up the hill one day to stand for a long time staring at a small grave already masked by fallen bark and leaves. When Billalong arrived one day—summoning him from the hilltop which marked his nearest approach to the hut—to bring news which struck him like a blow, it seemed, for all its pain, to release in him some dammed-up fury, and fill his life once more with fierce and savage purpose.

He made his preparations carefully. He dressed himself in his rarely-worn clothes, and, with the scissors traded long ago for salt beef at Green Hills, trimmed his red hair and beard as short as possible. He cleaned and oiled his musket and pistol, sharpened his knife, took a supply of ammunition from his dwindling stock, and hung the key of the hut about his neck. At the last moment some impulse made him pause to pick up from the shelf that curious necklace which his foster-mother, Cunnem-beillee, had worn so many years ago; it seemed, suddenly, at once a talis-man and a symbol, and he stood looking at the tarnished brass buttons threaded on their loop of human hair as if they held some secret which he must discover. Loneliness and fear for his freedom were now re-inforced by the bitterness of the tidings Billalong had brought, and because this necklace was intimately connected with the life his father had built in defence of *Them,* it seemed to Johnny that some mystical strength of hatred must lie in it to aid his own revenge. He hung it round his neck and went out, locking the door behind him. The shutter of the one window hung unfastened, for he had no fear of thieves; to turn a key was a mere ritual, symbolic of his ownership.

Billalong looked at him in sober approval as they clambered down to the river. Dyonn-ee might set out upon this business clad in white men's clothes, and bearing white men's weapons—but he understood the tribal laws, and, for all his strange ways, obeyed them when the need arose. When a man's woman is murdered, blood must be shed to avenge her.

* * * *

Patrick's head overseer appeared at Conor's door one morning to present a letter which, he explained, Mr. Mannion had given him a week ago, bidding him deliver it to Mrs. Harvey.

"A week ago . . . ?" Conor asked, puzzled.

"Aye, ma'am, before he set out on a journey, and he saying I should bring it to you only if he was not returned in a week."

"A journey? But I had expected him in Sydney about this time, for he said. . . . Where has he gone, Toole?"

The man eyed her sullenly. No love had been lost between him and the erstwhile mistress of Beltrasna since that day when she had found him flogging the convict, Finn, and, in a blind storm of rage, snatched the lash from him and brought it down across his own face. Perhaps it was some memory of that moment which made him finger his cheek as he replied:

"It's no business of mine, ma'am, what the master may do, and he tellin' me nothin'. But when I'm after seein' him set out with enough food to last him two-three weeks, I can't but guess it's for some place beyond the settlements he's bound."

"Who went with him?"

"He went alone, ma'am."

"*Alone* . . . ?"

"Well, ma'am, he left from Beltrasna on horseback with Jordan, but when they was a few miles up the river he sent Jordan back, leading *Mor,* and went on by himself entirely. . . ."

"On foot, Toole?"

"Aye, ma'am, carryin' his own musket and knapsack, and a roll of blankets, and if ye'll pardon the liberty, ma'am, it's no way for a gentleman to be travelling, and what the late master, God rest his soul, would never. . . ."

She interrupted him sharply.

"He left no other messages or directions?"

"No, ma'am. All he says is for me to bring this letter in a week's time—and there it is in your hand, ma'am, and me duty done."

"You return to Beltrasna to-day?"

"Aye, ma'am, when I've seen to some business at the stores."

"Very well. No doubt Mr. Mannion will have given me any neces-sary information in his letter. Good-day, Toole."

When he had gone she hastened indoors. Mark was in the school-room, where Desmond now sat among his pupils, and Emily was busy scrubbing out the kitchen. Conor sat down at her escritoire and broke the seal on the thickly-folded sheets; there were three of them, and Patrick's small, clear writing covered them closely.

"Since I had told you of my intention to visit Sydney in about a week's time from now, I send this by Toole that you may understand the reason for my not appearing. I should send it immediately were it not that I may return before the week is out, when I might tell you in person what I here relate, and perhaps add more. What I write will be dis-closed, I am confident, to no person other than Mr. Harvey, upon whose Secrecy I also rely.

"The thought of Johnny Prentice has long weighed heavily on my Mind, as you know, and for some time past I have been making expedi-tions in the hope of discovering some trace of him, but in this I was completely unsuccessful until one day about three weeks since.

"Upon that Occasion I was returning home, attended by a young labourer named Jordan whom I have lately employed, when, upon round-ing a bend of the River we came suddenly upon a native Woman lying wounded on the ground. I was about to dismount in order to ascertain the extent of her injuries, and render what assistance I could, when my horse reared in fright—thereby, as I believe, saving my life from a spear which hurtled past me. Jordan immediately drew his Pistol and cried out to me to take cover behind the rocks, which we both did, but in the act of retiring we heard a voice call loudly in the native Tongue from a slight distance up the hillside, after which there was, for some moments, com-plete Silence. From our shelter we endeavoured to scan the hillside, but could see no one; when, to our astonishment, the voice called again, but this time in English, bidding us put down our weapons. I replied, enquir-ing: Who was there? Upon which a young native stepped forward from behind some bushes where he had been totally concealed, and my Amaze-ment was increased upon recognising him as the eldest of those three native boys who, you will recall, appeared at Beltrasna on the afternoon of that day when my Father met his death. I had also spoken with him on a later occasion when he was in a canoe on the river below our Fields, and had no doubt of his Identity. I therefore put up my Pistol, and, calling upon him to approach, rode out to meet him, when a Conversation took place, of which the general Particulars were these:

"He had that morning been roaming abroad some miles east of the river with several other native men and two Women (of whom the poor Creature now lying before us was one) when they encountered three white men who attempted to molest the Women, and seized them, when an Altercation ensued, spears were thrown, and shots fired, one white man and a native being wounded. One of the women made her escape and fled, but the other, having scratched her captor's face and struck him with a stick, was brutally belaboured about the head and shoulders with the butt of a musket before the conflict compelled her Assailant to release her. The Encounter was not prolonged, and the natives were in the act of conveying her to their camp when they were alarmed by our approach, and one of their number had flung his spear immediately we came into view, imagining, perhaps, that we were sent out to apprehend them. The young native (who informed me his name was Billalong) now explained that upon recognising me he had called upon his companions to refrain from further hostile Action because—as he said—I was in the habit of giving maize to his countrymen when they assembled near my fields.

"All this had taken but a few moments to recount, and I then dismounted with Jordan to examine the condition of the wounded Woman. The poor Wretch was beyond mortal aid, but we washed and bound her wounds, and forced a mouthful of Spirits between her lips. While doing this my eye fell upon a ragged Cloth which she wore about her waist and hips, and I was aware of a sensation of surprise whose cause I did not at first examine in my Preoccupation. Nor, when she began in her stupor to utter a certain word repeatedly, did I pay any particular Attention, and it was not until some little time later, when she had at last expired before our eyes, that I perceived the significance of these things, and was persuaded that I had stumbled upon a person who had some connection with Johnny Prentice. For I found myself observing that the rag was of fine silk, and almost immediately descried beneath the grime which covered it, that it was embroidered with flowers, and with the initials 'C.M.'

"Your amazement upon reading of this will be no less than was mine upon seeing it, and you will readily imagine how my Thoughts flew to your scarf which vanished from Beltrasna years ago at the same time as my Father's Firearms. There has been for some time little doubt in my mind that Prentice was the author of that, and other, Thefts, and with his name resounding so clearly in my thoughts, there came upon me suddenly a recollection of the word that this unhappy Woman had uttered in her dying moments. It sounded like 'Dyonn-ee', but you will not, I think, consider me over fanciful when I say that the resemblance between that word, and the name of him whom I had been seeking struck me as more than accidental. And indeed other Circumstances supported this belief, for I have long suspected that the young man, Billalong, is also in some manner connected with Prentice.

No more took place on this occasion, and we parted from the natives to return home (for I did not wish to speak of the matter to Billalong in Jordan's presence, and determined to seek him out by myself at some *future time). But about a week later (and of this you will doubtless have heard something) a white man named Hassett was murdered at night near his Dwelling, supposedly by a Native, since he was speared. A few days after, another, whose name I have not learned, was attacked in the same neighbourhood and mortally wounded, though his cries brought upon the scene two companions who chanced to be passing the night in his Hut; one of these fired upon the Intruder, who made off, leaving a trail of blood behind him, but could not the next day be traced beyond a nearby Creek. Before he expired, this second man, while admitting that he was unable to see his assailant clearly, declared him to be no native, since he was clothed, and taller than the common run of those people; this was not supported, however, by the man who fired the shot (which appears to have found its target by luck rather than by marksmanship). But the Allegation, when I learned of it, aroused in me certain misgivings, which were increased when I was informed that the men who had been attacked were two out of three who had recently been involved in a brawl with a party of Natives, on account of having molested their Women.*

"I entreat you to imagine my emotions upon hearing of these Events. It is true that intelligence of them came to me only by those rumours which, as you know, pass from mouth to mouth among the common people, often losing accuracy in their Progression; but my Informant was my overseer, Dawson, who is a steady kind of man, and who had it from one whose sister is the widow of Hassett. Dawson, like most others, set aside the notion that the perpetrator of these deeds was a white man, arguing that they were clearly acts of revenge by Natives, and that the Victim of the second act had been deceived in his observation. I, however, had reason to think otherwise. I may tell myself that this curious chain of circum-stances provides no more than suspicions—yet when suspicions may be so readily reinforced by reason, must one continue to doubt? I cannot but believe that these, as well as earlier Outrages have been committed by Prentice in pursuance of a settled plan of revenge, and I ask myself: How far am I responsible? My mind discovers many arguments to absolve me, but I remain uneasy. Was my first blunder made in boyhood when I gave Ellen my promise to preserve the secret of her son's survival? When she took his guilt upon herself, was I wrong to remain silent, excusing myself with a reluctance to speak from mere Suspicion? If I speak now, am I not betraying a secret with still no more than Suspicion to guide me? How far must suspicion go before we Act?

"Yet is no action possible which does not involve betrayal? That I should feel such scruples concerning a promise made in the interest of my Father's murderer (for such I firmly believe Prentice to be) would strike many as absurd—or worse: and indeed it may be that the years have made him that kind of desperate Villain for whom the gallows is the only fitting end. He is an outlaw and An Assassin—yet he was certainly not so when, at the age of eight years, he was driven forth by my Father's severities, the harshness of his life, and the intractable independence of his spirit. But I shall not attempt further to explain what is, I confess, obscure and confusing to myself, trusting that your Sensibility, and your knowledge of the events which have occurred, and of what passed between him and me

in childhood, will render my actions comprehensible. Suffice it to say that my Reflections caused me so much Anguish of mind that I resolved to seek out Billalong immediately, and persuade him to lead me to Prentice, that I might endeavour to halt this dreadful train of violence and revenge. Accordingly, I set out yesterday at daybreak, for the place where we found the dying Woman, and, falling in with some natives, contrived (by repeating the name 'Billalong' many times) to prevail upon them to lead me to him. He, however, persisted with the greatest emphasis in denying that he had any knowledge of such a person as 'Johnny'. I am far from being persuaded of the truth of this, and shall redouble my efforts, for I am convinced that Prentice is in the neighbourhood, and bent upon a Course which can only lead to much harm for others, and to his own Destruction. Pray do not dismiss my notions as fanciful, nor my actions as ill-judged and Romantick. Yet do so if you must, and it will make no difference; for I cannot rest until I have found him.

"My reason for going alone you will readily apprehend. I shall be well supplied with food and other necessaries, and you need feel no concern for my safety."

Conor sat still, staring blankly at the signature crowded into a corner at the foot of the last page. A painful dread, born of some thought as yet but half formed, was gathering in her. The surface of her mind could not break away from the strange, absurd, incredible picture of her long-lost scarf about the body of a dying native woman, but all the time the obscure thought was taking shape, so that when the sound of children's voices came shrilly through the window as they clattered down the path, and Mark opened the door, he found her white-faced and agitated.

"My love—what is it? Are you ill—faint . . . ?"

She shook her head, pushing the letter into his hand. As he read she was confronting her fear, and knowing it to be not only fear for Patrick, but fear of something huge, implacable and apparently endless. Fear of cruelty which, once released, flowed on like a flood; fear of hatred which bred hatred; fear of injustice which spread like a plague, not halted even by death, proliferating like some malign growth through generations. How much tragedy had flowed from the fact that a child had been treated ill in this place twenty years ago! How much more might yet follow! It was this grim sequence which Patrick hoped to break. . . . An old childhood friendship, an old loyalty, an old promise . . . could faithfulness to these things overcome that which even death failed to conquer . . . ? She looked up as her husband laid the sheets of paper on her desk. He said, looking worried:

"You are afraid for him?"

"Has he not considered," she replied, clasping her hands together nervously, "that if this Prentice learns he is being sought by the son of a man whom he murdered, he will suppose it to be from motives of revenge?

Will he await the encounter? Will he not rather himself turn seeker—his old hatred reinforced by fear?"

"I don't doubt, my love, that Patrick has considered everything. . . ."

"He appeals," she interrupted rather wildly, "to my sensibility, and indeed I can in some measure understand. . . . Yet Prentice is a murderer, and I cannot see beyond the danger Patrick is incurring in seeking out such a man. And at such a time! He is fresh from the crimes he has just committed—will he not be desperate, and therefore doubly dangerous? Is there nothing we can do?"

"I could ride out after him. . . ."

"No, no!" She added hurriedly: "Absurd! He might be anywhere—we know nothing. . . . Even if you found him, could you persuade him from this mad undertaking?"

"Even if I could," Mark replied slowly, "would I wish to? Would you wish me to, my love?"

She was silent, and he went on presently:

"Shall we disregard Patrick's wishes and lay all the information we possess before the Governor? Shall we aid in bringing this murderer to the gallows, and thus ensure Patrick's safety?"

She sat staring down at her clasped hands. Safety. How everything had once conspired to keep her safe—and how bitterly she had rebelled! How safely Patrick himself had lived, only to say at last "I cannot rest . . ." and go out in search of danger. . . .

"No," she said. "No, not yet. For a time at least we must wait."

*　　　　*　　　　*　　　　*

Life was no longer dull for Emily, but now she sometimes found herself looking back with longing to the quiet time when a visit to the Market had provided the only excitement of her days. But its bell still heralded the event for which she waited all the week, for Joseph Dean was no lovesick boy to abandon his daily business for the sake of a wench, and it was only on Saturdays that his cart was to be seen trundling in along the Parramatta Road.

It was not love he had ever asked of his woman—fear pleased him better. But he was a fastidious bully, and disdained fear ready made for him. Like the gourmet who must prepare his own salad, he preferred a woman of spirit, in whom he could skilfully blend the ingredients of fear to his own taste. He liked to chill Emily's ardour with a sudden shadow of doubt; to arouse her passion, and then, with a word or a gesture, transform it into shrinking; to repel abruptly the confidences he had just invited. It amused him to tell her tales of tragedy and violence which, by subtle implication, seemed to threaten her own future; to leave her not quite sure whether his first convict servant had really been slain by natives; to hint that the woman now raving in the asylum at Castle Hill had once been young and lovely as herself; to imply that native women were as desirable as white ones, and less trouble; to take her unwilling finger in his hand and trace with it the scar on his forehead, as he described what he had done to the assigned servant who attacked him.

Yet he found himself in something of a dilemma. It was true that he intended marriage, for casual and temporary affairs could not satisfy his particular needs, which were so much more than physical. He had made it plain that he was a man of some worldly substance, and he knew from a long and varied experience that he was sexually attractive to most women. He could therefore, he supposed, afford to amuse himself with Emily in his favourite fashion without fear of losing her. But as the weeks passed he discovered that he could not entirely rely upon the respectable status and the material benefits which marriage would confer upon her; nor upon his capacity to arouse and satisfy desire. Emily might be a servant girl out of the Orphanage, but she would demand, he realised, more than that. It was not her shrewdness which disturbed him, nor her sharp tongue, nor the hardiness with which she overcame or set aside the doubts and fears he roused—these merely made the prospect of mastering her more piquant; it was the unexpected discovery that she was no friendless and downtrodden slut who would be willing to risk an unknown servitude—with solid compensations—in order to escape from one only too wretchedly familiar. During their weekly assignations in a secluded spot on the outskirts of the park, he had soon learned much of her employers, and he saw that she might well decide in the end that she preferred their protection to his.

"I must go," she would say anxiously, "I can't stay no longer."

"Why not?"

"The mistress might find me gone."

"What of it? She can but turn ye out, and ye've a husband waitin'. And no convict, neither, but a free man that can come and go as he pleases. There's no call to be afeard of the old woman."

Emily's astonishment at the notion of being afraid of Mrs. Harvey was swamped by indignation at hearing her called old.

"Old? She ain't old! Or not very—but thirty or thereabouts, and no other lady in the colony to stand near her for looks. Some says Mrs. O'Connell's handsomer, but she's like a doll beside the mistress, and that silly with her airs. . . ."

One night she wore a gay ribbon in her hair, and said proudly when he admired it:

"The mistress gave it to me."

He grinned knowingly.

"Or maybe you took it when her back was turned—eh?"

"I did not! It's new—not from one of her old gowns or bonnets, but new out of the shop! She bought it for me, and I'll thank ye not to be callin' me a thief!"

"Then ye're not like most that comes out o' that precious Orphanage. Did ye never steal? Come now—never . . . ?"

"Not from her." Emily's voice was sullen, and he changed his tone, pulling money from his pocket, and promising her a new ribbon every week if she wished it.

Once, rather anxiously, she asked:

"Ye've told me the truth? It's marriage ye mean?"

"Do ye set such store by the parson's blessing?"

"No-o-o. But the mistress. . . ."

And another night:

"I'm late—it was the master kept me back."

He asked sharply, stabbed by jealousy:

"What did he want with ye?"

"Don't—ye're hurtin' me! It was but to make me repeat me lesson again. . . ."

"Lesson . . . ?"

"Aye, he teaches me to read and write and figure."

He had pondered all this. These remarkably benevolent employers were, in a sense, his foes; yet it was plain enough, too, that her devotion to them inspired the only misgivings she felt for her surrendered virtue, and this, if he were patient, might serve him well. He reflected also that sometimes, when a servant was held in esteem by her master and mistress, her marriage was the occasion for a little present; he had been willing enough to take Emily for what he could see in her, but his bargain would be better still if she did not come quite empty-handed. . . .

One night she spoke of gossip heard in the Market that morning. He shot a quick glance at her, and replied:

"Aye, Tom Hasset's farm's but five mile or so from mine, and Luke Bates was workin' on a place a bit beyond—I knew them both well."

"Why do ye suppose the natives murdered them?"

"Because they're all damned murderin' heathen devils by nature—that's why."

"I heard tell they'd been after the native women—well, I reckon if that's the way it was they got what they'd been askin' for."

"Ye do, eh?"

"Yes, I do, and from what ye've told me I'd say ye'd best be mendin' y'r own ways if ye don't want to end like they did. I ain't got no use for men that go with native women."

"When a man can't get the white woman he wants, it ain't for her to blame him if he goes elsewhere." He peered at her closely. "What if the black devils did come after me next? Supposin' they murdered me before I'd put a ring on y' finger . . . ?"

In the dark he could not read her expression, but he thought she seemed agitated, and she was very quiet for the rest of the evening. And indeed it was but a week later that his patience was rewarded. It diverted him that Emily should valiantly assume a casual air so transparently false. Nothing was needed of him but silence to expose its falseness, so he remained dumb and unresponsive while her brisk tone wavered, her words faltered, and her pretence of hardihood collapsed. He let her weep for a time, ignoring the hand that reached out to touch his own—at first appealingly, and then in a frightened frenzy of demand. He said roughly:

"Hush y' noise, ye little fool—didn't I tell you it was a wife I wanted —and grandchildren? I'll go see the schoolmaster in the mornin' and we can wed when ye please."

"I've not said I'll wed ye for sure—there's other ways. . . ."

"Oh, aye, there's other ways—but ye'd not expect me to help ye there. Old Susy likes to see the colour of y' money before she lets y' in her door —and I reckon ye'd not be able to take that way anyhow, without y' mistress knew of it." He shrugged. "But ye can choose what ye'll do. I've wasted me time long enough—if ye won't marry me, there's others will."

"Ye want *me!*" She knew it was true, but her bewilderment found sudden expression in an urgent and despairing question: "Why?"

"Ye've got sperrit," he said, grinning at her queerly. "I've got no use for a woman without sperrit, and never had. What ails ye?"

She scrambled to her feet, her teeth chattering.

"I'm cold, ye great gowk, and no wonder, comin' out here these winter nights when I might be warm in me bed."

"Ye'd be warmer in mine. Well, will I see the schoolmaster in the mornin' and tell him it's marriage I mean, all respectable like the Gover-nor wants? Or will ye tell y' mistress ye've a bastard on the way? Mind ye, it'll not be looked on kindly in a schoolmaster's house, and there'll be those to say it's more than readin' and writin' he's been teachin' ye. I reckon it won't pleasure y' mistress to be hearin' tales the like o' that. Stop y' snivellin' now, and make up y' mind, for if ye've no use for me I'll be on my way in the mornin', and ye'll not be seein' me again. Will ye have me come, or not?"

"Aye," she said wretchedly, "ye can come."

*　　　　*　　　　*　　　　*

Billalong returned to camp about sunset. His wife greeted him with vehement complaints when she saw that he had brought nothing for the evening meal, but he ignored her, for he knew that Gocradoo had speared a wallaby which he would share. Exchanging a word or two with his friends as he passed their fires, he made his way to a small, bark mia-mia near his own, and crouched down at its entrance.

When Dyonn-ee, with a bullet wound in his side, had stumbled back to the camp to collapse in a faint from pain and loss of blood, the most potent spells of the medicine men had been required to preserve his life. Even when the evil spirits had at last been expelled, taking with them the fire which had been consuming his body, and the madness which had caused muttered, incoherent ravings to issue from his lips, he lay spent and weak, his hand always on the loaded musket which he would permit no one to move from his side, and his dark, burning eyes fixed upon the low doorway of his shelter.

Once, only a couple of days after he had been wounded, the red-coated ones had come, questioning the old men of the tribe in their rough, threatening way, shouting that two white men had been fatally speared by a native, demanding that all the young men be brought before them, that they might see which one had been wounded. And when all were found to be whole and unharmed, the soldiers had declared that they would search the mia-mias lest one might be concealed there; at this Billalong had grasped his spear tighter, and felt all about him the tense stiffening of his companions. But his wife had come quickly to whisper in his ear, and he had smiled, congratulating himself upon her quick wit, and told his friends with a gesture to remain still. When the soldiers stooped to peer into the dark mia-mia where Dyonn-ee lay moaning in an uneasy stupor, they saw only two women crouching over the swollen body of a third who lay upon a raised couch of skins; and Dyonn-ee's muffled groans were so mingled with hers, and with the shrill protestations which the other women immediately voiced at this intrusion, that they suspected nothing, and withdrew hurriedly. Since then no searchers had visited this camp, though they had appeared at others, and several young men carrying the fresh scars of some accident or honourable tribal combat had been savagely questioned and manhandled.

But by the time Dyonn-ee's sickness had abated, and he was able to hear and speak again, Billalong had another matter to relate. He had been disturbed by the persistent enquiries of the young white man from the great house down the river, for he knew that this was the home of Dyonn-ee's mortal enemies, and it was one of the proudest memories of his boyhood, as it was of Gooradoo's and Balgundra's, that they had all been privileged to play a part in the notable battle which had once taken place between these people on the one hand, and Dyonn-ee and the-one-who-is-now-dead on the other. Undoubtedly, Billalong acknowledged, Dyonn-ee had good reason to hate the white tribe known as Man-yun, after what had befallen his friend on that occasion; but it must be admitted that the young Man-yun who had questioned him was prefer-able to many of his countrymen, and showed some understanding of the behaviour which was seemly between man and man. He did not shout, threaten, or brandish whips and pistols when the natives crossed his property or landed on the river bank below his house; he directed his people to give them maize at harvest time; and he had done the best that could have been expected from one who was not a medicine man in his attempts to ease the dying moments of Dyonn-ee's woman.

The news that this young man was seeking Dyonn-ee had caused much anxious discussion in the tribe, where it was foreseen that a meeting of the two might have grave consequences. It was the young man's father who had killed Dyonn-ee's friend, and therefore, naturally, Dyonn-ee had killed the young man's father. Equally naturally, the young man was now clearly bent upon killing Dyonn-ee, but if he should succeed—so the argument ran—Billalong, and thus the whole tribe, would become in-volved; for Billalong must then, of course, revenge himself upon his brother's slayer. As matters stood at present between the black men and the white, such incidents were not desirable. The man, Ma-gor-ee, had several times conferred with the tribal elders, urging peace, and they had assured him that peace was also what they desired. They would not, however, endure wanton attacks upon themselves or their womenfolk without retaliation, and though the necessity for Dyonn-ee's vengeance upon his woman's murderers was deplored, it was not questioned. But this threatened development with Man-yun, declared the elders sternly, was different. Dyonn-ee had already shed blood to avenge his friend, and the matter was now honourably closed; it was the duty of every tribesman to do all in his power to prevent an encounter between these two.

Therefore Billalong was disturbed as he crouched before the mia-mia, for he knew that Man-yun was abroad again, alone, armed, visiting camps, seeking out natives as they passed in pairs or groups through the bush, and always asking, persistently, the same question: "Dyonn-ee . . . ?" Billalong had scarcely thrust his head through the opening when Johnny demanded sharply in the native tongue:

"Have you seen him?" He was supporting himself on one elbow, and his dark eyes were like caverns in his white face; but he was gaining strength every day, and this morning he had walked down to the river, leaning on Balgundra's arm.

Billalong shrugged. Dyonn-ee was as yet too feeble to set out upon any foolhardy errand, so there was no need for prevarication. Yes, he said, he had seen Man-yun—but Man-yun had not seen him. Where was he? Down the river on its western side, and making for the pool of flat rocks, escorted by Mur-gon and Bandaree. It seemed, added Billalong rather wearily, as good a place to lead him as any other.

He looked at his half-brother with concern and exasperation, reflecting that since he had already fulfilled the mission which had brought him from his mountain retreat, it would save everyone a great deal of trouble if he would now be satisfied, and return whence he came. But it was plain that this was not his intention. His code of vengeance, after all, was that of a white man, for it appeared to be of great importance to him that Ngili's death must be avenged not merely upon any member of her slayer's tribe, but upon the very three men who had caused it. Of these two were now dead, but the third—the scar-faced one who had become a scourge to the neighbouring tribes, and a terror to their women-folk—was still unharmed. For some weeks now the natives had willingly watched this man's movements that Dyonn-ee might the more easily surprise him when he was ready, and there was no man, woman or child among the dark people who would not rejoice to know him dead. But blood had already been shed to avenge blood; more was not necessary. . . .

"A few days," Johnny was saying, speaking now in his own tongue, and looking past Billalong with a strange, listening air as if he heard some distant summons, "and I'll be walkin' as good as ever." He shifted his hot, restless gaze to Billalong and said urgently: "I must knew where he is—all the time—every minute of the day. Aye, and the night, too. . . ."

Billalong threw out his hands argumentatively, but Johnny silenced his attempted expostulation with a few angry words, so he turned re-signedly from the hut to the fire where his meal was now preparing. One could not argue with Dyonn-ee, any more than one could argue with a storm.

Left alone, Johnny lay with open eyes, but it was not the bark roof of his shelter, touched by flickering gleams from the fire outside, that he was seeing. Still weak, he was apt to fall into a state between waking and sleeping when his mind created pictures rather than thought, spinning them from half-forgotten things—a glimpse here, a glimpse there, a scene with blurred edges, an episode unfinished. And though they ranged from childhood to manhood, every episode seemed the same—each one a single engagement in the unending war between *Them* and Johnny Prentice. When his mind created its pictures, it showed *Them* always as Mannions. Stephen Mannion, Patrick Mannion, it made no difference; they had ceased to be people, and become symbols of an oppressive power which would not let him live in peace either with it or away from it. It had driven him out and drawn him back, only to drive him out and draw him back again. . . . This was the inescapable cycle in which all his pictures seemed captured withdrawal and return. Dully hurtful as they were, heavy with resentment and the goading sense of injustice, they seemed but steps mounting towards an agonising climax—a picture neither blurred nor incomplete, but as cruelly definite and vivid as in the moment when it had burned itself into his memory for ever—the picture of Matthew Finn, his hands bound behind his back, being dragged up from the Bel-trasna fields towards the house, with Stephen Mannion and Patrick Mannion riding in front of him.

Finn had bidden him return to the place they had made together—and he had done so. Ah, but Finn had not realised that its river was a highway through the mountains, along which They would someday come tramping. He had not known that They would murder Ngili. But he had known that even freedom could lose its value in solitude—had he not said that it turned sour in the mouth, for there was no sweetness in it for any man alone?

It had turned sour in Johnny's mouth, and he was now tasting instead the sharp, fiery sweetness of revenge. There was nourishment in it as well as flavour; it was like good food and drink to his body, and he could feel it bringing strength back to him in a warm tide, so that his sagging eyelids suddenly flew open, and he thought clearly and fiercely that he need wait no longer. Until the fires died down, and the noises of the camp faded into silence, he lay still, listening, staring into the dark, nursing the hatred which was all the treasure he had left.

*　　　　*　　　　*　　　　*

Patrick woke in the morning to find a light rain falling. Perhaps it was as well after all, he thought, that he had agreed, despite misgivings, to accept the guidance of the two natives. Not only had they kept their promise to catch him a fish for his supper, but, when they looked up through the treetops to find the stars gone, they had immediately conducted him to this excellent shelter. Bidding him follow them, they had clam-bered about a hundred feet up the steep hillside from the creek, and then turned sharply along a ledge skirting a rocky promontory, beyond which they had come into this small cave. It was no more than eight feet wide from its back wall to the edge where the cliff dropped sheer to the rocks below, but its roof was solid rock, its floor dry, sandy, and approximately level. Here they had left him, and he had stretched out, wrapped in his blankets, and slept soundly enough, waking two or three times during the night to throw another log on to his fire. Now it was cold which aroused him, and he sat up stiffly and looked about. A sharp, east wind was driving the rain far enough into his shelter to reach the fire, which was hissing faintly, and sending shreds of blue smoke up from the larger of its still-smouldering logs. What he could see of the sky was a uniform, leaden grey, and with the wind in that quarter it might rain for days.

He decided as he opened his knapsack that he must return home; his food was almost exhausted, and a spell of bad weather would make this gipsy life he had been leading impracticable. Moreover, Miles might be arriving at any moment now with his bride, and it would be the height of discourtesy if he were not present to receive and welcome her. When that was done he would set out again, but for the present it was clear that he must abandon his search. It had already lasted longer than he had thought possible—and for that he must thank the natives. As he began to eat the last of his provisions he was reflecting that they were odd creatures, blending the crudest and most revolting of habits with a curious delicacy, difficult to define, but always apparent in their dealings with him or with each other. Without them he could not have pursued his search so long—and yet, perhaps, without them he might have pursued it more successfully . . . ?

He frowned. That had been the thought in his mind last night when he had hesitated to accept their offered guidance; and yet surely it must be a fanciful one? Had they really been as helpful as they seemed? Friendly—yes. Ready to guide him, ready to ferry him across the river, ready to carry his burdens, ready to share their food, ready to converse with signs, gestures, and stray words of English. But ready to help him find Johnny Prentice—or even Billalong? He had passed from group to group, always questioning. When he said: "Dyonn-ee . . . ?" they looked at him with amiable blankness. When he said: "Billalong . . . ?" they were all comprehension, pointing north, south, east or west, and urging him to accompany them; but when they arrived at their destination Billalong was never there, and they would shake their heads regretfully, and throw out their expressive hands as if to say that they had done their best. But could Billalong travel from one point of the compass to another with such astonishing rapidity? Patrick could not subdue a growing suspicion that when he asked to be led to Billalong he was, in fact, led kindly, efficiently and expeditiously away from him.

He finished his meal and stood up, stretching his stiff limbs, trying to remember how far down the creek he must walk to reach the river, wondering if he might there fall in with some natives who would ferry him downstream, and save him miles of walking. He picked up his musket, slung his knapsack over his shoulders, and turned to make his way round the shoulder of rock. And as he did so, Johnny Prentice stepped out from behind it.

Patrick stood staring at him. He had wondered once or twice whether he would recognise his old playmate now if he saw him; it was thirteen years since their last meeting. But there was no mistaking that blaze of unkempt red hair, that sharply-cut, angular face, or those hostile, challenging dark eyes. But he was surely ill . . . or mad . . . or both . . . ? He was thin to emaciation, his face so bloodless that its sunburn looked yellowish, and his eyes fever-bright. He was breathing heavily, and as he stood some dozen yards away, lifting his musket to his shoulder, he seemed to sway, and leaned against the wall of rock.

Patrick heard himself say sharply:

"Johnny . . . ! You know me . . . ?"

"I know ye!"

The voice was thick and slow, but the hatred in it sent a shock of warning through Patrick's body. He raised his own musket, but it was only halfway to his shoulder when Johnny fired. The report echoed from the rocks of the gully like the first splitting sound of thunder. Patrick felt a red-hot pain in his leg, found himself lying on the ground, and saw that Johnny had taken a few paces towards him, and that his eyes were murderous. He struggled to a painful position, half kneeling, half crouching, and reached for his musket, calling out a few desperate words which he could never afterwards remember. Then Johnny staggered and fell; his musket clattered to the ground between them; for a few endless seconds they were still, and watched each other.

At last Johnny moved. He pushed himself up on his hands and knees, gasping, and began to crawl. Now that the first shock of the encounter was fading, Patrick's mind began to work again, and he knew that at so short a distance nothing could have saved his life but the illness—weakness—whatever it was—that had made Johnny sway on his feet, and aim unsteadily with shaking hands. Now he was closer still, and the miracle would not happen twice. Pain stabbed him again as he threw himself forward, and they both reached for the musket together. Patrick's hand closed on it first, and he drew it towards him, raised it with difficulty, and threw it; they heard it fall on the rocks below the ledge. Johnny sank down on his folded arms, sweat streaking his face, and they became motionless again in a ringing silence that Patrick broke at last, to say, with a note of stupid incredulity in his voice:

"You would have killed me!"

"Aye!" Johnny's savage whisper was barely audible, and his eyes were on Patrick's musket.

"You killed my father!"

The little burst of words that came then from Johnny's lips in the same striving whisper seemed to exhaust his remaining strength, and his head sagged. "He killed Finn—ye both killed him!"

Patrick, already growing faint from loss of blood, felt a sudden wave of sickness and trembling. Somewhere at the back of his certainty there must still have been a doubt, desperately surviving—the ghost of a hope that he had not, after all, allowed an innocent woman to die. Kill, kill, kill, every killing but a prelude to the next—and there, on the ground between them, lay the instrument of killing. . . .

As he reached for the musket he was aware of Johnny's violent, convulsive attempt to rise; as he grasped it he heard himself utter an absurd, frustrated sound, half groan, half sob, because it was so heavy he could barely drag it towards him. He knew that Johnny had struggled to his hands and knees, but it was the musket, now, which seemed the enemy he must defeat before it defeated them both. He raised it laboriously and threw it after the other one, his arms weak and clumsy, so that it hung for a second on the edge before it fell, and, in falling, seemed to release him from some intolerable burden. He looked at Johnny, whose eyes had followed his action, and now met his own with confusion and uncertainty dimming, for the first time, their mad, implacable hatred, and whose whole body, robbed of the purpose which had lent it a last surge of strength, crumpled down on the sand, only its eyes showing life. The silence and stillness which claimed them again seemed less taut now; they watched each other half absently, and lay as if resting.

Patrick's sight was blurred and wavering; he stared for some time with detached curiosity at the red stains on the sandy ground near his leg, wondering why they moved. When he looked at Johnny again he saw that he was no longer watched. Johnny's eyes were still open, but they looked fixed and sightless; perhaps he was dead. Perhaps he himself would die here too. Perhaps there had never been any possible end to this business between himself and Johnny Prentice but death. . . . He tried to alter his position to one which would ease the throbbing agony in his leg, but the effort caused a drumming in his head, and a whirling blackness before his eyes. He collapsed face downwards, and when he regained consciousness Johnny had disappeared. Billalong and the two natives who had guided him last night were standing over him.

Billalong was puzzled, but relieved. He had felt no doubts about where Dyonn-ee had gone when, at dawn, his mia-mia was found empty, and a canoe missing from the river bank. *Aie,* he thought in alarm and exasperation as he bustled about collecting his spears and his firesticks, and calling upon Gooradoo and Balgundra to make themselves ready to accompany him, what a madman this Dyonn-ee was! Would any reasonable man set out upon a mission such as this before his wound was fully healed, and his legs strong enough to support him? Yet it was perhaps as well, for their chance of overtaking him would be the better.

But fast as they paddled in their three canoes, they saw no sign of him. Mur-gon and Bandaree, whom they encountered a mile or so down-stream, just about to embark in their canoes, had not seen him either—but they had been busy some distance from the river seeking a suitable tree to make a new shield for Mur-gon, and agreed that he might have passed unnoticed. Shaking their heads gloomily, they agreed to join Billalong and his companions.

The creek which flowed down to the river through the pool of flat rocks was too obstructed by boulders and fallen trees to be navigable for more than a couple of hundred yards, and they were making their way up it on foot, still half a mile from the cave, when they heard the report of a musket echoing down the gully. Man-yun's, or Dyonn-ee's? It was not only exertion which was making Billalong's heart thud heavily as he clambered at last round the ledge into the cave. Both there—and both lying still. . . . Both dead . . . ? But it needed only a second glance to tell him that both were living; and though it appeared that only Man-yun was wounded, it was over Dyonn-ee that he knelt first.

His companions, clustering round, exchanged exclamations of relief and wonder. Clearly the evil magic of sickness had taken possession of Dyonn-ee's body again, for it was burning hot, and he mumbled senseless words as they raised him. They must, declared Billalong, get him away as quickly as possible, before his enemy regained consciousness, and all this madness began again. Gooradoo and Balgundra, it was agreed, should take him back to the camp, where the spells of the medicine men must once more be exercised to preserve him. Hoisted to his feet between them, he could still walk after a fashion; when they reached the river and the canoes there would be no further difficulty. Billalong watched them go, and turned his attention to Man-yun.

The wound in his leg had been made by a gooroobera, the white man's stick-of-fire, but—as Mur-gon suddenly pointed out—no such weapon was visible. Man-yun, he said, had certainly been carrying his last night, and Billalong, frowning, replied that Dyonn-ee's had vanished with him from his mia-mia. They searched the cave, increasingly be-wildered, until Bandaree, peering over the ledge, summoned the others, and they all craned their heads to see the two muskets lying on the rocks below. Now one bewilderment was replaced by another. This was beyond comprehension. Either of the combatants might have secured his adver-sary's weapon and thrown it out of reach—but would he throw his own . . . ? Could such a thing happen in the confusion of combat . . . ? They became silent and rather sullen, having no taste for such mysteries, and reminded by this one that not only Man-yun, but Dyonn-ee, was a white man—one of those beings whose laws of battle were as absurd and irregular as all their other laws.

One thing was clear. They must remove Man-yun—return him with all haste to his own *towri,* and hope that (unlike any other white man they had ever known) he would be content to remain there. They looked at him; he had opened his strange eyes that were the colour of the sky on a fine day, and was trying to push himself up on his elbow. He said vaguely, staring up at them:

"Billalong . . . ?"

Billalong crouched beside him.

"Dyonn-ee . . . ?"

Their faces were blank, and they gave him no reply.

*   *   *   *

It was the climb down the hillside to the creek, and the journey down the creek to the river, which took up the greater part of the day. With one arm over Billalong's shoulder, and the other over Mur-gon's, Patrick made slow and painful progress among scrub and rock, his injured leg dragging, and pain blurring his sight; now and then, for a brief, merciful period, he lost consciousness entirely. Sometimes physical effort became confused with mental effort, and he strove to understand why a dream that he had seen Johnny Prentice should be so painful. Sometimes the rain, coming down harder now, soaking his clothes and streaming over his face, made him think that he was drowning, and he felt panic because his arms were pinioned, and he could not swim.

By mid-afternoon, when they came to the river, the natives were carrying him. They placed him in one of the canoes, and Billalong, crouching over his prone body, pushed off with his paddle. Gooradoo and Balgundra followed in their own canoes, and for an hour they travelled downstream until, in the fading light of the dull, winter evening when the rain had ceased and a watery gleam of late sunlight pierced the clouds, Patrick heard Billalong call out, and a voice reply in English.

The two men on the bank were settlers making their way home; they crawled out from beneath the dray where they had crouched to take shelter from the rain while they refreshed themselves with a drink from their rum flasks, and walked down to the river bank. They held their muskets ready and watched the river narrowly, determined not to be hoodwinked by the notorious artifices of treacherous heathens, but when they saw Patrick they broke out into a torrent of astonished questions which penetrated the confusion of his mind with a stab of warning. Soon he must speak, and say . . . what? The labour of thought was so intense that he shut his eyes, trying to separate the memory of fact from the phantasmagoria of delirium. His leg was injured. He clung to this fact, struggling with it until he related it to his dream of seeing Johnny Prentice. Blood. Yes, that was it; there had been blood on the ground near his leg. A dream could cause pain—but not blood. He heard the men questioning Billalong, and Billalong replying volubly—in his own tongue; yet Billalong understood and spoke English very well. . . .

The bottom of the canoe scraped mud, and he opened his eyes to see a branch above him, its wet leaves sparkling. A bearded face came into view beneath it, and another appeared for a moment, wearing an expression of curiosity which changed with almost comical suddenness to one of startled amazement.

"It's Mr. Mannion, be all the Saints! Mr. Mannion of Beltrasna!"

Patrick shut his eyes again as if by so doing he might ward off the inevitable question. The white men were muttering together; he heard one say: "Ah, what use to ask them? Ye'll get nothin' but a lot of their gabble, and likely all lies even if ye could understand it. We'd best get him up to the cart . . . come on, move him careful, now. . . ." He felt himself being lifted and carried. One of the men sharply ordered the natives aside. "All right—be off with ye, now, we don't need ye here!" The other said something in an undertone, to which his companion replied: "Nay—it's a bullet wound. Put him down a moment while I make a place ready in the cart. . . ." As they lowered him, Patrick heard the man call loudly and angrily: "Well, what are ye waitin' for? Didn't I tell ye to go . . . ?"

Go? Was Billalong, then, to disappear again—Johnny to be once more swallowed up by the bush—nothing achieved by all this, everything to do again . . . ? Patrick opened his eyes, turned his head, called weakly: "Billalong!"

But the natives had gone, and it was the white men who came into his line of vision again. One said: "There, Sir, ye'll do all right in the cart, and we'll have ye home in no time." The other asked: "That wound, Sir—how did ye come by that, now?"

"Don't know," Patrick mumbled, shutting his eyes again that they might not betray his lie. There was a pause, and then the two voices spoke incredulously, in unison:

"Ye don't *know* . . . ?"

"Did ye not see the rascal, then?"

Patrick answered with laborious care:

"No. Someone fired on me . . . from behind some rocks. Saw no one . . . natives found me long after . . . brought me here. Saw no one . . . no one at all. . . ."

*   *   *   *

The Governor and his wife were but a few days returned from a visit to Windsor when Conor, in response to a note from Mrs. Macquarie, called at Government House one wet Sunday afternoon; a fire burned brightly in the small parlour, for it had been raining since the previous morning, and the day was raw and chilly. Conor noticed that her hostess' eyes—looking bluer than ever in the transparent pallor of her face—had lost their twinkle, and indeed Mrs. Macquarie betrayed in her first words the crack in her armour of cheerfulness.

"I trust you won't find me poor company, dear Mrs. Harvey, for I've invited no one else to join us. I'm a little fatigued after our tour, but I felt the need for a quiet gossip with one of my own sex. Oh, I'm quite recovered, as you can see, but I have found it difficult to regain my spirits."

"I was so distressed, ma'am, to hear of your illness. I can't tell you how much sympathy I feel. . . ."

"You're very kind, my dear. I must not fret about it, but it's most disappointing and provoking, for I had been so careful! No horseback riding, not even carriage exercise—Dr. Redfern insisted! Ah, well! Fatigue one may avoid, perhaps—but anxiety . . . ?"

"The Governor's anxieties must be yours also, of course—and no doubt he has many."

"He's besieged by them. No single one in itself so grave, yet taken together they form a burden he's never free from—never! There's something here—I can't clearly describe it—which creates a feeling of insecurity, almost of a perpetually impending crisis. . . . Just lately Macquarie has been more affected by it than usual." She pondered for a moment, drawing her shawl more closely round her shoulders. "So many things to attend to, and yet no one satisfied! People like Mr. John Blaxland—so importunate . . . ! Since he arrived back recently he's given Macquarie no peace. He has been making all manner of complaints to the English authorities about his treatment here, and now returns to plague Macquarie—just at this time, of all others, when he was so harassed on my account, and so cast down by yet another blow to our hopes. . . ." She made a little rueful gesture. "Can you wonder that I'm not always able to preserve my own tranquillity when I see how much I add to his anxieties?"

"I wonder, ma'am, that you should forget how much you must also add to his comfort and happiness."

"Ah, that was kindly said, my love, but all the same. . . . You're right, though—I must not brood about it, or about other problems. Problems are but what a Governor must expect to meet with. And I would not have you think for a moment that I entertain any serious

misgivings—nor does Macquarie, I assure you. It's rather the multiplica-
tion of small trials which vexes him, and the constant *odour*—I can call
it nothing else—of concealed hostility and intrigue which so offends one
of his open character."

"It's as nothing—pray take my word for it—to what went on just
previous to Governor Bligh's arrest, and after it."

"Oh, that dreadful affair—shall we ever be quite finished with it?
We've lately seen the return of a number of those people who were
principally concerned in it, have we not? Captain Brabyn and Lieutenant
Lawson were both prominent in Colonel Johnston's party, I believe. And
Mr. Oakes and Mr. Gore and Mr. Suttor and the Reverend Mr. Fulton
are among us again—all of Governor Bligh's camp. I wonder . . . but I
must *not* anticipate commotions where none may occur! And I must not
waste this agreeable occasion in talking of such disagreeable subjects. Tell
me of your dear babe, pray. Children are the only riches I consider
worthy of regard."

"He's very well, ma'am—and very noisy."

"Desmond misses his sister, no doubt?"

"Perhaps—though he is of so amiable and placid a disposition that
he seems always contented."

"You still have the girl from the Orphanage?"

"Yes, but I fear we shall lose her shortly. She's to be married to a
settler in the Eastern Creek district soon."

"La, my dear, how tiresome for you! But you'll be glad to know
she's respectably settled, after the kindly interest you have taken in her."

Conor looked a little doubtful.

"I hardly know what to think about it. The man is in more comfortable circumstances than many, and I must own that his behaviour in
coming to my husband and declaring his intentions was very proper. I
suppose it's no bad match. Yet I can't feel entirely at ease about Emily
—she has seemed strangely distraught of late—quite unlike herself. But
I suppose some agitation and discomposure are not unnatural at such a
time."

"Natural or not, they're quite customary, I assure you. I've observed
it with my own servants many times. How did she meet the man?"

"At the Market. I spoke with him when he came to interview my
husband—a rough sort of fellow, but his manner was open enough, and
it seems he's industrious, and a good farmer, and not given to excessive
drinking like so many others. . . ."

"The girl may count herself lucky, I think. A free man, with property
and temperate habits! I only wish all our Orphanage girls could do as
well for themselves!"

"You are right, of course, but I still feel some slight misgivings. It occurred to me that the man was perhaps lacking in—in . . ." Conor hesitated, oppressed by a painful memory of the early years of her own first marriage. She concluded with a sigh: "A young wife stands in need of tenderness, I think. . . . But there—she declares herself willing, and I hesitate to dissuade her. . . ."

"I should think not, my dear Mrs. Harvey! Mercy, if we attended too much to the moods and vapours of young girls few of them would be married at all! And speaking of not being married, how is that obstinate bachelor, Mr. Mannion? My husband tells me that he has been spending some time in excursions beyond the river of late?"

"I understand so, ma'am." Conor, having unburdened herself upon the subject of Emily, felt and resisted a temptation to confide her anxieties concerning Patrick; for it was now a full week since she had received his letter, and no further tidings had come to reassure her. She deflected the conversation rather hastily.

"We're expecting his brother to arrive shortly. Miles left here nine years ago, you know. Patrick and I both received letters by the *Clarkson* with the news that he had recently married, and expected to obtain a passage for himself and his wife quite soon."

"My, how interesting that will be! Nine years, you say? He will be greatly changed. And his wife—you're not acquainted with her, I suppose?"

"Only through Miles' letters." Conor smiled. "I conjecture that the descriptions of a young man in love may be taken with some reserve. However, we shall soon have an opportunity of judging for ourselves."

"You're wise to await it," Mrs. Macquarie replied with a ghost of her old twinkle. "But tell me of your husband's school. His pupils increase in numbers?"

"Very considerably of late. And several of the free tradesmen and townspeople have enrolled their sons with us—which we regard as being one happy result of the Governor's humane policies, ma'am."

"I'm delighted to hear it. You know, he has for some time been turning over in his mind a plan for the establishment of a school for native children. To be sure, the idea may seem somewhat fanciful, but. . . ." ·

"Oh, no!" protested Conor. "I don't think it fanciful at all, ma'am, and I'm sure my husband would applaud it."

Mrs. Macquarie sighed.

"Sometimes I fear the Governor's performance will never overtake his plans, my dear—so many matters press on his mind, and he's compelled to move slowly, you understand, for every new venture involves more expense, which is not welcomed at home, of course. However, the question of the natives must be attended to, for though things go on fairly peaceably at present on the whole, there *are* disturbing incidents, are there not? And it's so important to keep them friendly, for what with absconders and hostile natives the more remote districts would be decidedly unsafe. . . . Why, Henry . . ." she looked up in surprise as Captain Antill appeared in the doorway, ". . . has the Governor released you so soon?"

"He has sent me with a message, ma'am—for Mrs. Harvey." The Captain bowed hastily to Conor. "I very much regret—I fear I bring bad news. Mr. Mannion's overseer has just ridden in from the Nepean—it seems that his master has been severely wounded. . . ."

"Wounded . . . ?" Conor was on her feet, pale and agitated, but it was not she who asked the obvious question.

"Wounded, Henry?" cried Mrs. Macquarie. "By whom? One of his convicts. . . ?"

"No, ma'am, the messenger says it happened in the hills west of the river."

"Ah!" exclaimed Mrs. Macquarie. "Natives!"

"Not natives, ma'am; it was a bullet wound, but it appears Mr. Mannion does not know who his assailant was. The shot came from behind some rocks, without warning, and he saw no one. But pray calm yourself, Mrs. Harvey, for we're assured that his life is not in danger."

Conor said slowly:

"He did not see his attacker. . . . He does not know. . . ." Seeing their eyes on her, she flushed slightly, and asked: "How did he reach home, Captain?"

"He was brought in late last night by two settlers, who found him being taken down the river by natives in a canoe. The overseer rode with Mr. Mannion's message to your house, ma'am, but finding Mr. Harvey absent, and being told by your servant that you were here, he . . ."

"He brought a written message from Mr. Mannion?"

"Yes—he is well enough to write, you see. But the man says he was bidden to deliver it only into your hands or Mr. Harvey's." Mrs. Macquarie checked Conor's blind movement towards the door.

"Come now, my love, you must sit down and let Henry bring you a glass of wine, for this has been a great shock. . . ."

"No—no thank you, ma'am—indeed I must go. I must drive to Beltrasna to-morrow, but in the meantime perhaps Dr. Redfern. . . ."

"The Governor," said Antill, "has already sent a message to Dr. Redfern begging him to ride to Beltrasna at once; he can be there by nightfall, or soon after."

"Then all will be well," said Mrs. Macquarie briskly. "Pray fetch Mrs. Harvey's cloak, Henry, and have the carriage sent round immediately. Now compose yourself, my love, and in a few moments Henry shall escort you home. An absconder, of course—my, we were just speaking of absconders as Henry came in! Have no fear—Macquarie will send out a detachment after the villain, and he'll soon be taken. Why, you're shivering, and pale as a ghost! Come closer to the fire, pray, till Henry returns with your cloak. . . ."

There had come to Conor a sudden poignant memory of her first husband's voice saying, as he prepared to ride out in search of absconders: "We shall have every man of them within an hour." He had captured but one, and that one she had seen a few hours later, hanging bloody and unconscious by his wrists from the flogging-post; that one had died before her eyes in the Beltrasna fields, spending his last breath in the pursuit of freedom. She could find small comfort in the promise that Johnny Prentice would be taken.

*   *   *   *

As his wife had prophesied, the Governor went through all the appropriate official motions in an attempt—unsuccessful, and not unduly prolonged—to track down the outlaw who had shot Mr. Mannion; but privately he considered that the young gentleman had invited his misfortune. To go out unaccompanied, unattended, on foot like a vagabond . . . ! Did he think the Governor had no better use for his military forces than to waste their time and shoe-leather in this fashion? Nevertheless he sent courteous enquiries for Mr. Mannion's health. When Dr. Redfern reported that there was no danger of the wound proving mortal, he expressed his pleasure. When the doctor added that it might cause a permanent lameness, he kept to himself the thought that such a disability could prove a boon if it precluded similar foolish adventures in the future.

He was, at the moment, a trifle impatient of independent explorers. Had he been a man to analyse his moods, he would have found this one as complex as most. He was not unaffected by the thought (which had also haunted his predecessors) that the legend of the impassability of the mountains had its value to an administrator who must keep a horde of felons under his eye. But there was also growing in him, with the daily exercise of autocratic power, a sense of possessiveness towards the colony which made him unwilling to allow any aspect of its development to pass beyond his own control. It was true that possessiveness bred a desire for more to be possessed; and not only duty, but inclination painted bright pictures of expanding territory. All the same, he would prefer the expansion to be directed by himself. If a few private individuals should push their way beyond the mountain wall, would not the dangerous thought be implanted in the minds of others that they could do likewise? In his own good time, therefore, in due order and with every proper safeguard established, he would break down this barrier himself. Meanwhile, it served its purpose.

But it was in the wind that Mr. Gregory Blaxland had notions of trying to effect a crossing, and there were reasons—though not of the kind to be immortalised in public despatches—why this prospect should inspire in His Excellency a certain peevishness not entirely accounted for either by his possessive attitude, or by his fears for the impregnability of his goal. It was true that on the occasion when the younger Blaxland had accompanied his party to the Warragombie, and propounded his theory that the mountains might be passed by keeping strictly to the summit of the main ridge, Macquarie had encouraged him, envisaging an expedition officially equipped, organised, and blessed. But that was before the return of Mr. John Blaxland; before the tiresome instructions from the home Government to investigate that gentleman's complaints of unjust treatment; before the commencement of that apparently interminable correspondence on the Blaxland brothers' capital and assets which was still plaguing him; before the conviction had matured in his mind that they had applied the favours granted to them in a manner which returned the least possible benefit to the colony. Having introduced themselves as agriculturalists, they had turned their whole attention to rearing cattle. The Governor had already made notes for an indictment of this pursuit which he would embody in a later despatch, and his objections to it were reinforced by a vague mistrust of grazing in general. Farming he could understand. It was stable and compact; large as some of the farming properties were, there was still room for them—and more. But grazing was different. It required vast areas of land. It made men restless, it made them wanderers, it awakened an insatiable craving for new country and new pastures.

It could not, therefore, be simply said that it was his possessiveness, his fear of an escape-route for the convicts, his suspicions of a profitable pursuit which might over-stimulate an embarrassing wanderlust, or his personal dislike of the Blaxlands which caused his present lack of enthusiasm for independent exploration. Each emotion reinforced the others—but all had been exacerbated of late by personal stresses which frayed his nerves, and magnified his anxieties.

In laying down their requirements for a Viceroy, no allowance could be made by His Majesty's Ministers for the cross-current of emotion which bedevil lesser mortals. He might suffer blow after blow to his ardent hopes of fatherhood; he might endure the keenest anxieties for his wife's health; he might pass night after night in restless vigil by her bedside—but the theory of delegated authority demanded that he remain unaffected by such trivialities. Life and nature were not, however, concerned with theories. To them His Excellency was a man like any other, susceptible to the ravages of worry, disappointment and sleeplessness, and they had blended these domestic trials with all his other doubts and annoyances to such effect that now the mere name of Blaxland was enough to cause him a spasm of irritation.

Such an attitude was reasonable in the sense that Nature itself is reasonable, operating through the inevitability of cause and effect, and seeking no other justification; but like most men, the Governor felt the need to justify his moods even if he did not trouble to examine them. Mr. Mannion's misadventure, having no connection with the enterprise said to be contemplated by Mr. Blaxland, had, nevertheless, for psychological purposes, the connection that both were exploration, and His Excellency was thus enabled to say inwardly, with a certain gloomy satisfaction: "You see . . . ? Nothing but a nuisance!"

But all this was no more than a slight shadow over a prospect which still looked bright enough. His most recent despatch from Lord Liverpool had been benign in tone, commending him in general terms for his administration, and, to his pleasure, confirming the appointments of Wentworth and Redfern which he had recommended. There had of course been the customary expression of pained surprise at the increase in expenditure; the customary hope had been expressed that no public buildings not strictly necessary had been commenced, and a note of caution had been sounded on the subject of roads. But his eye passed lightly over admonitions which might, if taken too literally, cramp and curtail his soaring plans. "*I trust that mere speculation of improvement will not induce you to incur any unnecessary expense. . . .*" Of course not; he knew his duty; the most careful economy would be practised. But roads and buildings—those two enterprises so brightly dear to his heart, and beyond all others the signs and portents of civilisation—surely *they* must be allowed as indispensable to a growing colony . . . !

*   *   *   *

Conor—but the day before returned from a visit to Beltrasna—was on her knees before a large trunk, taking out some clothes which had been folded away since her marriage, and consulting with Emily how they might be altered. ". . . for you know, I shall be quite at a loss when you have left me—I have little skill with anything but embroideries, and I fear even less patience."

"But ma'am, I could come and sew for you."

"You will have much to occupy you in your own house, I expect.

But perhaps you may do so sometimes, if your husband will bring you to Sydney."

She saw the quick shadow that seemed to pass over the girl's face whenever Dean was mentioned, and a hint in her eyes of the tears that lately were never far away. She went on hastily: "Oh, my, how thin and fine all these fabrics are! Why did I not favour something more useful? You know, Emily, in Europe the ladies will wear nothing else, even in the cold weather, and the doctors call the complaint it brings on the muslin disease. Of course in this climate. . . . What it is, child. . . ?"

"Oh, ma'am," sobbed Emily, "I don't want to leave you—indeed I don't!"

Conor sat back on her heels and spoke severely.

"Now Emily, compose yourself and be sensible, pray. You wish to be married, do you not?"

"Ye-es, ma'am, but. . . ."

"Is it perhaps that all has been arranged too hurriedly? You must not take so grave a step in haste, or before you have given it careful thought, and it's even now not too late to reflect again. Would you prefer to wait some months, until . . . ?"

"Oh, no, ma'am, I couldn't do that! I mean it's been read out in the Church, and Dean's spoke to the parson, and it's only a few days now. . . ." Tears overwhelmed her again. "It's just that I don't want to leave you, ma'am."

Conor sighed.

"If you are married of course you must go with your husband, so let us have no more of this very foolish behaviour. See, now, I've found what I was really looking for. Tell me—do you like it?"

Emily took her hands down from her flushed face and looked miserably from still-brimming eyes at the little sandal-wood box her mistress was holding out to her.

"Yes, ma'am, it's real p-p-pretty."

"Is it not? Take it, child. See the garlands of flowers carved on the top, and the little birds holding them at each corner."

"Oh, ma'am, it *is* pretty!" Emily examined it with curiosity and growing delight. "And there's writing on the sides. . . ."

"Turn it round and read it—see, it begins here in front."

Holding it up to the light from the window, Emily read slowly:

> "Diligent and prudent maid,
> Make your stitches small and neat,
> So you shall appear arrayed
> Fair and seemly as is meet."

"It's a workbox," Conor explained, "and it was given to me by my dear father when I was a little girl."

"Can I look inside, ma'am?"

"Yes, of course."

"Oh, law!" breathed Emily, entranced. "See the lovely blue satin! And all the little pockets for the reels of thread! And the needlecase, and the blue satin pincushion! And the scissors and thimble and bodkin all fixed in their own places in the lid . . . they look . . . My, ma'am, are they . . . gold . . . ?"

"Yes, they're gold, Emily. But I fear even a gold thimble never made me as good a sempstress as you are. So I want you to have this box as a present at your marriage."

"Oh!" whispered Emily, awed. "Me, ma'am . . . ? A gold thimble . . . ?"

Conor laughed.

"If you can get it on your finger, for it's rather small."

"Oh, I can, ma'am—see, it goes on beautiful. . . ."

"So it does—how fortunate! But we have spent far too much time over this trunk, and the master will be wanting his dinner before it's ready unless you make haste. Take the box, now, and put it away."

Emily scrambled to her feet.

"Yes, ma'am, thank you, ma'am." She paused in the doorway, holding her present tenderly in both hands, and her face was so radiant that Conor thought with relief: "Mrs. Macquarie was right—it's nothing but vapours!" Emily repeated almost inaudibly: "Thank you, ma'am," and disappeared.

Conor rose and shut down the lid of the trunk. She had found a new servant—a stupid, clumsy, cheerful girl called Hannah from a Hawkesbury farm—but she would miss Emily. She had suggested to Patrick that Dilboong and her child should be transferred to her from Beltrasna, putting forward as her reason that now, with Robert to tend as well as Desmond, she was in need of a nurse besides a servant for domestic work; but it was in her mind, also, that such a separation might be desirable not only for Patrick's sake, but for Dilboong's. She had been pleased that he seemed to approve the notion; that unfortunate affair was, apparently, over, and she felt sure that Dilboong would welcome a change which reunited her with Desmond, who had been her nursling. It should be accomplished as soon as possible—and then it would only remain for some charming and accomplished young lady to appear and capture Patrick's heart. . . .

Her mind was still full of the story he had told her, but there had been much more to tell than the mere story. Propped on his pillows, and still suffering considerable pain, he had found the telling difficult.

"Since this happened I have been asking myself what my object really was. I had thought it merely to find Prentice and avert further violence and bloodshed; to persuade him from a course which could only be fatal to himself in the end; even to offer him some different mode of life. . . ." He frowned. "Of that last I thought little, and never deeply—perhaps because I knew that it would lead me to an unwelcome conclusion . . . ? Can we thus declare ourselves . . . ? I see now that a whole cannot be unmade and re-fashioned in an instant by a good intention. Prentice is what he has become. Could I suddenly take into my service such a person—a stranger—from nowhere—unskilled in any trade—unaccustomed to the usages of our society . . . ? How should I explain him? There is no place for him in any life I could provide—it is no longer his kind of life. Then what did I hope to accomplish? By persuasion—exhortation—no doubt by the expression of high moral principles, to change him from an outlaw to—what? How does an outlaw live, save by behaving as an outlaw? What meaning can he attach to moral principles designed to guide us *in society*—of which he is no part? When I consider these things I realise that I was seeking him not for his sake, but for my own."

Conor had protested then:

"No, no—you are unjust to yourself!"

He shrugged and shook his head.

"I grant myself good intentions. I grant myself pity, humanity, a careless sort of benevolence. But I was content to assume, without adequate reflection, that my wealth and my station in life would prove as powerful in this matter as they have in every other. It's not easy for one in my class and position to admit helplessness. It's even less easy to confess that when I sought Prentice I went not with real favours or benefits in my hands, but in order to win my own peace of mind by offering him empty words. . . ."

She cried indignantly:

"You were prepared to offer him goodwill, Patrick. You have not only offered it, but proved it. He would have murdered you in cold blood, but when you could have killed him, justly claiming self-defence, you did not do so. You would not even then betray his name or his existence. Three times you have shielded him. . . ."

He interrupted with slight impatience:

"Three times I have assuaged my own conscience. Shielded him? In a sense that may be so. A word from me would have set the soldiers on his heels, and I did not speak it. But I think the hunt would have been unsuccessful. He has not survived for twenty years in the bush without providing himself with some safe place of retreat, and it's abundantly plain that the natives are his friends. No, I have afforded him no positive help; at best, I have merely done him the negative service of leaving him to his savage existence. And I can do no more." He went on, after a pause: "Yet how savage is it? You recall that we were never quite sure whether he could have made any contact with his father, the convict, Andrew Prentice, who had absconded some years earlier? We thought not, but in any case it could have been only the briefest, for the man met his death almost immediately after the child's disappearance. But there was some such contact; I have proof of it now."

"He told you?"

"Not in words. I saw it when I encountered him in the cave, though I did not think of it then." He smiled wryly. "There was little time for thinking. Perhaps you remember my father's account of the incident when the native woman and her child were in danger of drowning, and Andrew Prentice rescued them? You recall his description of a necklace she was wearing—one made of round, brass objects, like buttons. . . ? Johnny was wearing it about his neck; I think there could hardly be another like it. And he was also wearing a key. . . ."

"A key, Patrick?"

"A key—such as one used for the lock of a door. What does that mean? Nothing, perhaps? He has grown up among the natives, and we know that they wear all kinds of strange objects as adornments. But it suggests possibilities, does it not? A hut somewhere . . . ? Possessions . . . ? So I ask myself—how savagely does he live?"

The next morning, as though there had been no interval, he had returned so abruptly to the subject that she knew the night could have afforded him no respite from the inexorably turning wheel of his thoughts.

"What his life is, or has been, I don't know, save that it has held episodes of violence which should be—and are—repugnant to me. Yet I feel he has lived it to better purpose than I have lived mine. You protest? I have not lived my life; I have merely suffered it to carry me along—but his . . . ? Such as it may be, he has made it himself, and we may suppose from what we know that it has held some emotions less rude and uncivilised than we should look for in the life of a desperate outlaw, a brutal murderer. . . . In some manner he must have earned the loyalty of the savages who so steadfastly conceal and succour him . . . even felt, perhaps, some tenderness for the poor native woman he avenged. And it is plain—had you heard his voice when he accused me, you could not doubt it—that he cherished at least one friendship. . . ."

"Ah, yes," she had said sadly, "Finn. I can understand that he may well have found a friend in Finn."

*   *   *   *

The marriage of Emily to Joseph Dean was duly solemnized on a dull, midwinter day in the presence of Mr. and Mrs. Harvey. Emily had summoned to her aid that spirit which Dean had promised himself the pleasure of breaking, and maintained throughout the ceremony an air which was near enough to what might have been expected of a happy maiden on her bridal day. The pride she felt in the affection and solicitude of her late employers, and in the new gown of blue bombazine and the white bonnet trimmed with blue ribbons which they had given her, was real, however, and so apparent that Dean found it irritating. He resolved to teach her without delay that she was no longer the indulged protegée of gentlefolk, but a farmer's wife who must wear what he pleased to give her, and do as he commanded.

"Did they give ye nought else but the gown and the bonnet?" he demanded as they left the toll-gates behind, and set out in his cart along the road to Parramatta. "Ye'll have little use for such things now, and I daresay . . ."

He had been about to shatter her by declaring his intention of selling them, but the implied criticism, and his disparaging tone, made her interrupt hotly:

"Indeed they did give me more! The master gave me a writing desk —he said I write a good hand now, and I mustn't forget what he learned me; and Mr. Cowper gave me a Bible because he knew I can read, and bid me read a chapter every day, and so I will, for the practice, though it's hard to know what it means; and the mistress gave me a work-box. . . ."

He burst into a loud guffaw, inspired partly by genuine contempt, and partly by a desire to belittle skills which he could not claim himself.

"That's a fine lot of presents!" he jeered. "Ah, ye can trust the gentry to fool a little ninny with a lot of smiles and a lot of trash so they don't have to put their hands too deep in their pockets!"

"Don't ye call me a ninny!" she blazed. "It's no trash they've given me, but things the like of what they use themselves. It was the mistress' own father give her the workbox, and there's no lady in the land has one as good! The scissors and the thimble's real gold! Ye're a blockhead y'self, to talk that way!"

He looked at her with sudden sharp attention.

"Gold, eh?" His eyes slid to the bulky package lying between her feet. "Brass, more like," he sneered.

Then, as he had wished, nothing would satisfy her until he had stopped the cart while she untied cords, unwound wrappings, and displayed her treasures. Aye, he thought, fingering the trifles in the workbox, they were gold, all right. And the writing desk—that was worth something too; old, but handsome, made of some dark, sofly-polished wood, with elaborately chased silver corners, and a strong silver clasp. He allowed her to enjoy her little triumph for a while, watching her sardonically as she carefully re-wrapped and re-tied her package. Not until they were moving again did he remark casually:

"They'll fetch a pretty penny, I shouldn't wonder."

He glanced at her sideways. Her poke bonnet hid her face and robbed him of enjoyment until he noticed that her hands had begun to tremble in her lap. He went on reflectively: "There's a man I know from one of the ships that'll give me a good price for stuff the like of that."

Still she said nothing. His anger began to rise, but with it rose the pleasurable excitement he always felt upon confronting a stubbornness to be overcome. They went on in a tense, unbroken silence, and he thought: "Sulkin', eh? She'll find that don't answer!" It was twilight by the time they reached Parramatta and passed through it on to the western road; the sky was overcast, and it was growing cold. A few miles beyond the town he turned off along a disused cart track, and pulled up in a little hollow from which neither road nor habitation was visible. He tied the reins and climbed down.

"Ye can wait here," he told her. "I've a bit of business with a man that lives yonder over the hill." In the dusk he saw her quick glance about her, and read it as if she had spoken. Bound to him as she was, not only by the solemn ritual of marriage, but by the child she was carrying, she still felt an impulse to escape. Yet she had never before in her life been out of a town, and though she was afraid of him, she was also afraid of this unfamiliar solitude, of the long, deserted road, and the darkness closing in. She would wait, he decided, but another strand to hold her would not come amiss. He reached over and pulled the package from beneath her feet.

"No sense in leavin' vallybles where they might be stole," he remarked, tucking it under his arms. "There's plenty vagabonds roamin' about these parts that'd murder a woman for a gold thimble and think nothin' of it."

She said rather breathlessly:

"Ye'll bring it back?"

"Oh, aye, I'll bring it back—there's no one here could give me the worth of it." He turned and set off up the hill. Over its crest there was, indeed, a hut, but it had been long abandoned. The one for which he was bound lay a full half-mile beyond it, well hidden in the scrub, and occupied only on certain nights when its owner was in attendance to dispose of the product of his illicit still. Dean was, in general, no drinking man, but to-night he must keep out the cold and pass the time while his wife digested her first lesson.

An hour later it began to rain. Emily, already chilled to the bone, and terrified of the lonely night, peered anxiously up the hill, but there was no sign of her returning husband. Her gown—her lovely new gown —would be spoiled; already the brim of her bonnet was limp. Frightened as she was, she was angry too, and she resolved that he should not have the satisfaction of finding her helpless, soaking and bedraggled. The old sailcloth which he used to cover his farm produce in wet weather was lying folded on the floor of the cart among empty crates; she climbed over the seat and set about stacking these, and arranging the canvas over them to form a small shelter, into which, at last, she crawled, to lie curled up and shivering, with her head pillowed on her valise, and her precious bonnet placed carefully beside her, with a handkerchief to protect it from the dirty boards. It seemed to her that she lay thus for hours while the rain pattered steadily on the sagging canvas, and she dabbed at the drips which fell through it on to her soiled and disordered gown. After a time she sank into an uneasy half doze, and was aroused by a flash of lightning, followed by a loud clap of thunder. Almost immediately she heard Dean's voice calling angrily through the sound of rain which was now a downpour, and she thrust her dishevelled head out to answer him with all the pent-up fury of her long and wretched vigil.

"Aye, I'm here, the more's the pity, and here I stay! I hope ye're soaked to y' worthless bones! I wish ye'd have slipped and broke y' bloody neck! Where's me things?"

He was indeed drenched to the skin, cold, and a little drunk, though sober enough to be worried about the turn events had taken. He had not reckoned on the weather, and the creek between his farm and the road might be up over the track before they could reach it; though it would fall as quickly as it rose, they might well be stranded on the wrong side of it for as long as the rain continued. He threw the package in to her with a few snarling words which she could not hear, and climbed hur-riedly to his seat. She felt the cart jolt and sway along the track. By the time they reached the road the storm was at its height, and the rain a deluge. She was already bruised and jarred; two of the boxes had slipped, allowing the canvas to sag still more until it was almost on top of her, but it still afforded some protection. She did not know how long they travelled on the road; she was so tired, sore and unhappy that she wept a little, but passed much of the time in planning how she would hide her presents from him—dig a hole in the ground, maybe, and bury them—and then, though he raged and threatened, though he beat her, though he killed her, she would never tell him where they were—never, never. . . .

When the cart halted again she peered out fearfully, expecting to see some kind of house which was to be her future home and prison. But they had stopped, it appeared, somewhere in the bush. In the pitch darkness she could see nothing except that there were tall trees all about them; the rain had ceased, there was a sound of rushing water, and Dean was cursing furiously. Presently she heard him come round to the back of the cart; he began to rearrange the boxes, and did something with a long pole that lifted the canvas and held it taut, sloping from the middle to form a tent. Then he thrust his head inside and said:

"Well, we've a wait ahead of us till the creek goes down, so we'll make the best of it. There's room for y' husband in that snug little bed o' yours, eh?"

She struggled for a time. When she realised that this only increased his enjoyment the last of her youthful naïveté left her, and she developed, in the space of an instant, the bitter techniques of a more subtle resistance. He was in a black, raging mood when he left her at last, and she lay exhausted, seeing through the opening of the canvas that the first hint of dawn was lightening the sky.

It was almost full daylight when, after packing the soft, muddy bed of the creek with stones and logs, he got the cart across it, and up the slippery bank on the other side. She paid no attention to what he was doing, ignored him when he called angrily to her to help him, lay motionless and indifferent in a stupor of pain and weariness as he climbed into his seat once more, shook the reins, and flogged the tired horse forward. The sky was still heavy with cloud, and a thin, wet mist made the trees look ghostly. Only the creaking of the cart and the sound of the horse's hoofs broke the profound silence, and her eyelids were beginning to close when the sound of a shot startled her awake. Dean's voice uttered a kind of strangled shout; she heard something thud heavily to the ground, and felt the cart lurch as the horse reared and shied.

*   *   *   *

Johnny had chosen a spot where the track passed along the base of a small, rocky hillock, and here, on high ground from which he could see the cart approaching, and fire down upon his victim from a distance of only a few yards, he had waited, well hidden by a burnt-out tree-trunk, and a clump of wattle already sprinkled with early blossom. He had kept watch last night, cold and impatient, but dry enough in the lee of the rocks, until he realised that the cart could not cross the creek till its stormwaters fell. The delay was annoying, for he had planned to kill Dean and be on his way back to his own territory by morning; glimpses of white men working in their fields had made him strangely eager for the feel of a hoe or a spade in his own hands, and the sight of his own-turned earth. He toyed with the idea of surprising Dean at the creek, but decided against it; he was already as near to the road as he cared to go.

The mood of fury which had driven him from his retreat had cooled now. His encounter with Patrick Mannion had shaken him—not only because he had bungled it, but because it had confused his thinking. He had felt this confusion first when, lying helpless on the floor of the cave, he had seen the musket which could have killed him thrown away. Its effect was as yet no more than to arouse his old, instinctive desire to escape from what he could not understand, and to awaken a nostalgia for his own place, where solitude now seemed a small price to pay for freedom from the intolerable complications of human relationships. Yet having resolved to kill Dean, it did not even occur to him to depart without doing so, and therefore he had bided his time at the native camp, curbing his impatience, determined not to make, a second time, the mistake of attempting more than his strength would allow. Billalong had retrieved the two muskets from the rocks below the cave, but they were damaged beyond use, and Johnny had thrown them in the river. With the aid of the natives, he had stolen from outlying farms some seeds, nails, and a few small tools to take back with him, and these he had left in Billalong's care, wrapped in an old blanket stolen from a shepherd's hut; it was possible, he thought, that the cart for which he was now waiting would yield him further booty. Without a quickening of breath he had heard the creak of its approaching wheels; waited, almost with detachment, while it came towards him through the misty, morning light; and fired with implacable accuracy when the moment came.

He watched Dean's body slump sideways, fall heavily to the ground, and lie sprawling. The horse, after its first frightened plunge, stood quietly enough, so he jumped down the bank, bent over Dean's body to assure himself that his aim had been good enough, reached up to possess himself of the musket lying beneath the seat, and went round to the back of the cart in search of spoil.

The first thing he saw was a small, dirty hand on the end of a blue-clad arm, reaching out to push aside the canvas covering—a woman's hand. His heart, whose steady beat had not altered while he committed murder, now fairly leapt in his chest. Emily thrust her head through the opening, stared wildly at him for a moment, and then, retreating into her shelter again, began to scream. In the hushed, early morning silence of the bush the sound was so shocking that it threw Johnny into a panic; he wanted only to get away—far away—out of earshot, and he had actually turned to run before he realised that this woman had seen him, could describe him, could set upon his trail avenging settlers and soldiers who, for the first time, would know exactly what kind of man they were seeking.

He thrust his pistol in his belt, and examined the musket; it was, as he expected, loaded. Now the thought of killing made his heart pound and his hands shake, but as he turned back, holding his weapon ready, he was savagely desiring the death of this woman not so much because it would rid him of a danger, as because it would silence those nerve-shattering screams. He thrust the canvas aside and dragged her out; as she emerged, struggling, in a flurry of blue skirts and white petticoats, he had a glimpse of a tear-stained face and a pair of terrified dark eyes before her cloud of disordered hair hid them. She stopped screaming suddenly and bit his hand.

In shock and rage, he released her for an instant, and she made blindly for the bank. He stood stupidly, knowing that this was the moment to shoot her, while she was scrambling and stumbling up the steep, boulder-strewn slope, but so bemused and confused by the mere sight of her that he could only stare. She gained the top and plunged on through the low scrub, frantic with fear. A distraught glance over her shoulder showed her there was no pursuit, but she heard him call out, between fury and derision: "Where will ye run to?" Within the next few paces she had begun to hesitate. All about her there was nothing to be seen but trees, trees, trees. . . . There might be no one within miles to answer a cry for help. . . . She paused, gasping and sobbing, to look back again. He was following now, and she realised with despair that she could not hope to outdistance him—far less the musket if he chose to use it. She turned, trembling, to face him.

Had she known it, she was less afraid than he, but it took her some time to discover this interesting fact. He halted a few yards away, glaring at her with a ferocity which—with the man he had killed lying face downward nearby—she had reason enough to find alarming. She did not yet know that to Johnny nothing was more enraging—because nothing was more mysterious—than his own fear. He had very rarely been frightened since his early childhood, and then always by intangible things —by glimpses in himself or in others of incomprehensible emotions, by vague responses he had felt to the magic and sorceries of his native friends, by moments of receptive awareness when earth and sky and wind seemed to speak, and he, without understanding, knew that there was something to be understood. But now? What was there in a slight girl with huge, dark-ringed eyes, to arouse at once a terror which urged him to run as for his life, and a fascination which held him rooted to the ground, and began to send through him thin streaks of almost painful excitement? To desire a woman was a simple matter, and one which he was well accustomed to recognise in himself, but this agony of confusion which now possessed him was far more than that. He had not spoken to a white woman for more than twenty years. Sometimes, at Green Hills, he had seen them at a distance, eyed them with furtive wonder, lingered for a time where he thought one might pass; but since he had decamped as a child of eight from Mr. Stephen Mannion's house, the words which suddenly began to tumble incoherently from Emily's lips were the first a white woman had addressed to him.

"Don't ye point that thing at me, ye nasty, murderin' vagabond! Killin' people while they're goin' quiet about their business! A bush-ranger ye must be, like I've heard tell of—well, ye can put a bullet in me too, if you want, but ye'll hang for it if ye do, for me master and mistress'll never rest till ye're taken! And what's more, I'll haunt, for there's no hallowed ground here for me to lie, and them that lies un-hallowed allus haunts! Lucky ye were that I didn't get to me husband's gun before ye did, or ye'd have done some hauntin' y'self, never mind that I've not fired one off before! I'd have got ye all right, not bein' one of y' snivellin' women that takes on at a bang, only when I'm wakened out of me sleep sudden-like, when any woman might be put about for a while, and the more when she sees such an ugly, dirty, red-headed varmint. . . ."

"Stop!" shouted Johnny furiously, finding this deluge of shrilly-uttered words hardly less maddening than her screams. He waved the musket at her, and it was this gesture, aimless and distracted, which enlightened her. The incredible knowledge dawned upon her mind that he simply did not know how to proceed. For some reason he did not want to kill her, and he did not know how else to dispose of her. He did not even know what to say. Fear of death began to recede, but fear of life began gradually to return. What now? She eyed him warily. He was bare-footed, and wore, besides a pair of ragged and dirty trousers, nothing but two surprising and incongruous objects round his neck—a key threaded on a loop of hide, and a strange necklace made of old brass buttons. He was as tall as Dean, but less bulky, though his shoulders were broad, and his arms thick and muscular. His face, burned to a deep, reddish brown, had a wide, thin-lipped mouth, a straight nose, and dark eyes beneath brows which scored a black line across his forehead. His hair and the stubble on his chin were red. For a bloodthirsty bushranger, he looked oddly nonplussed and bewildered. She said tentatively:

"If ye let me go, I'll not inform on ye. . . ."

His senses came back to him. He had heard of informers during his clandestine visits to Green Hills while the rebellion was brewing years ago; he recalled Finn's guess that they had been at work when his plans to release Beltrasna prisoners went awry; it had been a word often on Finn's tongue, and spoken always with a depth of hatred and contempt not even exceeded in his references to *Them*. It rang now in Johnny's mind like a warning bell, and his face grew even darker. But Emily, anxious to conciliate, eager to prove her understanding of the desperate shifts to which men might be driven, went on disastrously:

"Ye've escaped, I reckon—well, there's many does, and some not taken. Ye'd be from a road-gang? Or maybe ye're no convict at all, but a sailor . . .? I've hear them say there's some that deserts the ships. . . ."

Her voice trailed off uneasily, for his expression was frightening. Sly devils, informers were, pretending friendship, feigning sympathy, cheating information from a man that they might sell it to his enemies. . . . He might have left her here to be found by some settler—to run off with her tale to *Them*. . . .

Suddenly he hated her. He took a few strides forward and grabbed her by the wrist. She struggled madly, struck him in the face with her fist, kicked at him, pulling, twisting, and straining against his hold—and began to scream again. He dropped the musket and hit her hard on the side of the head with his open hand; her screams were cut off abruptly as she staggered, tripped over her skirt, and fell; but Johnny's indecision was at an end. The situation was no longer mysterious, and therefore no longer alarming; his own action had resolved his perplexities, for this was, after all, a kind of scene with which he had long been familiar. Did it not represent merely the normal pattern of man's mating with woman, the ritual of his courtship, the preliminary expression of his desire, the appropriate demonstration of her reluctance? How many rebellious women had he not seen cuffed into docility—transformed by a display of male dominance into patterns of contented wifehood?

He stood looking down at her and breathing fast, shaken by the thought that he had a woman again—and a white woman, who would not flee from the evil spirits in his hut. . . . He said shortly:

"Get up, and we'll be goin'."

She was sobbing quietly, her face buried in her hands, but she looked up at this, and asked fearfully: "Where?"

"To—to. . . ." He had no name for his image of home. He said impatiently: "To my place where I live."

She was so puzzled by this that she stopped weeping, like a child whose attention had been deflected from its woe by some surprising sight. A place where he lived . . . it had a strangely settled sound, almost a respectable sound, difficult to reconcile with the notion of bushrangers, outlaws, murderers. . . . She asked suspiciously:

"What s-sort of place?"

"A place with a house—what would ye think?" He glared at her.

"Ye've got a house?" Her eyes strayed to the key on his breast.

"I said so—can't ye hear? And I'm wantin' to get back to it, so stop y' talk, and. . . ."

"Is it a . . . a farm?"

He bawled furiously:

"Aye, it's a farm! Now get up off the ground and come when I bid ye, or I'll fetch ye a belt that'll stop ye gettin' up at all!"

He hauled her ungently to her feet, making a movement as if to strike her again when she began to resist. She made no further attempt to release herself, but stood her ground, the tears drying on her cheeks, and said with determination:

"I reckon I must go with ye if ye say so, though it's not far we'll be gettin' before the sojers catch up with ye! But I'll not go without me things—aye, ye can hit me again, but till I get me things I'll not stir from this spot without ye carry me!"

He released her with a baffled gesture of irritation. Women! Men could never move without being delayed by their refusal to leave behind some coolamon, some digging-stick, some basket or bag, some child's toy or trifling ornament. . . ! Scowling, he picked up the musket and marched her back to the cart, noticing that though she passed round it to avoid the dead man lying on the ground, her sideways glance expressed aversion rather than grief or fear. He stood by impatiently while she dragged out her valise and her treasured package. He stared in astonishment at a third object—light, white, and curiously shaped, adorned with long strips of stuff that matched the blue of her gown; the women at Green Hills had been content with a kerchief tied over their heads, and he was dumb-founded when she set it carefully upon her head, and tied the blue ribbon beneath her chin. Its long, forward-thrusting brim completely hid her face, and in his curiosity he bent slightly to peer beneath it, realising for the first time that she was pleasant to look at; absurd, but pleasant. . . .

He pulled the canvas aside and hunted quickly through the contents of the cart. The crates were all empty and there was nothing that could be of use except a new iron cooking pot. This he snatched up hurriedly and handed to her, his mind already full of plans for the route he would take back to the river, and anxiety because his escape would undoubtedly be more difficult with the woman than alone. Under the seat he found ammunition, which he took, and a bottle of rum, which he ignored. He said sharply:

"Well, ye've got y' things—now come!"

He set off, only to turn in a fury when he realised that she was not following. She was holding the valise in one hand and the package under the same arm; the other hand held the cooking pot, and she was staring from it to him with an expression of surprised indignation.

"Would ye leave me carry a load o' things like this? Here, take y' cookin'-pot y'self! If ye can steal it, ye can carry it!"

He went back and stood over her menacingly.

"Do ye think I'll wait about and get meself taken while ye gabble foolishness? If ye don't want to end the way *he* did, ye'd best come when I bid ye—and come quick!"

He strode off again, outraged. A man went ahead, carrying weapons; a woman followed, carrying burdens. Such was the accepted and un-alterable rule of family life. He glanced back angrily over his shoulder; this time she was following.

*   *   *   *

Having prepared himself for difficulties and dangers to be overcome before he could convey his captive beyond the bounds of civilisation, Johnny was pleasantly surprised by the good fortune that attended him. On the other hand, he had not reckoned on the trouble that a white woman could cause merely by being a white woman; though he made irritated allowance for the skirt which encumbered her walking, he darkly suspected her of a deliberate intent to delay him. Her alarming con-spicuousness kept his nerves uncomfortably stretched; how could one hope to hide, if the necessity arose, in company with a creature who stood out from the shadowy monotones of the bush in a way which could not fail to catch the eye of even a distant observer? Also, it seemed at the be-ginning that she would never stop talking. She pleaded with him to walk more slowly; she complained of the weight of her burdens; she lamented that her shoes were hurting her; she paused to examine and bewail every new rent in her gown; she enquired over and over again how much farther they must go; she referred a dozen times to the soldiers who must even now be on their trail, and described in some detail a hanging which she had seen at Sydney. But by the time they came near the river, having heard no sounds of pursuit, nor seen any sign of human habitation save, in the distance, the ploughed fields of a lonely farm, she had fallen silent, and Johnny's anxieties were fading.

Soon after midday they fell in with his tribe, and he paused to collect his belongings, tell them of the success of his mission, and explain the presence of his astonishing companion. He noticed with a curious stirring of satisfaction that she seemed afraid, and stood close to him, as if for protection, though she was hungry enough by now to eat a little of the food they offered. She stared when he began to converse with them in their own tongue. It was clear to her that she was the subject of the discussion, for they looked at her with interest, and one young man presently came to squat beside her as she sat wearily on a log, and spoke, to her surprise, in tolerable English. "Billalong," he said, laying his hand on his breast. "Name Billalong. Good you go along Dyonn-ee, my brother." And two youths joined him, bending down to grin into her face, uttered strange words which appeared to be their names, and add, pointing to her captor: "Brother—brother." They chattered, then, among themselves, agreeing that this was a most happy solution to Dyonn-ee's wifeless existence, and the women clustered round her, grinning and gab-bling, stretching out their hands to touch the bright stuff of her skirt, bending to peer up the long funnel of her bonnet brim, and shriek with laughter.

She tried to draw away at first, repelled by their nakedness and dirti-ness, but she was so tired that she became, at last, almost indifferent, desiring nothing but rest and sleep. Already, once, she had privily dropped the cooking-pot as she walked behind Johnny, but it had struck a stone in falling, and the sound made him turn his head. He was so angry that she had feared he might make her leave behind, instead, her own possessions, so she had stumbled on drearily, and ceased to complain. It appeared now, when they began to move again, that some of these grotesque women were prepared to help her carry her burdens, but though she gladly surrendered the cooking-pot and the valise, she clung obstinately to her package, and walked on in the middle of a noisy group till they reached the river-bank. She learned, to her incredulous horror, that she was expected to enter one of the flimsy bark canoes, two of which were already pushing out.

Johnny pulled her forward.

"Ye'll not drown if ye sit still. But if ye struggle ye well might, and I give ye fair warnin' of it. Ye'll go with Gooradoo, for he's lighter than I am—but if ye play the fool and upset the canoe, he'll swim off and leave ye."

Gooradoo, who had manœuvred his craft into the soft mud, nodded beaming agreement, and immediately began an elaborate pantomime of drowning; his hands flailed the surface of imaginary water, his eyes rolled, he gasped, spluttered, contorted his face horribly, uttered a strangled cry and sank downward to his knees, his struggles growing more feeble till his outstretched arms seemed to hang and sway like weeds at the mercy of some drifting current. Amid the laughter and applause with which the natives greeted this performance, Johnny said peremptorily: "Get in!" Emily gathered her skirts together, picked her way through the mud, and obeyed, trembling.

They made camp after dark that night on a high ridge from which nothing could be seen but a confusion of tree-covered hills and gullies.

Emily was too exhausted to eat much of the food they offered, but too cold and frightened to sleep. She spent the greater part of the night crouching over the small cooking fire the natives had made, and feeding it from time to time with twigs. Once, believing them all asleep, she rose and tried to creep away, but Johnny, without moving, said: "Come back, ye little fool! Ye'd not find y' way by daylight—do ye want to fall over a cliff in the dark and break y' neck?" She returned to the fire and lay down beside it, weeping softly. She dozed a little, and woke at dawn, stiff and shivering, to find her captors already astir.

Here the women and several of the men left them; Johnny and Emily went on with Billalong and the two other young natives who had proclaimed themselves to be a white man's brothers. They walked all that day, save when she sank to the ground, sobbing that she could go no farther, and then they would allow her only the briefest of rests. The three young natives were friendly, and, after some argument which, she guessed, concerned the slowness of her pace, Johnny permitted them to carry the cooking-pot and the valise. But by nightfall, when the little party had descended a long, steep hill to the banks of another river, they set all their burdens on the ground, held a brief conversation with Johnny, turned back up the hill, and vanished.

The river, at this spot, ran no more than knee deep over a bank of stones and boulders, and Johnny, adding the blanket-wrapped bundle to his own load, which consisted of the musket, three spears, a wommerah and his firesticks, bade her pick up the rest, and without further ado, waded into it, signing to her to follow. She stumbled after him, her feet sliding on the slippery, water-worn stones, trying to keep her balance, and hold her skirts above her knees. Her sudden cry of distress made him turn to see her sitting in mid-stream, sobbing hysterically, the cooking-pot abandoned, the valise half submerged, but the package still held high and dry above the water. With an impatient exclamation he returned, retrieved the pot, hauled her to her feet, and guided her across with a hand beneath her elbow. She collapsed exhaustedly on the short, rough grass, still whimpering a little, and watching out of the corner of her eye while her incredible captor did mysterious things with two sticks, causing a thin smoke to rise from a little heap of shredded bark, which presently burst into flame. He ignored her when she came closer, shivering with cold, and spreading her wet skirts to its comforting warmth. By the time it was ready to cook a slab of meat which he produced from among a miscellany of other objects in the blanket, she was nearly dry. She ate a few mouthfuls, too tired to notice his silence. When she had finished eating she went down to the river, drank thirstily, and turned back to find herself suddenly pinioned in a clumsy, fierce embrace.

It was well after sunrise when she wakened the next morning from a sleep so profound that it seemed to have wiped out memory, and she lay motionless for a few minutes staring vaguely up at a blue sky. She felt bruised from head to foot, and every bone in her body ached; she was stiff with cold, though the old blanket lay over her, and the fire was still burning near her feet. She lifted her head cautiously, and saw Johnny squatting beside it, feeding flames which were made colourless by the sunlight, though beneath its touch his hair seemed ablaze. The thought of escape, which had hammered in her mind ever since her capture, now returned to her, but she did no more than toy with it for a moment. The river wound through a deep gorge, and its densely-timbered hills towered above her on all sides. Suppose that she could slip away unnoticed—suppose that, having done so, she could summon enough strength to evade his pursuit—how would she find her way? What would she eat? She realised dully that, desperate as her situation was with this murderous outlaw, it might well be more desperate still without him.

She lay still, therefore, watching him, perplexed by the thought that he could at once be her captor and her protector, and even more by the strange thought—hardly admitted beyond the outskirts of her mind—that, rough as he was, and harshly as he had treated her, she could feel in him none of that evil relish for cruelty which she had felt in Dean. This shadowy notion, combined with exhaustion and knowledge of her help-lessness, created a curious inertia, a resignation, almost an indifference. It was but forty-eight hours ago that she had been in the power of that other man, travelling with him to an unfamiliar destination, and praying for some miracle to release her; was she worse off now . . . ?

They moved much more slowly that day, for he no longer seemed to fear pursuit. This puzzled her, and she asked once:

"How much farther is it to this place o' yours?"

"Far enough."

She looked at him suspiciously. Born in a hovel on the Rocks, bred in the Orphanage where a knowledge of the country she lived in was not considered a necessary part of her instruction, she had seen, till now, nothing of the colony beyond a mile of Sydney Cove, and knew nothing save that there were distant farms, and mountains still more distant. But she possessed a full measure of common sense, and she knew that even the farms about Windsor, Richmond and Liverpool could be reached in a day. She enquired, watching him covertly:

"Ye say it's a farm ye've got?"

"Aye."

"With a house? And beasts, and wheat growin'?"

"Aye."

"And other farms nearby?"

"There's none but mine." He spoke shortly, as if unwilling to be catechised, but she persisted:

"I've not seen no road—how would ye get y' stuff to Market?"

"Market . . . ?" He looked at her with a frown, as if he did not understand, and her suspicion increased. She said with sudden sharpness:

"Don't think ye can fool me! D'ye think I don't know a lag when I see one? Farm! Ye're nothing but a convict that's escaped out o' one of the gangs—and for that I'm not one to blame ye, but. . . ."

"I ain't no convict."

"Well, maybe ye've been given y' ticket, or maybe y' time's expired. but if that's it ye're goin' the right way to find y'self back in irons—while they get the gallows ready!"

"I never was no convict."

"What are ye, then? Don't go tellin' me ye're a settler again, for I'll not believe ye. There's no farms out this far—on that I'd take me dyin' oath. Ye're a bushranger, an' all the bushrangers I've heard tell of was convicts that got away and took to the hills. And what's more, ye've been out a long time, for ye didn't learn to talk with the natives in a day, nor them tricks for makin' fire, either. And if ye'd not been a fool ye'd have let me go when I told ye I'd not inform, and neither I would, nor even now, for all ye've dragged me up and down hills till the shoes is fairly wore off me feet, and treated me the way no decent man should treat a girl, wed or not. So if ye've any sense, ye'll take me back, and. . . ."

She stopped, staring. They were skirting a hillside above the river; he had placed his load suddenly and quietly on the ground, and stepped to the edge of a flat, jutting rock, fixing one of his spears into its thrower. She saw his arm strain back and then shoot forward; there was a whir-ring sound as he launched the spear, and she saw its shaft flash in the sunlight like a long, straight streak of fire. There was a faint thudding among the dry twigs and leaves below, and she caught a glimpse of some-thing bounding along the slope. He turned upon her and exploded wrath-fully:

"Can't ye be silent for a moment? Talk, talk, talk, so every wallaby in a mile takes fright! Look at ye! Enough to scare every livin' creature, even without y' chatterin' tongue! Well, it's not much ye'll be gettin' to eat to-night, and ye can thank y'self for it."

It was, indeed, a sparse supper that they ate at dusk beside a small, shallow creek where it joined the river. They had not spoken for several hours, for Emily was offended, and Johnny wrapped in dark misgivings. To possess a white woman, it seemed, might prove more harassing than to possess no woman at all. Would Ngili have behaved so stupidly? Would she have plagued him with questions? Would she have sat apart like this, sulking, while he did the work? Scowling—pouting—shivering. . . .

He said uneasily: "Ye'd best come near the fire."

"I'll do very well, I thank ye," she said primly, "where I am."

"Ye're cold."

"If I am, it's me own business."

He moved irresolutely about, breaking sticks to place carefully over the flames. She watched him obliquely, and the thought came knocking at her mind again that he compared favorably with Dean. Yet she found it bewildering that with a man respectable by all the rules of society—a man who, though he had seduced her, had done so with the promise and intention of marriage—she should have felt far more lost and despairing than she did with this lawless outcast, this half-savage who did not behave as if he had ever so much as heard of a woman's virtue.

Another day passed, and another night. Several times she asked him his name, but to that question—though he answered many others—he would give her no reply. She thought he still feared that she might escape and betray him, but his reluctance went deeper than that—down to the primitive instinct, fostered by his life among primitive men, which taught that a man and his name were mystically and indissolubly united. Already he could feel her making mysterious claims upon him which no other woman had made, and instinctively he was resisting. To yield his name would be to yield himself.

He did not ask for hers, but used once, in calling to her, a word she did not understand.

"What's that ye said—*dulka* . . . ?"

He looked confused, and said shortly:

"It's one o' the Indian words—sky. it means."

"Ye weren't speakin' of the sky?"

"It's what they called ye—because of the colour of y' dress, I reckon."

She looked down at it, smoothing its stained and torn and crumpled skirt ruefully.

"Brand new, it was—an' look at it now! It'll need a deal o' mendin', and even then it'll never be like it was. Lucky I got me workbox still. . . ."

She caught her breath, the words no sooner out of her mouth than she repented them. He had shown no curiosity at all about her belongings, and by degrees she had forgotten to guard them all the time. Now his eyes followed her own panic-stricken glance to the package near his feet. She leapt up and snatched it away, prepared to die in its defence, but he only stood staring at her in astonishment for a moment before he turned away abruptly and sat down with his back to her, whittling with his knife at a piece of wood. She felt slightly foolish, and said presently:

"I was afeard ye'd take it from me."

"What would I want with it?"

He spoke contemptuously, without looking up, for he was deeply affronted. He could not banish from his mind the only lore he possessed concerning the life and behaviour of men and women together—the tribal life in which each sex had its own possessions, sometimes sacred, with which the other did not interfere. Yet he knew that this woman was different, and he was half abashed by his own application to her of rules and customs which belonged to another race. He glanced at her over his shoulder, and saw that she was untying the cords that fastened her mysterious bundle; he looked away again quickly.

There was a long silence. When he stole another glance she was busily stitching at one of the many frills of her skirt; a box stood open beside her. She looked up, caught him staring, and said in a conciliatory tone:

"Ye can look if ye like. I might as well sew up some o' the tears in me skirt while we're sittin' here, though . . ." she sighed, ". . . there'll be more before we're done."

Curiosity overcame his dudgeon; he edged across the rock and peered into the open box. She watched his face closely, looking for the gleam of cupidity which would re-awaken her mistrust, but she saw only wonder, and a sudden smile that changed his grim face to that of a boy. He was pointing at the scissors.

"I've some like those," he said, "but mine's better. Bigger. And one of them, too." His finger touched the thimble, and withdrew. Dumbfounded, she burst out:

"Better? *Better* . . . ? But these is *gold!*"

He looked at her blankly. Finn had spoken of gold, but always in a symbolical sense, as something upon which *They* built their power, and he could not immediately relate it to these pretty, shining toys. Such coins as he had handled had been of silver or copper, and he had not connected the thought of money with Finn's symbolical concept of gold. And Emily, observing his baffled expression, felt—for the first time in many hours—a chill of fear.

What kind of man could this be, who did not know what gold was? The implications were so staggering that she was almost incapable of thought. He was opening and shutting the box, examining its clasp and lock, tracing with his finger the delicate carving on its lid, and looking so fantastically like a child in his wondering absorption that she suddenly thought he must be crazy. That was it—a simpleton, a natural, like one of the girls she had known at the Orphanage, whose mind remained that of a little child, though her body grew beyond it. . . .

He was saying:

"What more have ye there?"

Silently she pulled the wrappings from the writing case and the Bible, and let him look, watching him the while with a painful curiosity. It was the Bible which captured his attention, and the excitement that flared in his eyes bewildered her. "Aye," he said in a low voice of suppressed passion, "it's a book—I knew a man that had a book—they took it from him, but he could say what was wrote in it. . . ." He looked at her unseeingly, and his eyes were wild. "They killed him, like they killed many others, but he said they couldn't kill what was wrote in a book. . . ."

She was terrified, convinced, now, of his madness. With some thought of deflecting his attention from an object which seemed to agitate him so strangely, she pushed the writing case forward, and opened it. He sat staring for a long time at the sheets of white paper, the pens and pencils and sticks of red sealing-wax, but blindly, making no attempt to touch them. He did not seem to know what gold was—he did not seem to distinguish between the Bible and any other book—perhaps he did not know, either, what writing materials were for . . . ? Suddenly she felt sorry for him in his ignorance and affliction, and spoke in tones of soothing reassurance.

"It's for writing." She took up a pencil. "Look, now, and I'll show ye. . . ." She placed a sheet of paper on the sloping lid, and wrote carefully: "Emily."

"That's me name," she explained, "so ye needn't call me by no heathen words no more." He looked calmer, and the moment seemed propitious, so she added: "I'd write down yours, too, if ye'd tell me what it is . . . ? Come, now—why not . . . ?"

His eyes searched her face slowly, but he made no answer. Feeling snubbed, and a little piqued, she was beginning to gather her possessions together when he leaned over abruptly, picked up the pencil, and wrote beneath her name: "Johnny Prentice."

Fine, sloping copperplate . . . ! Not the master himself could write a fairer hand . . . ! Prentice . . . The name stirred some chord of memory, but she was too astounded by his feat of calligraphy to pay it much attention. And as she sat in a maze of bewilderment he tore the paper savagely into small pieces and scattered them on the ground, his face no longer that of a child, but of a man whom it was easy to believe a murderer. Fear had caught him again, and set his fury blazing; he looked at the fragments of paper blowing about on the grass, and from them to her, his eyes sharp with panic. Ah, it was true what Finn had said—

you could destroy the written word, but it lived on in the minds of those who had read it . . . ! He said harshly:

"We been sittin' here long enough, wastin' the daylight . . . !"

Hastily she bundled her treasure together, and scrambled to her feet. He was very silent all the afternoon, walking faster than usual, and leaving her to follow as best she could, so that by the time they halted for the night she was almost staggering with weariness. He stretched himself out on the far side of the fire, and though she could tell from his movements that he was wakeful as herself, he did not come to her. Yet at daylight she opened her eyes to find him sitting but a few feet away, staring at her with a curious expression of puzzled anxiety. And when they set out again, he was carrying the cooking-pot.

Late that morning they came upon half a dozen cows and calves grazing on the river bank, but he passed them without comment, his face forbidding questions. It was mid-afternoon when he left the river and turned sharply up the steep hill that rose from its eastern bank. She toiled after him breathlessly—up, up, till her heart was pounding and her legs trembled. At last the ground flattened for a time, and he allowed a brief halt. She could see the river far below, winding away to the north-west through its deep, shadowed valley, and the hills beyond it brightly painted with a red-gold light from the westering sun. But soon after they had begun to move again she found, with dismay, that there was another steep hill ahead; and she plodded wearily at his heels, her eyes on the ground whose every yard, she had learned, might betray unwary feet with a slithering stone, a tough, protruding root, or a charred log half buried in undergrowth. So, when he stopped at last upon the crest, and she came thankfully to a halt beside him, and looked up, it was to find a scene spread out below which seemed like an apparition, con-jured out of nothing.

The valley, ringed on three sides by sheer cliffs, stretched out like a sea of undulating, grey-green billows, but at its nearer end, almost at their feet, the land had been cleared, and lay in a small patchwork of cultivation. Through it a stream ran down from the cliffs towards the river; she could see sheep grazing near it, and, in a sheltered pocket above it, a small, slab hut.

She found him looking at her intently, and seemed to feel a tautness in him. Neither of them could know that they were re-enacting a scene played many years ago in another place, when a native woman had read upon the face of another Prentice need for her praise of the home he offered. Emily was no native woman, and her first impression was that the hut only emphasised unendurably the loneliness of the surrounding bush, but she had a heart no less tender, and perceptions no less fine than Cunnembeillee's, and though her voice quavered slightly, she said:

"Is this y' farm, then? My, it's a fine big place!"

He seemed to relax, and waved his hand in a gesture that embraced the whole valley.

"Plenty o' land here. I can clear more if I want—it's all mine!"

She asked doubtfully:

"Was it Gov'nor Bligh granted it? Or Gov'nor King? How long have ye been here?"

He made no reply to that, and she thought that some of his tenseness returned. He set off down the hill, and she followed. She stood by while he unlocked the door with the key hanging round his neck, and then stepped nervously over the threshold, feeling bare earth still beneath her feet. She could see little at first beyond the path of light that had entered with them, but gradually she made out a table, a couple of benches, and two bunks built against the wall, furnished only with a few tattered, dirty blankets, and something that looked like the skins of animals. There was a door in one wall, but when she pushed it open and peered into another tiny room, she found it quite empty. As she turned back to him, tears of dismay were very close to her eyes, but his expression startled her so much that they dried unshed, for no one could have failed to read pride in it. She had abandoned all hope of understanding him; he might be a convict, he might be a settler, he was undoubtedly a murderer, and very likely a simpleton, but whatever he was there was some need in him as real as the need for food to a starving man. She put her valise down on the floor, set her package carefully on the table, and said:

"Well, I'm not sorry for a good roof over me head again, and a table to eat me food at—and a proper fireplace for cookin'. . . . Ye'd best light the fire."

*   *   *   *

Mr. Howe, who kept ready to his pen a stock of adjectives for all occasions, never failed to report a murder as shocking, dastardly, heinous, atrocious, unprincipled and outrageous, nor to imply that the horror with which all respectable people regarded assassins was no greater than their astonishment at learning that such fiends in human form could exist. It was, perhaps, because so many of the humbler colonists could not read, and were thus unaware of the emotions they should display, that they commonly received the news of murders with but little surprise, and had never betrayed less than when they heard of Joseph Dean's. They were more interested in the strange disappearance of his bride, though there were many who declared that business to be plain enough. Of a comely wench out of the Orphanage anything might be expected, and a lover might be assumed; some said she had killed Dean herself, and was now being concealed by the lover; others held that the lover, jilted for a richer man, had lain in wait for his rival, and abducted his bride. Officialdom attributed the crime to that convenient scapegoat, the absconder. A notice headed REWARD appeared in the *Gazette,* proclaiming that whereas Emily Dean, formerly known as Emily Rocks, had disappeared, the sum of twenty guineas would be paid by her former employers to any person who should give information leading to her discovery; but the best that anyone could find was a fragment torn from a frill of blue bombazine, not fifty yards from where Dean's body was discovered.

After a week or so gossip died; the soldiers and armed constables abandoned their aimless searching; a clerk in the Government office noted the name of Joseph Dean to be added to his return of births, marriages and deaths, paying it no greater attention than to remark that it was rarely a man was recorded as wed and dead with only a day's interval. And by all but Patrick Mannion and the Harveys the disappearance of a servant-girl was soon forgotten.

Mark rode to Beltrasna.

"You think this may be more of Prentice's work?" he demanded of Patrick.

"I suspected it at once, and now I'm convinced. I find that this man, Dean, was the third of that precious trio which caused the native woman's death."

Mark stared at him in dismay.

"You are sure? The fellow seemed decent and steady enough—sober, hardworking. . . . But it's useless now to regret what's done. We must find Emily, even if it means the end of your silence concerning Prentice."

Patrick said slowly, after a moment's thought:

"There's a search in progress, as you know. How would it be aided if I spoke?"

"They're wasting their time searching the settlements and the out-lying farms. . . ."

"They would waste more searching—that." Patrick nodded at the window which faced the river and the hills beyond. "They suppose the murderer to be an absconder; there are dozens of them at large—every week the *Gazette* publishes their names and descriptions. They are usually discovered still somewhere about the settlements, hiding in the bush, or harboured by their friends and accomplices. If they dare the uninhabited country His Excellency doesn't pursue them very far; he knows they have but exchanged one captivity for another. Consider, Mr. Harvey—what information can I give other than that which is supplied to any party searching for an absconder? A name—a description of his appearance. But, believe me, they will never be near enough to him to observe his appearance, or to demand his name. And they will learn nothing from the natives."

"Then what are we to do? We can't simply abandon the girl."

"We might serve her best by doing so. Prentice's motive in abducting her presents no mystery—she's a girl that any man might find desirable. But if her presence endangered him—if a hunt were prosecuted in which he were hard pressed, and found her an encumbrance. . . ."

Mark uttered a little groan.

"You're right, I suppose. But I might go myself—alone, as you did. . . ."

"I most earnestly advise against it. At the time I went I knew Prentice was in the neighbourhood, for I knew he had reason to be. There is now every reason in the world why he should be as far away as possible. Do you imagine he would keep so conspicuous an object as a white woman—and particularly one who is, we may suppose, an unwilling captive—in any area near to civilisation? And beyond there's but a trackless, foodless wilderness where he, with his knowledge and the assistance of the natives, could evade you for ever. . . ."

"All the same," Mark interrupted restlessly, "we must do something. How can we leave the girl at the mercy of a ruffian who might—you said it yourself—murder her as he has murdered others?"

"He won't murder her unless she endangers his liberty, and his liberty is not endangered until he is closely pursued. For the present you need have no fears for her life—and you may be sure that her virtue is long since past saving."

Mark said rather angrily:

"Virtue! Whatever may have befallen her, Emily is a good girl, and we need not speak of virtue. And there's another aspect to this business— the marriage was bigamous."

"The devil it was! How did you discover that?"

"It occurred to us that upon Dean's death, Emily, as his wife, became his heir. In case the unfortunate girl is still living, I felt it my duty to make close inquiries on her behalf into Dean's affairs, and from certain papers found in his dwelling it appears that he was married in England to a woman who was transported for theft under the name of Sarah Dane; whether that name was intentionally assumed, or whether it was merely an error I can't tell—as you know, many of the records are imperfect, not to say chaotic. At all events, Dean followed her here, and had her assigned to him—God knows why, but certainly from no motive of tenderness, for he seems to have treated her abominably. . . ."

"Can't she throw any light on the matter?"

"No—she's in the Government Asylum at Castle Hill—a raving lunatic. And poor Emily. . . ." Mark rose and began to pace about the room. "I blame myself bitterly. The unfortunate girl, if she still lives, is certainly being subjected to hardship, and perhaps to ill-treatment. I can't rest without making some attempt. . . ."

"I suggest that we await the outcome of this search. I don't for a moment expect it to succeed, but if it does Emily will be restored to you, Prentice will be taken, and the whole matter settled without our intervention. In the meantime, Miles' arrival is imminent. Redfern tells me it will be some time before I am able to undergo any arduous exertion, but when I can move freely again, we—you, I and Miles—could perhaps attempt a search."

Mark agreed reluctantly. "Very well—we must be content with that. If you are unable to come to Sydney by the time Miles arrives, what are we to tell him about the cause of your injury?"

Patrick shrugged.

"It was an attack by some unknown person—that will serve for the moment. If he is to hear the whole story, I prefer to tell him myself."

*   *   *   *

The *Isabella* anchored in the harbour on a crisp, mid-August morning, and among her passengers were two young gentlemen with their brides. About any member of the Macarthur family there seemed to hang a kind of effulgence reflected from the glaring personality of its redoubtable colonial head, and the return of his nephew, Mr. Hannibal Macarthur, would therefore have been at any time an event of some interest. It was increased by the fact that he had brought back as his wife the late Governor King's eldest daughter, Maria, who had been born at Norfolk Island nineteen years ago, and now reappeared in her native land for the first time since she had left it at the age of three.

But the sight of the second couple, when they came ashore with three servants, two horses, an elegant gig, a four-poster bedstead, a vast Irish wolfhound, a harp, and a formidable array of boxes and portmanteaux, created a minor sensation. Heads turned, tongues wagged, and old residents nodded. Mr. Howe, attending the disembarkation, notebook in hand, declared that he remembered young Mr. Miles Mannion well, and re-called how he had once, in company with little Miss Elizabeth King, invaded the office of the *Gazette* to inspect the printing press. "And," concluded Mr. Howe, watching the new arrival with benign interest, "a fine tall lad he was, even then."

Miles Mannion (of whom legend was to say that he stood six feet seven inches in his stockings, but who was, in fact, a full two inches short of that measurement) seemed, perhaps, the more fabulously large in contrast to his fair, diminutive wife, who clung to his arm and looked about her at the somewhat boisterous scene with timid grey eyes. Their arrival was not unheralded, for the *Mary Ann,* in whose company the *Isabella* had sailed, had reached port a few days earlier, and Mr. and Mrs. Harvey had driven down to the wharf to welcome them.

Mrs. Macarthur was there too, but though she greeted her husband's nephew warmly, the event of the morning was, for her, the bundle of letters just delivered into her eager hands. She seized a moment in the turmoil to glance hastily through one of them. Brief as it was, there was news enough to please her—good tidings of her mother, encouraging prospects for the sale of their wool, whose value, Macarthur assured her, was now established beyond doubt. *". . . wool of the quality of our most improved kind will sell for a Guinea a Fleece. . . . I hope there will be a large quantity to send by the* Isabella. *. . ."* Yet he was still speaking of their return to England. *"If you have the smallest apprehension or dread of coming home alone only say that it is your wish, and I will sacrifice every other consideration and come out for you. . . ."* Her eyes hurried on to linger over the last words: *"Till to-morrow, adieu, for I am weary and stupid. . . ."* How well she knew those dark fits of depression which alternated with his ebullience, and were, no doubt, the price he paid for the devouring energy and single-mindedness he brought to all his undertakings! Shaken by the adverse findings of Johnston's Court-Martial, shocked by news from the colony of Macquarie's policy, tormented by dyspepsia and gout, how much more readily he must now fall a prey to such dejection! She could read it in the anxious indecision his letters betrayed—in his almost nervous reliance on her judgment. . . . But Hannibal was addressing her, and she re-folded the letter hastily, reflecting that she would not be sorry to hand over some of the more tiring of her responsibilities to him. She bowed as Mr. and Mrs. Harvey, together with Mr. Miles Mannion and his bride, bowled past in their carriage. Mercy, how fast these children grew up!

The same evening Desmond appeared at his mother's side as she stood directing Hannah in the proper setting of the supper table, and announced with his customary placidity:

"Mama, there's a giant at the door."

"A giant, my love?" Preoccupied as she was, Conor spared him a glance of surprise, for Desmond was not given to flights of fancy. But her bewilderment was only momentary, and she laughed, patting his head as she hurried into the passage. "That isn't a giant, Desmond, it's your big brother, Miles. Ah, you have very rightly not waited to be admitted, my dear Miles—but where is Laetitia, pray?"

"Oh, I've not mislaid her. She was fatigued. She begs her compli-

ments to you, and asks to be excused. Is that Desmond? Come here, boy
—have you ever touched a ceiling . . . ?" For a dizzy moment Desmond's
fingers scraped the rafters; a little breathless, but otherwise composed, he
found himself on the floor again, and heard his mother's protest:

"But will she not be lonely—her first night ashore in a strange place?
This morning I thought she seemed a little—how shall I say it . . . ? A
little at a loss—alarmed, even . . . ?"

"Oh, she's a quiet little mouse, God bless her, but you need feel no
concern. She has her maid with her—a dragon called Johanna who has
been in her mama's service since before Letty was born; she frightens the
wits out of me. Letty has retired—I was permitted to kiss her hand—
and I don't doubt she's asleep by now. She's in the family way, you
know—which should shame Patrick into forsaking his single state. But,
confound it, what *is* this about Patrick? You tell me he has a bullet in
his leg . . . ? Some encounter with an escaped convict . . . ?"

"Come in, Miles, and let us talk in comfort. Yes, he has met with
an accident, but he will tell you of it himself when you see him."

"But how . . . ?"

"No, not in that chair, pray, for I doubt if it will support your weight.
My, how remarkably tall you have grown—but I knew you immediately
this morning!"

"Knew me? Damn it, I should hope so! Should I return to my native
land to be unrecognised by my family?" He leaned back in his chair and
eyed her with amusement. "So you defied them all to become a colonial,
and marry a schoolteacher! What a flutter there was among the old hens
at Beltrasna! 'She is mad!' says Aunt Hester. 'She is wanting in all
proper sense of her position!' says Aunt Abigail. And Grandmama taps
with her cane on the floor—damned cold and cheerless those stone floors
are, too!—and looks down her beak of a nose, and declares you will live
to repent it." He grinned. "But I see no signs of repentance, and you're
handsomer than ever! Where's your husband?"

"He will be here presently. Do not think that you are all the *Isabella*
has brought us. There is also, we trust, a parcel which he has gone in
search of, containing slates, primers. . . ."

He roared with laughter, looking curiously about the small room.

"I find this situation amusing, by Heaven I do! You know I have
often been begged to describe life in the colony, and I always replied
that I dare not do so, for whatever I relate there will be some other person
to declare exactly the contrary—and both will be true! Ladies may dwell
in humble cottages, and ex-convicts in mansions—yet the customs of
England survive, and one is merely conscious of an intermittent popping

sound as some ancient tradition explodes, or some sacred convention bursts like a bubble—am I not right?"

"So right," she replied with a smile, "that I find it hard to believe your only experience of the place has been that of a child. I should not have supposed, when you were thirteen years old, that you were so profound a student of society."

"Ah, I have been digesting my impressions in the intervening years. And conversing with colonials re-visiting their birthplaces. And reading between the lines of letters—particularly those of my brother, who provides a pretty example of a man attempting to face backward and forward at the same time. Damned philosophical, his letters are, which I take as a sign that either his liver or his soul must be disordered. Which is it, pray?"

"I've heard no complaints of his liver—and as for his soul—well, do not most of us suffer some discomfort in that region, Miles?"

"Not I!" he declared roundly. "And if Patrick feels a queasiness, it's merely because he wants a wife—and so I shall tell him. If he can find no colonial miss to suit him, he'd best return to Ireland and seek one there—he can do so without inconvenience now that I'm here."

"When shall you go to Beltrasna?"

"Why, to-morrow. I shall ride, of course, but Letty must go in the carriage. It's a plaguey nuisance, for we've brought out two of the finest mounts this place has ever seen—but the dragon won't hear of her riding in her present condition. I'll find few familiar faces at Beltrasna, I daresay—Toole, of course, and I believe Maria Prentice is still there? I trust marriage has improved her, for she was as lumpish a wench as ever I saw. . . ."

"And Dilboong," Conor reminded him.

"Dilboong! Ye gods, I had almost forgotten poor, ugly Dilboong! She'll be something of a shock to Letty, I fear, for the poor girl has conceived a violent aversion to the natives from those she saw about the town this morning."

"Will she be sufficiently rested to make the journey to-morrow?" Conor enquired. Miles looked at her in mild astonishment.

"Oh, yes, there's nothing amiss with her, you know, and she has the sweetest, most yielding nature imaginable. She knows I'm in a fever to get home."

*   *   *   *

Disregarding Mrs. Emmett's protests, Patrick rose from his bed for the first time since his mishap, and dressed himself with care to receive his brother and his brother's wife. The big bedroom, unused since his father's death, had been scoured, aired and polished; delicate china and massive silver long stored away had been brought out; the best table linen was even now being reverently unfolded by Mrs. Emmett, and Patrick had himself descended into the cellar to choose the wines. From the verandah he could see the carriage approaching, Miles riding beside it and his groom behind. Hattie hovered inside the front door, and old Morgan stood at the front of the steps with one of the stable boys—but eager as he was to greet his son, Shawn, it was not the carriage he was watching.

" 'Tis a fine beast, by the look of it, Sir, that Mr. Miles is ridin'—ah, it's no wonder, the way he was always one to know a good bit of horseflesh, even as a lad. . . ."

But his sentence ended abruptly in a cluck of shocked disapproval, for Miles, having caught sight of his brother, waved his coat over his head, bent down to say something to the occupants of the carriage, and set his horse up the hill at a canter. Heedless as ever, Patrick thought; but his greeting was warm when Miles dismounted, clapped Morgan heartily on the shoulder, flung his reins to the stable boy, and leapt up the steps to grasp his brother's hand. When his protestations of delight at his return were momentarily halted by the need for drawing breath, Patrick said, watching the carriage take the hill at a more sedate pace:

"I was mortified at being unable to greet your wife in Sydney; but Redfern insisted. . . ."

"My dear fellow, she understands, of course! A lucky escape you had, by all accounts, though what possessed you to go roaming the hills alone like a gipsy is beyond me—I had thought such indiscretions my own prerogative. What did you think of Maolmordha, eh? I'll wager there's not another to touch him in the colony! I bought Letty the finest little mare in Ireland—wait till you see her. . . . We brought a gig, too, but it was damaged during the voyage. . . . And Cheyne, the wolfhound I got for Letty—she doesn't like him, he's as big as a calf, but I never could abide lap-dogs—we've left him at Moore House for the present with my man, Doyle, but Sydney's too small for him, so he'd better come here. . . . By God, the place looks in fine trim—and the country we passed through —I never saw such promising crops of early wheat. . . . They tell me you had a good harvest last year, and expect another now. . . . How the trees have grown! And I see you've got those eastern fields under cultivation. . . . Ah, the mountains—they're waiting for me, eh? But I'll swear they're not as high as they used to be—nothing but hills—what's the matter with everyone that they haven't been crossed yet . . . ? We paid our respects to the Governor, and he sent his compliments—how does he shape . . . ? We heard all kind of tales—Hannibal Macarthur's shaking his head already—but damn it, one always hears tales. . . ." He bounded down the steps again as the carriage drew up. "Well, my angel, here we are at last, at last—and Patrick on his feet to welcome you . . . !"

He opened the carriage door with a flourish and handed his wife out. Her naturally pale face paler than ever with fatigue, her pregnancy apparent despite an abundance of shawls and scarves, Laetitia hesitated for a moment before ascending the steps to meet the gentleman who, leaning heavily on his stick, was limping down them to receive her. Enormous grey eyes were lifted to his; a cold, small hand was extended. Her first thought was: How like Miles he is! Her second: How unlike! But for the moment she felt little interest in anything beyond the thought of a bed to rest on, for she had been unmercifully jolted in the carriage; when his little speech of welcome had been delivered, she responded quickly to his courteous enquiry.

"I am indeed a little fatigued. The journey. . . ."

"You would like to retire to your room at once, no doubt. Hattie! Show Mrs. Miles and her servant to her room, and see that she has anything she may require. When you have rested, ma'am, I hope we may become better acquainted."

But Miles was protesting.

"No, hang it all, Letty, you can't desert me like this! At this won-derful moment! I have a thousand things to show you, and. . . ." He broke off, stared, and then roared out suddenly:

"Dilboong! Dilboong, as I live! Come out from behind that corner, girl, and let me look at you!" She hung back bashfully, but her wide, white smile transfigured her dark face, and tears of joy were pouring down her cheeks. He clapped an arm over her shoulders and turned her face up with a finger under her chin. "Grown up, by God—who'd believe it? A young woman! But I'd have known that grin anywhere, splitting your face from ear to ear! Don't say you've forgotten me, Dilboong? You remember me, eh?"

"Yessa, Mister Miles."

"Glad to see me home again?"

"Yessa."

"Ah, and it is home at last, for it's not everywhere one finds a Dil-boong! But I must see everything—everyone—and all at once. Patrick, your damned leg won't permit you to conduct this tour, so we must make it alone, must we not, my love . . . ?"

Patrick said nothing, his face carefully expressionless. Laetitia had paused in the doorway, patches of red staining the pallor of her cheeks, her lips fallen slightly apart in amazement and repugnance. Behind her stood Johanna, with a tight mouth and hands clasped over her stomach; it was she who spoke:

"Begging your pardon, Sir, the mistress is overtired with the journey. I'll take her to her room."

She put her hand beneath Laetitia's elbow, and they vanished into the house. Miles shrugged ruefully:

"A dragon, that woman, damned if she's not! Ah, well, it seems I must make my sentimental pilgrimage alone, for I'll not wait another moment. You've a horse I can use, Patrick—no, no, you needn't trouble to escort me—I've not forgotten my way to the stables."

Patrick drew his gold watch from his pocket.

"We dine at five."

But Miles had already taken the steps again at a bound, and replied only with an airy wave of his hand. Patrick turned slowly and limped indoors. Dilboong crept to the other side of the verandah, where she could watch the fabulously tall figure striding away, burnished by the afternoon sunlight from the crown of his shining, yellow head to the soles of his resplendently polished boots. She held her hands clasped tightly over her breast, and uttered almost inaudible sounds which were half moaning and half song.

*   *   *   *

By the beginning of summer Emily had settled down to domestic life with her abductor, but Johnny was still wrestling rebelliously with the discovery that white women were as restless as white men, and even more unpredictable. He was infuriated to find that even after he had brought her safely to his *towri* and installed her beneath his roof, she remained a problem. Surely a woman was a woman—her place clearly defined, her duties and functions exactly limited? She shared a man's bed, bore his children, and, for the rest, occupied herself with indispensable tasks about the camp. True, women were sometimes over-talkative, sometimes idle, sometimes shrewish; but a man need pay no more attention to such failings than to administer a rebuke or a cuff on the head when they threatened to plague him unduly. And it was understood that this did not disturb their essentially harmonious relationship, any more than a passing brawl made men forget the bond of their tribal brotherhood.

But this woman, instead of merely filling the niche left vacant by Ngili, seemed to threaten invasion of his whole life and thought. She would not be quelled, and she could not be disregarded. She did not merely inhabit his house, but took possession of it, upsetting many of its time-honoured customs. One of her first actions had been to gather together the old blankets and every garment she could find, and march off with them to the creek. When he followed, alarmed, he found her kneeling on a flat rock, punching and pounding them in the water, and she greeted him with a tirade because there was no soap. Soap? A struggle with his memory yielded a vague picture of his mother similarly employed, and of something in her hand which made a froth of iridescent bubbles; but while he strove with it his expression was so blank that she cried out in contemptuous irritation, calling him a dirty, good-for-nothing rogue who did not even know what soap was, and he retreated to the hut, angry and abashed. Every morning she straightened the purified blankets on the beds. She took the skins outside and beat them furiously with a stick, declaring that they smelt, and must henceforth lie upon the floor. But she would not even place them there until she had made an implement from a grass-tree shaft and a bundle of green twigs, with which she energetically expelled through the doorway a cloud of dust, and the accumulated litter of years. She complained when the goats and fowls wandered in, rising up with angry cries to flap her apron and hunt them out of doors. She moved a bench from where it had always stood to the other side of the hearth, and was able to give no sounder reason for doing so than to say, with decision, that it looked better. When, harassed and rebellious, he protested, she assumed an injured air, and asked: "Don't ye want y' house kept tidy?" He found that he dared not say no.

She produced what seemed to him a fantastic number of garments from the valise she had brought with her, hanging them carefully upon nails driven into the wall; sometimes, when she was not there, he fingered them, astonished at their whiteness, puzzled by their intricacy, and obscurely excited by an illusion that in touching them, he touched herself. On their arrival he had immediately reverted to his custom of going naked, for his few clothes were too precious to be worn unnecessarily, but she had been shocked at this, and made the meaningless remark that he was no better than the heathen Indians. Nevertheless, beside her own voluminously clad body, he suddenly felt the nakedness of his own, and began to wear every day his oldest and most ragged pair of trousers.

Yet she did not claim his attention merely by her sex, nor by her extraordinary activities. He found himself watching her for the mere pleasure of it, marvelling at the way the bright colour ran up into her cheeks when she was angry or excited; thinking how red her lips looked, and how dark her lashes against the whiteness of her skin; fascinated by glints of gold that the sun discovered in her brown hair. He noticed that one of her dresses (he did not know that it was but a faded cotton, well worn and mended) was the same colour as a sweet-smelling pink flower which grew on the hillsides, and once picked a spray to show her, holding it against her skirt; he knew a moment of almost painful happiness when she admired it, and pinned it in her bodice.

After a brief period of misgiving, he learned to appreciate her cooking. She had few utensils, but with them she contrived to produce a variety of foods whose excellence astonished him. Meat, in his experience, was cooked by being flung upon the fire; milk one drank straight from the bucket; eggs were broken and swallowed whole; birds and fish were wrapped in wet clay and buried in the red-hot coals; most vegetables were eaten raw. But from the pot simmering on the hearth there now came beguiling odours. Strange things were done with eggs and milk and honey, and the coarse flour which they made by grinding grain between two stones; meat was cooked with onions and potatoes; bones and barley were blended with vegetables to make appetising broths; creamy milk was poured plentifully over a thick, substantial porridge of whole wheat. With all this she herself appeared extremely dissatisfied, clicking her tongue angrily, raising her eyes in despair, crying: "Ah, if I only had some sugar . . . !" "For mercy's sake, how can I cook without salt?" "My, if we could get a butter-churn . . . !" But in this matter Johnny felt, as he sat down hungrily to a heaped platter, that he had no fault to find.

All the same, she talked a great deal too much, irritating him with the tireless persistence of her questioning. Not content with a physical intimacy, she sought to invade the privacy of his mind. His attempts to silence her with angry words, and once or twice even with a blow, only roused her to storms of tears, reproaches, and increased volubility; more-over, they disturbed himself. He found that he did not want to strike her; he did not even want to shout at her. He discovered in himself, with alarm and disgust, an actual impulse to abase himself for having caused her distress, and it was one such impulse which made the first breach in his fortress of reserve.

He had become resigned to her habit of moving things about in order to perform, with a bit of rag, a mysterious rite called dusting. He did not mind what she did with her own possessions, and had felt nothing but a mild astonishment when he saw her lift her workbox, her writing desk and her Bible each day to wipe the shelf upon which they stood, and then rub and polish them carefully before replacing them. After a few stormy scenes when she first laid hands upon his belongings, he surrendered; after all, he thought, she did them no actual harm. One morning, however, she lifted the necklace of buttons, and, instead of returning it to its appointed place, hung it round her neck, and turned, laughing, to face him.

He did not know how, when, or why it had acquired its mystical significance for him, but he knew that what she was doing was as intolerable and outrageous as it would have been for a native woman to treat with frivolity one of those sacred objects upon whose inviolability the spiritual welfare of the tribe depended. He knew that this was his totem, by virtue of which he was linked to his father, and to his ancestral past. He felt such a blaze of anger that his hands began to shake; he took one stride and seized her by the arm, snatching the necklace over her head and pushing her away so fiercely that she fell against the wall, the laughter smitten from her eyes, and the colour from her cheeks. And then, as rapidly as it had flared, his fury died. He stood holding his treasure, looking stupidly from it to her, and back again to it; suddenly it seemed a silly trifle, and the sound of her low sobbing as she passed her fingers over the arm he had so roughly grasped, filled him with a tumult of shame and sadness. He said uncertainly:

"I didn't think to hurt ye. . . ."

She sank down on the bench beside the table and buried her head in her outstretched arms. "It's nought to cry about," he urged placatingly, but she paid no attention, so he laid the necklace across her hand, and added with an effort: "Ye can wear it if ye want."

Her hand moved so that it fell aside, but it was not the sharp move-ment of temper, the angry rejection of an overture. Johnny—who never knew how much he had learned from his dark friends—had a native-trained eye for the nuances of gesture, and in this one he read desolation. It seemed to tell him that she was not really interested in the necklace; she had only made a playful pretence of adorning herself to please him— laughed to beguile and invite him. She was weeping not because he had taken from her something that she wanted, nor because he had hurt her arm, but because he had wounded some peculiarly feminine sensitivity which does not lightly expose itself to the danger of rebuff. Instinctively he dragged out his own most cherished reticences as atonement.

"I don't know why I set such store by it . . . it was something Cun-nembeillee used to wear when she was livin' with me father. She had it round her neck the first time I seen her, just after she and Billalong were near bein' carried away down the river, and me father was drowned savin' them . . . the natives tell of it in a corroborree they do, and the one that makes out to be Cunnembeillee always wears one like it, though the buttons is only shells. . . ."

Her face remained hidden in her arms, but he thought she was listen-ing. He sat down beside her, circling her shaking body with his arm, and plunged on recklessly:

"I wouldn't never have known about me father if it hadn't been for this thing. . . . I wouldn't never have known who made the fire or dropped the key, or who it was built the hut. . . . I wouldn't even have known that Billalong was me brother. I found out one day when I came on— on someone—a lad I knew before I ran away—and he told me. . . ."

She said from beneath her hair:

"I don't know what ye're t-talkin' about. What key? What f-fire?"

He rubbed his hand across his eyes, as if some blurring of the sight were obscuring his clear vision of a past grown legendary even to himself.

"It was when I ran away. I was hungry, for I'd had nothin' to eat but a crust or two since the day before . . . and scared, too. . . . I was no more than eight years old, mind ye, and cold and wet from swimmin' across the river and walkin' through the bush in the rain. . . . And I found a fire, and the key lyin' beside it. . . ."

One of her hands dropped down to cover his where it clasped her waist, and she lifted her head to stare at him through her tears.

"Eight years old—and ye ran away? Into the bush? For mercy's sake, how was it ye didn't starve?"

He said slowly: "I had the key."

It was more than an hour later when he went outside and sat down on the bench by the door—an hour in which pain and happiness had been strangely intermixed. It had been painful to remember that lonely, frightened child—but pleasant to feel her warm compassion reaching back into the past to envelop it. Companionship he had received from the natives, friendship from Finn, and a mild, docile devotion from Ngili; but tenderness had never touched him till now. He had been Ishmael for so long that the wariness, reserve and concealment which many incidents in his past had imposed as the merest practical precautions, had now become habits; to be alone and hidden seemed not only a matter of physical safety, but of spiritual necessity, so compelling that the exposure of wounds suffered in childhood now came as a revelation even to himself. Was this Johnny Prentice—this creature full of loneliness and fear, full of longing for comfort and reassurance, full of unshed tears and unclaimed love? He was afraid of what he had uncovered, not only of his life, but of his heart; and not only to her, but to himself. Yet as he sat there with the morning sun beating down on his bowed head he felt spent, but peaceful, in a relaxation and fulfilment not unlike the aftermath of passion. He knew that he would retreat from her again, gather his armour of caution about him, feel glad that he had revealed only fragments of his story, resolve to reveal no more. But beneath that knowledge a deeper wisdom was already whispering that he had begun to seek a union which could only be achieved by the abandonment of all reserves. He did not know whether it spoke in tones of warning or of promise.

Emily, for her part, had few reserves to yield. During the early weeks she had studied Johnny with a fearful curiosity which was only whetted by his uncommunicativeness. She was confused by the fact that he existed at all—apparently quite outside any of the categories into which she had supposed all human beings were divided—but also by her own inability to define her feelings towards him. Her fear was real, but she was bewildered when there appeared fleetingly in one whom she had seen commit murder, something which suggested the innocence of a child; she felt her hostility weakened by sudden waves of compassion, and could not maintain her resentment at his air of mastery when occasionally, by some small action, he seemed to offer her an awkward hint of homage. Agonies of loneliness possessed her; yearning for the sight of streets and people sent her into storms of temper and long fits of silent brooding; yet dreams of escape were revealed to her as only dreams, dissipated by the fierce, primitive protest of her body at the thought of leaving him. For the flame which Dean had lit was burning warmly now, fed by the youth and ardour of a man whose passion was direct, artless, unpoisoned by shame or cruelty. Freedom, for her, had always meant such freedom as she could make for herself within the prisoning walls of circumstance, and she was still largely governed by the habit of childhood, which parades rebellion while accepting the inexorable decrees of fate. Loudly as she protested, therefore—earnestly as she pleaded to be set free, fiercely as she argued and threatened, and stubbornly as she sulked—she was, all the time, adapting herself, transmuting dread into resignation, and resig-nation into something that was near enough to contentment.

But sometimes there were incidents which checked her growing con-fidence, plunging her once more into doubt and confusion.

"What was it," she asked him one night, "that ye hoped to get from Dean's cart? For it was little enough ye did get; the cooking pot—and me. . . ."

Oblivious of the coquetry in her last words, he said at once:

"It weren't for what I could get. I'd a score to settle with him—and with two other devils like him."

"Why—what had they done to ye?"

"They killed me woman."

He was utterly unprepared for the effect of this simple statement. Hours passed before she seemed able to accept the fact that another woman had shared the hut with him; days before she recovered from the shock of learning that her predecessor had been a native. But her mind was tenacious, and one point which had been temporarily obscured by the impact of a more personal revelation, re-emerged at last in further questions.

"What about the others?"

"What others?"

"The other two men ye said ye'd a score to settle with."

He was surprised. "I killed them too."

She said only: "Ye think nothin' of killin', do ye?" But she became very quiet for a time, and her face was pale.

She could not wholly reach him. Somewhere there was a wall behind which he retreated—a locked door. But after his outburst when she had had worn the necklace, she became calmer. She had learned little enough of his past life, but it was at last clear that he had never lived among white people from the age of eight, and she was thus provided with one solid fact which enabled her to shake her head at what puzzled her, and say inwardly: "No wonder!" But when his rage had collapsed so suddenly, when the necklace dropped across her hand, and his anxious tone, if not his words, begged forgiveness, she had learned something of far greater importance; the door was not irrevocably locked. True, he had opened it only a chink; true, he had slammed it again almost immediately. But now she knew that she had a key to it; he was only holding it shut, and every now and then it yielded a little to her pressure. She was able to smile to herself indulgently when she felt him withdrawing from her, for against his withdrawals she could set approaches and responses—a warmer tone, a kinder look, a service volunteered; sometimes, in the shielding darkness and on the crest of passion, he even used, clumsily, some term of endearment. They lost their wariness of each other, and the tension that had been between them slackened. She was now seriously troubled only by one dread in herself, and one resistance in him which she could not overcome.

She had for some time hesitated to tell him of her pregnancy, expecting, forlornly, to be met by some display of resentment, or even jealousy. But she was sometimes ill, and there had been no need to tell him after all; to her relief he appeared quite unperturbed—almost, indeed, uninterested, treating it as a matter too natural to require comment. But when their closer understanding encouraged her to confess some of the fears she felt of childbirth in this lonely place, he looked glum, uneasy and forbidding, as if she had transgressed some rule of proper behaviour. Her fears had grown as the weeks passed. Her knowledge had been gained only from her companions at the Orphanage, whose whispered tales of the pains and perils of maternity were, if not strictly accurate, well garnished with ghoulish details.

"How will I do," she once asked him desperately, "when me baby's born? There's no midwife here, not even another woman to help me. . . . Even the settlers' wives that live far out get a neighbour in to stay with them when their time comes. . . ." She was not yet voicing the root of her fear, waiting in an agony of hope for him to forestall her, but he was silent, and she struggled on: "Oh, I know there's some can't get another woman—there was one I heard tell of out near Castlereagh, and the creek came up so no one could get across to her—but she had her husband there, and he . . ." Her quick, bewildered glance showed him dark-faced and sullen. "But you . . ." she muttered and stopped, her heart wounded and her pride outraged by his unresponsiveness. His eyes had slid away; in this place of her greatest loneliness, he would not join her.

*   *   *   *

In Sydney the latter part of the year had brought its troubles to the Governor, and he climbed the stairs to his room one evening in October feeling unwontedly weary and depressed. Mrs. Macquarie had retired early, but when her husband entered she was still sitting up in bed with a book upon her knee, and a shawl about her shoulders. He seized this opportunity to read more attentively a letter he had received by the *Minstrel* from his friend Mr. William Wilberforce, but found some dif-ficulty in fixing his attention upon it. From across the passage there had suddenly broken out the loud, blustering voice of Lieutenant-Colonel Davey, conducting one of those regrettable altercations with his wife, to which she, poor woman, contributed nothing but an occasional mild and patient protest; and His Excellency suspected that in a room nearby their daughter was listening with an embarrassment which matched his own.

The thought of such a person in no less a situation than that of Lieutenant-Governor in Van Diemen's Land had begun to shock him within an hour of the gentleman's disembarkation. "I can't conceive," he had said to his wife half a dozen times, "why they made such an appoint-ment!" Certainly the fellow had been among the little band which first established the colony twenty-four years ago—but as a mere Lieutenant of the Marines, totally undistinguished. Of his career since then the Governor had as yet an imperfect knowledge, but he had already begun to feel that a man with so little regard for Order and Dignity might well be found wanting in Rectitude too. His appearance was slovenly, his deportment loutish, his manners uncouth and marked by a most unseemly ribaldry; moreover, he could not take his liquor like a gentleman. He was, in short, a clown, and His Excellency's reflections upon those who had chosen him (when they might have had his own dear brother, Charles!) were bitter and rebellious.

But bitterness had been gathering in him even before the lamentable Davey's shortcomings increased it. For the *Minstrel* had also brought him despatches from Lord Liverpool, and certain passages from these documents had been haunting his mind for days.

". . . it becomes necessary that you should transmit a more Satisfactory explanation than any that has yet been received of the Grounds upon which the unusual Expenditure has been sanctioned by you. . . . The only ground upon which a judgment can be formed at such a distance is upon Comparison of the total Amount of the Expence authorised by your Predecessors and yourself . . . and I regret that the only conclusion to be drawn from that Comparison is not in your favour."

Not in his favour! It would be simple enough, he thought indignantly, to keep expenses down by doing nothing! Simple enough to acquire a reputation for economy by patching the tottering public buildings erected in Governor Phillip's time, and handing them on in a state of increased decrepitude to his successors! Was no allowance to be made for the needs of an enlarged and ever-expanding colony? Had they not realised at home the disordered state of affairs which he had found upon his arrival—a disorder due not only to two successive and calamitous floods, but to the incompetence—or worse—of the usurping Government, which had stripped the stores of provisions, clothing, and well nigh everything else? Could they not envisage his predicament, arriving in a country thus depleted of food and other necessities, with eight hundred soldiers and some five hundred of their dependents, all of whom must be victualled at the public expense? Did they forget that he had been compelled, in addition, to supply the members of the New South Wales Corps and their families for four and a half months before their departure, and to supply six months' provisions for their voyage home? Did they not consider that the shiploads of convicts they continued to send out must also be fed and clothed, or that in granting land to new settlers he must obey the instructions the home Government itself had formulated, by clothing and victualling them for eighteen months? Was it not the height of unreason to direct that he provide suitable accommodation for the troops—and then censure him for the expenses thus incurred? Did they imagine that he possessed some Midas touch which could enable him to pay for all this without making inroads upon His Majesty's Treasury . . . ?

But another despatch had added to his disquiet. Proud as he was of the hospital now slowly rising, foot by painful foot, on the hill behind the town, it was causing him enough trouble without the addition of comments from his Lordship which were distinctly critical. His own earlier opinion that the free importation of spirits under a high duty would be sound policy, had apparently been so readily accepted that the authorities in England had lost no time in granting licenses to merchants who desired to export considerable quantities to the colony, and, as the despatch forcibly pointed out, an odd conflict between home and colonial policy seemed to have been created by his arrangements for the building of the hospital. "If the contract that you have entered into . . . has the effect of excluding them entirely from the Sale of that part of their Cargo they will have great reason to complain that on undertaking so distant a Voyage no intimation was given to them of the existence of such restrictions. . . ." His Excellency, said the tone of the despatch, appeared to have placed himself—and, more seriously, His Majesty's Ministers—in an embarrassing situation from which he must extricate himself—and, more importantly, them—as best he could.

"Extraordinary!" Macquarie exclaimed aloud as Davey's tirade gave way abruptly (for he was a good-natured oaf on the whole) to a burst of raucous laughter; but he was thinking as much of his hospital as of his guest. Was there no one else besides himself and his dear wife who could feel pride and a sense of achievement in the erection of useful buildings? Not even privately, however, did he quite dare to admit that he loved a building for its own sake, almost as one might love a woman, counting some additional elegance, some tasteful ornamentation as its natural right, and feeling it churlish to count the cost too parsimoniously. He said with some irritation as his wife glanced up from her book: "I'll be thankful when we can move to our new bedroom—we may be quieter there."

*   *   *   *

But he was permitted little quietude during the remainder of the year. The continued presence of his uncongenial guest—who could not, as yet, be packed off to Van Diemen's Land, and must in the meantime be treated with all honour and attention—was a perpetual annoyance to him. He had long and extremely important despatches to prepare before the *Isabella* sailed, and not only he himself, but his Secretary and the clerks worked late into the night. He called upon the Assistant Commissary, Mr. Broughton, to prepare a statement of the causes which had occasioned such greatly increased expenditure, adding his own detailed explanation, and a vigorous defence of his hospital contract. Though it appeared to be his duty to accept blame even for those expenses which the actions of his superiors themselves made inevitable, he permitted himself one faintly restive comment: "*As it is Your Lordship's wish to lessen the Expenses of this Colony, I must beg Leave to recommend that the number of Free Settlers sent out from England may be limited to as small a Number as possible. Every Settler Who Obtains Permission to Come out to this Colony Incurs a very Serious Expense to the Crown, which Your Lordship will perceive from a Perusal of the Statement I have transmitted respecting the Messrs. Blaxlands. . . .*" (And, thought His Excellency in parenthesis, may this tedious and unsatisfactory collection of documents cause you as much trouble as it has caused me!) "*I must also inform Your Lordship,*" he continued with some acerbity, "*that these Free Settlers in general, not excepting the Messrs. Blaxlands, Who are sent out from England, are by far the most discontented Persons in the Colony. They imagine they have done His Majesty's Government so very great a favour by Coming to New South Wales, that no Expense on the part of the Crown can repay the Obligation. . . .*"

He addressed himself also to what he regarded as the astonishing necessity for defending his construction of public roads—for Lord Liver-pool had declared that if the free settlers were not in a position to bear the cost of such amenities as wharves, roads and bridges, it might be assumed that the colony was not yet sufficiently advanced to need them. What was the use, Macquarie wondered, of the returns regularly sub-mitted showing increase of population, increase of cultivated land, increase of shipping, stock, and almost every other aspect of colonial life, if they did not show a picture of general development in which the need for increased communications might be taken for granted? "*Altho' there are many Opulent settlers in this Colony,*" he explained rather wearily, "*still the great Bulk of the People are poor, and as yet totally unable to bear any heavy Taxes or Burthens of any Description. . . .*" And whether the money were to come from the Treasury or from the colonial revenue, roads there must and should be. He set his teeth and continued obstinately: "*I confidently hope Your Lordship will approve of my Continuing to Construct public permanent Roads . . . two more great Turnpike Roads being yet essentially Necessary between the Town of Sydney and Liver-pool, and between the former and the River Nepean. . . .*"

For a moment there flitted before his mind the thought of Mr. Gregory Blaxland and his project for crossing the mountains—a project in which the recently returned Lieutenant Lawson was also betraying some interest —and he envisaged his road to the Nepean as not halted by that stream, but fording it to climb the foothills and brave the wild, craggy ridges on its journey to some unknown Eldorado. . . . For a moment the fancy excited him, but he checked it; if such a road were ever to be made, he thought, and the news of it were to be received in the Colonial Office without causing great personages to suffer apoplectic strokes, he would sorely need to be able to assure them of Eldorado as its goal.

The ink was barely dry upon the last fair copy of his despatch when His Majesty's Sloop of War *Samarang* arrived, bearing not only ten thousand long-promised dollars for the use of the colony, but also a less tangible cargo of trouble for the Governor. The dollars themselves pre-sented an immediate problem, for it was necessary to devise means of preventing their export from the colony; and though it was simple enough to conceive and order a machine for cutting a circle out of each coin, and stamping the two pieces thus produced with their respective values and the name of the colony, it proved less simple to construct it. In the meantime, while successive attempts were made, and successive failures reported, Macquarie's peace and the tranquillity of his capital were dis-turbed by the behaviour of the *Samarang's* captain and crew.

Like other Governors before him, Macquarie was shocked to find that it was not so much the control of degraded felons which occupied his mind and tried his patience as the control of respectable people. Felons were, after all, easily managed; the gaol, the lash, and, in the last resort, the gallows, might be relied upon to dispose of such recalcitrance as they displayed. But the intransigeance of respectable people manifested itself more subtly, and his own defence against it was limited to exhortations which could be ignored, the framing of regulations which could be evaded, and written complaints to his superiors which the disaffected could match with their own. The resentment and forebodings which had been aroused among them by his encouragement of emancipists were gathering strength, and wanted, perhaps, only the incitement and direction of a bold leader to make them articulate and challenging.

But disaffection on the spot was not the only danger he must fear; every ship that passed out through the Heads bound for England bore letters from his detractors to their friends and patrons, expressing views which, by devious ways, might come to the ever-listening ear of authority, telling tales of colonial administration at variance with his own accounts. Not only in public despatches, therefore, but also in private letters, it was desirable to make such counter moves as were possible—and here even his dear wife might play her part. Captain Piper, for example, was a popular fellow with a host of friends in England and a host of corre-spondents in New South Wales; a little policy might well be mixed with the gay banter of a lady writing to a gallant Captain. . . .

"We are all well here," scribbled Mrs. Macquarie rather hastily (for the despatches were about to be closed), "and the Colony continues prosperous; a small attempt has been made by some of the old Faction with a view as I think to make it appear that the colony is not quiet not-withstanding the absence of the old Head: All I have to say to you on that subject is that those who act with impropriety must suffer for it, let them be whom they may; which if they continue to be troublesome they certainly will. . . ." She glanced out the window to where the Samarang lay at anchor with the Estramina alongside, much activity dis-cernible as baskets of coal were loaded from the colonial vessel to the sloop. "But the probability is that the people will be quiet and all will go on. . . ."

There seemed to be some commotion on board the Estramina, and angry shouts echoed across the water. Mrs. Macquarie sighed and shrugged, wishing that people would, indeed, be quiet and refrain from quarrelling—though Captain Piper, who knew the place so well, would not, of course, imagine her to mean that any such idyllic state existed. But it must be made quite clear that nothing disturbed the peace save petty brawls and dissensions which might be regarded as normal, and with which His Excellency was quite capable of dealing. She was, she continued, being thus particular to Captain Piper since she believed that some of his friends would probably make more of the opposition to her husband than the facts warranted. ". . . it is," she assured him, "only a molehill, and a very small one too."

       *   *   *   *

Of all the activities which his situation demanded of him, the Governor enjoyed most his tours of inspection. He liked to hand his wife into their carriage and set off behind their two fine horses through the town, acknowledging the respectful salutes of the citizens and planning the further improvements he would make. He liked to drive along the street which bore his name, and alight for a few moments to observe the progress of the hospital, or to study an area of vacant ground, and reflect upon its eligibility for this or that new building. He liked to leave Sydney behind him and bowl at a lively pace along his turnpike road to Parramatta; and to set out thence with his bodyguard behind and his wife beside him, and a little retinue of congenial souls to bear him company, pausing here and there to admire a field of maize, enjoy a view, or exchange an affable word with a fellow-wayfarer, until he came to Windsor and his third colonial home—the stone cottage with its grounds sloping down to the river.

Such an expedition in December was marred for him, however, not only by the presence of the lamentable Davey, but by the accumulated annoyances of the past week which had left him in a mood of nervous exasperation not easily to be dispelled. The altercation on board the *Samarang* which had interrupted Mrs. Macquarie's letter-writing, had swollen into a heated wrangle between himself and its commander, Captain Case; for the pattern of colonial conflict (which each successive Governor must learn painfully from experience) was formed by a tendency to make its participants symbols of their respective classes or professions. A quarrel between a soldier and a sailor speedily became a quarrel between the Army and the Navy; a disagreement between a settler and a convict was soon an issue between the free population and the felonry; a dispute involving a native was apt to take on the aspect of inter-racial war; and should His Excellency find himself (as he often did) at variance with Mr. Marsden, there was even, in the reverend gentleman's attitude, a suggestion that the temporal power was presuming to array itself against the hosts of Heaven. Thus, dissension between Mr. Watson, the Harbour-master, and an officer of the *Samarang's* crew had been transformed in a twinkling to a clash between civil and naval authority; and the Governor's indignation upon learning that Mr. Watson had been summarily arrested and placed in irons on board the sloop had been met by Captain Case with the retort that while he allowed His Excellency to be His Majesty's representative ashore, he begged to claim for himself the authority of His Majesty's representative afloat.

For some time, also, there had been lying rather heavily at the back of Macquarie's mind the knowledge that a Select Committee of the House of Commons had been appointed to consider the whole question of transportation, and had begun its sittings in February. The outcome of its deliberations remained to be revealed, but he sometimes wondered uneasily what recommendations it would make, and what new policies he might be called upon to implement.

It seemed a final unkind thrust of Fate that even the smiling countryside, proclaiming in every field they passed a bountiful harvest and a promise of abundance, should add to, rather than ameliorate his anxieties. For abundance, here, brought its own problems and bred its own dissatisfactions, rumours of which had been reaching his ears of late. The colonists were becoming more and more forcibly aware that they inhabited a rich land; they were observing not only meat and grain far in excess of what the colony could consume, and wool now known to be commercially valuable, but the presence of other commodities such as timber, coal and whale-oil, which held alluring promises of profit. What was the use, they were enquiring, of producing all this if they could not sell it? Where was the market, once the needs of the colony itself had been satisfied? Sympathetically as Macquarie might hear such questions, he dared not answer them; he knew that it was no part of the rôle allotted to this humble colony that it should emerge as a trade rival to the East India Company and the independent merchants of the mother country.

By the time he returned to Sydney with his wife, his guest, and his train of attendants, he was tired. There was but a week to pass before Christmas, and in the midsummer heat the town seemed—after the open country and the peaceful, rural scenes of Windsor—drab, squalid, and more than a little smelly. He disposed of the most pressing business which awaited him, and retired thankfully with his wife to sleep for the first time in the new bedroom at last completed during their absence. He noticed with relief as he mounted the stairs that no sound came from the bedchamber of Lieutenant-Colonel Davey; perhaps he, too, had found the journey fatiguing.

1813

Laetitia Mannion, opening her eyes after a hot and restless night, found herself looking into a black, flat-nosed face not a foot from her own. She uttered a faint scream, and Miles started up from beside her.

"What the deuce . . . ? Letty, what ails you?" His voice became a roar: "Dilboong! What the devil are you doing, squatting there by the bed like a confounded gargoyle? Be off with you!"

Dilboong scrambled to her feet, tears of terror in her eyes. Every morning it was her duty to carry in the cans of hot water and draw the curtains aside, and this was not the first occasion when she had crouched for a moment to stare with wonder at the fair face of Mr. Miles' lady, at her pale, silken hair like corn tassels spread out over the frilled pillow, and her fine, dark brows arched over closed eyelids with delicate blue veins. This morning there had been a hand visible too—a white, frail hand wearing a ring whose diamonds glittered in the thread of sunlight that found its way between the curtains; Dilboong had remained longer than usual, held in tranced delight by the fiery flashes of colour that winked from it. Now she stood twisting her apron, her face puckered with alarm, her feet rooted to the floor; Miles, leaping out of bed in his nightshirt, was compelled to take her by the shoulders and thrust her unceremoniously out the door. He strode across to the window and pulled the curtains back with a clatter of brass rings.

"Good God, Letty, the girl's not a monster—she won't eat you! There, there, my love, compose yourself and I'll ring for Johanna."

Laetitia pushed her hands beneath the bedclothes to hide their trembling.

"No, no, pray don't. I'm quite recovered now. It was just that . . . the room was rather dark, you see, and I wakened suddenly . . . that black face so close to my own. . . ."

"Of course, my angel! I know you find the natives repulsive. I'm accustomed to them myself, but I admit that poor Dilboong's no beauty. Well, I'm astir, so I may as well dress and get out of doors. Just look at that sunshine! There's heat in it already—by midday it'll scorch like fire . . . ?"

There was a faintly nervous edge to her voice:

"One would imagine that you like to be scorched."

"By God I do! I like my heat hot and my cold freezing." He was dressing rapidly, strewing clothes and towels about the room, and dis-ordering the precise arrangement of her dressing-table. "Rain, now—let it be a deluge, not a drizzle. Give me a gale, and keep your zephyrs. The half-hearted irks me—the mild, the dim, the lukewarm—like this water, confound it! I like my spirits neat, my music loud, my lights bright, my women . . ." he dropped a kiss on her head in passing, ". . . beautiful, and my cards all aces."

She made no reply, but he did not notice her silence. Under the coverlet her hands were still shaking a little, and the morning's promise of midsummer heat which he had welcomed was already beginning to distress her. She had a momentary vision of herself waking in her parents' house in London to see a room that was familiar and all her own; and outside a mild, sweet sunshine touching the tops of the old elms in the Square. . . . Or perhaps it would be raining, she thought nostalgically—one of those soft, quiet drizzles that Miles so disliked. . . .

"You know," he was saying as he buttoned his shirt, "I'll confess that there was one disappointment in my homecoming—the damned place has shrunk. And they've tamed it. I went looking for a spot down near the northern boundary where we used to play—there was a burnt-out tree there that we could all get into—Maria and Andy Prentice, and Dilboong, and myself—and half an acre of bracken that stood higher than our heads. All gone—all under crops. . . . And the house, too—I'd remembered it as big, and so it is, as houses of its kind go, but not near so big as it seemed when I was a child. Someday I'll build a house for myself—for us—that a man can move about in, and rear a family in—a round dozen or so, eh, my angel . . . ?"

She said in a low voice, watching him wield his ebony-backed hair-brushes: "At the moment I do not care to look so far ahead."

"Why not?" He came to sit beside her, his great weight dragging the covers uncomfortably across her body. "When the first of our quiverful has made his appearance. . . ."

"Or *her* appearance . . . ?"

"Nonsense, my love—later on, perhaps. . . . Well, then, you shall come with me and look for a suitable site for our house—for it'll need to be carefully chosen, and as yet I've seen nothing that satisfies me. How does a mountain top strike you? Or a tall headland facing the ocean, so that at night one can hear the waves crashing on the rocks below . . . ? Well, we shall see, but it must be wild and spacious—I've no use for a pretty landscape—a hill, a dale, a brook, a lamb, a blue-bell. . . ."

"Miles," she said desperately, "was there not some talk of that girl going to Mrs. Harvey?"

"Girl? Oh—Dilboong. Why, yes, it was suggested, I believe, but the poor creature has become attached to this place. Patrick said she wept and begged not to be sent away, so both he and Mrs. Harvey. . . . Why, Letty, you're not crying . . . ?"

"No, no, of course not. . . . But I—I—indeed, Miles, I find her very . . . disturbing. Perhaps I'm a little nervous at present, but it puts me in a perfect frenzy to have her near me And she—she follows me about. I can never turn without finding her standing in some doorway or peering round some corner—staring at me. Have you not noticed it?"

"Of course she stares at you, my jewel—can you blame her? And I've certainly noticed that she runs to fetch your parasol or place a footstool for you, and her ugly face beams with delight that she can serve so exquisite a being! As for following—why, she has always followed. When we were children she was at my heels like a puppy all day long—and still is, for that matter, whenever I'm about the house. It's her way of show-ing devotion. Give her a wave and a smile, my love, and forget about her."

"I *cannot*. And just now it's not right that I should be agitated in this way. Johanna says . . ."

"Oh, you were startled for a moment—and not unnaturally, I allow —but there's no reason to be agitated about Dilboong. Why, she's the gentlest, meekest creature imaginable! When Julia and Desmond were infants she was their nursemaid, and a more tender and devoted one their mother declares she has never seen. Come, now, when you have watched her lavishing the same care on our own dear . . ."

"Oh, no, no, *no!*"

He laughed and patted her on the shoulder.

"Only try to keep Dilboong from a baby in the house! She adores them—it's a veritable passion with her."

Laetitia sat up in bed and made no reply for a moment. Then, with a slight crease between her brows, she said slowly:

"She does seem greatly attached to her own child—for whom I've been able to observe no father . . ."

She was arranging her pillows, and did not see her husband's quiz-zical sideways glance. He had refrained from comment upon a matter which Patrick seemed indisposed to discuss, but he had no doubt that Dilboong's child was his brother's, and it amused him that his wife had not, apparently, reached the same conclusion. What a little innocent she was, he thought fondly. And how scandalised she would be if she guessed that Patrick, for whom she had conceived such a high regard, had fathered a little black bastard!

". . . though it's plain enough," Laetitia was continuing, "that he must be one of the labourers or overseers employed here, and I wonder that any white man can so degrade himself, or that Patrick should permit. . . ."

Miles stood up and began rummaging in the tall mahogany wardrobe for a coat.

"Oh, come, my love, these little episodes will occur in such a place as this—you must not allow yourself to be distressed by trifles. But quite soon this tiresome period will be over—it can't be more than a week or two now—and then you'll be yourself again, and laugh at all these vapours and imaginings. Now, are you sure you'd not like me to ring for Johanna before I go?"

"Thank you—quite sure."

"Shall I fetch you anything? Your shawl? Your vinaigrette?"

"I have it here, and I think it's too warm for a shawl."

"Your novel, then? Here it is—and if I'm not able to offer you *La Belle Assemblée* I can at least provide the *Sydney Gazette!* There! Is all as you like it? Your pillows? The curtains? Then I'll be off, for I've time for a ride before I breakfast." He took her face between his hands and kissed her nose. "Macushla!"

She smiled, but her eyes were forlorn.

"Don't be so Irish, pray—it doesn't become you."

He asked from the doorway:

"Am I not Irish?"

"You're colonial," she said. The remark was not meant to be amusing, but she could hear him still laughing as he went down the passage.

She took up the novel, but was unable to fix her attention on it. Had Papa's misgivings been justified after all? Had she been a silly, romantic girl, blinded by Miles' remarkable handsomeness and his beguiling manners? Had Mama been wrong to support her against Papa's opposition, urging young Mr. Mannion's impeccable birth and his still more impeccable worldly prospects? "For we know," she had argued, "that quite apart from the Irish estates, property in New South Wales promises to become extremely valuable. I've been enquiring, and I'm assured there are fortunes to be made from wool. As for the undesirability of the place as a permanent home, I'm quite in agreement with you, but . . ." she waved her hand lightly and smiled, ". . . need it be permanent? If Laetitia herself is unable to adjust that aspect of the matter within a few years at most, I shall consider that she has earned her sentence of transportation for life!"

Now, holding her book before her eyes without seeing it, Laetitia was reflecting that she had already served five months of her sentence, and with each day its end seemed to recede farther into the future. It was not only that she felt little confidence in her ability to contrive a not too distant return to England—or even Ireland; far more disturbing was the fact that though she disliked the colony intensely, she was not even trying to escape.

She had no taste for rural life, and its days seemed endless—yet two weeks which she had passed in Sydney had been even worse. She could take no pleasure in a social round which seemed but a crude imitation of the life she had known in London; the town itself offended her, its few handsome buildings merely emphasising the poor appearance of the rest; it was impossible not to be continually aware of crime, poverty and other disagreeable things. There were some pretty drives, she allowed, and the water-picnics to some harbour bay or headland had the charm of novelty—but wherever one went one was likely to come upon those miserable, dirty, naked savages. . . . And where were there to be found congenial company and agreeable conversation for one who, like herself, had a taste for music, poetry and painting—who read the latest novels and saw the latest plays—who attended little soirees to meet the latest lion in the world of art or letters? True, Mrs. O'Connell played the pianoforte with some facility, and Mrs. Bent was the possessor of a voice which her fond, fat husband at least described as sweet and of great compass—but these were mere drawing-room accomplishments, and of no very high order either; one listened politely, applauded suitably, and that was the end. For the rest, there was that absurd ex-convict, Robinson, who recited his tiresome Odes upon the smallest provocation, and an academy of drawing conducted by another ex-convict. . . . No, she had been glad enough to escape from Sydney and return to Beltrasna where she could enjoy, at least, dignity, seclusion, and civilised conversation with Patrick. . . .

She turned a page hurriedly and read a few lines with determination before her thoughts again began to wander. They wandered, disconcert-ingly, to a memory of Mama saying, with a shrug: "It's perhaps a pity that Miles is not the eldest son, but . . ." And like a crash of brass and drums suddenly drowning a plaintive melody on soft strings, she heard them cry with shameless, passionate endorsement: "Yes, yes, a pity —a pity that Miles is not Patrick. . . !"

She dropped her book and, in a panic, snatched up the *Gazette* merely because it lay beneath her hand, and some kind of physical action seemed the only defence against her shocking thoughts. But what was there in this dreary record of paltry colonial doings to distract an anguished mind? The usual Government Orders, the usual reports of shipping, the usual account of vice-regal movements, the usual notices and advertisements. . . .

Her eye was caught by an outlandish name. *"Bennelong"*. Surely

Patrick had mentioned it only a few days ago when he was describing his earliest memories of the colony? Why, yes, this was Dilboong's father —the native whom Governor Phillip had attempted to civilise, and who had been taken by him to England. . . . Laetitia bent over the paper, holding it to the window so that she might more easily read the crude, smudged print.

"*Bennelong died on Sunday morning last at Kissing Point. Of this veteran champion of the native tribe little favourable can be said. His voyage to and benevolent treatment in Great Britain produced no change whatever in his manners or inclinations, which were naturally barbarous and ferocious. The principal officers of the Government had for many years endeavoured, by the kindest usage, to wean him from his original habits, and draw him into a relish for civilised life; but every effort was in vain exerted, and for the last few years he has been but little noticed. His propensity to drunkenness was inordinate; and when in that state he was insolent, menacing and overbearing. In fact he was a thorough savage, not to be warped from the form and character that nature gave him, by all the efforts that mankind could use.*"

Laetitia put the paper down and lay back on her pillows with a little shiver. Mr. Howe's valediction seemed to confirm the instinctive repugnance she had felt from the first moment when she saw those travesties of human beings about the town in Sydney, and the horror that had set her heart pounding not half an hour ago, at finding one of them so close to her. She had tried to subdue it, telling herself that she would become accustomed to them in time; recalling that it was said to be not uncommon for women in her condition to conceive violent aversions. But after all, was there not proof here that her instinct was soundly based? Drunken, insolent, menacing, overbearing—a perfect savage. . . . And this after all the kindness he had received, and all the advantages that had been lavished on him! Yet Miles could lightly propose that their own babe should be tended by the daughter of this creature! It was all very well for him to say that he had known Dilboong since their childhood, and to describe her as meek and gentle; here in her hand was proof that favours, benefits, indulgences and long association with civilised people did *not* obliterate the barbarous tendencies of savages. Suppose that in some fit of sudden and ungovernable rage, the girl should . . . ? No, no, Laetitia thought wildly, I shall not allow so much as one black finger to be laid upon my child . . . ! I shall insist . . . !

But with Miles it was difficult to insist, for he simply did not pay attention. He, for his part, never insisted, but merely assumed—and somehow what he assumed came to pass. Yet why should the decision be his? He was not the master here, and Patrick—so courteous and attentive, so full of understanding and sensibility—would surely listen?

*　　　　*　　　　*　　　　*

Dilboong closed the study door quietly behind her, and stood in the hall, trembling. On a table beside her a lamp had been set near a bowl of roses, and through the front door, standing open to admit the cool, night air, a moth had flown in to flutter round it. A few petals, dislodged by its restless wings, lay scattered round the bowl; Dilboong gathered them up mechanically, and wiped the polished wood with the corner of her apron. To her right the passage leading to Mrs. Miles' room was dim, and in front of her the one which ran to the northern wing of the house was in darkness save for a bar of light which came from the parlour at its far end. She stared fixedly at this light, crushing the petals in one hand, and pressing the other against her throat where a strange, breath-halting tightness had gathered.

It was not more than ten long minutes since Hattie had come into the kitchen where she was cleaning a row of boots and shoes, to say that the master required her presence in the study. Now she stood motionless, as if the world had become a place in which her feet could find no direction—a place so unfamiliar that she found herself listening intently, bewildered that for others life could be going on unchanged. In the scullery Maria was still busy with her piles of ironing; in the housekeeper's room Mrs. Emmett and Hattie were listening with respect to Johanna's tales of houses in which a black heathen and the daughter of a notorious murderess would not be found upon the domestic staff. Mrs. Miles was indisposed, and had retired early; Mr. Miles was writing letters in the parlour. Dilboong, with her hand at her throat, stood listening, hearing nothing but the tick of the tall clock across the hall, and waiting for something to happen.

Nothing happened but the slow, merciless clearing of her mind, shocked temporarily into confusion and stupidity. She was to leave this place. She formed the thought into words which formed themselves into a rhythm, as words frequently did, especially when she was greatly moved. Mrs. Emmett was unaware—and so, indeed, was Dilboong herself—that she was the daughter of a notable *youaragurrugin*, and the granddaughter of the greatest of them all; she had made it abundantly plain that in well-conducted houses servants did not go about singing, "if singing you can call it," she had added crossly, for the low, tuneless chants with their strange, primitive beat and their endless repetition had annoyed her extremely. So Dilboong's lips moved noiselessly:

> *"Dil-boong, Ma-ry,*
> *Away, away, away go,*
> *Away, away, away go. . . ."*

Like all her people she felt a close identity with the spot she had been taught to see as home. Sydney, her birthplace, was now hardly even a memory; this was her *towri,* and here her spirit lived. But it was also Mr. Miles' *towri.* Though he vanished for a long, long time, it was still his place, to which she had never doubted that he would return, and in which, with longing and indestructible patience she had awaited the day when she would look at him again.

To look was enough. To look, to follow, to serve—these had always been enough. To serve his lady was joy, for it was another way of serving him. Mr. Patrick was the master, and to serve him was duty, but Mr. Miles was the daylight of her life, and to serve him was happiness.

Now she was to leave him. Why? She was to go to the mistress in Sydney. "You will be happy there, Dilboong," Mr. Patrick had said— and indeed the mistress was kind, but how should she be happy there, having left her happiness behind? "There will be the mistress' children for you to take care of—you will like that, will you not?" But what of Mr. Miles' child? "There will be a good home for you and your baby." But was not this her baby's *towri* too?

She could not explain these things; she could only weep and plead while Mr. Patrick looked disturbed, and paced the room, and said at last, without looking at her: "I can't discuss it, Dilboong. The arrangement has been made, and it is best for—for everyone. Someday, perhaps, when Mr. and Mrs. Miles are no longer here, you may return. . . ."

What had he meant? As she stared stupidly he had made a little gesture of annoyance, as if his words had almost told something he had not meant to reveal, and said abruptly: "That's all—you may go now."

And she was left not only in agony, but without hope. To return only if Mr. Miles was no longer here? The bar of light from the parlour door widened, a tall figure moved out into it, and suddenly her feet knew where to go.

Miles stopped in astonishment as she ran down the passage and flung herself at him, clutching his sleeve, babbling incoherently:

"What's this? Stop clawing at me, girl, and speak plainly! Going away. . . . I'm not going away. . . ."

"Dilboong," she sobbed, "Dilboong, Mary, away, away. . . ."

"*You're* going away?"

"Not go! Not go away! Be here all time . . . !"

He frowned.

"Who says you're to go away?"

She moved her head in the direction of the study door. "Mr. Patrick, eh?" He shrugged. Patrick was a queasy sort of fellow, and no doubt the sight of his discarded mistress and his half-caste bastard was proving distasteful to him—destroying his sense of dignity, perhaps, now that he had a white gentlewoman beneath his roof! "Well, Dilboong," he said, "Mr. Patrick is the master, and you must do as he says, so . . ."

"No, no, not go! Dilboong, Mary live here. . . ."

"Come, come, you'll be glad to see the mistress again, won't you? And Master Desmond? And Mr. Harvey? Why, he taught you to write, don't you remember? And there's a baby for you to . . ."

"Not go—live here, do work, clean boots, wash dish. . . . Mary get big, do work. . . ."

"Let *go*, Dilboong! Good God, anyone would suppose you were being sent to Newcastle! If Mr. Patrick says you must go, you must, and there's an end to it."

But he could not release his sleeve from her grasp, and in the faint light he could see tears shining on her face as she renewed her frantic pleading. Confound it, he thought, it was hard on the poor wretch to be turned out after so many years. . . . He would have a word with Patrick in the morning—see if he could persuade . . .

But her wild flood of protestation had ceased. Into her mind had come, as a final hope, the recollection that she was a woman, and Miles a man. Once before, long ago when the mistress went away, and wanted her to go too, had she not known that she must remain in this place to which Mr. Miles would return, and had it not been Mr. Patrick's need of what she gave him that reprieved her? With a kind of clumsy desperation her clinging hands moved upward to Miles' shoulders, and she pressed her skinny body against his, offering her last argument.

So personable a young man could not be inexperienced in the arts of female invitation, yet for a second or two Miles failed to grasp her incredible intention. When he did, his reaction to it was as involuntary as the movement with which one flings off from the flinching skin a toad, a spider, or some noisome filth; it sent her staggering against the wall as he strode past her, muttering angrily: "God in Heaven, the girl's taken leave of her senses!"

She watched him turn from the hall, and stumbled after him. She saw the bedroom door open, and the light shone on his fair head for a moment before it closed. She had never lived among her own people, yet she knew that when the spirit dies and departs the body must prepare itself to follow; her instinct was to creep to her bed and lie down, turning her face toward the wall, thus to await the slow, inevitable extinction of a life no longer sustained by joy or hope. But she was among white people, who were able to walk, talk, and perform all the motions of living long after their hearts were dead. They would not allow her to yield up her life—they would rouse and scold her, and force food between her lips; they would perhaps lift her passive body and convey it to Sydney before it had time to escape into death. . . .

No sound came from the study; everywhere closed doors. The hall was quiet again, the tall clock ticking steadily, the moth still fluttering round the lamp. More petals were strewn on the table, but she did not notice them. One doorway stood open, and through it she could see moonlight shining on the river.

*   *   *   *

In Johnny's *towri,* as in that of Governor Macquarie, the season had been good, but Johnny, isolated from the benefits of civilisation, found this no embarrassment; indeed, he was nearer to contentment and tranquillity than he had ever been before. On fine, summer evenings Emily often took her sewing to the bench outside the door, and while he sat on the ground nearby, sharpening his axe or mending his fishing line, or repairing some damaged tool, they talked. Yet though he found pleasure in this companionship, it was the source, too, of the only uneasiness which still troubled him. By now she knew all the story of his life in the bush, and his association with the tribes, but of his contacts with civilisation he spoke guardedly. He told her of his father's escape, of the hut he had built in the hills behind the Cow Pastures, and of his own coming to it with Cunnembeillee and the small Billalong. He told of their life there with Milbooroo, and of the birth of Gooradoo, Balgundra, and their little sister, Gooburdi. He described Cunnembeillee's death, and the departure of Milbooroo with the children, so that he and Billalong had been left alone. He explained how the convict, Tom Towns, had arrived there, and how he had died; but when he spoke of Finn he left her to assume that this second convict had made his appearance in the same way. When she questioned him about his childhood in the settlements he dredged his memory, and found pictures which seemed to become clearer as he talked. He told her of his first friend, Arabanoo, whose death had left him consumed by a helpless, childish fury of grief; he mentioned his convict mother who had become the housekeeper and mistress of a gentleman—but when she asked him the gentleman's name he replied only: "Ye wouldn't know of him." He avoided, at first, any reference to his close, uneasy friendship with Patrick Mannion, and when his account of some incident made avoidance no longer possible, spoke of him only as "a lad". When she examined the once elegant brocade and rosewood footstool which he had stolen from the Beltrasna verandah, enquiring with surprise how so unlikely an object had found its way to this place, he said hurriedly that it was one of the things he had traded for his salt beef at Green Hills—and found his lie almost betrayed by his ignorance. She objected at once:

"But ye said they was all poor folks—how would a poor settler's wife be restin' her feet on a footstool the like of this? A bit of box, more likely! This is somethin' that's belonged to gentry." He was saved by her afterthought: "Ah, well, there's lots of queer things change hands, and in queer ways, too. Maybe they stole it, and got scared to keep it."

He found that every fresh tale opened the way to another—and sometimes the way was dangerous. What, she demanded, had become of Finn? Immediately he was in retreat again. It was not only a lingering caution which shut his mouth upon any mention of the Mannions, and warned him to say nothing that could connect him with a rich gentleman he had killed; it was still partly the old instinct to conceal himself, to guard in jealous privacy the hatred and the friendship which had been the main-springs of his life. Finn had been murdered, he answered her harshly, and would say no more.

In such fits of panic he told himself over and over again that silence, after all, was best; though she knew nothing of his past, and he nothing of hers, there would still remain the reality of their present life together, and the simple bonds of the flesh. But silence was not for Emily, and there were times when, all unconsciously, she dealt him wounds. No secret torments braked her tongue, and she chattered continuously of her life while he listened with almost strained attention, glimpsing through this tale of an unimportant orphan girl's existence, the shape of the society which had enclosed it. She sometimes teased him a little; having realised the profundity of his ignorance and her own far greater sophistication, she had found herself in possession of a useful goad for pricking an inflated male superiority which often irked her.

"Ah," she said one day, "ye should 'a seen the streets at night when the new Governor arrived! Bright as day, they were, with bonfires, and lights in all the windows, and pitchers of the King and Queen that beautiful you wouldn't believe. And the people walkin' up and down, shoutin' and dancin' and singin' till they fell down in the gutters. And the band playin' till near mornin'. . . ." She gave him a sly glance. "But there—I'm forgettin'! Ye've never heard a band play, I reckon, and I don't suppose ye know no tunes?"

In the evening hush it seemed to him that a thin, ghostly singing in his mind must be audible, and that the restless pain in his heart must communicate itself to hers.

> "O Paddy dear and did ye hear
> The news that's going round?
> The shamrock is forbidden now
> In all its native land."

It was the very voice of Finn's anguish and his memory ached with it, but she was unaware, watching him with bright, mischievous eyes.

"Do ye?"

"Aye."

"What tune? Can ye sing it?"

He kept his lips shut and his eyes on his work, but his brain was singing fiercely:

> "When laws can keep the blades of grass
> From growing as they grow,
> And when the leaves in summer time
> Their colour dare not show,
> Then I will change the colour
> That I wear in my caurbeen. . . ."

It was the very voice of Finn's defiance, and it seemed to Johnny that it filled the whole valley. He looked up at Emily, feeling their separateness, but unable, as yet, to take this step towards her. He said shortly: "The natives are always makin' songs—hundreds of 'em."

Alert though he was against her probing into his past, he relaxed when she spoke of her own; for though some reference might stir painful memories, he believed that no threat could come from there. He liked to hear her tell of the Orphanage, and the stealthy, vehement life of its small inmates, flowing secretly beneath the surface of a strict routine. Absorbed, he heard her describe the endless comedy and drama of the streets. Bewildered, he tried to envisage and understand the rituals of Divine Service. Himself accustomed to silence, her unconscious, nostalgic emphasis upon the sounds of civilisation intrigued him, and he tried to imagine an existence always full of noises—the clamour of the Market, cart-wheels and horses' hooves on cobbled streets, tramping feet and clanking chains as the road gangs went by, sawing and hammering from the lumber-yard, salutes fired from ships, and answered by the battery ashore, itinerant vendors shouting their wares, bands playing for parades, Church bells on Sundays, and even the silence of the night broken by the constable's purposeful tread, and his voice calling the hours.

When she spoke of the Harveys and her duties in their service he listened intently, his forehead creasing in the effort to reconcile her account of these kindly people with his own conception of employers and gentle-folk. She related proudly how the mistress had entrusted her with all the marketing, ". . . and how she'll be doin' now I don't know, for a slower lookin' lump than that Hannah I never did see!" She declared that no lady in Sydney had looked more elegant and beautiful than the mistress, even if the master was not as rich as some. ". . . mind ye, bein' good with me needle, she let me fix her gowns and bonnets. 'Emily,' she says to me, 'I won't know how to manage when ye've left me, for I'm no good with anythin' but embroideries.' (Ah, but she does them beautiful!)." She described her lessons with the master, and Johnny's thoughts went back to the flat rock by a creek which had been his only schoolroom, and to the escaped convict who had taught him to write. She told him of the games she had played with Master Desmond; of Miss Julia's departure for Ireland; of old Mrs. Herbert's death, and the birth of Master Robert. ". . . and Dr. Redfern never saw his bed that night, I'm tellin' ye, what with watchin' the old lady out o' this world, and fetchin' Master Robert in. . . ." And then, from these innocent matters, she passed on to speak of the rare, but exciting, visits of Mr. Mannion.

"Mannion . . . ?"

It seemed to Johnny as though, walking idly through pleasant fields, he had found a precipice yawning suddenly at his feet. What had this woman of his to do with the Mannions? She was chattering on:

"Why, yes, he was the mistress' step-son—didn't I ever tell ye that? A fine, handsome gentleman, too, though more stand-offish, like, than the master. His place is on the river—ye must have seen it—a big house called Beltrasna after their place in Ireland. Not long since he was shot at by some villain when he was out in the bush, and I can tell ye the mistress was in a fair takin' about it, but it weren't that serious that he won't have been walkin' again long before now. . . ."

This time the quality of tension in his silence did reach her, and she bent forward to peer into his face. "Why, ye look quite queer—what ails ye?"

"Nothin'. I used to know a Mr. Mannion, that's all. Put y' things away, it's got too dark for sewin'."

But to her a link between his past and hers was a matter for excite-ment and examination, and she did not long leave the subject unexplored. He was torn between the desire to guard his privacy, and the desire to venture farther and farther along the beguiling path she trod so gaily into a union where all things were shared; tormented by her assumption that where she gave her confidence so freely, he would not be niggardly of his.

He gave her half-truths.

"Mannion? Oh, I seen him in Sydney, walkin' around and talkin' with the officers. His son was the lad I told ye of that I used to play with sometimes. I reckon he'd be the same one that goes to y' mistress' place."

Her wits were sharp, and she asked:

"Ye spoke once of a lad ye met near the river—the one that told ye about y' father and the necklace . . . ? That'd be Mr. Patrick too, I daresay, seein' there wasn't many livin' near the river then, not in those parts. . . ."

"Aye," he agreed uneasily, "that was him."

* * * *

One evening early in the year she brought her sewing as usual to the bench beside the door. Only a few days earlier he had stared with astonished interest as she spread the best of her three petticoats upon the table, and, with infinite care, and much furrowing of her brows, cut from it a number of strangely-shaped pieces. Now, as he sprawled idly at her feet with his back against the wall, some of these were being transformed into a minute garment, and as they talked he was watching the gold thimble glint upon her finger.

They were speaking of convicts, of felonry, of the bitter, interminable war between high and low, rich and poor. Here, for all her wider experience, she found that he spoke with a confidence and conviction which surprised and faintly nettled her. She knew much of Finn now, but she did not understand that he had implanted in Johnny a habit of dealing with ideas. It puzzled her to hear crime discussed as a manifestation instead of as an incident, and poverty as more than a personal affliction; she could not treat justice as a conception when she saw it as Mr. Bent and a constable; she was bewildered and rather impatient when he seemed to suggest that flogging and hanging were demonstrations of terror rather than of terrorism. "It's because they're afeard," Johnny said stubbornly. "They're afeard o' them they flog and hang."

She shook her head in vigorous denial, her memory teeming with pictures of authority in full armour. The Governor, resplendent and commanding, flanked by his bodyguard, surrounded by his retinue, supported on all sides by every institution of the colony—by Mr. Wentworth's police, by Colonel O'Connell's soldiers, by Mr. Bent's unchallengeable Law, by Mr. Howe's *Gazette,* by the distant, but all-powerful King, and even, it appeared, by Mr. Marsden's God. Frightened? Only Johnny, ignorant beyond belief, and full of crazy notions, could imagine such a thing! What did he know? Why, she had *seen* authority at work —and in its most terrible guise, exacting the ultimate penalty . . . ! She retorted sharply:

"Ye'd not think that if ye saw them! Mind ye, I'm not sayin' the poor folks is afeared either—not all the time. Maybe there's plenty they'd like to say and don't dare, but they take their own back often enough, one way or another, and they ain't always caught. But when they are— well, I ain't seen no signs that the gentry's afeard of them! It's gaol or the cat or the gallows then. . . ." She paused for a moment, brooding. To the orphans execution had seemed—like the appearance of a new Governor or a plum pudding—an event which occurred normally if rather infrequently in life, but the scene which she was now recalling had remained more clearly in her mind than others like it, not only because it had involved a woman, but because, through her later association with the Mannion family, it had acquired a personal interest. "I tell ye," she argued, "I've seen it with me own eyes. There was a woman hung in

Sydney—oh, long ago, it must have been five years since when I was still nothin' but a child. We watched her go by when they took her from the gaol, with the crowd yellin' and pushin' around like they always do. We could see her quite plain—not a bad-lookin' woman, neither, for all she wasn't young no more—black hair, she had, and her eyes starin' sort of fierce, as though she didn't care. . . . What was her name, now . . . ? I forgot—but she was the one that killed Mr. Mannion's father—shot him down with a pistol, she did, on the verandah of his house—that place ye say ye've seen, called Beltras . . ."

He made a sudden, violent movement, and simultaneously the for-gotten name burst up from her memory, and struck her dumb in the middle of a word. Prentice! *That* was why it had seemed familiar when she saw him write it beneath her own on a sheet of paper . . . ! She looked at him fearfully. His head had jerked up and his muscles con-tracted as if to repulse some bodily assault; she saw the colour draining from his face, and a curious rigidity freezing it to unnatural stillness. "Prentice . . ." she said, and her voice was hardly more than a frightened whisper. "Why, that's *your* name—was she . . . ?"

"They hanged her, did they?"

She reached out timidly and laid her hand on his arm.

"Johnny. . . ."

"Hanged her for killin' Mannion, eh?"

He spoke calmly enough, but she could feel his arm trembling, and she thought his voice sounded as if it came from far away. He looked at her and said: "*I* killed him."

She could only stare, and he shouted suddenly: "Can't ye hear me? I say *I* killed him—not her, not me mother. . . ."

"Y' *mother* . . . ? The woman that was hanged . . . ?" She threw her sewing down and jumped up to crouch beside him. "Oh, Johnny, Johnny, Johnny . . . !"

"Why would they think she done it . . . ? Aye, me mother, but y' can spare y' tears . . . ye know how convict women live, I reckon. Maybe she counted herself lucky to catch the eye of a fine gentleman like Mr. Mannion. . . ." He repeated the name several times, softly, almost reflectively, and she asked, shivering a little:

"Was that—why ye killed him, Johnny?"

He seemed to ponder. Hatred was a plant of slow growth—perhaps its roots were there. But who thought of roots with the blossom in view? It was in the Beltrasna fields one hot summer afternoon that his hatred had come to its full flowering. He answered her remotely: "He killed Finn."

"Did she know—y' mother? Did y' tell her ye were goin' to kill him?"

"Tell her . . . ? I never spoke to her from the time I ran away. Never saw her but from across the river . . ." Emily felt a stiffening of the arm beneath her hand, ". . . except once—and then she didn't know."

"Didn't she even know you were livin'?"

His faraway stare focussed on her face, and his brows came together. "I never thought she did. But she might. There was one that knew."

"Mr. Patrick?"

"Aye, but I was thinkin' of someone else. Me brother, Andy—I got a white brother besides me black ones, an' a shiverin' stupid crawlin' fool he is, too! He knew, and he might a' told me mother, though I reckoned I'd scared him enough to stop his tongue. . . ." He was silent for a moment. She could tell that he was struggling with a new thought—almost feel and watch its growth as his arm began to shake, and a line of sweat broke out across his forehead. He pushed her aside and leapt to his feet, looking desperate and hunted, like one about to run for his life, and he cried out wildly: "Aye, I must a' scared him all right! It must a' been known that Mannion was shot with one of his own pistols that was stole from his house, and Andy knew who stole them—and helped me do it! But he never spoke to save her from the gallows . . . too afeard o' me, and afeard he might have to tell how he took me mother's keys to let me in the house. And Patrick Mannion, too. . . ."

His expression became wild, lost, bewildered; he rubbed his hand over his face, and his eyes looked blind. She stood beside him, terrified, and he began to speak again, though not to her, shaking his head slightly from side to side as if he might thus more easily release his thoughts.

"Aye, there was the two of them must a' known—and both keepin' quiet. . . . Me worthless brother—he was scared, but the other . . . the other. . . ."

"Mr. Patrick? But how could he know?"

"He did, I tell ye!" It was almost a shout, savage and desperate. "He said it himself when he was lyin' there in the cave with me bullet in his leg. . . ."

She cried frantically:

"What is it ye're sayin' now? What cave? When? Ah, for mercy's sake don't tell me ye were the one that . . . ?"

"Aye, it was me! And if I'd not lost me wits with sickness, goin' out after him when I was too weak to stand, and me hands too feeble to hold me musket steady, I'd 'a put the bullet in his heart instead. . . ."

"Ye'd have killed *him*?" Suddenly she was in a fury. "Why, ye're nothin' but a murderin' savage after all! How many have ye killed? There was the two ye told me of, and Dean that ye shot down before me eyes, and now ye say there was Mr. Mannion—and no fault of yours that there's not Mr. Patrick too! Well, the parsons say it's sin to murder, and I'll not argue it, but there's some that act to bring it on themselves, and I never held it against ye, knowin' what ye told me, and more that I'd no need of bein' told. But it looks like there's killin' in y' heart . . . for all I can tell it's me ye'll be wantin' out of the way next, now I know what I'd be glad to see ye hang for!"

He seized her by the shoulders and shook her violently, shouting: "Hold y' tongue, y' little fool . . . fool . . . what can y' know, out of an orphanage and a schoolmaster's house? Ye know that's a lie! Ye know I'd not harm ye! Ye'd be glad to see me hang, would ye? Ye can go, then—aye, I'll take ye meself and push ye back across the river where ye came from so ye can go runnin' to y' friends the gentry and inform on me . . . ! No, no, I'll not, don't take on so . . . ! Ah, now, be quiet, be quiet and listen. . . ."

She stood limp and sobbing in the circle of arms that had suddenly ceased shaking her to close fiercely round her body. "What can ye say?" she wailed. "If ye'd aimed to kill him because he let y' mother die for nothin'—but ye didn't *know* that . . . not till just now ye didn't know it. . . ." He said with desperation:

"There's much I didn't know. . . . Love, I'm findin' out there's much I still don't know. But all I know I'll tell ye—aye, there's more killin' in it, but not all done by me. . . . There was Finn that died too, and I seen them carry his body up from where they'd been floggin' him—him that was me friend, and found this place, and lived here with me. . . . Ah, if I kill it's murder, but if the Mannions kill it's punishment. . . ."

"But not Mr. Patrick," she cried. "*He* never. . . ."

"Ah—him! He was never one to do nothin'—only to stand by and watch. He was there when they took Finn, he knew what was bein' done. And when I'd settled with his father, d'ye think I forgot he knew I was alive? D'ye think I didn't know he might guess who done it? What did I care? He never seen me, he could only guess. . . ." He stopped for a moment, and when he went on his voice was urgent, beg-ging for belief: "I swear I'd no thought of killin' him then. . . . Let him leave me alone, and I'd leave him. . . . Let them all leave me alone and they'd hear no more of me. . . . But then they killed Ngili. . . ."

She interrupted angrily:

"Who's this 'they' ye talk of? It wasn't Mr. Patrick—he never even saw her!"

A sudden stillness fell on him, and several minutes passed before he said, out of a strained silence:

"He saw her. She was dyin' then, and past his help. . . ."

"But he tried to help her? And yet ye say. . . ."

His voice became sullen.

"He was lookin' for me. Weeks, he'd been lookin' for me, huntin' up and down the river, askin' the natives. 'Where's Johnny Prentice?' he'd say. . . . Out alone with his musket, lookin' for me, him that had helped to kill Finn, him that most likely knew I'd killed his father. . . ."

"So . . . ?" she whispered.

"So I went lookin' for him, and I found him." A tremor jerked his rigidly still body; he held her to him still more tightly, and she heard him say under a breath like a groan: "Ah, I don't know . . . ! Feeling his agony and bewilderment like a weight on her own heart, she murmured: "Well, never mind it then—it's done and past."

But he burst out:

"It'll not be past till I know. . . . Listen, listen, while I try to say what's been workin' in me mind till I'm near crazy every time I remember. . . . He could 'a killed me if he'd wanted. There I was, lyin' on the ground with no strength to move, and he had me musket—and his own. . . . And he threw them both away. . . ."

She pushed against his chest to peer up into his face. Twilight had deepened unnoticed, but she could see the line of his cheek and jaw silhouetted against the pale sky, lifted to it, as if he thought the answer he was seeking might come as readily from there as from the confusion of his own heart and mind. She knew better, and raised her hand to pull his head down.

"He knew ye, didn't he?"

"Knew me? He called me by me name, he said I'd killed his . . ."

"Hush, now. When they found him afterwards he said he didn't know who shot him. Ah, that surprises ye, but it's the truth, for I heard it from me mistress' own lips. He said he was shot at sudden like, from behind a rock, and never saw who done it. Why would he tell a lie like that?"

Unconsciously, she asked her question in the manner of Mr. Harvey, encouraging the correct answer to some schoolroom problem from a child who knew it, but whose confidence had failed. He peered down at her searchingly. "Come, now," she admonished him, "it's plain as day he's been tryin' to help ye."

He made a restless movement.

"Help me? Him? Me that killed his father—me that he never saw but once since we were children? Why would he care what comes to me, unless it was to see me hang?"

She said quickly:

"There's lots that goes on in children's heads that stays with them long after. Why, I can remember a little boy that used to play with me in the streets before I was took to the Orphanage, and even now it's like he was someone that belonged to me. Haven't ye told me about when you and Mr. Patrick was children together? And how he saw ye again by the river when ye was both almost grown, and knew ye, and called to ye, and asked ye to go home with him. . . ."

Johnny interrupted bitterly:

"Aye—to be his servant! To break me back workin' for his father, and be flogged for me trouble!"

"Must ye think of nothin' but what's bad? Mercy's sakes, can't ye see what's kindly meant, even if it's foolish—and foolish it was, I grant ye. Haven't ye thought that if y' name's not been put in the *Gazette*, and what ye look like written down for all to see, and a reward offered to any that can take ye, or even say where ye are, it's because he hasn't told? 'Why?' ye say! Are ye so taken up with hatin' that ye think there's nothin' else ever makes people do things?"

He was silent for a long time. It was almost dark, and very quiet; the trickle of the creek was audible, and frogs had begun to croak in the deep pool below the hut. Now that the door was wide open she knew that she had never really cared what lay behind it—only that it should be no longer shut against her. She waited, and presently his low, laborious voice began again.

"In Finn's book," it said, "there was a bit written about them that love mankind. 'What's love?' I says—for I didn't know, and that's the truth. Would ye tell me I don't know now? But ye said once I thought little of killin', and maybe that's true too. Lovin' and hatin'—they can live together like rich and poor can—but not at peace . . . I tell ye, not at peace." Again he was silent and again she waited, content to let him wrestle with his thoughts while she watched the first stars glimmer over his head, felt the cool, evening breeze on her hot cheeks, and his heart beating beneath her outspread palm. "If they're both in me," he said, "why wouldn't they be in him too? Why couldn't he mean well by one man he knew long ago, and still keep others o' the same sort livin' like chained animals in his convict hut . . . ?"

Once more a note of wildness had crept into his voice and her hand moved soothingly on his breast; but she was responding to the tone, and not the words. "Finn knew it well enough," he said, quiet again. 'Let ye never be wastin' time,' he used to say, 'hatin' people. Save y' hatred,' he says, 'for the evil that's in them, and keep some back for the evil in y'self.' There was plenty he said that I didn't rightly understand when he said it—or even now. But things come to ye . . . aye, they come. . . . There's good and bad together in a man, I reckon, and if ye hate the bad there's the more reason for not turnin' y' back on the good. . . ." She felt him hold her a little away from him, as if trying to see her through the darkness, and he added quickly, on a note of wonder and discovery: "But ye know that, don't ye?"

"Me?" She looked up, startled, having lost the track of his thought long since. She was very near her time, and wearied by the long, hot summer and the heaviness of her body, but so long as she could feel the tenseness going out of him she had been content to stand within his restraining arms while he talked. She could pursue her own thoughts, which were of more practical matters than love and hatred, fear, cruelty and kindness, and in the last few moments they had turned anxiously to the cooking pot which she had left simmering on the fire. Ah, he was a queer one, this Johnny—and how his aimless talk of good and evil had led him so abruptly to herself she could not imagine. But he sought, apparently, no answer to his question, merely saying, as his face came down to hers: "As well for me that ye do!"

*　　　　*　　　　*　　　　*

From the celebrations in honour of the Queen's birthday, Patrick had intended to excuse himself; but on the morning of the hot, January day when they were to take place, he changed his mind, ordered his horse, and set out for Sydney. For a week of nights two faces had come between him and sleep, and when he slept at last they still drifted through his dreams—the more horrible because, for all their brutal contrast, they seemed sometimes the same face. Dilboong's, made uglier in death than in life by river mud and slime, had yet expressed a certain peace: Laetitia's, still lovely despite a shock which increased its pallor almost to transparency, had been one branded by horror. Yet sometimes, in his dreams, the black face was hers, and Dilboong looked at him from one magnolia-fair; and sometimes Laetitia's was fair, but frightened, begging him for mercy, while Dilboong's wore the soft radiance of one who knows herself black, but beloved. For how many months—or years—might not he and his brother's wife have denied to themselves what each had seen betrayed a hundred times by the other? How ruthlessly, he thought, tragedy rips away pretences! Had it not been so he might have tried to spare her—even to excuse himself; but in those moments when they confronted each other—no mask on the face, no guard on the tongue, truth at last between them—only true words would come.

"It was because—she was to be sent away?"

"Yes."

"It is my doing then—I caused it?"

"You and I."

Since then he had not seen her. She had kept her room, from which even Miles was mostly banished. Johanna, dour faced, would say only:

"It's unlucky, Sir, that she should have had a shock just now, but she's as well as can be expected." And this morning in the early hours he had heard the womenfolk astir, and Miles had come to his room at day-light to sit on the edge of the bed, yawning, and say: "It's over, God be thanked, and Johanna says Letty's sleeping. A boy, of course—I was allowed to look, but my impression is vague. Two eyes, two hands, a mouth, and—if you stretch a point—a nose. An extraordinary creature, upon my word! Well, I'm going back to bed, for I've hardly slept yet, and by the look of you I think you haven't either."

This morning, as Patrick stood on the verandah, having given Toole his orders, he had noticed Mary sitting alone in the middle of the stone-flagged yard outside the kitchen. She had spent most of her life astride Dilboong's hip, and it was thus that he was accustomed to see her. Now, watching her, he knew her solitude to be more than physical, and won-dered with pain and dread what was passing in her mind. Never again would he be able to say, for his comfort, that savages and children were lightly touched by grief; where there was a mind there was the capacity to suffer, and even in that babe, not yet three years old, there must be, at least, the awareness of some lost security and comfort. She sat quite still, her bare legs thrust out before her, nursing a rag doll and staring at the ground; was it some trick of an imagination too much stirred by self-reproach that made him see in the curve of her mouth and cheek an infantile copy of his own? It was then that the place had suddenly become unendurable, and he had walked across to the stables as rapidly as his limp would allow.

*   *   *   *

He had passed through Toongabbee when, to his astonishment, he was overtaken by Miles. He asked at once, in sharp fear:

"What is it? Is Laetitia . . . ?"

"Letty? Why, no, she's improving every hour. Why?"

"I was surprised to see you—I thought you might perhaps wish me to send out Dr. Redfern after all."

"Not the least necessity! No, I merely decided to give you the pleasure of my company."

"You're coming to Sydney? But did not Laetitia ask you to stay with her?"

"Oh, that was yesterday when she was feeling low, poor girl. She's happy enough this morning—dandling the infant and reciting to Johanna every masculine name under the sun. Did she but know it, the child's already as good as christened Richard Lachlan Patrick Francis Miles Alexander. . . ."

"Don't be absurd!"

"Absurd? Never was a name chosen with more policy! Lachlan for obvious reasons; Patrick—no, not for you, but for our late Grandpapa, in the hope that our Grandmama's purse-strings (which she keeps devilish tight when I'm around) may be loosened for him; Francis for you, since your first name is already bespoken; Miles for me, from sheer vanity; Alexander for Letty's Papa, who is still not entirely reconciled; and Richard because I fancy it. But for God's sake let's not talk of babies— I want to speak to you of something else. I propose to cross the mountains, as you know. . . ."

"You're thinking of joining Mr. Blaxland's party?"

"I'm thinking of nothing of the kind; I shall go alone."

"Alone? You must be mad!"

"Not at all. I've been considering what you told me of that fellow, Prentice, and his familiarity with the natives. Reflect, now—what is it that one needs on such a journey?"

"A number of things, I imagine, such as . . ."

"One thing only—food. For a brief journey a small supply—but this journey may not be brief, and therefore a large supply. What then? Immediately one is compelled to take horses, carts—even to establish depôts, as Barrallier did—and before one can blink one has a veritable cavalcade. . . ."

"You exaggerate."

"Always—but don't interrupt me. The solution is to go alone, and unburdened."

"Living on what, pray?"

"What do the natives live on?"

"Nothing that would be to your taste, I think. Grubs, snakes, half-raw meat, birds and fish, eels. . . ."

"I'm not unreasonable. If I can't eat well-roasted beef I'll eat half-raw wallaby—if I can't have grouse I'll make do with jackass—failing caviar, I'll even try grubs."

Patrick looked at him.

"Granted that such fare would support you, you may find that the mountains are not lavishly supplied with it."

"That may well be true, and it's the reason why I have been assiduously cultivating the acquaintance of the natives in the past few months —including your friend, Billalong."

"You have met with Billalong?"

"Several times, though I took care not to enquire for him, or to mention Prentice. It's my opinion that he's half white."

"You think so?" Patrick looked up quickly. "It had not occurred to me, but now that you suggest it. . . ."

"Where are your eyes, man? He's a full two inches taller than any of his companions, a good deal more robustly built, a shade or two lighter in colour, his nose is less flat, and he has calves; I never yet saw a native whose shanks weren't straight and skinny as a beanpole. But let that pass for the moment. You think he's in close touch with Prentice?"

"I feel sure of it."

"Then he knows where the fellow lives, and I'd wager you Maol-mordha against nothing that it's somewhere in the mountains."

"And if it is?"

"If it is, there's a route to it."

Patrick said sharply: "Do you want a bullet in your leg too?"

"By no means—I expect to find much use for my legs. I mean to go, in the near future, to Billalong, and tell him that I wish to be led to Prentice. He will, no doubt, ask me why, and . . ."

"You're mistaken," Patrick interrupted dryly. "He'll look you in the face and swear that he knows no such person."

"In that case," replied Miles, unruffled, "I shall look him in the face and tell him he's a damned liar. Pray don't make trifling objections, Patrick. I shall next speak of the servant-girl—Emily, was that her name?—who is with Prentice. . . ."

"Suppose she is not with him after all?"

"My dear fellow, why must you create difficulties in the face of all the evidence? She *was* with Dean when he was murdered. Dean *was* murdered by Prentice—yes, yes, an assumption if you like, but good enough for me. For the rest—well, you have seen the girl, have you not?"

"Of course I have seen her, many times."

"I'm told she's as comely a little wench as ever swung a dishclout. Is it likely Prentice would not . . . shall we say appropriate her?"

Patrick said grimly: "He may have murdered her—he takes murder very lightly."

"Oh, come, come, he could find a better use for her than that. Take my word for it, she's with him. I shall explain, I say, to your dark friend that I have been entrusted with a letter to this girl which I must place in her own hands."

"What letter?"

"One from our former stepmother, of course—I shall secure it from her later. I shall assure Billalong that I'm not asking him to betray their hiding place, but merely to tell Prentice that I wish to deliver this letter —when, where or how I care not, so long as it is into the girl's own hands. If he will contrive this, I will go alone and unarmed to any meeting place he may appoint—conducted, of course, by Billalong—and taking with me anything (within reason) that he may desire. And I shall add that he may, if he pleases, keep the appointment surrounded by the warriors of every tribe in the colony, all bristling with spears like porcupines. . . ."

Patrick gestured irritably with his riding whip.

"You're joking, of course—the whole plan is fantastic. And, in God's name, what would you achieve by it? It would not take you across the mountains. It would not release that unfortunate girl."

"I should make Prentice's acquaintance, and perhaps develop it. Now mark me, Patrick, I'm not as wild and irresponsible as you imagine. If I believed that this fellow were no more than a wanton murderer, do you suppose I should be prepared to keep this secret of yours? Believing that, would you keep it yourself? I've considered his story as you told it to me very carefully, and I have found that he does not kill wantonly, or even for personal gain. There are no less than six murders which we either know or suspect that he committed, and if we take them one by one, assuming him to be guilty in every case, we find that we have here a man whose acts of violence, however sordid and brutal, are not actuated by self-seeking, but by a deep sense of injury. A man, too, who has grown up from early childhood among people whose code, in these matters, is different from our own. I want to talk to him. What shall I gain, you ask? I shall hope to gain a guide and an established head-quarters somewhere in the mountains; I shall at least discover something of the girl; and I shall, I think, complete the task you began—the task of reaching some accommodation with Prentice which will free his mind from this obsession of hatred and revenge." He glanced sideways at his brother, adding mentally: "And yours, I trust, from an equally disastrous obsession of remorse!"

Patrick was saying angrily:

"You talk like a lunatic! This man is dangerous—maddened, as you yourself admit, by a spirit of hatred and revenge. I take it that you would not attempt to conceal your identity? You would go to him openly as Miles Mannion?"

"Of course."

"Mannion is not a name he likes. He *might* keep the appointment with you—but the girl would not be with him. He would take what you brought—including the letter, which she would never see—and shoot you down in cold blood without a moment's hesitation."

Miles shrugged.

"It's barely possible—but I think it of all things the most unlikely. You have made it so. He well knows that when he was himself unarmed and helpless a Mannion could have shot him—and did not."

Patrick said, staring: "Gratitude? You think him capable . . . ?"

"I think such a man as I have described is capable of almost anything
—including gratitude. Yet I take but little risk; Heaven has seen fit to
make me larger than most men, and in a hand-to-hand encounter. . . ."

"Now I know you're mad. He will be armed, and you will not. He
will be attended by his friends, and you will be alone. . . ."

For the first time Miles showed a trace of impatience.

"You have been so occupied with your sense of culpability that
Prentice has become to you no more than a symbol of your guilt, and
you have failed to consider him as a man. He's revengeful—we're agreed
on that. Reflect, though, that one ingredient of revenge is always pride.
A man without pride doesn't resist injustice or indignity—he grovels, he
fawns, he licks the boot that spurns him. Oh, I concede you that revenge
is not a pretty thing. Say, if you like, that it's a debased and undisciplined
pride that resists by murder—but still, it's pride. And a man with pride
does not accept his life at the hands of an enemy without repaying the
debt when an opportunity occurs. Even if he determines, in spite of all,
to kill his enemy, he will at least do it upon equal terms. Don't you
see that my invitation to him to surround himself with supporters is in
the nature of a taunt, or a challenge? Believe me, if he keeps this rendezvous at all, he will see to it that not even Billalong is present. He
won't trust me—no. From some distant vantage point he'll watch to
assure himself that I do, indeed, come alone and empty handed. And
when he has satisfied himself as to that, he will join me—alone and unarmed like myself."

Patrick said thoughtfully:

"You spoke of offering to take him anything he required. Does a
man with pride accept gifts from his enemy?"

Miles let out a roar of laughter that made the horses shy.

"Bravo! Of course he does not—that proposal is merely another instance of my incomparable guile. I want an *answer* from the fellow, not
contemptuous silence. Could any man of pride resist the opportunity of
saying to his enemy: 'I want nothing from you'? Should his answer be
any other, then he's not the man I think him, and I should reconsider
my strategy. I like my life, Patrick, and I have no intention of throwing
it away."

"I don't yet understand," Patrick said after a brief silence, "how all
this furthers your aim of crossing the mountains. You speak of Prentice
as a guide, and of his retreat as a headquarters—yet you spoke earlier
of going alone—and living on grubs."

"How do I know where his retreat may be, or how much farther I
must go to cross the mountains? He may choose to accompany me—he

may not; he may, or may not, provide me with food. But I intend to cross the mountains in any case, and I'm merely assuming that my chance of doing so will be improved if I can find, somewhere in that wilderness, a man who is already familiar with it, and who evidently has the means of subsistence. Instead of setting out from here, my starting point will be much farther forward. And should hunger drive me back, it need drive me no farther than there. Come, now, admit that it's a capital plan! I can see no flaw in it."

"I can see a dozen," Patrick retorted gloomily. "Prentice may simply ignore you—indeed, I think he will. Or he could satisfy his pride, as you call it, by sending you a message to the effect that he wants neither your gifts nor your company. Why should he consent to meet you?"

"If he did not, I think his pride would still be itching. I shall have issued what is, in effect, a challenge; if he does not accept it, shall I not think him afraid?"

"You attempt to read his mind like a book," said Patrick, "but I think you may find it written in a foreign tongue. His life has been . . . peculiar. However, granted that he meets you, what in God's name do you imagine will make him conduct you to his hiding place?"

"My persuasive tongue. I've induced people to do unlikelier things —why, I even induced Letty's Papa to accept me as a son-in-law! But in fact I care little whether he does so or not—so long as he will direct me on a practicable route, and provide me with food; he could do that without betraying his retreat. 'Sir,' I shall say to him, 'I am not interested in your present arrangements, your future plans, or your past activities. I am, however, interested in finding a passage across the mountains, and I seek your assistance.'" He paused for a moment, cocking an eye at his brother, but Patrick merely shrugged, and he went on presently: "I'm also hoping much of the girl. It will depend on whether she ever hears of me, or the letter I bring; and that in turn will depend on what sort of relationship has developed between her and Prentice. But of one thing I'm sure: if she hears of this letter she will use whatever powers she may possess—be they wiles, stratagems or influence—to get it. The situation seems to me to promise all kinds of diverting possibilities."

"Diverting . . . !" The word exploded in a tone of such bitterness that Miles raised his eyebrows, and for a full ten minutes they rode in silence, Patrick staring blankly in front of him. Was his already overloaded conscience to support another burden? Was he to contemplate responsibility for his brother's death? And, to add a final twist of torment, must he suffer an evil whisper from some dark corner of his mind, urging that his brother's death would leave Laetitia free . . . ?"

He burst out furiously:

"I wish to God I'd never mentioned Prentice to you at all! I oppose the whole plan—it's preposterous! You would be risking your life upon a string of suppositions—and damned far-fetched ones, too. I can't believe that you seriously intend it, but if you do, you're worse than mad. Have you no thought for Laetitia and your son? Can she claim no consideration at all?"

Miles regarded him with amiable astonishment.

"Pray don't be so vehement in this heat, man! Letty has always understood that the crossing of the mountains was to be one of my first tasks upon our return. She has always known that I can't abide being stuck in one place for more than a few months at most. I shall install her and the babe and Johanna at Moore House, where she'll have plenty to occupy her with dinners, and cards, and balls and visiting; she'll have friends and advisers in the Harveys, to say nothing of your brotherly attention and counsel. And in a few weeks—months, maybe—I shall reappear, covered in glory and blisters. . . ."

Patrick said shortly: "It's useless to talk to you."

After that he returned only brief answers to Miles' flow of cheerful conversation.

*   *   *   *

The Governor's fifty-second birthday had found him tired and a trifle irritable. The hot, midsummer months had been crowded with business and exertion. The *Spring Grove* had brought—along with tidings that Bathurst had replaced Liverpool at the Colonial Office—the usual bundle of despatches whose multifarious instructions must be attended to. Arrangements for the removal of the last settlers from Norfolk Island had involved the hire of the transport *Minstrel* at a cost of twelve hundred pounds—and Macquarie was, by now, nervous about expenditure. He had been unable to circulate his new currency, since no satisfactory machine for cutting the dollars had as yet been evolved. And he was not yet rid of Captain Case.

The *Samarang,* having sailed early in the new year, reappeared in port the next day, leaking so badly that a survey, just completed, revealed the need for extensive repairs; since Captain Case consistently disregarded port regulations by allowing his seamen to roam about the streets on Sundays, bringing their liquor ashore with them, and thus—whether they drank it or sold it—disturbing the peace and sanctity of the Sabbath, Macquarie found this development extremely irksome.

The settlers had fulfilled his worst forebodings by using the opportunity afforded by the customary New Year addresses of loyalty, to set out in black and white those dissatisfactions which he had known to be brewing in their minds. The sight of a colony bulging with surplus food had produced the inevitable desire for a larger market, and their request that he would be pleased to sponsor and recommend the Memorial which they proposed to submit to His Majesty's Government on the subject was, to say the least, embarrassing.

As each day developed his acquaintance with Davey, his misgivings increased, and he had just completed and signed a set of Instructions so detailed and so comprehensive as to leave that gentleman little latitude for independent action when he arrived in Van Diemen's Land. He said grimly to Campbell as he scrawled his signature and threw down his pen: "If I'm to be held accountable for the state of those settlements, then Davey must be accountable to *me!*"

The building of the hospital, which he had once seen as an inspired combination of astute business, practical utility and aesthetic achievement, had become but a source of interminable wrangling between himself and the contractors. And to add a final burden to an exhausting month, there had been, even for his gregarious soul, too many large social engagements for such hot weather.

Early in February some respite at least was vouchsafed to him when Davey—less armed with than shackled by his Instructions—departed for Hobart Town. But as one task was completed, others crowded in upon him, and he had reason to be grateful to the happy chance which had provided him with so energetic and capable a Secretary. It was time now for Mr. Campbell to muster the two hundred male and female convicts on the deck of the newly-arrived *Archduke Charles,* and for himself to inspect the males in the gaol yard after their disembarkation. Attended by the Captain of the transport, the surgeon, and the Superintendent of Convicts, he walked slowly between the two long lines of prisoners, enquiring whether they wished to make complaints of their treatment during the voyage, consulting with the Superintendent as to their disposal, and pausing at last to deliver the brief address which, from constant repetition, now came almost mechanically from his lips.

"You have sentences to serve for offences against the laws of your country, but when these have been concluded no account will be taken by me of your past lives. I am concerned only with the manner in which you conduct yourselves in this colony. It is at all times my endeavour to make it a home—and a happy home—to the honest, the sober and the industrious. That is all; the Superintendent will arrange for you to be conveyed to the places where you will labour."

The ranks stirred and shifted as the men stooped to pick up their bundles of clothes and bedding. Macquarie mounted and rode home to breakfast, feeling—as he always did when this particular duty was behind him—an odd sensation which was half relief and half disappointment. How much of what he said had been believed? Those eyes, watching his every movement . . . ! That expression which, looking from blue eyes or brown, from young faces or old, printing itself with equal sureness upon a thousand different sets of features, was always the same . . . ! It was compounded of many emotions; sometimes hatred was uppermost, sometimes fear, sometimes despair, sometimes envy, or contempt, or curiosity, or a fawning servility, and sometimes, even, a sardonic amuse- ment. But it was always, in total, the same expression, and its message was separation: You in one world, I in another. It made him feel that his words were bewitched in mid-air, and reached the ears to which they were addressed bearing some meaning quite different from his own; or perhaps no meaning at all. He was no believer in equality, and the years had not mitigated the abhorrence with which, long ago, he had once written of "the infernal and destructive principles of Democracy". Yet in speaking to convicts and to natives he tended to raise his voice a little, as if trying to call across some gulf from whose depths mistrust, like a cold wind, blew the warmth of sincerity from his words before they could span it.

He was the Governor of a penal colony, and as such it was his duty to see that malefactors served the sentences passed upon them in England, and to inflict other penalties for offences committed here. His soldierly mind explored the matter no further; duty was a word like a full stop. Theft, violence, murder—these things, he supposed, must be expected in such a place as this. When they occurred he sent out across the gulf from his own world the old, stern demand for observance of its law, threatening punishment to those who defied it, promising rewards to those who, by betraying their fellows, would support it; and he was shocked when there came back from the world of the dispossessed the old, fierce assertion that there no crime was so base and unforgiveable as the crime of informing. He could see only chaos in that other world; it did not occur to him that in the jungle of misery and punishment there operated a kind of jungle law with its own powerful traditions and its own rough justice; that those from whom much had been taken, would take back what they could; that the refinements of learning, and the luxury of entertaining abstract principles had been bought from life by the in- habitants of his own world, but paid for in the other; and that the inhabitants of the other had evolved their own code in their own defence.

Yet his heart had never been soldierly, and he could not punish with- out feeling some distress. He realised, too, that while violence and in- subordination among the felonry and the poorer settlers were directed less against his own authority than against authority in general, a strong and vindictive opposition to himself was gaining strength among the higher ranks. The ever-growing army of emancipists was breaking down the old colonial pattern which knew only the felon and the free, and the "exclusives", who had lived so snugly and profitably within it, were now noting with resentment that His Excellency seemed not only to accept, but to encourage its disintegration.

Macquarie felt their hostility, and understood the reason for it, but both dignity and policy dictated that he should not allow the conflict to become an open brawl. Many a time, as he exchanged greetings with Mr. Marsden, with Dr. Townson, with Mr. Nicholas Bayly or a dozen others whose sentiments, he knew, were not accurately reflected in their civil smiles, he had congratulated himself upon having so far been spared the inflammatory presence of Mr. John Macarthur. At the end of March, when Macarthur's ill-fated catspaw, George Johnston, returned from England, Macquarie received him with his customary genial courtesy; nevertheless he observed with some relief that gentleman's prompt and discreet withdrawal from the public eye to the seclusion of Annandale. One, at least, of the faction which had opposed and thwarted Governors for twenty years, appeared to have learned his lesson. The others, he suspected, were biding their time, and doing what they could, meanwhile, by complaining of him to their friends at home; that young nephew of Macarthur's, for instance, was doubtless sending pretty tales to his exiled uncle . . . !

But he had stated his policy clearly enough to his superiors, and it had been approved; he was hurt and harassed by opposition, but not yet alarmed. His mind, neither complex nor adventurous, could conceive no alternative to a society breeding crime from harshness, suppressing it with harsh punishment, and thus breeding more crime—but it was, within the limitations imposed by such an acceptance, an intelligent mind, and a just one. Intelligence showed him the impossibility of keeping the emancipist class in perpetual segregation, and his sense of justice recoiled from the very thought of attempting it. But it was perhaps mostly in compensation to his unsoldierly heart for the harsh laws which duty compelled him to enforce, that what had been undertaken calmly as a policy, was developing into a passionate crusade.

*　　　　*　　　　*　　　　*

Johnny, passing out with the pail in his hand to fetch water from the creek, had left the door ajar, and a fresh, sweet breath of dawn wind blew in over Emily's face, rousing her from a stupor of exhaustion. The hut was close and over-warm, though the fire had burned down to ashes on the hearth; outside the air was crisp, for in the mountains even February nights could be cool, but the sun was just rising over the eastern cliffs, and already, here and there, the locusts, celebrants of summer heat, were greeting it. Emily stared out through the doorway, and though her newborn daughter lay in the curve of her arm, all her attention was fixed upon the rim of the sun as it slowly lifted; and she noticed with astonishment as the blazing circle rode clear of the cliff line, that its circumference enclosed not merely a static brilliance, but something with all the fierce, dancing, shimmering mobility of flames.

To see it thus, discovering it with her own eyes, and all unaided, gave her a curious shock of pleasure and excitement, for hitherto her relationship with the heavens had been unfortunate. The terrors of a time when, as a little child, she had huddled in some gutter or doorway, cowed by the immensity of night and stars, had taught her to keep her eyes upon the earth; the discourses of Mr. Marsden, proclaiming a God armed with thunderbolts of punishment, whose unsleeping and censorious eye observed her every thought and action, had taught her that the sky was inhabited by an Authority whose power differed only in degree from the temporal power which haled men to the lash and to the gallows. Night and day, sunrise and sunset, wind and lightning, moon, stars and thunder—these were all parts of a mysterious Creation whose very magnitude and mystery had at last repelled wonder, and intimidated her mind into a wary, qualified acceptance of what she neither understood nor welcomed. They were the pageantry of God, the demonstrations of his power, the heavenly counterparts of bugles, banners and parades. Such things were threats; they were warnings to the humble, reminders to go softly, to transgress secretly, and conceal the rebellions of the heart.

But now, as she watched the sun climb the sky, it seemed no longer a flaunting of celestial authority, but something as near, as useful, as much her own as the fires Johnny kindled for her cooking; and it delighted her, not only because it was beautiful and strange, but because she was still alive to see it. The dread which had possessed her during the past few weeks seemed wiped away, and she was wearily but peacefully content to lie staring at that fragment of the world before her eyes, knowing herself part of it.

The misery of those weeks was already half-forgotten, for hers was a nature which hastened to put sorrow behind. Yet, while it lasted it had been more poignant than any sorrow she had known. She had won so much from Johnny—why did he stand stubbornly aloof from her now, in her worst fear and loneliness? As her time approached she had found reserves of courage, and made such preparations as she could. He seemed disturbed, watching her furtively, but now it was she who had withdrawn; sometimes, lying wakeful in the dark, she had thought that she could feel death approaching, and gathered her forces to resist. Last night she had ignored his unwilling question, not from hostility, but from the concentration of her thought upon the hours ahead; it was without either surprise or bitterness that she had presently found him gone. She lay alone in the hut, watching the shadows thrown by the firelight flicker on the walls, and the long night was black with pain and striving, silent but for the sounds of effort that drove between her locked teeth. Towards dawn she had seen the light flicker in a sudden draught from the opening door, and she had screamed—for by then her mind was confused—thinking that the vast shadow that swooped towards her across the wall could be no other than the dark angel of death.

Now, growing drowsy, she turned her eyes away from the door. There was no knowing why Johnny did things—why he had left her alone, why he had returned. But he had returned, and she no longer felt forsaken. "Ah, he's a queer one!" she thought, and fell asleep.

*   *   *   *

When he had hauled the pail in and set it beside him on the bank, Johnny remained squatting on his heels, motionless, as if calling on the stillness of his body to aid him in composing the tumult of his mind.

It was suffering the shock which any human mind endures when a law, hitherto unquestioned and sufficient, is revealed as mutable. He had learned something of the white men's laws as they affected property, and as they defined the obligations between man and man; he had even learned from Finn something of an ethical law which dealt, apparently, less with what was than with what might be. But for guidance in the relationship of man with woman he had neither found nor sought any other authority than the tribal law of his dark friends. In such a matter—concerning as it did not merely incidents of behaviour, but the very source and perpetuation of life itself—how could there be any law save one? And that law had no place for a woman who feared childbirth, and who, instead of jealously guarding her rights, sought to draw a man into affairs which lay properly in the sole custodianship of her own sex. Women, by native law, were not slaves; they had their inviolable rights, their honourable duties, their assured place; many a domestic wrangle witnessed during his life among the tribes had made it clear to Johnny that they did not hesitate to assert themselves. But between the spiritual life of male and female there ran a rigid line of division which each sex accepted as impassable. On the lower levels, defining tribal custom and behaviour, the law was shared by both, but when bodily needs had been met, and tribal organisation shaped, there remained still the quest of the mind and the hunger of the spirit; to man his mysteries, and to woman hers.

Yet Emily had upset in many ways his notion of what was permis-

sible between the sexes, and Johnny's sense of outrage had become confused by a growing doubt. Now she had somehow brought about his
involvement in the ultimate female mystery, and the astounding truth
which was holding him motionless in the flowering daylight was that he
had found there no mystery at all, but merely a woman whose suffering
became, because he loved her, his own.

He rose and took the brimming pail, glancing up as he did so at
the sun-crowned cliffs, and thinking that it would be another hot day.
But there had been good rain lately, and the stream was running fast.
He had harvested his wheat, his vegetable plots were flourishing, and
there was abundant feed for his beasts; they would live well enough
through the coming winter. He climbed the path to the hut and, entering, stood looking down for a moment at Emily asleep with her sleeping
child.

*　　　　*　　　　*　　　　*

March had begun, but the reluctantly dying summer still punctuated
cooler weather with days of fiery heat. Johnny, returning to his hut at
noon one day, paused as he waded across the creek, crouching to drink,
and to splash water in handfulls over his face and head. When he
straightened again he did not immediately go on, but stood for a few
minutes with the stream running round his ankles, looking down into the
pool without seeing it, a sharp frown between his eyes.

It was almost a month since Billalong had arrived with a strange
message from a man who proclaimed himself to be the brother of Manyun
—a man, declared Billalong (carelessly indicating the sixty-foot ironbark
under which they stood) as tall as a tree, whose name was Mi-el. And
Johnny, despite the complete unexpectedness of such tidings, had found
himself saying without a moment's hesitation: "Aye, I know—what of
him?"

Even as he spoke he had wondered at that sure and instant recognition. Years ago he had seen Miles Mannion sometimes with the other
children—his own brother and sister, and the little black girl—when he
was watching the Beltrasna fields from across the river. But the younger
brother, unlike the elder, had not lived in his thoughts, or played a part
of any real significance in his life.

Yet had he not . . . ? Thought had discarded him, but memory was
more tenacious, hoarding a picture which it had thrust suddenly to the
forefront of his ·mind—the picture of a baby in his own mother's arms
and at his mother's breast—a foster-child upon whom she had lavished
more tenderness than she had ever shown to him. It was a jealousy so
stifled at its source, so hardily denied by a defiant urchin who acknowledged
no hunger for love, that in all the years since he had barely thought of

that more favoured child. But he had not forgotten, and his voice was made harsh by the thrust of an old pain. "Aye, I know—what of him?"

Billalong explained. For a few moments Johnny had been disturbed by the implications of the message. If they knew that Emily was with him they must know, or at least suspect, that he had killed Dean. There was danger in that—but after all, it was a familiar danger, and his defence was still what it had always been. They might suspect, or even know what they pleased about him, so long as they did not know where he was. He was mentally shrugging the whole matter away when recognition of another peril lying unobserved in the heart of this message struck him like a blow. In a kind of panic he had told Billalong to return to his tribe, to avoid this man, and to come again at the next waning of the moon for an answer. Since then he had known no peace. The turmoil of his mind made him physically restless, and Emily noticed with surprise that he had suddenly begun to work with insane energy. He was morose and abstracted, answering her briefly, or in words that showed his thoughts were far away. His lean body grew leaner, the skin seemed tightly stretched over his jaws and cheekbones, and two deep furrows settled between his brows. Though Emily herself slept soundly, she had several times wakened to find him gone, and heard him prowling restlessly outside.

All day as he worked his brain struggled, and at night he was no nearer to decision. Yet he must decide. How to answer this message— or whether to answer it at all . . . ? But also, whether Emily should hear of it . . . ? His old fear warned that she should not. She was his, like his land, like his hut, like his cattle, like all his possessions which They would take from him if they could. Say nothing, this fear urged him; do nothing, ignore this message, let it be no more than a breath of speech given to the air and dissipated, and everything will remain unchanged.

But would it? He knew that it would not, for there was now in himself a new thought which moved forward relentlessly from the back of his mind, pushing all other thoughts and fears aside, forming itself, at last, into a pitiless question whose answer no one knew but Emily. He was asking it now as he stood looking down into the clear water.

Why was she here? Only because he had brought her, and she could not escape? Strange that he should never have asked himself this before, living in a blind and heedless happiness until this sudden intrusion of her world in the shape of a message and a promised letter had made him attempt to see with her eyes and feel with her heart. She was here— as surely and safely imprisoned by the bush as she could have been by any key; and he, whose whole life had been given to preserving his own freedom, he who hated the enslavers, he who had learned from Finn the misery of captivity, was her gaoler. How sharply he had searched her face in these last tormented weeks! Why that look of sadness? What was she thinking of, staring at the hillside, but seeing, surely, something else? How much did she long for the life she had left behind—the noise and bustle of the Market; the gossip of a town; a kitchen with many pots and pans; other women to talk to; china dishes, shining mirrors, bright lamps, music . . . ?

He stepped out of the water on to a rock that felt warm beneath his bare, wet feet, and hesitated again. To-morrow Billalong would come, and still he had made no decision. The fear of losing her was like a dull ache, but the fear of keeping her against her will was like a streak of intolerable pain. He began to walk slowly up the path towards the hut.

*   *   *   *

The meal was over, and still he had said nothing. She had sat alone on the bench outside for a little while, and he could hear her crooning absently to the baby. Presently she came in, walking listlessly, and lay down on the bed, putting the child to her breast. After a time she turned her head to find his eyes on her, and asked tartly:

"What are ye gawkin' at? If ye've nothin' to do, can't ye be still? Pacin' and fidgetin' about like that! And eatin' nothin' but a few bites of the food I get for ye! For mercy's sake, what ails ye lately?"

The question burst from him.

"Would ye go away from here if ye could?"

But it was barely beyond his lips before he knew that he was cheating her—and himself. It was no vague "if" that he must set before her, but full knowledge of an event which could certainly take place, and which she could, if she wished, use to escape from him, unless, by force or guile, he prevented it. He added hurriedly: "Wait, now—don't answer till I tell ye somethin' more."

He stood on the far side of the room and told her, watching her face disturbed by a series of emotions from which he could learn nothing. Amazement—that, of course; an excited joy which chilled him and set him stumbling over his words; sudden terror—what was it she feared?

"So there it is," he finished heavily, feeling his bodily weariness and sitting down on the bench with his arms across the table. "They know ye're with me, and . . ."

"How can they know? Guess, maybe, but that's all. Ye say Billalong never told?"

"He done what he always does. Said he didn't know me—never saw no white woman."

"But Mr. Miles didn't believe him?"

"Said Billalong was lyin'. 'That's the message,' he says, 'and ye can take it or not, as ye please.' So Billalong brings it, and he'll be back again for me answer—to-morrow, maybe."

She cried incredulously:

"Answer? Ye'd never answer it?" He could see the terror in her eyes again. "Ye'd not be such a fool! Don't ye see, if they get no answer at all, they'll begin to wonder were they right . . . ?"

He rose and crossed the room to crouch beside her.

"Don't ye want the letter?"

"Oh," she sighed, "I'd like the letter, and I'd like the mistress to know I'm not dead, nor forgettin' her, but . . ."

"Why wouldn't ye have me go, then?"

"Are ye crazy? Haven't ye done murder?"

"Ye said ye reckoned Patrick Mannion didn't want to see me taken —d'ye think this brother of his feels different?"

She clutched his hand.

"Ah, I don't know, but why should ye take the risk? Can't ye see that maybe they might feel different about it now—because of me? Maybe it's the master and the mistress tryin' to get me back—not knowin' how things are. . . ." She paused, and added crossly: "What is it ye're thinkin' with that smile on y' face, as if ye're *pleased* they're after ye again?"

He turned her hand over, playing with her fingers and keeping his eyes on them.

"I'd not want to smile too soon. Listen, now. I could meet this Miles Mannion, takin' you and the baby along with me. And I could say to him: 'Here's the girl, but there's no need you should give her the letter, for she'll be goin' back with ye to . . ."

She snatched her hand away and he lifted his head abruptly; now the question had been plainly put, and he found the plain answer in her eyes.

"Ye don't want to go? Well, then, there's no need to trouble our-selves more—I see the way of it plain enough now."

"Ye see it now! Wasn't it plain enough from the start, ye booby? Look what ye've done, gettin' me in a state so the baby's upset too! Makin' a to-do out of nothin', when all that's wanted's a still tongue and a bit of sense! *Now* what are ye grinnin' at?"

He stood up and went across to dip a mug of water from the pail and drink thirstily. He no longer felt tired. He wiped the back of his hand across his mouth and said:

"I'll get the letter for ye—why not? I can meet him in some place that'll not give him a hint of where we are." He silenced her attempted interruption. "Don't start arguin' now, for me mind's made up." For a second or two he paused to examine and savour the intoxicating truth of this statement. Doubts were gone; he felt full of confidence, queerly excited, impatient for the arrival of Billalong so that he might set in train arrangements for a meeting to which he now looked forward almost exultantly. She snapped:

"Don't ye try to stop me speakin' me own mind! He'll not give ye the letter—didn't he say he'd give it only into me own hands? And if ye think I'm goin' traipesin' around the country carryin' a baby with the nights gettin' cold and all . . ."

He said with sly enjoyment: "Then maybe I'll have to take it off him."

She rose up on her elbows, flushed with anger.

"Now you mind what I say, Johnny Prentice. I know ye hate the Mannions, and maybe ye had cause once, though it was never Mr. Patrick harmed ye, nor Mr. Miles neither. But if ye go lookin' for trouble when there's no need, and maybe endin' up with losin' that black temper of yours and shootin' . . ."

"There'll be no shootin'." He sat on the edge of the table and looked at her, wearing an odd expression of suppressed triumph. "I want to see him—that's all."

"Mercy on us—*why?*"

He made a quick gesture, half impatient, half exuberant, and said with a grin: "To get y' letter."

"Ye're crazy! Would I care about the letter when . . ."

"Letters!" He was grinning even more widely, possessed by a restless and reckless excitement. "Well, I can write letters meself! I'll write one for Billalong to take, and I reckon that'll surprise him, for he'd not think a savage like me could write! Aye, and what's more, I'll write it on a bit of that fine paper of yours out of y' case, so he needn't do no more guessin' about whether ye're with me. . . ."

"Have ye lost what little wits ye ever had? Why can't ye let well alone, and . . ."

"Don't y' trust y' Mannions after all?" He was rummaging in her writing case, setting out paper and pencil on the table. "Come, now, what'll I put down?" He sat on the bench and she watched him angrily as he bent over his task, the grin fading from his face as he addressed himself to the effort of composition. He looked up at last and read out with satisfaction: "'In three days from when you get this I will be at a place where you will be took.' And I made me letters so careful that even y' schoolmaster couldn't do no better."

She ignored him. He said regretfully, studying the page:

"There was marks Tom Towns used to make under what he'd wrote —lines, they were, curly lines lyin' just so; but I never learnt how to do them."

"Ye're talkin' like a fool." She turned her head away sulkily, and then turned it back. "And when ye write a letter ye should start it with 'Sir'. Ah, stick it in the fire, love, do, and let's forget about it all."

"It says all I want without no Sirs." He looked up and met her eyes; she looked away quickly but he had seen the tears in them and he said: "There's nothin' to fear. I'll have no weapon in me hand, and neither will he, for I'll make sure of that before I let him see me. Would ye have me act more frightened than he does? If it's y'self he's lookin' for —and I reckon it is—I'll tell him ye're well enough where ye are. And that's all there is to it."

He stood up and went across to the bed. "Ah," she cried, locking her arms round his neck as he bent over her, "ye're crazy, right enough!"

*   *   *   *

Billalong arrived next morning. Emily, well accustomed by now to his habit of avoiding the hut, saw him appear on the hillside and called to Johnny who was working in the field across the creek. As she returned to her household tasks she glanced at the letter and the pencil lying where he had left them on the shelf. The natives, being innocent of pockets, frequently carried small articles twisted in their hair, and Johnny had considered Billalong's convenience by tearing off the unused top and bottom from his sheet of paper, folding the remainder tightly, and tying it round and round with thread from Emily's workbox. She went to the door again and looked out. Johnny was still on the far side of the field, and taking his time. She ran back to the shelf, untied the thread hurriedly, and smoothed the paper out on the table. There was a narrow blank strip along one side of the sheet; she snatched up the pencil.

*   *   *   *

Conor had at first shaken her head when Patrick suggested that she and Mark should pass a few days at Beltrasna with the children; the school, she objected, allowed no time for such visits. But he had renewed the invitation several times, and Miles now seconded it, adding Laetitia's solicitations to his own. "She's bored to death, poor girl, but she declares herself not strong enough to come to Sydney yet. I confess my ignorance of such matters, but I'd not have expected maternity to be so prostrating an experience."

He sounded a trifle impatient, and Conor remarked:

"Perhaps Laetitia's constitution is not robust; she looks rather frail, I think."

"I grant you that—eggshells and rose petals look no frailer. But she has danced me to a standstill in London many times, and she has never known a day's illness. As for Patrick, he's become a veritable misan-thrope! Beyond riding out with Toole and appearing at the dinner table, he emerges from that study of his only to go to bed. I tell you, the place is like a tomb!"

"You have received no answer to your message to Prentice?" Mark asked.

"Not a word, not a sign. I shan't wait much longer.—I hear that Blaxland and Lawson are determined on the trip, and that William Wentworth is to join them. They're taking servants and horses."

"And you still mean to go alone, and on foot?"

"Certainly alone, and probably on foot. But in the meantime, Sir, I do beg you to relieve the intolerable tedium of life at Beltrasna for a few days at least. You surely don't profane the Sabbath with lessons, do you—or Good Friday? So give your pupils only one day's holiday, and come to us on Thursday . . . ?"

"My love . . . ?" said Mr. Harvey.

"Well. . . ." said Conor.

"Excellent!" cried Miles. "Ma'am, I rely on you to convince Laetitia that she can't lie indefinitely on a sofa fanning herself. And you, Sir, must assure Patrick that studiousness is a virtue only up to a point—from his ex-tutor it will come better than from a younger brother who was never studious himself." He added, looking half puzzled and half amused: "It's poetry he writes, I believe? I've not been honoured with a sight of it myself, but he showed Letty some not long after we arrived. She pronounced it full of merit and sensibility, and she has some taste. She used to grow quite animated discussing such things with him, but of late they hardly speak."

"You mean they have quarrelled, Miles?"

"Good God, no! Nothing so vulgar and healthy! They both just immure themselves in their rooms—I can't get near enough to Patrick to quarrel with him myself."

"I think," said Conor, "that Patrick was deeply affected by poor Dilboong's unhappy end. Perhaps it is that . . ."

Miles spoke with sudden violence:

"And not only he! I was myself affected—and the more so since I have reason to believe that I was at least partly responsible—but I'm damned if I propose to be haunted by remorse for the rest of my life. What's past is past. I will not have my future hampered by vain regrets. . . ." He broke off, shrugged, and laughed. "You see this atmosphere of gloom is making me quite testy! If I'm to be home by dark I must set out—but I have your promise that you will come on Thursday?"

"We shall come," said Conor.

*   *   *   *

It was early when they set out from Sydney, and they reached Beltrasna by mid-morning. Patrick, still limping slightly, came out to welcome them. Miles, he explained, had ridden off some hours ago to Woodriff's Farm whence, so they had learned, the Governor was to leave that morning with his wife and a party of gentlemen to inspect Emu Island. "He suggested, Sir, that you and I should join the expedition later, if you would care to do so?"

Laetitia, who rose late, did not appear till they were seated in the dining-room for refreshments; she looked frailer than ever, and Conor noticed that she ate little, though she talked with what seemed a slightly forced animation. Patrick, however, confined himself to such remarks as courtesy demanded, sitting sideways at the table so that Robert—who had reached him after an arduous journey round the vast rectangle of mahogany—could clamber on his knee to inspect his watch and his waistcoat buttons. Between amusement and annoyance, Mark found that the constraint was infectious. He was oddly conscious of Stephen Mannion's portrait looking down haughtily from the wall in front of him; the house, he thought, was too full of memories.

They still pursued him when he stepped out with the others on to the verandah. There, standing in its old place, was the table at which he had taught the studious Patrick and the inattentive Miles; he could not but remember Dilboong, creeping up on her bare feet to peer over their shoulders at the forbidden mysteries of learning. He hastened to agree when Patrick once more raised the question of their ride.

The ladies, having watched them depart, settled themselves in chairs facing the sloping fields and the river. Johanna, appearing with her mistress' fan and needlework, reported that Maria had come to take charge of Mrs. Harvey's children, and went off again with Robert in her arms and Desmond at her heels. Conor, recalling how often in the past she had sat there chafing at her idleness, smiled at the pleasure it now gave her to do nothing. Far down the hill she could see a few convicts at work under the watchful eye of Toole, and presently, from behind the house, and walking slowly down the avenue between trees now tall enough to shade it, came Maria with a group of children.

"Six of them!" exclaimed Conor. "And your own dear babe inside makes seven—Beltrasna is quite a nursery, is it not? But how one misses poor Dilboong! It was always she who cared for the children before."

Maria had Robert in her arms, and her own little son, Simeon, was clinging to her skirts. Desmond was running on ahead with Samuel Dawson, while Samuel's eldest brother, Timothy, hung back to wait for the tiny, dark-skinned girl who toddled unsteadily in the rear. "What a tall lad Timothy is growing," Conor remarked, "and how inattentive he is to poor little Mary. You know, Laetitia, it seems no time at all since Dilboong used to run about these fields with Miles."

Laetitia's head bent lower over her needlework. Conor, glancing at her, sat up in astonishment and concern, for a tear was sliding down her cheek.

"Why, my love, what is it? Have I said something to distress you?"

Laetitia looked up, hesitating and twisting her sewing round her fingers. She said at last: "It was I, you know, who caused the death of that native girl."

"You? Oh, nonsense, my dear Laetitia . . . !"

"It was I who insisted that she be sent away."

"No, no, you're quite mistaken—it was spoken of before you ever arrived."

"I know. But she had begged to be allowed to remain, and Patrick had agreed. He—he altered his mind because I asked it." She blinked tears from her eyes and said painfully: "You see, I am not able to—to adjust myself. . . . It is a weakness, a lack, I am sensible of, and yet I cannot overcome it. But when this terrible thing happened I felt that because of this lack I may not only suffer myself, but from ignorance and cowardice may cause others to suffer. . . . As I did then . . . Dilboong . . . and Patrick—for he has been greatly distressed by it. . . ."

Her voice trailed into silence. It was but a week or two ago that there had come to her, in the middle of a wakeful night, the thought that Patrick was the father of Dilboong's child. Next morning she had gone in search of Mary, and stood for a few moments studying the soft, still babyish face almost furtively. Yes, there was a look, despite the pale brown skin . . . the shape of the brows, an elusive something in the line of cheek and chin . . . in the sunlight the tips of her curls looked almost fair. It was plain enough now. And, having seen it at last, she began to see much more. Dilboong's face was clearly in her mind again, wearing an expression for Miles which it had worn for no one else—a look whose adoration had seemed but to add a rather repellent absurdity to those black, ugly features, a smile whose joy in his mere presence had seemed, on those thick lips but a ludicrous grimace. Must she believe, then, that this creature had been a woman like herself, with feelings like her own? It had plunged her into an agony of humiliation to realise, reluctantly, how very like her own Dilboong's unhappy situation had been. For if the black savage had shared Patrick's bed and borne his child while her love was all for Miles, had not the white gentlewoman shared Miles' bed and borne his child while her love was all for Patrick? She had snatched at the word love as if it were a balm that she might apply to her wounded self-esteem; there, at least, was a difference, for while Dilboong had merely been desired, had not she herself been loved? But she was soon wondering, almost with detachment, whether Miles had ever loved her; whether, indeed, he was as yet capable of love. She fell back on the thought that where Dilboong's love for Miles had been an absurdity too fantastic even to be recognised, her own for Patrick was not unrequited. But this could lend her little comfort. And already in his constraint and his withdrawal she could read condemnation of the use she had made of his love. She looked up wretchedly at Conor, and spoke again out of her thoughts:

"Oh, I wish to condemn myself—indeed I do! Yet when I try to do so I find that I am thinking with abhorrence not of myself but of this place, this country, as if it were an enemy. I don't understand it, and in consequence I don't know how to act in it. I am repelled and bewildered by many things which, to Miles, seem ordinary—even our eyes and ears seem to see and hear differently. . . . In London, ma'am, the difference in our natures was not as apparent as it is here. I cannot see beauty where he sees it. Sounds which to me are painful, give him pleasure. Those dreadful insects in the trees—can you believe it, he woke one morning when they first began their piercing din, and cried out: 'Ah, there's music!' Oh, *pray* don't smile! These are small things, but they show me a chasm. I believe I'm not by nature heartless, and the thought of that poor girl torments me—yet I am still disgusted by her people—their savagery, their dirtiness, their nakedness. . . . And I'm not devoid of pity, yet I cannot see convicts working on the roads without noting the brutishness of their faces, and being thankful for the chains that control them. And when I learn that every day such men are being freed to take up land, and advance their fortunes, and even to be received into society. . . . Does not all this alarm you, ma'am?"

"It interests me," said Conor slowly. "As for brutish faces, my love, a lifetime of dirt, hunger, fear and ignorance does not improve the human countenance."

"Would you tell me," cried Laetitia passionately, "that if we strike the chains from these men, and feed them, and wash them, and teach them all that—that Mr. Harvey knows, let us say—they will become as he is?"

Conor found herself laughing.

"Do you believe in miracles, Laetitia? I do, most profoundly, since I contrived to free my mind of the notion that they occur like a flash of lightning—for indeed there's nothing that takes place more slowly than a miracle. No, I should expect to see no sudden transformation. Yet if all these remedies should be applied patiently and for as long as were needful, I think it might be found that a miracle had occurred—not only affecting the children or grandchildren of those whom you despise, but our own also. . . ."

Laetitia said, staring:

"I don't ask for miracles. I want only a life in which I can be myself. For though I don't claim perfection, ma'am, yet I won't admit that my faults are as great or as grievous as this place makes them appear. Oh, I don't know how you can accept so calmly! Look at your own children down there beneath the trees—who are their playmates? The sons of an overseer—a servant; the grandson of a convict woman who murdered Desmond's father; a child who is the grand-daughter of a notoriously violent and drunken savage . . ." she met Conor's eyes, and plunged on vehemently: "and also—yes, I know it—the daughter of my husband's brother! Does that not but add to the horror of the association? I *cannot* reconcile myself to the thought that someday *my* son . . . And yet Miles only laughs, and waves my fears aside. I do not blame him for it—I blame this place where he was reared, and where such things can happen."

"My dear Laetitia," Conor said with a trace of impatience, "you are talking very foolishly. What happens in this place is what we cause to happen—unless we choose to except such things as the insects in the trees. It is all strange to you, my love, but you will become accustomed to it soon. And you are fortunate," she added, "in that you have the support and comfort of a happy marriage to aid you in adjusting . . ."

She broke off, startled. Laetitia was looking at her, and the look was all denial. More plainly than she could have done it in words, she was saying that her marriage could give her neither comfort nor support; but she was saying something else as well. She was not only denying, but asserting—not only repudiating, but claiming. And she continued to meet Conor's troubled eyes with a hint of defiance in her own as she said:

"I may become accustomed, but I shall not become reconciled. For that I may not blame the country, I cannot blame my husband, but I will not, either, too bitterly blame myself, for I could be—I am sure of it—a good wife to . . . to a different kind of man. . . ."

Suddenly she was weeping. "I have said too much," she murmured incoherently, standing up and fumbling for her handkerchief. "Pray excuse me—I am tired—I am not well. . . ."

Conor watched her disappear into the house. *I could be a good wife to. . . .* She had broken off in time, but surely an unspoken name had filled that momentary pause? Patrick . . . ? Through the still air Conor could hear the voices of the children, and in the midst of her agitation and dismay she found herself thinking that they sounded no different from those which had come, years ago, from Miles, Andy, Maria, and Dilboong; no different from those which would come, someday, from other children still unborn; not the voices of any particular children, but childhood itself made articulate, renewing in each generation the damaged joy of life.

She rose and picked up her hat, thinking that she would go down and join them. But she found herself walking in a different direction—to a hillock near by upon whose crest she presently stood looking down at a grave marked by a plain slab of stone which said only:

MATTHEW FINN.

d. January 26, 1808.

＊　　　　＊　　　　＊　　　　＊

Laetitia had not re-appeared by sundown when the men returned. Conor, having seen Robert to bed, and left Desmond eating his supper beneath the eye of Hattie, went out on the verandah to find her husband and Miles coming up the steps. Patrick, she observed, had ridden down the hill to where Toole and Dawson were mustering the convicts for their march back to the huts; she could see him talking to the head overseer as the men shuffled into line. The sun was already behind the hills, but it had left the sky ablaze, the fields flushed with rosy light, and the river a brazen streak on which a single native canoe made a black speck moving downstream.

"You have had a pleasant ride?" she enquired, and Mark answered:

"I had almost forgotten how pleasant such rides can be. The Governor and Mrs. Macquarie both sent you their greetings, my love, and regretted that you had not accompanied us."

"Old Sandy was in capital form," Miles declared, throwing Laetitia's sewing over the arm of her chair and seating himself, "and bursting with plans and projects, as usual. That's a fine stretch of country that we rode over—they say four or five hundred head of cattle could graze there all the year round. Sam Marsden was with the party—smug and garrulous as ever—and Cox, and of course Maclaine and Antill. . . ."

Conor said suddenly:

"Look, Miles. . . ." She was shading her eyes and pointing towards the river. "A native has landed from that canoe—see, he's walking up the hill towards Patrick. Do you think it might be . . . ?"

Miles leapt to his feet.

"My reply from Prentice, eh? At last! But confound it all, at this distance and in this light I can't tell whether it's Billalong or not."

"You had best contain your excitement," Mark said. "It might be any native—though I must say he walks with an air of purpose. And yes—Patrick is riding down to meet him. . . ."

Miles slapped him exultantly on the shoulder.

"It's Billalong, not a doubt of it! Look, he's giving something to Patrick—what the devil would that be?" He glanced over his shoulder at the door, and lowered his voice. "Where's Letty? I don't want her to know of Prentice or of Billalong—it would only agitate her."

"She is occupied with the babe," Conor said, "and she begged to be excused from joining us at supper. She's a little indisposed, and means to retire early."

"Good!" said Miles blithely, and was unaware of two quick glances. The knot of figures near the river had broken apart; the convicts were a black line moving slowly round the hillside, flanked on either side by an overseer; the native was walking back to his canoe, and Patrick was riding up to the house. The sky faded as they watched him approach, and the dying glow seemed to take with it not only light, but warmth; suddenly it was dusk, and the scene, with every feature and outline unchanged, yet seemed to Conor utterly transformed. Now the deserted fields looked bleak and lonely, the river cold, the dark hills behind it steeper and higher than they did by day, mounting towards heights that still guarded secrets. She turned to pick up the shawl that Laetitia had left hanging over the back of her chair.

"Well," she heard Miles say urgently, "what message do you bring me from our friend?"

Patrick reined in by the steps; he was looking down at something between his fingers, and there was a brief pause before he answered: "A piece of paper."

"Paper? You mean a letter?" Miles' face fell. "Wasn't that Billa-long? But Prentice . . . ? Don't tell me the fellow can write?" He ran down the steps and held out his hand. "What are you waiting for, man? Where *is* this bit of paper?"

Patrick dismounted as Morgan appeared round the corner of the house to take his horse. When they were alone again he still stood hesitating, and Conor thought that the look of boyishness which had so long per-sisted on his face was now quite gone.

"Before I give it to you," he said, "let me urge you once more—whatever it contains—to abandon this absurd plan of yours, and . . ."

"Good God, you're a veritable prophet of doom!" Miles cried im-patiently. "Give me this precious bit of paper, and spare me your warnings!"

Patrick gave it to him, and they came up the steps together. Miles turned it over in his fingers curiously—a tiny, tightly-folded object, damp and discoloured.

"Folded up like a *billet doux*," he remarked, "but there the resemb-lance ends. Dirty, more than a little greasy, and wound about with thread. . . ."

"Thread?" asked Conor sharply.

Mark produced a penknife from his pocket. "After all, thread could be procured from many people. You'll get it open more quickly, Miles, if you cease fumbling, and use this. My love, don't allow yourself to become agitated before it's necessary." But even his calm voice had a faintly nervous edge as he added: "Miles, if there's anything written there, pray read it, and relieve our suspense."

As they watched him, they were expecting anything but amusement. Yet as he turned the paper this way and that to read, his knitted brows rose slowly in astonishment, and his smile, at first faint, widened until, at last, he looked up fairly shaking with laughter.

"Oh, yes," he answered their enquiring eyes, "it's from Prentice, and your Emily too, ma'am. As a scholar she does you some credit, Sir, though where Prentice learned his penmanship I'm damned if I can guess. But you recall, Patrick, that I offered to take him anything he required . . . ?"

"I do," replied Patrick quickly, "and I recall your confidence that he would ask for nothing."

"Nor does he—in his own hand, at least. I had not reckoned upon the fact that the sternly practical and acquisitive sex would not lightly pass such an opportunity. Oh, God, it's too rich! When I go to meet this dangerous outlaw of yours—this ruthless abductor of an innocent female—this revengeful savage—this murderer—do you know what I'm to take him? *Soap!*"

"Soap?" echoed Patrick blankly.

"Soap!" declared Miles, throwing himself into a chair that he might laugh in greater comfort. "Here, take it, Sir, and read it for yourselves, for I must enjoy this at leisure before I turn to its more serious aspects!"

Conor and Patrick leaned over Mark's shoulder to decipher the words in the failing light. Written in a large, neat hand, one sentence occupied the centre of the page: *"In three days from when you get this I will be at a place where you will be took."* Along the side margin was a longer message in a smaller, rounder hand:

"Sir, if you pleas will you give the letters to Johnny becaus i have got a baby and can not come to get it but i thank the mistress kindly for writing it and send her my respecs and the master to. Sir i take the libety to ask you will not tell about Johnny he is not a bad man tho he has done bad things we have a farm and live well sir we only want to be left aloan and would you kindly bring some soap becaus of the baby and Oblige yours respecfully Emily."

"A farm . . . !" said Mark.

"A baby . . . !" said Conor—in her eyes the absent expression of one engaged in mental calculation.

"In three days . . . !" said Patrick, staring at his brother.

"Soap . . . !" murmured Miles ecstatically—but he was laughing alone.

And his jest was forgotten as he met Patrick's eyes and sat up in consternation. "The meeting-place! Confound it, Patrick, have you let the fellow go off without . . . ?"

"No. He said he would return to-morrow morning, soon after sunrise —he refused to come any nearer to the house." Patrick threw his hat and riding whip down on a chair and burst out angrily: "For the last time I beg you to abandon this absurd undertaking. If you don't care for your own safety, do, at least, consider Laetitia. And if that thought doesn't move you . . ." the bitterness of his tone made Conor glance at him uneasily, ". . . will you not pay attention to the appeal of this girl? They wish only to be left alone." He began to pace the verandah with his swift, limping stride. "And for myself I should ask nothing better than to forget that Prentice ever existed! You spoke of reaching an accommodation with him, and I did the same, once—a useful phrase, conveniently vague! What accommodation is possible between his kind and ours?"

"And what 'kind' is he?" asked Miles, amused.

Patrick stopped to stare at him.

"The son of two convicts. . . ."

"I was not referring," Miles interrupted, "to his ancestry. You don't know what 'kind' he is, nor do I, but I, at least, propose to find out." He turned to Conor. "You'll provide me with my credentials, ma'am, will you not?"

She looked up from the letter with a start. This baby certainly could not be Johnny's; was it Dean's, she wondered, or had Emily entertained some younger, faithless lover, so that she had felt compelled at last to grasp at an unwelcome offer of marriage? However it might be, Conor was thinking guiltily that she had failed the girl, and there was a moisture in her eyes as she raised them from the torn fragment of paper.

"Credentials? Oh, the letter. . . . Yes, I shall write it, Miles, upon one condition."

"And that is?"

"That we shall all, here and now, swear that should you discover where this hiding place, this farm of theirs, is situated, we will do nothing, and say nothing that might betray it."

Miles shrugged.

"Willingly; I've no wish to disturb their rustic idyll, I assure you. I wish only to be first across the mountains—and now also—I confess it —to make the acquaintance of this fellow who appears to kill his men and tame his women with such remarkable facility. You have my promise, ma'am. Patrick asks nothing better than to wash his hands of them, and I see from Mr. Harvey's face that he's quite of one mind with yourself.

So pray write me your letter to-night—including in it, if you like, an assurance of our silence. And may I beg you to complete your kindness by escorting Laetitia to Moore House when you return to Sydney, and doing all in your power to make her sojourn there pleasant and diverting . . . ?"

"She does not," said Patrick with cold distinctness, "care for Sydney."

Miles replied easily:

"She was indisposed when we were there before, and in no mood to care for anything. It will be different now." He jumped up ener-getically. "I'll go now and tell her that I set off to-morrow to cross the mountains—her ignorance of the country and her faith in my capacity for doing what I want to do are such that she'll think it as good as accomplished. Though I daresay she'd tremble for my safety if she knew that I was going to be guided by a savage to a rendezvous with an outlaw." In the doorway he paused to address Patrick's back. "You see, my dear fellow, how wise was my decision to travel unencumbered? I have but the simplest preparations to make; a musket, a blanket, a letter—and, of course, some soap. . . ."

He grinned at them, and was gone.

*   *   *   *

Billalong stopped and held out his hand for Miles' musket.

"I take now, give back another time. You wait. Dyonn-ee come."

Miles handed over his musket and sat down thankfully on the rock, wiping his arm across his forehead, and looking up at the young man who, for the past three days and two nights, had been his sole companion. It had amused him to discover in this naked and untutored savage a gaiety and lightheartedness which matched his own carefree temperament, and though Billalong had set a pace which allowed little time for conversation, they had reached, Miles considered, a very tolerable understanding. During their halts for food and sleep the young native had been loquacious enough, but his knowledge of the English tongue was singularly erratic. He had understood without difficulty Miles' questions about fire-making, the art of hunting game and finding food, native customs, and his own manner of life, answering them readily, and falling back on pantomime and demonstration when at a loss for words. But any question about Johnny Prentice had found him armoured in impenetrable obtuseness, and he had seemed quite unable to comprehend queries about the topography of their journey. Though it was clear enough that the steep, wild country they had traversed, and the cliffs which had obstructed their progress, made detours necessary, Miles still suspected that he had been brought to this place by an unnecessarily circuitous route.

At all events, he reflected, looking about him, Prentice had chosen the spot for their meeting well. The river which they had reached must surely be the Wollondilly—but what part of it he did not know. At this point there was a long, straight stretch; it ran broad and shallow between wide, grassy banks, and in the middle of it lay the large expanse of bare, flat rock upon which he was now seated. He wondered, glancing round at the hills that towered above them on every side, from which one Prentice was now watching.

Billalong remarked with a chuckle:

"You tired feller—come long way, walk quick."

Miles threw his coat down on the rock—he had been carrying it most of the time—stretched his legs out in front of him, and considered his boots, soaking wet from the shallows through which he had waded to the rock, and already the worse for the rough, stony distance they had covered. He replied amiably:

"Tired, my friend, and hungry. If Johnny is to be late for our appointment you had best leave me a morsel of that—that substance we breakfasted upon. I shall not enquire its nature." He cocked an eye at Billalong who was listening with evident pleasure and interest to the sound of the unfamiliar words, but already responding to one which he had understood."

"You all time much hungry." He deposited beside Miles on the rock a slab of seared meat wrapped in soft bark. Miles eyed it, smelt it, and enquired: "When will Johnny come?"

A subtle movement of hands and shoulders and eyebrows proclaimed that Billalong would not care to anticipate the movements or intentions of Dyonn-ee. He picked up the musket and stepped from the rock into the water.

"Dyonn-ee come," he repeated encouragingly, "you wait."

He waded knee-deep through the rippling shallows, climbed out on to the bank, and crossed it to the fringe of the bush. He turned with a gesture of farewell, and clambered up the slope into the shadow of the trees; for a few minutes he was visible less as a man than as a movement in that dappled shade, and then he was gone. The pleasant noise of water rushing over stones emphasised a silence of which Miles now, for the first time, became aware; the hills, covered from foot to summit in their dull, quiet green, bounded the vision on every side; high above them an eagle hung like a black speck in the sky. It was mid-afternoon, but already shadows from the western hill were reaching out towards the rock.

Miles found that he was no longer resting; every muscle in his body had become tense. Prentice's strategic skill in appointing this particular place for their meeting—which at first had won only his amused acknowledgement—now seemed sinister. Alone on a bare rock in the middle of a river, he could be seen from any point of the compass—seen, or fired at. . . . He felt intolerably exposed, and beat down a sudden impulse to wade for the bank, and dive for the shelter of the trees.

He stood up and began to patrol the rock restlessly. He told himself that Prentice was *there*—or *there*—behind that rock, that tree-trunk, that broken stump, that tangle of scrub and vines; and he watched his chosen spot intently until something that was almost like a physical sensation in the middle of his back made him turn sharply to face the other way. It was nearly an hour by his watch—and the shadows had crept to the rock—before he saw something move on the western bank far up the river; a second or two later he saw that it was a man, emerging from the scrub and rocks at the foot of the hill.

A tall fellow, Miles observed, walking quickly and without hesitation, empty-handed, bare-footed, wearing nothing but a faded pair of trousers. Once, as he came nearer and passed through a streak of sunlight, his hair flamed, and the upper part of his body—which had seemed in shadow almost as dark as a native's—betrayed that reddish tint which the fair skin at last reluctantly accepts from the unwelcome sun. He came abreast of the rock, and halted. Miles went to its edge, and across the shallow, glittering water they faced each other for a moment in silence.

It was hardly possible, Miles had been reflecting, to think much of an unknown person without forming some mental image of him. An outlaw, a desperado, a murderer, a son of convicts, a lifelong companion of savages—it was not unreasonable, surely, to picture such a person as ruffianly in appearance? He had been prepared for rags or nakedness; for the demeanour, half furtive, half defiant, of a man who knows himself fugitive and outcast; for the dirty, unkempt, wolfish look of one who had never known the amenities of civilised life. Before him, it was true, stood nakedness sketchily covered by one garment which was little better than a rag, but there the accuracy of his mental picture ended. This man was neither dirty nor unkempt, and his demeanour, far from being furtive or defiant, was a blend of confidence, composure, and something else, even more surprising, which Miles glimpsed for a moment, but could not name. Johnny stepped into the water, waded across to the rock, and stood just beneath it, his thumbs hooked into the leather thong which served him for a belt. Miles, looking down at him, asked:

"Your name is Prentice?"

"Aye."

"You will hardly recall me, and I have but the slightest recollection of you. . . ."

Suddenly he felt a wave of irritation. He was tired and hungry, and he had just passed through an hour of acute nervous strain. He had assumed that this interview would be conducted and dominated by himself, but Johnny's unexpected appearance and bearing had already shaken this belief, and the odd word which now sprang to his mind as he met a direct, unmoving gaze, seemed so absurd that it threw him into momentary confusion. Authority . . . ! Where the devil should such a man get an air of authority? With just such an air might Patrick stand before a stranger on his property, waiting for him to state his business. Goaded by an unfamiliar and enraging sense of discomfiture, Miles completed his sentence coldly: ". . . yet certain events have served to remind my family of your existence from time to time."

Johnny replied briefly: "I've not forgot any of ye, neither."

"You killed my father, and you tried to kill my brother. May I ask whether you have the same designs on me?"

"Not unless ye cross me."

Miles stared at him.

"You're remarkably confident. Are you alone, as I am, or have you friends concealed about us in the hills?"

Johnny's thumbs pressed downward a little harder over his belt, but his tone was still colourless.

"Ye see me. I'm alone."

Miles hesitated, and grew the more angry from his hesitation. He was puzzled again by that elusive expression which he had glimpsed before, though how it manifested itself through the fellow's taciturnity and his impassive countenance he could not tell. It was something held down tightly beneath his composure—excitement—eagerness—a kind of elation . . . ? Yes, it was surely elation, and Miles, suddenly conscious again of that sensation in the middle of his back, wondered whether it were the elation of a man who has successfully lured an enemy into a trap. He found himself glancing uneasily about, and heard Johnny say:

"Ye've no need to look around. Even Billalong's far from here by now." He stepped out of the water on to the rock. "I've come for the letter. When I've got it I'll give ye food, if ye want, and put ye on the right way back."

("And, by Heaven," said Miles, recounting the story later to Conor, "you'll hardly believe it, but it was the sight of a darn in the fellow's trousers that restored my good humour! It spoke of domesticity, and a kind of innocence so incongruous . . . !")

He said:

"I'm obliged to you. But the letter is for Emily—I'm to deliver it into her own hands."

"She bid ye give it to me."

"Ah, so you know that! I was not sure if you were aware that she had added something to your note."

"She told me—after it were sent."

Miles burst into a spontaneous shout of laughter.

"Feminine guile is something we must all learn to suffer, it seems!" Johnny, glancing sideways at the package lying on the rock, remarked imperturbably:

"And she told me she'd asked ye for soap. Well, if she wants soap she can have it for all I care. For meself, I ask for nothin'." He stared hard at Miles and repeated with emphasis: *"Nothin'!"*

"Not even silence?"

Johnny stood for a moment without replying, his head bent, his eyes fixed on his bare feet and the wet patch that spread round them on the rock. "For meself, not even that," he said at last, without looking up. "All me life I've been hidin', and I reckon I could still hide—alone."

"But you are not now alone."

It was at this moment that Miles felt he had come upon something of significance, yet later, when he described the interview to Patrick and the Harveys, he made no mention of it. He had uttered a simple observation, to which Prentice had replied with a simple: "No." Young Mr. Mannion might notice an air of confidence and authority, an air of suppressed elation; in Johnny's suddenly raised eyes he might see those emotions, uncontrolled for an instant, expressing themselves in a look which was one of naked triumph; but it would be years before he understood the cause. It did not occur to him that Johnny was no longer outcast, but cherished, no longer frozen by loneliness, but warmed by companionship, and no longer bedevilled by hatred, but fortified by love; for it had not yet occurred to him that a woman was more than a pretty possession and an agreeable bedfellow. Therefore, struck and startled by the queer, fleeting blaze in Johnny's eyes as he uttered his bald "No," Miles asked quickly:

"You have other companions? Absconders, perhaps, who have joined forces with you? I ask this merely because it might affect a plan I have in mind. . . ."

"There's none but me and Emily. But we want no plans. We want nothin' but to be left in peace."

"So far as our silence can ensure it, you shall be. However, I wish to ask your help in a certain business of my own." He paused, but Johnny, still standing with his thumbs tucked into his belt, merely waited. "I wish to find a route across the mountains."

Johnny's eyes narrowed, but he remained silent, and Miles continued:

"I don't know where your retreat may be, but I have assumed that in all these years you will have become familiar with country which is

285

unknown to us in the settlements. If so, you may be able to give me information of a route. . . ."

"No."

The word came out flat, hard and final. Miles considered him.

"There is at this moment," he said at last, "an expedition being prepared to find such a route. It may succeed, or it may not, but even if it does not, others will follow until a way is found. I don't propose to join it. What I want to point out is that sooner or later, the mountains will be crossed. You can do yourself no harm by aiding me to cross them first."

Still Johnny had nothing to say, and Miles went on arguing.

"I'm asking you no questions; but somewhere in the hills you have a place where you can live—a farm, if we are to believe what Emily wrote. I don't necessarily want to see it, or even to know where it is, unless it might be of use to me in my undertaking—and of that you are the judge. You may have my word, and my brother's word, that your hiding place would never be revealed by us should we discover it. I tell you I want *only* to cross the mountains."

Johnny shot him a quick glance, oddly amused.

"The promise might make y' crossin' of little use to ye."

"I don't know what you mean. But if you will guide me—or direct me—on a route which will take me to the other side, I'll risk whatever disadvantages there may be."

"Why don't ye go with the party ye say's gettin' ready?"

"There are several reasons. All my life, since childhood, I have wanted to be *first*. Call it pride, if you like—vanity, stubbornness—it doesn't matter. And besides . . ."

But Johnny, with the expression of sardonic amusement deepening in his eyes, interrupted suddenly:

"First, eh?"

Not since his childhood, when some cold blast of reality had swept away a cherished fantasy, or some ruthless adult edict had destroyed his coaring plans, had Miles felt so abrupt and violent a sense of deflation. He gazed blankly at Johnny, realising that in assuming achievement to be the prerogative of his own class, he had actually failed to see the implication of his request. He said flatly: "You, I suppose, have been . . . ?"

"Aye, but I wouldn't claim to be the first. There's been natives crossin' back and forth maybe for hundreds of years."

"Oh, natives—yes. . . ."

"And there's been escaped convicts in the hills from time to time, though they stick close to the Nepean, mostly. But I'd not like to say there was never one that found his way to the other side. Why not? It ain't hard."

"Not hard? It's been attempted many times. . . ."

"Ah, they make it hard!" Johnny spoke with impatience and contempt. "I've seen it—here in this same valley. . . . Ye know where we
are?"

"I judged that this is the Wollondilly."

"Aye. And up this river years ago there was a man came explorin'. . ."

"Barrallier?"

"I never knew his name. But he came with a crowd of others—
convicts and soldiers—and they had a waggon, and bullocks, and they
built a hut, and some of 'em went on loaded down with food till they'd
eaten what they had, and then back to the waggon for more. . . .
Wearin' themselves out for nothin'! I could 'a gone," said Johnny dis-
gustedly, "twice as far in the same time, and gettin' me food as I went."

"Ah," said Miles with interest, "you have hit on another of my
reasons for not joining an expedition. It has struck me that dependence
on our own food has been a handicap in the past. That turned my
thoughts to you—for though I suppose I possess as much bodily strength
and endurance as a native, I can't claim to be familiar with their methods
of procuring food. Nor," he added, with a wry glance at Billalong's
odoriferous slab of meat, "do I find their fare palatable, though I'll eat
it if I must. But you—so I reasoned—are well known to the natives, and
practised in their arts. I also dared to hope what has now been confirmed
by Emily's letter—that you might have established some secure retreat
which (if I could persuade you to agree) would furnish me with better
supplies; and also serve me as a setting-out place, and a refuge to which
I could return in an emergency."

Johnny squatted down on his heels. He picked up a pebble and began
tossing it from one hand to the other. The sun had gone from the valley,
and it was growing chilly. Miles put on his coat, but Johnny, half naked
as he was, seemed impervious to cold. He asked at last: "Does y'
brother know ye came to meet me?"

"Certainly—and he disapproved strongly."

"Aye . . . ?" Johnny glanced up, and then back at his pebble.

"His own last encounter with you," said Miles, "made him apprehensive for my safety."

"Why did ye come, then?"

Miles sat down on the rock. Suddenly impatient, he reached out his
hand and intercepted the pebble in mid-air. He flicked it away into the
water, and said:

"Let us understand one another. For years you have conducted a kind
of feud against my family. You thieved from us, you abducted one of
our convicts. . . . I presume you *did* aid Finn's escape . . . ?"

"Aye, he was workin' by the river, and I took him off in a canoe."

"You attempted to abduct others, and finally you murdered my father We need not go into your reasons for all this—they seemed sufficient to you, no doubt. But I tell you plainly, Prentice, the past bores me. I don't care for the way it accumulates ancient grudges and fruitless hatreds that impede the present. You may see me, if you wish, as a member of a family you hate—and therefore hateful. I may see you, if I wish, as my father's murderer—and therefore as an enemy. But I don't wish. I wish merely to see you as whatever you may be. I came here mainly because I want your help; but also because it was only from a meeting that I could discover what you are. You will perhaps now tell me why you came?"

"I reckon," said Johnny slowly, "that I came for much the same reason—to get rid o' what's past." He glanced up at Miles from under his brows, and asked: "Ye still want to cross the mountains even if ye're not the first?"

Miles laughed rather ruefully:

"I should at least anticipate Will Wentworth! Yes, I still want it."

"Y' brother didn't shoot me when he might 'a done it easy enough. Maybe I owe ye somethin' for that. Ye speak of promises, but . . ."

Miles produced the letter from his pocket.

"No doubt Emily has spoken to you of her mistress, Mrs. Harvey?"

"Aye."

"Then perhaps her word will carry more weight than mine. She showed me this letter, and bade me show it to you if the need arose.

Johnny took it and read, his lips moving slightly as he spelled out the words with care.

"My dear Emily,
The letter which was sent to Mr. Miles, and to which you had added some lines of your own, was delivered to him, and shown by him to me. To know that you are alive and well has greatly relieved my Mind, and Mr. Harvey's too. I assure you that we (and I speak also for Mr. Mannion and his Brother) harbour no ill-will towards your Companion, and you need have no fears that your Dwelling, wherever it may be, would be betrayed by us should Mr. Miles discover it. Of this you have our most solemn Assurance.

I am astonished to learn that you have a Babe, and think that I now discern the reason for what I may call your unwilling Determination to accept Dean as your Husband. I fear that, after all, I did not sufficiently command your Confidence. Yet I dare to hope that in the strange Fate which has befallen you, you may discover the Happiness which will always be desired for you by,

my dear Emily,
Your sincere Friend,
Conor Harvey."

"You are satisfied?" Miles enquired, and Johnny looked up.

"It's plain enough."

"You are willing, then . . . ?"

"I'm willing, but—ye'd have to make a choice. There's two ways ye could go. One's not easy—ye'd have rough country that I've lost meself in before I learned the way of it. And I'd not go with ye, for I'll not leave me place so long."

"That's no matter. I want but two things of you—information of the best route, and food."

"Food. Aye, there's the trouble. If ye went this way ye'd get but little, even with y' musket. I might get Billalong or one o' the other natives to go with ye, but they don't like that country—and when natives don't like what they're doin' often as not they just stop. And even the food they'd get wouldn't hardly keep ye goin'. . . ."

"Well," Miles interjected impatiently, "what of the other way?"

Johnny pondered for a long moment, staring at the water with eyes at once thoughtful and amused. "I could take ye most of it meself," he said at last. "It's easy enough walkin', and ye couldn't miss the way after I'd left ye. I could give ye food to carry, and there's more to get without much trouble. . . ."

"Good God, man!" exploded Miles, "where's the difficulty, then? Let us go by this easy way, and set out immediately!"

Johnny looked at him squarely.

"I said before it might be of little use to ye when ye've done it." He eyed Miles' bewildered face, and explained with a faint grin: "That way, ye'll pass right by me doorstep."

For a full minute Miles sat staring at him. Then, with a furious exclamation, he jumped up and began to stamp about the rock, coming at last to a halt again before Johnny, who had risen, and now stood in his old attitude with his thumbs in his belt, and a glimmer of derision in his eyes. "You mean," Miles demanded incredulously, "that if I go this way I cannot speak of it? I can cross the mountains—but I may not announce that I have done so? I can find a route—an easy route—and reveal it to no one else?"

Johnny said laconically: "That's how it'd be."

Miles began to laugh. Johnny, watching him, felt his own still-hovering grin not only widen, but change at its very source. Getting rid of what was past meant, to him, much more than calling a truce between himself and the Mannions. Hatred, bitterness, envy, resentment and revengeful-ness were all burdens he was now ready to discard, and he had come to this meeting to confront a Mannion without caring—to test, and prove, and exult in his new freedom. But he had anticipated, nevertheless, some

289

satirical amusement from the spectacle of a Mannion, helpless and discomfited, and he had deliberately lingered in his hiding place, reading
from afar in Miles' every movement the stress he was enduring; half
hoping in his heart to see him yield to a panic which would set him
struggling through the hills, foodless and weaponless, until it pleased
Johnny Prentice to succour him. But he had not expected the interview
to yield him such exquisitely derisive triumphs. *First* across the mountains . . . ! Yet by the time he learned of that desire he had heard Miles
laugh, and, in a queer shock of pain, it had reminded him of Finn; his
relish, as he had killed that fantasy with a word and a look, had been
oddly transient. This second jest, he found, as he watched Miles enjoy it
with his head back, his mouth wide open, and his laughter waking echoes
from the surrounding hills, was changing its flavour, but losing none of
its piquancy for that. For Johnny Prentice was no longer laughing at
his enemy, but with him; and if the enemy were not thus miraculously
transformed into a friend, he was, at least, the only man of his race, save
Matthew Finn, with whom he had ever laughed.

"I'm fairly caught!" Miles was declaring. "I confess that this is a
development which had not occurred to me. Come, now, is there no
solution? You advise against the other route—which would take me, I
gather, so far from your retreat that my promise need not embarrass me?"

Johnny shrugged.

"Try it if ye want. Ye might get through. But if ye died on the
journey back ye'd not be able to tell what ye'd done, neither."

Miles made a wide gesture of philosophic resignation.

"I'll go with you and make the best of my predicament. You're right
—I could think of nothing that would embarrass me so much as to die.
But, by God, if I remain much longer on this accursed rock I'll be
compelled either to eat that unsavoury morsel of Billalong's or to die of
hunger."

Johnny kicked the meat into the river.

"I can give ye better than that."

"Good; pray take me to it. My musket . . . ?"

"I've a camp not an hour's walk away. I told Billalong to wait there
to go back with ye."

Miles asked curiously: "Does he always do your bidding?"

"Natives," said Johnny, stooping to pick up the package of soap,
"don't do nobody's bidding unless they feel like it."

"Apparently he often feels like doing yours."

Johnny replied briefly: "He's me brother." He stepped down from
the rock and began to wade across the shallows. Miles swung his blanket

over his shoulder and followed, halting when they reached the western bank, and Johnny turned north along it.

"But you came from upstream," he objected.

"Aye," said Johnny dryly, "but now we go down."

*   *   *   *

When they reached the hut Miles was, to his astonishment and chagrin, almost exhausted. It was the pace at which they had travelled rather than the nature of the terrain they had covered which made the journey arduous, for Johnny had ruthlessly curtailed their periods of rest, barely halting to eat and drink, making camp only when dusk was deepening to night, and bestirring himself at dawn to set out again. They came to the hut after dark when nothing was to be seen of its approaches or surroundings. Miles was too weary to do more than eat the rough but plentiful meal which Emily set before him, and note, with a flicker of interest, that she was, indeed, a comely wench. Wrapped in his blanket, and with a few wallaby skins between him and the earth floor, he slept in the bare, inner room of the hut without moving, for ten hours.

He felt refreshed—though a trifle stiff—next morning when, stooping beneath the doorway, he stepped out into the crisp, autumn dawn and looked about him. Sunrise came late to the valley, lying shadowed behind its eastern rampart; the sky's darkness had faded to pallor, and the pallor was slowly beginning to glow with a blushing warmth against which the crest of the cliff line stood out in harsh and jagged silhouette. As Miles watched, the colour deepened to a blaze that touched the highest summits with a radiance like pale fire, spreading downward till the lower slopes turned golden, and the sheer face of rock below them was no longer black, but purple. He could see much of the valley now, and he studied it with interest, noting its inaccessibility, poised at a level midway between the river below and the tableland above; he observed in the immediate foreground the evidences of Johnny's husbandry, and recalled the cattle they had passed on the river flats the day before. But it was to the heights above the valley that his eyes returned again and again, and he felt that odd stirring of excitement which troubles and enchants a man when he comes upon a spot that seems his own.

His motive in seeking new country had been—unlike that of other explorers—romantic rather than practical. He still liked drama, as he had liked it in the days when Andy and Maria and Dilboong had played their subordinate parts in the imaginary adventures whose hero was always himself. But he was compelled to admit that there could be little that was heroic in his present enterprise; he was subdued by the reflection that it had disconcertingly lost both the spice of danger and the promise of glory. He would not be first across the mountains; even if he were

291

second, he could not claim the honour, or reveal his route; even if he could reveal it, there would be little in his exploit that could be turned to advantage. Somewhere up on those heights that skirted the northern end of the valley, Lieutenant Lawson, Mr. Blaxland and Mr. Wentworth would very soon be toiling westward, and he knew that if they were successful the settlements would burst the barrier that had held them circumscribed for so long, and a tide of land-hungry men would flow inland—not along his route, but along theirs. More than his promise, he now realised, would ensure that, for the river route, easy as it was for a man on foot, would present insurmountable difficulties to a road-maker.

His journey, then, had no importance from a public point of view—though that, he admitted candidly to himself, had never been a strong stimulant. It was not wider pastures that he had really sought, but a wider background for his own personality, and a new set of sensations. Some new sensations he had already experienced; the newest was his attitude to Johnny, curiously compounded of liking and hostility. Cattle —sheep—fowls, he thought—all stolen. He had noticed in the hut, with quite absurd annoyance, a footstool upon which he could remember seeing his Cousin Bertha's tiny. feet neatly placed. Everything stolen—even Emily! Miles belonged to the possessing class which had no mercy on thieves, and one part of him resented Prentice the thief even more strongly than it condemned Prentice the murderer. But there was another part which saluted audacity—and this rogue had been nothing if not audacious. Miles was conscious of an inclination to excuse even robbery if it were committed with an air.

He said to Johnny as he was finishing a hearty breakfast in the sun outside the hut:

"You said, I think, that I should have to do no more than follow this river to find myself beyond the first range of mountains. What then?"

"There's more hills, but none to maze ye like those up yonder. Beyond them ye'll come on another river flowin' north-west; ye can count y'self across the mountains then. Likely ye'll see some natives, but I reckon they'll not trouble ye if ye don't trouble them."

"Food?"

"Ye can take some with ye, but there's no want of game there. I'll give ye a line for fishin'. When will ye start?"

"To-day," said Miles rather restlessly. "At once."

*　　　　*　　　　*　　　　*

"I met Blaxland in the street this morning," Mark said to his wife as they sat at supper one evening early in May. "He tells me the expedition is to set out in a matter of days. If Miles is to win his race it will be with but little to spare."

"Did Mr. Blaxland appear confident?" enquired Conor.

"He was confident enough, but a good deal put out. He said he called at Government House to announce their departure, and was received rather cavalierly. It appears the Governor wouldn't see him in the morning, but invited him to dinner, and the matter was not even mentioned until Blaxland himself brought it up just as he was leaving. Then the Governor wished him success—but Blaxland thought his manner cool."

"Oh, that might well be so, I should think—they don't like each other, you know. And besides, don't you recall that I told you Mrs. Macquarie was taken very ill on Saturday, and is still seriously indisposed? *Another* of those misfortunes that they have suffered before! It's no wonder Mr. Blaxland found the Governor's manner reserved, for he must be beside himself with anxiety, poor man! Have you heard any details of the expedition, my love?"

"Only that William Wentworth and Lawson are going—it seems that Lawson is another who has for years cherished an idea of attempting the journey. They're taking horses to carry the food and ammunition, and servants, and dogs—a very different affair from Miles'—and perhaps more prudent, too. How long is it now since Miles left?"

"More than a fortnight. I fear Laetitia is growing anxious. Miles always spoke of it so lightly that at first I really believe she imagined it to be no more than an extended ramble in the hills. But lately, of course, there's been so much talk about this other expedition that she begins to realise the difficulties and dangers."

Mark asked after a pause:

"What is being said, by the way, of his absence? For of course it must have been remarked in this gossip-ridden place."

"Oh, as to that," Conor replied, "I'm really very displeased with Miles!" But he noticed that she was smiling, and reflected that Miles' misdemeanours were apt to be found amusing, or even endearing. "He disappeared," she continued, "so hurriedly that matters were not properly discussed or arranged; but it appears that he told Laetitia not to mention that he was making an attempt on the mountains, and when she asked him what she *was* to say, he merely remarked in that careless way of his: 'Say what you please, my love—say I'm collecting botanical specimens. . . .' "

"Botanical specimens! Why, he barely knows a waratah from a mimosa! He's no George Caley, and everyone knows it. What possessed him to bid her give out so nonsensical a story?"

"Oh, I daresay he didn't really mean it, you know, but Laetitia is inclined to take things in their literal meaning." Conor looked troubled. "The whole country and everything in it appears fantastic to her—and

Miles, instead of helping her to overcome her confusions, merely laughs, and waves them aside. Devoted as I am to the dear boy," she sighed, "I must confess that when he's in pursuit of some object of his own, he pays little attention to the difficulties he may be creating for others."

"Has Laetitia had occasion to use this absurd tale?"

"She did so once or twice, I believe—but I advised her to say in future that he's remaining at Beltrasna to assist Patrick for a time. Not that I think that sounds very likely, either. . . ." She sighed again, and added absently: "Poor Laetitia—I fear she is not altogether happy."

*   *   *   *

On the eleventh day of May—having heard that the long-projected expedition was to set out that afternoon—Patrick rode down to the ford at Emu Island. He was not only curious to witness a departure so different from his brother's, but glad of any excuse to absent himself from the house, which now seemed intolerably silent and deserted. He had not long to wait before he saw the party moving towards him—nine men, four heavily-laden horses, and five dogs. Lieutenant Lawson of the Veteran Company—at thirty-nine the senior member of the expedition—was walking ahead with young Wentworth, while Mr. Blaxland, conversing with two other gentlemen (who, Patrick presently discovered, intended merely to accompany the explorers on the first stage of their journey) followed close behind. The four servants brought up the rear, leading the horses. "What Miles would call a 'cavalcade'," thought Patrick as he watched them approach.

The party came up, and greetings were exchanged; during a little desultory conversation Patrick observed William Wentworth's thoughtful eye upon him. Mr. Blaxland, whose high spirits appeared to have induced one of his facetious moods, remarked jovially:

"I begin to fear that our arrangements have been deficient, Mr. Mannion. We should have brought Hannibal Macarthur—and some elephants!"

"I don't doubt you will conquer our Alps without them, Sir," replied Patrick. "At all events, I wish you good fortune."

"We may need it," said Lawson, "but we shall at least be proceeding according to a definite system—which is more than can be said of our predecessors."

"You intend to keep between the heads of the gullies, I believe?"

"Exactly, Sir. We shall keep the streams that empty themselves into the Grose upon our right, and those that feed the Western River on our left, so that we shall be always on the main ridge. At least the walking should be easier than what Caley has described to me."

"Where do you intend to make your first camp?"

"We shall go only to the foot of the mountains to-day. Would you care to accompany us so far, Mr. Mannion?"

"I thank you, but I must return home; and I shall not detain you now, for it's growing late, and the evenings are short. My best wishes for your success."

He watched the party begin to cross the ford. Young Wentworth, lingering, broke away from it, and returned to stand beside Mor, looking up at Patrick with his slightly crooked gaze.

"Your brother is well, Sir?"

"Very well, I thank you."

"His botanical researches progress satisfactorily?"

"I beg your pardon . . . ?" said Patrick, puzzled.

"I understand that he is collecting specimens. It's to be hoped," pursued Mr. Wentworth politely, "that his scientific enthusiasm will not tempt him too far afield. To the other side of the mountains, for example . . . ? Farewell, Sir; when we return triumphant I shall give myself the pleasure of describing our adventures to you—and to him."

Patrick stared after him for a few moments as he splashed across the ford to join his companions, and then, with a shrug, turned Mor's head towards home. As he rode up from the bank he noticed a native youth at a distance, loitering down towards the river, and watching the group of men and horses; no doubt, Patrick thought, he would appear by the camp-fire to-night begging food, or such other trifles as might catch his eye. Balgundra, however, knew that a party of white men, with horses so heavily laden, and moving with such an air of purpose towards the mountains, would be of interest to Dyonn-ee, and by the time the explorers broke camp next morning, he was far away.

* * * *

Miles returned to the hut eighteen days after he had left it. He was ragged, and his boots were tied together with kangaroo hide, but he had suffered no worse hardships than a wrenched ankle, and the discomfort of wet clothes during a day or two of rain. He had been able, as Johnny had predicted, to provide himself with ample food, and he had seen no natives, though he came several times on the still-warm ashes of fires, and knew that they were near.

He said to Johnny:

"If you knew of this country, why the devil didn't you move to it? It's far finer land than this."

"Maybe that's a good enough reason for me stayin' here. There won't be no one botherin' about this for many a year after they've found that." But he knew it was not the only, or even the main reason; this was his *towri*, his tribal home, and the place to which Finn had bidden him return.

He added, half to himself: "There's other things ye want of a place besides a livin'."

Miles, with a mouthful of food halfway to his lips, paused and looked hard at him.

"I have been thinking that myself. The country out there . . . Amazing! Rich, open, well-watered—they'll descend on it like locusts when they've found it. But I want something else. . . ."

"Ye don't *want* more land—rich land?" Johnny sounded unbelieving, and Miles said quickly:

"I didn't say that. I should have said, perhaps, that I want something *more*. Rich land means wealth, which is always welcome. But it won't run away. I can afford to wait till it's open for settlement. In the meantime, I want. . . ."

He stopped, frowning, and continued his meal for some time in silence. It disconcerted him to realise that what he wanted was a magnified and transfigured version of Johnny's outlaw life. Not to be a fugitive—not to hide. . . . But to do what more cautious and prudent men would never do—to break away from the pattern—to ignore frequented paths, and make his own. . . . He was seeing Johnny's life adjusted, enlarged, smoothed and polished, shorn of its rudeness, bedecked with civilised comforts—transmuted, in short, to something more suitable for himself. The isolation of this tiny hut had excited him—but not the hut itself, not its meanness, its obscurity; Miles Mannion might please to be solitary, but he would never please to be unnoticed. The sense of distance from the civilised world had stimulated him—but he reflected with satisfaction that it was largely illusory; he might choose to withdraw at intervals, but he would never choose to be a hermit. The sight of a white woman in this primitive wilderness had intrigued him—but Emily belonged to a class which must expect to live in rough surroundings, and thus the situation was robbed of some of its piquancy; how much more striking would be the contrast between such a wild environment, and Laetitia's delicate and sophisticated beauty! He saw himself alone—but accessible; remote—but conspicuous. No hidden valleys for him, therefore, but some commanding height past which (at a respectful distance) there would some-day run a road to link him with the world; no hut of bark and logs, but a fine house of solid stone to burst upon the view of travellers, and make them rub their eyes. *Here* was Johnny Prentice, obscurely poised between the river and the mountains; *there* would be Miles Mannion, flamboyantly poised between the coastal settlements and the rich inland. The best of both worlds—nothing less would do. . . . He found that he was staring through the open doorway at the cliffs.

"If you will extend me your hospitality a little longer," he said at last, "I should like to make another brief exploration—of the heights up yonder."

Emily, who was busy at the fire, turned round in astonishment.

"Law, Sir, you won't find nothin' up there! Johnny's been, and he says it's only rocks and trees and great, awful precipices!"

Johnny, who had been watching him with curiosity, asked abruptly: "Ye're lookin' for a place to live?"

"Live . . . !" cried Emily, scandalised. "Mr. Miles? Up there? Don't talk so foolish—how could a gentleman like Mr. Miles live in a place like that?" She was agitated by Johnny's ignorance of what was suitable for gentry. Miles cocked an eye at her.

"Why not, Emily?"

"Why not, Sir . . . ? Because there ain't nothin' *there*! And it's mortal cold in winter, too, and the wind's somethin' cruel. And the soil's that bad ye couldn't grow no crops. . . ."

"I shouldn't need to," Miles replied, "if there were a road."

"A road. . . ?" There was fear as well as incredulity in her voice. Miles answered her, with his eyes on Johnny:

"I think there will be a road—someday. Perhaps soon." He rose and went to the door. "You know of a way up those cliffs, Prentice?"

"Aye."

"Then I shall beg you to show it to me to-morrow."

*　　　　*　　　　*　　　　*

But next morning a cold, sleety rain was falling, and it was not until the following day that the weather had cleared sufficiently for Miles to set out. Johnny had been thinking hard, not only about his guest's peculiar desire for a habitation in the mountains, but about the predicted road. At first he had felt anger—that old, familiar anger whose origin was fear; he had cursed himself for bringing Miles to his retreat, and even, for one raging moment, reflected that a dead man could cause no trouble. But that mood had passed, and he had pondered the business more soberly. Though he wanted neither a road nor a neighbour, he realised that in time the road would come; if a neighbour must come with it, let him at least be a well-disposed one.

So he said, when Miles had been provided with food by a still-puzzled and disapproving Emily: "I'll go with ye as far as the pass—it ain't easy to find." But they had been walking for barely an hour when they encountered two natives who—consumed by curiosity about this white man whose head topped Dyonn-ee's even as Dyonn-ee's topped theirs—announced their intention of accompanying him. Johnny turned back, therefore, and Miles went on with his self-appointed guides, one of whom was a slight, elderly man bearing many combat scars, and the other a robust youth who amused himself as they proceeded by memorising and repeating English words. They were, Miles had observed, well known to Johnny, who had addressed them as Boorah and Murrunga.

They climbed, at last, up a steep, narrow pass, darkened by over- hanging rocks, and wet with flying spray from a waterfall. It was already late afternoon when they emerged from it, and toiled up the slope to the crest of the ridge. Here the trees, though tall, seemed to live embattled; broken branches told of snow, blackened trunks of fire, and distorted shapes of wind, but high in the air they fluttered their sparse, glittering leaves, throwing a flicker of shadow on the low-growing scrub, and on the grey rocks whose every crevice sheltered some small, toughly-rooted plant. Miles walked forward with the natives, taking no thought of direction, since he was less looking for a place than hoping it would appear. And they had been walking less than half an hour when they came again to an edge of the cliff line where Miles halted, staring.

From the heights on which they stood, a narrow isthmus ran out to join another tableland to the south, and on either side of it, dropping sharply from the base of its sheer cliffs, lay a valley. To the west Miles could see the one he had just left, bathed in the warm, yellow light of the setting sun, and at his feet the second stretched away to the east beneath a luminous blue haze until it was stopped in the far distance by another ring of cliffs. Out of it a great, rounded mountain rose solitary from purple depths, its crest still sunlit. With the few native words he had learned Miles asked his companions its name; "Korrowal", they said, and he stood looking at it for a long time while the sinking sun threw cobalt shadows into the creek bed that scored its massive top, painted its cliffs with a brief splendour of red and gold, and then vanished, leaving him to confront a lonely, but majestic waste, cold, silent and remote.

There was no lack of shelter, and they camped that night in one of the many caves that honeycombed the rocks. Miles woke at sunrise to find the western valley gone—buried beneath a sea of white mist so dense that it looked solid; marvellous, he thought, that somewhere beneath that motionless cloud-sea, Johnny and Emily could still be breathing. But the eastern valley was clear, its blue pure, delicate and elusive, and the sun was just touching the top of Korrowal. As Miles watched, a faint breeze from the west began to stir the mist dammed back by the isthmus, and now the sun caught the surface of that white sea so that it seemed capped by restless, rosy waves. A few vaporous wisps drifted across the dividing wall, and drawn by some downward current of air, slid over the eastern cliff face. More followed, faster and faster, rolling up in billows and spilling over the edge, not floating down, but pouring hard and fast like water, so that the wall was lost beneath a rushing cataract that glowed like pink dust in the early sunlight. Miles, still staring, demanded of the natives the name of this place on which they stood; it had no name, they tried to explain—it was merely a high place. *Illalangi,* they repeated— *illalangi,* a high place.

When there was nothing left of the mist in Johnny's *towri* but a few shreds between the folds of the hills, and the strengthening sun had dispersed it in the eastern valley, Miles said that he was ready to return; he wished to go no further. They climbed down the pass again, and it was soon after midday when they reached the outskirts of Johnny's domain. They found him at work, splitting one of the logs he had sawn from a felled tree, and surrounded by a group of young native boys who were stacking the wood to dry—but who, upon seeing their fellow-tribesmen and the white giant, immediately dropped their burdens, and stood at gaze. A plume of smoke came from the chimney of the hut, and far away on the hilltop beyond it another drifted up idly from among the trees. Johnny, leaning on his maul, asked:

"Have ye seen all ye want?"

"For the present, yes—and it pleased me."

"It's a fine sight," agreed Johnny, stooping to pick up his wedges, "but I reckon the explorin' party that's set out'll be lookin' for somethin' more than fine sights." Miles asked quickly:

"The expedition has set out, you say? How do you know?"

Johnny jerked his head at the distant thread of smoke.

"Balgundra. He seen 'em movin' off from the river, and come to tell me. Hi, ye little devil—put that down!" He retrieved his axe from one of the small boys, and, running his thumb tenderly along its edge, asked: "Would ye say they'd get across?"

"Who knows? You're afraid they might stumble on this place?"

"They'd be stumblin' well out of their way if they did. And there's not many passes down into this valley, neither—I only know of two meself besides the one ye took. Emily'll give ye somethin' to eat; I'll come after ye when I've had a word with Boorah, here."

Only when he was halfway across the field did Miles stop dead for a moment, realising that he had been, in effect, dismissed. He thought irritably: "Devil take the fellow!" Again that air of authority! Yet what was authority without orders? Johnny gave the natives no orders, yet—though they came and went as they pleased, and abandoned at will any labours they might choose to undertake for him—it was plain enough that they were useful to him. Miles was still pondering this as he sat down to the meal which Emily placed before him, and it was a mere extension of his thought which made him ask her suddenly:

"Am I to tell Mrs. Harvey that you are content here?"

"Oh, yes, Sir, if you please. Not that there ain't some things I miss, Sir, but I do well enough with what I got, and I wouldn't want to go back."

He looked at her curiously, and meeting his eyes, she came quickly to the table, resting her hands on it and leaning towards him.

"Sir, there's those gentlemen that are lookin' for a way across the mountains—I'm afeared they might find us. . . ."

"You're well out of their path, Emily."

"Yes, Sir, so Johnny says—but if they did . . . ? Or if not them, then someone else—some time. . . . Johnny's no convict, Sir, nor never was. Maybe it ain't regular that he took this place without it was granted to him, but there's no call they should hold it against him when it's so far, and no one else wantin' it. . . ." She darted a look at the door and lowered her voice. "It ain't really *good* land, Sir. I never was on a farm before, but I've heard talk, and I've seen the things the farmers bring to Market from the Hawkesbury, and we don't grow nothin' like it here. But it's good enough for us, Sir, and I reckon the way Johnny's worked on it makes it his. . . ."

Miles raised his eyebrows; though he felt some sympathy with Emily, he could not fail to see this point of view as a heresy fraught with peril to those who could afford to buy their land. He interrupted:

"As to that, it would be a matter for the Governor if ever you were discovered. He's a kindly sort of man, and I daresay some arrangement might be made. . . . But that, I think, is not your real danger, Emily. What was done beside a certain cart on a lonely track was hardly 'regular' either—and your presence here suggests very clearly who was the author of that deed."

She went white, but faced him without moving.

"No one knows anythin' about that," she said, "except me. *You* don't know nothin'." There was actually a threatening note in her voice, and she had forgotten to say 'Sir'. He replied with a shrug:

"My dear Emily, it's a fair assumption. . . ."

"*I* say it weren't Johnny!" She leaned closer, and her eyes were fierce. "I say someone else shot Dean—someone that never saw me because I was hid in the back of the cart, and I never saw him, neither, because he ran away too quick. I reckon there was more than one might have had reasons for killin' Dean. *I* say I got lost afterwards, tryin' to find me way back to the road. . . ."

"On a track? Come, come, Emily . . . !"

She hit the table angrily with her hand.

"No one expects a woman to have sense! I was in a state, and I wandered off the track. And some natives found me, and took me to the river, and Johnny was there, and I came here with him. . . ." She paused, glaring at Miles, and added menacingly: "That's what *I* say! Can ye say any different?"

He began to laugh.

"It's a damned unlikely tale—but, by Heaven, no more unlikely than the truth. . . ." She cried furiously: *"Can ye say it's not the truth?"*

"No," he said, suddenly sober. "No, indeed I cannot. And now, Emily, pray let me do justice to this excellent dish, for I'm half starved."

She was smitten, all her fire quenched, and tears in her eyes.

"Oh, yes, Sir, I've kept ye from y' dinner!" She retired, blushing, to the fireplace, and was still busy there with her back to the room when Johnny entered a few moments later. He seated himself astride the bench opposite Miles, and remarked:

"I'll know sooner than the Governor does if they've found a way across the mountains." Miles looked up from his meal.

"How so? Do you intend to dog their footsteps?"

Johnny swung his leg over the bench as Emily placed a platter before him. "Not me. Boorah and Murrunga, and a few others from the tribe'll do it better."

*　　　*　　　*　　　*

The rough cairn of stones was evidently the work of a European They stood round it for a time, debating whether it had been erected by that same explorer whose marks they had found a week ago, cut into the bark of a tree; on one side of it the stones had been displaced, and Lawson suggested that this had probably been done by natives, curious to discover if anything were hidden in it—but they could do no more than conjecture. They agreed, however, that it must mark the farthest point reached by its builder, and that from here they would, in all probability, be upon ground never before traversed by white men.

Such encouragement was welcome. They had been out nine days, and covered only about eighteen miles; to follow the main ridge was not, they had discovered, as easy as it sounded. Often narrow and always tortuous, it wound its intricate way between the heads of steeply-sloping gullies, and from the beginning the heavily-laden horses had moved slowly along it, impeded by stony ground, dense scrub, and closely-growing saplings. The third day had found them in a patch of forest land with good grass and water, but a few miles farther on they had been halted by a brush so thick that they had attempted a detour, only to find that every subsidiary ridge they followed ended in cliffs, or led them far down gullies. The horses several times fell under their loads, and the men, baffled and exhausted, had returned at last to pass the night in the forest land, resolved to cut their way through the brush in the morning.

301

With no knowledge of where they might again find water or feed for their beasts, they had decided to leave them behind with a couple of men, and cut a track forward until a spot suitable for the next night's camp was reached; but after clearing a path for five laborious miles, they had been forced to return, weary and unsuccessful, to their base. Next day they had tried again, and won two more miles, but still there was no grass, and again nightfall found them back at their old camp, chafing at the delay and fatigue caused by walking backward and forward over their route. The next day, being Sunday, they had rested, but at night the dogs, excited by the howling of dingoes near the camp, had barked continually, so that there was little sleep for the men. A horse had broken loose, and had to be pursued next morning more than a mile back along the way they had come. Having had an idle day in which to reflect upon difficulties already experienced, and imagine worse to come, they were all gloomy.

Determined to escape from this spot, they had loaded the already-burdened horses with as much grass as they could carry, and pushed on along the track they had made to encamp in the afternoon between two deep gullies; it was only by clambering six hundred feet down a ravine that they had been able to fetch up just enough water for the men; the horses had gone thirsty that night.

Next day they had once more prepared their track, gaining a mere mile and a half, and returning to their camp dejected. And to-day, having traversed a ridge no more than twenty yards wide, with steep, rocky gullies dropping away on either side, they had for the first time seen the settlements far below them to the eastward, and presently discovered this pile of rocks by which they now stood.

Thus far, at least, some other European had been before them. The thought that they, unlike the builder of that cairn, were not at the end but still near the beginning of their journey, gave them fresh heart; and the sight, when they pushed on, of a swamp covered with tussocks of coarse grass like rushes, and intersected by a stream of good water, put them all in better spirits than they had been for some days.

They were climbing all the time, and the air grew sharper. One of the men fell ill, and struggled on in feverish misery. There was still no good feed for the horses, but they lived on the reedy grass of the open swamps which now seemed a feature of the country, and in these there was always water. One night the dogs set up a furious barking, and they heard something run off through the scrub; they thought at first that again a horse had broken loose, but all were safely tethered, and they assumed that natives had been about the camp.

Soon they were travelling along a bleak, high upland, bounded on the south by a tremendous and continuous wall of perpendicular cliffs that rose from the chaos of tumbled hills and valleys a thousand feet below. Young Wentworth, who had a taste for geology, studied the strange rock formations, speculated upon the fearful convulsion of nature which had produced this awe-inspiring scene, and coveted specimens of the stones and minerals which might lie below, fallen from the cliff face. Leaving the horses and provisions in the care of three men, the rest of the party attempted a descent. They tried gullies, and found themselves peering over the edge of some rocky platform from whose lip a thin stream of water fell vertically to the talus, and thence found its way to creek beds which betrayed their presence below only by lines of dark shadow, sinuously winding. They followed ridges out to their farthest point, and began to make their way down over loose earth and slipping stones, between vast rocks and along narrow ledges until, again, a precipice was at their feet. "Wings are what we need," Lawson remarked morosely as they scrambled back wearily to the heights.

They made three more miles next day, and cleared a path forward for four more. When they woke next morning to proceed along the prepared way, the valleys were full of mist from which, here and there, a few hilltops higher than the rest emerged like islands. Slowly, as the sun climbed, it began to disperse, and the depths were visible again, veiled in their curious, translucent blue. In the afternoon while they were at work marking and clearing the next stage of their journey, they heard, quite close to them, a sound as if someone were chopping a tree; the dogs barked and gave chase, but the men could find no one. Murrunga, as he plunged, panting, down a trickling stream through a steep little gully, determined to keep a better distance in future; white men he could easily elude, but he did not like dogs.

The country was still rough, and the prickly undergrowth still thick, but the convenient swamps persisted. Now, below them, the explorers could sometimes see the fires of native camps, and once, looking out towards the south, they idly noticed a thread of smoke rising from behind a fold in the hills, many miles across the valley; but the fine, blue, wavering plume that rose from tribal fires was a familiar sight to all colonists, and there was nothing to tell them that this one came from Johnny's rough, stone chimney.

Eighteen days after they had set out they found themselves on the brink of a precipice, and facing the sunset; this time, however, they were gazing down at what appeared to be comparatively open country, with tall trees and good grass. They found, after some searching, a pass some thirty feet wide between high rocks, leading on to a hill so steep that they looked at it in dismay. But they tried it next morning, and though they cut a narrow trench with a hoe to keep the horses from slipping on the stony, treacherous ground, they were still compelled to unload the animals, and themselves carry the burdens. They reached the foot at last, and went on, jubilant despite their fatigue, through country where the grass grew three feet high, until they reached a fine, clear rivulet which invited them to rest.

They were all, to some extent, ill; their clothes were rags, their shoes badly worn, and their provisions running low. Not only distaste for the salt meat they carried made them rejoice when the dogs killed a kangaroo. Here the weather was much colder than on the eastern side of the range, and what they had imagined from a distance to be sand, was found to be grass, burnt brown by severe and continuous frosts. Yet it was pleasant next day to walk over open, well-watered, undulating country after struggling along the dry, scrubby ridges of the plateau. For two days a party of natives had been moving a couple of miles ahead of them, and now they came upon abandoned fires. Following down the rivulet, they reached its junction with another larger stream, flowing very fast from the north-west over smooth, red-brown granite stones. This, they agreed, must flow into the Western River, and thence into the Nepean; but Boorah and Murrunga, watching with their companions from a distance, saw they had no intention of following it.

A few miles farther up its course three isolated hills were visible, one, higher than the others, on its right bank, and two on its left; in the afternoon, having climbed to the summit of the tallest, the explorers looked round them and saw land which, they judged, would feed the colony's stock for the next thirty years.

It was the first day of June when they turned back. Better country still might lie beyond the next range of hills, but they had discovered enough; the route had been found, the way was open. They toiled up the precipitous pass again and set out eastward; to speed their progress they now had a trail to follow, their previously used camping sites ahead, and—not least—the knowledge that their food would not last for many more days. The miles which had been so slowly won on the outward journey were covered as fast as they could push themselves and their flagging horses. On the fourth day one of these fell exhausted, and there was a long delay while they transferred its load to other beasts, and got it on its feet again; but by nightfall they had reached the end of their marked track, and here, in that patch of forest land where they had been so long halted, and so bitterly discouraged before, they now made camp cheerfully. A road, said Lawson, would be a simple matter, and no doubt a communication could be made from it to the Coal River district. This range, they agreed, was formed by nature as a defence against invasion.

And—of more immediate importance—they had proved that it was traversable by cattle. They had succeeded, and they felt that ebullition of the spirits which so pleasantly follows a physical ordeal surmounted; they could almost enjoy their present discomforts—their aching muscles, their blistered feet, their scratched hands and their uneasy stomachs—for to-morrow they would breakfast by the Nepean, and then, in a few more miles, there would be soft beds, fresh food, soap and water. Mr. Blaxland recalled that it was His Majesty's birthday, and they all agreed with the utmost cordiality that it was a pity they had no wine to drink his health.

Next morning—feeling themselves even nearer to home from having clearly heard, during the night, the noises of domestic animals from the farms below—they set out early in high good humour. But the mountains, having let them through, held one more lesson in reserve. From here they had no track to follow, and for hours they blundered among ridges and gullies—within sound and almost within sight of home, but lost. Nothing remained of their provisions but a little flour, and their spirits fell as the day passed and they realised that they must spend yet another night beneath the sky. It was late in the afternoon by the time they saw the river below them, and made their toilsome descent to it. Hungry, exhausted, and suffering a sharp reaction from premature triumph, they made their last camp on its banks.

"For my part," declared young Mr. Wentworth, glaring malevolently at the dark foothills, "I would name this as the most abominable and fatiguing day of the whole journey!" Wearily, they all grunted their assent.

*   *   *   *

The interest aroused among the colony's inhabitants by tidings that a way had at last been found across the mountains, partially accounted for the absence of official jubilations; Macquarie had no wish to encourage a premature drift of settlers to some as yet unproved domain where they would be beyond the range of his watchful eye. Moreover, it was not certain that the mountains had been completely crossed. The explorers themselves expressed doubt, though they claimed with confidence to have overcome the worst obstacles, and were emphatic as to the value of the country they had found. The Governor, therefore, contented himself with congratulations to the leaders of the expedition; and it was noticeable that Mr. Howe's brief account in the *Gazette* described the adventure merely as "a trackless journey into the interior", and forestalled too feverish enthusiasm with a cool reference to fine, level country "which time may render of importance and utility".

It was not only caution, however, that restrained His Excellency from immediate preparations to follow up this interesting discovery. Like most administrators, he had learned that the petty affairs of each day—though soon to be buried and forgotten beneath the accumulated petty affairs of a thousand to-morrows—nevertheless demanded an immediate attention which, frequently, could be spared to them only by making more momen-tous business wait. A few limited agricultural settlements might suddenly find themselves confronting a gateway flung open to a continent—but this did not diminish the tyrannical pressure of routine duties upon the Governor; nor the importunities of individuals who conceived their prob-lems too pressing to admit of a moment's delay; nor the clamorous in-trusion of events whose importance a month would obliterate, but whose claims upon his notice could not, for the moment, be ignored. The mountains, having awaited conquest for twenty-five years, could wait a little longer.

Thus, in the weeks following the explorers' return, their exploit was, perforce, relegated to the background of the Governor's thoughts. The ship *Fortune* entered the Heads almost simultaneously with their re-appearance in Sydney; Captain Case was still plaguing His Excellency, not only about repairs to the *Samarang*, but by the general intransigeance of his attitude; there were two hundred new convicts to land and dispose of; there were readjustments to be made in the Commissary's Depart-ment; Mr. Bent was being extremely importunate about the erection of a new Court House which should be worthy of his dignity; there was a despatch box filled with documents of more than usual interest and im-portance; and the *Minstrel* was awaiting completion of his own despatches before setting sail for England.

At the moment it was the despatch box which held his attention. He was informed that a state of war now existed between His Majesty's Government and that of the United States of America; this, though naturally interesting to a soldier and a loyal subject, seemed of less concern to a viceroy than certain other documents. A remarkable private letter from Under-Secretary Goulburn made him raise his eyebrows and recall, with some self-congratulation, the restrictions which he had placed upon his deputy at Hobart Town. That the Colonial Office should warn him to keep a sharp eye on ex-Colonel Johnston was not surprising; but that it should, apparently, more than half expect the gentleman appointed as Lieutenant-Governor of Van Diemen's Land to make improper use of his authority, and indulge in peculation of public moneys, was not so easily explained. Mr. Johnston was still behaving in a very quiet, in-offensive manner—but what might not Davey be up to? Macquarie could not but feel a trace of rebellious irritation against his superiors. It was understood that his colony was designed to be a receptacle for rogues—

but were they not going a little too far . . . ? One expected roguery among convicts; one accepted it with resignation among the lower class of settlers, and with grieved astonishment among the upper; but one had hoped, at least, to find one's immediate lieutenants above reproach!

He snapped to Campbell:

"They don't seem to realise the problems that distance creates in this country!" And for a moment he found himself imagining yet another distant settlement—a new one beyond the mountains, administered by some other deputy for whose misdemeanours he would also be held responsible. It must come, of course—and soon; but his desire to see the colony extend was sometimes accompanied by misgivings, caused not by fear of his own inadequacy, but by dread of restrictions and handicaps imposed upon him from across thousands of ocean miles. Ah, if he could but be unfettered—if he could but make his own appointments, form his own policy, draw freely from some less parsimonious Treasury, and govern this country in the light of his local knowledge and his large benevolence—he would make of it a veritable land of Canaan . . . !"

But for all his playful talk of "my realm" and "my subjects", he knew that he was a subordinate, and the despatch box yielded another document to remind him of it. He read with sharp interest the voluminous report of the Select Committee of the House of Commons upon the burning question of transportation.

It was not so bad as it might have been, he thought. He was profoundly relieved to learn from his despatches that the Committee's unfortunate recommendation that the Governor should be assisted by a Council had found no favour at all among His Majesty's Ministers, and he hastened to endorse their views. It was pleasing, also, to find the Committee urging the distillation of spirits within the colony—a measure which he himself had already advocated. The present surplus of grain, and the consequent discontent of settlers unable to dispose of it had caused many of them to mutter that they would not trouble to grow what they could not sell; wheat had fetched as little as five shillings a bushel in the Sydney market of late, and farmers were feeding it to their pigs. A distillery, by absorbing this surplus would, he argued, not only stimulate the flagging zeal of the settlers, but yield a better spirit than that commonly imported, and also return a considerable revenue to Government.

Perhaps the most gratifying of all the news that reached him at this time was the assurance that the colony's Courts of Justice were to be remodelled. On the subject of trial by jury, Bathurst posed a series of weighty questions. How far would the peculiar composition of society in New South Wales allow such an innovation? Were there enough settlers suitable to act as jurymen? Might they not, in so small a place, bring with them into Court passions and prejudices incompatible with their duty? If settlers were to sit in judgment upon convicts, would not the great principle of the institution—that a man must be tried by his peers—be violated? And, on the other hand, would free settlers be content to see convicts act as jurymen?

To this last Macquarie had his answer ready. A convict was one thing; an ex-convict quite another. "*While a Man is under the Sentence of the Law he is not eligible to be employed in any place of Trust.*" But an ex-convict must take his place in society, sharing both rights and duties with free men. "*. . . he should in All Respects be considered on a footing with every other Man in the Colony, according to his rank in Life and Character.*" But the Governor had no illusions; he knew that with many persons such a policy would not be popular, "*. . . but in My humble Opinion, in coming to New South Wales they should Consider that they are Coming to a Convict Country, and if they are too proud or too delicate in their feelings to associate with the population of this Country, they Should Consider it in time, and bend their Course to some other Country. . . .*"

In the matter of the re-modelled Courts he had another request to make. Still in pursuit of perfect accord, he was ready to do anything which might remove the slight, but troublesome constraint which seemed to persist in the manner of Mr. Bent. He wrote, therefore: "*I take the Liberty to Name and strongly recommend to Your Lordship Mr. Jeffrey Hart Bent (Brother to Mr. Ellis Bent, the present Judge Advocate here) for the Appointment of Assistant Judge.*" He declared his belief that Mr. Jeffrey Bent was a lawyer of some eminence, and a gentleman of good sense and conciliatory manners; and he touched upon the harmony which would undoubtedly prevail in a legal department administered by two devoted brothers.

In his despatch he embodied reports and suggestions which, he trusted, would inspire approval in Bathurst. The abundant harvest and the increase of livestock had enabled him to reduce the price of meat and grain received into the public stores; while he explained and defended certain sharply criticised items of expenditure, he hastened also to mention new duties imposed upon various articles of merchandise produced in the colony, which, he asserted, must greatly increase, "*. . . and I hope the period is not now far distant when I shall be able to defray a Considerable proportion of the Expences of the Colony out of the Revenue collected here. . . .*" With such cheering hints to sweeten the pill of further requests, he pointed out the necessity, in the meantime, of continuing to build streets, roads and bridges. The many months which must elapse before replies to despatches could be received was frequently an embarrassment—but sometimes a convenience. A Governor might have his own way for quite a long time by saying: "May I do this? Meanwhile, until I receive instructions, I shall do it." But for this matter he needed more than months; let the authorities but acquiesce for two more years, he pleaded, and he would have completed all the roads and bridges which the colony required.

He set forth his views upon the necessity for corporal punishment, reported the evacuation of Norfolk Island at last completed, and the machine for stamping the centres from his dollars at last functioning. He renewed his pleas for more clergymen, more schoolmasters, more paper for Mr. Howe's press, and more medicines for the hospital. These, and other matters, were at length dealt with to his satisfaction, and he ended rather exhaustedly: "*I have particular pleasure in drawing Your Lordship's attention to the Reduction in Expences of the Colony in the last two Quarters; and Your Lordship may rest assured that my utmost Exertions will be constantly directed to Economy. . . .*"

The voluminous document was ready, together with its mountain of returns, statements, accounts, requisitions and other enclosures; the hands of Mr. Campbell's clerks could never be idle, but they knew a brief respite as they dropped pens, and gathered duplicates and triplicates into orderly piles. The despatch box was put on board the *Minstrel* almost at the moment when the town was thrown into an uproar by a more than usually outrageous murder.

Whatever hopes might have been entertained that the appointment of a soldier as Governor would tend to improve the discipline of the colonial garrison, had not been fulfilled; for some time past Macquarie had been compelled to notice that the behaviour of the soldiers left much to be desired. Now, when two Lieutenants—having put aside their uniforms—stepped out one evening bent upon amusement, and attempted the seduction of a young sempstress who lodged in the house of a respectable couple called Holness, they provided a crisis which made His Excellency demand with urgency and indignation the removal of the whole regiment.

". . . *several of those,*" he wrote, "*whose Military rank and duty alike require them to restrain acts of insubordination and resistance to the Civil Authority, are the foremost in trampling down all Order, and exhibiting Scenes of disgraceful riot and confusion to the dread and terror of the peaceful inhabitants of this place. Having premised so much, I am now to acquaint Your Lordship that at an early hour of the night of the 30th Ulto. a very peaceable and unoffending man in the lower ranks of life, called William Holness, was murdered in the streets of Sydney by Lieutenants McNaughton and O'Connor of the 73rd Regt. . . ."*

Painful and revolting as were the naked facts of this affair, the Governor found its sequel even more disturbing. The officers, committed for trial before a Criminal Court, found themselves convicted merely of manslaughter, and sentenced to nothing worse than a fine of one shilling each, and imprisonment for six months. If the Governor was shocked, the populace was furious. "*This Sentence*," wrote Macquarie, "*being in direct variance with what was generally expected . . . excited a Public sensation of strong surprise and much indignation. Neither could the popular Sentiment be suppressed or restrained that 'little Justice could be expected towards the Poor whilst the Court consists of Brother Officers of the Prisoners at the Bar.' In fact, my Lord, the present construction of the Criminal Court is such as must necessarily excite a popular if not a just feeling against its decisions; especially when, as in the present Case, some of the Members who constitute that Court were the intimate friends of the Prisoners.*"

The incident gave point and urgency not only to the need for a revised system of justice, but to the uneasiness he had been feeling about the regiment for a long time. This colony offered too many temptations to a soldier—temptations which, on the one hand, caused him to forget the duties imposed on him by his uniform, and on the other invited him to magnify the privileges he might claim from it. This was an old evil— almost as old as the colony, and growing stronger with the years. Civil authority was not popular among men who either recalled personal experience of periods when military juntas had held undisputed sway, or had imbibed a nostalgic tradition of such times. Their pleasant sense of superiority had been reinforced by the activities of officers whose influence increased with their increasing possessions, and was consolidated by their position as members of the Courts. It was hardly to be wondered at, Macquarie reflected, that the arrogance of the higher ranks should be reflected in the lower, and attitudes aped as well as pursuits. His report on the Holness murder included an urgent recommendation that in future no regiment should be allowed to remain longer in the colony than three years.

This business, and the preparation of detailed and documented complaints against Captain Case, occupied much of his time during July and the first half of August, when the *Phœnix* was to sail. Glancing through a duplicate of his earlier despatch—now well on its way across the ocean —he paused for a moment on one of his opening phrases. ". . . *this Colony and its several Dependencies are at present in a state of profound Peace and Tranquillity. . . .*" He thought of the insolent Captain Case and his rowdy crew, of Davey, roistering (and perhaps worse) at Hobart Town, of footpads terrorising travellers along the Parramatta Road, of the always precarious relationship between whites and blacks. He saw the inimical stare of the "exclusives", and the handsome, haughty face of Bligh's implacable daughter. He heard the protests of disgruntled farmers; the sullen mutterings of the hospital contractors; the perpetual undertone of denunciation which his policies aroused; the voice of the widow Holness as she knelt in the dust crying out: "He's dead!" and that of McNaughton answering: "If he's dead, let him be dead, and be damned!"

But he knew that these disturbances were not the source of that faint chill, that pang of apprehension which had halted his eye as he read; he had the weapon of his authority, and he still trusted it to quell commotions. He was glimpsing want—that enemy of peace which no authority could over-awe, no proclamation subdue—and for some months now he had, intermittently, felt that warning chill.

For the usual autumn rains had not fallen, though every week they had been expected, and expectation had held anxiety at bay. Winter had begun—and continued—in an unbroken sequence of cloudless days, and his wife, seeing how restlessly he sometimes watched the sky, said reassuringly: "Why, it must rain soon, my love—fine weather cannot last for ever!" But still the days marched up from behind the Heads out of a golden sunrise, hung glittering over the dusty landscape, and marched away to vanish in a crimson glow behind the mountains. Increasingly anxious, Macquarie instructed the District Magistrates to make a survey of the colony's grain, and reserved an amount sufficient for those who must be victualled by the Crown. Presently he would issue regulations designed to prevent waste and extravagance; and he would reduce the standard, both in weight and quality, of the colonial loaf. . . .

He picked up his pen and sat tapping it thoughtfully against his chin. He must send some kind of despatch by the *Phœnix*, though there was little to report since the sailing of the *Minstrel*. Must one report the appearance of a spectre . . . ? Surely it would be routed, long before the vessel could reach England, by plentiful Spring rains? Yet perhaps it would be wise to make some reference to the possibility of a future scarcity—attributing it, as he could justly do, to the improvidence with which the population had disposed of the last harvest's bounty. He wrote carefully:

"*Altho' our last Harvest produced a Redundance of Grain, more than Sufficient for a Year's Subsistence of double the present Population if well husbanded, Yet, owing to the lazy negligence of the lower Order of the Settlers, and their inexcusable profuse Waste of Grain . . . there* is *now a great Scarcity Induced, and I am Concerned to add that the Quantity in the Country will with great Difficulty subsist the Inhabitants until the next Harvest. . . ."*

And what of the next harvest . . . ? That was in the hands of Providence; but as he looked out the window at the brilliant sunshine, he was thinking how slowly, under cover of blue, beguiling days, drought could creep in and take possession.

*   *   *   *

Winter passed into Spring, and still there was no rain. At the end of August the *Gazette* was gloomily reporting the death of many cattle, bogged in the mud which was all that remained of their usual drinking ponds. The days gathered heat as Spring advanced, and the farmers, watching their poor crops, or the bare ground where seed had perished in the earth, predicted a harvest of no more than eight bushels to the acre instead of the customary twenty-four. Now the price of wheat received into the Government Stores must be raised again, but even this inducement failed to bring in adequate supplies. The wealthier colonists foresaw a still further rise in the price, and held back their hoards. "And how have they been placed in this favourable position?" Macquarie raged bitterly to his wife. "By Government, which has granted them land, and stock, and labour, and every other kind of indulgence! By Heaven, if they don't see their duty and come forward with grain at a reasonable price, I shall tell them I can fill the stores from abroad at half what I must pay here!" But he knew there could be no immediate relief by such means; wheat which he did order from Bengal in October could not arrive for many months. Now, when the *Earl Spencer* reached port, he looked with disfavour on the two hundred new convicts mustered for his inspection; they seemed no longer hands that would help him to build, but mouths that must be fed. For some measure of consolation, the despatches and private letters which the vessel brought contained good news—and none more welcome than information which revealed that his request for the removal of the 73rd Regiment had been unnecessary; arrangements were already in train for its transfer to Ceylon. Very gratifying, too, was a reliable, though unofficial assurance that he was certain of promotion to the rank of Major-General. And though he had cherished a hope that his brother might step into O'Connell's shoes when the 73rd was withdrawn, he could not but rejoice at the tidings that Charles had become betrothed to an accomplished young lady of considerable fortune, and had no further inclination for colonial life. "All the same," he said to his wife, "Charles did me an ill turn when he told Bathurst he didn't want to come out; I might have been spared that fellow, Davey."

But he could find no real respite from anxiety, and he began to hate the sun which, day after day, filtering through smoky air, shed a hot, yellow light over the town and the surrounding country. From his house at Parramatta he could see the red glow of distant fires. As he drove or rode abroad he passed muddy hollows which had once been ponds, dry gutters which had once been streams. Every day more sheep and cattle died, and the air was noisome with the stench of rotting carcases.

It was clear that the limited area between the sea and the mountains would no longer support the colony in a bad season, and his thoughts turned more and more to the country which Blaxland and his companions had discovered beyond that blue barrier of hills. Even during the dinner party which celebrated the sixth anniversary of his marriage, he was a little absent-minded; even the joyful knowledge that his dear Elizabeth was once more pregnant, and continuing remarkably well in spite of it, could not banish anxiety from his mind for more than moments at a time. He had settled more and more farmers on the land—and the land was failing him. His task was to produce a self-supporting community, and while Nature smiled he had felt himself to be advancing victoriously towards that goal. But Nature was no longer smiling—and who knew when she would relent . . . ? He must look ahead—he must have more room. . . .

One hot day, after a hot and wakeful night, he instructed Campbell to send for Assistant Surveyor Evans.

*   *   *   *

The *Earl Spencer* had brought letters for the Harveys, among which was one from Mark's mother, which concluded: "*You will forgive me for not writing at greater length, my dear boy, for I have been a little indisposed, and confined to my bed these last few days. Your letters, and those of your dear Wife, are my greatest Joy; pray give my fondest love to her and to your little Robert, whom I still hope to see someday before I die.*" Another from his uncle, and dated two weeks later, informed him of her death, and of his inheritance of her modest income.

From Ireland, Julia wrote:

"*My dear Mama,*

I am very well and I have a Poney and a new riding Habit it is very elegant, green Velvet and a hat with a Feather. My Cousin John is engaged to be married to a Lady of Titel, she is rather handsome but I do not like her as she teases me and calls me a Colonial which makes me very Mortafied. I have a French governess her name is Mademoiselle Dupre she does not like Boney but when I say he will get beaten by the English she cries. She is silly. I am having lessons on the Harp and the Pianoforte.

I remain, dear Mama,
Your affectionate Daughter,
Julia Mannion."

Conor smiled, and sighed, and put the letter away. The busy life which she had so ardently desired was now hers, and if there were little time for reflection, there was also little for repining. The school had so far increased that one room was hardly large enough to accommodate all its pupils, among whom the sons of many free artisans and tradesmen now sat side by side with the sons of convicts. Mr. Harvey, however, was more than the mentor of his scholars; by imperceptible degrees he had become unofficial adviser to their parents, and it was a rare day upon which no harassed man in shabby clothes presented himself at the door with a question, a problem, a baffling document, or a request that the schoolmaster would be so good as to write a letter for him. And, encouraged by the men's reception, the womenfolk had begun to appear, begging the favour of a word with Mrs. Harvey. In her little parlour Conor listened to tales of poverty, illness, desertion, cruelty, drunkenness and prostitution. She learned much of hardship, but much, also, of the stoicism, and even the humour, with which hardship could be met by those who expected nothing else. She fretted at first that she could no longer dip her hand into a bottomless purse to relieve all their pathetically small—but grimly pressing—financial embarrassments. She passed through a mood of despair when she realised that every tale might be multiplied endlessly, and that the purse of charity, however generously its strings might be loosened, could never balance the deprivations of the dispossessed. She gave what she could in money, food, garments, advice and sympathy, and began to feel that in the last she had found something that offered hope. She looked at it for a long time with disbelief. Sympathy—how barren an offering to a wife whose drunken husband contributed nothing to his family save blows! To a mother, whose son kept bad company, and would surely end on the gallows! To a bride deserted, a girl forced by poverty on the streets, a widow struggling to maintain her children! Yet it was this, far more than her alms, which loosened their tongues, and freed their tears, and swept away that mistrustful and half defiant reserve with which, at first, they faced her. And it was this, perhaps, that must always open the way for changes that improve the lot of man; for the heart stirred the mind to seek solutions, and the stirred mind, in turn, exploring and expounding, provided that accumulating reservoir of facts and knowledge upon which other minds, goaded by uneasy hearts, could draw. But she cried restlessly to Mark: "It's too slow—too slow!"

There were other demands upon her time. Laetitia, though she had become fairly intimate with Mrs. Bent, Mrs. O'Connell, and some of the other ladies, still frequently descended from her carriage at the Harvey's door. Miles, upon his return from his mysterious excursion, had played the devoted and attentive husband for a time, but he was irked by domesticity, and preferred the company of his own sex. His popularity was such that Conor, knowing something of colonial entertainments, at first feared that he might be led into intemperance, but he seemed able to emerge from even the most prolonged festivity still strictly sober.

Yet did he not, she wondered, so far surrender himself to his sensations that they produced a kind of intoxication? Had he not, for example, seen something, felt something in the mountains which was now working in his blood as potently as any liquor? She thought of a day soon after his return when he had come with Patrick to tell them of his adventures. Patrick had heard the tale already, and he sat silently while Miles retold it, holding his hands out to the wood fire that burned on the hearth. But one thing, apparently, he had not heard, for when the telling was over, and the discussion had ceased, Miles, with a yawn, had remarked casually: "And I saw, also, the place where I shall build my house."

Patrick looked up sharply.

"What house?"

"My house, man—my roof-tree, my home."

"On the banks of this river . . . ?"

"No river banks for me! Now summon this poetic imagination of yours, my dear fellow, and picture a hilltop from which a thousand other hilltops fall away . . . distances that melt into the sky . . . a scene of such vastness and grandeur that it would almost repel one if it were not for the blue. . . ."

"Blue? What are you raving about?"

"Blue. They're called the Blue Mountains, are they not?"

"All mountains are blue at a distance. But you're not proposing to live in the heart of the mountains, I suppose?"

"Why not?" He had looked round with an amiable smile at their three astonished faces. Patrick snapped:

"I could give you a thousand reasons why you should not. Can you give me one why you should?"

"Certainly," replied Miles promptly. "Because I want to."

Patrick put up a hand to shield his face from the fire—and perhaps to hide the angry frown that Conor, nevertheless, had seen. Mark enquired cautiously:

"With what object? It seems the soil is not . . ."

"There's no soil," Miles assured him cheerfully. "Sand and rocks."

"You have no idea, then, of cultivation?"

"You couldn't grow a turnip."

"Cattle—sheep . . . ?"

"No pasture."

"And the climate, Miles," Conor had interjected, "is it not very severe?"

"Devilish severe, I believe. Wild, bleak, bitter, and swept by gales. Prentice tells me that snow lies on the ground in winter. That's the place for a house to defy the elements! Hewn stone, of course—there's no lack of that—with three-foot walls, and chimney places where you can burn logs as thick as a man's body. And doorways that I shan't crack my head on every time I pass through them. . . ."

Patrick asked, with rather unnatural calm:

"Have you considered the dangers, the inconveniences, the isolation?"

"Isolation—ah, yes, there's the feel of solitude there!" He paused to sip his wine, staring over the glass into the fire. "More than solitude, though. It's as if time has stopped. And I've seen. . . ." He paused, and the silence extended until Patrick prompted at last, his voice a trifle ragged with irritation: "Well?"

Miles addressed himself half absently to Mark.

"There are eagles, Sir—I'd judge them seven feet from wing-tip to wing-tip. Prentice says he shot one that was more than eight feet. They float over the hills, and play in the wind. . . . One has not thought of eagles as playful birds, but I swear they play—they hover over those deep ravines, and a draught takes them and they rise on it, blowing sideways. . . . And then they soar up and up till your eyes smart with trying to watch them, and you wonder what they see. . . ."

"You were beginning to tell us," Patrick interrupted, "what you had seen."

"So I was." Miles drained his glass and set it down on the table beside him. "I've seen my house as an eagle would see it. Alone. White in the blueness. And in the dark, one light showing. . . ."

Patrick pushed his chair back and rose suddenly.

"Eagles, so I understand, retire at night to their eyries upon cliffs; I doubt whether they would appreciate this solitary light of yours. I think you're mad—but I know you're obstinate, and what gives me concern is the prospect, however remote, that you could consider settling Laetitia and your son in so unsuitable—so preposterous a place. . . ."

"There's a waterfall nearby," Miles said, oblivious. "My native guides called it something like *goodoombah*—which I suppose to be a word representing the sound of its waters thundering down the cliffs. But far more strange and striking was what I can only describe as a mistfall. . . ."

"You'll excuse me," said Patrick to Conor, "if I take my leave? It's growing late, and I should be in Parramatta before dark—the roads are no longer safe for solitary travellers."

"Parramatta?" Miles looked up in surprise. "But you'll be passing the night with us at Moore House, will you not?"

"No," said Patrick baldly, and departed with little ceremony. Conor, having sped him on his way, returned to the room to find Miles replenishing his glass. "Upon my word," he remarked, mildly aggrieved, "Patrick's growing confoundedly testy! I believe he'd quarrel with me— if he could."

Since then the Harveys had seen little of Patrick, though Miles rode occasionally to Beltrasna, and remained for a few hours or a few days as his inclination dictated. He reported that there, as elsewhere, the crops were failing, and a field of maize had been destroyed by fire. "I told Patrick he'd do better to turn his attention to sheep or cattle, and prepare to take up land across the mountains when the time comes—but he wouldn't listen. 'I'm content here,' he says—though I'm damned if he looks content! I believe he views that place as if it were already some ancestral home that he's bound to preserve unchanged—but in Heaven's name, to what end, if he remains a childless bachelor? Of my father's three sons, ma'am, I declare I believe Desmond is the only one who is not slightly mad!"

Conor smiled, but she thought there was some truth in the remark. Desmond was now, at nine, one of his stepfather's most diligent and promising pupils—a grave, even-tempered child with an enquiring and tenacious mind. An announcement recently of the arrival of the colony's first steam engine had captured his interest, and he was impatient to see it erected on the site which had been granted to its owner near the shores of Cockle Bay; in the meantime, he valued his acquaintances according to their capacity for informing him upon the mysteries of steam power. How big was the engine? How did it work? Was it true that Mr. Dickson would use it to saw timber as well as to grind wheat? What else could steam engines be used for? Conor, hastily diverting these questions to her husband, privately considered Desmond to be a child of quite remarkable intelligence.

But it was the baby, Robert, who claimed all her attention in the last months of the year. An attack of dysentery reduced his sturdy body almost to skin and bone, and he recovered slowly. The cot where he lay, fretful and feverish, became Conor's world, and for the first time the gossip of the colony failed to interest her. She heard with indifference that Mr. Deputy-Surveyor Evans had set out with two free men and three convicts to make further investigations of the country across the mountains; she paid little attention to reports that the prospect of an heir for His Excellency seemed more promising than ever before. It was not until mid-December, a few days before the second anniversary of Robert's birth, that Dr. Redfern was able to pronounce him out of danger, and go away philosophising to himself about the sly ruthlessness of single-minded Mother Nature. How artfully she filled the minds of prospective parents with bright pictures of joys in store for them, and encouraged the fond optimism that ignored terrors and torments! He looked up at the lighted windows of Government House as he passed, reflecting that not even the sight of the wasted little body he had just left, and the drawn, exhausted faces of Mr. and Mrs. Harvey, would abate the ardour with which the Governor and his wife were inviting similar agonies. And indeed, at that moment, His Excellency was seated in his high-backed red leather chair, writing with cautious elation: *"My dearest Elizabeth has this day completed the sixth month of her Pregnancy—and is—thank God!—in very good health and doing very well! N.B. Mrs. M. felt the Child she is now Pregnant of quicken for the first time on Thursday the 21st of Octr. last—and it has ever since continued very lively!!!"*

*   *   *   *

But such pleasant reflections could not dispel for long a growing worry about Mr. Bent. The Governor had endeavoured to meet that gentleman's pressing desire for a new Court House by suggesting, as long ago as July, that funds for its erection might be raised by public subscription, and he had himself given not only five hundred pounds from the Colonial revenue, but sixty pounds from his private purse. Nothing like the necessary amount, however, had been contributed. Now it had come to his knowledge that Mr. Bent had been expressing himself in a most vehement and unbecoming manner upon the Governor's failure to withdraw labour from other public works, and set it to the construction of a building in which the majesty of the law—and the dignity of the Judge Advocate—might be suitably housed.

It could no longer be denied that Mr. Bent was becoming very difficult, and his manner was distant to the point of offensiveness. Moreover, he had of late been flagrantly disobeying a Government order. The agreeable custom observed by many civil officers who were also owners of farms, of betaking themselves for several days at a time to their country estates, had been causing so much neglect of their duties that Macquarie had forbidden it without his express permission. This prohibition had been duly observed by every officer except the Judge Advocate who—despite the overwhelming pressure of business of which he so often complained—continued to absent himself at will.

Throwing down his pen with an abrupt, impatient movement, and tapping irritably with his fingers on the arms of his chair, the Governor resolved to have a long, serious conversation with Mr. Bent.

*   *   *   *

Meanwhile, Mr. Evans with his party—which included a man named James Burns, who had accompanied the former expedition, and was now to act as guide—moved rapidly westward along the backbone of the Blue Mountain ridge. It was part of his task to make accurate measurements of distances, but this he decided to postpone till the return journey; while the horses were fresh, he would push on as fast as possible, and, should their food supply become exhausted, it would be simple, on the way back, to send a man ahead with a horse for replenishments. Along the track laboriously made by Lawson and his companions, the men made such good progress that they stood, on the morning of the sixth day, at the brink of the towering cliff line which abruptly ended the ridge, and by midday they had accomplished the descent without accident, if not with-out difficulty. Here Evans providently stowed away a week's provisions in a crevice of the rocks, and they set out upon the next stage of their journey. The horses, weary and hungry, took new heart when they found themselves in a valley full of good feed, and by one o'clock the party halted to make camp on the bank of the rivulet that flowed down from the mountains behind them.

A day's rest to refresh the horses and themselves afforded an oppor-tunity to explore the surrounding country. *"There are small Meadows clear of Trees,"* recorded Mr. Evans, *"and good soil with chains of holes of water; in wet weather they are connected with each other by small streams which lead to the riverlett. . . ."*

By next evening, after travelling some miles down the stream, they reached its junction with the larger one coming in from the north-west and flowing away to the south; after following it up for a mile or two, Burns declared that they were now at the farthest point reached by the previous expedition.

From here it was unknown territory. Day by day the country grew steeper again, and ahead loomed another range of hills. The horses, their backs chafed by heavy loads, were troublesome, and tired easily. The river began to lead them so far north of west that Evans forsook it, and the party struggled at last to the top of a high ridge from which, to their delight, some forty miles of open country were visible to the west. Cheered by this prospect, they descended into an extensive valley watered by another fine stream.

But this one flowed west. Now they were across the watershed, and could confidently claim to have passed the mountain barrier. Despite an interval of bad weather, the descriptions which Evans penned for His Excellency grew daily more enthusiastic. *"I am more pleased with the Country every day; it is a great extent of Grazing land without being divided by barren spaces as on the East side of the Mountains, and well watered by running streams in almost every Valley."* There was an abundance of game, and it was only necessary to drop a line into the river to catch a fish; the men sat contentedly at night grilling them over their fire, and even the dogs feasted.

The horses' backs were still sore, but they were growing fat on the rich pasture; the men were on an allowance of bread—much of their supply having been spoiled by rain—but they had so little trouble in securing ducks, fish and kangaroos that they hardly touched their salt pork. The river led them through a tract of fine land with flats stretching out a mile on either side, but, having passed through this, they came upon another, still more extensive. *"I cannot see the termination of it North of me; this soil is exceeding rich, and produces the finest grass, intermixed with a variety of herbs; the hills have the look of a park and Grounds laid out; I am at a loss,"* protested Mr. Evans, *"for language to describe the Country."*

Yet he was not really at a loss. He was an astute public servant who knew that there were certain niceties to be observed in the naming of such topographical features as did not, by some obvious peculiarity, name themselves; it was but seemly—and politic—to ensure that the most impressive should bear the most illustrious names, and that, in punctiliously descending order, the social hierarchy should be reflected in a hierarchy of mountains, plains and rivers. The three hills which so suitably marked the limit of the previous exploration must, of course, be called after Blaxland, Wentworth and Lawson; to an eminence crowned by a huge rock, Mr. Evans could without presumption give his own name, for it was conspicuous without being either commanding or important. But he had been holding other names prudently in reserve, and now, in his enthusiasm, he could produce one to imply all that magnificence which his pen could not describe. *"I named this part Macquarie Plains,"* he wrote, and felt that he had done justice to the locality, to the Governor, and to himself. The lesser plain through which they had just passed was, he judged, fine enough, and yet at the same time sufficiently inferior, to be called O'Connell Plains. But the stream from which a meal could be plucked as fast as hooks were baited, had already become, by mere usage, the Fish River.

Under a heavy and lowering sky they proceeded down this stream next day until they found themselves halted in the fork formed by its junction with another of almost equal size which came in from the south; with one eye on the jagged streaks of lightning which split the sky, Evans called it, rather hurriedly, after the Governor's indispensable Secretary, and led the way up its banks in search of a ford. The storm overtook them before they had gone two miles, and they made camp, but the next morning broke clear and warm, and they continued their search for a crossing. But there was none to be found, and they set to work upon the construction of a bridge over which their baggage could be conveyed. They dragged two forked logs as far into the water as they could, and then drove them into the mud, laying another log crosswise in the forks; several of the men swam the river, and made a similar gallows-shaped erection on the other side. They felled trees, and rolled them down the bank, securing one end with a rope, and allowing the current to carry the other end across. Two of these were at last laid, with much labour, from one gallows to the other, and two more from each gallows to a bank. They passed the baggage over successfully, and swam the horses across, holding them against the force of the current by a rope from the opposite bank. Tired, but elated, they set off again downstream, and reached the junction as the sun was setting over a vast expanse of smiling country, fresh after the rain, and green to the tops of the distant hills.

By next night, when Mr. Evans addressed himself to his journal again, they had travelled eight miles along the river through country which delighted him more at every step. *"I have called the Main Stream 'Macquarie River'. At 2½ Miles commences a most extensive Plain, the hills around are fine indeed; it requires a clever person to describe this Country properly. I never saw anything to equal it. . . ."* The river, they judged, sometimes overflowed the wide flats on either side of it, where the lush grass grew thick and high; it began to wind now, and they found themselves walking south of west instead of north of it, as they had done the day before. There were emus, though the dogs refused to chase them, and geese, though these were so shy and wary that none could be shot; but ducks were plentiful too, and many went into the cooking-pot. *"Nothing astonishes me more,"* wrote Mr. Evans, *"than the amazing large Fish that are caught; one is now brought to me that weighs at least 15lb., they are all the same species. I call the Plains last passed over 'Bathurst Plains'. . . ."*

But soon they were among hills again, and though the pasture was still good, the soil was stiffer, and more rocky. The river wound between rocky bluffs, and Evans became concerned for the horses, whose backs were still sore. *"I do not know what to make of the River,"* he complained. *"Its course seems so irregular, the direction to-day has been from SW to NE; the hills are so very high and close, that from any one of them its run cannot be distinguished."* The horses were flagging, the men limped painfully in worn-out shoes, and on the sixteenth day of December Evans decided they had gone far enough. *"I am now,"* he wrote, *"98½ measured Miles from the limitation of Mr. Blaxland's excurtion. . . ."* He paused, staring at the river. Where did it lead? To the western coast? He thought so, and hoped someday to follow it there, through country such as that they had already passed. Now, captured by the beauty and the richness of the land, and stirred by the idea of a future which would surely be built in it, he really felt the inadequacy of his words; he had the vision, he had the pen and the paper—but words would not sing for him. Well, he said to himself as he went on setting down his limping phrases, let others do the singing; I've found them something to sing about, by God! He finished, and from the rock where he sat looked down at his companions, busy round the fire where the evening meal was being prepared. There was still sun on the hilltops, but here the light was failing, and a faint mist hung between the craggy banks. As always when one paused to listen, and detached one's mind from the moment's tasks, silence and solitude seemed qualities of the land more characteristic, and perhaps even more significant, than its rivers and mountains, its rocks and pastures, its trees, plains and valleys. This fabulous, fertile area, teeming with game, watered by fast-flowing rivers alive with fish—where were its inhabitants . . . ? Mr. Evans picked up his pen again and wrote slowly: "*I conceive it strange we have not fell in with the Natives; they are near about us as we find late traces of them; I think they are watching us, but are afraid and keep at some distance.*"

1814

1814 came in on a blast of scorching wind. Sydney looked drab and dishevelled; the grass in Hyde Park was dusty, and the Tank Stream low; the thermometer at Government House hovered round 100°, and old residents declared they could not recall so fierce a January for ten years past. Under a steely sky, even the harbour had lost its colour. In the outer settlements the farmers, having seen their wheat crops fail, now watched their stunted maize bend before the withering blast. South Creek was a muddy gutter, and bushfires filled the air with smoke.

Evans and his companions greeted this malignant New Year from the crest of the Blue Mountains, up whose precipitous western rampart they had toiled the day before; and as they pushed eastward along their former track, they, too, were in country that had been swept by fire. It had seemed arid enough when they passed through it on their outward journey; now they looked uneasily at a desolate expanse of charred tree-trunks and still-smouldering logs, counting themselves lucky that they had not been on this cliff-bounded ridge when the flames roared over it. The under-growth had been burned away, and the naked, stony ground was deep in ashes. Boulders and long stretches of flat rock, hot from fire and blazing sun, scorched their feet, now shod clumsily in kangaroo skin. Bare branches of what had once been thick scrub tore their clothes, and every twig that brushed them left a smear of charcoal; they moved in a swirl of fine ash, lifted and scattered by the wind, and wiped their blackened arms across their sweaty faces. Save for their remnants of clothing, they might not have been easily distinguished from Boorah and Murrunga, who had never been far from them in the last few days.

But they were soon past the neighbourhood where, had they chosen to turn aside, they might have come upon the route down into Dyonn-ee's *towri*, and the two natives now had their own problems to consider. There was little enough game to be found on the heights at any time, and now none at all; if they were to eat that day, they must get down into their own valley. They watched the white men—who, as Murrunga pointed out to his companion, now looked as black as themselves—vanish eastward along the ridge, and then retraced their steps to the head of the pass.

Evans and his party plodded on. The cuts they had made on the trees to mark their route had mostly been obliterated by fire, and it was necessary to make them again; it was harder than ever to find feed for the horses, and though there was still water to be found in the reedy swamps where they camped at night, they were always thirsty. Yet the fires, for all the discomfort and inconvenience they had caused, had cleared the ground, and made not only walking, but the measurement of distances, easier. As the six men limped down the last slopes towards the Nepean, Evans was calculating that they had travelled some hundred and fifty miles.

*　　　*　　　*　　　*

By the *General Hewitt,* which reached the colony early in February, John Piper returned, now retired from the Army in order to take up his appointment as Naval Officer, and he made haste to wait upon Mrs. Harvey. He had not seen Julia since delivering her safely into the hands of her aunt in London, but he had heard of her from friends in Ireland; out of a bare statement that she seemed a pert and pretty miss, he contrived the kind of tale which a mother might find comforting, and, this friendly duty done, settled down to give and receive gossip.

He had travelled on the same vessel as a detachment of the 46th Regiment, which was to replace the 73rd, and it had been followed in a few days by the *Windham,* bearing O'Connell's successor, Lieutenant-Colonel Molle.

"He's an old acquaintance of the Governor's, I understand," Piper said, "but from what I know of them both, I doubt whether their friendship will prosper here."

Conor sighed, and her husband remarked upon the apparent impossibility of agreement between Governors and Lieutenant-Governors. "There's always something to disturb the harmony. What do you expect it to be in this case?"

"One hears rumours, occasionally," Piper replied. The Harveys exchanged a glance of amusement at this understatement, for the amiable Mr. Piper probably knew more of the intricate personal relationships which played so large a part in colonial politics than anyone else. It was greatly to his credit, Conor reflected, that he did not, apparently, use his knowledge to make mischief. He continued now:

"We all know the Governor's views about emancipists, and it seems that most of the officers of the new regiment don't share them. In fact I'm told that Molle himself urged the Mess, before their arrival, to pass a resolution not to associate with convicts or ex-convicts."

"We may assume," Mark interjected dryly, "the usual reservation—'except in the way of business'?"

"Oh, quite, quite! But I foresee difficulties if they're asked to sit down at Government House with someone who has worn felon's garb in his day, no matter what his earlier history may have been. Which reminds me of a convict on our ship, ma'am, who, having come down in the world, may live to go up again like a rocket if the Governor's policy is pursued. And, by Heaven, like a rocket he would go, too, for a more pompous, self-assertive, explosive little fellow I never saw! Greenway, his name is—an architect from Bristol, who had the misfortune to be only too apt with his pen. He takes pains to inform anyone who'll listen that he comes with a letter from old Admiral Phillip, commending him to the Governor. I trust His Excellency won't try to seat him at dinner next one of his military shipmates. However, we needn't anticipate trouble—it will find us soon enough. Tell me of this new country beyond the mountains—Evans has lately returned, I believe, bursting with enthusiasm . . . ?"

"We heard something of it from William Wentworth," said Mark, "before he went off on his voyage to the islands. What appears to have impressed him most is the fact that the mountains form a barrier of some strategic importance; he seems to envisage a few holding them against invading thousands."

"From what I hear," Piper remarked, "we shall ourselves provide the invading thousands—and I don't imagine our dark friends will attempt to hold the mountains against us. But Evans extended the first discovery a good deal further, I hear."

"I know little of that," said Mark, "beyond what has been published in the *Gazette*. It's certain that there's good country to be settled there —and I'm told Lawson and his companions are to get a thousand acres of it each."

"No doubt they earned it—and may earn it all over again when they take possession, for it'll be a rude kind of life for many years to come."

"Perhaps, Mr. Piper," Conor suggested rather mischievously, "you yourself will be among the pioneers when the time comes?"

"I, my dear lady?" Piper laughed. "No, no, I prefer a town, with lively company and good entertainment! My appointment, of course, keeps me at Sydney for the present, but I have no taste for the wilds in any case. A grant of land somewhere on the shores of the harbour would please me better."

He ruminated pleasantly for a moment. The post of Naval Officer was arduous enough, for it would be his task to collect all harbour dues, wharfage duties, and taxes on imported goods; to board each vessel on its arrival, inspect its papers, and receive the Governor's despatches; to see that smugglers were frustrated, and that no convicts were spirited away on outgoing ships. But it was also lucrative, for he would receive five per cent. of all moneys he collected, and already he had been impressed by the progress made during his absence in the business of the port. Trade was increasing, which should increase his income; but better still, worldly comforts and elegancies were now available, upon which an increased income could be very agreeably expended. "Ah, well," he concluded cheerfully, "someday I may have my wish, and in the meantime I must be content with my modest cottage down by the Cove. I see great changes here, Mr. Harvey. The roads have improved beyond what I thought possible; I hear there's a new one to Liverpool just about to be opened."

"They are improved in one sense," Conor remarked, "but not in another. Of late they have been so infested by robbers and footpads that it's no longer safe to travel alone. The bushrangers have been very active round Liverpool. It disturbs me when Miles and Patrick ride to and fro alone between Sydney and the Nepean. . . ."

"Miles, my dear ma'am, should be a match for any half dozen bushrangers, and I don't doubt that Patrick would give a good account of himself too. But I'm told that outlaws are not the only peril of the wilds nowadays; they say the natives in the Nepean district are becoming more hostile than formerly."

"For that," Mark replied, "I think the settlers are not without blame. There have been some ugly tales of their barbarities, and I know the Governor is greatly concerned. . . ."

Piper chuckled.

"The Governor, my dear Sir, is at the moment concerned only with his approaching felicity. Oh, yes, ma'am, he performs his duties valiantly, I allow—but there's an absent look in his eye. When our Crown Prince is born, no doubt he'll be able once more to fix his whole attention on matters of state."

*   * · *   *

To the thirty-eight guests assembled for dinner at Government House some weeks later, the absent look in His Excellency's eye was very apparent. It had not been expected that their hostess would appear, for the whole colony was perfectly informed upon the progress of her pregnancy; but Mrs. O'Connell whispered to the ladies that the midwife had been in attendance all the afternoon, and a general air of suspense made the conversation fitful. With so interesting an event pending, the company was loth to disperse, but at eleven o'clock—when, it was noted, Dr. Redfern disappeared—departure could no longer with decency be delayed. Indeed, the Governor's celebrated hospitality seemed to have deserted him, and he fairly hustled his guests to their carriages. The clock was striking the half-hour as the door closed behind the last of them, and its minute hand was creeping towards midnight before Colonel and Mrs. O'Connell, who were passing the night in the house, reluctantly retired.

Impatient as he had been for solitude, Macquarie was suddenly afraid of it as he stood irresolute in the deserted hall. Was it only this morning that these silent, empty rooms had been thronged with the civil and military officers—that Bent had read Molle's Commission—that he himself had administered the customary oaths to his new Lieutenant Governor? It seemed a week ago, or even longer, for the scene was already hazy in his mind; he discovered with astonishment that what he was really thinking about was Master William Macquarie Molle. True, the infant was not yet christened, but he knew that it was to bear his name, and as he thought of it the fear born of so many disappointments was creeping up behind his joy like an enemy poised to strike. He felt, at this moment, no appropriate benevolence towards Master Molle—only the latest, and surely not the last, of many children to be named in his honour—but a vague sense of injury and resentment. How lightly other men were able to take their parenthood! Could Fate be so malevolent as to rob him, at this last moment, of the child whose name would be Macquarie by right, and not by courtesy? His hope had mounted steadily during these months when Elizabeth had seemed so well; his confidence had strengthened as Redfern assured him that all was progressing as it should. But now, with the clock loudly ticking the moments away in the unbearable silence of the house, hope and confidence alike deserted him. He moved slowly towards the door of his study, and the hand he raised to open it was not quite steady.

Quick footsteps sounded on the floor above his head, and he turned sharply towards the stairs. Redfern was there, in his shirt-sleeves, his face one wide, congratulatory smile. "A boy, Sir!" he announced jubilantly. "It's a boy!"

*   *   *   *

For Johnny, too, it had been a bad summer, but one of anxiety and discomfort rather than of hardship. He had never really feared hunger, for he was still not only Johnny, but Dyonn·ce, to whom the land would yield enough sustenance to support life, even if all the foodstuffs of the white men failed. The river still ran, though rocks and sandbanks were now visible which had once been hidden under fast-flowing water; fish and eels still flickered in its deeper pools, wild birds and beasts still came to drink at it, and he had his spears. Yet this confidence, which would once have kept him carefree, now did no more than arm him against the ultimate fear of starvation, for he knew that life at so primitive a level was not for Emily and the child.

With the coming of autumn the heat abated, but there was still no rain save for a few brief thunderstorms. The creek below the hut had long ago—for the first time in his knowledge of it—stopped running, and he must climb down its steep, dry bed almost halfway to the river before he could fill his pail at a large rock basin, normally fed by a waterfall, and fringed by a thick growth of ferns. Now there was not even a drip to replenish it, and the ferns were dying as the water fell away from them; but since the overhanging rocks and trees still kept it a place of dense shade and slow evaporation, he judged that it would serve him for a few more weeks.

His main anxiety was for the sheep. There was little pasture for them, and they must graze farther and farther afield, searching the stony, timbered ridges for coarse, tussocky grass. The cattle he had long ago driven down to the river where they could fend for themselves, for there was still good feed along its banks, but the sheep must be yarded each night to preserve them from dingoes, made bold by hunger. Despite his care, a few had been killed, and he had found the carcases of young lambs with their eyes picked out by crows. His harvest of wheat had been poor, and the small field of maize now ripening in the cooler and later season of the mountains was parched and sparse; but he was not bedevilled by economics, and what he grew was there to be eaten. There was still milk, though he had to climb down to the river flats to get it, and toil back up the hill with a full pail; there were eggs, though not so many as formerly; there were a few vegetables, and he could kill a beast when he needed it.

But he left the bush creatures alone, even abandoning his old custom of catching fish from the river. The local tribe of natives had always kept to the northern end of the valley, and the river banks below it, but when fire swept over their *towri* in the early summer, they had been driven nearer, establishing their camp barely a mile from his hut. He had lived too long among natives to fail in understanding their need to follow their food, and he knew that there were days, in this cruel season, when the hunters returned empty-handed. Emily, watching the glimmer of their fires at night, protested: "They'll spear the sheep!"

"When ye're hungry," said Johnny, "ye take food where ye can get it. I aim to see they ain't hungry." So he left their food alone, and gave them, more than once, a freshly-killed carcase only partially devoured by dingoes; and when the women came with their children to stand on the far edge of his fields, he put a few potatoes in their baskets, or filled their coolamons with grain. "We could'a done with it ourselves," Emily said, frowning. But as the long, hot summer passed, she realised that there was, between Johnny and these naked heathens, an understanding which served both very well, and she no longer objected when he refused to fish, and even allowed a native child, sometimes, to drink from his milk pail; for it was clear that he not only dispensed favours, but received them. The natives always knew where the sheep were grazing, and even shepherded them now and then, turning them homeward as the afternoon shadows lengthened. The men sometimes gave him a duck or a fish when their hunting had been successful, and the women brought the thin, dark, sweet wild honey in their wooden vessels. And when tidings had come from them of the second expedition across the mountains, arousing in her once more an anxiety which had almost faded, she recalled words spoken once by Johnny, and felt some reassurance: "Many's the time I've known white men to go explorin' around the Nepean years ago— but they never went nowhere without the natives was watchin' them Never fear we'll be taken by surprise—I tell ye no white man could come within ten miles of the hut without I'd know of it. I got eyes and ears all over the valley."

Yet her feeling for her dark neighbours remained tinged by a faint hostility, for there dwelt in the Johnny who was hers another man named Dyonn-ee, who was more elusive, and sometimes it seemed that the natives understood him better than she did. Often, without doubt, he understood them better than he understood her. But the cause went deeper still. She knew that girl-children were less seriously regarded among the natives than boys, and, with the impetuosity of half-knowledge, assumed this to mean that they were less loved. She always felt angry, baffled and forsaken when Johnny became Dyonn-ee, and—as she expressed it to herself—"thought native"; she blamed this perverse native thinking for his obvious indifference towards her child—not only a girl, but a feeble and ailing one. All this was in the forefront of her mind where she could see, if not always control it. What she had not admitted to herself at all was that her own love for a child of Dean's could only be painful and jealousy protective because it was half unwilling. The spontaneous passion of her maternal love was already directed towards Johnny's child, now moving in her body.

But to Johnny himself—who "thought native" in nothing so much as in such matters—all this was unsuspected. He was the head of the family which served him for a tribe, and his woman's child had its right-ful and unquestioned place beneath his roof. If he had paid it but scant attention, he was being neither white nor native, but merely masculine. It was too small and frail to be bounced or tickled; it did not laugh or gurgle, and even now, a year old, it made no attempt to stand or speak. His interest would awaken in response to the first indications of dawning independence; a baby was its mother's business; time enough for a father to step in when it became a person. And so little was this fragile creature a person that it had never even acquired a name; Johnny with detachment, and Emily with a half-guilty tenderness, called it merely "the baby".

Johnny was thinking of it as he set off at dawn one morning with his two pails for water and milk. It had been ailing for some time, and its fretful crying had disturbed his night. The fierce, unremitting heat of summer had sapped what little strength it had, and even the return of cooler weather had not revived it. This morning, as he looked at the tiny, wasted body which Emily was bathing, he had thought that it must surely die.

He had finished his milking, and was setting out to climb the hill again, when he noticed a native approaching up the river, bedecked in feathers, intricately painted with markings which proclaimed him an emissary from his tribe, and bearing, as an ambassador his credentials, a message-stick; not until he was within twenty paces did Johnny recognise him as Billalong. The native, having returned his greeting, began immediately to speak in his own language—for it was not fitting that he should tell of Balgundra's death in the tongue of Balgundra's murderers. My brother, the brother of Gooradoo, he said with careful circumlocution, is dead; he was killed by the Beerewolgal. Johnny, who had not been conscious until then of the sounds about him, now heard the water running over stones at his feet, and a soft stirring in the needle-like foliage of the trees above his head. It was one of those moments—now growing rare—when he seemed to receive all life and the whole world with his normal senses, and one more; a moment such as those, long ago in boyhood, when, with a strange, sick excitement, he had watched tribal ceremonies, and felt magic near. He looked at Billalong, but the familiar face was a mask, all expression obliterated by the sharp contrast of white clay streaks and circles on dark skin. "Dead?" he muttered.

They squatted together on the grassy bank—the barefooted white man in his ragged trousers, and the naked savage, ceremonially decorated—and for the first time Johnny was aware of their unlikeness. He found himself wondering, too, with seeming irrelevance, when he had ceased to squat native-fashion on both heels, and learned to sit as he was sitting now, on one heel only, with the sole of the other foot on the ground. and his arm bent across his knee.

During this blazing summer, Billalong said, life had been even harder for the Nepean tribes than for those in Dyonn-ee's valley, for there were now large areas taken by the Beerewolgal over which the men might not hunt, nor the women forage, without peril from the muskets of the settlers; nor were the lands still remaining to them as rich in game as formerly. But—as Dyonn-ee understood—these were not the only problems caused by the continual encroachments of the white men. There was a life not of the body, bound up with certain places in any *touri*—places which had been sacred to the tribe for countless generations, and from which its members could not be separated without losing touch with their ancestral past; places where their spirits had dwelt before birth, places where rites were performed, places to which the women must go, seeking the spirit children they would bear. All this, of course, Dyonn-ee knew . . . ?"

Billalong's tone held the mere shadow of a question, but it hung uneasily in the brief silence that followed. An echo hung there too, and they both heard it—Johnny's angry, contemptuous voice saying: *"Spirits! Magic! I tell ye there's no such thing as spirits!"* Never, even as a child, had he been able to identify himself completely with that mystical life which was as real and necessary to his native friends as the food they put into their mouths; but it had touched him, and though he would not share their magic, he had made, now and then, something that was near enough to a magic of his own. There had been, he remembered now, a place—an overhanging rock above the west bank of the Nepean—where once, long, long ago, he had found a fire burning, and a key lying on the ground; it had seemed for years peculiarly his own, as if some part of him had died there, and some other part had been born. Had he not jealously preserved the key and the necklace? Had they not become for him objects not unlike the *churinga* of the tribal elders, linking him to his father, who was all the ancestral past he had? And if he passed by that place even now, would he not pause to look at it with a strange nostalgia, as at some old home, long abandoned . . . ? "Aye," he said, not looking up. "I know."

Billalong nodded soberly. Because of these things, he went on, the tribes were going hungry, not only in body, but in spirit. Anger was rising. Young men had been going out in force to plunder the farms, taking pigs, corn, clothing, and anything else they could secure. A few days since, a large party, including Gooradoo, Balgundra and himself, had been raiding the cornfields of a settler when it was fired upon by three soldiers, and Balgundra fell dead. The other natives had immediately attacked the soldiers with such speed and fury that they had no time to re-load their muskets, and were compelled to flee. . . .

Johnny could feel the old excitement of violence throbbing in him, but he was also painfully aware that his brain seemed to stand aloof from the turmoil of his blood; he wanted to kill the man who had killed Balgundra, but he knew that he could no longer purge himself of hatred thus. Billalong was continuing:

Let Dyonn-ee have no misgivings, however; the white tribe had promptly paid in blood for the blood of their brother, for he himself, with Gooradoo and their friends, had gone out next day and attacked the hut of a white stockman, killing him and his woman. . . .

Johnny's hand, hanging over his knee, moved suddenly in a sharp gesture; he stared at the mask, enraged by this primitive doctrine, and yet feeling, at the same time, envy, and even awe, of a people to whom the complexities of life were still so simple.

And now, Billalong explained, he had been sent by his tribe not only to tell Dyonn-ee of these things, but to speak with the natives of the valley. For the white men were still seeking new country. They had sent parties across the mountains, and the tribes which now dwelt un-disturbed in such valleys as this, and on the plains beyond, would not remain undisturbed much longer. Had not Dyonn-ee himself declared that the Beerewolgal would be content with no less than everything? Therefore messengers had been sent out to many tribes, summoning them to a great meeting; they would confer about what was to be done, but already there was a strong inclination among the younger warriors to appoint a time when they should fall in force upon the white men and destroy them all.

Johnny sat staring into the river.

"Ye can't do it," he said at last, in English. Billalong watched him from eyes fantastically circled by white clay. "Ye can't fight muskets with spears," Johnny went on slowly, and moved his hand to check Billa-long's attempt at protest. "Not for long, ye can't. Ye can't fight thousands with hundreds. When it comes to killin' ye're but babes compared with them. Look, boy," he said with sudden urgency, "I know. It ain't only here they kill—they do it in other countries—across the sea. . . . And not only black men, neither, but other white men like themselves. They want . . ." He paused, struggling for the words which he knew Finn would have found so easily, and Billalong, leaning forward, anxious for a revelation of the mysterious impulses which moved white men, de-manded: "What they want?"

Johnny hesitated. Of all that he knew about his countrymen's society, there was little that sprang from his own observation and experience. Yet it was upon vague childish memories that he drew now, seeing himself— a skinny, ragged child, sly and predatory—haunting the convict hovels and the military tents of the early settlement, listening to the talk of his elders, learning that to possess was the ultimate goal of men, and money the road to it; stealing as they stole, lying as they lied, cheating as they cheated, watching sharply for every opportunity to add to his own small, hidden hoard of coins. . . .

"Money," he said; but he knew the word a failure even as he uttered it. And indeed Billalong objected instantly, with impatience:

"Money? No good to eat. You got money, you don't eat—you not touch, not want. No good."

"Land's money," Johnny said slowly. "Sheep and cattle are money. You sell them and get money—then you buy food with it, and clothes, and wine, and more land, and more sheep and cattle, and you get more money to buy more food and wine. . . ."

Billalong exploded in a native exclamation of scorn. "That silly talk!" He relapsed into his own tongue again to utter a flood of angry rhetorical questions. Is a man tall enough to cross the mountains at one stride, that he should need so much land? Has he more than one body, that he should desire enough clothing for ten men? Is his thirst so great that he would drink a river dry if it ran wine instead of water? Is his belly so large that all the cattle in the Cow Pastures could not fill it? He broke off abruptly, and looked hard at Johnny. "You white man," he said, speaking the white man's tongue again, "you not want all that."

Johnny glanced at him, startled, for it was the first time Billalong had ever plainly referred to his whiteness. "Aye," he agreed heavily, "I'm a white man, and there's many another like me that don't want no more food than he can eat, or more land than he can use. But they ain't the ones that count. It's the ones that have the money you got to look out for."

But Billalong denied this vehemently. On the contrary, he said, it was not the great white men dwelling in the great houses who oppressed his people, so much as those who dwelt humbly in huts on the small farms. When Ma-gor-ee visited the tribes he spoke fairly, with civility, offering friendship. Other great men, when they appeared at the farms, rarely offered insults and violence; it was the humble people who dwelt there all the time, who were making tribal life insupportable. Johnny held his head in his hands, defeated by the complexity of the argument.

"Many of them's servants," he said, "and the farms ain't theirs. Even when they're called free, and work their own farms, they're still servants. . . . Aye, they'll still touch their caps to the gentry. They do what they're bid, and what they've been taught, and bad enough it is. But I tell ye, don't try to match white men in killin', for they'd shoot ye down till there wasn't a man left in the tribes could hold a spear. They don't care that ye'd kill a score of soldiers—or a hundred—they can get plenty more. Sometimes," he said, staring into the rippling shallows at his feet, "it's come into me mind that they'll go on killin' till they destroy themselves. . . ."

Billalong began to speak at once—no longer in English, which he found inadequate for the expression of ideas, but in his own tongue, which lent itself with dignity to such matters—and Johnny listened with bent head and aching heart, for he could hear strange echoes of Finn. Such an end, Billalong declared with grave matter-of-factness, was of course to be expected, and had often been discussed in the tribes. For it was well known that the Beerewolgal had two laws which were irreconcilable—one which enjoined mercy, peace and brotherhood, and another which ordained this killing which Johnny described. Two conflicting laws were clearly the same as no law at all. There could be no peace in the hearts of lawless men; and men without peace in their hearts could live only with weapons always in their hands. It seemed very likely that they would destroy themselves in time. Yet since there were so many of them, their self-destruction might be long delayed, and in the meantime, his people must defend themselves. . . .

"Defend y'selves . . ." Johnny said, standing up abruptly. "Aye, defend y'selves—if ye can. But if ye don't want the tribes to be left with nothin' but women and children—and maybe not many of them—don't do no attackin'. I've warned ye."

He walked off and left Billalong sitting there. He climbed slowly back up the hill, thinking of Balgundra, remembering his birth in that other hut on the heights between the Wollondilly and the Nepean, where he himself, as the reincarnation of its builder, Andrew Prentice, had occupied so strange a position of authority. When the natives fled from it after Cunnembeillee's death, he had felt that they deserted him; now he almost wondered if he, by renouncing their law, had not deserted them. Balgundra—a baby, staggering after him as he left the hut, wailing to be taken too. . . . Balgundra—a little boy, proud when Dyonn-ee noticed him, and taught him to hold his spears. . . . Balgundra—an older boy, one of his faithful allies in that ill-fated enterprise which had cost Finn's life. . . . Balgundra—a youth, guarding his secret, bearing his messages, watching his enemies, helping him back to camp after that meeting with Patrick Mannion. . . .

Balgundra, his friend and tribal brother—now dead.

*   *   *   *

The 73rd Regiment sailed at the beginning of April amid all the excitement that such an event must naturally cause, but Macquarie performed his part in the farewell ceremonies rather perfunctorily. Even the moment when he saw Bligh's daughter go aboard the *General Hewitt*, and knew that at least one social irritant was being withdrawn from his domain, now seemed hardly important enough to arouse the relief he had long expected from it. It was but another official occasion to be hurried over as quickly as decency would permit, so that he might get back to the room where his son lay sleeping. Many times a day he climbed the stairs during snatched pauses between his duties to enquire how the infant fared, and to question the two nurses narrowly about the slight, griping pains which it seemed to suffer.

Suddenly it became clear that the child was ill; Dr. Redfern, summoned from his bed near midnight about a fortnight after its birth, arrived at Government House to find Macquarie awaiting him at the head of the stairs, looking haggard. His grey hair was dishevelled, the gown he had pulled on hurriedly over his nightshirt robbed him of his customary dignity, and his eyes were pleading—almost humble. As his own winced away from them, Redfern thought that if His Excellency could confront a mirror now, he might recognise that look as one often bent upon himself by some accused wretch, hoping against hope for clemency. He seemed to have lost his authority; no—not lost it, but stripped himself of it, that he might thrust it on the shoulders of an ex-convict doctor. The doctor assumed it, not without some sardonic recognition of its transience.

"You had best get some sleep, Sir."

"No, no, I can't sleep. The child is. . . ."

"Then at least some rest. You can do nothing now—and will be able to do nothing later to support and calm your wife, if you are too much fatigued. I must insist, Sir."

"Well . . . you are right, no doubt. But you will call me if . . . ?"

"You may rely on me to do so if necessary."

"You'll stay the rest of the night, of course?"

"Of course, Sir."

"Yes, yes—I have every confidence in you, my dear fellow—every confidence. . . ." He went away down the dim corridor, walking like an old man.

But in a week the child was sufficiently recovered to be privately baptised, and Redfern, standing with his wife among the little group gathered in the bedroom to witness the ceremony, noted that the Governor had not only reclaimed his authority, but added something to it. He was careful to explain that it was his wife's wish that their son should be called by his name—and no doubt that was true, for her eyes were hardly less maternal when they rested on him than when they contemplated the child; but anything else would have been unthinkable, for his possessive pride and triumph were plainly written on his face for all to see. Lachlan Macquarie! A good name, no longer to be immortalised only by streets and rivers! A grand name, now to be borne safely forward for another generation by living flesh and blood! Redfern found himself recalling many glimpses he had been afforded of the Governor's Scottish pride in his clan, his fierce sense of duty and responsibility to all its members. To such a man, fatherhood in the personal sense must, of course, not only have an added meaning, but permit a more uninhibited betrayal of emotion; yet so deeply rooted and urgent a paternalism could not be fully expended upon a clan, or even upon a son. No doubt it had coloured his attitude to his regiment, and to comprehend it was to see many aspects of his vice-regal administration illuminated. Stern and indulgent, severe and benevolent, rejoiced by good behaviour, and deeply wounded by recalcitrance, he might speak the language of the ruler— but always with an undertone of the parent. "By God, yes," thought Redfern as he watched His Excellency holding the child with the confidence and aplomb of one who had been nursing children all his life, "the man's a born patriarch!"

*　　　　*　　　　*　　　　*

Somehow, through all this turmoil of personal anxiety, the necessary official duties had been performed, but Macquarie could now attack his work with zest. In the despatch he was preparing he had much to report —the departure of the 73rd, the arrival of the 46th, the state of agriculture, the inadequacy of the military garrison, and a host of other matters. He must comment upon that curious information received by the *Windham* about a man named Jorgen Jorgenson who claimed to have knowledge of a French plan for attacking the colony. The fellow had served for a while on the *Lady Nelson,* and therefore knew something of the place, but the home Government evidently placed little credence in his tale; nevertheless, it was a strange echo from that occasion, years ago, when Captain Baudin's two ships had appeared at Port Jackson during a voyage, as they declared, of scientific discovery. Governor King, reflected Macquarie, had had his doubts at the time; for himself, he thought it certain that Bonaparte would have been glad enough to wrest this promising outpost from the English if he had not been kept too busy in Europe. The rumour would serve, at all events, to emphasise his urgent request for an increased military garrison.

There was also the important news to be conveyed of Mr. Evans' expedition, and his discovery not only of new and fertile land, but of a westward-flowing river. "*Under Your Lordship's Approbation, I propose to Name this New Country 'West-more-land', but I shall wait Your Lordship's Commands on this Head before I give it any distinguishing Name. For the purpose of rendering this new Tract beneficial to the Settlers at as early a Period as possible, it is My Intention to Cause a Cart Road to be constructed over the Blue Mountains to the Commence-ment of the first Plains. . . .*" He need not fear censure for this; it would be no mere local road for the greater comfort of pampered colonists, but the highway to Eldorado of which he had dreamed. All the same, he made it clear that he was mindful of his instructions to spare the Treasury. ". . . *The Expence of constructing it I mean to defray out of the Colonial Funds. . . . When this road shall be so far completed as to admit of a Provision Cart passing over it, I mean to proceed myself through this new Country. . . .*"

How soon could that be? Evans said three months from the date of the commencement of the road, but that was perhaps optimistic if reports of the ruggedness of the mountains were to be trusted. It would take time, too, to find the right person for directing the work, and to make all necessary arrangements. Early next year, possibly; and by then his dear babe would be sufficiently strong to be left in the care of a nurse, and Elizabeth could accompany him. . . .

He thumbed through his papers; what next? Some account of affairs at Van Diemen's Land—they had had a good harvest there, fortunately, and he had instructed Davey to purchase all surplus grain and send it to relieve the settlements on the drought-stricken mainland; public works, and the urgent necessity for a new Court House—Mr. Bent was growing very restive! Education and religion; more doctors for the remoter settle-ments—ah, for a score like that excellent Redfern!

That name gave his thoughts a different turn, and he pushed his official papers aside suddenly: he would amplify all these points at some later time, and deal with others too. For the moment he felt inclined to allow himself the indulgence of dwelling upon more intimate things. He took up his pen and drew his private memorandum book towards him, his mind ranging back over a pleasant, memorable day, with twenty-three guests sitting down to a christening dinner after the formal baptism of their infant and the Molle's at St. Phillip's. The pen moved steadily and without haste upon a congenial task. ". . . *the healths of the two young Christians were drank in overflowing Bumpers. Young Molle was present —but our little darling being asleep at the time their Healths were drank, and having been a little griped during the afternoon, it was not thought prudent to disturb him on the occasion of his health being drank.*" Yes, a very pleasant day, full of joviality and good cheer. But the serenity which had been reflected on his face as he wrote the words, became clouded by a faint frown as he read them over. Was there a hint, an absurd, unintentional implication that his son was a weakling—less robust than the Lieutenant Governor's. . . ." He dipped his pen in the ink again, and wrote firmly: "*Our darling Babe is only 1 month and 3 days old this Evening, whilst young Molle is 4 months and 7 days old to-day.*"

* * * *

The *Catherine* and the *Three Bees*, both from Ireland, arrived early in May. Toole, having journeyed to Sydney in search of a couple of likely new labourers for Beltrasna, took one look at the wasted and scurvy-ridden convicts lined up on the deck of the *Three Bees*, and turned his back on them. "Is it an infirmary we're supposed to be runnin' here?" he demanded contemptuously of the Superintendent. "Or maybe a charity home for old men? Nine dead on the voyage, ye say? Well, the rest of 'em don't look but half alive to me; I'd not be troublin' meself with such rubbish." He took charge of a packet of letters addressed to Mr. Mannion, and returned to Beltrasna in a bad humour. Patrick, seated in his study late that afternoon, deciphered with some difficulty a couple of sheets, crossed and re-crossed in his Aunt Hester's spidery hand, which informed him of his grandmother's death at the age of eighty-five, and described her funeral at considerable length.

"*As you well know,*" he read, "*her resolute Spirit and her remarkable grasp of Affairs have enabled her to direct the Estates despite her great Age; but altho' I trust I should not be found Wanting in a similar Spirit, my time has been, and still is, wholly occupied with my domestic, Charitable and Religious Duties, which have permitted me no opportunity to familiarise myself with Matters which should properly be the province of a Man. As for your Aunt Abigail, she is entirely Useless; nor would her health, or mine, permit us to undertake so grave a Responsibility. You will therefore, I trust, see the imperative necessity for your early Return —permanently, we hope, but if your Conscience permits you still to persist in your absurd Exile at Botany Bay, at least for a period sufficient to set Affairs in order here. I should be failing in my Duty to the Family did I not add that you would do well to devote some time during your Visit (if a mere Visit it must be) to finding a suitable Wife. . . .*"

Patrick threw the letter down and went out on to the verandah, puzzled by his own surge of rebellion. What kept him here, after all? He had seen many things happen in the colony, and although he had held himself aloof from active participation as far as he might (or perhaps because he had held himself aloof?) he had seen them with a painful vividness which made him part of them. He had seen the houses advance, and the trees retreat. Beltrasna itself had been an outpost, but now there was a new frontier across the mountains, ghostly as yet, drawn only in men's minds, but soon to be marked, as all frontiers must be, by more rising houses and more falling trees.

Did he want to go on watching it, or could he now be content with a land in which the only frontiers left were those of the mind and the spirit? Why not? They were the ones that mattered, after all. Yet while he stood looking at the hills he realised that the pushing forward of this new land frontier was by far the most important and exciting of all the things he had seen happen here. It was an end—and a beginning.

The colony could never be the same again. There would be a shift of policies, a shift of population, a shift of aims and attitudes; everything was suddenly in flux, and anything might emerge from it. They had taken a country for their own purposes, but now it seemed that they had themselves been appropriated. They rejoiced at having broken down a barrier which had shut them off from riches, but perhaps they were triumphant for the wrong reason. Perhaps, now that there was no barrier, they were confronting something which would demand as well as give—demand more than labour, more than fortitude—much more. . . .

They had barely begun to know this land; had they ever tried to learn it, or had they merely attacked it savagely with axe and plough? A rape, he thought—all taking, and no love. But they would have to learn it now, as the frontier, retreating inland, drew them after it like a magnet. They would have to forget that the sea had once been always at their backs, an escape route, a line of retreat, a reminder to nostalgic hearts that home was far away. They had tried to make a war between themselves and the land, counting cleared acres a victory, and new dis-covery a conquest; it was not a war, but a bloodless capture, and they, as yet imperfectly aware, the not unwilling captives. They had made a little gaol for felons, but now they were all prisoners, and their sentence was to learn that their gaol could be a heritage. No war, and therefore no conqueror; victory was always an illusion, and when men spoke in terms of warfare with this or any other land, they were talking the language of fools. Wrecking or building, spoiling or husbanding, taking or giving, they must come to terms with it in the end—and that, regard-less of land frontiers, was a business for the frontiers of the mind.

Suddenly he knew that he wanted very much to stay; and in the same moment, knew that he must go. He had avoided Laetitia as much as he could, but the very avoidance, in this small community, must in time become conspicuous; and when they met he could not trust his eyes —or hers. He tried to tell himself that time would extinguish this flame between them, and knew that it would not. He tried to think that Miles would someday tire of colonial life, and then he himself could return; but the faint, brief laugh which he heard himself utter, ended that fantasy. Miles would not pause to ponder the sense of urgency, the stir of adventure, the lure of unknown places which would presently rise like a fever in the colony—he would merely feel them, and plunge. He would set out to raid the future—and no doubt the future would impose its discipline. But it was certain that he would never turn his back upon a stage so richly set for his own spirited performance. "And if he will not," Patrick thought, "I must, and my exile will be permanent."

Exile . . . ? Despite his thoughts, it still startled him that the word should come so naturally, and he began to cast about in his memory for the time when it had changed its meaning in his mind. He could find no hour, or day, or year, but while he searched the past his eyes were finding an answer in the present, looking with a kind of hunger at the river and the hills which imperceptibly, day by day, had claimed him. I must break away from them, he thought, I must go home, home, home (his mind repeated the word, testing it), and find myself a wife, and do my duty to posterity. . . .

A movement seen from the corner of his eye made him start and look downward. Mary, with a doll dangling by one foot from her hand, was standing beside him, staring solemnly at the river as if to discover what had so absorbed his attention. She looked up at him and, finding his eyes upon her, fixed her own hastily on the floor. He had no gift for talking to children, and rarely addressed her, but now, troubled by her shyness, and struck anew by that subtle, fleeting resemblance to himself, he said:

"Your doll is broken, Mary."

She lifted it and studied its armless torso, but made no reply.

"Would you like a new one?"

She clutched it tightly to her chest and backed away from him, looking frightened. He stretched his hand out, thinking to reassure her, but she turned and fled—making for cover, he thought painfully, with her treasure. Why should she trust him? To her he was master, not father. He could ensure for her a home, protection, kindness—and his presence could add nothing more; indeed he would harm her less by giving little than by attempting too much.

But as he watched her vanish round the corner the thought came to him that he could not, even if he would, withdraw wholly from this place. He could go, putting the country behind him for ever, but through Mary the life he had lived in it went on. As he turned to go indoors he was wondering why that thought should give him comfort.

*   *   *   *

Mr. Howe, like other editors, found that news was apt to descend upon him in a deluge after weeks when he had been hard put to it to fill his columns. The publication of proclamations, Government Orders and official announcements occupied much of his space; the routine reporting of weekly events claimed more, and allowed him but little exercise of his gift for dramatic narration, laced with moral and philosophical comment. Even the most brilliant social events—vice-regal balls, dinner and levees, or entertainments at the homes of the wealthy colonists—had settled down into such an unvarying pattern of elegance, tastefulness and liberality, and were so monotonously attended by the same persons of the first respectability, that he could have penned his descriptions of them —and sometimes did—before they occurred.

As a good newspaper man who understood that a few rich adjectives can lend colour to even the most colourless events, and who would never write "end" if he could write "termination", Mr. Howe did his best with such material; but an occasional outrage was undoubtedly a godsend, and his perpetual hope that a really robust sensation would occur was as ardent as the Governor's hope that it would not. To aggravate his frustration, there were many promising stories which he must not tell— budding rumours which must be nipped by a frosty silence when he might so easily have nurtured them with words into a brave, full-blossoming scandal. There had been but recently the matter of a library donated at Mr. Marsden's request by philanthropically-disposed persons in England for the instruction and moral elevation of the colonists. Mr. Howe had published a letter from a correspondent signing himself "Free Settler", who enquired where this library was to be found; the revelation that it was unobtrusively housed at the back of Mr. Marsden's dwelling in Parramatta had caused the reverend gentleman to declare affrontedly that the library was not a public one, but merely a collection of books to be lent out at his own discretion, and to demand the name of this officious busybody. But this the Governor would not direct Mr. Howe to reveal, though there were others besides Mr. Marsden who whispered that he was none other than His Excellency's secretary. Mr. Howe remained silent and inscrutable as the Sphinx, but whatever he might have disclosed, the increasing coolness between the Governor and Mr. Marsden was no secret. He had never forgotten Macquarie's insulting suggestion that he should act with two ex-convicts as a Trustee of the turnpike road; nor had he forgiven the Governor's failure to consult him as the colony's leading agricultural expert; Mr. Howe, who was experienced by now in assessing the significance of apparently trivial and passing disputes, regretted his inability to reveal this one as a straw showing the direction of a rising wind.

But in May and June there was no dearth of news. The natives, whose principal function in his eyes had hitherto been to provide him with opportunities for displaying a sprightly vein of humour, had lately ceased to be amusing. They had made several attacks on Mr. Cox's Mulgoa property, showing an astonishingly reckless disregard of the muskets brought out to drive them off; and within the last week a horde said to have numbered nearly four hundred, had descended on Mr. Campbell's farm, making off with a quantity of food, and leaving the overseer with a spear in his shoulder.

Mr. Howe had barely prepared his account of these outrages when the *Catherine* and the *Three Bees* arrived, bringing news of a resounding defeat inflicted on Napoleon's armies. Imperative as it was for a loyal colony to make much of such tidings, the interest they aroused could not, in the nature of things, compete for long with the interest of events nearer home. Boney might challenge the whose civilised world—but that world was far away, and close at hand naked savages were challenging the white men's possession of their land; gloriously as a soldier might fall before Boney's cannon, a colonial settler could not but feel that his own possible death from a native spear, inglorious as it might be, was still a matter of more pressing concern. By the following week hostilities in Europe were forgotten, and Mr. Howe was again preoccupied with hostilities in New South Wales.

"*Our public duty once more lays us under the necessity of reporting violences between the natives and ourselves. . . .*" The events he related had already been described to Johnny Prentice by Billalong, but Mr. Howe, whose business it was to reflect—and sometimes even to anticipate —vice-regal views, added a confident assertion that the Government would spare no effort in ascertaining by which side the first act of aggression had been committed. Meanwhile, the situation remained uneasy, and he judged that it would provide at least a few more incidents for his columns in the weeks to come. But before this prediction could be fulfilled, a sensation worthy of his greatest eloquence occurred in the capital itself.

* * * *

It was about a week later that Patrick rode in from Beltrasna to tell his brother and the Harveys of his impending return to Ireland. To announce that he meant to remain there permanently would, he foresaw, involve him in explanations, and possibly in arguments; it would be simpler to leave undisturbed their assumption that he was going only for a visit. "I heard the *James Hay* was about to sail," he said to Mark and Conor, "so I came in to send a letter by her, but it appears she's still delayed. I shall go on to Moore House presently to talk things over with Miles; he'll have to curb his restlessness and settle down at Beltrasna for a time."

"It will be useless your going to Moore House just now," Conor objected, "for Miles isn't there. He set out early this morning for Windsor to see Mr. Cox, and he said he would not be back before sunset. You had best dine with us, and go on to see Miles afterwards. You can discuss everything with him at your leisure, spend the night there, and make an early start for Beltrasna in the morning."

Patrick frowned; he was right—it was becoming difficult to avoid Laetitia.

"I want to get back to-night. There's a good deal of uneasiness about the natives along the river at present, and I don't trust Toole to handle them." He added rather irritably: "What does Miles want to see Cox for? I thought they were barely acquainted."

"Perhaps he merely wanted a ride to Windsor. But Patrick . . ." Conor's voice was anxious, "I wish you would not ride alone at night— indeed the roads are no longer safe. It cannot really be necessary for you to return to-night." Mark asked:

"You have had no trouble with the natives at Beltrasna, have you?"

"None at all, though Toole says one of them menaced him with a spear the other day. I shouldn't be surprised. He resents my orders that some maize is to be handed out to them, and his manner shows it. They're in no mood to stomach insults at the moment."

"I never liked Toole," Conor said slowly. "Why don't you dismiss him?" Patrick shrugged.

"He's a surly brute, but too useful to be dismissed lightly—particu-larly if I'm to be away, for Miles is quite inexperienced. Well, if I may take dinner with you, I'll call at Moore House later as I pass by, and hope to find Miles returned."

As he rode through the streets soon after five o'clock he noticed an air of excitement among the people, many of whom were hurrying in the direction of the cove. There was a smell of smoke in the air: "Some house on fire, perhaps," he thought, but was too preoccupied to be greatly interested. He hoped to find Miles at home, but he was conscious also of a small pulse of hope which could only beat so urgently because he thought that he might not, and that he would then find himself, through no fault of his own, alone with Laetitia.

He was surprised—and not altogether pleased—to see Shawn Morgan standing with Flora and Mrs. Bodley in the street outside the house as he rode up; that the servants should stand gossiping by the front gate was but another instance of that odd, colonial laxity that often irked him. He was even more astonished to see Johanna, with the baby in her arms, walk down the path to join them, and he was no sooner within earshot than Morgan said:

"It's glad we are to see you, Sir, for we've been a bit uneasy, like, with the master away, and . . ."

"Beg pardon, Sir . . ." it was Mrs. Bodley, bobbing an agitated curtsey, "is it true there's a hundred casks of gunpowder on board?"

"Gunpowder?" repeated Patrick, staring. "Where?"

"You've not heard, Sir?" cried Flora. "Why, it's all over the town, and they're sayin' we'd best get out into the country before . . ." All save Johanna began to speak at once, and Patrick cut in impatiently: "What is it, Shawn? What's amiss?"

"Why, it's the *Three Bees*, Sir—she's on fire down there in the cove. They say she'll blow up for sure, Sir, the way she's got all her guns loaded, and casks of powder on board."

Patrick turned in his saddle and stared at a column of smoke rising from behind the buildings near the cove.

"Where's your mistress?" he demanded. Johanna spoke for the first time:

"She's in her room, Sir. She was feeling poorly, and she's taking a rest."

"Does she know of this?"

"No, Sir, and won't unless there's need. She smelt the smoke and asked what it was, but I told her it was a fire on the North Shore."

"Very well. Don't alarm her—it's probably of no consequence. I'll ride down and see what is happening."

He found as he rode that he was now moving more and more against a stream of people hastening away from the water as fast as they had formerly hastened towards it. But there were others still crowding the shore when he reached it, to stare at the burning vessel near the Government Wharf, and among them he found Mr. Howe, torn between professional enthusiasm for a spectacle rich in drama, a certain aggrieved peevishness that it should present itself on a Friday evening when his next day's issue was almost ready for the press, and a very human concern for his own safety. It appeared, he told Patrick, that the fire had begun in the hold, and burst into fierce and uncontrollable flames when the hatches were accidentally raised. The crew, vividly conscious of gunpowder stored close to the blaze, had hastily abandoned the ship. "And they've cut her adrift, Sir, for the wind's from the south, and they hoped it would take her out from shore. But as you can see, she's just swinging about this way and that—and God knows what will happen when her guns go off."

Frenzied activity was apparent on the other vessels in the cove as their crews hauled in anchors and prepared for removal to safer berths. "I imagine," said Patrick, "that only buildings near the shore would be likely to suffer damage. How are they loaded?"

"Some with ball and some with shot, they say. But when the fire reaches the powder . . ." Mr. Howe shook his head lugubriously, "why, Sir, the blast may shatter the whole town!"

"Hardly, I think. How much is there on board?"

"Some say thirty casks, and some say over a hundred—but whatever it is, the situation is not pleasant, Sir. No, by Heaven, it's not pleasant at all—a burning ship cast loose, as it may be said, in the middle of a town, with her loaded guns pointing this way and that, and the whole vessel likely to explode at any moment . . . !" And Mr. Howe, as if suddenly alarmed by his own description, hurried away, calling over his shoulder: "It's none too safe here—any moment, Sir—any moment . . . !"

Patrick, looking away from the glare of the fire to watch his hasty retreat, saw that many other people had reached the same conclusion, for the shores were almost deserted. He decided that they were right, and made his way back towards the lower end of George Street, noticing that the swift twilight of a late Autumn day had fallen while he faced the burning ship, and that the lambent glow of fire on smoke-laden air made the dusky street look not only darker, but oddly forbidding. Carts and carriages were making westwards towards the Parramatta Road, impeded by pedestrians who overflowed the footpaths, and Patrick, momentarily caught in a throng of people, was frustrated in his attempt to turn down Bridge Street and seek a quieter route. Mor was nervous; disturbed by the smoke, the glare, the unaccustomed press of people jostling his flanks, the vehicles full of shouting men and half-hysterical women, and the subtle infection of excitement, he shied and baulked. Near the corner of Hunter Street Patrick caught a glimpse of Mark Harvey gesturing to him from the side of the road, and was beginning to edge his mount in that direction when a child ran across just ahead of him, and a cart, swerving to avoid it, crowded Mor into a group of people who immediately began to push and shout. The horse reared, plunged, and fell; Patrick heard a woman scream just as his head struck the cobblestones.

The scream seemed to merge into a deafening bang. He tried to sit up, but someone was holding him down with arms so soft and warm that he found it agreeable to submit. He asked hazily: "What was that?" A voice, soothing as the arms, murmured surprisingly: "Oh, my love, my love . . . !" He opened his eyes and saw Laetitia's face close to his own, but his head ached so fiercely that he closed them again, and found himself in the middle of a long, difficult dream about a fair-faced woman named Dilboong who, when he tried to reach her, withdrew into a room whose door shut in his face with a resounding bang . . .

He started up again, the bang still echoing in his ears. Laetitia was still there, and this time he did not sink back on his pillows under her gentle pressure. He looked about the room, fighting his confusion, collecting his wits, and asked at last: "Was that one of the guns?"

"Yes." She rose from her knees and sat down in a chair by the bed; her eyes avoided his, and contemplated her hands, lying folded on her lap. "They have been going off for some time," she said, and he replied stupidly, resting on his elbow: "I meant to take you out into the country."

"Pray don't disturb yourself about it." She gave him a faint smile. "Mr. Harvey thinks we are in no danger at this distance."

"No." He tried to think, but was troubled by the memory of a voice saying: *"My love, my love!"* and by his inability to separate it with confidence from his dream. "No," he repeated, "but I thought you would be alarmed."

Her eyes met his; they looked at each other for a long moment, and she said at last:

"I have been alarmed—for you."

The room was in darkness save for one candle burning on a small table beside her. He sat up, swung his feet to the floor, and put his head down into his hands until his giddiness passed. "What time is it?" he asked.

"It must be after seven. Mr. Harvey had you brought here almost an hour ago."

"Miles—is he back yet?"

"No."

"Mark Harvey?"

"He has returned home. We sent Shawn for Dr. Redfern, but he could not be found."

"There was no need—it was nothing. Mor came to no harm?"

"No, no. Shawn took charge of him."

"What happened to the ship?"

She lifted her shoulders in a slight shrug. It told him with sweet but frightening explicitness that there had been no room in her mind for the ship. "I don't know," she said indifferently. "Its guns keep going off—a dozen or more—I don't remember . . ."

She was looking down at her hands again, so he allowed himself to stare. In the candlelight she seemed more beautiful than ever before, but her mouth was sad, and he thought there were traces of tears on her cheeks. Feeling his eyes on her, she raised her own, and once more there was that wordless interchange, that unspoken confession and response. He said uncertainly: "Laetitia . . ." and she interrupted quickly, her voice faint and nervous: "You should be resting—pray lie down again."

"No, no, I'm perfectly well." He felt his heart thudding as if he had just escaped a danger, and stood up. His head was indeed much clearer—clear enough to tell him that those words still haunting it had been no part of any dream. But his abrupt movement had caused a momentary return of giddiness, and he stumbled a little. She put her hands on his arms to support him, uttering an exclamation of distress; it seemed by no will or action of their own that they were suddenly standing tightly clasped. He spoke her name again with a questioning desperation: "Laetitia . . . ?" She answered him at once with the same quiet murmur he had heard before: "Oh, my love, my love!" A kind of trance fell on them then, as they stood motionless in the dim room, saying no more, finding in silence and immobility a refuge from decision, a magic to halt time, and postpone the perils of forbidden love. It was the muffled crash of a distant explosion that broke the spell, making the pale flame of the candle jump and waver, bringing back to their reluctant minds awareness of a world outside. Almost at the same moment there came a soft knocking on the door, and Johanna's voice said: "The master's just riding up, ma'am; he's talking with some gentleman along the street."

*　　　*　　　*　　　*

Miles found Shawn bringing Mor round to the front of the house, where Patrick and Laetitia stood side by side in the lighted doorway.

"You're not going at this hour, Patrick?" he demanded. "I guessed I'd find you here or at the Harvey's, for I rode over to Beltrasna, and they told me you were in Sydney. A lucky chance, too, with all this uproar going on, or Letty might have joined the exodus from town. But I see you're quite composed, my love. Take that horse away, Shawn, and mine too—Mr. Patrick will be staying the night."

"No," said Patrick shortly. "I'm riding home at once."

"Good God, man, why? Letty, you complain that nothing happens here, but by Heaven, when I reached Parramatta and saw the stream of people coming in from Sydney I thought Boney's troops must have landed! But they're all trailing back again now, and looking a trifle sheepish, too, I assure you. My love, I trust you now realise the peculiar charm of this place, where the natural order of things is reversed, and only the unexpected can be looked for. Show me anywhere else in the world where the inhabitants of a town are bombarded by one of their own ships lying in their own harbour! And I must choose this day to be absent! What a spectacle she must have presented, turning round and round like a teetotum, and solemnly discharging her guns in all directions! Piper got a ball through the parlour window, I'm told, and another sailed over Blaxcell's place, but from what I can learn no one suffered so much as a bruise. . . ."

"Your brother," said Laetitia from the doorway, "was thrown from his horse, and brought here unconscious."

"The devil! Yet you talk of riding home to-night, Patrick! Don't be a fool, man!"

Patrick, with a formal bow of leave-taking to Laetitia, came down the steps and took Mor's bridle.

"I tell you I'm perfectly well—the fall was nothing." He asked, to forestall further argument: "What happened to the ship?"

347

"Oh, she's drifted over on to the rocks off Bennilong's Point, and there she's quietly burning away in the most peaceable fashion. They think water got at the powder before the fire did, so the explosion was something of an anti-climax," Miles chuckled. "Those who prophesied the town would be laid in ruins don't know whether to be relieved or annoyed! I'm thirsty, Letty. And starving. Patrick, for God's sake come indoors and let's take some supper. Your housekeeper said you came in to see me, and now you insist on disappearing the moment I arrive. . . ."

"I had wanted a word with you," Patrick said, mounting, "but it can wait another occasion."

"Why the devil should it? I want to talk to you, too. I've been with Cox—it seems the Governor's serious about this road over the mountains. Cox says it's to be begun immediately. When it's progressed far enough, I want you to come with me, and . . ."

"That won't be possible," Patrick interrupted. He looked over his shoulder at Laetitia, standing silently in the doorway. Cruel to tell her thus, without warning . . .? Cruel, after those brief, wild moments of bewitchment, to reveal, in words not even directly addressed to her, the coming years of separation . . . ? All life is cruel, he thought furiously, and the hopeless attempt to be merciful, of all cruelties the worst! "I shall not be here," he said harshly. "I'm going back to Ireland."

He rode out into the street without even a farewell gesture, and set Mor at a canter towards the Parramatta Road.

*   *   *   *

Late in May and early in June, settlers were reporting that tribes from other parts of the country had joined those that dwelt along the Nepean banks in the neighbourhood of the Cow Pastures; some said they came from as far distant as Jervis Bay—a harbour in which the boats of white men had always met with an unfriendly reception. They were quiet at present, but a rumour grew that they intended to begin an attack upon all whites "when the moon shall become as large as the sun". Settlers formed themselves into bands, and kept night vigil, watching the thin crescent of the moon grow towards the full splendour it would attain when June was nearly over.

Macquarie's desire for peace between his countrymen and the natives, though based on the natural benevolence of his temper, was now, for other reasons also, stronger than ever. A road over the mountains seemed day by day not only more attractive to his imagination, but more urgently necessary; he would not now feel easy until his colony had spread over an area which offered at least a chance that drought in one part need not mean drought over all. Natives displaying the aggressiveness which had characterised them in the past few months, might prove troublesome to a lonely party of roadmakers.

He set to work to impress upon black and white alike the need for amity, and ordered an enquiry before a Bench of Magistrates—a solemn, formal enquiry with native as well as white witnesses—which he trusted would demonstrate to both sides the seriousness with which he regarded this unhappy situation. When June was half over, fresh and horrible material was provided for its deliberations. A party of white men, it appeared, having come at night upon the wife and two children of a native named Belugally, all sleeping, had shot them, cut an arm from the woman's body, stripped the scalp from her head, and, finding one of the children still alive, had beaten its brains out with a musket. They had left the corpses as a salutary example for the natives to note next day, and the natives, having noted them, attacked and killed two of Mr. Broughton's servants at his farm in the Appin district.

Macquarie knew it to be but one incident of many, set apart only because it was, if not the first case, then at least the first that had come to his knowledge, in which murder had been accompanied by such ferocious sadism. How many other such crimes, he wondered, had been—or might still be—committed in the lonely bush under cover of darkness, and shielded by a conspiracy of silence? As the scion of a Highland clan whose members had, in the past, exacted blood for blood without waiting upon legal formalities, he could find it in one fiery corner of his heart to applaud the prompt and savage retaliation of the natives; but as Governor he could not afford to indulge in such heady emotions. He glimpsed uneasily the swift, demoralising influence of fear, spreading its infection among black and white, turning his agricultural outposts into bloody frontiers, and leaving his farmers with muskets in their hands more often than hoes.

In the Government notice which Mr. Campbell handed to Mr. Howe for publication, he referred to the legal enquiry which, ". . . *although it was not sufficiently clear and satisfactory to warrant the Institution of Criminal Prosecution, it was enough so to convince any unprejudiced Man that the first personal Attacks were made on the Part of the Settlers and of their Servants.*" He mentioned the natives' habit of helping themselves to grain, and acknowledged that this provided cause for complaint by the settlers. ". . . *But whilst it is to be regretted that the Natives have thus violated the property of the Settlers, it has not appeared in the examination of Witnesses that they have carried their Depredations to any alarming Extent, or even to the serious prejudice of any one Individual Settler.*" He urged patience and forbearance; he condemned wanton acts of cruelty; he reminded his countrymen that the natives were, like themselves, entitled to the protection of British Law; he recalled that "with the exception of a few slight interruptions", they had lived at peace with the white men since the foundation of the colony. "*The Governor,*" he continued, "*has lately taken much personal pains to impress this Circumstance upon the minds of several of the Cowpastures and other Natives, and point out to them the absolute necessity of their desisting from all acts of Depredation and Violence . . . and he has had strong assurances from them that unless they be shot at or wantonly attacked (as in the case which occurred lately at Appin, wherein a Native Woman and her two children were, in the Dead Hour of Night, and whilst sleeping, inhumanly put to death) they will conduct themselves in the same peaceable Manner as they had done previous to the present Conflict; they have at the same time the fullest Assurance from the Governor that any Complaints they may be disposed to make to him will be duly attended to. . . .*"*

This, he hoped, when read throughout the colony during Divine Service, would produce a calmer mood in his white subjects; the attitude of the black ones must depend on the effectiveness of his parleys with those wrinkled old men who, through the crude and halting English of native interpreters, aided by the polished and eloquent language of their own signs and gestures, had assured him that peace was no less their desire than his.

At all events, the full moon waxed and waned without further trouble. His road must be begun, and he thought that he had found the man to make it. Mr. William Cox of Clarendon, near Windsor, had already volunteered his services, and early in July Macquarie summoned him to a final interview. This ex-paymaster of the New South Wales Corps was a robust and vigorous fifty; his grizzled hair receded from a formidable forehead, and merged with side-whiskers which lost themselves in the folds of a high, white cravat. His nose was large, his chin jutted beneath a straight, close-shut mouth, and his eyes were arched by brows which —since one was slightly higher than the other—lent them a faintly quizzical expression. Macquarie, as in duty bound, had considered his colonial history, which was, like most colonial histories, chequered. There were still those who contemptuously recalled his association with the Irish rebel, "General" Joseph Holt, in whose company he had first voyaged to the colony fourteen years ago. He had had his financial troubles which, perhaps, had not served him ill, for his bankruptcy had brought about his suspension from military duties, and withdrawn him to England during a period when he might otherwise have become embroiled in the mutinous proceedings of his turbulent regiment. Now, having resigned from the army, he was a magistrate, a prosperous farmer, a practical, intelligent man, and—not least—the father of a large family which included six sons. Macquarie, studying him across the desk as he put his views with brevity and decision, decided that here was no unreliable will-o'-the-wisp, no merely self-seeking adventurer, no intriguing trouble-maker, and no fool; but the solid head of a well-rooted colonial family, with some experience already of road-making in his own district, capable of handling men, and—as a sound agriculturalist—possessing full knowledge of the importance to the colony of such a task as this. By the time the interview was over, Macquarie was toying with the notion that he had found not only the man to build his road, but the man to administer, someday, those distant settlements to which it would lead.

*   *   *   *

Cox rode home that night and plunged into preparations. He converted a cart into a caravan for his own use, and recruited his company, choosing men who had been some years in the colony, and who were accustomed to field labour. There were, to begin with, thirty in all, who would be reinforced or relieved by others as occasion arose. They included, besides twenty convict labourers, a blacksmith, a carpenter, a miner, an overseer of tools, a doctor, a constable, two bullock drivers, and two superintendents; of these last, one was Burns, who had accompanied both the previous expeditions, and the other a man named Lewis, who had been one of Evans' party. A sergeant, a corporal and six privates of the Veteran Company would repel possible attacks by natives, and guard against any disposition on the part of the convicts to take advantage of their isolation in the mountain wilderness.

It was a clear, frosty July morning when Cox rode to the appointed rendezvous on the river bank opposite that tract of land hitherto known as Emu Island, but now to be called Emu Plains. By two o'clock his party was assembled, and carts had arrived from Sydney and Richmond with clothing, tools and provisions which must be examined and checked against the Commissary's return. They made camp there that night, and at daylight next morning set to work. It was still early when Patrick rode down with Miles, who was spending a few days at Beltrasna, and the steep east bank, as they approached it, seemed swarming with men, and littered with gear. They paused to watch the storeman loading blankets, shoes, suits of slops, bags of corn and biscuits, casks of pork, flour and sugar; axes, picks, crowbars and grub-hoes had been distributed; the smith had set up his forge; on the ground about the carts, methodically stacked, was an assortment of indispensable articles, from gunpowder to medicines, and from a grindstone to a supply of cobbler's thread. The Governor, determined not to have the work hampered by idle curiosity, had repeated his order that no one might cross the river without a pass, and a military guard was to be stationed at the ford.

"You're well equipped," Miles remarked as Cox paused for a moment beside them.

"Well enough." Cox shouted an order to one of the bullock drivers and watched till it was obeyed. "Yet I judge," he added in his dry way, "that my best equipment is invisible."

"Indeed? And what's that?"

"The Governor's promised emancipation to those of my labourers who work well and willingly. They're all volunteers, too."

Patrick looked at the gang working on the bank leading down to the ford. "From what I see yonder," he replied, "I should say they're bent on earning their reward. Well, Sir, we'll follow the news of your progress with interest; perhaps we may even have an opportunity of hearing of it from yourself?"

"I'll be riding back and forth. And the store carts will be returning all the time for more provisions. I hope to be finished by the end of the year, if all goes well."

Patrick and Miles remained for a while, watching the work and exchanging a few words with others who had come to see the beginning of this momentous task. As they rode back to Beltrasna, Miles remarked:

"The end of the year. . . . When you return from this wild goose chase of yours, you'll see great changes in the colony."

"No doubt," said Patrick, and was silent for a long time.

*　　　　*　　　　*　　　　*

Five days later the road had crossed the river, and was creeping steadily across Emu Plains towards the foothills. It was no broad, smooth highway that Cox aspired to build over the range at breakneck speed and in the depth of winter, but a mere track for carts and waggons, a route for stock, a lifeline between the coast and the interior. He would follow Mr. Evans' line, as Evans had followed that of his predecessors, because that tortuous ridge, winding its way between the heads of plunging gullies, was the only practicable line, even for a man on foot. But on it he must cast about, as a man on foot need not, for the easiest grade, the widest flat, the place where he could skirt an outcrop of rock instead of blowing it up and clearing it away, or pass between trees instead of hewing them down and grubbing out their roots. He went ahead with Lewis, marking it out to a selected spot—some five miles beyond the river on the lower slopes of the mountains—where his first depôt must be constructed. In three more days the road was beginning to nose its way up the foothills. The grade was steep, the ground rough and stony; all day the grindstone whirred, for the timber was tough ironbark which turned the axes. Two carpenters had been sent forward to erect a tent hut at the depôt and prepare it to receive provisions, and the stonemason was at work on its chimney. There had so far been but one casualty when, during a high wind, the limb of a tree had fallen on one of the labourers. By the first of August, when Cox returned from a brief visit to Clarendon, he found the road completed to the depôt, where a store-house furnished with a strong lock, received the remainder of the provisions from Emu Plains."

The men had been working well and cheerfully despite a few early mutterings about the meat ration, but some tension was apparent between the two overseers, and Cox was not altogether surprised when Burns, surly-faced, presented himself with a grievance.

"Beg pardon, Sir, I've had word from Lewis that you want me to set the three that are fellin' trees in front to fire makin' . . ."

"Well?"

"It's this way, Sir, that I'll take me orders from you, but . . ."

"Don't be a fool!" snapped Cox. "Can I be everywhere at once to give every order with my own tongue? I'll send them by anyone I choose, and I expect to see them carried out."

Burns, scowling, turned away, but he was soon back again, his expression darker than ever, to announce: "If that's the way of it, I'd sooner be leavin'."

Cox turned on him angrily. Perhaps, he thought, the fellow had some notion that he, by reason of having travelled this route twice before, could claim a kind of seniority over Lewis, who had made but one journey; or perhaps some old quarrel still rankled. At all events, the men nearby were listening, and Cox had no intention of allowing them to think that he was prepared to argue with malcontents. He said promptly:

"Take yourself off, then, and the sooner the better. Give up your arms and ammunition to the constable, and I'll tell Gorman to strike you off the stores. You're discharged."

He watched the man presently walking off down the track towards the river, and cursed. He would have to send Lewis in to get another superintendent; he had a man in mind named John Tye, who had been with Evans' party.

Natives were heard nearby next day, but they remained invisible. The working gang was now at the entrance of that thick brush which had so long delayed Mr. Blaxland and his companions; its roots were tough, interlacing beneath the stony surface of the ground, and twining them-selves about buried rocks. The men swore and sweated as they grubbed them out, but by the end of the week the road had moved forward to the end of its ninth mile, and along it Mr. Hobby, late of the New South Wales Corps, came riding to act as assistant to his former comrade in arms. The next week brought a new difficulty, for the storeman reported supplies of meat and sugar almost exhausted; Lewis was despatched with a message to the Governor, while another rider sped to Clarendon with a letter from Cox bidding his wife send out immediately three hundred pounds of beef. But they were through the brush, and they had the satisfaction of proving their road's worth when, after only two days, a cart came in from Clarendon with a side of beef and sixty cabbages.

Now they were on the twelfth mile, in a patch of tall timber; they measured a felled tree which was eighty-one feet to the first branch, and another more than fifteen feet in circumference. Water was available every mile or so, but in small quantities, lying in shallow pools or trickling thinly among mossy boulders in some deep gully off the route. Shoe leather was wearing out, and one of the men turned cobbler. Ahead of them now was more rough ground, climbing a high, rocky hill at which Cox looked with some misgiving. They had won sixteen miles when they attacked it, but he saw that their rate of progress must receive a check here. From the sheer, rocky bluff on its western end they must construct a kind of causeway down on to the ridge again, some twenty feet below. September was almost half over before, in a grateful glow of achievement, he inscribed in his journal a less laconic entry than usual: "The bridge we have completed is 80 feet long; 15 feet wide at one end and 12 at the other; 35 feet of it is planked, the remainder filled up with stones. . . . At the left there is a side wall cut from solid rock. At the right where the ground is lower, we have put up a rough stone wall about 100 feet long, which makes the pass to the bridge quite a lane. It is steep from the top of the mountain quite to the lower end of the bridge, a distance altogether of about 400 feet. . . . It is now complete—a strong, solid bridge, and will, I have no doubt, be reckoned a good-looking one by travellers that pass through the mountain."

*   *   *   *

Meanwhile, in Sydney, two ships had arrived together. They had fallen in with each other off the coast, and it was a skeleton crew of volunteers from the *Broxbornebury* which brought the *Surrey* into port, for upon the latter a fever which had caused fifty deaths was still raging. In later years, Macquarie was apt to feel that both vessels had carried pestilence; but upon that July day, as he bestirred himself to order quarantine for the *Surrey,* and the segregation of her people at an encampment on the North Shore, he was far from suspecting that the *Broxbornebury's* most important passenger, Mr. Jeffrey Bent, would in time appear to him more dangerous and malignant than any fever.

It happened that when the ships were reported to be entering the harbour, he had just finished reading, with some astonishment, a letter which was, in a sense, connected with the young man at that moment assembling his possessions and his many documents in readiness for disembarkation. The Governor had made an occasion for his serious talk with the Judge Advocate, but it had failed to restore harmony between them. for that gentleman was full of grievances, among which the fact that no suitable Court House had been provided for him seemed the most bitter. Macquarie, alive to the dangers of an open rift between himself and so important an officer (and willing to allow, also, as he looked at Ellis Bent's puffy, pallid face, that poor health might affect the temper and the judgment), subdued his indignation, and, with as much mildness as he could summon, ventured to hope that Mr. Bent would, upon reflection, see the injustice of his complaints. But Mr. Bent had his own reasons for being beyond the reach of conciliation. Despite his handsome salary, he was suffering financial embarrassment arising from speculation in currency notes; and since he had himself, soon after his arrival, framed the Proclamation in which the Governor forbade this practice, he was in no position to state frankly the source of his moodiness. He withdrew, offended and irreconcilable, and thenceforward had appeared at Government House only when duty compelled it.

But the Governor had continued to ponder the matter, for a new Court House was needed—and not only as a shrine for Mr. Bent's immoderate self-esteem. Court business was increasing all the time—indeed His Excellency often remarked testily that he had never known such litigious people as these colonists—and soon Mr. Jeffrey Bent would be here to take his place as Judge of the Supreme Court, to be established in accordance with the new Charter of Justice. Macquarie, never happier than when he was considering a new building—began to seek plans for a new Town Hall and Court House against the time when he should be permitted to build it. But during the last year or two, as the hospital progressed by fits and starts in a clamour of argument and recrimination, he had learned from bitter experience how little he knew of the craft of building. There was, he realised, a limit to what he could do with a vision, when he must rely entirely for its execution in bricks and mortar upon carpenters, stonemasons and bricklayers who could look him in the eye and advance technical objections which his ignorance did not permit him to refute. It was more than four years, he reflected bitterly, since he had twice earnestly requested the home authorities to send him an architect immediately—but they had sent none.

Yet had they not . . . ? He recalled a brief interview some months ago with a new arrival, pale and debilitated after his voyage on that unhappy ship, the *General Hewitt,* but still walking with something of a strut, still betraying in his bearing some hint of a man whose confidence in himself remained undamaged. Yes, they had sent one—little as they knew it. . . . Perhaps he might try the fellow—make some small test of his skill . . . ? He said to Campbell:

355

"That man who came out on the *General Hewitt*—what was his name . . . ? Green? Greenwood?"

"A convict, Sir?"

"Yes, yes, an architect of sorts—a little red-headed oddity who came with a letter from Admiral Phillip. I gave him a ticket-of-leave on account of it. . . ."

"Oh, yes—Greenway, Sir."

"Send him this drawing; tell him to copy it."

He had now just read, with raised eyebrows, Mr. Greenway's response.

". . . I *will immediately Copy the Drawing Your Excellency requested me to do, notwithstanding it is rather painful to my Mind as a professional man to Copy a Building that has no Claim to Classical proportion or Character. . . .*"

"God bless my soul!" ejaculated His Excellency. " 'requested' him . . . ! 'painful to his mind'. . . !" He read on in growing wonder, not unmixed with displeasure. Mr. Greenway proceeded to educate him by quoting at some length from what he described as an "Elegant Treatise" upon the subject of architecture; he pointed out that a worthy building might often be erected at a lesser expense than a mean one, and added reprovingly that when public works were in contemplation, this point should be seriously considered before hasty decisions were made. He declared that the Governor now had an opportunity to adorn the town with a public building in the classical style, and promised to exert himself in the construction of one which neither his own, nor His Excellency's posterity would have reason to condemn. . . .

"Tchck!" said His Excellency, nettled, and threw the letter across to Campbell. "Answer this; tell Mr. Greenway that when I request— confound the fellow!—when I *command* him to copy a drawing, I wish to receive a copy of the drawing, and not a dissertation upon architecture!" But beneath his annoyance there was actually a faint stir of excitement. Had he found in this cock-sparrow someone who *loved* buildings . . . ?

It was at this moment that the arrival of the two ships was reported, and in the business of arranging a suitably impressive reception for Mr. Jeffrey Bent, the presumptuous convict architect was temporarily forgotten.

*　　　*　　　*　　　*

Emily's son had been born on a bitter night in July. "It'll be easier this time, I reckon," she had said hopefully to Johnny, facing this second childbirth in better heart because, with mind and body, she welcomed it. But it was not easier, and when Johnny opened the door for a few moments soon after midnight to fetch in more logs for the fire, her eyes recorded a picture of the world outside which remained to haunt her mind throughout the hours of pain. There was a full moon above the valley, and beneath its white, chill radiance cold ceased to be merely a sensation, and became a visible enemy, freezing all sound and movement. She muttered confusedly: "I wish the creek was runnin'." He replied: "We got plenty of water," but she felt wretched and injured because he did not understand that what she wanted was the sound—any sound which would prove that something stirred in that dead world outside.

In the morning there was a hard, white frost on every leaf and blade of grass, and the rising sun shone palely down on a scene where there was still nothing moving but a thin, straight thread of smoke from the chimney of the hut, and another from the hilltop south of it. Inside the hut, too, it was quiet and still, for Emily was asleep, her face white and transparent from exhaustion; on her arm the newborn child was asleep, but preparing for his first essay in living with small, sucking movements of his lips; in a bark crib on the floor by the hearth the nameless baby girl was asleep, her tiny, claw-like hands twitching, and her brow puckered, as if the effort of remaining alive haunted her very dreams; and on the second bunk, face downward with his head on his folded arms, Johnny was asleep too.

It was an hour after sunrise when he stirred, sat up, and peered round the dim, close, smoky room. It filled him with a sharp uneasiness, a sense of revulsion, and he rose quickly and went outside, treading softly past the crib where, he knew, the baby girl would wake only to wail. As he stepped out into the sunlight he saw the smoke on the southern hill, but he took his pail and set out for the rock pool in which, thanks to a few passing thunderstorms, there was still water.

He was thinking of spirits. Such things did not exist—but they had kept Billalong or Gooradoo out there in the freezing night when there was a hut nearby which offered shelter. Such things did not exist—but he knew that the natives of the valley whispered that Dyonn-ee's little girl, who could neither walk nor talk, was proof that they did; for how should the birth-spirit prosper in a place cursed by the spirit of death? And he knew that last night, while Emily was achieving in a long ordeal of agony that which women should achieve with no more distress than could be forgotten in an hour, he had felt them there himself.

They were gone now, but he was left with the memory of a fear that angered him, as fear always did. It was late in the morning before he walked up to the hill, and though he could tell himself with truth that he had been too busy to go earlier, his refusal to hurry to a rendezvous with a native expressed an obscure resentment towards what was still native in himself. It was Billalong who sat on his heels beside a small fire, cooking a pigeon wrapped in clay; Johnny placed on the ground

357

a few hot potatoes which he had pulled from the ashes on the hearth, and they sat side by side to eat as they talked.

Billalong had come to report the commencement of the road, but when he had described the bullock carts, the men, the tools, the quantities of food and equipment, and the soldiers stationed at the ford, he passed on to his own affairs. Hostilities between his tribe and the Beerewolgal, he said, had ceased for the present; but he said it sombrely, adding that for his part the vengeance he had taken for his brother's death had not erased his hatred of all white men. And Johnny, made nervous and irritable by the stresses of the night, and by the odd conflict they had caused in him, said sharply:

"Ye're half white y'self!"

Billalong did not raise his head but he stopped eating, and darted a look at Johnny from beneath his brows. Johnny, still driven by that obscure anger, went on:

"We've never spoke of it—why should we? But ye must know it well enough. Ye're alive this day because y' white father pulled ye and y' mother out of the river, and drowned himself to save ye from drownin'. Yet ye talk of hatin' all white men! Hate me, then—I'm y' brother, and I'm white!"

He knew that he was thus angrily claiming his whiteness because he half feared the persistence in himself of qualities and impulses which belonged to a different race. He looked sideways at Billalong, who was eating again now, but in whom, with those very qualities, he could feel a painful turmoil and confusion; he found himself saying in that dropped, defeated tone of one making unwilling confession: "Ah, what's it mean, anyhow, the colour of y' skin? Mine may be white, but for all that I reckon I'm half black. . . ."

He felt the truth of this as he watched Billalong finish eating, wipe his fingers on his thigh, and sit motionless with bent head, staring at the fire. For he found that he could follow the thoughts which must be striving in that head, and feel the frightening sense of loss that they aroused. The corroboree was false, the legend was false, the red-headed one had not returned from death to take his place again with the tribe as a child named Dyonn-ee. The mystery was gone, the miracle broken. Perhaps it had gone long ago, and he had clung to its shadow, knowing that the loss of one mystery is the first step towards the loss of all. Not only he, but every member of his tribe, had known this dread as the white men, foes of mystery, closed in upon them, invading not only the land that gave them bodily sustenance, but the unseen, spirit world of their beliefs. It was this, far more than the sticks-of-fire, which was dangerous to his people, inflicting doubts like wounds, so that their very will to survive was injured, and a strange, cold apathy possessed them. Had the Beerewolgal, then, a law to give them in place of their own lost law . . . ?

Billalong looked up, and said, laying his hand on his breast: "Black man." He laid it on Johnny's and said: "White. You live with my people, I live with my people." He asked slowly: "We live with your people?"

It meant much more, Johnny knew, than mere eating, sleeping, working. It meant living in the tribal sense, sharing not only food and shelter, but privilege and responsibility, plenty and hardship, song and dance, law, legend and faith. He answered reluctantly: "Not now . . ." and paused, fumbling in his mind for the concept Finn had left him of a world where such things might be. It was somewhere, that world, if only in his heart and other hearts, but he did not know how or when it might be reached. He did not even know how to speak of it, so he repeated heavily: "Not now—not yet . . ." and Billalong, without reply, began to pull the clay-wrapped pigeon from the embers.

Since then neither Billalong nor Gooradoo had visited the valley. From time to time Johnny heard news of the road's progress from natives of the local tribe who climbed up through the pass to the plateau and crept silently at night about the camps of the white men, or watched them from distant hilltops; he decided that when the work had reached a point level with his own valley, he would go up and reconnoitre for himself.

Emily spoke often of the road, and sometimes he saw her looking up at the eastern cliffs, her brows furrowed, as though she expected at any moment to see ominous signs of white men's activity against the skyline. "It's not up there they'll be takin' it," he said, grinning at her ignorance. "There's nothin' out that way to interest 'em—it don't lead nowhere. They're makin' for the plains, and they'll get there along that ridge yonder." He nodded towards the distant, northern cliffs. "And they won't be turnin' aside for anythin', ye can depend on that."

"Maybe they'll follow down the river this time," she said fearfully.

"Not they. We're safer now than we was a year ago when they was still lookin' for a way. Now they've found it they'll stick to it—and I've been thinkin' maybe we'll live the better for that. There'll be people goin' back and forth with carts and waggons loaded with things that might come in handy. . . ."

She interrupted in terror, smitten by the memory of a cart halted by a shot, and a dead body lying on the road beside it: "No, no, ye fool! Ye've done enough killin'!"

"Ye can take without killin'—and take I will!" His eyes were hot

359

and angry. "That's their way, ain't it? Take, and take, and take! Who d'ye think'll get the land when they've made their road to it? The likes o' me? A bit here and a bit there, maybe, but it's the gentry'll get the best and the most—and it'll be them that sends the big lots of sheep and cattle over, and the best-filled waggons. But they'll not go over in a day. They'll be sleepin', or leavin' their carts to go down the gullies for water. Will ye say ye'd not have me handy for a chance like that?"

Emily would say nothing of the kind. If she still felt misgivings they were caused only by the thought of possible danger to Johnny. She shrank from killing, but robbery, in her world, had always been an expedient frequently necessary, usually excusable, and in certain circumstances entirely commendable, just as in other circumstances it was unthinkable. She troubled herself less about the road as the winter passed, for she was busy with her two children. The boy, though robust, was troublesome, displaying from the first a tempestuous will. Unlike the girl, he did not wail, but shrieked; he squirmed and strove in Emily's arms, nipped her breasts between his toothless gums, arched his body strongly when she laid him down, kicked his legs, and flailed the air with his hands. The little girl seemed better since his birth, as if she had found, at last, something in life to capture her interest, and stimulate her to small physical efforts; she learned to say a few words, and began to walk when she realised that she could thus reach the baby's side to touch his hands and feet.

"We did ought to have called her somethin' too, poor mite," Emily said during one of the many discussions she held with Johnny while she sought a name for the boy. "We could call her for me, and make it Emmy to be different." The boy she finally named Andrew. "Ye say ye never cared nothin' for y' father, but I reckon it's nice to call a boy for his grandpa; makes it seem like he had a family, and I never had no pa meself—not to know about him."

Johnny made no objection, but he felt some uneasiness. He himself no longer feared the evil magic that lay in a dead man's name, but it was still real to Billalong and Gooradoo, whose continued absence was beginning to disturb him. But living as they did, he reflected, in a place of death, perhaps it made but little difference that his son should bear a forbidden name. Nevertheless he felt a vague relief when the little girl —who had already changed her own name to Memmie—changed her baby brother's to Andy.

*   *   *   *

From the causeway which had cost so much time and labour, the road-makers had moved forward at a better pace through country still blackened by last summer's fires, but showing in every charred tree-trunk the rosy shoots of new Spring growth. The road climbed laboriously to an eminence from which the fields and houses of Windsor were clearly visible—a high, wild, rocky plateau, bounded on the south by sheer cliffs. Reconnoitring ahead of his party, Cox found, two miles farther on, a patch of flat ground where, among reedy herbage and scattered boulders, tall, spear-like shafts of the grass-tree stood out against the sky, and a stream of clear water flowed from an ice-cold spring. Here, at the twenty-eighth mile, he set his men to work upon the erection of a second depôt, and then, leaving Hobby and Lewis in charge, himself set out for Windsor where, as magistrate, he must attend the Governor at the annual muster.

He crossed the river at the ford, and rode on to Windsor through countryside still parched by drought. During the second week in October, while he was still at Clarendon, light rain fell, but Macquarie, though he welcomed it, and dared to hope it might afford the farmers some small relief, found greater comfort in Mr. Cox's account of his labours. He had need of it, for his troubles were increasing. Mr. Jeffrey Bent had no sooner stepped ashore than he began to complain. He demanded a house at Government expense, and also desired to be provided with Chambers—to which, he declared, English Judges in distant settlements were always entitled. Macquarie, protesting that he had no authority to grant such indulgences, offered to rent a house for him on condition that he would repay the Government if, on application to the home authorities, the expenditure should not be sanctioned. Mr. Bent declined with some hauteur, but rather grudgingly accepted the offer of two rooms in the Barrack for Chambers. The despatches he had brought for the Governor had not been helpful in the matter of a Court House, merely suggesting that one of the wings of the new hospital might serve as temporary accommodation for the Courts—an arrangement which, Macquarie foresaw, would be received by the brothers with further storms of protest. Another new arrival, the Reverend Benjamin Vale, was also loudly voicing his discontent, having been given to understand—as he tirelessly assured the harassed Governor—that he would have his own Church and parish, a cultivated glebe, and a well-furnished parsonage, with servants, fuel and rations provided by the Government.

Such expectations were at the moment particularly unfortunate, since the same ship which brought Mr. Vale had also brought peremptory instructions that the practice of allowing Government servants and store rations to the families of civil officers must end forthwith. This edict, already published abroad by the Governor, was causing much discontent; indeed, it was not without a sigh that Macquarie had sternly performed upon his own household that painful operation known locally as being taken off the stores.

More disturbing than anything else, however, was his suspicion that in Jeffrey Bent those persons who were making his emancipist policy the ostensible reason for opposition to his whole administration, might find a powerful champion. Bathurst, while supporting its general principles, had nevertheless sounded a note of caution. "As those who have been desirous of counteracting your Measures have selected the Admission of Convicts to Society as their main point of Resistance, you will I am sure see the Necessity of not compromising your Authority by exerting it on a subject where Resistance may be so well cloaked under a rigid Sense of Virtue, or a refinement of Moral Feeling." His Lordship's admonition was ambiguous; he spoke of convicts, whereas Macquarie's plea had always been for emancipists. But to Mr. Jeffrey Bent the distinction appeared to be invisible, and the fact that Molle and his officers shared the same view, not only with the Bents, but also with Mr. Marsden and many other people in places of official or financial influence, made the Governor feel that strong forces were mustering against him.

It was with relief, therefore, that he listened to Cox describing the progress of his road. Here was achievement in its simplest, its most manageable form. The intangible obstacles which impeded him in other undertakings—greed, hypocrisy, intolerance, slander—could not, alas, be rapidly and finally demolished, as were the obstacles of this one, by axe-blows or blasts of gunpowder. He found it strange that this report caused him more pleasure and excitement than other tidings which followed him to Windsor; beside the glorious news that the tyrant, Bonaparte, had at last surrendered and suffered banishment to Elba, the tale of a cart-track creeping forward over the mountains should have seemed, he thought rather guiltily, more paltry than it did.

*   *   *   *

Cox returned from Clarendon to find the road completed to the thirty-ninth mile, but Lewis, who had gone forward to inspect the spot where they must attempt a descent from the western end of the ridge, met him with a long face.

"Be damned if I think it's possible, Sir," he said. "It's as near as makes no matter to a precipice, and there's no way round that we could find. There'd be a good half-mile or more to get down—and all blocked with cliffs like walls, and rocks the size of a house." He glanced up at the sky. "I don't like the look of the weather, neither."

Cox shrugged, and set all hands to the road, including the carpenter, the stonemason and the blacksmith; the sooner they got forward to this precipice, the sooner they would get down it. He sent off a letter to the Governor demanding more gunpowder and more ropes, and watched the sky, feeling uncertain whether rain were to be welcomed by Cox the farmer, or dreaded by Cox the roadmaker. The wind, growing ever stronger and colder, blew it up at last, halting the work, soaking the men's clothes and blankets. The lighting of fires and the cooking of food became a tiresome labour. They were enveloped in a driving mist that blotted out everything beyond a few yards of where they stood. The wind shifted to the east, but the rain continued to pour down, and the only busy hands in camp were those of the cobbler. Lean and bedraggled horses, urged on by cold, wet, dejected men, plodded slowly up from the depôts with rations, and returned empty for more; the bullocks were now in such poor condition from heavy labour and lack of good feed that they were unable to work.

On the last day of October, when patches of blue sky were showing through the flying clouds, Johnny climbed up through the pass with Boorah, Murrunga and three other natives. Emily, knowing of his intention, had argued, protested, and even wept until, grinning to himself, Johnny had arranged a little demonstration to quiet her. Returning one night after having been absent since midday, he had received from her an account of how a party of natives had appeared on the hill south of the hut, and remained there in full view for more than an hour.

"So ye didn't know me?" he asked slyly, and though she was angry at being tricked, she was also reassured. She realised now that though Johnny, alone and clad, was obviously a white man, Johnny as one of a group of natives, his hair and skin plentifully smeared with charcoal, would always pass at a distance for one of them. "It ain't only that I look the same," he said. "It's because no one thinks to see a white man like that. I reckon unless somethin' puts 'em on guard, people always see what they're expectin' to see."

Now he emerged from the pass with his companions and climbed to the backbone of the ridge. It did not take them long to find the road-makers, for the ring of axe-blows sounded sharply in the clear, mountain air, but they were content to observe from a distance the tents and the caravan silhouetted against the sky on the summit of a hill, and the dark shapes of the labourers moving among the scrub and rocks beneath its western brow. Johnny watched them for a while, toyed with the notion of trying to steal something from them while they slept, and decided that better opportunities would occur later, when parties were not attended by a military guard. He reached his hut again by nightfall, just as Mr. Cox was recording in his journal that a group of natives had been seen that day.

Next morning the sun was bright and the sky cloudless, but Cox was worried as he looked about him. The great valleys to the south were full of mist, and it lay like white lakes in the shallower ones to the north— beyond which, he knew, the ridge must end at the brink of more cliffs rising from the Grose River. It made no practical difference to his task, that surrounding ocean of white cloud, but it sharpened his sense of being marooned on heights from which there might be no way of descent for a road save the way they had come. He sent three men to scout along the southern cliff-line, but they returned at night with the old, familiar tale of subsidiary ridges which had stopped them abruptly with nothing under their feet but empty air; or dark, steep gorges they had followed down until their streams became waterfalls, leaping into space. Next night Cox climbed into his caravan and wrote doggedly:

"November 2. Fine morning. Thunder, with light showers. Sent three men again to examine the descent of the mountain and ascertained that there is no other way than the bluff originally marked. To-morrow I intend going to survey it, as a road must be made to get off the mountain."

Must. From now that word was the answer to every problem. Must, must, must. He set off at six o'clock with Lewis and two other men for the western extremity of the ridge. He stood for a long time staring down at the rocky, precipitous slope, and at the comparatively flat and open country below it. This was worse—much worse—than he had expected. Vast boulders would have to be blasted out and cleared away in the early stages; both to right and to left the face of the hill fell away into steep gullies, and could only be negotiated by a road winding in a series of sharp, circular turns. The surface of the ground was covered with loose stones; he dislodged one with his foot, and watched it crash down, glancing from tree-trunks and setting other stones rolling till it disappeared from view, and only the sound of it, still smashing and thudding through the undergrowth, told him that it had not yet reached the bottom. He moved out to the edge of an overhanging rock, and tried to trace with his eye a possible route. To get down, he was thinking, was one thing—and bad enough; but how would a laden waggon get up such a grade?

Lewis said, as if following his thought:

"If we get the carts down this, it looks like they might have to stay down."

"We could make a road," Cox said slowly, "that a cart could get down empty, or very lightly loaded . . . but I judge there's no possibility it could come up again with any load at all. It'd serve for stock . . ."

He looked out over the country below, remembering Evans' glowing account of the rich plains beyond, and shook his head with a movement half rueful and half angry. "By God, it's a great drawback to this new country! We'd not be able to bring in any produce—only sheep and fat bullocks. . . . The sheep could be shorn in the mountains—driven down to the second depôt, maybe, and waggons sent in to fetch the wool. . . ." He turned back from the rock impatiently—all that was in the future; for the moment his task was to get some sort of road off this accursed hill. "Well," he said, "we're here, so we might as well go down and find this rivulet of Blaxland's."

It was sunset by the time they scrambled back up the mountain, and the western sky was blazing. Cox, exhausted, sat on a rock at the top and faced it, his thudding heart returning to a normal beat, the sweat drying on his body, the trembling in his knees slowly ceasing. It was the first time he had felt that he was no longer a young man, but it was the first time, too, that his task had challenged him with difficulties great enough to stimulate the almost exhilarated obstinacy which now possessed him.

The party had moved its camp during the day up to the forty-fifth mile, and he plodded back to it with his companions through the gathering dusk. His day was not yet over, for there were details of organisation to be attended to. The storekeeper had arrived with a load of provisions, and the news that fresh Government bullocks had reached the first depôt; Cox sent a man back to bring up the lame and worn-out beasts—which must be got down into the good pasture below as soon as possible—consulted with Lewis and Tye upon a variety of matters, issued a few orders, visited the tent of a man whose arm had been injured by a falling tree, arranged for the Sergeant to return to the river for an extra horse and cart, and climbed at last into his caravan, to make, despite his weariness, a long entry in his journal. *"Put up the forge,"* he finished, *"for the blacksmith to repair all tools for the Herculean mountain. Issued to all hands a gill of spirits."* Sound tools—warm bellies—willing hands; he could make no other preparations.

In the dispiriting hour of dawn, when the wind had risen again, and a cold drizzle was falling steadily, he woke, and thought: "Of course there must be another way down—it's only a matter of finding it." But when the day was over, and he reached once more for his journal, his entry was brief: *"Sent three men to examine all the ridges and gullies to the north, offering a reward if they found a better way down. All returned successful. Removed to 47 miles."*

Next day found him again examining the descent; it must be here, or nowhere. The men were all at work behind him, despite the rain that fell unceasingly, and the bitter, east wind. Down on the coastal plains it was now summer, but here winter was not yet routed, and he knew that cold, discomfort, and the prospect ahead were casting a gloom upon his party. One man had sprained his ankle while bringing water up from a gully off the road, and another was ill. Cox had heard talk of natives, though none had been seen of late, so he had set the blacksmith to making pikes; he did not expect attack, but weaponless men were nervy. Lewis took a party with dogs down to the forest land, and came back with a large kangaroo. At least, thought Cox, they would eat fresh meat that night.

*   *   *   *

All over the coastal settlements it was raining too. The Governor, having attended Divine Service, and disposed of such other duties as the Sabbath could not render avoidable, was spending an hour or two with his wife and son. But even young Lachlan could not wholly distract Macquarie's mind from a business which had been rankling in it for the past month; Elizabeth, having made one or two fruitless attempts to turn the conversation, resigned herself to being an attentive and sympathetic listener.

"I can't understand the Bents," he was protesting. "It's beyond all belief that they should meet my efforts to satisfy them so churlishly—and with such transparent disingenuousness!"

"Oh, Mr. Jeffrey . . . !" exclaimed Elizabeth with a sniff, "I don't trust him at all! But don't you think, my love, that he has probably worked on his brother's mind until the poor, silly man really believes that it might be injurious to his health to have the Court House in the hospital? I won't say that Ellis is a *malade imaginaire,* for it's true he is not robust—but he has always appeared to me to be excessively preoccupied with his ailments."

"My dear Elizabeth," exploded her husband, "the apartments I took them to see are quite separated from the other parts of the hospital by a very thick stone wall, as you must remember from your own inspection. And the entrances are not only separate, but a considerable distance apart. All the same, my love, it's not only their reluctance—nay, their *refusal* —to accept the arrangement that shocked me, but the manner of it. Most peremptory and ill-natured! And it's downright selfish of them to demand the building intended for Dr. Wentworth instead, for he has obviously a greater necessity for being quartered near the hospital. It's not as though it were a more suitable building for a Court House—indeed it's much less suitable, though it has all kinds of domestic conveniences— which is why Mr. Bent wants it. He's thinking merely of his personal comfort!"

"Very likely," Mrs. Macquarie agreed, but she spoke absently, for she was thinking that there might be more to it than that. She had heard

366

Mr. Jeffrey Bent let fall some remarks which made it clear that he was not prepared to stomach ex-convict attorneys. Oh, this perennial dispute, this evergreen source of conflict! She was uncomfortably conscious of it as a growth with strong roots, and she knew that it was being tended and cherished not only for its own sake, but in order to make of it an effective ambush from behind whose shelter her husband's enemies might more safely attack him. Let there be but one such issue, she reflected, and the stubbornness and resentment of each party would be increased and sharpened by the almost instinctive reactions of the other. Thus, when Macquarie, observing his emancipist guests being cold-shouldered by the rest of the company, took pains to pay them some additional attention, he lent colour to the whisper that it was not merely equal treatment he accorded to ex-felons, but preference. Already, she knew, he was be-coming hag-ridden by the knowledge that complaints on this score were being made by individuals to the Colonial Office, and reinforced by other complaints (such as this one about accommodation for the Courts) which might, in time, by sheer numbers and persistence, arouse doubts in high places of his capacity—or even his integrity.

What of Mr. Marsden, for instance? There was that little disturbance about the library, and there was the matter of the Government Order which he had declined to read in Church, suddenly discovering—ridiculous man!—that such a practice was "irregular and improper", after having acquiesced in it without protest for years. And there was his use of an unauthorised version of the Psalms, which Macquarie had felt himself compelled to forbid, pending instructions from London. Perhaps it was just as well, thought Mrs. Macquarie with a sigh, that he was about to absent himself from the colony for a time, and set off for New Zealand to convert the heathen—though (as her dear husband often remarked) it was odd that he should choose to exercise his missionary endeavours so far afield, and pointedly ignore the poor, naked heathen on his doorstep. Of course John Campbell, who couldn't abide the man, declared it was all a question of trade, and that when Mr. Marsden pronounced the colonial natives to be so inferior a race that it would be a waste of time to attempt their improvement, he really meant that they were so lacking in useful crafts and commodities that one could not do business with them. But however that might be, he had powerful friends and supporters in England, including Mr. Wilberforce. . . .

And what was Mr. Hannibal Macarthur saying? For the present he was not openly hostile, but Mrs. Macquarie suspected that this might be because his exiled uncle wished to gain Macquarie's goodwill, and thus pave the way for his return—perhaps even wished Macquarie to intercede for him, and obtain the revocation of that clause in his Instructions which had ordered Macarthur's trial before the Criminal Court of the Colony for his part in the rebellion. Yet civil as Mr. Hannibal might be, he was one of those who greatly resented the terms of the hospital contract, who criticised Government policy at almost every turn, and to whom, in short, no Governor would be acceptable unless he ruled the colony for their exclusive benefit. . . .

And what was Lieutenant-Governor Molle saying? And his officers? And the tiresome, disgruntled Mr. Vale? And the Blaxlands, and the other Gentlemen Settlers? And that crew at Hobart Town where, from all accounts, things seemed to be in a pretty state, what with that dreadful Davey's shocking behaviour, and the island infested with desperate bush-rangers . . . ?

Yes, there were plenty of ill-disposed people on the watch for in-cidents which they could use and magnify, not only in reports to the home authorities, but in their own minds, thus justifying to themselves a rancour which had a different and deeper cause. Mrs. Macquarie stole a glance at her husband's face, and found it still heavy with a troubled frown.

"Oh, bother the Bents, my love!" she exclaimed, laying the child down on the bed. "Just look at our darling, pray—how beautifully he sleeps! Don't you think there has been more colour in his cheeks these last few days?"

Some of the lines smoothed themselves from the Governor's face as he stooped to look closely at his son. But his wife, though no hint of it appeared on her face, was still worrying. She could no longer think lightly of molehills; they began to seem ominously like mountains.

*   *   *   *

The townsfolk in their homes, the settlers in their farmhouses, the shepherds in their solitary huts, the convicts beneath whatever roof they might find themselves, and even the malefactors in gaol, could watch the rain with satisfaction. But on the barren, sandstone heights more than three thousand feet above sea level, it was less welcome to the roadmakers, huddling round fires beneath lofty, overhanging rocks at the end of the ridge. In these caves they could at least dry their clothes and bedding, and find shelter at night from the rain and the cold, east wind, but the weather had affected their spirits and their health; two men had been sent back to Windsor, and four were suffering from feverish colds and aching limbs.

A beginning had been made on the road down the mountain face, but illness and wet weather were hampering the work; and Cox chafed at its slow progress. It had been a long and arduous task to get the lame, half-starving bullocks down the steep and treacherous slope; one, quite blind, had blundered into a ravine from which it had not been extricated till next day, and in the process a bullock-driver had been injured. Picks rang against rock as they were driven into the iron-hard ground. Men grunted and strained as they dragged on crowbars and large levers to turn them out of the way. The blacksmith worked from morning till night repairing broken or blunted tools.

It was now mid-November. During a respite from the rain the sun shone down with a grateful warmth, but the wind was still cold, and the nights bitter. Among craggy rocks the tree-trunks rose tall and straight to a canopy of leaves that filtered the smoke from cooking-fires, and the dust of blasted earth; through the strong smells of burning leaves and acrid gunpowder crept the elusive scent of pink flowers that grew in profusion down the slope, among a carpet of ferns now scarred by rolling boulders and the debris of construction.

"*November 18. Hard at work on the rocks this day. Kept our six pickaxes at work; and W. Appledon (a sailor) fixed the blocks and tackles to trees and got a most capital purchase to turn out an immense large rock at the side of the mountain in the way of the road, which he performed well. . . . The rock would have cost me at least 5 lb. of powder to have blown it up. . . .*"

Soon the fine spell ended with wet mists that turned to a drizzle, and from a drizzle to heavy rain. Three men were sent out with a week's rations to re-mark Evans' route to the Fish River. The bullocks, turned loose in the good pasture below, strayed, and could not be found for many days. But all the time the road inched down and forward perilously— now a deep cleft blasted through cliff whose newly-exposed face showed rich colours and marble-like veinings; now a narrow ledge, buttressed by tree-trunks, clinging to the side of the mountain; now a stone-filled causeway leading to a log bridge across some minor gully.

"*November 26. Light rain the whole day. Wind east-south-east; blowing very hard at times, and quite cold. The men kept at work the greater part of the day but so much wet for so long at a time makes them quite cheerless. . . .*"

Spirits lifted a little the next evening when the three men returned from the Fish River, bringing with them not only alluring descriptions of a country very different from the harsh and barren tableland, but also, in earnest of luxuries to come, a few remarkably fine rock cod.

"*November 29. A dirty morning. Got a tree 55 ft. long and 9 ft. in circumference by the men in the woods into place as a side piece below the bridge, and joining the rock, which is the last we want for this job. Men stuck very hard picking and grubbing the rocks and forming the road. Fine evening.*"

Early in December the road was completed after a fashion to the foot

of the mountain, but not yet in a condition to allow the passage of horse-
or bullock-drawn vehicles. Cox's caravan and a cart, therefore, were taken
down by man-power, with logs dragging behind to serve as brakes, and
Cox himself, accompanied by Hobby, set out on horseback for Johnny's
river, upon which the white men had not, as yet, bestowed a name. They
rode along its banks searching for the most favourable spot to build a
bridge, but—as Johnny had predicted—they were interested in it only as
an obstacle to be crossed, and Cox paid its course no more attention than
to remark that it must empty itself eventually into the Nepean.

He was elated now to find a ridge nearly three miles long which ran
from the foot of the mountain to the spot where he proposed to bridge
the river. Another week would see the road down the pass completed,
and it now measured fifty miles from Emu Ford. But the men were
restless again; he suspected that some of them were thinking of their small
holdings, and wondered how their scanty harvests were being got in. . . .

*December 5. Wrote to the Rev. M. Cartwright to send two or three
of the gaol-gang to cut and house Tindall's wheat (about three acres)
at the Nepean. He has a large family and it is his all. He could not allow
himself to go in as many others would fancy they were entitled to the
same indulgence . . ."*

On one of those clear, perfect mornings which so waywardly inter-
vened between days of cloud, wind and rain, the caravan and a bullock
cart moved forward to the junction of the river and the rivulet, and Cox
prowled up and down the banks of each in turn. The approaches to the
river at the spot where he had intended to bridge it were rocky, and he
decided at last that easier grades and better ground would compensate for
the labour of bridging both. Having reached the foot of the mountain,
and ground less hard and stony, the road was fairly racing down the slope;
by the end of the first week in December it was finished to the rivulet,
and the next day saw both bridges begun.

*"December 9. All hands employed at the first bridge before breakfast.
At 9 a.m. took all hands to the second bridge, and before dinner got one
of the side pieces, 45 ft. long, about 100 yards down the river, and fixed
in its place without accident. The other side piece we got by felling a
tree across the river, about 60 ft. long, and that was also fixed. After
dinner gave all hands a gill of spirits. Several of the men appear to be
inclined to give in and shirk work, the greater part of whom, in my
opinion, are quite as well as myself. Gave them a reproof in earnest,
which I expect will make them well by to-morrow. A cart arrived on the
mountain with stores."*

Next day the first bridge was completed. The party was now split
into three sections—a handful of men still putting the finishing touches
to the road down the pass; another group, under Mr. Hobby, camped

forward at Mount Blaxland, and forming a stretch of road along a line already marked; and a third gang working on the second bridge. The advantages of the spot chosen for the crossing did not include suitable timber; trees must be felled higher up, and great logs drawn to the site by bullocks, or floated down by men working all day in water. Cox counted himself lucky that the weather, though still unsettled, had grown warmer.

He set out himself on horseback with Hobby, Lewis and two other men to inspect the country between Mount Blaxland and the Fish River. It was rough and hilly, and the route indicated on Evans' chart proved, to his disappointment, impracticable for a road. They explored other ridges and valleys all day, and rode back into camp at sunset, tired and un-successful; but the bridge was progressing well, the party at Mount Blaxland was moving steadily towards the sixtieth mile mark, and, four days later, the road down the pass was reported complete.

Early afternoon of the next day saw the bridge finished. At either end a strong, log causeway, filled with stones and covered with earth, led on to it; the bridge itself was forty-five feet long and fourteen feet wide, and Cox surveyed it with pride before giving orders for the whole party's removal next morning to Mount Blaxland. The immediate problem was now to fix a route over the hills to the Fish River—the river that flowed west, the river which would be their visible proof that the water-shed had been crossed, the mountains set finally behind them, the way made open to a known land of promise, and who could tell what else, beyond?

"*December 18. At half-past 7 went forward on horseback to examine the road from hence to the Fish River. Found the country very hilly and rocky in many places. . . . Fixed on the road, except going up the hill, which must be avoided if possible . . .*"

It was hot now—hot and sultry. The cloudy skies split with lightning, and thunder rumbled continually. Provisions and tools were slow in coming forward. One of the men was very ill, and had to be sent back in a cart, with the sergeant in attendance. But Cox had found a route skirting the hill he had wished to avoid, and the road would now have moved forward fast had it not been for the obstructing creeks. In a dry season he might have taken them too lightly—for they were minor streams —but the rains had set them flowing briskly, and the progress of the road became punctuated by bridges, bridges, bridges. . . .

"*December 20. . . . Finished the woodwork of the largest bridge, and got on well with the other.*

"*December 21. . . . Finished both bridges this afternoon, and removed all hands one mile and a half on, where there is another bridge to build . . .*

"*December 22. . . . Finished the bridge this day by 3 o'clock. . . . Re-moved one mile and a half at 3, where we were brought up again by* another run of water. Set to work on a bridge, and got all the large timber in its place before dark . . .

"December 23. . . . At noon, having finished the bridge, removed about half a mile forward, and began another bridge. . . . On account of the Parramatta team being sent in, we are obliged to get the timber for the last six bridges by the men . . .

"December 24. . . . Finished a very good bridge at one o'clock. Went on after dinner half a mile and began another bridge. This bridge required great labour to fill it in with timber at the ends before the earth was put on, as the ground was swampy from springs . . ."

But now there were ninety miles of road behind them—already a much-frequented route. On the mountains Johnny, scouting warily along it, would hear the approaching hoofbeats which heralded a constable riding up from Sydney with messages from the Governor to Mr. Cox; or, lying hidden, he would look down on a waggon going forward from the second depôt with food, or a team of bullocks being taken back to Parramatta, or a group of discharged labourers plodding eastward beside a cart, or a soldier bound for Sydney with Cox's latest report. There were spots along this road, he thought, very favourable indeed for essays in plundering, and he spent some time in an investigation more thorough than any he had ever troubled to make before, of the cliffs that surrounded his own valley. By the time he returned to his hut he had learned three more routes, widely separated, by which he could climb down from the heights into his own territory, and marked down half a dozen snug caves in secluded gullies to which he might retreat in an emergency.

    *   *   *   *

The departure of the *Somersetshire*, in which Patrick had taken his passage, had been delayed, and he now seemed poised in a state of uncomfortable suspension between one chapter of his life and the next. All his preparations were made, and his boxes packed, but no one seemed to know when the ship would leave. During the later months of the year Miles had been spending much time at Beltrasna, familiarising himself with the management of the estate, but towards the end of November he left for a visit to Sydney, and on the first day of December a messenger arrived from him with news that the vessel was expected to sail in a couple of days.

Patrick went away to his study to complete the arrangement of his papers. Already he felt cut adrift, the house no longer his own, the fields —at which he presently sat staring through the long windows on to the verandah—no concern of his. For weeks past, as he performed some routine duty, he had felt that he was doing it for the last time; now he had come to the end, and knew himself without anchorage.

Only one thing remained in the room which was, in a personal and intimate sense, his own—a brass-bound box standing open on the desk beside him; into this he had packed a parcel containing his poems and essays, and the pile of journals in which, for sixteen years, he had recorded the story of his colonial life. He found himself eyeing it with a strange uneasiness, thinking that if he could be said to have lived his life at all, he had lived it on paper. It was all there—and much that concerned the lives of other people too. If I were to die, he thought, it would be Miles who would someday open that box, and read what, perhaps, ought not to have been written. Papers could be burned. Secrets—his own and those of others—could be secured by reducing them to ashes and a wisp of smoke. . . .

He moved impatiently. This was mere morbid brooding—a result of that melancholy which arose from the dread that once again, by the negative means of silence and retreat, he was building tragedy in another's life. Yet how could he serve Laetitia now—except by silence and retreat? No word had passed between them since that night, and none could pass save, at the end, the barren phrases of formal leave-taking.

And that, strangely, was his greatest torment. He could bear to be passive, but he could not bear to be inarticulate; he could, if he must, renounce love, but that he should be forbidden to express it was intolerable. That he should be compelled not only to leave her, but to leave her in ignorance of himself, his life, his mind; that he should survive in her thoughts only as one loved, and never as one known; that she should be left with the memory of no more—or little more—than his physical presence, and build herself, perhaps, in her need for more, some fantasy of a Patrick Mannion who never had existed; these things roused in him a storm of rebellious frustration, even of jealous fury, as if that self he might some day become in her imagination were a rival with whom she would betray him.

He must speak to her once more. Yet when he contemplated meeting her again, speaking with her alone, in the knowledge of imminent separation, he knew that it was impossible. Telling himself with bitterness that he must fall back upon his old compromise, he took up his pen as a man might take up a weapon to end his life, saying "I should not", and "I must". He began a letter to her, but erased the words as swiftly as he wrote them, discarding page after page, and becoming still at last, staring at his paper, baffled by the discovery that he could not begin to reveal himself without speaking of Johnny Prentice. *I am a man who, unable to look on misery unmoved, yet lacking that decision and that ruthlessness which generate action, has been haunted by a sense of guilt.* What would she make of such a statement, knowing nothing of two children discovering, at play, a dark abyss between them? What could it mean to her, knowing nothing of a promise made and kept, though the gallows took an innocent woman, and men were murdered? She would understand— had understood—what Dilboong's death had meant to him, and even tried to free him of some blame by taking all upon herself. If he said to her: "To me even love cannot come innocently," she would think she under- stood that too. But she could never understand that his guilt was a cumulative anguish, or that, in flight from it, he felt more guilty than before.

He thought suddenly of his brother, and envied him. Not for Miles that agonising acuteness of feeling which so stretched the mind that all the world could invade it, making one both victim and oppressor, loading upon one both suffering and guilt. Were these the steps to moral im- mobilisation—passivity—guilt—remorse—and the hairshirt . . . ? Ah, to plunge through life like Miles, without a backward look!

He was writing again when Hattie tapped on the door to tell him that his dinner was served, but it was merely a verse that he had accom- plished—a few trifling lines that hinted lamely at all he might not say. He smiled slightly as he read it over, caring less than he had ever cared before that his Muse was a modest one who had never dared the heights of Parnassus; he knew that to Laetitia, in the coming years, some visible, tangible object that had passed from him to her, would be a treasure and a consolation—and that sufficed.

In the doorway he paused and looked back at the box, uneasiness stirring in him again. He returned to the desk, picked up his pen, and wrote rapidly on a sheet of paper: "In the event of my death, this box with its contents is to be delivered to Mr. or Mrs. Mark Harvey of Sydney, New South Wales." He signed his name, and stood looking down at the page, annoyed with himself for yielding to so curious an impulse. Yet there were many uncertainties in a long voyage such as that he was about to undertake, and there could at least be no harm in this precaution. . . . He laid the page with the writing uppermost on top of the parcel in the box, closed the lid down, and locked it, putting the key in his pocket before he left the room. When he had nearly finished his meal, he sent Hattie to fetch Mrs. Emmett, and said when she appeared:

"My ship is about to sail, so I shall ride to Sydney to-morrow—tell Morgan I shall leave about ten o'clock. The cart must be ready to take my baggage in by seven in the morning, and there's one more small box from my study to go in it."

"Yes, Sir, I'll see to it, and I'm sure we all wish you a very good voyage. Will Mr. Miles and his lady be coming here at once, Sir?"

"Very shortly. Pray have everything in readiness for them. And Mrs.

Emmett . . ." he spoke without raising his eyes from his plate, ". . . you understand that the child, Mary, is to have every care and attention during my absence?"

"Oh, yes, Sir," agreed Mrs. Emmett, exchanging a quick glance with Hattie. "Yes, indeed."

*   *   *   *

But on his arrival in Sydney next day, Patrick learned that the *Somersetshire* would be still further delayed, and was not expected to sail for a week. Mrs. Bodley informed him that her master and mistress had gone driving with a party of ladies and gentlemen to South Head. where (Mr. Miles had bidden her say) they trusted Mr. Mannion would join them, and accompany them later to dinner and cards at Mr. Palmer's.

Dismayed, Patrick left his horse with Shawn Morgan, and went out again into the hot, dusty street. A week! He had been prepared to spend one night at Moore House—but a week . . . ! He began to walk slowly down Pitt Street, and realised presently that he was looking about him with that strained attention which, for all its care, often fails to fix a scene as firmly in the mind as the less conscious glance. What I shall probably remember in my old age, he thought, is not this, but Sydney as I saw it in my childhood—yes, as I saw it from the deck of the ship that brought me here. He stopped at the corner of Bridge Street, hesitating, feeling more than ever alone and at a loss. He resolved suddenly that he would pay his farewell call upon the Governor, and then, having visited the Harveys, return to Beltrasna. Curiously heartened by the decision, he walked briskly up the hill to Government House, and was admitted promptly; Macquarie rose hospitably from his chair to greet him.

"Ah, Mr. Mannion, we see you in Sydney all too seldom—and now you come only to say good-bye! Pray be seated, Sir. I wish you *bon voyage,* but even more ardently a safe and speedy return to your native land!"

"It's not quite my native land, Sir," replied Patrick, "though some-times it seems so, from my long residence in it. You are thinking of my brother, I believe."

"So I am, so I am! Yet you were a mere child when you came here first, so I insist upon stretching a point, and numbering you among the native-born—a company in which I rejoice to include my own son, Sir! It's a fine land, this Australia—for I hope the foolish name of New Holland will soon fall into disuse—a land of great possibilities, just now opening up before us. I've been looking over my reports from Cox . . ." he gestured at the papers on his desk, ". . . who seems to be getting along capitally with his road. By the time you return to us there'll be settlements out there beyond the mountains, and perhaps other important discoveries made."

"No doubt there will, Sir." Memory rushed up at Patrick out of the past, and, on an impulse, he said: "I recall a day soon after our arrival here when I accompanied my father and Mr. Dawes for a walk. Just where we went I can't remember, but it was a hill from which we could see the mountains in the distance, and I asked my father what was on the other side of them. . . ."

"Ah? And was he a good prophet, Mr. Mannion?"

"I fear he was a very poor one, Sir. He thought there could be no country there more fertile than that of the coast, and he based his belief upon the natives—arguing that only a barren land could produce people so utterly savage, and incapable of any civilised arts."

"Perhaps we shall prove him wrong there, too," remarked the Governor. "I recall that you once expressed the view that they might achieve some small degree of education, Mr. Mannion, so you'll perhaps be interested to know that I propose to establish an institution at Parramatta for native children. I've had some interviews with Mr. Shelley—the missionary, you know—who is ready to undertake its management." He rummaged among his papers and studied one of them for a moment. "According to this estimate of his, it can be done at quite trifling expense. And I have ideas about settling some of them on the land—we may make agricul-turalists of them yet. But I must not detain you with what my dear wife terms my daytime dreams. . . ."

Patrick said as he rose:

"I have recently heard something of this plan of yours, Sir, and I believe you are inviting private subscriptions to further it. If I might have the pleasure of handing Mr. Campbell a small contribution. . . ."

"Very handsome of you, my dear Sir—it will be put to good use, I assure you. I'm well aware that you are one—among too few—who has always treated these poor fellow-creatures with kindness and humanity."

Patrick took his leave, and was passed on to Mr. Campbell. When he stepped out into the street once more, the Governor's last sentence was still nagging at his mind. Ah, Dilboong, Dilboong . . . !

When he called again at Moore House, Mrs. Bodley came to him in a flutter.

"Mercy, Sir, is anything amiss? I thought you were going to join the master and the mistress . . . ?"

"I find I must return to Beltrasna this evening. Pray make my excuses, and tell Mr. Miles I shall come in to Sydney again next Thursday— unless the ship is delayed further."

"Yes, Sir."

"Has the cart arrived with my baggage?"

"Oh, yes, Sir—it came in just after you were here before, and every-thing's been taken up to your room. You'll take dinner, Sir, before you go?"

"Yes, if you please. Is Johanna here?"

"Why, yes, Sir, she's upstairs with Master Richard."

"Pray tell her that I wish to see her for a moment when I have dined."

He was glad to rest in the cool house, for it was hot outside, and he was tired. When he had finished his meal he returned to the parlour and stood by the window, watching the old convict gardener raking up leaves from the grass. Johanna entered so quietly that he was unaware of her presence until she said from behind him: "You wanted to speak to me, Sir?" He turned sharply.

"Yes. I want you to tell your mistress . . ." he chose his words care-fully, ". . . that there were circumstances which made me feel it advisable to return to Beltrasna until the ship sails."

"Yes, Sir." Her voice was neutral. "The mistress will be disappointed. If I may take the liberty, Sir, it's not many people's company she can take pleasure in here. I'd not be surprised if she wished she was going back to England too."

Patrick felt himself flushing. Was the confounded woman daring to suggest that he should run off with his brother's wife? Was she hinting that his brother's wife would go? However it might be, he must use her to solve one problem that had been perplexing him. He was determined not to see Laetitia alone again—yet how else could he give her the verse which was all he had to give? He took it from his pocket—a narrow strip of folded paper, sealed and unaddressed. "This is for your mistress," he said abruptly. "Pray give it to her." He knew from the glance she gave him as she took it that there was no need to urge discretion, and the knowledge brought anger as well as relief. He left her without another word, walked out of the house, and turned his steps towards the Harvey's cottage.

He found Conor alone, lying on a sofa in the parlour, but they were presently joined by Mark who said, throwing himself rather wearily into a chair: "So you were not in a mood for cards, Patrick? I hear that Miles has bestirred himself to arrange a round of diversions to while away your week in Sydney."

"I shall not be a week in Sydney," replied Patrick, "or even a night. I'm going back to Beltrasna this evening."

"But . . . !" cried Conor, and stopped. He saw a troubled glance pass between her and Mark. "I'm sorry," she said presently, "for we had all hoped to see something of you before you sailed."

He turned the conversation by speaking of Mary.

"I have left instructions with Mrs. Emmett that she's to be well cared for. Miles and Laetitia also know my wishes—but you'd be doing me a favour, ma'am, by seeing her now and then, and giving me some news of her in your letters. Later on some tuition might be arranged for her—I should not wish her to be quite untaught. . . ."

"But my dear Patrick," Mark exclaimed, "she's nothing but a baby! You will have returned yourself long before she's of an age . . ."

Patrick, cursing his unwariness, said hastily:

"Yes, yes—of course—I did not mean . . . I was thinking of the future." Conor, looking at him closely, asked:

"How long do you expect to be away?"

"I don't know—it's impossible to say."

His eyes met hers, and saw that they were dismayed. He realised that she knew, or guessed, his intention never to return, and the reason for it, but he did not care. She would say nothing; one cannot, he thought, with an impulse towards unmirthful laughter, speak recklessly from mere suspicion. . . . Silence—he knew something of that, its safety, and its dangers. It was not his tongue that he had found unruly, but his mind which, firmly as he might discipline his tongue, had still insisted upon speaking, even if its words were imprisoned between the closed covers of journals, strait-jacketed in paper, bound with cord, entombed in a box under lock and key. . . .

Conor said almost pleadingly:

"I trust it will not be too long, dear Patrick, for I think you have been here for so many years that you will not adjust yourself easily to another kind of life."

He shrugged, and asked: "Have I ever adjusted myself to this one?"

She shook her head slightly, uncertain and distressed; it was Mark who replied rather sharply with another question:

"Will you adjust yourself better to any other? Life itself has never been adjusted—here or anywhere. There are smoother surfaces, I grant you, than we see in New South Wales, but I think you will never be deceived by surfaces again." He added carefully: "I think you are right to go; but I believe you would be wrong not to return."

"Have I said I would not return?"

"Not in words. You say little in words—but much without them to those who have known you as long and as well as I and my dear wife. We can assure you—can we not, my love?—that there's happiness to be found here, little as either of us expected to find it once. I recall a day when I stood and looked at the ships in the harbour, and longed to leave this place for ever. I recall my mood of apprehension—of despair

378

—on that day when poor Dilboong was the innocent cause of my banishment from Beltrasna. . . ."

Patrick looked up quickly.

"Dilboong? What had she to do. with it?"

"Did you never hear that tale? She wrote a letter to Miles—a pathetic,
ill-spelt document of a few words, expressing her hope that he would soon
return—and begged me to send it for her. Your father was displeased.
I spoke rashly and with some heat—of that and other things—and within
two hours I was on the road to Sydney, already half regretting my outburst. . . ." He sighed. "Poor Dilboong, she was always deeply attached
to Miles."

"Yes," said Patrick mechanically. He rose, adding something about
the hour, and the long ride before him. Of course, he was thinking—of
course! Why did I never see it? Strange, Dilboong, that of all those
about me I understood you least—you, whose pain was, like my own,
the pain of loving without hope. *Someday, when Mr. and Mrs. Miles are
no longer here, you may return.* . . . What a humble hope it was that I
took from her!

Conor was saying:

"Yes, I fear it is time you set out, Patrick. I do hope I shall see you
again before you sail, but I'm likely to be *hors de combat* at any
moment, you know—and babies show some lack of consideration in timing
their arrival."

"Another of the native-born," he remarked, smiling, as she took his
hand and pulled him down to kiss his forehead, "in whom His Excellency
takes so benevolent an interest! Pray name it for me, if it's a boy."

He walked back to Moore House, went round to the stables for his
horse, and presently rode out again, turning his back on the town, and
his face towards the setting sun. It was almost dark when he rode up
to the toll-bar on the outskirts of Parramatta, and passed through it on to
the western road. From the first rise he could see the distant mountains
silhouetted against a sky which still held, faintly, the afterglow of the
vanished sun; in a field nearby someone had been burning a felled tree,
and he breathed the smoky, aromatic fragrance deeply, thinking: That is
something I shall not smell again. The dark blue vault of sky became
pricked with stars, and he studied them as he rode. There's Orion—but
I shall find him again in northern skies—and not standing on his head. . . .
Sirius, too; why do we call him the Dog-star—surely the natives were
happier in naming him the Eagle, so high and bright and fierce . . . ? But
I shan't see Canopus again—nor the Cross. . . .

*   *   *   *

A farmer, setting out early for Market the next morning, found him lying face downward at the edge of the road, a few miles past Toongabbee. He had been shot, but he was still breathing, and he lived for an hour after he had been conveyed to a hut on the outskirts of the town. Miles and Mark, accompanied by Dr. Redfern, galloped out from Sydney, but he was dead before they reached the hut, and it was from there that the funeral procession set out for Parramatta.

The assassin—a sailor, whose name had for some time appeared in the *Gazette* as a deserter from his ship—was taken the same day, before he had had time to rid himself of Mr. Mannion's gold watch, and a handsome sum of money. The trial was prompt, and the execution took place as the *Somersetshire* was passing through the Heads to the open sea. That night Conor slept deeply with her newborn daughter beside her; but Laetitia lay awake, dry-eyed, with the words of a verse to keep her company.

          *   *   *   *

Johnny, having made himself familiar with every yard of the road between that point where it began to be readily accessible from his valley, and the bridge where it crossed the river to vanish into the hills beyond, set out for his hut, well satisfied. A fine thing, a road was, to keep men from prowling! Explorers might be dangerous to him, but travellers were not—particularly the kind of travellers who would be using this road for many years to come. He knew from Emily's gossip, and from conversation with Miles Mannion, that the mountains had acquired among colonists a reputation more grim than they deserved. Perhaps the authorities had been willing to let the legend grow; perhaps they had even fostered it. At all events, it existed, and those who set out along the new road would do so resolved to cross the inhospitable heights as fast as their bullocks or their horses could take them. All their thoughts would be fixed upon the kind, fertile plains beyond, and they would see nothing in the wild hills and gorges which might tempt them to turn aside.

He was thinking thus as he climbed down the pass at noon of a hot, December day. He paused to rest for a while by the creek that ran out from it, and it was mid-afternoon by the time he reached a hill from which he could see his hut and his fields; although he was hungry, and impatient to be home, he stood looking down at them, and felt the anguish that always assailed him when he thought of Finn. For it was Finn's place far more than it was his. It was Finn's discovery, the fruit of Finn's thought, the affirmation of his faith, the means to his purpose—and it was still incomplete. Johnny found himself recalling, and soundlessly repeating, words which had not been spoken in that place since one night, many years ago, when Finn had uttered them, and he himself, a bewildered young savage, had listened with resentment and alarm; words from Finn's book which Stephen Mannion had taken from him; the book now ashes, most likely, and Finn dust, but the words still alive. *O receive the fugitive, and prepare in time an asylum for mankind.* . . .

He knew as he said them to himself that not only this place, but he himself, Johnny Prentice, was Finn's creation. He had been an outlaw. Not merely what "they" would call an outlaw—no doubt he was that still. Not merely an outlaw from white society, but an outlaw from all society; for he had accepted from the natives what was of use to him, rejecting all else. He had thought only of taking; admitted no restraints; sought nothing but the satisfaction of his immediate needs, and the assuagement of his appetites. It was Finn who had made him feel the sterility of solitude, Finn who had released him from his preoccupation with himself. It was Finn who had shown him that happiness was more than pleasur' able sensations, and bequeathed him funds of knowledge upon which he was still drawing every day. It was to Finn, he saw now, that he owed even his relationship with Emily—for there had been no comprehension of love in the outlaw he had been. It was Finn, in short, who had taught him to give and to think, and as he walked on slowly down the hill he found that he was considering the road again, but no longer purely in terms of what he could take from it. Now, when he imagined the carts and waggons, they were not merely loaded with goods for him to steal, but driven by men about whose lives and fate he began to wonder; now that long, winding ribbon of cleared earth was not only a route by which possessions would flow into the hands of Johnny Prentice, but a road to that future which he had never glimpsed until Finn showed it to him. He did not know what it held, nor how it could be shaped; he darkly suspected that "They" would do the shaping. But already there was a new quality in his attitude to the part that he himself might play, and his mind stumbled among thoughts of men who would pass along that road not to inherit the promised land, but as captives—men who might, after all, be ready to turn aside into a wilderness, however forbidding, if there they might find freedom.

He came up towards the hut from the creek—now flowing again with its old, pleasant sound among the rocks—and halted in surprise. Away on the hillside to the south there was the smoke of a fire, but what startled him was the sight of Billalong standing at the doorway of the hut with Emily. He called, and she ran a little way down the hill to meet him.

"He's just come," she said, and he's brought his woman and his two children—they're up there by the fire. He says he's goin' to stay here." She asked, puzzled: "What's he want to do that for? Ain't he frightened of the spirits any more?"

Johnny thought, as he walked on up to the hut, that Billalong was undoubtedly frightened of something, but he stood motionless, watching his half-brother approach, and there was something besides fear in his eyes. "I come," he said without preamble as Johnny stood before him. "Bring Moolabaru. We stay here, make hut, not go away more."

Johnny stared at him. He was wearing a pair of patched, but still-ragged trousers, and an old coat without either arms or buttons—stolen, Johnny supposed, from some shepherd's hut or lonely farmhouse. Clad thus, with the tribal markings on his body hidden, it seemed more notice-able that his features were sharper than a native's, and his skin lighter. He had spoken with decision, but there was a tenseness in his attitude which suggested a stubbornly contested desire to flee. Johnny said to Emily:

"Ye'd best get him some food he can take up to the woman and children." He waited till she had gone indoors, and turned again to Billalong.

"Now," he said, "what's come to ye? Why do ye want to stay here?" But even as he spoke he understood from the baffled wretchedness of the dark face confronting him that there were matters here too complicated for Billalong's English, and he repeated his question in the native tongue. He was tired, so he sat down on the bench by the door to listen, watching a long trail of small, black ants hurrying across the bare ground into the grass beyond. Billalong squatted on his heels, and what he said came to Johnny like an echo, for he felt that he already knew it all. A man must have a home for his body, but he must also have a home for his spirit. In his *towri* Billalong had once had both—a roof, a fire, a woman, but also a law, a legendary past, a mysterious future, songs and corroborees for delight, rituals to dedicate his manhood. Now it was different. He looked at the black men, and knew that he was black—but then he looked at the white men and knew that he was white. Could he be both? Their laws were different—and which law was his? Many in his tribe felt an uneasiness, but he, who was half white, felt it more than they. He grew angered by their magic, and said there was no truth in it; yet he, who rejected it, felt its truth, and they, who made it, felt its falseness. He had thought of these things, and it had come to him that only in the *towri* of Dyonn-ee, who had said that he was half black, could Billalong, who was half white, find a home to be at ease. . . .

Johnny glanced at him from under his brows, and thought: "Ye don't look at ease." He asked whether the woman did not fear the evil of this place, and Billalong, with a flare of impatience that faded quickly to dejection, replied that she did fear it, but she feared other things also, which they had left behind. And the fear of evil magic, he added flatly, was not now as it had been before. There was a change among his people. . . .

He fell silent and looked sullen, as if tired of trying to explain what he did not understand himself. Johnny was silent too, knowing the change to come from white men who lived unscathed in forbidden places, and violated with impunity laws which black men had always believed inviolable. Fear might survive, but it was now accompanied by doubt. While the powers of evil magic had been too terrible to challenge, they had remained certain and absolute; now, by the reckless, lawless Beere-wolgal, they were challenged every day—and failed. Billalong and his family, it appeared, were in flight from the unendurable spectacle of mystery dissolving.

The thought of flight had set a whisper stirring in Johnny's memory again. From over there, not a hundred yards away, there seemed to come Finn's voice saying those words he had been recalling half an hour ago, and in reply came his own, harsh and suspicious, demanding: *"Fugitive— man running away . . . ?"* Well, there were more things a man could run from than whips and chains. He said: "There's room here for more, I reckon, and work too. We can start buildin' a hut for ye to-morrow."

    *   *   *   *

Cox had spent Christmas Day beside the Fish River, planning yet another bridge. The spot which he finally chose for his crossing-place was again deficient in suitable timber, but he had brought forward four men to begin assembling the best that could be found, leaving the rest of the party at work on the road and bridges behind. An excursion to the westward a couple of days later had revealed country which seemed to threaten no particular difficulties, and he had returned to camp encouraged —not only by this, but by the sight of lush valleys of green grass, finer than any he had seen in the colony before.

Now they were in country where the rations could be supplemented freely with fresh food; kangaroos, emus, wild turkeys, ducks and pigeons were plentiful, and the river teemed with fish. The men, when he mustered them in the mornings, looked cheerful, and though the weather was still unsettled, he no longer had to record that progress was delayed by illness. Along the river bank there was excellent grazing land, and in front of them lay not only the rich valleys he had seen, but others which Evans had described. True, he must be prepared for some further set-backs, some unforeseen problems, but he was in a mood to make light of them; there could be nothing as bad as what lay behind.

He was at peace with the world as he sat in his caravan one morning making notes for a report to His Excellency. Outside the sun was shining from a cloudless sky, and the world looked clean and brilliant after the rain. Down on the bank Tye was giving out tools to the men who were employed cutting timber for the bridge; that work should go on faster now, Cox thought with satisfaction, for two more men had come up to them yesterday after having completed the last of the ten bridges between the end of the mountains and this spot. A week to finish the one they were now beginning—perhaps less—and then on again to the end. He felt a stab of excitement. He had imagined the end before, but it had always seemed far away, separated from him by time, distance and un-known obstacles; now it seemed quite close. Every stage completed had found him still looking forward; it would be strange and exhilarating to stand at last and look back—at some hundred miles of good, serviceable road. To-day he would go out again with a small party to Campbell's River and make a thorough survey. He decided that he would now finish his report of proceedings up to this time, but wait until his return from the reconnaissance before sending it. No doubt there would be even better news to add.

He took up his pen and marshalled his thoughts soberly; for it would be a report, and no shout of triumph. His mind had already returned from its brief glance at a successful climax, and was busy with the practical details of the moment. But it was a long time since there had been so pure and vivid a morning—crisp through its warmth, promising the dry, noonday heat of the inland, astir with a faint breeze, full of elusive scents and agreeable sounds—and his attention wandered to it. He had noted, in a hurried way, many interesting and pleasant things as they toiled westward—the deep, dreaming blue of the mountain gullies, the strange, tall ant-hills of the ridges, a handsome flower like the laylock, a pliable timber which he fancied might make good cart-shafts—but there had been little time to admire the beauties and the curiosities of nature. Now, with the open journal beneath his hand, he found himself turning from his report to write:

"*December 29. A fine morning, which the birds seem most to enjoy on the banks of the river. The shrubs and flowers also are extremely fragrant. Left six men preparing materials for the bridge across the main river. The remainder at work bringing up the road. . . .*"

ALSO BY ELEANOR DARK

THE TIMELESS LAND

First published in 1941, Eleanor Dark's classic novel of the early settlement of Australia is a story of hardship, cruelty and danger. Above all it is the story of conflict: between the Aborigines and the white settlers.

In this dramatic novel, introduced here by Humphrey McQueen, a large cast of characters, historical and fictional, black and white, convict and settler, brings alive those bitter years with moments of tenderness and conciliation amid the brutality and hostility. All the while, behind the veneer of British civilisation, lies the baffling presence of Australia, a timeless land that shares with England 'not even its seasons or its stars'.